LIFE IS SWEET AND BITTERSWEET

Jerry A Grunor and Janice E Grunor

Live Life To The Fullest!

iUniverse, Inc.

New York Lincoln Shanghai

Life Is Sweet and Bittersweet

iUniverse books may be ordered through booksellers or by contacting:

iUniverse
2021 Pine Lake Road, Suite 100
Lincoln, NE 68512
www.iuniverse.com
1-800-Authors (1-800-288-4677)

ISBN: 0-595-33532-2 (pbk)
ISBN: 0-595-66961-1 (cloth)

Printed in the United States of America

LIFE IS SWEET AND BITTERSWEET

CHAPTER AND VERSE

▼

A novel jointly written by Father and Daughter,
of the lives we all have led in some way or another…
or would have loved to have led sometime in our lifetime.

It involves love, intrigue, mystery and suspense,
with a cast of characters
that could only happen in your wildest dreams.

CHAPTER 1

▼

LIFE COULD BE A DREAM

I have learned that as you get older, food plays a most important part of your life. At age 40, or more, you are either trying the Atkins Diet or some other diet, because you have high cholesterol, lots of rolls and handlebars, and your neighbors and friends tell you that this diet is better than that one. You have to stop eating bread, meat, potatoes, carrots, milk, and chocolate. You are to eliminate alcohol and no more smoking cigarettes, but to brush your teeth with a tar resistant toothpaste. You are to cut out all carbonated sodas, do not use Sweet & Low, no more tomatoes, eliminate lettuce and cucumbers as they are acidic, and back away from orange juice as this is acidic as well. Coffee and tea are no-nos, and shellfish is absolutely bad for you.

No more salt, no more pepper, and no more sugar. Sweets and in-between snacks will make you fat. Eggs are bad for your indigestion and your cholesterol. Bread is mattress stuffing and you must not sip from straws. You have to throw away all the chewing gum and sucking candy you stored up in your car.

If you are caught drinking wine, beer or a martini, you will definitely lose all of your friends, as these are not trendy things to do. Even your family will not talk to you anymore. Life becomes frightening as you get older. It is not sweet and loving anymore.

No matter what you do, you are pushing the button to oblivion and living this way is definitely not fun. No matter what you do, others will tell you that you are totally wrong anyway.

So what do you do with yourself? You can always eat last week's People Magazine or munch on the Classified Section of the New York Times. You may want to have some Power Bars, only to find that they are so expensive, that each bar, if you read the ingredients carefully, contain all of the stuff you were told not to eat anyway. Each diet tells you to eat different kinds of food. So what do you do with your eating habits without killing yourself? If you decide on any one of the diets, who is to say that you will not be killing yourself and enjoying it less?

Now you go to the supermarket to find something to eat. You walk down each aisle pushing your little supermarket cart, looking at all of the colorful little boxes of food, and reading all of the ingredients. You find out that even potato chips have less than 1% fat and some have no cholesterol, and the 'Ridges' are better to eat than the 'BBQ'd' kind, but are twice as much in price.

The leanest meat, without all that fat, is quite expensive, even more so than the meat with all of the fat. The skinless chicken is exorbitant, because the butcher took the fat off by himself. The Halibut is out of sight only because it is frozen since they only catch this fish in November. Try finding fresh Halibut in the middle of June.

So you keep walking the aisles looking for a food that is palatable, reasonably priced, good for your cholesterol count, easy to boil, not too fatty, has a lot of protein, easy to digest, and not dated last year. Most of all, you really want something that interests you. Does this exist, I ask you? Who are we kidding? There ain't no such animal in the entire damn supermarket.

There, before your eyes, you see a disaster. There she is, a cute little old biddy, about 85, somewhere in the neighborhood of five feet short, and as innocent as all get-out. She is loading her cart with, of all things, Chips Ahoy. No…it can't be. She can't do that. This will literally destroy this nice old lady who is already chomping at the bit that when she gets home, she will have the snack of her life. It may be the last snack that she will ever have in her life. And she is doing this all to herself. Hasn't she read about the high cholesterol count or the amount of sugar in chocolate cookies?

You wait until she turns her body back toward the shelves, and you, very nonchalantly, squirm over to her cart. Without a sound, you remove the box of Chips Ahoy and place it back on the shelf. When she returns back to the cart, she slowly moves her little body back down the aisle not realizing that you just may have saved her life. What a happy moment for you. You are patting yourself on the back and are feeling good all over. You may have given this woman about ten more years to live out her pathetic life with her not even suspecting what you did. You are so proud of yourself.

You cannot believe what you had done. You actually did something nice for a change. You realized the density of the problem and did something good for a stranger you never met before in your life. As you start to walk slowly away, pushing the cart down the aisle, a thought comes over you. For being such a good guy and helping a fellow human being, you deserve a reward. Why not? You earned it. So you think for awhile and then it hits you.

You are going to reward yourself with something that is small and not so toxic that you feel will not jeopardize your health. You gradually walk back to the shelf and grab that box of Chips Ahoy and throw it into your cart. But that is dessert. You need some nourishment. So you walk down the aisles, looking for something for dinner. Let's see now, how about some eggs for breakfast, fried chicken for lunch, lobster or shrimp for dinner, a salad with all of the fixins', a bottle of Chardonnay and maybe a Vodka Martini. You need to have a smoke afterward, and oh yes, where do they keep all of the soda?

Upon reaching the checkout, out of the corner of my eye, I caught the little old lady just leaving, and I wondered, "Did she realize that she did not get her cookies or did she notice and then return for another box? Or did she say 'The heck with it!'"

In all reality, she probably chalked it up by imagining that she had them and they weren't missing at all.

Does this mean that I too will forget or not even notice my cookies being swiped from my cart when I reach her age? Or will someone save my life as I saved hers? Will that really matter to me? Or, on saving her life, in return, do I now have the responsibility to continue 'saving' others? Am I destined to be a person who looks out for others, when they grab the wrong 'cookies', so to speak? For some strange reason, I was probably looking at myself in the very near future.

Driving home, I continued to think of the old lady. Was my concern about her life just a reflection of my own coming of age? When, after a certain point in your life, do the smallest of things mean so much more than the biggest issues in the world? Because in reality, there is very little we can do on a larger scale. Are all the so-called 'cookies' we choose always going to have a consequence?

If they do, is it just another analogy for everything else we choose? If women were 'cookies' for instance, have I always chosen the ones with the most chips or the ones that were the sweetest? Or have I been conservative and picked the 'cookie' with the least fat content, and thought that it was best for me? Is everything just an analogy for something else we do?

I put a lot of thought into my actions that day, and decided that I would do something for the greater good, and begin making it my mission to help others see the errors of their ways. I went straight to the computer and signed up to teach at a local college where I can use my previous education as a Psychologist/ Health Advisor/Chef. In actuality, I am sort of a chief cook and bottle washer so to speak. It might be nice to educate adults on the choices they make when they are shopping or creating in a world where consumption and sales have little or no interest in the consumer.

Again, my pride got a boost and I felt that I was on my way to doing something for others. Up to this point, it would have gone unnoticed if I had not seen that little old lady and her little box of 'cookies' with all of the yummy chips. I decided to reward myself with a Yodel and made a beeline for the shopping mall.

I made it to the mall, although it took nearly forty-five minutes to find a parking spot, which was at least a quarter mile away in this huge parking structure. I also noticed how some people kept circling the mall trying to find a parking spot that was close to the department store building. I noticed their cars going around and around so many times, that it became an obsession with them.

I just wondered if they ever made it into the building at all. That is too, too tiring to watch. Why can't people just park, take a little stroll from their car, and realize that it would get them to the mall much faster?

I finally got into the mall, and there were so many people skirting about, looking for some store to shop in, without even knowing why they came to the mall in the first place. Going to a mall could be so stressful, an obsession for many, a waste of time for others. Where do you go to first? Do I go to Macy's, Nordstrom's, Lord & Taylor or Sears? Or do I just walk around and check out the little boutiques, making believe that I am looking for something? I have no idea why I am here. Does anyone? If I were looking for clothes, it would take too long to try them on. The sales people are all over you, and you feel obligated to buy something even if you do not want to.

The malls were not only built for adults. They are hangouts for teenagers. The developers knew that when they built the malls. There are all types of teenagers who come to the mall, and they are looking to meet other teenagers, who are also on the prowl. When I was a teenager, we hung around candy stores in Brooklyn because we did not have malls. We met girls at parties or in school. Now, it is a different ballgame.

There are tons of teenagers who have a much greater lot to pick from. The clothes are different and the language is something out of a Spike Lee movie. I have a hard time trying to understand the lingo nowadays. The teenage girls all wear jeans that are two sizes too small, and you can see their little asses jutting out. Their tops are more revealing to emphasize their newly formed breasts. And the lipstick is so bright, that it would take hours to wipe it off their mouths. Their hair is hanging wild and loose, and they have so much eyeliner on, that they look like the wife of Frankenstein in heat. If only their parents could see them. And if they did, they would probably not even say a word. Today's parents have a totally different outlook on their teenage children than when I grew up.

"David, be home by six for dinner." "David, make sure your earlaps are down when you go out in the cold." "David, you are a teenager now, so act like one."

Heck, I never knew what a teenager was supposed to act like, except what my mother told me. When I found out that my teenage years were different from hers, I felt that I was becoming a mature adult. I was no longer that little boy that my mother tried to keep telling me I was. I was *her* little boy!

The adult females take along the adult males to buy them the clothes so they can show them off to their female friends. The men just go along for the ride, and of course, to pay for the clothes. The females always forget to take along their credit cards and give their male companions a sweet smile by asking them if they could use their credit cards. Their thought is to then pay them back when they get home. And if the guys are asked how the clothes look on their spouses or girl friends, they would be hinging on a total breakup if they say that the clothes do not look good.

You are wrong if you agree or disagree, so the best thing to do is to not say a word. The men are better off going shopping by themselves, otherwise they would be questioned why they are buying that black leather jacket or tight fitting pair of jeans.

"Are you trying to impress the women?" "Aren't you too old to wear such clothing?" "Why on earth are you buying that for? It will only hang in your closet for years."

Just to watch the people and listen to the comments could drive anyone up a wall. But I took along my little pacifier with me. Yep, I took along a chocolate chip cookie. That will give me that added sugar to make my day go by easier and less painful. You must have a little sugar when you go shopping or you will be dragging very quickly.

So I am eating this delicious cookie when a young woman stops me and asks, "Where did you get that cookie?"

Heck, what is this? I can't even enjoy my own cookies without being stopped by this idiot. "I brought it from home."

"Do you know where they sell cookies like that in this mall?" she asks.

How the heck should I know? I just got here. Why is this becoming such a big issue? Why can't I even enjoy taking a little sugar while I dig my way through the crowds? I stare at her, hoping she will go away.

Drool runs down her jowls like a bulldog at dinnertime. Her eyes remained glued to my luscious little cookie with the chocolate chips just waiting to be eaten.

I thrust the cookie at her. "Take it."

She can't believe what I had just said.

"Take it?" she asks. "Take it? How could you give me a half-eaten cookie from your mouth? That is disgusting. I cannot believe that you would actually do that." She turns in a huff.

I just stared at this incredible woman who must have weighed in the neighborhood of 450 pounds, wearing tight jeans, which the Grand Canyon would have looked so pale compared to her huge mountain of paradise. I shrug and tear off another bite.

What could be more astonishing? What else would I find at this mall? Who else would stop me and give me a hard time? Where can I go just to be by myself and find a little peace? Is this what I get for going to a mall after spending a grueling forty minutes parking my damn car? Should I have stayed at home on my computer and just had gone on the internet instead of going to the stores? Do I really want to educate people on the choices they make? Now where did I put that package of Yodels?

On my last go-around, I thought, while I was there in the mall, I might as well stop in the book store and pick up a few journals on psychology and philosophy. As long as I had signed up to teach students, I may as well refresh my memory and not look like an uneducated smart ass. If I quote a few good sentences from some paragraphs, I might just get away by sounding educated and experienced. One can only hope. It is all in the delivery and I can do that. Not that I ever underestimated my intelligence, but I simply have to remember what the new generations of empty minds had caused the reason for my teaching such a class.

I approached Barns & Noble and saw that it was very busy. Knowing how I feel about crowds and my most recent incident in the mall, I did not want to encounter another person wanting from me. So I hi-tailed it out of the mall with my last cookie in hand and attempted to locate the vehicle that brought me here. Oh, I just knew that this was going to be another one of those journeys.

At that moment, I realized what fear of the unknown is all about. It felt like it took about a half hour to get into the parking structure, but no telling how long it would take to get out. Thank goodness for the fact that I savor every morsel, unlike others who devour cookies in one swallow. I felt the cookie in my hand, as I took it from my pocket, like a rattle in a baby's fingers. This was my own, personal safety net. The idea of thinking of the forthcoming traffic, this entire experience left me feeling rather empty.

Again I asked that same old question, "Why did I ever come here in the first place?"

After many attempts to maneuver my way past others who were also looking for their own cars, or trying to pull out of the garage, I had to think what floor did I park my car on? What kind of car was I driving? Why was I having a senior moment? Who will be the next nuisance while I am trying to leave this place? All of these questions were swirling around in my brain, either from anxiety that started to make me laugh at it all. You know what? I still had my sense of humor and this was keeping me sane.

Guess I must have gotten that from my father. He had a great sense of humor and kept everyone in stitches, except my mom of course. She was too serious of a person to laugh at anyone's jokes. So today was not as bad as I thought it was. Now, I had to find my little car and get the hell out of here. I walked, what seemed to be the length of a country road to a level that I could only hope that my car was on. Upon turning the corner, my eyes caught what I assumed to be the most beautiful face I had ever seen.

No, it was not my cuddly mom with her womanly charm and smiley face. It was someone who just knocked the living heck out of me. The most beautiful person I had met in quite some time. My heart was pounding and I was not able to get all of the right words out, but there I stood, admiring this very pretty woman. For some reason, as I stood there in awe of this tall, about five feet, ten inch model, I guess I was hoping that she would be attracted to me. After all, I stood nearly six feet tall, average weight, good looking, charming and rather intelligent. So I just looked at her and smiled.

She too stood there facing me as if we had our eyes locked on to each other. I could not recall where I had seen her before, but she seemed so familiar. I almost wished I could have said, "Wow, it has been a long time. How have you been?"

But it was not someone I had known before. In fact, it was a face from a cover of a magazine or a movie picture. She had turned the corner too quickly as well, and bumped right into my shoulder.

She then turned to me and said, "Oh, excuse me."

"No problem," I responded. I quickly tried to continue the conversation so she would not disappear into the darkness of the concrete walls that filled the garage.

I then remarked, hoping to get a response, "This is not an easy place to find your car, is it? I mean, look at all the cars, and there must be about four floors, and miles of cars just in this garage alone."

I was thinking that by talking to her, and asking her a question, it would make her stay a bit longer. I felt that if she had any class, she would have responded to my question.

She turned again in my direction and gave me a smile. Then, as she shook her head, I could hear a slight giggle coming from her beautiful lips, "No it isn't, and I think that I am lost."

I felt relieved that there would be more to talk about. I pretended that I too was lost, and though it was not far from the truth, I felt the need once again to come to the rescue of a maiden in distress. "Let me help you find your car."

Why did I feel such a warm passion for this woman? I did not even know her name or where she came from. But she was the most attractive woman I had ever met. The car angle seemed to be working.

I approached her and asked, "what kind of car are you driving?"

She very shyly glanced back at me and replied, in a most provocative, yet sexually quiet tone of voice.

"I drove here in my two door, silver gray BMW. It's so small, I may not be able to find it among all of these giant SUVs."

I was fumbling for my keys, trying not to look too harried nor taken back by this wonderfully groomed, almost statuesque-like woman, who was so dramatically dressed in her tightly fitted red blouse, and the cutest mini jeans that just ended half way up her thighs. I could not take my eyes off hers, except when I glanced at her pink, almost curled up lips.

Wish I had an extra chocolate chip cookie to offer her. Nah! That would have been too gosh.

"Let me see if I can help you locate your car, Miss," I said, trying to sound almost stern as if I was a parking attendant, without showing any anxiety or sounding too forward.

"By the way, my name is David, and yours?" I said almost sheepishly. "I—er—mean, what is your name?"

I just didn't know what was coming over me. I was gloating over this beautiful young woman and felt so weak inside that my heart was pounding, my legs were crumbling, and my mind was going a mile a minute. Why did she suddenly appear out of nowhere? Where did she come from? Is this something that was meant for me?

"I'm Julie, and thanks for helping me, David. I feel so silly here."

"Don't worry, Julie" I interrupted. "We will find your BMW, I promise."

I could not believe how I was acting, and I wanted to say, "I promise to find it for you and never let you go."

But of course, I would have sounded like a complete moron. So I kept to my conservative nature and continued to pretend that I had the situation under control. Imagine if she was the one I had been looking for all of my life. Imagine after going to the mall, where, at first I felt a complete sense of emptiness, I would find complete fulfillment with this total stranger.

Thinking back, I have always been this way. When I met my wife, I was biking on the boardwalk in Santa Monica. She happened to be there with some friends, as I was. We started chatting and before long, we dated and we got married in a period of six months. Of course, this was quite a few years ago, and she has since passed on, due to a most unfortunate sickness.

Being a widower for over two years now, has made me wonder if I could ever find true love again as I did with Martha. We spent over 17 years together, mostly blissful, other times a bit argumentative. But we were together. We married very early, I at 24 and she was twenty one.

My mind raced faster and I knew that I had to make a move by not letting this beautiful woman get away. I could procrastinate longer, but then she might think that I could not help her. Or I could hurry and find her car, and she could be impressed with my ability to locate her missing car.

We walked up and down the garage and my eyes could not decide whether to look for the gray car or look at her wonderful figure. Of course, she was more intent on finding her car than carrying on a conversation with me, and I understood that. But, secretly, I hoped that she would find me utterly attractive and pursue this romantic interlude. So I thought. I was dreaming. I was hoping. I was in the twilight of my life right now, and so was she.

"Ah, there it is." I heard the words from her luscious lips, and my heart sank.

Oh dear God, what could I have done in this split second to see her again. My fantasy was coming to a close. The end of the dream seemed so near. I watched as she quickly walked to her gray BMW and I followed her, remarking, "Let me at least make sure that all is okay before you take off."

My last ditch effort. I did not want to lose her. I needed more time and I wanted a positive feedback from her. Boy, was I green around the edges. I was like a school boy, meeting his first date in class.

She nodded and turned around, her hair swinging over her shoulder, as if in slow motion. I thought that I was going to pass out by her exquisite beauty. I must have been crazy but I kept thinking, why was I acting like a teenager in love for the first time. Naturally, I thought, it had been quite some time since I had had a woman in my life.

My hormones, all what were left of them, were raging in ways that were even foreign to me. I watched as she opened the door and then faced me, holding out her pretty soft hand, her thin fingers, coated with red painted nails. I took it and felt the warmth of a body that I had hoped would grab me and take me to where she was going.

I had to calm down however, and shook her hand, and smiled. "I'm glad everything is okay. Have a great day, Julie."

"Thanks, David," she replied. "I do appreciate your help and you have a great day, too."

She let go of my hand and got into her car and shut the door. I stood there for what seemed like ten years, but knew I had better move away and start looking for my own car. I immediately thought of following her and see where she was going. But she pulled away rather quickly, from the parking spot.

And as I was about to turn the other way, I heard the window open, and her sweet voice echoed.

"Hope to run into you again, sometime, but maybe under different circumstances." And she giggled sweetly and drove away.

I wanted to respond with something, but could not come up with the right words at the time. I was so taken by her, that my mind went blank. I saw her waving, and she then rolled up her window and drove off. I eventually located my car but not nearly quick enough to follow her. I succumbed to the fact that this was a dream and I could only relish the moment, and only hope that the last ten minutes of my life would get me through the horrendous traffic that I was about to face.

Days later, I was still thinking of Julie. Everywhere I went I looked for her in every gray BMW, to see if it was she driving it. I was hoping that I would have a chance to see her again. I did not have any idea as to what I would say to her, but I knew that if I had the opportunity to see her again, I would not let her go. I had a lot of time to think of her, as my life had come to a point where I had only the activities that I decided to do, and was financially able to do what I pleased.

Years ago, we made a killing in the stock market and the fact that I had been employed as a Health Advisor for the School System for 20 years, my benefits and pension well took care of any needs that I had. I also had retirement pay from my stint in the Navy. I was a bad dude in one of the most elite branches of government you could imagine.

After Martha's death, I took solace in the fact that I was destined not to marry again. I managed to have dated two nice women on occasion. Both also lost their husbands and both knew about each other, as we were all friends for years and basically, we kept company because we had something in common. Funny, how 'death' becomes a common thread with people, and sometimes, it brings to you, a most unusual passion.

Although this may be true, the passion I felt for the stranger in the parking garage was much greater than I had felt for any woman, except Martha, may God rest her soul. But honestly, I didn't remember having my groins awakened to that degree as they were in the parking garage that day.

I decided to take some time off and take a trip to Las Vegas. What a city with its bright lights, the hustle and the bustle, and the sounds of chips bouncing on the tables, with people yelling and screaming over a ten dollar bet. That is for me.

I kept thinking of Julie and what may have happened if only she called out to me that I should contact her by saying, "David, here is my phone number. Call me."

But that did not happen. I was not happy continuing on with my relationships with the two women, and I needed to be with someone else. I needed to start an entire new life, to get rid of the baggage that had tagged along in my life for the past couple of years. I needed to first find myself, to be happy within my soul, and be able to express my happiness and love upon another. This unexpected meeting with Julie had somehow opened up my eyes as to what I needed in life, and what was best for me. If it were not Julie, it would be someone else. I needed to find out for sure.

I packed my two suitcases, made reservations at the Venetian Hotel, and decided to do some gambling, see some shows, walk the streets, and get to where the action was. What a great spot to either hit it big with great memories or just go home, a beaten man, without a lust for life, without some memories that I was able to call my own. I hopped into my car and headed north on the I-15.

Las Vegas is truly a city that never sleeps. This is the home to three of the top convention centers in the country. The Las Vegas Convention Center is one of the largest exposition facilities in the world. And the Sands Expo Convention Center, conveniently connected to the Venetian, where all of the prettiest women, from all over the world, come to. The Las Vegas' newest convention center facility, at the Mandalay Bay Resort and Casino, is probably the most breath-taking hotel on the strip. Just imagine browsing the stores of Paris, Rome, New York, Cairo, Venice, and the South Pacific, in just a few short hours.

You are traveling all over the world when you come to this city. Las Vegas has the venue where the hotels were designed to replicate the great cities of the world. You can find a mix of designers, renowned retailers, and boutiques, plus the most beautiful women from all over the world. From boutiques to unique, fuzzy dice, to Ferragamos, everything you could possibly want is found in Las Vegas. That is where I decided to go and have some fun.

Living in southern California, I would go to Las Vegas often. San Francisco and New York City have traditionally been considered the nation's top dining destinations. But these days, Las Vegas is America's hottest spot for foodies. Long famous for its 'all you can eat' buffets, the city is famous for its growing roster of gourmet restaurants. It doesn't matter what time of year you go to Las Vegas, people will always be dazzled by the array of unmatched entertainment offered here, on the strip, every season. A steady stream of celebrity performers, spectacular shows, and special events fills marques at dozens of the city's theatres and arenas.

I love Las Vegas, with its famed stage extravaganzas that continue to put the 'spectacle' in spectacular, with high-kicking showgirls, eye-popping special effects, lavish costumes, and stunning sets. You have everything from musical megastars from every genre and generation, master impressionists, illusionists, and superstar comedians. This was for me.

This is what the doctor ordered, and I was picking up the prescription to give me the extra 'oomph' that I needed to get me out of the doldrums that I was in. I was going to visit the City of Lights. Whatever your taste is, whether it is the Imperial Palace, the Aladdin, Caesars Palace, the Flamingo, the Las Vegas Hilton, Mandalay Bay, Paris, the Riviera, the Stardust, the Tropicana, the Venetian or the MGM Grand, or any other fabulous hotel, or whatever your heart desires, you will find it in Las Vegas. This is paradise in heaven, as long as your money holds out, and your credit card still has a balance.

The trip was long and agonizing to do alone. The road to Barstow, through Riverside was boring, with lots of traffic and I knew that I needed to stop for a break and have some lunch. The weather was balmy, quite cloudy, a bit humid, and I was just keeping to the speed limit, not pushing it. It would have taken about five hours from home. I was not in any rush. Whatever was going to happen would happen. I had no time schedule, no one to meet, and not a worry in the world.

I just kept the car purring along on the freeway at a moderate speed. I was hoping to find some kind of adventure in the desert and was looking forward to it. After two and a half grueling long hours, my stomach was growling. It was getting close to noon, and I was approaching Barstow, a town filled with shopping centers, lots of gas stations, and fast food restaurants. It is the halfway stop between Los Angeles and Las Vegas.

My journey was beginning, and where it was going to take me, only fate would have a hand in it. I was ready for anything. Martha was no longer in my life. Was that it? Did I still have a guilty conscience about being with another woman? Hey, it has been two years, and Martha would want me to start a new life. I really did want to start a new life, but something had held me back all of these years. Maybe that was it. It was my love for Martha.

But I just could not get Julie out of my mind. Did I say the wrong thing? Did I act like a fool? Was I not macho or romantic? Who knows! I was me, and that is whom I am. Just another guy trying to do the right thing! Just another memory in a life of ups and downs! Who knows! Maybe next time, if there is a next time, I will be more forward and ask the girl for her number.

Yeah…that's it! I was learning from my own mistakes. Next time, I will be the kind of person I always wanted to be, but never had the chance to do it. Well, now all that will change. I am going to a city that never sleeps. Who knows! I may be lucky and not find any time to sleep or to gamble. Las Vegas, here I come!

But first, let me grab some fuel for my gas tank and some fuel for my tummy. Then we can fantasize later.

I drove to the nearest service station and refueled the tank, and noticed a small diner up the road. The best part of being in a small diner is not just the menu with so many options, but the waitresses who are friendly and can chat it up if need be. Since I had been driving for a while, it would have been nice to have a conversation with a friendly face, and if she was cute, that would even be better.

It would make a good start to my new life if I could practice opening up more to strangers. When 'good' gets involved, there is a certain warmth that goes with it as well. Here I was, in Barstow, only half way to paradise. And I was on a roll. I had that sense of excitement, knowing that in a few hours, I would be in Vegas.

I drove up to the diner, parked my car and walked in and sat down at the counter. As always, it was the more personable choice to make if you wanted to have a good chat. The big burly cook walked around with his dirty apron, and the waitress seemed to be tremendously busy with other customers. This did not fair too well with my new beginning, as I was counting on opening up to strangers. But I was determined to test the waters anyway. One of the older waitresses leaned over the counter as if she thought that I could not hear her too well, and asked if I could be helped. Now there was a loaded question. If only she knew.

I ordered coffee and a ham sandwich, and then asked her, "So how's it going for you today?"

She gave me quite a stare as if she thought that I was out of my friggin' mind to ask such a question. I was hoping that she would respond further for my need of conversation. Finally, after pouring my coffee, she took a deep breath, sighed most elegantly, and said, "Very busy…can't believe the crowds coming in."

She rolled back her eyes and walked away. I knew that she would be back, at least with my sandwich. One could only hope. I was getting quite hungry. It had been a long drive so far, and I still had to go through the desert.

I looked around the room and noticed how many different types of faces there were in the room. I wondered how their lives took them to this same point and time as my life took me. There were older faces with blank stares, and younger faces with mouths that never ceased to move, even between the bites. There were young families that seemed overwhelmed just being here in Barstow, even with their own activity at their table, making sure that their kids were having some lunch.

I was pleased that I was by myself, not having to deal with any of the inconveniences that were at other tables. I might have been alone, but I was happy, at least to the point where I could say, I did not have to explain anything to anyone, or be expected to be there for anyone. Or was this just an excuse for not having anyone to be with and to love? Was I purposely hiding behind my excuses, or was it truly what I wanted? I had hoped that I would find this answer on my journey in the desert.

After lunch, and failing at the attempt for conversation at the counter, I ventured back to the car and hit the road. I was on the second lap of my journey to the Venetian Hotel, with anticipation and excitement that was before me. Something inside of me was yearning and something new and wonderful was about to happen. I just knew it.

I finally made it to the California and Nevada border. There was Whiskey Pete and the other three hotels, with lots of cars. I drove through and got to Jean, Nevada. I drove by more hotels, and found myself just an hour away from the Las Vegas Strip.

As I came down the mountain, I could see the lights of all of the hotels in Las Vegas. Another thirty minutes and I would be there. This was the entertainment capital of the world. Each hotel was more beautiful than the other. And they kept on building more and more hotels, from the very first that Bugsy Siegal had built in the fifties, over fifty years ago. And now it is the place to go to, little did he know then. Just seeing the lights of the hotels got my body excited and I couldn't wait to get there.

CHAPTER 2

▼

LOVE IS A MANY SPLENDID THING

I checked in and threw my luggage down on the bed and headed right back downstairs to the nearest Crap Table. I found a spot on the end and waited for a few minutes to see when the best time was to jump in and be a part of the action. I stood at the ten-dollar table and played a few hands and won close to eighty bucks and was very pleased with myself. The room filled up, and the noise grew louder, with screams of joy as well as disappointment. After two hours and three drinks later, I knew that it was time to head out.

I took a stroll on the strip, and looked at the bright lights and the enormous neon signs. It was all very overwhelming. The thought of what it might be like to continuously maintain this kind of city, day and night, would sure keep a lot of people busy. I could only imagine all of the stories that occurred, and the lives of those that were changing at that very moment. I knew before I would call it a night that I would want to play one more game, and drink one more brandy. So I headed to Caesars Palace, where to my amazement, I found a second wind come upon me. I knew that I had made the right choice. This moment was going to change the rest of my life.

For some reason, Caesar's Palace has always been one of my most favorite hotels on the strip. If you want to find pretty faces, they are here. Not saying that they are all staying at this hotel. But this is *the* place to meet women. The Venetian is a wonderful hotel, with its sunken suites and lush decorations. Although it is a bit pricey, it is a great place to bed someone down for the night.

The din was beyond expectation, loud, nearly ear throttling, to a point that you could not even hear anything. The people were excited, laughing, trying to talk loudly over everyone else's conversation. So I just coasted from table to table, trying to find a little opening where I could slither into a place to lay down my chips. I always made it a point to be at the end of a craps table, so I could see more of the betting and the faces of the people.

There was a spot at this table, and I gave the guy wearing a black suit, two crisp one hundred dollar bills. He gave me twenty, ten-dollar chips and I placed them in the small slots before me. I looked to see how the betting was going. Was the table working for the bettors or not, or was the action against the house?

I placed ten dollars on the Come Line. Lo and behold, a seven came up. I tried it again. Then the number six was thrown. So I played the numbers for odds, and even laid a ten-dollar bet on the hard six. I looked like I knew what I was doing. And I loved to watch the other gamblers, as they followed the same routine over and over again.

The men handling the money for the bets were quick, courteous and looking to make some good tips by helping the bettors win. That is how they make their tips. But, of course, eventually, even after winning a few games, reality sets in and the bettors will eventually lose all of their chips regardless.

As I am watching the play, I noticed that a new bettor had arrived on the scene. She just slinked in next to the person on the right of me and she was all set to place some bets. She was a long-haired blond, with a tight fitting black sweater and white slacks. Another pretty face, I thought, not overly angular, but sweet looking. I had a good view from where I was standing and was enjoying this new addition to the table. She was trying to figure out how to bet her chips.

"Can I get you something to drink," a voice came over my shoulder.

It was the cocktail waitress wearing her cute little Roman outfit, carrying a tray, a notepad and a pen.

"Yes," I responded. "I think I would like to have a brandy."

As she started to walk away, I then said, "Oh, by the way, see that blond next to this gentleman? Ask her what she would like and just say that I offered to take care of it."

Now, we all know that drinks are free in the casinos, but this was an opportunity to get her attention. If she would only look over to my direction as I was not exactly next to her. There was too much action at the table to get her attention. I was having fun with the game of dice, so why not approach some pretty young lady and try my luck with her? Who knows? I may wind up with some company for the evening. Heck, this is Las Vegas, the city that does not have any clocks. The night was young. And I was venturing out to find me some fun and perhaps a little sex afterward.

She looked up at me as the cocktail waitress moved away from her with her drink. She smiled, but then she had to concentrate on her betting. I did not even have a chance to smile back. She was so engrossed in placing her bets that I felt a little foolish. So I waited until this big guy who stood between her and I would walk away.

But everyone was so intense on betting, that there was never going to be that opportunity to get closer to her. Perhaps I could have asked him to move into my spot and I would squeeze next to her. But that would mean taking his chips and moving them into another slot and that may break his luck pattern. That was not a wise thing to do at the moment. I was getting a bit frustrated as to what I could do to get closer to her.

So I watched her and watched my own betting. It was kind of difficult to do as you could lose the concentration and not know what was happening on the table. Craps is a game of concentration. You bet the way the dice is thrown. You bet either with the bettor or with the house, the Come Line, or the Don't Come Line. The money was going back and forth. The people were hoping to make their point and win some money. There was yelling and screaming from the other side of the table as the dice thrower was getting the momentum to a boiling point.

"EO-ELEVEN", he shouted, as he laid down several five dollar bets. "I am looking for a Six," he yelled. "But I will take anything that will pay me money."

He was looking to hit pay dirt by throwing his number. I was hoping to make some headway with another cute number, one with blond hair and a black top that revealed a nice figure. Everything is relative. If I were to win my bet, there would be a better chance for her to look at me. If we both reached for our chips at the same time, we may touch each other's hands by accident. I needed to get her attention.

I 'accidentally' rolled one of my ten-dollar chips to her on the felt. It landed right in front of her. Now I thought that this 'accident' would get her to look at me. But those casino guys are right there. 'Johnny-on-the-Spot'! He reached over and retrieved the chip for me and placed it in front of me. What a guy! No wonder they make good tips. So I naturally thanked him, although he broke up my little plan. (Schmuck). Now I had to think of something else to get her attention. As I put the chip back in the slot, I looked up, and the cute little blond smiled at me once again.

Her eyes were as blue as a perfect sky. She winked at me, and I took that as 'thanks for the drink'. I did not want to make any wrong moves because I felt that I had it in the bag if I played my cards right. The big guy in between us finally grabbed his few chips and quickly went on his way. Ever so smoothly, I glided to his spot and continued with my game, and waited for her to speak first.

After a minute or so, she turned to me and said, "You seem to know this game quite well. I'm impressed. And by the way, thanks for the drink. I'm Christy."

She held out her hand for me to take it. It was the least of the things I wanted to take from her. I shook her hand but had to continue to focus on the game or else I would fall behind or decide that it was time to quit.

"I'm David," I replied. "It is a pleasure to meet you. With regards to the drink, you're quite welcome."

But what I really wanted to say was 'you are quite welcome in my bed any-time.'

We both continued to play our individual games commenting on occasion, and cheering for the other when we won. As a nice gesture, she would sympathet-ically rub my shoulder when I would miss a number. But each time she did, my heart jumped out of my chest, and my slacks felt a bit tighter where it counted. I thought that maybe I could purposely lose so I could get more of her touch, but thought better of it, and didn't. During the next half hour, my mind no longer could focus on what I needed to do to win, only to win this lovely blonde in my bed.

I finally got up enough nerve and asked her, "Interested in trying our hand somewhere else, say as a team effort?"

How bold of me. But this was the whole intention of leaving the table, and opening up another game of chance with this woman. This was a way of becom-ing a whole person once again. I felt revived and excited that I was now able to be a person that I had always admired in others. I used to marvel at those who could be so courageous and take the initiative, go for the brass ring, and wind up with the prize for the evening. My friend Mario was like that.

I looked at Christy and she was extremely focused on her game. I decided to hold out a few more rounds to see where she was headed. I then noticed that she too had a grasp of the game of Craps, and that was a good sign. Christy was an intelligent woman, and a pretty one to boot. This was a definite 'go' in my book.

It took her a good ten minutes to respond, but she did so by saying, "I'd love to try my hand elsewhere, David. Lead the way."

I was ecstatic. She actually was pursuing my proposal and I had a chance to make it with this gal. We grabbed our remaining chips and headed to the cashier to check out. As I walked just a bit behind her, I noticed her legs, the rear end, and the way she walked. I was impressed with this woman. Her stride was sexy, and the way she held her head up high, showed confidence. I was in heaven.

I could not think too far ahead, which could have been my downfall. I just decided that I would take each minute as it came. I wanted, at that moment, to be someone that I only dreamed about. I wanted to be that someone who could land a beautiful woman such as she was. I almost had to pretend that I was a different person for now, and eventually take on the personae of this new guy forever.

We got our money from the cashier and she turned to me sweetly. "Let's go back to my hotel. I am staying at the Luxor. They have good tables there and it might not be so crowded this time of night."

Of course I said yes, and followed her out into the street. I thought she wanted me to lead the way. Mmm…guess I was with a woman who knew what she wanted, and I was just hoping that it was going to me by the end of this evening. We started to walk on the Strip and the crowds were only slightly starting to decrease. I knew from my last visit to Vegas that after midnight, the people are a very different breed from those who roam the streets in the afternoon.

Only the die-hards, and those who have won big, keep mulling around. Of course, there are the sore losers who want to start a fight and need some psychological guidance. But in this case, my mind could not focus on anything analytical. I was completely enthralled by this blond and the fact that she was in control of her destination and hoped that it would be me.

"So, David, where are you from?" she asked, as we walked to her hotel.

"I live in Dana Point, in Orange County, in southern California," I replied. "And you?"

"I'm originally from Boston, and just love this place! I now have a place in Irvine, also in Orange County," she said, as the excitement was building, and so very appealing. She actually lived about twenty minutes away from me.

I hated to have to disappoint myself by getting to the bottom of things too quickly, but I finally had the courage to ask her if she was here by herself or with others. I had to know if I was wasting my time, or did it really matter? Was she with a group, a boyfriend, a bunch of girls from the east or the west coast, or by herself? I hesitated, but knew my time was limited. I did not want to make the wrong move and make a complete fool of myself if I were to proposition her to go to bed with me. So I went for it anyway.

"Are you here by yourself?"

We were crossing Las Vegas Boulevard. The traffic was busy as usual, even at this late hour, and I took her arm as if I were her Sir Galahad.

"Thank you, David," she said with a smile. "I came with two other girls. They decided to see a show but I had been there, done that. I just needed to spend some time by myself. We are all staying at the Luxor Hotel where we are headed. And where are you staying at?"

I was somewhat relieved except for the fact that they may all be sharing a room together. Boy, you gotta think of all these things before you actually take a woman to bed. Especially if she invites you to her bed! It was getting all so complicated and stressful. This whole thing could have turned out to be a big nothing. But I kept with the program and could only hope for the best.

"Oh, I have a suite at the Venetian Hotel but I prefer to gamble elsewhere," I replied. "Did you know that the percentages of winning at the Venetian are one of the worst of any of the hotels?"

"No, I did not know that, David," she answered with a most pronounced smile. "I am not a true gambler in any sense of the word. I just like the action. I spend a few bucks, have some fun, and then it is time to do something else. I hate to lose. I don't know anyone who doesn't mind losing. Yet, we come here thinking that we are going to win the big easy. Not me. I come to Vegas to take a break from my job and get away from the same old mundane things."

She continued. "And are you here on business, or did you leave your little wifey back at the spa in the hotel?"

Now I was getting mixed vibes from her and I had to keep my cool. We had crossed the street and people were walking in all directions, looking up and down, to the left and to the right. The fountains were spurting out tremendous waterfalls. We could hear sirens in the distance, the air was humid and I was getting hot. Was it the humidity or was it this lovely young thing on my arm with whom I had not let go yet.

I sort of glanced at her white pants and the curvature of her ass and it was exciting to watch, as she took one step after another. Her long blond hair kept swaying back and forth on her face, and she had this great complexion about her. There was quite a pause before I was able to respond to her. I was sure she was waiting for me to tell her if I was alone or married.

"Christy, I decided to come here for a break from work," I explained. "You see, my wife died nearly two years ago and all I do is work, day and night. I teach psychology at a junior college and with all the term papers, and preparation that I have to go through, it was time to get away and relax my brain for awhile."

I hoped that this would get her sympathy a bit. Perhaps, being a teacher and writer, it may have turned out to be a turnoff to her. Maybe she expected me to say that I was a president of a design-engineering firm, and that we were working on the latest software for humanity. It was always difficult for me to find the right words to say to women when you do not know them. I just didn't have too much experience in these kinds of situations. I was basically never out looking for anyone since I was married to Martha for many years.

We were passing some of the hotels, and people were all over the street. Some seemed happy, while others appeared to be down on their luck. The horns were honking, the people were literally scrambling for space on the walk paths, and Christy and I were just walking along, close to each other, holding on to the moment.

"This is wonderful, David," she finally remarked. "You sound like you have it all together. A psychology teacher! Wow! I took psychology as a minor and found it fascinating. Are you going to try to psycho-analyze me later?"

I took this as a good sign. I took it as we would spend some time together later. Now, how was I going to play this out without showing my hand? Boy, it was so much easier taking high cholesterol crap out of someone's cart at the supermarket. I didn't know if I could do this and get away with it. I decided I may as well just be me, and let the chips fall where they may. This was only the first night. I had plans to be in Vegas for three nights.

I thought to myself. 'Just go with the flow, David, and try not to fuck it up.'

"Actually, I am good at teaching and love to work with students," I exclaimed. "But the fact of the matter is that I turned down many jobs with large companies in human resources because I felt that I have a talent to guide youngsters, and teach them how to think for themselves. This is why I chose teaching."

The conversation was getting a bit too off course. We were approaching the Luxor Hotel and I was ready for a drink.

As we walked through the doors, I politely approached the subject. "You know, Christy, after that walk, I would like to have a drink at the bar. I need something refreshing. Come with me to the bar so we could just sit and get acquainted. I would truly like that. It has been a long day and I am not sure if I want to stand at the craps table right now."

"By the way," I added, "are your friends all sharing the same room at the hotel?"

She did not look at me at that moment, but chose to sit at one of the empty seats at the bar. She took out her wallet and placed a fifty on the table as if to tell the bartender that she wanted to play the poker machine. By playing these games, all drinks are free. Was this simply a good gesture to me so I would not have to pay for her drinks, or was it that she had class and knew how to treat a gentleman?

"Actually, we are all staying in our own rooms," she responded. "I suppose you might look at this as an act of independency. And who knows, some of us may want to party while others do not."

The bartender came and we ordered drinks. We each put some money into the slot machine in front of us, and it was time for me to make the next move. Either, I was going to score and party, or I was going back to my hotel room, alone. Deep down inside, I knew that I was not good at this. Just a homey, looking for a good time! But then again, aren't we all? Was this why she chose to ask me back to the Luxor where she is staying?

"I would love to party with you, Christy, if you are willing to party with me."

What a dumb shit thing to say, I thought afterward. If this line was going to turn her off, I was going back to my room and watch television for the next three days.

I could see that she looked rather surprised, although she was not facing me. She kept putting quarters in the poker machine and her eyebrows lifted. Her lips looked as soft as silk, and I kept having this desire to feel them on mine. It was late, and I was being bold. But I felt that I had nothing to lose by asking her that question. I waited patiently, like a schoolboy and his first crush, and all the background noises became mute, if only in my head.

My heart palpitated, and the sweat from anticipation was building, not only under my arms, but I felt the wetness beginning to formulate on my forehead. The last thing I wanted was for her to see this. I brushed my hair with my hand, and rubbed my pants to relieve the slight moisture I had felt. What was I so goddamn nervous about? I was a grown man looking to get laid. Basically, that was it in a nutshell.

She stopped what she was doing, and turned to me.

"David, you are a sweet man, and I like you, for how little I have known of you. Perhaps we can finish our drinks and get to know each other better. I will be here for the next couple of days and who knows…" She paused, and looked back at the machine. "Maybe there is a party that is just right for us, somewhere."

She smiled slightly, but I knew that she might have felt that I was moving too fast for her, or did she have something else up her sleeve?

I felt totally embarrassed, and wanted to make a mad dash for the nearest exit. I knew that I had to be a gentleman and maintain a level of cool, if only she would say more. I needed to reestablish what self-esteem had been diminished. But, why was I feeling so insecure? It was so easy for me to take control in the supermarket, to decide for someone else, that what she was buying was not in her best interest. And then, meeting a stranger in a mall garage, and chatting it up, it felt so natural at the time.

I thought, with Julie being just as attractive as Christy, why did I feel so disconnected in my own mind and body? Could it be that it was almost 2 am and I had not eaten anything but a sandwich all day? Now, several cocktails later, I was feeling either weak or just tired. Or was I just not ready or experienced enough to say or do the right thing?

Surprisingly, like a bolt of lightening coming out of the sky, Christy put her hand on my leg, and turned to me and gave me a soft kiss on my lips.

She looked into my eyes and smiled so beautifully, and said, "Just because you have been so nice, and that I feel comfortable around you, David. I hope you don't mind."

I took her face with both of my hands and held her gently, imagining that I was holding porcelain china, and looked into her blue eyes that reminded me of the sea and the sky all in one.

"I think you are very attractive, Christy, and there is nothing more I would like to do than to get to know you better. If it pleases you, perhaps we could find a more private place to get better acquainted?"

"David, please, let's not rush it!"

Was she some kind of tease? Was she playing with me? Why was I not getting the feeling that I had to remain calm, although my groins were ready to explode all over the bar stool? I pulled back with a slight look of disappointment, and she noticed my doing so. But I didn't want her to, and that was a mistake on my part, I thought. We sat in silence for a few minutes and I ordered another drink and asked her if she wanted one too.

"How about if I make us a drink in my room," she replied. "We can talk there?"

Before I knew it, I was following her to her room. It looked like a million other hotel rooms, but I knew that there was something different about her room. Was it because it was her room, a room filled with feminine clothes, lightly colored suitcases, lots of cosmetics on the bathroom counter, perhaps something that I had not seen in a long while?

But it did not matter to me. All that mattered was that I did the right thing and made this woman feel for me and invite me to her room. The anxiety of that thought may still have not helped my confidence any, but I thought it best to remain centered and calm and go with her lead. She told me to relax and she would fix us a small drink from the little bar in the cabinet.

"Boy, isn't it amazing how much they charge for these little nips?"

Another dumb ass remark! I must have sounded like a young kid who never got laid in his life, yet lied to his friends that he was no longer a virgin. Oh well, live and learn!

Time had passed. I opened my eyes and it was a bit dark so I could not see anything. Where was I? What did we do this evening? Did we actually make love? How come I could not remember anything that had occurred? Was I too intoxicated to realize the feel of her body next to mine, her warm breasts against my chest, those lovely lips pressing against my own? Did we have sex or did we both just lie down and go to sleep?

I looked at the clock on the dresser and it was close to 6:00 am. I walked toward the windows, and from a crack in the drapes, I saw the thin outline of a sunrise that was creeping out of the sky, above the other hotels in the distance. As I pulled the drapes open, ever so slightly, I looked into the morning sky and I could see the Needle Dome, the Paris Hotel's Eiffel Tower, and a vast desert in the distance. Morning was upon us, and the evening past was just a blank. I followed this strange woman to her room and I was not sure what we did here. And I looked down at my body and I was not wearing anything. I just walked out of a woman's bed, naked, and I was not sure whether or not we had engaged in sex at all.

How many goddamn drinks did I have? Was I totally drunk not to remember if I got laid or was all this a dream? I must have been dreaming if I could not remember what had happened. And I wondered if Christy would tell me if she enjoyed whatever I did or did not do to her in the past few hours. I felt like a stupid Shmuck!

"Hey big guy," whispered a voice from the other part of the room. "Are you okay? What's ya doin'?"

I looked back to the bed and it was Christy, half asleep, pulling the covers over her body, and just barely getting out of never-never-land. She looked so gorgeous just lying there, with her beautiful face, her long blond hair and her long bare legs, half out of the covers.

Now I was feeling more conscious than I did before. I wondered if I was feeling up to making love to her. And this time, yeah, this time, feel the sensation that I wanted to feel.

"Hi love," I responded. "How do you feel this morning?"

She just smiled at me and turned the other way. She was still out of it. I thought I had better hit the john and grab a pee while she was still in dreamland. I hedged my way past the bed and headed toward the bathroom. Her black sweater was on the chair by the desk, the white pants on the floor next to her shoes, and her panties were closer to the bed. This woman whom I fell asleep with was absolutely, positively totally naked. I hope I had a good time, although I did not remember a damn thing. Boy, was I a total idiot. Better take a pee before I let loose down my leg.

The bathroom was clean except for her toiletries on the sink, a few bottles of cologne and perfume, box of Q-tips and lipstick, toothbrush and toothpaste, and some mouthwash. That was what I really needed. I flushed the toilet and used one of the new bars of soap and then washed my mouth with the sample bottle of mouthwash. As I came out of the bathroom, Christy was turned toward me and once again was giving me one of her sexual smiles that really got to me last night.

"How's my big guy this morning?" she again asked. "Are you feeling refreshed or do you want to get back into bed?"

"Maybe I should not have taken a pee," I thought. "The big guy ain't so big no more."

I turned toward her and walked to the bed and sat down. "I feel wonderful, sweetheart," I replied. "It was so great to spend the evening with you, lying next to you, and falling asleep with you in my arms."

What was I saying? I had no idea what I did, let alone fall asleep with her in my arms. So I thought it was a good line and continued.

"Let me lie down next to you and give you a back massage," I said.

I slowly moved under the covers and placed my chest against her back. I ran my fingers through her hair and pressed my body close to hers. She just lay there, not saying a word. So far I must have been doing well. How the hell did I know? I was just reacting out my fantasies and hoping for the best. Maybe this time, I would know what I was doing and not wake up without a clue as to what I may not have done the night before.

"David," she again whispered to me. "You are so loving! I am so glad that you came to bed with me last night. I really enjoyed having you next to me and keeping me warm and comfortable. I just enjoyed knowing that you were there and that we were both able to fall asleep without any problem. Thank you for spending the night with me."

In my wildest dreams, I was a bit perplexed at all of this. How easy it is to take a woman to bed and have sex with her, to simply play with a woman, and remember what you did and enjoy the memories. But this was something else. I had a memory like a minute. What the hell happened that made her feel so good? It was best not to ask her.

Maybe it was time to take advantage of the moment and do what came naturally. I really wanted to know how it felt to make love to this woman.

So I took my hands and started to massage her back, up and down, from side to side, in little movements, then in sweeping curves. All the while, my body was aching to make love to her. I knew that it would come sooner or later. I just had to keep my cool and everything would take its due course. I just knew it would. Now why the hell did I answer Nature's call? It would have been an immediate love making. I tried to see if I could get this thing back up to its potential and show her what I had. I was ready for action and was hoping that she was too.

"A refill, sir?"

The waitress looked tired but she was ready to serve. The restaurant was already bustling with people ready to start their day. The Venetian Hotel has this fine restaurant for breakfast and they have a menu fit for a king. I watched in awe, as the waitress was running her trays up and down the counter. Then there is the little French cook, wearing what looked like a dirty apron that he probably had on the day before. He kept coming out of the kitchen looking at the people, and then going back to prepare more food. They must have lots of cooks back there.

This is a rather large restaurant with lots of tables. I just felt more comfortable sitting at the counter than at a table. The tables were set up for two or more parties. It was late morning but I really needed this cup of warm, herbal tea. I sat there drinking my tea and had the newspaper folded neatly in front of me. I was still in amazement. I had a most delightful morning, with a beautiful, yet unfamiliar woman, wrapped around me.

She kept her long legs holding me tightly, while I felt her body that had this fresh scent of lilac flowers that could have been newly picked from a garden. There was her long blond mane touching my skin and swaying with her every movement. We had made love this morning, but she did not want to join me for breakfast. Oh well, it was closer to lunch anyway. I was not that hungry. I was completely full in another way. Christy had brought me an immense feeling of satisfaction unlike anyone I had been with before. Well, there was this woman in Hawaii…but that was over two years ago.

I kept remembering the way she kissed me, gently on my neck, after I massaged her back. She then turned over and curled up around me, and caressed my shoulders so tenderly. We did not talk during our pleasures and though she moaned from joy afterward, we still did not mention whether or not we had made love the night before. After two orgasms and an hour of passionate post-oral play, we lay spent on the wet, steamy bed, and stared at the ceiling.

I did ask her if she was okay and she simply said, "Wonderful, David, simply wonderful."

I then got up to dress and asked her to come to breakfast with me. She said that she better get out and locate her friends, whom she had snubbed the night before and whom might be worried that they had not heard from her. We hugged and kissed before I left her behind, and we exchanged our phone numbers to our hotel rooms, and our cell phones, just in case.

In case we wanted to get laid again later, of course.

After experiencing a night of the unknown and an early morning of delightful sex, I felt lost in a cloud. I was not sure whether or not I would want to call her, or I would just chalk it up as a one-nighter.

I had felt a strong affection for Christy, yet I still knew very little about her. I was successful in my endeavor for pleasure, but there were unknown gaps that would possibly stress me out by my making mountains out of molehills. Perhaps, it was not necessary to question her, but simply enjoy the experience of the moment. As I sat on the stool in the restaurant, sipping my second cup of tea and eating some dry toast, I kept eyeing my cell phone, thinking that I should call her and meet her later for another go around, if she desired. I didn't want to push it, but the thought of another evening with Christy sure sounded much better than to sit at a slot machine or stand at a Crap Table by myself.

I left the restaurant and went up to my room. I thought it best to get her out of my mind for the time being so I could think clearer on what I was doing here. I suppose what bothered me the most was that we did not talk much in the way of feelings, let alone where we would go from here. Was I so out of the loop that a one-night stand could be erased so easily? Or was I stuck in a time warp where even a passionate encounter with a stranger could lead to more pleasures in the future and be a meaningful relationship? Just as I entered the room, my cell phone rang. I looked down to see the number. It was her!

My heart skipped a beat and I almost started to pick up on my emotions, but caught myself. I let it ring one more time before answering.

"Hi sweetie!" Was that too much to say? I wondered.

"Hi David! It's Christy. We were wondering, my friends and I, if you would like to meet us for dinner. They are dying to meet you."

I smiled with a wide grin, and though I remained calm, I was so elated that she called me. "That would be wonderful, Christy. Where and when?"

We discussed where…at the Bellagio Restaurant, and when, would be around 6 pm, and then we hung up. My cloud nine was even bigger than it was before. I was elated. I sang some love songs in the shower and gathered some great looking clothes from the drawer in the dresser. Ah, the new pair of white pants had not been worn yet. And I loved my deep purple shirt, which would truly make me look sexy. That was the key. I had to look good.

I also thought of buying her a gift with a nice card, and to make plans for our future trips if and when we were going to see each other after this week. I would have loved to bring her back home to meet my little Maltese dog and she would have fallen in love with him. Women love little dogs, especially a little Maltese. I truly wanted to spend every evening of my life, wrapped around her gorgeous body.

Yet I wanted to make a lasting impression on her friends and have them say to her, 'Boy, you have a winner, here, Christy.'

Truthfully, I really wanted to skip dinner and be back to where we were only hours before. Under the covers, searching each other's body and arousing each other like it was heaven on earth. I thought about how her picture would look on the mantel over the fireplace and how pretty her eyes were when she gazed into mine. I thought about the way her lips stuck to mine like glue, and how her tongue nibbled at my ear, and she knew exactly what she was doing to get me excited.

I remembered how she rubbed her long, soft fingers down my chest, and the slow motion of her body, moving like a symphony up and down on mine. She was playing my song, over and over again in my mind. I also thought of the way she smiled and opened and closed her eyes. Oh boy, I did remember a lot of things. I was thinking like a school kid on his first date. I also thought that I better not think that I was falling in love, or someone had better shoot me right there, on the spot. I looked around the room, and thank goodness, there was no one there but me. For a guy in his forties, I sure acted more like a teenager who just experienced his first sexual encounter. I took a deep breath and started to get dressed.

It was late morning, and I was wide awake from a wild evening and morning. I needed that hot tea that I had earlier, plus the dry toast was great. At least, I had something in my stomach. I was not even hungry, but I needed to walk around and cool my jets for a while. I had this unusual energy that was making me feel like a total man today. I didn't know if it was the fact that I scored last night and this morning, or maybe, just maybe…it was something else.

"Wonderful, David." Those words kept ringing in my head.

I had hoped that this was not a one-night-stand. It was too good to just die and not do it again with this woman. I stood there, staring at the walls in my hotel room before I decided what I should do today and kill some time before I would meet Christy and her friends. I looked at my body and it was pretty lean for a mid 40ish guy, who had slight graying hair, standing nearly 6 feet tall, and a fairly good physique. The suite was beautiful, sort of a Roman setting, made for a king. They even have bathrobes hanging in the closet, like togas for the Roman soldiers. I felt like I had conquered my quest and was a Roman soldier ready for more action.

In one way, I was glad that Christy had called me. But to meet her friends for dinner was not something I had in mind. I called her 'Sweetie' when I answered the phone, and that was a bit much, even for me. Was I getting smitten over this woman who gave me the pleasures of life? Why were her friends dying to meet with me? Why did I consent so easily to meeting with her friends? What would happen if they thought that I was just another 'shmuck' with earlaps?

I decided to look for my pair of comfortable Lorenzo Banfi shoes that were made in Milano, that I had bought for special occasions. I had some time to kill so I decided to go to the Hotel shops, perhaps find a nice gift for Christy. The shops are so exquisite at the Venetian. Each one tells a story unto itself, and the atmosphere is so relaxing.

I walked through the shopping mall, looking in all of the windows. What do I get for Christy, I thought. I was thinking of a piece of jewelry, a sweater, a blouse, a pair of Italian sunglasses, or a lovely card? While casually strolling in this land out of Venice, I looked up into the sky, and the top of the ceiling was a pale blue with white clouds, giving the appearance of being outdoors. I was indoors, but there was this ambiance of being in Italy, walking in the streets of an Italian City, with outdoor cafes and Italian speaking sales people.

It was then that I saw the place that was so unique and had all of these hundreds of great looking fifteenth century masks. That was what I would get her as a friendship gift. So many to choose from, in beautiful color, in black and white, big ones, small ones, happy and sad faces, and they were all literally so beautiful. I walked through the store until I found the two that I thought were outstanding. The total price was about six hundred and fifty. I thought, so what! I was going to make a statement in front of her friends. I was going to look like a prince among thieves. I just wanted to make a good impression so I could take Christy back to the room and make love to her again and again.

I deposited the masks up in my room until it was time to go to dinner, and decided to head back to the casino. I had enough time to relax, hit the tables and have some fun. I did not do so badly the day before as I had some winnings left and decided to try my luck at the crap table once again. Knowing that the odds are not as good here at the Venetian as they are in the other hotels, so they tell me, it just did not matter. I was sitting on top of the world. Now I could sit on top of my game and enjoy throwing the dice, making the odds or just crapping out. I already scored last night, and anything else today would only be icing on the cake. So I headed toward the tables.

CHAPTER 3

▼

LUCK BE MY LADY TONIGHT

Passing through the slot machine area, I thought I would try my luck at the machines. I found a quarter machine that was empty. You need to play three quarters, and you have a better chance to win more money. But you also lose three times as much if you are not lucky. Just another way for the casinos to get your money faster! The slots are basically the best way to lose more money than you may realize. That is why they are called 'one armed bandits'.

'Oh, what the hell, let me try this machine' I thought, as I stopped at one of the Elvis slots that gave you a chance to spin the wheel for an extra bonus. I deposited a hundred in the slot and I had all of these plays to last for a while. So I started to play the machine. Pressing the button to spin the wheel did not take too much effort, which probably an idiot could do in his sleep. I wouldn't have been surprised if some people sat there, pressing the buttons while sleeping at the machine. Every few seconds, you just press the button. Seventy-five cents per spin seemed to go very quickly. How come I was not getting a win here? How boring it was.

"Can I interest you in a drink," said this nice young thing, carrying a tray. "Would you like a cocktail?"

I thought that it was a bit too early in the day to start drinking and paused. Then a voice two seats over remarked, "When you finish there, could you get me a vodka martini?"

I looked over to where this voice was coming from. There was this rather bright, red-headed, full busted, feisty young thing, with two large white cups of quarters, placing her change in two machines, while watching the wheel spin around and around. She was intent on winning a lot by hoping that her chances would double by using the two slot machines.

"I would like an ice tea, please," I said.

I just could not handle any liquor at this time. My stomach was still feeling the pain of all the drinks I had last night. I was not used to this shit. Boy, you sure can develop a taste for alcohol here in Vegas. The drinks are free and all you do is tip the waitresses. A little rest in the gut was what I needed, not chest pains.

"Hey, is that all you are having?" said the feisty haired young thing, who had the gall to even try to put me down.

Heck, I got laid last night to the best looking woman in Vegas, and this little pain in the ass was making a mockery of me for ordering some ice tea.

"Hey, it is none of your fucking business what I am having, okay?" I said with authority.

Now she would know that I was not such an idiot. I was not going to buy her a drink. Nor was I going to sit there and be intimidated by her stupid remarks. My goddamn dick was still sore as hell and my groins were aching all over from the night before. I just wanted to relax and find some alone-time before I met the women for dinner. Who the hell was this bitch anyway, getting off like that to me?

"I am so sorry," she replied. "I did not mean to upset you. I guess I am having a hard time at the slots. Ice tea is good."

What the hell was this? Why was she picking on me? Did I look like a wimp or what? What were her intentions? I did not need to get involved with her. I could have just as easily cashed in my quarters and walked to another machine. I already found my lover for this trip. Why did I want to respond to this woman? But she was so cute, sitting there, with her knees crossed, her long red hair hanging over one shoulder, and her body was a complete knockout. Maybe she didn't mean anything by it. Maybe I was becoming too paranoid and over protective. I had to cool it a bit and take a deep breath and forget the stupid remarks. Both hers and mine!

"That's okay," I reassured her. "I am sorry for using such language. I was just in some other time zone. Okay?"

"Hey, handsome," she said without a moment to lose, "get your cute little butt down and relax. This is Las Vegas and I am also here to just enjoy the trip. I do not need a lesson in vulgarity but I do apologize if I upset you. So let it go at that."

She sounded sincere and I was not sure how to handle this. I slowly leaned back on the seat and introduced myself.

"My name is David," I said. "I am here for a break from teaching and it has been stressful, so I needed to get away from it all. I just wanted some peace and quiet, and I did not expect to hear from anyone like you telling me what I should or should not drink. I feel totally embarrassed for using four letter words and talking so much to you."

She looked at me with her deep black eyes and just stared. I could see that I again spoke too much and made a complete jackass out of myself. I could be so dense sometimes that I could just crawl up into a shell never to be heard from again.

"So what else is on your mind, David?" she asked with a roving eye on my body, the other in my head.

Here was one tough little bitch who was getting my craw. I just didn't know where to take this. I then started to continue to play the slots and tried to ignore her. What was I getting myself into? Who was this little impish hot tomato who was teasing me with her questioning, and why did I want to go there? I really didn't. As a matter of fact, there was something about this gal that bothered me. I could not place it, but maybe it was going to come to me later. I just knew that there was something not Kosher here. So I went back to my slot machine, trying to find out why I had not won a game yet. There was another push of the button, and another three quarters down the tube. Boy, it did not take too much talent to do this.

"Hey, David," she again muttered. "I asked you a question. What's the matter, the cat got your tongue?"

Jesus Christ, who was this bitch who wouldn't leave me alone? Why was I the chosen one for this annoying person to bother? I really didn't need this shit. In a minute, I was going to get up, cash out my quarters and get away from her. I took another deep breath and just sat there and decided to see where this was going. For some strange reason, I was getting curious.

I turned to her and threw a question back to her. "Are you having a good time at the slots? Are you staying at this hotel? Should I be able to call you by any specific name?"

I thought that I may as well play the game and see where this was going. I was not looking for another woman to keep my crotch hot and heavy. If my questions burned her soul, that's tough. So I thought of being a macho kind of guy and take this to the limit. I really did not care. But she really may have been a nice person and I may have been acting like a jackass.

"Yes…and yes…and you can call me Rita", she answered as she held out her hand for me to shake.

Her hand was sweaty and I couldn't get over how red her hair was. It looked like a flaming fireball of wild curls. I leaned back into my chair and hoped that it was not going to take too long for my second encounter with Christy. I looked at my watch. I still had a lot of time to kill before I was to meet her friends for dinner. I had mixed feelings on this. But after presenting the beautiful masks that I had bought for her, at our dinner, I was sure to make a lasting impression. At least I would show that I had some class.

And again, Rita rambled on. "So, David, what is up with you anyway?"

More interrogations, and her tone was starting to rub me the wrong way. There was something brash and derogatory about this broad. I just could not put my finger on it. Speaking psychologically, this was a trait that would normally make me run for the hills.

I turned to her with a deep sigh and replied. "Look, Rita, is it? I am a bit busy and I am not in the mood to chat it up at the moment. I'm sorry."

I just did not feel like making conversation nor what this woman thought of me and whether or not I had any manners. I also did not care if I would use the "F" word again if she didn't get the hint. I would not apologize the next time I did.

As I again went back to my slot machine, there was this whining voice once again. "Hey, that's too bad. I think you are quite a handsome devil, and I really like those shoes. Where'd get them, here at the hotel?"

Mmmm…now she was flattering me and I liked it. So maybe I would be a bit less angered and try being nice. Perhaps it was the better way to ease out of this situation with this pest.

"Why thank you," I said. "I have plans this evening and I want to look my best."

Why was I telling her this? She was suckering me into more conversation and I began hating myself for it. I could have easily gotten up and walked away, but something made me stay, perhaps wanting more compliments. She slid over to the chair next to mine and brought her two buckets of coins with her. She then leaned so she could face me, putting her two hands on my legs.

"David, I know we just met, but you are really turning me on. There is something elusive about you. I certainly can overlook your previous rudeness, if you want to come with me for a good time."

Jesus Christ! What the hell was happening here? Was I dreaming this or what? I wanted to wake up if I was. But then again, how often did I get a chance like this, two days in a row. And tonight, might make a third, if all goes well. I thought about it and thought about it. She looked impatient, but again, I didn't care.

"Well, what's the problem, David? Wouldn't you like to have a good time with me?"

"Rita, I am flattered, but I just don't know…"

"What's not to know, David? I am here and you are here, and we could go right to my room, right upstairs and have a good time,"

She seemed a bit tipsy already, not even three in the afternoon, and her eyes were glowing with that blackness I had seen earlier, that could either be frightening or extremely exotic. Should I have gone with this interesting, yet, aggressive redhead I thought, and have a fling before I go on my way to yet another fling? Should I have told her to go fuck herself yet again? The idea of flipping a coin crossed my mind, as I was holding a bucket of nearly a hundred dollars worth.

I even reached into my bucket to grab one but I turned to her, saying, "Thank you, Rita, for the lovely invite. But I'm on my way to dinner shortly. Perhaps we can make it another time?" Perfect, I thought. I gave an acceptable out.

"Well, okay. Here is my room number in case you should change your mind." She ripped off a piece of paper from something in her purse and jotted down four numbers, 1432, with a signature of 'call me when you are free, Rita'.

I took it and said thanks, and she got up and grabbed her buckets and left the slot area. I took a deep breath, and it seemed that was all I had been doing anyway, in the past twelve hours. I had felt a sense of relief, but also an excitement.

If what transpired later on did not pan out to my liking, I always had a back up. Not bad, considering up until yesterday, I was down on my luck with the ladies. Pleased with myself, I walked over to a crap table to kill the couple of hours before meeting Christy. I decided to use my new self-confidence to meet new women and make more friends.

I thought of giving away the small piece of paper with Rita's room number to some other poor soul who may have been looking for someone like Rita. I looked at the paper, and on the reverse side, it had an address in Pacific Palisades, southern California with the initials, CM. Oh well, I thought, it was probably nothing important. Maybe that was where Rita came from, I thought. Or, there was the possibility that the person living at this address may have been a friend of hers. I was smiling loudly, and very anxious to start my new life. I had a plan, I had a date, I had an invite to meet new women, and I had nice shoes. I was the man!!!

The crap table was pretty busy, lots of business type suits, some Midwesterners, a few lovely looking southern ladies, a couple of old timers, and a very tall black guy, perhaps a basketball player for a college. I was watching the action before I decided to throw down some money. How were the odds playing? Were the players making money on hitting their points? Which way would I bet? I watched and followed the betting.

Nothing too erratic was going on, as the players were just standing there placing their five and ten dollar chips on the numbers. That is all there is in Craps. It is a numbers game, and you don't have to be a mathematical genius to figure out how the table was playing.

The business suits were pretty quiet, while the people from the Midwest, perhaps somewhere in Montana or Arkansas, with their southern accents, were shouting and having lots of fun. The older people were playing cautiously while the southern ladies were throwing their chips at almost any number and doubling on the bets. The tall black man next to me was so intent on placing his bets all over the board, that he held many of his chips in his hands, trying to decide what to do and when to do it.

I then reached into my pocket and drew out a hundred dollar bill. This seemed like a friendly table to play Craps. I asked for five-dollar chips and again watched the table. I decided to bet on the Come Line and the thrower of the dice landed the number ten.

It was a difficult number to get again, and I assumed that the number seven would come out sooner than the ten. So I played the odds on five, six, eight and nine. They pay about six and seven to five and I felt that they were safe bets. I also played the hard ten, two fives. It is much more difficult to get two fives which make up a Hard Ten, then a six and a four, or a seven and a three. Odds are about eight to one. Not bad. If I was lucky, I could make forty bucks sooner than make the five dollars on the number. So I waited until the thrower of the dice aimed the little square cubes toward the rear of the table.

Six was the number. The throw won me a total of six dollars. I was ready to be more daring. I looked at the other players. They were so intent on the game that no one was looking up at anyone else. All eyes were glued to the board. There was a buildup of excitement and the bettors were getting anxious for the next throw of the die.

"How are you doing, handsome," a little voice came from the back of my right side.

I was hoping that it was not Rita. I just did not want to be faced with her again as I needed my space, my alone time right now. I was going to meet Christy and her two girl friends soon, and I just did not need complications. I turned, and it was her.

"I knew I would find you at the crap table. You just did not get enough of this yesterday, did you?"

My God, it was Christy. Thank God, it was not Rita. And, oh my God, this would have been a disaster if I was with Rita while Christy came along.

"Hi, sweety," I said joyously, sputtering my words with emotion and relief. "What brings you to the Venetian Hotel?"

I turned toward her, attempting to kiss her on the cheek. "And how are your friends doing? Aren't we going to join with them very soon? I mean...we ARE going to all meet for dinner soon, aren't we?"

"Oh yeah," she said with her cute smile. "I was just making sure you were not getting into any trouble down here, that's all."

Any trouble, I thought. If she only saw what was going on just a few minutes ago. That would have been the end of a dinner and a wonderful romantic evening. And those masks! What would I have done with the masks?

"Well, I figured that I would just get in a couple of games before we met, as I may not get a chance to gamble later on," I said with hopeful pleasure and tried to open up a door of opportunity with her.

"You are right, David," she replied. "We may be too busy catching up on some unfinished business from this morning. By the way, how does fish sound to you? We were thinking of some seafood later. Suzie wanted to try this restaurant at the Bellagio that serves this great Ahi, and Julie is a vegetarian. You don't mind, do you? I am sorry if I did not ask you what kind of food you would prefer. I suppose we can go elsewhere if you'd like?"

"Nah, anything is fine with me," I quickly responded. "But I have to watch my betting right now. Do you feel lucky?"

I remembered a line from a 'Dirty Harry' movie that I thought was apropos.

"I am waiting for the ten to hit. Two fives would be great. I put some money on the hard ten. Have any feelings on how the dice will roll?"

Just then, an eight was thrown. Another six dollar win for me. I decided that this may be a good roll of the dice and wanted to play it out and see what would happen. Concentrating on the game and trying to listen to Christy was a bit much, even though I really liked this gal. She was pretty, and witty, and charming and polite. The game was picking up speed as more and more chips were being put down on all sorts of numbers. The dice thrower was feeling lucky. The action was increasing and I just wanted to take Christy around and give her a great big hug.

"If you'd like, we can go after the number comes out, or a seven which would end the game," I asked, sounding like a guy who was hot to trot on his first date. "I would rather spend some time with you than stand here and get into the game. We have some time before dinner anyway, right? Do you have to meet the girls beforehand or just show up at six? We can meet them at the restaurant, right? We don't have to meet them at the Luxor Hotel, do we?"

Whew, I needed to slow down a peg and give my vocal cords some rest. I was carrying on so, that I forgot about the game. Just then, the ten hit. Damn! It was a soft ten, not a hard ten. The guy threw a six and a four. Oh well, I won the point but lost my five on the hard ten.

"How about taking a walk with me around the casino and tell me about your friends?" I asked, as I picked up my winnings and placed them in the slot in front of me.

She nodded, and I quickly scooped up my chips, threw a five dollar chip to the house, and we both walked to the cashier to trade them in for cash. It was fun being with Christy and I was glad that I already put on one of my favorite shirts that complemented my neatly pressed white slacks and my new Italian shoes. I really felt good. As I admirably looked at Christy, she was wearing a lovely white sweater resting on her beautiful frame, and powder blue pants that made her curves look so fantastic when she walked. I was proud to be with her. She had that attractiveness that provoked roving eyes from other guys who couldn't help but notice her lovely figure.

I still had to go up to my room and get the masks before we headed away from the Venetian. It just felt good walking with Christy, looking at the other tables, and the people placing their bets.

We noticed a woman at a blackjack table, with five one hundred dollar chips, as she was doubling down with a seven and a three. That move would cost her another five hundred dollars. The dealer had a picture face card showing. With half the cards in the deck, ten and above, the dealer probably had twenty. But the woman had to draw one card and got a nine. Nineteen was good, but not with a picture face card belonging to the dealer. When all of the cards were dealt to the other players, he opened another face card, a King, and she lost. One thousand dollars down the drain! Not even a sigh. She went back to betting another five hundred dollars.

"So who are Suzie...and, I forgot the other girl's name?" I asked. "Are they good friends of yours?"

"Suzie works in Los Angeles as a film editor and I have known her for many years when I used to live in Encino, in the valley. We used to travel a lot together and she is really a nice soul. Julie lives in Orange County, and is a lawyer in this well-known law firm. You might say that she is really dedicated to her work. She has just come out of a difficult relationship with someone who also is an attorney. It was hard on her, but she felt that it was best to break it off. She and I play tennis together when we get a chance. She also plays golf, and loves to go bike riding in Big Bear and Lake Arrowhead."

Suzie and Julie! Sounded like two good friends of Christy's. I had a strange feeling that they were also as attractive as Christy. But, we shall soon see, I thought. My mind started to picture what they looked like. Then, as we were walking, a funny thought hit me. I met a Julie in the parking lot a few days ago. She was one of the most attractive women I had ever seen. But, it is such a common name, so maybe it was not the same person. Yet, the possibility was there. Nah, I thought, not this Julie!

My mind started to wander about that lovely woman I helped in the parking garage, who was looking for her car. Then she drove off and I could not even get her out of my mind, not until I met Christy. She was something else. What were the odds that Christy's friend could be the same woman I had met in the parking garage? If I were a betting man, I would not take that bet. Something told me that this could turn out to be a most interesting dinner.

"David?" the voice next to me called out. "Are you okay? You seem to be in deep thought, like somewhere else?"

"Oh, I am fine, Christy. I am just letting my mind relax as long as you are here by my side. It is fun to walk the casino with you and look at the other people gambling and having fun as we are. You are having fun, aren't you?"

And my mind went back to the parking lot and to that beautiful face from the cover of a Hollywood magazine.

The likelihood of her being the same beautiful woman from the garage might have been too much for me to handle, but I was almost wishing it would turn out to be her. I thought, maybe a little complication in my life right now could be just what this guy needed.

I turned to Christy, and said, "I need to make a stop in my room. Do you want to come?"

Boy, if she only knew. I also thought of convincing her to stay once we got there, forego dinner, and make up some good excuse as to why she blew off her friends. Yet, again, she could tell her friends that this new guy she met is just sooooo insatiable, which was not far from the truth.

She turned to me and said, "I…David, I would love to come with you."

Oh boy, was I ever ready for this treat. I was ready for Christy again. I didn't want to wait 'til after dinner. I wanted her right now. It could have been the picture of Julie in my mind, or the obvious fact that Christy was also incredibly stunning.

We went to the elevator and were the only ones in it. Just as the door closed, we grabbed each other and started kissing. Before long, I was reaching to remove her blouse. With my right hand, I pressed the stop button in the elevator. Then I reached for the zipper on her skirt. Soon, I was tearing off her white satin panties and throwing them as far away as I could in the tiny space of the elevator, which may have had a capacity of eight people. The sweet smell of her luscious body, the taste of her soft skin didn't take much persuasion to put my lips all over her. It was such spontaneity, and within moments, we were both completely naked, and all over each other.

As we pressed our bodies against each other, I became hard as a rock, and shoved my penis into her. The fluids were exchanged almost immediately, and it felt so wonderful. We both cried out as we reached our climax at the same time. There was no talk, and no thinking, as we both felt the urge and did it. Imagine! This spontaneous combustion of hot passion exploded right in the hotel elevator. I was glad to have pressed the 'Stop' button. What a great spot for sex.

Having little time to savor the afterthought, it was best that we started to button and zipper up, and to comb our hair. I needed to take deep breaths to refocus on the moment, and found myself coming back down to reality. I felt like we just sucked the air out of life if only for a few brief moments. I was panting and found it a bit difficult to zipper up my fly. My white pants had a few creases now, and

there were a few spots on them from the floor. Who gave a shit! We just committed an act of sex in the Las Vegas Venetian Hotel elevator. Whew! If only Otis
could have seen us doing our thing!

With what just happened in those few moments, I was exhilarated and
shocked with myself, but mighty pleased. Even with very little communication,
we connected and it felt incredible. She was a red, hot fireball of energy, a great
way to start our evening together. When we got to my room, she leaned in to kiss
me and whispered.

"David, you are wonderful." We hugged each other again.

"I am really enjoying your company very much," she continued. "I just don't
know if we should continue this after our visit to Vegas is…I mean…I think that
you are terrific, and…" she waited and took a long pause. "I should tell you
something though."

"Oh no! Am I not going to like this?" I thought. Was this already the beginning of the end of a great moment in my life?

"David, you are going to hate me for this." She leaned back on the bed, looking up at the ceiling. "I am actually here for my engagement party. My friends
decided to take me to Vegas as a last singles getaway. I am so sorry, David, but I
have been feeling so fabulous with you."

She looked half ashamed and half enjoying herself, as if it was a coup, and she
used me as a pawn in her game.

"I thought it best that I come out and tell you before we get too emotional."

Before we got too emotional, I thought? What the fuck were we already doing,
before getting too emotional? Don't we normally get emotional over having sex
at night, next in the morning, and then again in the elevator. Now we were going
to meet her friends in an hour or so. What was all this about?

"Well, then," I said with a deep sigh, not knowing how to handle this at the
moment. "I guess we ought to head out to dinner."

My mind was confused, but my body felt great. I didn't know who was going to win this race. When I finally reached the realization that Christy wasn't going to be someone permanent in my life, I was hoping that her friend was going to be that same Julie whom I had met in the parking garage. Or, should I have just hoped that I was able to get my money back on those masks. Then, there was always Rita, good old Rita. There was time to worry about all of this after she brought me to meet her friends at dinner. At that moment, I didn't know what I had going for myself except one sore dick that I was able to call my own.

The two masks were in a box, surrounded in popcorn wrapping, in the corner of the room. I walked to the box and then passed it by. Why give them to Christy now? Who was I kidding? Was this some sort of game that she playing with me, as her last ditch effort before her big day? I decided to bypass the box and walk toward the windows, sort of disappointed in the turn of events. Perhaps it was just a passing fancy with her.

So what did this all mean? Was I really that good, or maybe, I was just a patsy who happened to come along and give her the last bit of freedom before her commitment to whom ever this guy was? I decided to play along to see where all this was headed.

"I am very happy for you, Christy," I uttered, as I bit my tongue, realizing that this woman wanted a last fling before she bed down with a new husband for, perhaps the rest of her life. "I do hope this was a memorable occasion for you as it was for me. You are truly a lovely person and I am sure that you will make him very happy."

"You are making me feel very sad," she responded. "I was hoping that you would understand."

How could I have understood what people do, having been married to the same woman for so many years? They invite you to their room and want to make love to you. They act sexual and enticing in bed. Then they are eager to take you in their arms and shower you with lots of affection. I really did not expect this from her. But then again, I was here on a visit to another planet. Las Vegas is the city where anything can happen. And I just had not one, but two happenings, one with Christy at the crap table, and the other with Rita at the slot machines.

"Well, to be honest with you, my dear, I am a bit disappointed," I said honestly. "I was hoping that we may have had something there that could have lasted for more than a day. I mean, maybe a week or two, or a month at least."

"I know this may sound selfish," she responded, as she sat down on the bed once again. "But I was afraid to tell you when we first met. I like you and I feel so comfortable with you. I just came with my friends as a last singles get-a-way, you know, a last hurrah, before I get to tie the knot with him. His name is Chuck, a rather intelligent man whom I have known for God knows, a lot longer than I have known you."

She continued to ramble on. "I thought that I could start a good life with Chuck. He is extremely wealthy and lives in a large house in Malibu, another house in the Pacific Palisades, also having a ranch in Phoenix. His family has been involved with politics for quite some time, and he is very friendly with many political people high up including congressmen and senators. I just needed some status in my life and he asked me to marry him. But, there is more to this than you think, David."

I just listened and didn't say a word. I watched her as she explained her new life, sitting on the bed, as I stood before the drapes. Here was this lovely woman, a model, a raving beauty, who was telling me that she wanted more out of life than many men were able to afford to give to her. Was there more to this than I was to believe? Was she carrying his child? Were they both gay and both hiding this from other people?

Was there a hidden motive as to why she wanted this type of life if she may not love this dude? Yet, I was looking at a woman in pain, not really happy to be a part of Chuck's social circle, the glitz and the glamour, the parties, the society and the celebrities. I was looking at a woman who was not really happy at all.

"Is this what you really want out of life," I asked her. "Or is this an escape?"

"David, don't ask me that," she said, sitting there with her head in her lap. "I was hoping that you would understand. I really don't know what I want. All I know is that I do not want to wind up with nothing in my life. I know that I am attractive, and have a decent body and all that shit. But I want financial security and a future."

So that was what it boiled down to. She was a woman who wanted financial security. Her future husband may screw like a toad out of water and would probably use her good looks just to show her off to his stuffy chums as they make their way into social circles. But is this what Christy truly wanted out of life?

"Perhaps you can try it on for size," I asked. "Then if it does not fit well, you can leave. After all, nothing is forever."

Christy looked up at me and started to cry. I may have hit a nerve. She was so beautiful, so innocent, so loving, that I had to go over to her and sit down next to her, put my arm on her shoulder and pull her close to me. I felt her pain, perhaps a future that was so uncertain. I just had to offer my feelings to her, and it also was my own feelings of love. Who the hell knew the answers? I found myself in such a muddle of affairs, that at this point anything was possible.

I quietly placed my lips on hers and squeezed her toward me. She responded and gave me her body, and pressed her lips against mine. I could feel her breasts against my chest and had to put my hands all over her body and take her one more time. I moved her down on the bed and started to caress her body, my hands moving as fast as I could take them, from her chest, to her thighs, across to her stomach. I reached under her top, and felt the nipples of her warm, firm breasts, and started to get excited all over again.

I really wanted to make love to this woman once again and the hell with her future husband. I knew that if I could get beyond the pain, I would be on top of her, taking her clothes off, getting it on with her as we did last night and in the elevator. I knew that all I needed was a little more time with her to forget her future groom, her social activities after her marriage, and her life in the upper crust. I was going to make love to Christy at least one more time. I wanted to make love to this woman. I wanted this woman, and I was going to take her now.

We lay spent from the hot passionate desires we had felt for each other. We were both lying on top of the damp sheets, taking deep breaths, trying to come back down to earth. Her luscious body was next to mine, and her head was leaning on my chest, as I rubbed her beautiful hair.

"Christy," I called out to her as if I had to bring it up, but I had no choice. "I was wondering if you still feel the same way about your finance now? There is definitely something going on here, between us, and if you tell me that there are no feelings on your end, I will back off."

She turned her head toward me and smiled. It was a smile that I could have fallen in love with, but knew it would not work for me. If she could cheat on her soon to be husband, so close to the wedding, and only marry the bastard for status and money, then who is to say that she would not have a similar agenda with me at a later date. Of course, that would be nothing other than passion and sex. Hey, wait! Wasn't that supposed to be enough for any man to handle? Ha, ha. So what was I laughing about? I was about to lose a woman whom I was falling in love with. Was it truly love, or just a quick hit in the sack?

"Sweetheart, I'm not really sure how I feel about Chuck at this moment in time." she tried to explain to me, in her quiet voice, almost apologizing for getting me involved with her. "All I know right now is that you make me feel extremely good."

As she started to rub her fingers on my chest, she looked at the clock on the night table, noticing the time and became startled.

"Oh my God, David, we are so late."

She jumped up in a scurry and started to put her clothes back on. I reached over to her. "Oh Christy, let's call your friends and stay here for a few more hours and talk. What do you say?"

She got rather agitated with my question and replied abruptly. "No, I really want to meet them, whether you want to come or not. We can see how it goes and maybe, come back here later."

Maybe? Gee, it was sounding more and more like the rather finalistic send off one lover gives to the other. We then dressed and headed back down the elevator. I recalled our little romp in the elevator only an hour or two before, and then our passionate connection up in my room. If it were the last time that she and I were to be together, it would be a memory I would not soon forget.

We ran up the street, dodged not only the cars that were parked in the street, as traffic was at a standstill, but we also moved in and out of the people who were just walking along the streets.

It was a good twenty minutes before we arrived at the Bellagio. We quickly walked up to the hostess of the seafood restaurant and she told us that we were expected an hour ago. She also stated that she was most certain that our friends were going to be happy to see us. Like, how did she know all this? I always disliked people who made assumptions.

Christy leaned into my ear and quietly spoke ever so slowly. "They probably have an idea why we are late."

There, in the corner of the elegant, yet modest restaurant, were two of the loveliest women I had seen in a long time. They both got up to introduce themselves. The smaller of the two, Suzie, held out her hand and I took it and gave a peck on the back side of her palm, almost apologizing to her that we were late.

"A pleasure to meet you, Suzie!"

Then, as I turned to shake the hand of the other lovely creature, my heart skipped a beat. Was it really her? Was I dreaming? Was it the woman in the parking garage? Right there, in front of me was the goddess from the mall, Julie. I could not believe it and was so elated at that moment that I completely forgot that I had just made love, not once, not twice, but three times, to the woman standing right next to me.

"David? What a coincidence!" She smiled warmly and shook my hand out of amazement. "This is such a small world. What in heaven's name would the odds be that we would be running into each other at a dinner table in Las Vegas?"

Julie was right. The odds were high, but on this night, they surely shined on me. I sat down in between Julie and Christy, and Suzie sat across from me. Christy had not said a word as yet, and I was getting very curious as to what she might say. But I knew that she would be a lady nonetheless.

I assumed that in a public place, there was very little chance of a scene if she wanted to take it to that level. She kept eyeing me, while Julie was chatting it up

about the day at the mall where we had met, recapping how we were both looking for our cars. Suzie was laughing with every word being extracted from Julie's
lips, and her giggles were a bit too much for me. Well, two out of three were not
so bad. If I were to make a wager at this point, I would have to say that my odds
were spectacular that I would be in Julie's arms before the night was over.

"So tell me, David," quipped Julie, with her precious smile, elevating her
bright white teeth, looking so radiantly beautiful. "How did the two of you meet?
Did you just bump into each other here in Vegas or did you know Christy before
this trip?"

She was as cunning as an attorney would be, and working in a law firm would
have rubbed off on her so easily. You wonder why people do not trust attorneys.
This one was cute, but deadly to 'wit'.

"Well, we just met here in Las Vegas", I replied. "After our little meeting looking for our cars at the shopping mall, I decided to take a breather from my work
and spend a few days here. I met Christy at one of the crap tables yesterday, the
day I arrived."

Christy was sort of embarrassed or else was stunned that Julie and I had met
before.

Christy then added. "David was so engrossed at the crap table when we accidentally bumped into each other late afternoon yesterday, about the time when
you girls went to see the show. Even today, I thought I would look for him at the
crap table realizing that he was having such a good time as he did yesterday. I was
afraid that he may have forgotten about our dinner tonight and I did not have his
phone number. I found him at his hotel in the casino while I was taking my afternoon walk at the Venetian. Then it took about twenty minutes to get to the Bellagio to meet with both of you."

I did not think that her excuse was working too well. Julie was too clever not
to pick up such a 'cock 'n bull' story. And Suzie was just getting a kick out of all
of this. A pretty young thing, with dark brown hair, about five feet six, thin, a bit
busty, as I could not tell if they were real or just phony boobs. It didn't matter. I
was really concentrating on Julie, my next conquered woman for the evening.
After all, there was no guarantee that I would ever have sex with Christy again.

But here I was, sitting with three gorgeous looking women like I was the star, the celebrity. Obviously they were all happy to be here with me. They all looked so stunning in their outfits. All were in their late twenties or early thirties, and were just a trio of beauty. And they were all having a good time. The only thing that crossed my mind was that I was not sure if Christy was feeling a bit of uneasiness through all of this. I could sense that she tried to avoid being questioned by her friends. After all, she was an engaged woman.

"Christy told us that she met you yesterday and that you were a doll," Suzie said, followed by her usual laugh. "We are just teasing you David, so don't take this seriously. Now I could understand why she invited you along to dinner, with us girls. You are a cutie. Ha! Ha! Ha! Ha!"

Was this embarrassing or what? Now I was a cutie. I felt more like a commodity. Maybe it was in the cards to do all of them, at the same time. I suppose that would have been a blast. But, I couldn't see myself in that situation. It would be better to do them, one at a time, I thought. Let's see now, Christy was great. Then there was Julie, who could even be better. Better than great? And then, there was busty Suzie. I bet she could have bitten my thing off with her laugh, if she wanted to.

"So what have you girls decided to have?" I asked. "I must apologize again for being late, and you are all probably so hungry. Suppose we all peruse the menu and see what the chef recommends tonight?"

"Oh, that's okay," replied Julie. "I just love sitting here, watching all of the folks as they come into the restaurant. Each one has a different story to tell, just like the four of us. So, David, did Christy tell you that she and this guy, Chuck are tying the knot soon? Suzie and I took Christy to Vegas to celebrate her last time as a single woman."

Whew, there was no pissing around with this Julie. She just got to the point. I rather like that in a woman. About time I met someone who gave straight answers. I always hated people who played silly games, and tried to go around the truth. By the time you finally get a straight answer out of them, it was too exhausting to even care.

"Yes," I answered back, with a grin just to show her that Christy and I were not on the make, nor forming a relationship, but just an acquaintance, having met at the crap table in the casino. "It seems we both like playing craps, and after our little gambling, and a few laughs, we had a few drinks at the bar. That is when Christy told me about how you guys took her to Vegas right before her pending marriage to Chuck."

That must have taken some pressure off of Christy. She looked over to me and gave me a smile. I was back in the good graces of her now. I protected her from any further questions Julie may have had. So now it was time to order some cocktails, then some great seafood. I certainly started to have an appetite realizing that I only had some dry toast for breakfast many hours ago. Here I was, among three beautiful women, all seeming so eager to have a good time. Or, at least, I was eager to have a good time with them. I felt like I was in heaven. So I just let it fly and took one moment at a time. I came to Vegas without any expectations, and I already had met four women in no time. Not too shabby.

While the three gals were talking to each other, I just nodded and smiled. Then a thought came to mind. Suppose, just suppose, a man was to take three women to bed at the same time. Do you use the same condom? Do you have time to change condoms? Do you have time to put on any condoms? How stupid a thought! Wonder what a guy would do in this case? Oh well, I did not think that this would come to pass. I did not think I could handle this anyway.

"How about a cocktail before dinner?" I proposed. "I also recommend some white wine to go with the fish What would be your pleasure? Suzie, suppose you go first and decide. At this point, I think we all need a drink."

Julie, the vegetarian, looked at me as if she did not drink and acknowledged my question by telling everyone that white wine would be good for her and would go well with the seafood we were about to order. Suzie then agreed. I turned to Christy and she was in deep thought, but managed to turn toward me.

"David, why not pick out a good bottle of wine for all of us. After all, you are the man at the table and we are just three sweet things out with a man-about-town who probably knows all about wine. Here David, here is the wine menu. Pick out something that you feel will make us all giddy and funny."

So now I was taking charge. I rather liked that. I reached for the wine list and opened it up. I went down the list of sweet and dry wines, bottles from thirty to three hundred dollars. Whew! Some of those bottles looked a bit steep for no more than five or six half filled glasses of wine. I chose something dry and moderately priced. It was a rather nice vintage that was about fifty dollars. I waved to the waiter and told him that we would start with this bottle of wine first.

The conversation started to quiet down as we began to know each other, and things were going quite well. I suggested the Captain's Special that contained crab legs, a lobster tail, boiled veggies, a baked potato, and some hot bread. After I received a nod from Julie, meaning that it was not on her diet, I then suggested another plate, boiled sea brass or the trout. They sounded good too.

After going through the menu, we all decided what we wanted. By then, the waiter came back with a bottle of wine, four glasses and a wine opener, a bucket and a white towel. He opened the wine bottle and poured a little of the wine in a glass and handed it to me. I twirled the glass and then moved it to my lips. I took a sip. I immediately thought of Christy's lips touching mine, and the glass of wine started to taste warm and delicious, almost humanly good.

I then grabbed the cork, and it was moist. Never accept a bottle of wine, if the cork is dry. So far, so good!

"This wine tastes good and I am happy with its fragrance," I said joyfully. "I hope you girls will enjoy it."

I acted as if I knew what I was doing. I was just trying to make an impression with each of the girls. First there was my lover, or former lover, Christy, who loved me but was marrying Chuck. Then there was Julie, who recently broke up with her boyfriend and may have been on the loose for another one.

And then, there was Suzie, this pistol-packin' mama was something else. I kept glancing at her just to look at her body. It was muscular and so very tight, that her breasts were shooting out of her tight sweater like melons in a supermarket.

The supermarket! Better not go there. Not to the supermarket, and not to Suzie. I had better concentrate on Christy and Julie. Either one could wind up in my bed at the Venetian when the dinner would be over. And then, on second thought, there was always Rita. Lovely Rita! Wherever the hell she went to. I was ready to consider a midnight swim afterward or a splash in the spa. I wondered if the girls would like that?

We were working on the second bottle of wine. The conversation was lively. Our small, yet intimate booth that sat off to the left of the restaurant was a cozy choice. We were satisfied with our meal, and the waiter asked if coffee and dessert were on our agenda. We weren't ready for dessert it seemed, by the mutual shake of the heads and Julie's slight brush of her hand. She was such a straightforward gal, a trait I really enjoyed about her.

As soon as the waiter disappeared out of sight, I felt Christy's hand reach for my knee under the table. She gave me a small wink and a tender squeeze with her hand. I started to imagine being in the hot tub with her or a swim in the pool, under the moonlit sky feeling an ever so slight breeze. Being with this lady, I knew that I would enjoy myself no matter what we did.

We were listening to Suzie as she told us a story about a work incident a week earlier, and we laughed and enjoyed her cute little antics, although her laugh needed some repair work. Then, out of the blue, I felt another hand on my other knee. It was Julie's. Oh God, I thought, what if they knew what the other was doing? I did not know where to put my eyes, but thankfully, Suzie kept us focused on her tales of woe. I continued to look straight ahead at Suzie without being too obvious that I was forming a bulge between my legs.

I had each of my hands touching each of theirs' and knew that this could not continue without some control on my part as to what I should consider next. I decided that I would accidentally drop something on Christy's side and would have to lean over to pick it up. I would then whisper something sweet and invit-ing in her ear. I felt that I would have a better chance with her, having been with this woman over three times already. I also knew that my time was limited so I had better make some closure with her and make it good. Then I could move on to Julie if Julie was still available.

As I knocked over my cloth napkin that was sitting on my lap, I leaned down to pick it up. Christy took my lead and followed me to the floor. Julie's hand left the knee that it was on and I was able to be face to face with Christy half way under the table.

"Can we meet in my room tonight, babe?" I asked, as boldly as I possibly could, but ready for any rejection from her.

She smiled at me and shook her head slightly. My guess was that she liked the idea and she returned back up to the table before me. As I started to resume an upright position, I noticed something rather strange under the table. The sound of Suzie's voice was still rambling on, but her hand was firmly gripped around Julie's hand under the tablecloth. There was more than one secret at this table. Were they actually lesbians? Was either of them bi-sexual? I had no idea what they were doing. Perhaps it was best not to find out.

I got back to my upright position and noticed that Julie's hand did not return to my knee, nor did Christy's. But I received a nod from Christy and that was good enough for me. I knew that the night was going to be most entertaining, if, perhaps, we all could go for a swim as well.

Okay, I thought to myself, where was I going with this? Christy wanted to meet me later, perhaps for a swim or in the spa. Julie, that gorgeous looking woman was holding hands with Suzie, probably an over-sexed or bi-sexual, or homosexual woman. Were they both under the same sheets or was I reading into all of this in a wrong way? I was not sure of the players or even the scorecard. This was even more difficult to figure out than playing a game of golf on a course with narrow fairways and the rain coming down in buckets.

"Hey, let's have some coffee or tea, or a brandy," I said. "I think we can top off this evening with something sweet and wholesome. What do you say, kids?"

Julie and Suzie looked at each other and they both started to laugh. Christy was just looking at me as if I had struck a nerve. Better still, I think she had struck a nerve...mine. And it was hanging loose in the wind right now, perhaps looking for some direction. Maybe it needed some sort of a road map, as this trip had many winding twists and turns. Little did I know that it was only the beginning of a long and winding road.

"That is a wonderful idea," replied Suzie. "Hey Julie, how about a Khulua or a blackberry brandy?"

"I am ready for anything that is sweet on my tongue and easy to go down," Julie responded.

Everything out of her mouth was a tease. I wondered how it would feel going into her mouth. She sure knew how to throw her sex around, even orally.

"David, I think I will have an Anisette. How about you, Suzie? That would be a great after dinner drink after all of the fish we had. Sound good, David?"

"You chose a good one, Julie," Suzie remarked, as she put her hands to the top of her sweater and slowly moved them down the sides of her breasts. "I am getting a bit flushed and will need to get some fresh air soon."

I had the waiter bring over four Anisettes and some coffee. The next thing I felt was Christy's hand moving up my leg and into my crotch. I nearly gasped as I took a sip of the drink and my mouth almost dropped into my glass.

"Taste good, David?" she asked. Wonder what she meant, my drink or her grabbing my crotch so hard that I nearly cried out with pain. Maybe she watched me as I glared at Suzie's big boobs as she massaged them and it made her jealous.

"Just what the doctor ordered," I said as I just sat there trying not to flinch.

The next few minutes brought lots of laughter from Suzie, a louder tone of voice from Julie, and lots of fingers belonging to Christy up and down my legs. I was waiting for the next shoe to drop, turning to Julie and Suzie.

"So what are you girls lining up for this evening? Have anything interesting in mind?"

Now that was stupid of me but I just had to act nonchalant and not let on that the two of them may be lesbians and may want to spend the rest of the night under the same sheets. If this was turning out to be a crazy evening, I did not know if I could handle all of this. I looked at Julie, then at Suzie. Then I glanced back to Christy.

"I have an idea," remarked Suzie. "Why don't you join us in the gym later and we all could go for a swim. A midnight swim would be great. I think you would look kind of cute in a bathing suit, David, or maybe in your Sunday suit. Whatever suit suits you. Care to meet us later at our pool at the Luxor? We could also come to visit you at the Venetian?"

"Wonderful idea, Suzie," Julie chimed in. "David, you can show us how good you are doing your back stroke."

I knew I made a mistake. I then grabbed Christy's hand under the table as if to get a cue from her, and I did.

"Well, big boy," she said. "You opened up the door and let the cat in. Now you will have to go swimming with us."

Christy was humored by the conversation and I just got caught with my hand in the cookie jar. They were having fun with me and I was the patsy. But, I decided to play along them and be their playmate for the evening. I turned to Julie and Suzie.

"Your idea sounds great. I will tell you what. After dinner, I will go back to my hotel, pick up my bathing suit and meet you at your pool at about eleven thirty."

Christy was overwhelmed with my response.

"And I will need a walk after this dinner. Suppose I stroll with you back to your hotel so I can walk off some of this food. Is that okay with you, David?"

Julie looked at me with her bright eyes and lovely smile, and Suzie just tilted her head and laughed, realizing that Christy and I may take in a quickie before we head back to their hotel. What the heck, perhaps Suzie and Julie would also take in a quickie themselves. And if I was lucky, I could have time for a quickie with Rita. Hey, I was not sure what I was thinking, but the evening was turning out to be more interesting than I had hoped. Anything could have happened and I was here to have a good time, maybe a wild time. The check came and I reached for it.

Julie also reached for the check and said, "I would not think of having you pay for all of us, David. Let's split it three ways as this is supposed to be a treat for Christy anyway. Is that okay with you?"

Heck, it was better than paying the damn check all by myself. We each put in ninety dollars and started to leave. Suzie was first to get up from the table and it was then that I noticed her cute little buns in her tight mini skirt, which was as high as the middle of her thighs. She was something else. Her big busts kept moving up and down as she walked toward the door of the restaurant. She was carrying a little black purse and was wearing black high-heeled cowboy boots. I couldn't help but look at some of the patrons who also were watching this little stick of dynamite light up the room as she walked out. This was a character.

Julie was in back of her, right in front of me as Christy was just in back of me.

Julie turned around and quietly whispered, "I am so glad that we had a chance to meet once again, David. I am looking forward to seeing you later at the pool. I just love to swim. I do hope that you can make it as I would like to see you later."

I felt like I was going to be raped by these women. I had hoped that I had enough strength to carry on as best I could. As Julie walked briskly out the door, I turned back to Christy and just sighed.

"I hope I made a nice impression with your friends, Christy. One never knows how people react to your choice of words or if they really mean what they say. I do hope that you are pleased with the evening, so far?"

I got a big grin out of Christy. She told me that they loved me for my being a good sport. She took my arm as we walked into the hallway and toward the casino of the Bellagio. She needed to feel that I was still in her corner. I moved her arm closer to mine, and as we waved goodbye to Suzie and Julie, we started to walk toward the front of the casino and out through the main lobby. It was homeward bound, back to the Venetian Hotel for a little fun and relaxation with this woman. I felt that I needed to get away from her two friends for now.

I could not wait to reach the hotel and take the elevator up to my floor, throw my shirt off and undo Christy's clothes. I wanted this woman now and I knew that she wanted me as well. We had enough time to make love before we headed back to her hotel and meet with Suzie and Julie. And if we did not make the swim and decided to stay in my room for the duration of the evening, that would not have been so bad either. It was a cool, refreshing evening.

CHAPTER 4

▼

I HAVE A LOVE, ONE HAND, ONE HEART

The streets were busy with people, and we heard the pirates at Treasure Island, the waterfalls at the Mirage, the noise of the cars, and the people lining the streets of the Las Vegas Strip, the most popular street in the world. This was indeed a town of lights and people, of action and history, of new friends and love lost. And this was going to be a most memorable time for me. I was acting like a young kid on his first date, and I had three young ladies who were crazy about me, and were about as sexy as anything I had ever seen in my life. I just was not sure at the time if they were straight or lesbians. Who cared? I surely didn't.

But I was with a woman who was beautiful and full of life. I was falling in love with her. I would do anything to take her away from this guy Chuck because she wanted to be with me. I needed more time with her and was hoping that somehow, all of this could win her away from him. She did not love this man because she made such beautiful love to me and I felt her sincerity and her loving touches to my body. You just can't do that unless you really wanted to.

The humidity was still pretty high up in the numbers, as was the temperature, and I was getting hot from the walk. We were nearly there, and the long steps up to the main lobby of the Venetian Hotel seemed like they never ended. What a pretty hotel. We entered the lobby and it was crowded with people, some snapping pictures, others checking in, while others just lost in space. And there was a lot of space to get lost in. For a big place, it was cool, not as humid as the air outside. I felt a little relief from the cool air as my shirt was starting to stick to my back.

We needed to get to the elevators leading to my floor and then to my room. We started to walk briskly and did not even lose a step as we headed across the floor of the lobby. Pretty soon we would be at my room and I would be able to relax and cool off. Perhaps a quick shower, and then I would have Christy all to myself. We approached the elevators leading to my floor.

"Hi, David!" I heard a voice to my left. "How are you doing? I have not seen you all day. Where have you been? I was hoping that we would meet this evening." It was Rita. Jesus Christ!!!

There she was…that red-haired, big-mouthed, sex-pot, a fireball of energy and with a mouth that just would not quit. I did not know what to make of her but there she was, standing right in front of Christy and me.

"Hi Rita, How the hell are you?"

I introduced the two ladies but didn't go any further hoping that she would just go away. I didn't want to bite off more than I could chew, especially with two other women pending in the wings, (by the pool anyway). I thought it best to make this meeting quick, if at all possible. It didn't seem to be that way, however, as Rita kept rambling on and on and didn't even notice that my arm was entwined around another woman, or did she? After about twenty seconds, I looked at Christy who thought that this was a scene from a comedy. She too didn't know what to make of all of this.

Rita was dramatic, a bit tipsy, nothing new, as she was the same way earlier today. She was over exaggerated and far beyond the energy I felt to keep up with her. I kept hearing Christy giggling under her breath as we all walked into the elevator. The thought occurred that perhaps, Rita was following us? I truly had no idea, as my mind was full of fun and love, and the fact that I had spent a lovely dinner with three beautiful women.

Who was to say what each of them was up to? One was engaged, but not to me, and yet I had sex with her more times than I could have imagined, under the circumstances. The other two might have been lesbians, one of whom broke up with someone, a male or female, I was not sure. The third of the group had the cutest ass and the weirdest laugh I had ever heard in my life. Looking at this, I also knew that Rita was not going to join Christy and me in my room, not in her Goddamn lifetime.

We got out of the elevator and the three of us started to walk in the same direction.

Finally, Rita said, "I will hook up with you guys later," as if we were all long, lost friends. "I have to meet someone. It was so nice to see you, David and meeting with you," directing her comment to Christy.

Christy then turned to me and asked, "A friend of yours?"

"Yeah, sure," I responded. "We go way back to the stone age, perhaps to the beginning of time."

Better that she not know who this little bitch was and how I met her, and leave the door open for another passing of time with the redhead. Sometimes, you never know if you need a backup. I was hoping that it would not be a necessity, as I did not want to lose Christy. She was good about the incident and took it in stride knowing not to question me any further.

We got to my room and we both took a deep sigh, and sat on the bed. It had been a long day, a big dinner, lots of drinks once again, and it was definitely tiring listening to Rita. My body was slowing down a bit. Christy also sensed this and started to rub my shoulders after I took my shirt off. We hugged and nibbled on each other's neck, all the while fondling each other. I just loved touching her hair, the way it felt when I put my fingers through it. I enjoyed the smell of her neck as I kissed each beautiful inch of her tender flesh. She looked so beautiful, with her gentle strokes of her long delicate fingers massaging my back, soothing the rough edges of my body. Christy was fantastic, very experienced, and I was most impressed and desirous of her to get naked. I started to take off her white top, when she pulled my hand away.

"David, I want to explain something to you, if I can, about Julie and Suzie, before we venture to the pool to see them."

Perfect timing, lady! I was not thinking of chatting right then as I was getting into the right rhythm for lovemaking and sex. But, I have always been a gentleman, so why change? I removed my hands from Christy's body and sat back to listen to her. She went on to explain that Julie was not a lesbian as I may have thought. And although she knew that I saw both Julie and Suzie holding hands under the table, I might have gotten this impression. Julie was simply good friends with Suzie and with her. Nonetheless, Suzie was gay and she believed that she, Suzie, was being a huge comfort to Julie by having just broken up with a male friend after a long, torrid relationship. They have been friends for many years, Julie and Suzie. Christy also mentioned that sometimes Julie will swing, but not for a commitment.

Okay, I was getting the scoop on the two girls. It made sense to me, and now I wanted to continue where we left off with Christy. But just as I was about to do so, there was a knock on the door. Why couldn't I just take our clothes off already and there would not have been any reason to be disturbed? When I went to the door, thinking whom ever it was, I would tell them to come back later, and I would put out that little sign on the door that read 'Do Not Disturb'.

I opened the door and there was this big burly man, with a suit and a tie that hung in disarray, and a voice that expressed total displeasure. He brushed his way through and shoved me aside as if I was a piece of lamb chop hanging in the butcher's freezer, and then he went straight to Christy. Standing before her, with one hand on her arm, he spoke in a very heavy southern accent.

"There you are my honey pie. I think you should come with me…NOW!"

He pulled her arm so she had to get up off the bed, and as she rose, I heard a loud antagonizing word…"Chuck…"

I made a move toward him as he started to pull Christy toward the door at which time she turned toward me and shook her head, as if to tell me not to do anything. I watched as the two of them left the room. How did he know where Christy was? My thoughts were all over the place. I watched this huge frame of a man come charging into the room, grabbing Christy, sounding like a gangster with big hands and a rough demeanor. How did he know my room and who led him there?

In a quick flash, I thought back to the dinner with Christy, Julie and Suzie. They were all so loving. Did any of the other girls tell Chuck where Christy was? Did they know what room I was in? They were friends, and I did not think that they would call Chuck and tell him that Christy was with another man. Close friends do not do that. So I tried to believe that it could not be them. Was she being followed? How did he know what room she was in and when she would be there?

I sat down on the bed and all of these thoughts started to flash though my mind. What was going on here anyway?

What were Julie and Suzie doing, until Christy and I would meet with them at their pool? Were they engaged in sex or just enjoying each other's company? So Julie was not a lesbian. Thank God! There was hope for me yet. And that little cracker-box, Suzie was gay. What a group. Was it possible that they went both ways? Was that what Christy was implying to me? I could just imagine how they were spending their next few hours before we were supposed to come by.

There was Suzie, trying to get it on with Julie, and Julie was not ready for this right now. Perhaps it was best that I was not there because the thought would break my heart. Maybe I did not want to see what was happening between the two of them, as this would really have gotten to me.

Julie was a most attractive woman, and as a professional working in a law firm, she definitely had smarts. She was bright, almost too quick for the average Joe, but I certainly appreciated that demeanor in any woman. She truly knew how to handle herself. Christy said that Julie's breakup was with a man. Was it really a man, or was it with a woman? All I wanted to do was have some fun, and this was becoming a big nightmare. So what's wrong with a male wanting to rock his nuts? After all, I am human. I am a male. I needed the release in life that comes with having sex the normal way.

I tried to imagine what was going on in their hotel room between Julie and Suzie.

"So what do you think of David," asked Suzie. "He sure seems like an okay guy. Kind of cute and cuddly, and he is attracted to Christy."

"Well," replied Julie, "I am just wondering what would happen if Chuck ever found out that Christy is having a thing for David. You know how Chuck can be, a very macho character, involved with the mob, and a big house in Pacific Palisades overlooking the Pacific Ocean and all that. He must have control or he will lose his cork. I am so glad that we are here and he is there right now. Honestly, I do not think that Christy really loves Chuck and would like to get out of this, one way or another."

"Remember Christy telling us that Chuck is involved with prostitutes, the numbers, and drugs, and that he has had guys, soldiers, who go out and 'whack' people who were late in payments?" Suzie reminded Julie, as she sat on the king size bed in their hotel room. "I do not think that this is the life for Christy and she should find a way to get away from him. Chuck is a dangerous man and could do harm to Christy if he found out that she is with someone else."

"You are right," Julie responded. "It is time to call it a day. You know how I feel about these things. And I feel guilty because our law firm represented some of these assholes against the state and federal governments, and I was the one who introduced Christy to Chuck about nine months ago. Then we all went to the party at his estate and Chuck just went 'ga-ga' over Christy. He knew that he could not have me as I am in the law firm representing his bogus companies. That would not have been Kosher, by no means. So now we have a situation with Chuck and Christy, with Christy and David, and we are in the middle of something that could become a major problem for all of us."

Suzie decided to take off her top and relax. She unhooked her bra and allowed her large breasts to fall freely down her chest. She then took off her mini skirt and felt free and easy. Julie watched her roommate and took the hint. She also took off her top and then her shoes. It was time to relax and not get too much into an uproar over something that was out of their control, at least for now.

"Care to give me a rubdown, Julie," asked Suzie.

Julie looked at Suzie, wearing only her panties, displaying her big breasts and her muscular legs, as if this might be a good way to relax. But instead, Julie took a deep breath and walked into the bathroom.

"I need to take a pee, after all of the wine we had," she said. "I don't know about you, Suzie, but I cannot hold too much liquid for too long, and we had quite a bit. Don't you need to get rid of some of the fluids in your body? You can sure keep the juices flowing for a long time. I know that I can't"

The noise of the toilet was drowned out by the sound of the air conditioning. As Julie walked out of the bathroom, wearing only her pink panties, Suzie remarked astonishingly.

"Gosh, Julie, you really have beautiful tits, I must tell you. Mine are too large and heavy at times. Yours' are perfect. So how does it feel not having Richard the Lion-Hearted around any more?"

Julie walked to the large windows in the room and just sighed.

"Well, it was for the best. He was a partner in the law firm and decided to get involved with things that I was against. Dear old Richard was the one who brought in Chuck and his people as clients. He thought it would be good for the firm. It was not for me. Even his lovemaking got tiresome. He was always drunk and became abusive, and I just did not need that in my life. He blamed it on the hours he had to spend at Chuck's house, devising ways to keep the government off of Chuck's back, as well as the FBI and the attorney general's office. I do miss being with a man, Suzie, but I am better off without that kind of relationship.

"Did you know that Richard was asked to leave the firm because his association with Chuck was getting all of us involved in criminal affairs? The partners told him, 'that was it!' They just about had enough of all of his shit, his drinking, his late hours, his gambling debts and his whoring around with Chuck's girls. I just did not want to be dragged down with him either. Three years was a long time but it was time to move on. I am happy that I have you and Christy as friends. It kept my sanity. If I could only meet a man like David, a teacher or a person with a decent, honest job, it would be great. No taking any office crap home with us, only a good, clean relationship."

Suzie looked down at her body and then grabbed a cigarette out of her pocketbook. She lit one up and turned to Julie.

"I hope all of this works out for you and for Christy. I do not know if I can ever be happy with a man."

Julie walked over to Suzie, as she watched the smoke come from her lips, only half painted with the pink lipstick she had put on hours ago.

"I can understand, Suz. Sometimes, men are such a handful of fuck-ups."

They both giggled and had the same vision in mind, that being the passionate carnal nature of a woman holding a man in her hands. Julie continued.

"Chuck is so domineering and I was always a little bit doubtful of my intent to introduce them together. But, he seemed nice enough, although I just didn't know him all that well. I thought he was charming in a masculine sort of way, though Christy always seemed just a bit nervous being around him. Yet, I felt that she could take care of herself."

Suzie's eyes drifted toward the window and started to shake her head with disdain.

"If I didn't like women so much, I might have been able to deal effectively with a man. But, once bitten, twice shy. No sense in beating a dead horse."

They were in hysterics. Their afterglow of the two bottles of wine and the meeting of the stranger, 'Mr. David of California', had left them giddy, and they kept making jokes with regards to the oddities of men in general. They laughed and carried on, and finally made their way down to the pool, after a few caresses, a few touches, and several small pecks on each other's lips. There was nothing too sexual, but only as a friendship. The comfortable flow of women together, such as Suzie and Julie, without the underlying intentions or the expectations, showed intimacy as friends, not as lovers, and both women were elated for the others' maturity to handle such casual and mature affections. They even held hands in the elevator but did not make it a public showing as they kept as much privacy as they could, amongst themselves.

When the elevator door opened two floors down, both Julie and Suzie were expecting people to be standing in front of the door. There was no one there. Just as it was about to close, a hand reached over to hold the door open.

"David! What are you doing here?" Suzie said, shocked to see me, looking like I was in shock myself.

"Hi Girls, I guess I got on the wrong floor. I was coming up to see you..."

"What's wrong," interrupted Julie. "You look a bit stressed, and where is Christy?"

"I just had a very intense encounter with Christy's fiancé, Chuck, I believe that's his name. He found out where my room was and came looking for her." I continued, breathing heavily as I had just run from the Venetian to the Luxor in less than twenty minutes.

"He took her with him. We didn't have a chance to speak. I tried to do something but she nodded to me that I better not, and he waved his fist in my face. So I grabbed my wallet and left the room."

"Oh my God!" the two girls said in unison.

"I left her alone and they ran out the door. I do hope that she will be okay. I feel a little guilty, but what should I have done? I just didn't know what to do? And I am not sure how he found her in my room in the first place? Do you?"

"Oh David, we were afraid this might happen. We were just talking about this earlier," Julie patted my back for comfort.

"I realize that you may feel awkward allowing Christy to go with Chuck but you did the right thing. Chuck is someone you just do not want to fool around with. He would sooner kill you than let you go home in one piece if you know what I am talking about. You do not want to get in this man's way. So just relax and let's work this out together, okay?"

"Look, Julie, I do not think that Christy loves this Chuck. She told me that she had doubts about her relationship. But I do wonder how he knew about Christy and me in the first place. Did any of you tell him about us?"

Suzie shook her head no, and said, "Gosh, Dave, it is such a coincidence that we were just saying how she has always been nervous around him, even after so many months of being with him. I am sure that if she wants to break off with him, she will. And we have not been in contact with Chuck because we hate his guts. He is a cruel dude all right."

They hit the main level and headed toward the pool. I then asked, "Has she ever done this type of thing before, you know, cheating behind his back? If she truly does not want to be with him, why stay in this relationship?"

Julie laughed. "Well, you just do not walk away so easily from Chuck. But I am not sure what Christy has done in the time she and Chuck have been together, David, but I would not put it past her either. She has been a bit elusive, even with us. But it is probably best that you did leave your room when you did to sort out what had happened."

"I suppose I am glad to get out of this alive." I uttered with nervousness. "This Chuck is one big dude all right."

I felt that I could play on their sympathy. I thought that if this interlude with Christy was too dangerous to continue with, that perhaps I would be able to get involved with Julie. And if Julie and Suzie wanted to do their own thing together, I would not have minded if I just watched the two of them in action. I was not sure how involved I got with Christy or if she truly wanted to get away from Chuck.

Everything was moving so quickly. Perhaps the best thing for me to do at that time was to move on to something else before I ruined the rest of my vacation. I thought, the hell with it, life goes on. There are many more women to conquer in this world without getting my ass kicked in by someone like Chuck.

We walked onto the pool area and it was empty for the exception of one eld-erly woman who was just leaving. We had the room to ourselves. Just then, my cell phone rang. I got nervous and my heart started to beat with intense, that I nearly fell into the pool. I picked up the phone from my belt and said 'hello'.

It was Christy. I turned to the girls and they knew as well. I spoke into the phone.

"Hi Christy! Are you okay?"

"David, I am fine." She spoke rather rapidly. "Just listen. Let me speak and do not say a word. I told Chuck that I had to cash in my chips before we left, so he went back to my room to pack my things. I just had to call you."

"Are you okay?" I again asked. Just then, Julie grabbed the phone from my hand and started to talk to Christy.

I could not hear what she was saying as she walked away from Suzie and me. I thought it best to just let them work it out by themselves. I may have had a chance to get out of this one way or another, and maybe Julie would be the answer. I truly did not want to get into any more dangerous situations, and maybe it would have been best to just spend the rest of my time with Julie and Suzie. Perhaps I had gotten in way over my head. What did I know? I was just a teacher, not a CIA or a secret service agent. So could this have been my final lap on the quest for the weird and the unusual? I was back in my thinking mode. I was thinking of what was next on my agenda aside from trying to make the most of my last few days and my trip to Las Vegas a most memorable one.

"She's coming over." Julie interrupted my thoughts as she got me back to reality. She gave my cell phone back to me, and started to pace back and forth by the pool.

"She's what?" Suzie said excitably. "She is coming here? When? Where do we meet her?"

"She's decided that she is going to leave Chuck and stay here, and she wants to talk to you, David." Julie then asked me to talk to Christy.

Oh, shit. Just when I thought I had everything worked out, I was going from the pot into the fire. What to do from here, as I only had moments to decide. I could have stayed and chatted with Christy and hoped that Chuck would not come looking for her, which I felt he would. Or I could excuse myself and go back to my hotel, check out, find another hotel to stay at, or just go home. I had many options. But whatever I decided to do, I had to make up my mind right then and there. No time to think.

I spoke to Christy for a moment and she asked me to be there for her. I told her that I would help her if she wanted me to. There was this little part of me that always seemed to reach out to people who needed help. We then hung up.

"Girls, do you know where the men's room is?"

They both pointed in the direction of the locker room, and I excused myself, with the intention of not returning. I was not going to turn this issue into a disaster. I was going to run far away from all of this. Christy or no Christy! Julie or no Julie! I would return to my room, pack my stuff and move out of the Venetian and go to another hotel where no one would be able to find me. I had had enough of all of this crap.

I left the pool area, not even saying goodbye to the girls as if I was heading for the can. I ran as fast as my legs could go without having a heart attack. I did not want to appear like a man afraid of another man, especially if that man was a gangster.

But I was not about to put myself in this kind of situation again. I got away from all of this, years ago and I chose not to do this ever again. And this man was twice my fuckin' size and could cause me to have a very short life. I could imagine that the bulge in his pocket was far different than the bulge I have had in my pocket for the past few days. It was not his other friendly fellow, but his 'Rosco' that he could do a lot more damage with, than I can do with mine.

I got to my room and nothing was rearranged. I put all of my things together and headed to the checkout. It was time to find another place to bed down for the night and get away from all of this madness. I did not want to be with any more flighty nymphomaniacs or happy lesbians, or hot-to-trot gay women who could have really done a number on me by having their fiancées come lurking at me in every corner. I needed a place of safety for a day or two and then head on home.

As I approached the check out counter, I heard a voice. It was that same fucking voice that seemed to plague me all day. Why was it, that wherever I was, I would hear this voice in my ear that was enough to rattle one's brain?

"Checking out, David?" It was my friend Rita. Always there, no matter where I was, so was she.

"Yes, I am. I think I will try something new for the remainder of my trip," I said, trying to ignore her.

But she curled her lips and then pursued by persistently asking one more question.

"Interested in a drink before you change your plans?'

That was exactly what I needed, a brandy to calm the nerves. I was getting too old for this shit, but not too old to have some fun, even if it was Rita who I might indulge with this evening, before it was over. I decided not to check out yet. Who knows, with what has happened in the past few hours, my experience in Vegas could turn out to be a blast yet. We headed to the lounge. Something told me that it was not over yet.

What was I doing with Rita anyway? She was the last person I expected to meet up with again. How come she always seemed to show up at the wrong time? Why was I going with her to the bar when I really needed to get away from this mess I got myself into? I just had a bad feeling about all of this. I wanted to check out but here I was with this redheaded beauty who always seemed to be there for me when things were not what they were supposed to be. We sat at one of the tables and ordered some wine.

"This has not been a good day for me, Rita. Things have gone from bad to worse." I muttered, almost feeling sorry for myself.

She gave the waitress some cash before I even had my wallet out. Oh well, maybe I should have let her pay for the wine. At that point, who the hell cared? She seemed harmless enough, but I was getting this uneasy feeling about all of this. Why did Rita always seem to appear just when problems began erupting?

Who was this girl who seemed to ask so many questions and did not offer any substance? It was time to lay all of the cards on the table and get some answers.

"Who are you, Rita?" I asked. "Where do you come from and why do you ask so many goddamn questions? Why is it that you seem to appear when I least expect you to? Every time I turn around, it is fucking Rita, rambling on like you are a thorn in my side."

I glared at her and things were not making any sense to me. Yet, I had this uneasy feeling just being around this person. I grabbed her neck and moved her to me.

"Rita, are you mixed up with this guy, Chuck? Are you working for him? I want to know what the hell you are up to and I want to know now?"

I allowed her to take a sip of her wine. I also raised my glass to my lips and things were beginning to compute as if I was downloading a file and waiting for it to come onto the monitor. I reached into my pocket and pulled out a piece of paper. It was the piece of paper that Rita had given to me early this afternoon. I looked at it again and it had her room number, 1432. It also had the message, 'Call me when you are free' and it was signed, Rita. The address shown was in Los Angeles. Was this the address of someone I should know? Who would Rita keep calling while she was in Las Vegas? I then decided to find out what the hell was going on here.

"Rita, take your drink and let's go. We are going to room 1432, your room."

We moved into the elevator to go to her floor and I pressed number fourteen. I asked her if she knew who Chuck was and if she was involved with him. We were alone and I kept my hand on Rita's neck, as she squirmed and cried out.

"Hey, David, take it easy. You don't know what you are talking about. I don't know anyone named Chuck. I am here just for a few days and you are coming on to me as if I am a spy for the FBI."

I realized that I was hurting Rita but would not release her from my hold.

"Rita, I am going to ask you again. I want you to tell me what you are up to? Why are you spying on me and who hired you to keep tabs on me, or the woman I was with? Just tell me the fucking truth or I will break your Goddamn neck."

The elevator stopped at the fourteenth floor and we got out. I told her to take us to her room or I would definitely eliminate the flow of air from her throat. She had no choice as I had a choke hold on her that would have snapped her neck. We got to her room and she opened the door and we went in. I threw her on the bed, placed my luggage on the floor, and sat down next to her. She felt the pain in her neck, and realizing that I had a strong hold on her, she started to back down and cringe each time I pulled her neck tighter. I had a strange feeling about this bitch and would not let up at all. My gut feeling told me that she was responsible for many of the things that happened to me that day.

"Okay, Rita, I am waiting for the truth. No more Mr. Nice Guy," I said. "Time is running out. Did Chuck hire you and are you following his girl, and that is how you got to me? Are you the one who told Chuck about Christy and me? Tell me the truth, Rita, or I swear, I will break your stinking neck and stop your breathing right here and now. You have three seconds before I pull the plug and squeeze you to death, you little bitch."

Rita was in a hold and she knew that if she responded with a wrong answer, I would angrily disengage her pretty little head from her shoulders. She asked me to let up so she could speak. I did so only with a warning that if she was going to play games with me, I would not give her a second chance.

"Okay," she replied. "Yes, I know Chuck. He got me a great job and I owed him one. He asked me to follow Christy and then I found you. The two of you were having an affair and I told Chuck what I had seen. I told him what had happened and he told me that he would come to Las Vegas. I followed you to the Bellagio and saw you with the three women. I knew that there was something going on and this was something that Chuck would want to know about.

"Chuck was going to pay me a lot of money to spy on his girlfriend and then I saw an opportunity to cash in on you too. He could cut you off so fast, that you would not know what hit you. He is a gangster and I did not want to go against him. I am afraid of him. I saw a way to make a quick buck or he would have cut my nipples off and that is the way he operates. He is an animal."

I saw this frightened young woman whom I held by the neck, shaking and very scared of what may have happened to her if she did not do what Chuck wanted her to. She was definitely scared of Chuck and now she was opening up to me. Perhaps we would be able to work something out where I could get back at this big shlub and get Christy back. Christy called me on my cell phone and said that she wanted to leave him. That was good enough for me. I should have stayed at the Luxor and met with her, but something told me to get back to the Venetian Hotel. Now I found out how Chuck got to us. But I know that you do not leave a gangster like Chuck. I needed a plan to get Chuck out of Christy's life forever. And out of mine for that matter.

I had to think hard and fast, and I needed Rita to act as my shill to get Chuck in a certain area so I could get to him. Did I want to kill him? That was a thought. I never killed anyone in my life, at least not in the past twenty years. I don't count what happened in my previous life, before marrying Martha, my loving wife. But too many people were at risk here and I was trying to resolve an issue that affected the lives of some pretty darn nice people.

As I sat back and relaxed my hold on Rita, I thought what in blazes was I thinking? I just met this girl yesterday and already I was involved in something that was probably way over my head. But it was also my head that I was concerned about. Chuck now knew that I had an affair with Christy and he would be coming after me as well. I knew that I had to act quickly, or someone was going to pay the piper. I had to get Christy out of this and at the same time, get me out of this. So I had to devise a plan.

"Rita, you and I are going to sit down and we are going to get both of us out of this mess. Are you willing to work with me? Just say yes or I will tighten my grip on your fucking neck so hard that you will never see tomorrow. Do you understand what I am saying or do I have to rearrange your life right now?"

Rita was scared. She was afraid of me and she was also afraid of Chuck. I got her in a position that was not too pleasant. I needed her for my plan and decided to give her some slack by telling her that I would be able to free her from this overgrown humanoid and then she would be able to go back and enjoy a lifestyle that was more befitting to her. She would not have to fear Chuck ever again. I was hoping that she would cooperate.

I looked at this woman, a most interesting species, with great breasts, and a face that was cute and innocent. I was hoping that my demands would sink into her devilish little mind that what I was about to do would free her, and Christy, and me, from this guy who everyone seemed to be afraid of. I was going to commit a crime of some sort and it was just another experience in my life as a simple, nice guy, who just wanted to meet a lovely female to have a relationship with. Now I was having a relationship with four women and one guy. Boy oh boy. I felt like this escapade was getting to be more like a mystery. Why does life have to be so complicated? Did I really want this? Was this going to be the end of my teaching career?

I sat on the bed thinking about how my life was getting more and more complicated. Why can't we just meet someone, fall in love, and live happily ever after? Why do we have to go through so many hardships and do what we need to do to make our life safe and secure? Now I was going to be part of a scenario that I had no idea how it was going to turn out. Here I was with Rita, a sexy woman with a body that wouldn't quit, and I was threatening her to work with me so I can be with another woman whom I thought I was falling in love with.

First things first! I grabbed my cell phone and found the number of Christy's cell phone. I called and let it ring. Once, twice, three times. I called the number again and a voice answered. It did not sound like Christy's. "Hello…"

"This is David," I said. "I would like to talk to Suzie." It was best not to ask for Christy under the circumstances.

The person on the line paused and said, "David, this is Julie. Where are you? I took Christy's phone from her when it rang, thinking that it may be Chuck. Are you okay? What happened to you?"

"Julie, I went back to the hotel and learned how Chuck found out about Christy and how he got to my room. It was that red haired gal who Christy and I had met in the elevator earlier in the evening. She followed us since yesterday because Chuck hired her to do so. I am fine. How is Christy?"

Julie put Christy on the phone. I moved away from Rita but told her to hang loose and not to leave the bed. I walked to the window for better reception and heard Christy on the phone.

"David, I am fine. I am with the two girls in their room. Chuck would not know about them and where their room is. I am so glad you called. I was worried about you. Will I be able to see you later? I told the girls that I do not want to go back to Chuck. He is a maniac and he is a dangerous man."

I pondered a bit and then spoke with conviction, having decided to take charge.

"Christy, stay with the girls for now. It is too dangerous for me to come after you as I may be followed. I will stay in touch with you by phone and you can call me on my cell phone. Let's just cool it for now and let me come up with a plan and get back to you later."

"Okay, David," she said, feeling a bit tired from all of this. "I will stay here with Julie and Suzie until I hear from you. Please be careful. I am so glad that you called. I was really concerned."

I faced the window and glanced back to Rita, then replied to Christy.

"I will call you later, Christy. Good bye."

I then put my phone away, and walked over to the bed. Rita was still sitting there with her face looking down at her lap. She then picked up her head when I sat down. She was so motionless, but still looked like a very pretty woman. She smiled at me and reached out to my face.

I saw this woman who was so noisy before, and so solemn now that it felt like I was with another woman. I held her hand and apologized for hurting her. She understood and just put her hand around the back of my head and smiled, moving me closer to her. Her shoes were already off and she just fell into my chest. I grabbed her and pulled her top off. I felt her warm breasts as she kept close to my body and allowed me to do anything I wanted. I was hungry for her body. I decided to make love to her and I did believe that it was what she also wanted as well. My mind told me one thing, but my body reacted differently. I felt the urge to get this fireball into bed, and I did.

I reached in the back and untied her bra and took it off. I then pulled her down on the bedspread and unhooked the snaps on her pants and pulled them off of her legs. Yanking off my shoes, I unbuttoned my pants and my shirt, and pulled them both off. I took Rita under the covers and spread her legs apart and started to make passionate love to her.

I put my face on her breasts and was ready to get inside of her. She was already wet so it did not take too long to find the right spot in her. I must have come about two times, and saw in her face, that she was going at it, hot and heavy herself. I was willing to try coming once more. What a piece of ass. Rita certainly knew how to give it all she had and she did. I sucked her nipples, and felt her body, from her legs, to inside her thighs, right up to her breasts and she touched me all over like an angel.

She was good, damn good. Rita knew how to make her man happy. She was making me happy. It was so easy for both of us to reach our climax. She did not fight me off at all, so I kept at it until all of my desires, and all of my anxieties were satisfied. I needed this after all that had happened. I kept my lips close to hers and she embraced me with her arms, and wrapped her legs around my body. We made love for at least an hour. We would have continued to make love but the phone rang. She reached for the phone and picked up the receiver.

"Hello," she muttered. It was Chuck.

"Where the fuck have you been, Rita?" He said as I had my ear close to the receiver. "I lost Christy and I need you to help me find her. Get your fucking ass down here to the lobby and find her, Goddamn it. I want you down here now. Do you understand?"

"Okay, Chuck," she replied. "Let ME take care of finding David. YOU should be concerned about finding Christy. But if you want me to find both of them, I will get on it. We'll meet in the lobby in forty five minutes."

Chuck seemed content with her answer and hung up. She took a deep breath and knew that she bought herself some time. Very unlike Rita to answer back they way she did, as she had told me that Chuck did not like others making decisions for him. He had to have control in the 'family', she said. I took this remark in the sense that she meant 'Mafia-family'.

I put my clothes back on and even though I felt incredibly relieved having just indulged in passionate raw sex, I was still concerned about Christy. She had the beautiful face of an angel, unlike any other woman I had ever known, except, maybe Julie. Though Rita was a fine, hot and passionate broad, there was no love there. I just wanted to be inside the dark, comforts of a woman, the depths of escape and pleasure. Rita satisfied my needs at the time, but I wanted my lady back in my arms. At this point, 'that lady' could have been Christy or even Julie. What the heck! I would take them both.

Rita asked me if I had come up with any ideas as to how we were going to handle this mess. I thought for a while and felt that there had to be a way to get this straightened out without having to kill anyone. It was the last thing I needed on my resume, let alone in my memory. There were too many obstacles, but I knew that if I came up with something where everyone could win, there would be no need for bloodshed.

I told Rita that I needed some time to think.

"I am going to take some time to work this out, Rita. I will call you in an hour and we will meet somewhere to discuss this. Give me your cell phone number if you will not be up in your room. Here is mine just in case. We have to stay in touch, no matter what."

I did not want her to know where I was going. So I took control of the situation and reinforced my threat into her brain that she had better answer her cell phone or there would be hell to pay. She agreed and I left her to the uncomfortable task of meeting with Chuck in the lobby. I snuck out the back exit and slipped through some side streets, all the while, holding on to my two small pieces of luggage.

I still had not checked out from the Venetian, as Chuck and his boys would have spotted me, and I was feeling like a fugitive. Was this what my idea of a relaxing vacation had come down to? I had found myself in a bit of a mess. Yet, on one hand, I was enjoying the unexpected excitement that was luring me into a world of intrigue, mystery and injustice. It had been nearly twenty years since I played these kinds of games.

I tried to rid myself of those memories and lead a normal life. It had been twenty calm years, and I was a sort of happy guy, being with Martha, my dear wife, until that fateful day when she died of cancer. That tore me apart. My entire world collapsed. I never thought that I could be as happy ever again. I cried for weeks and we never even had a chance to have children due to her long, endearing problems. It was meant to be, I suppose. I would not know what I would have done if we did have children. I just kept on teaching and going about my life as if time would heal all wounds. It had been a most stressful time for me.

Now I was in a situation once again that was stressful. I was hoping that Martha was watching over me and guiding me through all of this as she guided me throughout the mourning of her death. It was so difficult cleaning out the closets and the dressers of all of her things. That was more stressful than anything I was in at Vegas, and nothing could be as bad as losing a loved one. I have missed this woman and missed the love that she always gave to me. I missed that part of my life. And for two years, I was leading a most unproductive life that did not mean a damn thing to me.

How ironic that unexpected circumstances had led me into the arms of a total stranger, trying to detach herself from a tyrant, a mobster. Here was this big bad dude who just might have been on the verge of losing control when he found his fiancée with me in my room, and was tailing me while I was trying to hide from him. For the first time in a long time, I was putting my life on the line for a stranger. Unlike saving a little old lady in the supermarket from filling her face with a high fat count from a bag of cookies, this was a bit different. This was more of a matter of life and death. Was I ready for this? It has been so long since I encountered such intrigue and was called upon to do this kind of a job.

You never know everything about life. You may not have known that Winston Churchill was born in a ladies' room during a dance, or that Al Capone's business card said that he was a used furniture dealer, or that Maine is the only U.S. state whose name is just one syllable, or that the full name of Los Angeles is 'El Pueblo de Nuestra Senora la Reina de los Angeles de Porcuincula. Does anyone care if all fifty states are listed across the top of the Lincoln Memorial on the back of a five dollar bill? Or a dime has one hundred and eighteen ridges around the edge? Or in England, the Speaker of the House is not allowed to speak? Or that there are three hundred and thirty six dimples on a regulation golf ball? Does anyone really care at all?

Why are these things not important to people? Why is life so strange and unpredictable? Why do we love a challenge and want to help others whom we feel are helpless and don't even know they are? Is this why we were put on this earth, to try to accommodate others or to give ourselves that edge against those who do not know that they are helpless?

I have tried to understand life and have always tried to do what I thought was right. I found myself walking the narrow streets away from the Strip and kept an eye out for someone who might be following me. I tried to blend into the shadows of the buildings, and watched the footfalls of my strides and remained cautiously alert.

I finally found a small hotel on a side street, off the Strip and knew that it would not be the most likely place for anyone to find me. I then would have to check out of the Venetian immediately to end all ties from that hotel by remaining invisible. It was best if I made sure that they had no idea what I was up to or where I was. This trip still might have turned out to be a lot of fun, I thought, once I solidified my plan to save Christy.

I settled into a modest room, nothing compared to the one I just left, and called Julie on Christy's cell phone.

"So how are you girls doing?"

"David! Where are you? Are you okay?" she sounded frantic, responding to me.

I could not tell whether Julie was actually frantic or just going nuts trying to outguess Chuck. I thought back just a few short hours before, when the four of us were dining and laughing at the restaurant.

"I'm good, Julie. Are all you girls there, together?"

I had to get an assessment of where the girls were and what kind of frame of mind they were in. If we as a group were going to conquer the big bad wolf, we needed to be on the same parallel. I felt that this was a mission that enabled my testosterone to definitely grow again as it did when I did this kind of work before. I was good in those days. Nothing got past me. Even in terror, I still had erotic thoughts about Christy, yet I had to remain in control. I knew that the girls were counting on me.

Julie came back on the phone. "David, I must tell you. Christy got impatient and left to go looking for you. I'm afraid for her. Chuck has goons everywhere in Vegas now, looking for her and for you. No telling where she is. She took my clothes and tried to disguise herself so as not to look like herself. She may have gone to a phone booth to call you on your phone. So if your cell phone rings, it may be her."

I too felt a pang of frantic nerves and told her to remain calm and to stay put. We hung up, but before we did, I told Julie that I would keep the phone clear. If I heard anything, I would call her back. What the heck was I supposed to do now? Just then, my cell phone rang. I thought that it might have been Christy. It was a number I did not recognize with a California area code. It looked like the same number that was written on that scrap of paper Rita had given to me when we first met at the slot machines. I quickly pulled it out and it was. It was Chuck's phone number.

I pressed the 'talk' button and heard this rasp sound on the other end.

"David, this is Chuck. I am with Rita and I am looking for Christy. I am not in a good mood right now, and I want Christy back. If you have her, you better bring her to me."

It was a voice of anger, of panic, and of desperation. I thought for a moment, and then replied.

"Chuck, I do not know where Christy is. And, as far as my being interested whether or not you find her, I am not. That is not my concern. But if I do by chance meet with your finance, tell me where you are and I will bring her to you."

I needed to know how to contact him and find him if I had to. My better sense was to let him think that I was bowing out of this mess. It was best to tell him that I wanted out and did not want to tangle with him or his cronies.

"This is how it is, my friend," he said, as he started to raise his voice, angrily. "If I do not find her, I will find you. You got into something way over your head and I am not about to forget what you did to my Christy. I am with Rita now and I have my people looking for Christy and you, and we will find you both. And when we do, there will be hell to pay, you understand? You are a stinking lowdown son-of-a-bitch that needs to know that you have fucked with the wrong person. You do not know what you got yourself into. You do not know me but you soon will. You understand, you 'prick'?"

I asked Chuck to give me his own cell phone number, as Rita would probably keep her own phone. I again told him that I would contact him if and when I knew where Christy was, and that I was on my way out of Las Vegas. He was in a piss poor mood and was not about to let this thing go away. I felt safe being out of the Venetian Hotel but I needed to know where Christy was. I wanted him to think that I was leaving so he would not keep looking for me. But, I was going to find him and put a stop to this. He gave me his cell number and I hung up. There was no need to continue any further with this conversation. I sat in the room and waited until I heard from Christy.

Did Rita turn against me? I had no idea but I could always reach her and find her later. I first needed to find Christy, so I sat in the room smoking cigarettes and watching TV. It must have been an hour or so. The time was past midnight. I could not sleep but I was getting tired. I tried to close my eyes but there was too much on my mind. I tried to relax yet I was on the edge of frustration. Then the phone rang again. It was Christy.

"Where are you?" I asked her. "Are you in a safe place where no one could find you?"

Christy started to cry. She sounded nervous and I could sense that this girl was frightened and needed me.

"David, I am okay. I am at 'Circus Circus' at one of the phone booths. I needed to find a safe place. Where are you? Could you get me or could I come to you? Just tell me where you are so I could be with you."

I pondered over this very carefully and told her that I would go to her. I just did not want to tell her where I was or she might lead Chuck and his boys to me if she was being followed. I thought that if I went to her, I could case the area that she was in, somewhere in the southeast end of the casino. She told me that she was wearing a blue baseball hat, the kind that Julie would wear playing golf. She had on a denim jacket and black pants, and tennis shoes just in case she had to run from one place to another. I told her to stay there, hidden by the slot machines and just play for the next hour until I got there and would find a safe place for her.

I took out some jeans from my luggage, a pair of tennis shoes, and a black t-shirt. I changed my clothes and had an old golf jacket that I put on. I also had a baseball cap to partially hide my face. While dressing, I thought back to the time I was in the Navy Seals, stationed in Nicaragua and we had an assignment to get Manuel Noriega out of Panama. This was a secret mission and there were about fifteen Seals, all experienced in the art of war and covert operations.

This was what I was trained for and vowed that I would never again do this kind of work. It was tiring and dangerous, and I saw many people killed, both on our side and the other side. The politics in our country were just as bad as in any other country, and I felt that we, the men and women of the armed forces, were pawns in a battle of wits. But I followed orders and we hit the beach secretively and had a mission to accomplish.

We were to take out the elite guard that protected Noriega and take him back to the states. This was a delicate operation, one that only the Joint Chiefs of Staff and very few units knew about. It was a pitch-black night and we had to get to Noriega's palace unseen. There were too many obstacles before us, and any fuck-up would have hurt our mission. We moved about undetected and hit the streets like shadowy figures, no noise, not even a whisper. Each one of us had headsets and a way to contact each other but we were only allowed to do so if there was something before us that would get in our way. The unit had to go many miles inland and up the coast. We had just so many hours to do this as there was a sub waiting for us to take us home.

As a back up, we would call in the choppers and find our escape that way. The Navy Seals were trained like no other cadre in the armed services. The Delta Force and Rangers were good, but we were the finest and best-trained men in all of the United States. The excitement and the unexpected just kept your blood churning all of the time. It took at least three years and heavy training for me to get my first assignment and this was a big one. They said that I was good but I sometimes had my doubts. There were so many who had seen combat before me. I was new and still wet behind the ears, but longed for this kind of action ever since I joined the team. Now I was in the thick of it and I loved every moment right down to the sweat pouring down my face, and the stink of the jungle habitat all around us.

We trained hard, and learned how to use our hands in combat by taking all sorts of martial arts. Heck, that was over twenty years ago. I wondered if I still had the skills just in case I needed to use them now. I was like a machine then, a fucking soldier who was not afraid of doing my thing. It was a great exercise in fruition and I pulled through with flying colors. Now, twenty years later and fifteen pounds heavier, I may not have the same kind of quickness that I had, and my reflexes are probably a hell of a lot slower. But what the heck, I was trained by the finest, to be the best.

This training came in handy as the fifteen of us slowly moved through the countryside that dark and chilly night in this God-forsaken country. It was the United States that put Manuel Noriega into power. Just like Sadam Hussein, Osama Bin Laden, and other dictators in countries around the world, we seemed to find drug czars who took money from the United States, built up a powerful army, developed acres of drug plants, and created a distribution of the drugs throughout the world. All of this came on the bankroll of the United States of America.

We were the culprits that planted the seed to put these people in power. Then we come along and want to take them out to show the world that we are the good guys. And here we are, opening up the roads so that the marines and the rest of the cavalry can come in and take Noriega back to the states and place him on trial for drugs. It was all a political game and we were the chosen pawns to show the world that we were tougher, smarter, and had the guts to take out any leader that would not conform to our way of democracy. We were the soldiers, the professionals. We were the striking force that made it all happen.

This was not what I joined the Navy Seals for. Having read stories regarding the independence of Israel, there were many such leaders who gave their lives for the independence of a free state. Prior to becoming Prime Minister of Israel, and during the years of his long service in Parliamentary opposition, and the three years of his participation in the Government of National Unity (1967~1970), Menachem Begin was commander of the Irgun Avai Leumi, fighting for the liberty and independence of Israel, and indeed the survival, of the people of Israel. He always indicated that it was a higher task to lead the fighting patriots in that unequal struggle, under the heaviest of odds possible, of the few against the army. I remember reading his quote:

"When a man fights for freedom at the incessant risk of his life, he identifies himself completely with the very idea of liberty. Such identification is possible only once in a lifetime."

Israel was finally declared independent as a state when the City between the walls fell, in Uyar 5708, the year 1948, and the Irgun Zvai Leumi had broadcast this message:

"...There was no surrender in the Old City, but a battle waged with supreme courage which returns us to the days of yore of our people, when it's sons stood on the Temple Mount, and together with it went up heavenwards in flames. This fight and this courage strengthen our hearts on this bitter day; they give us the confidence that the liberators of Judea and the redeemers of Israel shall yet return to the Temple Mount, and shall yet raise our banner atop the Tower of David."

My parents named me after the Tower of David. I felt a strong strength of belonging, of doing what was right. And I joined the Navy Seals to help make our country a better place to live in. I wanted to be like Menachem Begin, to fight against tyranny and for freedom. I wanted to think that there was so much good in the world, that I could make a difference if I joined the best outfit and do my part in taking out the bad guys. I wanted a total world of freedom.

So here I am, in the middle of a struggle to get rid of a dictator that we put in power, and take him back to stand trial for his crimes. How ironic. It was our job to pave the way for the marines to come in and take Noriega back to the U.S., and imprison him. And we, my fourteen comrades and I, were here to do a job to make our country look good in the eyes of the world. We crept along the countryside and did just that, and we opened the doors so that our boys could overtake the cancer that was hurting this country. We accomplished this feat, without much resistance.

We were the elite group that made all of this possible. We captured the leader of the drug cartel and brought him back to the U.S and he still remains in prison today. This is what I was trained for. This is what I did. And the Sadams and the Bin Ladens of this world would live on, because we could never find them. Sadam was finally captured, a poor and wretched soul. Most of the enemies we supported at one time or another, became poor and wretched because we forced them to become that way.

Now I would meet Christy at Circus Circus and find a way to get her away from yet another tyrant, a mobster who needed to be stopped in his tracks. This time, I did not have the backing of the Navy Seals, the cavalry of the Delta Force or the Army Rangers. I needed to do all I could to get this guy to go away. But first, my priority was to find Christy and make sure that she was safe and sound. I needed to take her away from Chuck, as I would have done years ago.

CHAPTER 5

▼

HOW DEEP IS THE OCEAN...HOW HIGH IS THE SKY

I headed to the Circus Circus Hotel and Casino and wanted to look around before I approached Christy, whom I was hoping would be at the slot machines as I told her to. I thought I was falling in love with a woman whom I did not know but I had this yearning, this desire, to be with her and protect her from all possible dangers. I walked into the casino and looked around cautiously and went to the area that Christy and I set up as our meeting place. I kept my eyes peeled for any scrounging looking people who might also be looking for her, as well as for me. We both had baseball hats on, and we both dressed like beach bums from Laguna Beach or The Hamptons. We were going to find a way to get out of this situation one way or another.

I took my time and just walked very cautiously, as I got nearer to the slot machine area that Christy was supposed to be at. I looked around and saw people putting their coins in the machines. I saw lots of people holding buckets of change as they tried to find friendlier slots to put their change in. I watched the people, and tried to notice any odd looking characters in the area. When you go to Las Vegas, nearly every character is odd looking, even you to others.

I approached the exact area where Christy was supposed to be and looked for a woman in a baseball cap. I walked up and down the aisles and there were so many people sitting, facing the slots. It was going to be hard for me to find her, and I supposed that was a good thing. It was going to be hard for Chuck's people as well. Slowly, I walked up and down the rows of slot machines, until I spotted a woman in a baseball cap at one of the machines at the end of an aisle. I walked toward her and was hoping that it was Christy. Leaning over, trying to see her face, I whispered in her ear.

"Christy, is that you? If it is, just keep on playing the slots and wave your hand at me."

The beautiful, long thin hand waved at me, and continued to play the machine. She wore light colored painted polish on her nails, and her hat, just covering her blue eyes, did not give her away, as her hair was tied neatly in a bun under the cap. If it weren't for the polish on her nails, she would have passed as a man. She wore black denim jeans and cute little tennis shoes, with a button-down shirt tucked inside, and a big belt that looked two sizes too big for her. Julie's clothes, I bet. Perhaps her curvy body may have revealed her sex, but who would be looking at it, under such an unattractive outfit? I remembered her beautiful body, how it was so warm, up against my own. That was something I could not forget.

If it were not for the fact that I enjoyed the immense pleasures of this woman, I probably wouldn't have been there at that moment. I was getting in deep with this woman and her trials and tribulations of her life. It was unlike any other moment of passion I had had, even with Martha. There was no comparison. Martha did not bring out the animal beast in me although I loved her dearly. Even in the military, I had been in my prime and yet, it did not even come close to being with a woman as sensual as Christy. My entire life had led me to the gems of this woman. Was this all worth being with her? Or was I going to find that there will be something more to her once I was able to escape this charade?

Looking into her eyes, I almost wanted to melt as I had a need to kiss her and tell her that everything was going to be better than before. We would eliminate

Chuck's hold on her and resume our normal lives. Normal? What the heck was that? It has felt like years since I had been home, living a normal life. Being in this fantasy land, and the overwhelming commotion had made it nearly impossible to remember my being in my own home, only two days earlier.

For the past two years, I had been living in a world with nothing but memories surrounding me. Until that day at the mall, meeting a beautiful woman in the parking garage, I would not have had the urge to get out of Dodge. This gave me that opportunity to be a man once again. The stresses of my last two years transformed me into a different person. The stimulation of going to Las Vegas, meeting fabulous women who enjoyed flirting with me, and possibly my falling in love with this woman who was sitting next to me.

I felt the obligation to save her from a man who was a bully, and the possibility of my becoming the super-hero in my own comical sense of the word. Who knows? The joke may have been on me. I had to remember what it took for me to conquer and save the distressed. That is what I was good at. I needed to reboot that time frame by thinking of a quick idea for our next move. I was taxing my brain for answers and I needed them right away. I had to get back on track as if I was a weapon of the Navy Seals who flirted with danger continuously.

"David, so wonderful to see you," she whispered under her breath as she kept putting quarters in the slot machine in front of her, not once picking up her head. "What the heck are we going to do?" she said, trembling.

I rubbed her back, and thought of the time she did the same to me in my room the night before. If only we were back in my room again, and there was none of this 'cloak and dagger' to contend with. My wishful thinking was to be back in bed with Christy but I knew that I had better concentrate on our escaping from this crap. I had to put my mind in high gear, and get out of here as soon as possible, or we both would be dead. I knew though, that it was not going to be easy. I did not know what kind of pressure Christy would be able to handle. I figured out that she always had a need to run, and I wondered how long she was running like this.

She told me that it was because of me that she finally got enough nerve to leave Chuck. Perhaps this was so, but maybe I really didn't have anything to do with it at all. Maybe Christy had done this before and Chuck always came to rescue her from her own demons. But she had not known Chuck for too long, so it could have been something in Christy's past that made her do this. I did not think that Chuck was an easy person to compromise with, especially if he was so well connected. I also did not believe that Christy had been strong enough to leave him sooner and that he somehow had a strong hold on her.

I would have liked to think that I was the reason but I certainly did not want my act of bravery to be in vain. If I was to risk my life for this person, it had better be for the reason that she wanted me in her life, and not just to use me. Nothing would be worse than a chump on a mission of mercy. In my past life, I was sent to save men who were fighting for a much larger cause, the courage to fight for a nation, I was now in a position to save a woman but had no idea how I was going to do it. I just could not think logically at the time, for something was missing in this puzzle. I turned my head for a moment, and there she was coming toward us. How anyone was able to find someone in this crazy town was beyond me.

I shook my head and thought, 'this was unbelievable'. She never ceased to amaze me. It was Rita and she appeared out of nowhere. Just when I thought that Christy and I had good cover.

"David," she muttered quickly. "This is what is going down. Listen up. Chuck is on his way. He found out where Christy is and he is out for blood. I truly suggest that you leave here immediately. I will detain him as long as I can. He knows you came here to find her, whether he got wise to you by tapping her phone, or his boys spotted you somewhere."

I stood there and listened to her rambling on and tried to keep up with her every word, as she kept speaking a mile a minute. Her eyes were bugged out and she kept fidgeting with herself. Phone taps? Was I followed? How the heck did they do that? They must have really known what they were doing, and I had better get smart, real fast.

"Okay, Rita," I said. "We'll go now and I will be in touch with you."

I immediately grabbed Christy's arm and we started to move away from the slots. I did not know where I was headed but we just had to keep on moving away from this place, and from Rita. We moved in and out of the crowds and sped up our pace, heading toward the exit. We looked around to see if we were being followed. These guys were good, whoever they were. I knew that I had no time to waste. It was now or never. I had to make some sort of a move. What if Chuck's people had every exit covered? Would I surrender Christy to them? I had hoped that I had a clear chance to escape this web of entanglements and find a better shelter for both Christy and me. We walked quickly to the east exit of the casino and saw the streetlights just outside of the doorway.

Deep down inside, I secretly had hoped that there would be a confrontation between Chuck and me. What would I have done if there was one? Actually, we did have a confrontation, but I stood there like a dummy because Christy told me not to say or do anything to Chuck. I grabbed my things and ran. That was not what I was trained for. I never ran before in my life. Next time, it was going to be different. I would confront this guy and somehow, someway, end this madness.

We stood outside on the sidewalk. Christy leaned into me and squeezed my hand.

"Oh David, what are we going to do?"

I just did not have an answer for her, yet. As we stood there, I kept hearing this constant honking from behind us. I hated to turn around thinking that it might be Chuck and his boys, and maybe it was not for us. But everything was starting to bother me as I felt like a hunted animal. It was dark and it must have been after two in the morning. There were two beeps, then three in a row, and a faint voice yelling.

As I turned to look where the racket was coming from, I saw Julie waving her arms from the driver's side of a car, while Suzie was sitting next to her in the front seat. Their car, Julie's BMW, was behind two other cars, two taxicabs. I told Christy to look behind me so she too could see the girls waving at us. My hunch was they heard from Christy from Circus Circus and came to rescue her, probably right before or right after Christy called me. She yanked my arm to go with her toward the car the girls were in. We quickly got into the back seat and at this early morning hour, traffic was moving quite fast. We sped onto the main road and after we caught our breath, I opened up the conversation.

"Okay girls, now that we are all here, where are we going?"

"It is so late, we probably need some sleep," Suzie remarked. For once, she was right. We were all good and tired.

I looked at Suzie, then at Julie who was driving, and suggested they pull down one of the side streets into the parking lot of the motel I was staying at. Julie parked the car and we all went into the room that I had my luggage in. It was a safe bet and we could all grab some shut-eye until morning. The only thing that was certain was that we all needed time to rest and think about what we intended to do. It was muggy in the room so I flipped the switch and put the air conditioning on. There were two double beds, so Julie and Suzie took one, and Christy took the other.

I needed to wash my face and grab a smoke so I did both in the bathroom. I locked the door to the room with the chain and we were able to see Julie's car from the window. It was as safe as anyplace right now. We were all exhausted and everyone just wanted to lie down and close their eyes.

I thought about how Rita always seemed to show up when you least expected her. I thought about this as I got into bed, next to Christy who was fast asleep. I was thinking of a plan. I had to get to Rita. I needed to know what was going on here and how they seemed to track us down. I needed to check out at the Venetian. We also had to get back to the Luxor and get the girls' clothes packed and to take their suitcases from their rooms.

Next, I thought of calling my old buddies from the Navy Seals whom I stayed friendly with. They were tough and knew how to handle this, and I needed a good, strong team to go after Chuck. During the past twenty years, we were always there when any of us needed each other. If that was what it took, then that was what I needed. I just did not want a guy like Chuck, hanging over my head. It was time to fight back and put all of this to rest, once and for all.

Morning came and I got up. I headed to the shower and changed into some light clothes as it was going to be another hot day in the desert. The girls were also up when I came out of the bathroom, and each one had to use the facilities. I told them to stay put and if they wanted some breakfast, Suzie should go and get it and bring it back to the room. I also said that I had some phone calls to make and was putting together a plan to get us out of this mess. They did not ask how as I just told them that I was going to get some friends to help us, and that I needed to do a few things in the morning.

I headed back to the Venetian Hotel and went to the fourteenth floor, Rita's room. I knocked and Rita came to the door.

"Yes, who is it," I heard this voice, as if the body had been awakened from a deep sleep.

"Open up, Rita, it is David."

Rita opened the door and she was in a black negligee, probably just got out of bed. I sat down on the chair by the desk and I needed some answers from her.

"Rita, how did you find us at the casino at Circus Circus last night?"

Rita told me that Chuck had people all over the strip and he was determined to find Christy. One of his people had followed Christy when she left the Luxor Hotel and tailed her to Circus Circus. When I showed up, Chuck was notified and he was going to meet us there with his people. He told this to Rita and she ran to warn us. I thanked her for her telling us to leave when she did.

She also indicated that Chuck had gone back to Pacific Palisades in southern California as he had some business to take care of. He told his people to hang around awhile but Vegas is such a big place, there was no way he would hope to find Christy and me unless if by accident. We seemed to cover our tracks pretty well. Yet, they found us anyway. Rita was scared and wanted out of this and was willing to work with me to get Chuck to forget about all of this.

She told me that she was leaving Vegas today and was going home. She lived in Irvine, not far from John Wayne Airport in Orange County. There was nothing more she could have done and Chuck felt that she failed and he was not pleased with her trying to help him locate Christy and me.

I took down her home address and phone number and told her that I would contact her when I got back to southern California. She also gave me the address of Chuck's home in Pacific Palisades plus his phone number, and that he would be there all of this week. I offered to pay for her room to show my gratification but it was already taken care of. Chuck prepaid it ahead of time. Now I had to check out of my room and help the girls gather their things, and check them out of their hotel as well. What was supposed to be a relaxing vacation for me, turned out to be a nightmare. I had met many characters during this visit to the Vegas Strip and I thought about what might happen in the next few days.

Rita was not such a bad person after all. She was lovely to look at, even in the morning, and she had such a marvelous body that just accentuated her negligee. If I had time, I would have loved to grab her and fondle her breasts, and make love to her. But my better judgment told me to let it go. There would be another time, another place. I had too many things to do this morning and I needed the time to take care of them. Today was checkout time for all of us. Las Vegas would have to wait for another time, and I still had to contact my buddies who could help me out of this unfortunate mess that I got myself into. As a team, we used to brainstorm and come up with great plans of action. I needed that brainstorming now.

I kissed Rita on the cheek and told her that I would call her in a few days. I then went downstairs and checked out of my room. There was no need to go to my room as I may have encountered some of Chuck's thugs. After that, I found a phone booth in the casino and called Kyle, hoping that I would catch him at home. Kyle was the leader of our team. Captain Kyle Mclean, or 'Cappy' as he preferred to be called! He knew how to organize the unit to do what was right and we did what was expected of us. Kyle was trained as a ranger and then was part of a group that excelled in hand-to-hand combat and taught us how to handle ourselves as Navy Seals. The phone rang and he was not home, but his wife told me to try him at his office.

I called the stock brokerage firm and asked for him. He finally got on the phone.

"David, it is so great to hear from you. I thought that you were enjoying yourself in Las Vegas? Get a chance to gamble or just relax at the shows? How are the women there, my friend?"

I told Cappy the story, about meeting Christy, her two friends, Julie and Suzie, the unpredictable Rita, and the encounter with Chuck. I needed to have this guy whacked and I needed the help of our friends. The Navy Seals were trained to do this and knew how to take care of these kinds of problems.

He told me to meet him at his home the following evening and he would make contact with the other guys and have them at his home as well. That was good enough for me. I now had a team of experts to go after Chuck. I had the most elite team of professional killers you could ever hope to find. And we were trained by the best. Now I had to change my whimpish ways and start thinking like a Navy Seal once again.

I went back to the motel, told the girls to get dressed and that we were going back to the Luxor to get their things and check out. We drove into the garage and Christy stayed in the car with Suzie. Julie and I first went to Christy's room to pack her clothes in her luggage and we brought everything to Julie's room where we packed Suzie's and Julie's stuff and placed everything in their luggage. Julie checked out of both rooms and we went back to the car in the garage. They drove me to my car that was parked at the Venetian and we decided to head out of Vegas and toward Los Angeles. I followed them in my car and we stayed pretty much the speed limit.

Within two hours, we came to Barstow and decided to have some lunch. We filled up our tanks with gas and sat down at Denny's for a quick lunch and discussed all of the things that had occurred yesterday. It was time to just sit back and relax. We started to laugh at the different things we had done, and all the while, watching over our shoulder for any nasty looking thugs that might come through the door. The lunch was good and there were no incidents. What do you expect at Denny's? I paid the check and we climbed into our own cars and started to drive toward LA. So far, so good!

We felt safer as we were getting closer to San Bernardino and then to Riverside. The familiar areas were welcome to me and we just talked back and forth by cell phone. Suzie was driving and Christy sat in the back seat, while Julie was up front with Suzie. We were safe and sound and I would follow them to Julie's house where Christy would stay for the night just in case they were watching her home. Julie was certainly an intelligent individual. If all went well, I was thinking of taking Christy back to my place where we could bed down together if she wanted to.

It was about 4 pm and we arrived at Julie's. I followed them into her home, a nice townhouse that had lots of room. We unloaded Julie's and Christy's luggage and Suzie said her goodbyes, got into her own car that was parked on the street, and took off. The three of us sat down on the sofa and breathed a sigh of relief. We were home, safe and sound. And I was sitting with two of the most beautiful women I had ever met in my life. I told them of my meeting with my friends the next day and the two of them just wanted to know more about me and who I was that I could have such friends in my life.

Julie took out some wine and we just relaxed and opened up to each other, whom we were, some history about our past lives, and how we were all becoming friends. This was the first time we were talking about ourselves to each other. It was nice to hear about their stories, as I was sure that it was interesting to them to learn a little more about me. Things started to become a little clearer in my mind.

Christy started to open up first. She was the most shy out of the three of us, but she also had more wine than any of us. I turned to Christy and asked her to tell me more about herself. I was not trying to pry into her life, but she began to say so much that it made it possible for me to have a better understanding about her.

She was relaxed on the couch, one leg tucked under the other, with her glass of wine in one hand, and the sweetest smile on her face, as she spoke to us.

"Listen, guys, I was never one to share my soul with anyone, except when I met Chuck. But I feel so comfortable now, and so relaxed. It was such a great idea to come here."

Christy continued. "Listen, Julie, first of all, thank you for opening up your home and for being such a good friend and for making me feel safe, and letting me vent. I know that I have put you guys through a lot, and I wish Suzie had stayed on so I could tell her this. But I know that she had things to do."

Julie was sitting next to her and gave her a big, warm hug. The women looked so beautiful together. I suddenly got the urge to get in on this action, but I didn't pursue it. Mentally, I took a picture of them and forever I would be able to see them embraced in this loving hug.

Christy continued to speak, and the more she did, the more I wanted to make love to her. I had to focus on her words, but I was continually imagining the both of them in bed, naked, and I wanted them to devour every inch of me. I knew that Christy was talking mostly to me as she had revealed her life to Julie before, having been friends for so long. I not only felt honored to be the recipient of her life story, but I was feeling very horny, all at the same time. I had to remember to keep my 'rocket' in my pocket. This was not the time. But it was 'hard' to do that.

"When I met Chuck, I was young in my thinking about life, and I felt taken in by his power and his control. He made decisions for almost everything we did. I grew up with a father that was not there, because he was always working. I had to take control of the family, tend to my younger siblings, and make all of the adult decisions. My father and mother had divorced when I was a young teenager and we had lived with my father. As I grew older, I got tired of all that, and all I wanted was someone to take of me for a change. I met Chuck through Julie just about a year ago as he was a client in her law firm and he invited us to a Christmas party at his home."

She then turned to Julie and winked, but I knew that she never resented her friend for introducing her to Chuck.

"It was a moment I would never forget," she continued. "Chuck took me in his arms that night at the party and promised me the world. He bought me gifts I had never imagined I would ever own. He took me to places that I had never been to, and showed me a world that I only dreamed about. I was his queen and he was my king. But things started to change. I found out who Chuck was and the things he was involved in. He was a ruthless man and I was his toy to play with."

Christy then stood up and walked toward the bar and filled her wine glass once more. I thought that she had had enough, but who was I to judge.

"My family was sort of wealthy, but my Dad had other plans for his income. My Dad liked to dabble in the stock market and buy commercial buildings and other real estate. Many times, it never panned out and he lost money. When he made money, he was off with other women and left us kids to fend for ourselves. He left my mom and she had to work two jobs, and all that jazz. I had to take control of my younger sister and younger brother. Well, let's just say that she, Kathy, is happy somewhere in Paris and I haven't heard from my brother in a couple of years. He has his own agenda and we haven't spoken to each other for many reasons I do not care to discuss."

She shook her head, and I could see that there was another story there but let it alone.

"But it was my sister, Kathy who introduced us to Suzie, actually. Isn't that right, Jules?"

"Yes," Julie jumped in and took it from there as I turned my head around to face her. Julie was sitting on the other side of Christy, on the couch, also with her one leg tucked under her. I had a great viewpoint from the chair across the way and could watch both of them, as they were so heavenly to look at. Like two little pixies, each holding a glass of wine.

"That's correct," Julie said, and both girls started to giggle.

The wine was relaxing them, but I knew that there was a good tale coming. So I got myself situated, filled my glass with some more wine, and asked Julie if she had some snacks.

I was still a bit hungry even after our trip to Denny's. Maybe my appetite was not for food. Perhaps I was hungry for them, but that was not an option at that point. I was the observer and they were telling me very intriguing stories about themselves, and who they were as people. I did not want to miss any of it.

Christy went back to her story.

"Suzie is actually from Paris originally. She came to the United States to a convention and met my sister, Kathy who was at the same convention. They became friends, and soon after, Kathy went off to Paris. We thought she was going to Paris for work. She came back for a visit one winter, and brought Suzie with her. None of us knew that Suzie, or that even Kathy were gay. She introduced Suzie to Julie and me, and we just loved her. They had broken up about a year later and Suzie stayed here while Kathy went back to Paris."

I could see some tears assemble in Christy's eyes as she told the story.

"It is rather simple actually. Suzie became a great friend to us. She may be a bit eccentric, but she makes us laugh all of the time."

Julie brought in a tray of cheese and crackers and little finger sandwiches. Now here is a woman who can do more than just one thing at a time. Talk, listen, comment, pour some wine, and then make cheese and sandwiches. I was impressed with Julie from the very beginning. I wondered if this was how she was in bed with a man, able to do more than one thing at a time. A few hours went by, and after a few glasses of wine and some snacks, I was getting either a bit restless or feeling a bit woozy from the wine. Christy began to talk about her life with Chuck again, when I thought it best to interrupt her at this point.

"I'm sorry to break in, sweetie," I said. "I would love to take a walk, if you don't mind, girls? Maybe we need a bit of fresh air and watch the sun go down? How does that sound to both of you?"

They both loved the idea and they each went upstairs to find something else to put on for our stroll. I watched them walk up the stairs, with their long legs, and their sexy strides, constantly talking, and taking each stair so delicately. I was in awe. Two such beautiful women and all I wanted to do was to follow them and make love to both of them at the same time. I shook my head with these thoughts as if I had better cool my jets.

I could not imagine how this was possible, not now. Perhaps I could make an advance while we were walking or I could lead our conversation to the point where they would have to respond to me whether or not it was a possibility. I wanted to find out if this was in the cards. I had to make love to at least one of them, although both would be ideal.

The odds for both were extremely slim, but I might have had to roll the dice and try anyway. Heck, I just left Sin City and I was still thinking in terms of 'odds'. So for one last gamble, I was going to go for it. Maybe if they were both not interested, at least, maybe, it would get me the hell out of this mess. If they were offended that I suggested it, they might ask me to leave them alone. Did I really want that? I had to think about this. Was it worth the gamble? I pondered over the odds and considered rolling the dice.

We headed out into the yard area. The grounds were well kept and the condos were clean and freshly painted. I was walking in the middle of the ladies and I wanted to grab their hands, but knew better of it. I listened to each of them talk and giggle, and I jumped right in.

"Hey girls, is there a place nearby where we can sit on a bench and watch the boats? Where is the nearest harbor?"

Now this was Irvine, an inland city off the I-5 Freeway. So we jumped in Julie's car and headed to Newport Beach. We drove down Jamboree Road and it was just a short, fifteen ride to the ocean. Julie turned down Pacific Coast Highway and parked in front of the harbor where these tremendous sailboats and yachts were docked.

"Oh David, this is a beautiful spot. Let's walk. I will lead the way."

Of course, Julie loved to take control. She would be the initiator in bed if you let her, I thought. She would direct what action to take in our lovemaking, and would be like my Navy Seals buddies who make the plans and execute the action. She would talk about the outcome, analyze the scenario and size up the people. She had what it took to make things happen. I could have made it appear as if it were her idea. Perhaps that was best. I started to make my move.

"Julie, have you ever been married?" I asked.

"Yes, David," She replied. "I was married many years too soon, and many regrets later. I do believe that I married for the wrong reasons, and after finding this out, I had to start my life over again. I have been single for many years, and prefer it this way. I dated one of the partners in my law firm but that only lasted a short time. We split up when he brought Chuck and his company into the firm as a client, and things started to go downhill after that. After we broke up, he was also asked to leave the firm. I have many good friends and I have just met another. You! You have been terrific, David. I really appreciate all that you have done."

She reached for my hand and squeezed it, and I held onto it a little bit more. I turned to her and took her in my arms. If she was in control as I thought she was, my risk had better pay off.

I looked into her eyes, so close for the first time, and she had the most beautiful face. Christy was pretty, but Julie was beautiful.

"Thank you, Julie. I think that you are terrific too."

I gave her a small kiss on her lips and started to pull away, even as she held on. At this point, Christy had walked further ahead, and we had stopped in our tracks. It didn't seem to matter to Christy that we were hugging. She was in her own little world and didn't even look back at us.

"Listen, Julie," I started to comment. "I realize that you know that I have been with Christy, and how that turned out. I don't want to continue to be the culprit of bad tidings. I think that she is lovely, and quite fascinating, but the more time I spend with her, the more I will be getting into a mess that I really do not want to be in. I had called my buddies to help us out and we will meet tomorrow evening to look into this situation."

I continued. "But it is really because of me that it has gone on this far. I feel very responsible for all of this. I find you extremely attractive, ever since we met in that parking garage, and if…."

Julie put her hand on my mouth. She didn't want me to finish my sentence.

"David, please don't feel badly about any of this. I truly believe that it would have happened with or without you. It was just your lucky day. I would love to get to know you better, perhaps later, when things have calmed down a bit."

We both agreed that this was best and we caught up to Christy, who found a great bench on the lawn for us to sit and watch the yachts anchored quietly, floating on the still waters of Newport Beach. I was in heaven. I felt like jumping on one of those boats and sailing away, taking Julie with me. We would head out to sea and have a wondrous time together. But that would mean that I would have to leave Christy behind. And seeing that I was mostly responsible for the situation we were in, I thought that I had better fix it, and fast.

The sun was setting. It was close to 7:30 pm and we wondered where the day had gone. We all stared out into the horizon and for a while, none of us said a word. We watched as hundreds of pigeons, wrens and penguins circled the waters in search of food. The fishing boats were making their way back and the sailboats, with their masts fully blown, were slowly heading toward their slips at the dock. It was peaceful and very still. We just sat there and stared at the beautiful surroundings.

"You live by the harbor, don't you David?" Julie asked. "I love to be by the water and lie on the beach and get a tan. California has such great beaches, Huntington Beach, Seal Beach, Newport Beach, San Clemente, and so many others."

I kept looking out at the sunset and replied.

"I live down in Dana Point, right next to San Juan Capistrano where the swallows come out. It has been a city since 1989, and is about six square miles with a population of about 35,000 people. I enjoy it, as it is quiet and very serene. The people are truly great and care about their city. There is a local paper called the Dana Point News that comes out every Thursday with news about the City. Have you been there?"

"Yes!" she replied. "I have spent many days surfing at Doheny Beach, and also Capo Beach. I just love it there. It is much cooler than in Irvine and it is only about twenty minutes south. How long have you been there?"

"Well, let's see now," I thought. "It has been around seven years. I could bike ride along the San Juan Creek Trail and be at Doheny Beach in five minutes. It is good exercise for me and I love the coolness of the ocean air as the sun does not even come out until early afternoon due to the overcast."

I continued to talk about myself to Julie as if she was truly interested in me.

"Only problem is that it is far from Los Angeles if I have to go there. Since I teach within a twenty minute drive or so, I really don't mind the morning traffic."

Christy was coming out of a so-called coma as she had been staring at the ocean for a long time, and finally decided to join in the conversation.

"You know, David, I would like to go to Dana Point and see the ocean. I think I need a change of scenery right now. You don't mind, do you? I mean, would you take me there?"

I turned to her and told her that I would, one of these days.

"No," she stated emphatically. "I mean tonight. Could you take me to Dana Point tonight? I think I would like to see the harbor and the boats in Dana Point this evening. Could you take me there and show me around?"

I looked at Julie and she smiled at me.

"You know, David, that would be good for Christy. Perhaps she needs to sit by the ocean and get all of her thoughts together. Anyway, I have things to do to get ready for my day at the office tomorrow. This way, Christy can have some company. You did say that you wanted Christy to meet with your buddies tomorrow evening anyway, didn't you?"

I didn't know if I was getting the brush off from Julie, but at this point, I could see that she may have been considering her friend, rather than having a future relationship with me. She gave me the go ahead by putting her arm around Christy and was thinking of her concern rather than ours. I thought it was noble of her and I decided to do it.

"I think that you are right, Julie. I have plenty of room in my home and in this way, Christy can relax and not be alone. We will just go back to your place, pick up our luggage and I will take her to Dana Point."

We stayed for a little while watching all of the boats come in, and then we headed back to Julie's home. Christy headed to the bathroom and this gave me an opportunity to speak to Julie.

"I was looking to get to know you better, Julie. I had no intention of taking Christy back to my home. I hope you understand that before I take Christy back to my place. I am doing this because you had asked me to."

I made it sound as if I was doing this for her.

"David, you are always so sweet. A naughty boy sometimes, but you are sweet. I want you to take care of Christy until we can work this entire matter out. Take her with you to see your friends and perhaps, they will have a better angle on how to cope with this guy Chuck so we would not have to be bothered with him ever again. And another thing, it would be good for you and me to know that we shall have this understanding between us. I like you David, but until we can get Christy safe and sound, we could never have anything else than what we have now. I am asking you to do this for me as a friend. We need some closure on this and then we can talk again."

It seemed like Julie was keeping the door open. That was fine with me. She trusted Christy and was beginning to trust me. I didn't know if I could trust myself. I had the 'hots' for both of them and for the moment, it did not matter who I went to bed with. What the hell, they both are gorgeous women and I already had Christy. I was waiting for the chance to have Julie also. Just then, Christy came back into the room and was gathering up her things.

"David, I feel so much better now. I am looking forward to a quiet evening with you and want to see how you live. Let's go. I want to see the boats at your harbor and maybe we can grab a bite to eat at one of the local restaurants."

We hopped into my Jeep and headed south along the I-5 Freeway. The sun was gone, and it was getting late. Food was not something that was on my agenda. We turned off Camino Capistrano and headed into the heart of Dana Point. I parked the car in the garage and took both Christy's luggage and my own into the house. She followed me inside. I asked her if she wanted to go to the harbor and she replied by saying that she wanted to see the highest view of the ocean.

We drove up Blue Lantern and parked close to the Chart House, where we could see the entire harbor and all of its boats. Although it was dark, the moon cast a bright stream of light over the ocean that shone on the boats at the harbor.

It was so breathtaking, even for me, having seen this sight hundreds of times before.

"This is so wonderful, David," Christy said as she just stared out into space. "I love it here. I could see why you live here. This is one of the most beautiful spots in all of California. I just want to stand here and admire all of the beauty."

We stood outside of the car, looking at the ocean with the moon leaving a long brightness across the sea. The sounds of birds were heard in the distance, and the water seemed so motionless. This was indeed a paradise to live in.

"I am happy that you are happy, Christy," I said, feeling a sense of relief for her after all that we had been through together. "I just want you to be happy and enjoy life as we all should. This has been a moment in time that I will never forget."

We stood motionless, as if staring into space. There were cars coming and going up the hill but none stopped. All of this was ours. The smell of salt water, the stillness of the ocean, the specks of dark dots in the sky that were the birds, seeking some food, the coolness of the air, and a beautiful body next to mine.

"David, do you like me? I mean, do you really like me?"

I thought for a few seconds and replied.

"Christy, I think that you are so beautiful that I enjoyed every moment we had spent together. I truly enjoyed making love to you and always looked forward to doing it over and over again. I just treasure those times we spent under the covers, touching your body and letting myself go, right into your arms. You have given me the most pleasure I have ever had with any woman I have been with. I was not afraid to let my control go."

"David, take me in your arms and hold me," she whispered as we embraced our bodies, while overlooking the ocean.

She moved her leg between mine and ran her fingers through my hair, moving my head close to her. She gave me passionate kisses on my lips and wanted me to squeeze her body into mine. I was feeling the same way I did the first time we made love and the anxiety was still there. This woman was hot. And I could have her if I wanted to. She wanted me and I would be foolish if I did not take her back to my bed and have sex with this lovely creature with so much fire.

We embraced a bit more then got back into the car and headed toward my home. I opened up the windows and sliding doors to air out the place. I then gave her a quick tour and told her that she could use any of the three full bathrooms, two upstairs, or one downstairs, as they all had showers. I went into the master bathroom, took off my clothes and turned the shower on. I reached for a clean towel and placed it around my waist.

I then brought out some new towels for Christy and gave her a new bar of soap thinking that she would also want to shower in the other bathroom. I then went into my shower as the water was becoming nice and hot.

I thought that I might have a great evening with Christy under the covers and this would be a good ending of a long day. I let the water go over my body, through my hair, and lathered my body with soap. It felt so good and I was starting to feel clean all over. I then heard the shower door open. My heart stopped. I had no place to go but just wait for the person to make his move. I was startled by this and turned toward the door. I saw this body coming toward me and moved to the back wall of the shower. I was not used to someone opening my shower door and it sort of surprised me when it did open. I was relieved when I saw the figure coming closer to me, as the heat of the shower made the room misty and unclear. It was Christy and she decided to join me in the shower.

CHAPTER 6

▼

COME TOGETHER, RIGHT NOW, OVER ME

Her beautiful body slid into mine. The mist in the air, and the hot water felt amazingly erotic. She had her arms wrapped around my shoulders and I caressed her soft sensual body. She leaned down to my erection and with her voluptuous mouth, encountered me and took it upon herself to enjoy and devour every inch she could feel inside of her. She was tender and sweet, and not as aggressive as before, and I liked that. I felt like I knew her a little better, and even so, her taking the initiative did not frighten me at all. I had never experienced this kind of lovemaking in the shower before, not even with Martha, as she would not have thought of such pleasures. I was not as forthcoming with Martha as I was with Christy either. I was definitely a new man.

My trip to Vegas had proven to be quite productive and it was an awakening for me. Although there still were areas of uncertainty to tend to tomorrow, my mind was free of that for the moment. I was enjoying the desires of this magnificent beauty, and Christy was bringing me to peaks of pleasure, that gave me this elation of life, and it was like being in heaven.

She came back up to me and kissed me on the lips. I grabbed both of her legs and wrapped her around me as I entered into her. The moment was hot, like the burning timbers of a forest blaze. The hot water did not even exist as I only felt the heat of Christy's body as I moved in and out of her. She seemed to have it really bad for me, and without hesitation or need for further foreplay, she appeared to only want to please me.

I could have come in a heartbeat, but then I would not have enjoyed all that she had to offer. I let myself go deeper inside of her for what seemed to be eternity. I felt like this big stud, able to hold my own, as if I was an actor in a porno movie, and patted myself on the back, literally speaking of course. I knew that I could do it, but I didn't realize that I had this flaming desire in the shower.

This was quite arousing to me and I reached a new level of lovemaking. Christy then slowly bounced up and down on me, and I felt as if I was in a dream state. Unfortunately, I had visions of Julie on and off, doing this to me, and tried not to feel guilty for having them. For a brief moment, I imagined Julie was there and I was feeling her breasts up against mine, my penis inside of her, not Christy, and her hot body holding on to me as tight as Christy was. I was fantasizing about another woman as I was making love to someone else.

This only made me more excited and I came inside of Christy as if I was being drained. Every time Christy touched my balls, it just made me more excited, and I had to come more and more until there was nothing left and my body grew limp from the force that came from within. The shower kept cooling me off.

The water soon began to get cooler as we were in there for quite some time. I reached over to turn the nozzle off, but Christy grabbed my hand and whispered.

"Don't…. don't leave me."

Okay! If that was what Christy wanted, we would continue under the cold water. I just experienced another new love making as well, I thought. She cried out in joy and moaned and screamed several times, but I only concentrated on not blowing this trip I was on too soon. After several minutes, I couldn't hold out any longer and went for it again. She screamed even louder. I was actually surprised at the level of her vocal chords, though the acoustics in the shower only made it sound louder, having an echo effect. I was thinking that maybe, my neighbors heard her and might be rushing over to see if something was wrong. I had better calm her down and make our way into the bedroom.

She would not leave the shower. She wanted to continue long after I had finished and she seemed out of control. I wanted to make sure that I was not imagining this, so I turned the water off, ice cold at this point, and said to her.

"Come, my darling, let's move to the bed and go under the covers."

She was not going anywhere. I stood back from her and saw that her eyes were all glassy, and she looked completely out of it. I picked her up and carried her to the bed.

Standing over her, I could not have imagined what had happened to her. She lay on the bed with her eyes closed and she did not say a word.

"Honey, are you okay? Christy, please say something."

I was afraid she was asleep or unconscious, or she took something that made her lose all sense of herself. I was in a panic and knew that I had to do something as I was never in this kind of predicament before. I saw her purse on the floor and turned it upside down to see if she took something. If I could find any bottle or signs of pills, I would know what to do. Two small packets of some unknown substance lay on the rug.

I did not know what the heck they were or how she got them. All I knew was that I was in trouble if I had to call emergency. The last thing I needed was to have the closest of kin notified and have to come into contact with Chuck once again. I was not prepared for this bozo right now so I had to handle this my own way. I thought of calling Julie as she would know what to do.

But then again, I would have to explain to Julie that Christy and I were making love in the shower and that could very well end my friendship with her. I was damned if I did and damned if I didn't. It seemed that ever since I met Christy, my life had been one dramatic episode after another. Maybe my best bet, I thought, was to drive her to the hospital myself. I could then drive away, after I dropped her off. It also occurred to me that I could also drive her to Julie's house. Did I have time to do this? Would Christy die if I didn't react at that moment?

I immediately dried my body and hers. I put on my clothes and put hers on her body. I put those two packets of substance into my pocket and carried her to the car. I was going to take her to South Coast Medical Hospital and let the doctors look at her. The trip only took ten minutes and I needed to save her life. While they took Christy to the emergency room to look at her, I called Cappy and told him what had happened. He drove to the hospital and we looked at the two packets that belonged to Christy. He was sure to tell me what they were without bringing in the police.

"This is CPC, Coke or Crack," he said. "It seems your girlfriend was taking these drugs as a stimulant to help her out of some misery. Were you not aware of this, David?"

I looked at Cappy and realized that Christy may have been a dope addict. Having a boyfriend like Chuck, anything was possible. I went in to see the doctor and told him that she may have taken some drugs and that he should take a biopsy or a blood test. They had Christy in the emergency room for a few hours, and Cappy stayed with me in the lobby. I told him what was going on and that we needed to get after this Chuck and stop all of this nonsense once and for all.

Cappy told me that he had at least six of the Navy Seals, our long time buddies, coming over that evening for a meeting. I reached in my wallet and found the piece of paper that Rita gave to me with Chuck's address and phone number on it. I handed it to Cappy. Then Cappy spoke to me in his usual authoritative voice.

"Look David, I did some prelim on this guy. I called the 'Moose' and he told me who this character is."

The Moose was Monty Maynard, our IT technician, a research and data guy. Anything you needed to know about anyone, Moose knew how to get it. He was good. He could get into CIA files and hunt down any kind of data and come up with just about anything you needed to know about anyone and anything.

"Moose told me that this Chuck is Chuck Manzione, a new type of hood who has taken over the drug market in California. His father was a soldier in the old Teflon Don Gotti's family. His grandfather was a driver for Carlos Gambino years ago. Chuck is trying to reorganize the family under his rule and has many politicians in his back pocket and he is a vicious bastard who would stop at nothing to rejuvenate the family under his leadership."

At least we had some background on him and the wheels were turning. It was best to know whom we were going after and find the weak spots in order to put him away. Cappy was good at organizing and I knew that he still had the power to do so. With the rest of the Seals, we could put an end to Chuck and the police would only welcome the loss when we did.

"Look, David," he continued. "This Chuck has to go. I checked with some of our friends in the FBI and they have been after him for a long time. His entire organization has been under suspicion for a while and if we put him away, no one would care. I got many of the boys coming over tomorrow night and we can work out our plan of attack to go after him."

I felt relieved. Now we knew whom we were going up against. The guys were experienced in this. I thanked Cappy and he left as he had to get up early and get to his business. He ran the management company for a large stock brokerage firm in Los Angeles and they started very early in the morning. I then sat down and waited until I heard from the doctor. Two hours had passed and I just sat there, thinking about how we, as Navy Seals, handled situations years ago.

It was dark that night in Panama, and we were closing in on Noriega's palace. We had to open up the doors so that the marines could go in and get that scumbag and take him back to Washington to stand trial. We each had an assignment, and we entered the palace through separate doors. We had to take out some of the guards quietly, by using our knives or choking the dumb shits by twisting their necks. Cappy was first to enter the palace. The rest of us followed as we surrounded the building. We had the latest naval night vision goggles, communication gear, small arms and other weapons, developed by engineers at the Naval Surface Warfare Center (NSWC) in Crane, Indiana. Crane's primary function was to acquire a wide array of parts for the U.S. Navy, ensuring naval superiority.

Crane boasted a labyrinth of buildings and munitions bunkers, dedicated to researching and developing batteries, radar systems, night vision sensors, chemical and biological detection, small arms, radiation hardening equipment, pyrotechnics, microwave tubes, and printed circuit boards. The Seals were the first to test these products and this gave us the superiority over other rogue groups, which made us the best fighting force in the world.

As we moved silently into the palace, we realized that Noriega was probably upstairs in one of the bedrooms and we had to take out a lot of his men. One of our guys disconnected the electricity and it was dark, except for the vision we had from the night vision goggles. We slowly crept along the walls of the downstairs' rooms, eliminating any of the guards who were there, and climbed the stairs leading to the upstairs bedrooms. Not one shot was fired. We were trained to use our hands and whatever else we could, without using our guns.

When we arrived upstairs, we had many bedrooms to enter, before we would find Noriega. We traveled in twos, silently but cautiously. After going into many of the rooms, it was the team of Scott and me to enter the room where Noriega was. He was shacking up with one of the women in his entourage and was on top of her when we walked to his bed. Scott grabbed Noriega and quickly tied his mouth up with tape so he would not scream, and I looked down at his bitch and she was totally scared out of her mind.

She had the biggest pair of tits I had ever seen and had this sweat from Noriega's body all over her. She was completely naked and I felt like getting a piece of this but there was no time. Even then, I loved fucking the women. I was younger and so Goddamn horny, I needed to rock my nuts whenever I could. I guess I had my share traveling around the world as I did. In every corner of every city, of every country, there was some piece of ass I had left my mark on.

I taped her mouth, tied her up to the bedpost and we left with Noriega. We took him downstairs and tied him to one of the dining room chairs in the big room. Cappy notified the marines that Noriega was captured and that the building was secured and they were free to enter the building.

Our job was done here but we had other missions to follow, one being in Afghanistan. It seemed that a rebel was causing some problems there and he was somehow involved with the bombing of planes and buildings around the world. Our job was to find out about him and report to the Pentagon. He was an unknown entity but his terror was expanding and he seemed to be involved with these terrorist acts. He was a strange dude as I never heard of him before but our

job was to track him down. Our next mission was to capture this unknown terrorist, Osama Bin Laden and his group called the Al Qaida..

I was taken out of my thoughts by a tap on the shoulder. The doctor returned
and sat down next to me.

"Mr. Burns, your lady friend is doing fine. We found a little blood clot and we
were able to take care of it. She also had some drugs in her system but we neutralized that as well. I suggest we keep her in the hospital for a few hours. Why not
go home, get some sleep and come back later on in the morning. I am sure that
she will be just fine."

I was worried that he would report this to the police but he reassured me that
when Cappy told him that this was a secret mission for the Navy Seals, he would
not file this report. He too was in the service years ago and recognized a growing
danger to this girl if it ever got out that she was on drugs and was in hiding from
gangsters. I felt good about this.

I drove home, did not call Julie, but went to bed feeling a sigh of relief. Cappy
came through again as he always did. I also felt comfortable having friends like
Cappy and the rest of the guys. We were still a team after all of these years. I had
a growing sense of protectiveness and I was getting back into the game once
again. Once a Seal, always a Seal!

After nine hours of blissful sleep, and God knows, I truly needed it, I just lay
back on my king size bed feeling quite comfortable, actually. It occurred to me
that I had not been alone for quite a few days. I found myself with many beautiful women and it was exuberating. I enjoyed the trip to Las Vegas, but it certainly
was a pleasure to come home and find peace and solace, here in my own bedroom. I found myself rejuvenated with a sense of freedom that I had not felt
before, or at least for many years.

I believe that I accomplished something within myself, getting out of the
period of time that I was almost feeling sorry for myself, after losing my wife to a
disease that nearly rocked me out of my own life. I was getting free from the
attachments of my own past, and found myself engaged in the lives of others.
Although I no longer thought of myself as being glued to the images of my previous life, I was beginning to sense that I was able to move on, and to be someone

who was able to create a new life with someone else. Who that person might be, I didn't know.

I thought about Christy's seduction in the shower the night before and it was an incredible time. She was so hot that she wound up in the emergency room. I was so hot that it was unbelievable. There was nothing appealing to me to further deal with these problems except for the fact that it got me involved. I needed to get out of it so I would be able to go on with my life without any interference from a hood like Chuck. I thought of calling Julie and asking her to meet me for lunch, but I wanted to see how Christy was doing.

For some reason, although I really liked Christy, I had this sensation that I would rather be with Julie. She was intelligent and classy, full of life and awfully sexy. I really loved her in that red dress she had worn when we strolled at the harbor in Newport Beach. I loved her seductive nature in the garage at the mall. I thought how intelligent she was and how she seemed to be able to handle things in a most logical manner. I enjoyed touching her and holding her in my arms. Her lips were luscious and I wanted to be able to spend time alone with her. There was going to be a time when I was hoping all of this was going to happen and I thought about my future with her.

One might have thought that her friends may have been dysfunctional, like Christy, for instance. But even there, I adored Christy for who she was and how she affected me sexually and intimately. She was a different kind of woman and I found myself falling in love with her. This was indeed a tremendous time for me, especially for finding out who I was and where I was going. I was beginning to recognize the change in me and I liked it. I was becoming a new me. It felt really good.

After my shower, I phoned Julie at her office. She was probably swamped with work and quite busy, but I didn't care. The phone rang in her office and then I heard her sweet voice that immediately filled my body with an immense passion and a strong desire for her. I didn't know if she realized what kind of power she had over me, or purposely did it to amuse me. But Julie did say that before we could move closer together, we had to get rid of any problems that were in Christy's life. Such was a typical woman's move. If it were up to me, I would convince her that all this waiting was a waste of time, and that we should get it on NOW. I wondered if her attraction to me was as strong as mine was for her.

"Hi David," came that sexy voice over the phone. "It's so good to hear from you. I am so swamped with work, you wouldn't believe. I will probably be here until midnight this evening. And how is Christy doing?"

I told her about Christy's mishap the night before and that I left her to rest at the hospital. Julie thought I did the right thing as we both needed rest after the ordeal in Vegas and the five-hour trip home. I really wanted to see her but knew that tonight was taken as we had this meeting at Cappy's house. So I thought about another night during the week.

"How about dinner one night this week when you are not so busy with your work?"

I just didn't want her to feel obligated so I thought of using some reverse psychology. Yet, I was certain that she would pick up on it.

"That sounds wonderful, David," she said. "How about calling me tomorrow so I could see where I am with this work. And I know that you have things to do yourself, so it would be best for both of us to clear our calendar, our minds, and just have a relaxing evening."

Julie sounded great and she was happy to tell me what was happening at her law firm.

"Oh, by the way, the partners received a call from Chuck this morning, wanting to know where I was. He didn't waste any time trying to get me. He is a character, David, and I just do not like him."

Chuck was trying to get to Christy through Julie but I was sure that Julie would not tell him anything. She continued.

"When I got on the phone with him, I just told him that we parted company and that I had no idea where she was."

"That was a good 'heads up'. You did well, Julie," I commented. "Now that gives you an out. Let him locate Christy on his own. You don't have to be bothered with that guy. You have enough to occupy your time".

We hung up and I felt a sense of relief knowing that I touched base with her and she was happy to hear from me.

I thought I had better contact the hospital and find out how Christy was doing. When I had called, I was told that Christy had left and they could not tell me anything else since I was not family. But they did say that someone had picked her up and drove her from the hospital, as the car was parked out in front. They had to escort Christy in a wheel chair as it was hospital procedure, having had some tests and she was under sedation for a while. I wondered if Chuck had found out where she was or if Christy had called Suzie or one of her other girl friends.

Since Julie had not mentioned this to me, I assumed that she did not know so I did not bother calling her. I had Suzie's number in my wallet and scrambled to find it and then called her on her cell phone. Suzie seemed a bit distant and not that interested in knowing about who picked Christy up. But she did ask how she was, after I told her that Christy had gone into the hospital for some tests. Suzie did not hear from Christy ever since she left Julie's house, but we did chat a bit about our trip in Las Vegas. She was getting her house together and would return to work the next day. We hung up on a good note, and I told her that I would keep her posted how Christy was. But I was stumped as to whom might have come to the hospital and picked Christy up.

I went about my day, cleaning up the house, first downstairs, then upstairs. I had laundry to do, make some phone calls, prepare some lessons for my teaching in a few days, and after two hours of this useless drudgery, I decided to call my friend Stephanie. She was free for lunch so we met at the harbor. Stephanie was an old friend of mine whom I had known for years, during the time I was married to Martha. She would come over the house and helped me take care of Martha during this time of crisis.

Her husband, Tom had some problems with Lymphoma, a disease that produces additional white blood cells, and he was battling this for years. We discussed some of the bittersweet memories we had, reminiscing about our lives and the turn of events during the past two years since Martha's death. She sounded exactly the same as she did when I had last spoken to her about a year before, reminding me of a simpler, yet somber time in my life. I was now at a stage in my life, being more secure than I was back then, and did not want to let the history of my past come back to haunt me.

She was thankful that I had called her and we met at one of the restaurants overlooking the harbor. I listened to her go on about her new life and how she kept busy with the kids, while Tom had taken things easy, working at home as a writer. He always wanted to write novels and stuff for television, and now he was finally doing it. Her children were grown now and they attended high school, while she worked at the Chamber of Commerce office just a few blocks from her home. I then asked her if she and I could take in a movie sometime when we both had a few hours to kill.

Stephanie and I used to sit downstairs at my home while Martha was resting up in the bedroom. She had filled a gap that was missing in my life at the time, but I now had new interests, having met Christy and Julie. Since Stephanie was still married, there was no need to pursue her, but keep our relationship on a friendly basis only. Secondly, I was feeling that I needed something in my life that was much different than what I had had in the past. We had talked at the table in the restaurant for over an hour, when my cell phone rang. It was Christy.

"Hi David. Now don't be angry at me. I am fine and with a girl friend of mine."

I was relieved to hear that and asked her how her friend found her at the hospital.

"Oh, Patty is an old friend of mine and I contacted her this morning to tell her where I was and she picked me up and took me back to her house in Mission Viejo, not far from where you live. You know, just about six miles north on the freeway"

"Christy," I asked, "does Chuck know your friend, Patty?"

"Yes, David," she answered. "I told Patty everything that had happened. But she will not tell Chuck where I am and he doesn't know where she lives. I'm fine, David, really fine. I do have to apologize to you for my behavior. I told Patty all about you and how nice you have been to me. I have been out of control for so long, David but I am starting to see the light now. Please come by and pick me up. I want to go back to your place now. Let me give you Patty's address."

My heart felt heavy as I had this incredible need to rescue this woman from the cruel world and bring her back to me. I told her to stay put and would be at Patty's house within the hour and take her back to my home. This way, I would know where she would be and we can go to Cappy's house later without being late. I felt that there were other problems, mental problems with Christy, but I could not worry about that now. If she were on drugs, she would have to correct it or die. Perhaps Chuck had such a strong hold on her for so long that he got her interested in drugs.

Stephanie and I finished our lunch, and she went back to her job, not even asking me what that was all about. Stephanie knew not to meddle in my affairs the same way that I would not do so with her. I went home, finished the laundry, and whatever else I was doing before I met Stephanie, and drove out to Patty's house. It was a nice, private neighborhood, not far from the lake and she lived in a gated community where there were lots of pretty apartments. I parked in front and walked to the front door.

Patty opened the door and I saw this nice looking young woman, nearly 40, with such a great big smile. She welcomed me in her home and we sat awhile, until Christy turned to me and asked that we go. Christy and I said our goodbyes and headed, not to my home, but to the harbor. I think we both needed to sort out some things before we went to Cappy's. We stood around the rocks overlooking the ocean, with the docked boats on either side of us.

"Once all of this is over, let's take a boat ride to Catalina Island or even further, okay David?"

I smiled, and nodded positively. I then turned to Christy and asked her if she was on drugs, and she said that she was. Chuck had influenced her to try some drugs and now she wanted to stop this habit. It was not as bad as I thought as she had not taken any drugs for weeks, but still had these pains and headaches that made her feel weak and disjointed. I gave her a great big hug and bought her an ice cream cone. We walked along the ocean's edge, watching some of the smaller boats going out and coming into the channel. It was a nice, clear day and the weather was always perfect by the ocean, much cooler than in the inland cities.

Dana Point had its own overcast and the feel of a quaint town that never grew like many of the other nearby cities. It was rustic and had many different types of neighborhoods that consisted of apartments, townhouses, individual dwellings, some sitting high on top of the hills, and others that were huge mansions that were simply magnificent. Real estate in Dana Point was really expensive and they ran out of space to build any more homes.

There was one builder though who thought that he could control the town by buying seats on the city council until one year, that too blew up in his face. Two independent women beat out the two candidates that the builder had spent nearly $250,000 on, and that was the end of his dominance in Dana Point. I was happy to see this take place. The people finally recognized the fact that the builder was a pain in the ass and they did not fall for his direct mail pieces that crucified the two women who ran independently. For a small town, Dana Point has some pretty sharp residents. God bless them!

Christy was calming down and she was back to her usual self, which made me happy. We headed back to my place and I fixed a glass of wine for her. I showed her around and we sat outside on the back patio for a while, admiring the trees, the little birds that would come by and visit the birdhouses that I put up, and sang their pretty songs. It was a most relaxing time for both of us. We then went inside and I took Christy around and gave her a great big kiss. Tonight, she was going to tell us all about Chuck, the layout of his house and anything else that she could remember that would help us hit this guy hard and fast. I wanted this over as soon as possible. The only way to eliminate this cancer was to cut it out entirely.

"Christy, is there anything I can do for you? We have a couple of hours to kill before we go to Newport Beach and visit with Cappy. How about a sandwich or some hot tea? Would you like to lay down for awhile before we go?"

Christy turned to me and acknowledged that the part about lying down sounded good. She asked me to take her upstairs and she sat down on my bed. She motioned to me to come and sit down next to her. I had my body up against hers, and she snuggled even closer. She then put her hand inside of my leg and moved it toward my penis and touched me ever so slightly as if to awaken the sleeping giant. I looked into her eyes and saw this little girl who wanted some love and without saying a word, was trying to tell me that she wanted me at that moment.

I put my arms around her and we both moved our bodies on the bed, and Christy was ready to make love to me again. How could I resist such a beautiful woman? We took our clothes off, got under the sheets and she immediately got on top of me and straddled my body. I moved my hands up her sides, to her breasts, and placed them on her nipples, cupping them as she bent down and moved her lips onto mine. We suddenly found ourselves wrapped tightly around each other and we started to make love.

It was so easy with Christy. She had a body that was made to love and I was glad to be the recipient of this. I just loved the way she could get me to do anything I never thought I was capable of doing, and enjoying it as much as I did. This was something that I shall always remember about Christy, no matter what would happen in the future. We just lay there, making passionate love for the next couple of hours. It was sweet and gentle lovemaking and so relaxing.

Julie was in her office working on files when the outside receptionist called her to tell her that a Mr. Chuck Manzione was in the lobby to see her. She was taken back by this abrupt visit from Chuck and was not ready to see him, as she had so many cases to work on and type up the briefs that the other attorneys had left for her. It was late in the afternoon and she still had at least six or eight hours of work to do. As she moved her papers on her desk to get up, her door swung open and it was Chuck and one of his hard-nosed looking henchmen, standing in the doorway.

"I just came by to talk to you, Julie," he said. "I need some information on this boy friend of Christy's who I met in Las Vegas. I would like you to tell me everything you know about him and how I could find him. Then I want you to tell me how I could find Christy. I promise not to hurt you but I am looking for answers, so do not give me any jive talk, okay?"

"Please, Chuck, take a seat." Julie pointed to one of the two leather back chairs in front of her desk. He did not move but stared at her with the dark eyes of a tyrant.

"Please, Chuck, sit down." She repeated her plea a bit softer in tone as she simply wanted to make him feel comfortable and not have to look up at him as he stood before her.

Julie did not want a confrontation with Chuck and knew that her office would not appreciate it if she were involved with him as he was a client of the firm. They had simply had a bad history with him for the past year or so, and she knew that she had better quiet him down. The partners also felt that other prospective clients did not go with them due to the firm's ties with mafia people and they were always in the news media, trying to settle suits against the federal government on behalf of Chuck's companies.

Business Week Magazine called them the most arrogant group of attorneys around. The law firm had tried, on numerous occasions, to find Chuck another law firm to handle his affairs but he refused to consent to their wishes. This was his way of telling them that he was in control, not them. And the law firm was only there to guide him as to how to get his corporate affairs and his image out of public view. But he had to make all final decisions, and it was his word and his power that were controlling them.

"Listen, Julie, just listen to me and shut up." Chuck remarked to Julie as he kept his voice low so it did not trickle out of her closed office. "You bitches are all alike. Give you some authority, and the next thing you do, you think that you can control men. Well, don't even go there. You are nothing without men. And your law firm wouldn't be where it is today without us. We spent millions to your firm and now you will listen to what I have to say to you. I want you to meet with me at Angelo's this evening for a drink. Be there at 10:00 sharp."

He left the office and she knew that he meant business. She didn't want to go and talk to him but it also was not a good idea to avoid him. He would only be back and find her, and get others in her office involved, including any of her friends. She was also aware of the meeting that Christy and I were having with my friends this evening and she knew that she had to let them know that Chuck was badgering her and was still seeking Christy and me out. His pride was hurt and you do not hurt the pride of a lion when he thinks that he has you under his control. He had to feel that he was 'King of the Jungle'.

Julie then picked up her phone and called me as I was still at home with Christy, and time was getting closer to meet at Cappy's house.

"Hello?" She heard my loving voice and wondered what I was doing with Christy at the moment.

"David, this is Julie. Chuck came to my office and wants me to meet him tonight and threatened me to tell him where you live, what you are doing with Christy, and he wants answers. Obviously, you have gotten to him and he feels like he is losing control. I don't want to meet him, but I am afraid. I would like to tell him that you and Christy are not here, but had left to go on a trip, perhaps back to Las Vegas, or San Francisco, or even Barbados, for all I care. Tell me what you want me to do because I am scared and I don't like being in this position. Is Christy there with you, David?"

"I really did not want you involved in this, Julie. Let me think for a minute." I responded, as my mind was going a mile a minute.

"If you go, he can persuade you to tell him anything under pressure. If you don't go, he might do something nasty. If he heads back to Las Vegas to look for us, that will give us more time and I am afraid that he may want you to tag along and then you are stuck with him. But if he is in Vegas, maybe we can go through his place for some proof of what he is involved with and take him down that way. And by the way, Christy is here and she is doing fine. She is feeling much better now and we have to leave soon for my meeting."

I told Julie that I would call her back as she had some time before she had to meet with Chuck. Julie had this uncanny ability to foresee the future and was able to put things in their proper prospective. Her skills, by working in one of the top law firms in the city, enabled her to work with keen minds and learn how to analyze the facts quickly and with resolve. It was time to get dressed and go to Cappy's. I had to think about Julie's situation before we left and tell her what to do.

The phone rang, and Julie thought that it was my calling her with some additional thoughts on this issue.

"Julie, it's Rita."

How this woman was able to track Julie down was something else. She was the most remarkable woman I had ever known. Julie related this conversation to me later on.

"Julie, I need you to realize that Chuck is aiming to not only kill David and Christy, but you as well, for getting involved by taking Christy to Las Vegas. His demon-like mind thinks that all of this was pre-arranged and that you had a hand in getting Christy away from Chuck and bringing her to David. He might be stopping by to see you today if he hasn't been there already. I just wanted to give you a 'heads up'."

My goodness, thought Julie, this girl knows everything that is going on here. She spoke into the phone.

"Thank you, Rita. I was just about to head out for the day. Yes, Chuck was here a few minutes ago and he left. He wants to meet with me tonight and I do not think that this is a good idea. How do you know all of this and why are you calling me?"

Chuck had telephoned Rita and he told her what he was going to do. If it meant killing Julie, then that was on the agenda. In Rita's mind, he was a sick individual and he knew that Christy had friends at Angelo's which was a singles-getaway bar and grill. Rita also told Julie that many of his drugs were manufactured in Las Vegas out in the desert, where he had some large warehouses that stored the stuff.

Julie asked Rita if she knew where in the desert the large warehouse was, and Rita gave her some vague directions that led to locations outside of Henderson, although no one suspected anything. Henderson was growing in leaps and bounds and it was composed of senior citizens who were the majority residents living there. They would never suspect that anything like that was going on. Between the hot desert temps in the hundreds in the summer, and the heavy rains and dust storms in the winter, the retired seniors had all they could do by staying indoors or going to the slots at the casinos and spending their social security checks. They just did not care and would never think of questioning anything else that was happening around Las Vegas.

Julie did not know whether or not to trust Rita. She just asked questions and let Rita do the talking.

"Julie, I like David, and think that you girls are getting a bum shaft. Chuck has threatened me enough and my life is worth shit anyway. So just take this as advice and whether you believe me or not, that is up to you. If you need to speak to me later, here is my phone number. I suggest you tell David what is going on and protect yourself against this son-of-a-bitch."

I was just about ready to leave my place with Christy and go to Newport Beach to meet with Cappy and my Navy Seal buddies, when I decided to call Julie to tell her to meet me there as well. I didn't want anything to happen to Julie. I then called Cappy and told him what had transpired between Chuck and Julie. Cappy felt that Julie should make the ten o'clock meeting with Chuck but she would have company with her. Three hours was enough to discuss a game plan with the guys, and Cappy would send Mario with Julie to Angelo's before she would meet with Chuck.

This way, Julie would feel safe, and Mario could watch the situation very carefully as he was a good advance man, and knew how to handle things by himself. This would also give us a way to keep Chuck in sight and know where he was at all times.

I then gave Julie directions to Cappy's home and told her to go there right away. Julie also told me that Rita had called her and warned her that Chuck might kill Julie if she didn't do what he wanted. My own intuition was correct. I felt for her and did not want to take any chances on her being hurt. What could truly happen in a public place like Angelo's with all of the single people mulling about, trying to pick one another up, drinking, talking wildly about each other, and having fun?

But, I was talking about Julie's life here and I didn't want to chance her being in danger. Cappy thought that everyone was like him, a Navy Seal, ready to take on the world. That wasn't Julie. She was still a classy lady.

I then called Rita and wanted to know about Chuck's association with Angelo's and why he would choose such a place to meet with Julie. Rita told me that across the street from Angelo's, was an Italian Club and Restaurant called

Fiorentello's, which Chuck used to make all sorts of deals with other mafia people. By the time he was fifteen, he killed someone in this restaurant and was never caught. He later went on to buy the place and had an apartment upstairs that he used for his evening pleasures.

Rita also told me how he had brought her to that room, although she had blatantly refused. But his forcefulness to take her to bed caused her much pain and she was forced to help him with his business as well. For her services, she received money to buy her own place, her own car, and just be there when he wanted her. She became his go-fer and he had a strangled hold on her for a long time.

But Rita had another plan. Her comment to me was, why jeopardize Julie's life when she could meet Chuck instead. Knowing Chuck for many years, having enjoyed the connections, the money, the power, the protection, and how she sold her soul for all of this, she felt that Chuck had a hold on her and would believe her, no matter what she would say. Although he was like a bull in a china shop, she still respected him. She thought about that night in the hotel room and if she did not do what Chuck wanted her to do, he would have killed her right then and there.

I was happy that I told Julie to get to Cappy's. I thought that Rita's plan made sense, but thought about having Mario there anyway, just in case. Rita was also afraid for Julie's life and felt that there was a 50-50 chance that Chuck would harm her.

"David, if I tell Chuck that I heard from Julie and that she got tied up with the lawyers in her law firm, he would believe me. I really think he would. But do not have Julie meet him tonight. I don't trust him"

I thought that she was putting herself on the line. Yet, I preferred her suggestion anyway, instead of having Julie meeting with Chuck, even with Mario next to her. Why blow the cover right now. Perhaps Mario could still be there, keep an eye on Chuck, and report back to the team.

"Okay, Rita, let's go with your plan, but I want you to report back to me afterward and tell me everything that happened. You have my cell phone number, right?"

Rita was content with this new plan as she just wanted out, like we all did. She felt more comfortable knowing that Mario would be close by and she would call me later to give me all the details. I took Christy and we headed to Cappy's house.

Julie also took her car and went to Cappy's, but I had called her in the car and told her of this change of plans. She certainly appreciated my getting her out of this and felt relieved.

We had many plans of action to contemplate with, over at Cappy's. We both were glad that Rita was willing to go meet with Chuck and hopefully, was going to be able to lie through her teeth most convincingly. So far, everything was working out fine and now we had to go after Chuck and his illegal operations and either arrest him or kill him. Either way, we had to take him out. Julie was hoping for this to happen as quickly as possible. Her law firm would appreciate the outcome, and not have to deal with him anymore. Christy sat in the car and smiled at me, feeling secure, not knowing what was to happen next. My adrenalin was working overtime and I was able to start calculating moves as if I was back in the Navy Seals.

CHAPTER 7

▼

BEFORE THE PARADE
PASSES BY

Christy and I arrived at Cappy's at around seven and the other guys were already there. There were seven members of our old Navy Seals squad. Cappy was the leader, a brilliant organizer who led us into many battles and we always seemed to fair out well. He was our mentor and trained us well throughout our training and took us from one mission to another, without hesitation. He knew his stuff and not only organized the battle plans, but was always there, leading us.

Cappy's wife was a doll. She had prepared little tuna and ham and cheese sandwiches, and there was beer, some wine and cold drinks. We sat in the huge den overlooking the bright lights of the community and of the ocean. Cappy knew how to live well, as he remodeled this beautiful home as he only wanted everything the way he saw fit. Nothing was too much for Cappy. He had to have what he wanted and that included his family, this home, and all of its furnishings.

Cappy had been at the heart of driving American capitalism to where it is today. He became a consultant in the stock market, and part of what motivated him was his raw ambition and a desire to become wealthy. As a leader of this stature, he has always had a vision and an ability to persuade large numbers of people to buy into whatever he was selling.

We never really thought that we should worship at his feet. But he deserved to be singled out because of what he had accomplished in the Navy Seals and the fact that because of his wisdom, the regulatory climate was much more benevolent, and globalization was taking place more rapidly than ever before. We may not attribute his success to family pedigree, but his tenacity and aggressiveness as well as his drive and savvy were what made him one of the most recognized CEOs around.

He would pass comments that the bar raised substantially for public company directors who would be held much more accountable and would have to work much harder than in the past. As a consultant to many companies, and sitting on the board of directors at his company, he felt that the government had aggressively attacked the wrong problem.

"The new law's certification regs are causing CEOs and CFOs of public companies to avoid risk (new investments, new products) because the rewards for a failed risk can be jail or massive law suits," he would say. "Until the public business community can determine the extent of SEC and DOJ enforcement, the risk-taker will lie low."

Cappy was always a risk taker but felt that the incentives of going public were swaying in the wrong direction, and the liabilities were dramatically increasing. With the financial markets the way they were, there was ZERO reason to take a company public given the lack of cash and the amount of financial liability. He felt that the CEOs were increasingly confident about the overall economy, but they seemed deeply distressed by the regulatory and financial climate. He also preached that CEOs no longer had a choice.

The NYSE rules were clear. All listed companies must perform an annual assessment of the board and the audit, compensation and nominating/corporate governance committees. And companies must publish guidelines describing the evaluation process. Cappy was good in his new profession, just as he was on the battlefield as a Navy Seal. He was a leader and knew how to work the crowd and make them understand that what we fought for was for the good of the country.

He rose in the capitalistic society as a leader and a great spokesman for the market.

Cappy was strong in his convictions and had the ear of the many companies whom he spoke to. The risks many companies were now taking would be an erosion of credibility. If sensitive issues were raised and then swept under the rug, directors would review the process as a sham. When he spoke of growth rates disappearing or a U.S. trade deficit, he provided an important stimulus and gave the world a chance to rethink its position as a world leader. I understood Cappy and knew that he loved being in charge, as he was on the fields of battle.

There was Moose, a little, scrappy guy who knew everything about computers. He was our Research and Development IT analyzer who always found solutions on how to beat the odds. He then became a technician for many of the computer organizations and helped them develop software that was sold internationally and made these companies rich and famous. He carried his laptop around with him no matter where he went. If anything needed to be sought out, just ask Moose. He not only carried our team through deep analysis and computerization, but he also fought well on the firing line.

In his years with the Seals, Moose developed expertise in engineering and electronics that had made his background and resume read like he was the leading guru in today's world of technology. He wanted to work with the PCB industry at the beginning of the computer age to ensure its survival and competitiveness. Because of his traveling to Asia, it is no accident that electronics is one of Asia's biggest exports.

Foreign governments such as China, Hong Kong, Taiwan and South Korea have targeted PCBs as a strategic manufacturing technology with his assistance, and now are investing heavily to support this industry by building more manufacturing facilities in these countries, than we had done in the United States. A new dawn was appearing as we no longer had that 'Yankee Ingenuity'. Instead, our once cold war opponents were experiencing their own 'Chinese ingenuity.'

Indeed, with the number of domestic PCB manufacturers shrinking, while the numbers of foreign manufacturers were growing, it is possible that the U.S. military would be buying its parts from foreign companies in the very near future. Moose had this foresight years ago and cashed in very early and made millions. As ironic as it seems, in the next ten years, we may need to go to Mainland China to get our top secret military electronics manufactured. It is with great respect that I admire this most versatile individual.

The New York Time in June, of 2004, had reported about lockboxes and Iraqi loot that was found in throes of the battle in Iraq with a trail that led back to the Feds. This was part of the problem of our government and how many of our own politicians and worldwide banks were getting involved with laundering money.

In 2003, a United States Army sergeant broke through a false wall in a small building in Baghdad on a Friday afternoon and discovered more than three sealed boxes containing about $160 million in neatly bundled $100. bills. Later that day, soldiers found more cash in other hideaways near the Tigris River, in an exclusive neighborhood, that elite members of Saddam Hussein's government once called home. By the end of the evening, they had amassed 164 metal boxes, all riveted shut, that held about $650 million in shrink-wrapped greenbacks. The cash was so heavy, and so valuable, that the Army needed a C-130 Hercules cargo plane to airlift it to a secure location.

Just two days later, on Sunday, April 20, 2003, Thomas C Baxter, head of the legal unit of the Federal Reserve Bank of New York, read a brief news account of the discovery. Most of the money that turned up in Baghdad was new, bore sequential serial numbers, and was stored with documents indicating that it had once been held in Iraq's central bank. One fact particularly bothered Mr. Baxter: the money had markings from three Fed banks, including his own in New York.

Moose got involved with this and realized that the money trail led back to politicians, banks throughout the world, and to the mafia and drug cartel. He was already assigned to this project and our good friend, Chuck Manzione also had a hand in laundering the money, as did the drug cartel, with the help of some people in the State Department.

Iraq, of course, had been subject to more than a decade of trade sanctions by the United States and the United Nations, so large piles of dollars, especially new bills, were not supposed to have found their way to Baghdad. Mr. Baxter went around with his head up his ass asking, "How could that happen? Not only with U.S. sanctions, but with U.N sanctions. How could that happen?"

Mr. Baxter and the New York Fed, along with the Treasury Department and the Customs Service, immediately began an investigation into Baghdad's currency stockpile. The continuing inquiry offered a rudimentary road map of illicit dealings—including lucrative oil and drug smuggling—in Iraq and neighboring countries during the Hussein years.

The investigation led quickly to the vaults of four Western banks that were among a select group handling the sensitive task of distributing freshly printed dollars overseas: the Bank of America, the HSBC Group, the Royal Bank of Scotland, and UBS. Several other commercial banks and foreign central banks, which the Fed did not name, also served as stopovers along Baghdad's money trail, according to a written account Mr. Baxter provided to the Senate Banking Committee.

None of the four main banks the Fed scrutinized had sent currency directly to Iraq. But as the inquiry wore on, investigators learned that UBS, Switzerland's largest bank, had transferred $4 billion to $5 billion to four other countries that were under sanctions: Libya, Iran, Cuba and the former Yugoslavia. The funds came from laundering drugs.

Over an eight-year period, UBS employees had quietly shipped the money to those countries from a vault at the Zurich airport undetected by Fed auditors who made regular visits to the site.

Finally, the Federal Reserve Board fined UBS $100 million for the currency violations. It was the second-largest penalty ever levied by America's central bank, surpassed only by a $200 million fine imposed on the Bank of Credit and Commerce International, or B.C.C.I, in 1991 for violating American banking laws. The B.C.C.I case was part of a global investigation of fraud and money laundering.

Moose told us that the money came from the sale of drugs, and the mafia gave out huge percentages to the banks to launder the money. This money was then shipped to foreign countries for safe-keeping and deals were made with the foreign leaders to store the money for future use. In turn, they were given huge sums to purchase arms and other weapons of mass destruction, to fight their enemies. One of the enemies they would be fighting was the United States.

UBS's transgressions didn't appear to be in the same league as those at B.C.C.I. Several people briefed on the transfers said most of the UBS transactions involved currency exchanges for the Cuban tourism industry; such transactions angered Washington, but did not evoke security fears in most of the world. After all, many countries in Europe, including France and Germany, had oil ties with Iraq and they didn't want to get their hands dirty and therefore stayed out of the game.

A handful of lower-level UBS employees were said to have doctored trading records that misled their employees and American officials. All of them had been fired or had left the bank. UBS had not been charged with any crimes in the matter. Neither had anyone from the banks, the State Department, or any drug cartel or mafia linked organization. Not until now. Now we had a chance to break into this tightly wrapped plan and finally put an end to what has been happening all over the world. And there was no one who could want to stop us, unless they wanted to be exposed for fraud and illegal acts against the country. Moose knew the players and had an open door to get around them.

A former Fed official, and others involved in the investigation, who were hung out to dry, had indicated that the hefty fine reflected the Fed's displeasure at having been misled by UBS employees for so many years. Members of Congress had accused the Fed of being asleep at the regulatory switch, an added incentive for a marquee-size fine at a time when regulators of all stripes had come under fire for overlooking abuses and excesses on Wall Street.

Yet, UBS's trades with Libya, Iran and Yugoslavia, and the investigation into how hundreds of millions of dollars circumvented sanctions and regulatory barriers on their way to Baghdad, were hardly trivial affairs. The irony was that this happened during the Clinton administration, when Yugoslavia was at war, and we had a chance to go after Osama Bin Laden and failed to do so. There was more money laundered during this time that involved the Middle East, than any other time in the history of mankind. There were many people who got rich, and left the administration for private positions.

Of the $680 billion in cash that the Fed now has in circulation, more than $400 billion, or nearly 60 percent, is outside the United States. That overseas supply, particularly in economically unstable regions, is the financial lifeblood of businesses, and even of pensioners who stow dollars in mattresses. The authorities constantly monitor that supply to keep counterfeiters from tainting it, and hub banks like UBS play a pivotal role in ferreting out currency forgers.

Those billions overseas, however, also grease the wheels of more nefarious commerce-arms trafficking, smuggling and the timeless crafts of political graft. The trail of the cash that soldiers found in Baghdad remains murky. A senior Treasury Department official who supervised investigations of Saddam Hussein's finances said that investigators thought the funds were part of about $1 billion that Mr. Hussein's son Qusay looted from Iraq's central bank hours before American-led forces invaded in early 2003. Qusay Hussein, who was killed in a shootout with American troops in July of 2003, oversaw the Iraqi government's oil smuggling, according to a report published in 2002 by the Coalition for International Justice, a Washington group that monitors human rights issues.

From 1996 to 2003, the United Nations controlled Iraq's oil profits, which were intended to be used for food and other goods for Iraqi civilians. The United Nations has defended its stewardship, but the General Accounting Office estimated that oil smuggling and kickbacks linked to that program allowed Mr. Hussein to steal about $10 million.

Moose confirmed the story in the Times that The United Nations appointed Fed Chairman, Paul A. Volcker, to lead a panel investigating possible fraud in the oil-for-food program. The Treasury Department said that a large Syrian bank that did business with major American banks helped divert and disguise oil-for-food funds stolen by the Hussein government.

The trail of names led to people in the State Department, and to some outside interests, one now known as Chuck Manzione. His name kept popping up in all records of deals that were involved with money laundering overseas.

Mr. Baxter was grilled about the monitoring of currency the Fed shipped overseas, and about the challenges that arise when some people, like UBS's former employees, cover up their use of the money. Tracing bank notes once they are outside the United States is one of the fundamental problems. When Baxter began tracing the Baghdad funds in 2003, he first acquired serial numbers for some of the notes and turned over that information to Fed currency analysts in East Rutherford, New Jersey. Analysts linked this to twenty four cash shipments the New York Fed made to special vaults it had at HSBS in London, and Bank of American and UBS in Zurich.

After American forces in Iraq discovered an additional $112 million in hidden cash, on top of the $650 million they had already found, the Fed's cashiers tracked it to the same vaults and to a Fed vault at HSBC in Frankfurt, a Royal Bank of Scotland, a vault in London, and to other locations the Fed has not disclosed.

All of these overseas vaults are part of a Fed program that begun in 1996 to combat counterfeiting, retire worn-out dollars and keep currency circulating, especially during emergencies. For example, the vaults were opened when the Year 2000 computer problem caused banking jitters in 2000, and again after the September 11, 2001 terrorist attacks in New York grounded planes that would have normally delivered cash abroad.

Until the mid 1990's, American currency was relatively easy to forge, compared with most other leading currencies. Its colors were not as varied, it did not bear watermarks or special security bands, and its linen and cotton composition was much like that of another currency still widely used by counterfeiters to mint fake dollars: the Hussein-era Iraqi dinar.

Though successful counterfeiting is usually short-lived, and fakes are just a minuscule portion of the bills in circulation, there are moments when near-perfect copies, known as super notes, circulate for uncomfortably long periods. Phony $100 bills are the forgers' favorite. A rash of forged $100 bills have hit the streets in the past few years and it is being traced back to a group of people tied in with the mafia. That group of people once again has a name linked to it, namely Chuck Manzione. Chuck Manzione has been linked with laundering and counterfeiting, as well as drugs and prostitution.

In 1996, the Treasury Department was about to introduce a new, more secure $100 bill into circulation in Europe, aware that the note would be eagerly snapped up in the booming Russian economy. Also aware that sophisticated Russian criminal groups and forgers would pounce on the newly minted bill, the American authorities wanted a safe harbor in Zurich to monitor it. Republic Bank, an American bank that had once handled those duties, was leaving the business.

UBS was eager to make inroads in Russia, so the Fed contracted its services.

By the end of May, 2003 based on Baxter's testimony, nearly all banks contacted by his team about the money found in Baghdad had identified the countries or parties with whom they had traded dollars. The exception was UBS. According to Baxter's Senate testimony, UBS initially told the Fed that it did not track the serial numbers of currency it traded and that Swiss law precluded its identifying of specific trading partners. Eventually, however, UBS agreed to identify countries. Iraq was not on the list, and that it appeared to satisfy the Fed until the following month, when one of its auditors made a routine visit to Zurich.

It was then that UBS gave the auditor a report showing that eight shipments of dollars had been sent to Iran, a country under American sanctions. UBS said that its trading had been a mistake. A month later, Mr. Baxter and the Swiss Federal Banking Commission began a deeper investigation. By October, 2003 according to Mr. Baxter's testimony, the Fed had learned that UBS had also traded currency with Cuba and Libya and that employees had covered up the Cuban transactions.

Mr. Baxter revoked the Fed's contract with UBS on October 28th. About a week later, UBS told the Fed that it had also traded currency with the former Yugoslavia, which was under American sanctions. UBS declined to comment on its transactions with Libya, Yugoslavia and Iran.

UBS, in cooperation with the Fed and the Swiss authorities, then began an internal investigation and over the next six months, investigators interviewed forty eight UBS employees, often more than once. They had also reviewed several thousand documents, including e-mail messages.

UBS reported the results of its investigation to the Fed on April 16, 2004, and the Fed levied its $100 million fine on May 10th. Only a handful of UBS employees conducted the trades, and none took bribes or received extra income from the transactions, that they could find, according to a senior investigator with the Swiss Federal Banking Commission and several others briefed on the matter.

But some on Capital Hill indicated that there is more to be learned about the UBS transactions. Although Mr. Baxter's team quickly identified the source of the cash found in Baghdad, it was still not clear how it got into the hands of the members of the Hussein government. Obviously, there was a middleman involved and the name that kept coming up, time after time, was Chuck Manzione.

Jordan and Syria, two neighbors of Iraq, were routinely accused by Western politicians and law enforcement officials of helping Iraq flout sanctions during the Hussein era. But both countries had repeatedly denied those accusations.

The Los Angeles Times reported that some of the currency found by American soldiers in Baghdad had been sent to Iraq's central bank by the Jordan National Bank. But, this was disputed by a Jordanian official.

On May 11, a day after the Fed fined UBS, the federal government issued trade sanctions against Syria, saying that it supported terrorism. The same day, the Treasury Department shut off access to the American banking system for Syria's main state-owned bank, the Commercial Bank of Syria, citing suspicions that transactions at the bank were used to finance terrorism and launder money related to the United Nations oil-for-food program.

Numerous transactions that may have been indicative of terrorist financing and money laundering were referenced to a reputed financier for Osama bin Laden. Again, that reputed financier was alleged to be Mr. Chuck Manzione.

According to the Treasury Department, Iraq's state oil agency maintained accounts at the Commercial Bank of Syria through which oil-for-food money was diverted. Imad Moustapha, Iraq's ambassador to the United States, in an interview, indicated that the Syrian bank had about $265 million in funds legally deposited there by the Hussein government. He denied all accusations of money laundering and other financial improprieties involving Syria and the Hussein government, describing them as "politically motivated" and part of a "campaign of disinformation about Syria."

The Treasury Department document said that the Commercial Bank of Syria maintains correspondent accounts with a few American banks. Though not named in the document, the banks are Citigroup, J.P. Morgan, and the Bank of New York. The American banks declined to comment.

Although the documents said that unnamed American-based accounts appeared legitimate, it also said that "suspicious wire transfers, totaling more than $1 million" moved through those accounts on their way to the Syrian bank. Although the Fed just seemed to take UBS at their word as to where they traded money, showed some of the Fed's regulatory weaknesses. Obviously, as long as the bottom line matched up, the Fed didn't seem to worry that much about where the money went. UBS falsified documents and the Fed did not show the proper due diligence.

Regulators walked softly around the accusations of money laundering and the two biggest such investigations of the late 1990's, involving Citigroup and the Bank of New York, did not result in any regulatory fines and stalled after investigators hit dead ends in gathering evidence outside the United States. Although September 11 changed some things!

Suspect financial activities that were once perceived as an exotic form of white collar crimes are now looked upon with a tangible threat in mind: terrorist financing.

For instance, the Riggs National Corporation is mired in an investigation of suspect transactions in its banking accounts and, like UBS, has found itself saddled by federal regulators with a hefty fine—$25 million—for regulatory violations. Riggs had denied any wrongdoing.

Gaps in the global banking system, that may have posed national security risks, had been overlooked by the country's leading regulators. Mr. Baxter had stated to the House Financial Services Committee, that the mistakes the Fed made in its examination was because the old audit admonition of 'Trust, but verify' was not followed.

Based on this report and what Moose told us about the reach of Chuck Manzione, I figured that due to an accidental meeting with Julie, and then with Christy, my involvement with Chuck and his organization came at a time when the government was ready to crack down on him. Yet, there were too many tangibles and many people in government and the banking system would have to stay away from this so as not to be a part of the landslide when we would take him down. Obviously, we were going to have a free rein and no one was going to interfere with our plans.

Mario was our wonderful Italian buddy who loved to cook and make it with the women. You would never find him without his Ermenegildo Zegna, Canali, Armani, Brioni Zanella, Hugo Boss, Cole Haan, Bragano Moreschi, or Gravati fashionable clothes. As sharp he was as a dresser, he caught on to any situation as quickly as anyone I have ever known.

He decided to test the waters by going to France and Italy and export their clothing, and after spending over ten years in Europe, building an international group into a financial powerhouse with operations in 130 countries, Mario decided to get into management and deliver such great results that broke records all over the place. As commander of the company he worked for, he wouldn't ask any one to do anything that he would not be prepared to do himself. He was ready to discuss business any time, anywhere, and he expected his top executives to be equally available. Using his brain as a sponge for knowledge, there wasn't much time to sleep and if you didn't think about details, you were not going to have a long term plan. Mario was our thinker, our guiding light when it came to formulating out a plan of attack.

He could be exacting and short on patience, but he can be equally driven to take care of his team. He always told us that the greatest thing you can leave behind, is a legacy of a team that is great now, but will go on to even greater heights. Mario went on to become a legend in his own right and can still run circles around those who try to beat him at his own game. He now directs companies, from retail to restaurants, that make money, hand over fist and he has made a darn good living at being who he is and will always lead others in finding the gold at the end of the rainbow.

Then, there was Mike. He was the star athlete in high school, in college, and then as a Navy Seal, and was very proficient in martial arts. Mike nearly turned golf pro but could never make the cut. He had a two handicap and just loved the game. So now, he is the golf pro at a few of the better golf courses in Orange County and gets paid quite well, teaching the game and playing in the amateur tournaments around the west coast. Mike was the ultimate warrior, always excelling in anything he had done, but he had a light side as well. He loved to tell cute little stories.

"So how are you, Mikie? How is your golf game going?" I asked him.

"Well, little buddy, I was playing golf at Pelican Hill last week and saw a strange thing." He proceeded to tell us a story that sounded so real about this nun who was sitting with her Mother Superior chatting after she played eighteen holes.

The sister said, "I used some horrible language today and feel absolutely terrible about it."

"When did you use this awful language," I heard Mother Superior ask the nun.

"Well, I was golfing before and hit an incredible drive that looked like it was going to go over 250 yards, but it struck a telephone line that was hanging over the fairway and it fell straight down to the ground after going only about 100 yards."

"Is that when you swore, Sister?"

"No, Mother," said the Nun. "After that, a squirrel ran out of the bushes and grabbed my ball in its mouth and began to run away."

"Is THAT when you swore, Sister?" asked the Mother Superior again.

"Well, no," said the Nun. "You see, as the squirrel was running, an eagle came down out of the sky, grabbed the squirrel in his talons and began to fly away!"

"Is THAT when you swore, Sister?" asked the amazed elder Nun.

"No, not yet. As the eagle carried the squirrel away in its claws, it flew near the green and the squirrel dropped my ball."

"Did you swear THEN?" asked the Mother Superior, becoming impatient.

"No, because the ball fell on a big rock, bounced over the sand trap, rolled onto the green, and stopped about six inches from the hole."

The two nuns were silent for a moment.

Then Mother Superior sighed and said, "You missed the fucking putt, didn't you?"

We all laughed and started to eat some of the sandwiches and drank the beverages that were on the coffee table. I noticed that Christy was feeling more comfortable being among the guys, and I looked around the room at the rest of the Navy Seals. Some had put on a little weight, some had thinner hair, but by and large, these guys were bigger than life.

Sean was now an attorney, working at a high priced law firm in a tall building in Newport Beach. He was a great criminal lawyer and had a mind of a genius. He told us a story of a famous basketball athlete who was traveling to Colorado for some tests on his bad ankle and stayed at a hotel overnight before returning to Los Angeles. The news reported that he coerced a woman to have sex with him in his hotel room.

A week later, the Sheriff's office of Denver put out an all points bulletin for him as he was charged with an unethical sex conduct and had to post $25,000 bail. He flew back to Denver and was released in his own cognizance and returned to his wife and child. The papers and the TV media really played this up but good, as he was a seven year veteran of the NBA, and had a squeaky clean image, with endorsements that netted him nearly seventy five million a year. This incident could have tarnished his career as well as his endorsements.

He hired Sean's law firm to help him out of this mess. With Sean's help, they discovered that while having some blood tests at the hospital, the nurse took extra blood and placed it in her possession. She saw an opportunity to get this guy and possibly make some money off of him. While having some drinks at the hotel lounge and talking to some of the other guests, two women approached him and made offers to him to take them back to his room. The nurse's girlfriend was the more aggressive of the two. The famous athlete turned them down and remained in the lounge with the guests as he was having a good time, telling them about the many playoffs his team had won, and how he tried his best to get them there.

The second woman had gone to the police and accused him of literally having sex with her against her will, in his room and they sought him out after he had returned to southern California. When Sean's firm got involved, Sean led the team to Denver and found out about the nurse taking the additional blood and giving it to her friend who made the sexual gestures to the athlete in the lounge. It seemed that she put some of the blood in her vagina and went to the police station and demanded that tests be made.

With sworn testimony from the nurse after she was told that she could be jailed for abetting a felon by faking the evidence and accusing someone by lying to the police and the district attorney's office, both she and her friend were themselves jailed and the famous athlete was able to walk away without any damage to his career.

I am amazed at all of the many stories that are told about athletes and their going to hip bars, fooling around with women, getting divorced by their wives, are on drugs and are in a shootout with others. Many do not survive and their celebrity status only puts them in harm's way if they choose to bite at the Devil's temptation. Others remain unscathed throughout their career and never fall into this trap. Sean has represented so many athletes in the past twenty years that he is well known in the legal sense of the word. We are thankful to have him as a part of our team.

Then there is William. 'Billie Boy', as we referred to him, was our arms specialist. He knew everything from any kind of munitions, including tanks, guns, knives, explosives, radar systems, biological weapons of mass destruction and any kind of military arms, from the Pentagon to Iraq. Billy was not afraid to take risks, whether on the battlefield in Afghanistan or at a conference with generals and secretaries of states. He used to feel that even though our officials at the Pentagon were increasingly confident about the overall game plan of the wars we were in, around the world, they seemed deeply distressed by the regulatory and financial climate.

Many of the government requirements, Billy used to say, will undoubtedly become de facto requirements for all major battles, both across the ocean, and even at major corporations, as they become adopted as the yardsticks for measuring "good governance."

His intellect in the arms war distinguished himself from others as he was quoted as saying, "Poor board assessments can backfire, but good ones yield real benefits."

He was referring to improper arms warfare and how we would go to battle in other parts of the world, not knowing the kinds of weapons we would be up against. Billy has spent two decades building American international retention and the arms race of the U.S. into a financial powerhouse. He has earned the respect of the Joint Chiefs of Staff, and the Pentagon for years, and it was certainly good to have such a powerhouse on our team. No one knew more about munitions than he did.

I looked at Jules, a former tennis player, a dropout from college at 17, and an enlisted man in the United States Navy. He left the service when we all did and managed to get into foreign affairs, working as an assistant to ambassadors and as an aid to congressmen and senators. He learned a lot about the political lifespan of those who work for the government.

His favorite comment was, "There is nobody who's indispensable and they will run in a different way, but the country won't collapse when there is new thinking and a new management team there to pick it up and run with it."

Jules realized that the reason why we lost the edge in the arms race, or the space race, or in world leadership was because we got complacent with ourselves. We were great yesterday, but many of our leadership roles have disappeared, and you look at the reasons why. It always comes down to complacency. Our leaders failed to manage change. They failed to recognize that things were not going to stay the way they were. He looked at the future, not the past.

He used to say, 'Who cares what your record was for the past five years? The people, the citizens of this country want to know what you are going to do this year and next year, and the year after.'

Jules became a professor at one of the great universities and had written books on the struggling American dream and its policies abroad. He became so involved in political science that he thought of running for office in Congress. He has seen the administration and the house members scrambling to comprehend a whole new set of rules and get new policies and procedures in place. They could not afford to make mistakes.

The scandals in the past few years had so tainted politics and the people demanded a public response. The stock market was affected as was the economy, and it would take a long way to restoring public confidence. We seemed to be spending most of our time covering our ass rather than look at the whole picture. Jules would have made a great politician, and if there was time in his schedule to run, he surely would win.

Last, but not least, is Dickie. As a reporter, then an editor for major publications, he made his mark by covering the ethics of companies when it wasn't gosh to do so. Thanks to his great reporting while others shied away from these topics, Dickie was one of the first to report on the financial scandals at Enron, World Com and elsewhere. This new coping with understanding and carrying out a slew of new federal regulations aimed at preventing further corporate wrongdoings, had led to longer board meetings, a doubling of directors' and officers' insurance rates and more employee time devoted to the business of compliance rather than the business of business.

In the end, the Enron debacle had cost its customers millions of dollars. The new rules of corporate regulations consisted of the composition of audit committees to penalties facing corporate chiefs-turned-scoundrels, up to millions in fines and twenty years in prison.

Dickie's editorials and articles won him a place by the side of not only the members of both houses in Washington, but the President of the United States as well. It would take a long time to restore investor confidence, and the stock market went way down. His meetings with Alan Greenspan and others only added to the lack of stimulus in the country and the response from many were that we were going to be spending most of our time covering our ass. Many boards of companies were asked to do serious house cleaning, and new rules were devised to examine the duties of all committees.

The corporate world was under scrutiny, and Dickie was reporting all of the facts to the media, making appearances on CNN, MSNBC and Fox News. His reports on companies forced a new breed of whistleblowers and employees were asked to make confidential and anonymous complaints if they suspected financial impropriety.

There was some anecdotal evidence that many executives were taking heed of the certification provisions and scrutinizing financials more carefully before signing off on them. The considerable challenge for CEOs of companies of all sizes, was to successfully repair the damage to corporate reputation, while not letting that distract them from the business of growing their companies for the future.

Dickie decided to crack down on Wall Street and the corporate leaders. It would have taken the government five years or more to get through the backlog of corporate fraud cases. He became Washington's man of the hour when he took on the assignment of looking into corporate fraud and the shenanigans that were going on. He questioned whether his role was meant to be aggressive, or whether the White House would be satisfied with the hand-slapping of a few prominent wrongdoers. After all, many of the wrongdoers were heavy financial supporters of the President of the United States.

Dickie would tell me that when the scandals came, a weakened SEC was faced with a daily stream of headlines, most from out of his corner office, as chief editor and associate publisher. It took a special breed of CEOs to repair the damage caused by corporate implosion. New CEOs found themselves in extreme situations and had to fight for credibility with employees and middle management, investors, customers and regulators.

They had to quickly understand what went wrong and identify a path out of the morass. They had to reform wounded cultures and become white knights who would be able to slay the dragon of poor performance while restoring a sense of honesty. They must be willing to work long hours and must have the stomach to constantly make tough decisions even while employees and shareholders were distrustful, while rebuilding an organization. Companies worked on new strategic and operational plans, and they would be used as a touchstone to examine previous practices.

As Dickie once said, "Most CEOs are good at what they do. It's when things start going sideways, that they are very poor."

As a proficient editor, Dickie addressed all issues and eventually every newspaper in the world was tracking and reporting the issues and accusations.

He reported in an editorial that "if people have the background and character to stomach the pain, the demands, and the difficulty of taking over true corporate fiascos, it can be worth the effort."

With this came anti-American sentiment in Europe and many companies in the United States started to close down due to a poor economy. He always came out with great statements, such as the one recently. "Superstar CEOs are like high-stakes poker players. They think fast, act fast and bluff with impunity."

Dickie had the right approach in defining what went wrong in the big corporate world. Publishing has always been his love and he had always fought his way to get the right story out in the public.

"Functions that used to operate one way in the past will have to operate a different way in the future" he used to say, and he meant it.

Just as he now was in his job as editor, he was that way in the Navy Seals. He always knew the right things to do and with his fortitude, we were able to brainstorm like top management executives and pull off all of the missions we were on without a hitch. Thank goodness we had a guy like Dickie, as well as the rest of the team. We sure were the elite Navy Seals and no one was better than us. We were the superstars of the armed forces. Now we are here tonight to plan out another type of mission. Perhaps it was a mission of mercy or something that we were able to accomplish without any effort at all. We had the power.

"David, are you there?" asked a voice from behind, and awakened me from thoughts of yesteryear. It was Christy, and the boys were going to ask her what she knew about Chuck and his regime. It was time to formulate our next mission.

I told the guys of this new development, with Chuck and Julie, and that Rita was going to meet him in her stead. Cappy agreed to my allowing Rita be there in place of Julie but wanted Mario to also be there and keep tabs on the situation. Just then, the doorbell rang. It was Julie. Everyone looked at her as if she was a goddess and welcomed her. Cappy's wife put her arms around her and made her feel warm and offered her some sandwiches and a cold drink. Julie looked around the room and saw these strong looking guys, knowing that they represented the Navy Seals. She also went over to Christy and gave her a big hug. Both girls looked so beautiful that it seemed more like a fashion show than a showdown.

"Hey, I'm impressed," said Mike. "If you were going to get involved with women, you certainly chose two of the most beautiful young ladies to get involved with. I certainly like your style." He nodded approvingly to both Christy and Julie.

"I did some research on this here Chuck and his organization, guys," Moose cut in. "And I came up with a lot of stuff on him and what he has been involved with for the past twenty years. He has built a cadre of people and drug affiliates from Liberia, Columbia and Ecuador, to Afghanistan, Iraq and Panama."

Moose continued. "He grosses about five to ten billion in drugs every year and he has built an empire that involves political figures, lawmen and corporate people who gained a lot of power by using his influence to make substantial gains in their own right.

"Manzione's influence has penetrated nearly every aspect of the corporate world and politics, and he has been using their clout to move his drugs around the world. He has had ties with Castro, Saddam, Bin Laden, the Hamas in Palestine, and some prominent figures in show business, on capital hill, and in the electronics industry, mostly in Hong Kong and China. He is something else, my friends."

"Have you thought how we could take him down," Mike asked. "I mean, if he is tied in with so many people, wouldn't we hurt them as much as we hurt him? And what would the long term effect be after all this comes to a head?"

It was time for questions and many of the guys had the answers. It was just a matter of putting everything together by gathering all of the information as to how we were going to proceed to take down Chuck and his gang. Obviously, what we learned many of the big shots in Washington who knew him and benefited by him, as well as in the corporate world where Moose had a foothold, could not and would not do a damn thing to stop us. They were in too deep and knew that if it got out that they were using mob money to finance their own personal assets, it would be the end of them.

Billy Boy, our arms professional did some homework on Chuck as well, and gave us a scenario on his military might in the Middle East and how he financed some of the terrorist nations for a place to build up his drug factories which became the intellectual manipulation of all chutzpah, including benefiting from developing business opportunities and providing a hidden outlet needed to develop, manufacture and distribute the largest drug operation ever assembled.

His financing was responsible for the design and manufacture of some Airbus variants overseas, with facilities that included the new Skin and Stringer Manufacturing centers, which is regarded as state-of-the-art. His money crept into Lockheed, Boeing, Honeywell, Ceradyne and many other large companies that reaped the benefits of producing diamond machines for incorporation on the Lockheed Martin missiles. Fuselage sections of Airbus variants would be traveling by sea from Hamburg to Mostyn Docks near Liverpool to collect the wings for the variants and then sail south to Bordeaux, and the components would be unloaded on to a barge to be taken down the River Garonne to Langon, with the final leg of their journey being by road to Taulause.

The tail plane would be transported by sea from Airbus Spain's Cadiz facility to Bordeaux, France. What this was leading to was supplying terrorist countries with warfare that even the Israeli Aircraft would not be able to knock down.

These companies had no idea what was happening only that they had monies to build integrated propulsion systems that were to reach a new level in the aviation industry, far exceeding what was there now.

Powering brushless electric motors were part of a new specialization and with the possible control of torque, position, and speed, as well as higher power ranges, who ever would control these types of weapons, could eventually control the skies. With the volume of its cargo hold, high cruise speed, and intercontinental range, Airbus claimed that the A400M would significantly increase the load carrying capability of the aircraft it would replace, while retaining their essential tactical, short, and soft field operating characteristics. The U.S. Navy was keeping close watch on what was happening and was only hoping that these new specs would not fall into enemy hands. After all, just who were our enemies now?

Billy went on to say that the first of two Mars exploration Rovers (MERs), Spirit, was launched by NASA aboard a Boeing Delta II from the Cape Canaveral Air Force Station in Florida. NASA was getting short on funds from the American government and needed additional financing, thus Chuck's company, through intermediaries in the government, helped NASA move forward with their dream of going to Mars.

The NASA 'robotic geologists', which were on the way to Mars carried five scientific instruments, including a panoramic camera and microscope, plus a rock abrasion tool that would grind away the outer surfaces of rocks to expose their interiors for examination. They would navigate around obstacles as they drive across the Martian surface, traveling up to about 130 feet each Martian day. Each Rover's prime mission was planned to last three months at different sites on Mars. These missions would continue NASA's quest to understand the role of water on Mars. This was NASA's dream…to send a manned mission to the Red Planet one day.

With help from our mafia buddy, and using our government for a potential Mars expedition in the future, he also retained friendships with terrorist nations and traded off money for land, money for arms, and money for friendships. Not ours, but his. With companies like Boeing, Dunlop, Smiths, Ametek, PCB and National Instruments, they were able to move forward and develop products for the aerospace industry without ever knowing where the extra cash came from, as the government failed to tell them it did not come from the U.S. mint, but from some sleazy drug czar who had been making money distributing white powder to our schools, our family members, and our children.

This was blood money, and we had to stop all of this before it was too late. It was already out of hand, and the doctors and attendants at hospitals were not helping matters any, as they too had access to drugs and either gave or sold them to their friends and drug seekers.

"That is why I want to get into politics," quipped Jules. "I see a need of honest politicians once we take out all of these scumbags who seem to control our government, our schools, our businesses, the stock market, and our lives."

Jules was very bitter over what was happening in this country and how we look the other way every time something is mentioned that may lead to allegations to a person like Chuck Manzione. His network of people stretched all over the world. If we take out the big man, the rest of the system will topple and we can then sort out what is right from wrong. Until that day is here, we will constantly fight the battle of truth against lies, against right from wrong, and from surviving against destroying what we thought we had in the way of a good life in supposedly, the best country on this planet.

"The way I see it, we have a lot of information against Chuck, but we need to formulate a plan as to how we are going to take him out once and for all," added Cappy. "And if others are taken down with him, so be it. We just let the chips fall where they may. Sean, give us a report on Chuck's operation and what you see as the weakness areas that we should concentrate on. We need to hit him where it hurts the most and that means right in the fucking gut."

Sean took out a portfolio and started to read off some of the things that would help bring Chuck down. These were his assets and liabilities and we were getting this from one of the best attorneys in the business. He had friends in all of the right places, including the attorney general's office, the administration in the executive branch of the government, and both he, Cappy and Moose had been working on this for awhile now, even before I approached Cappy with my problem.

Little did I know that Cappy was asked by the CIA, the Secret Service, and some of the upper echelon of the FBI, that they wanted his team to take out Chuck's network across the country and overseas. Little did I know that these guys were working on a plan for nearly a year. Now, with my coming to Cappy for help, he felt that it was time to move the calendar up a few notches. He had very silently contacted each of the guys to gather information together until it was time to strike. The time was approaching to take down one of the most notorious terrorists we had ever encountered.

Cappy left me out of the loop due to my wife's passing and he felt that I may not be ready to be part of this team. I had become too soft, and he felt that I had lost my nerve. He needed a team of strong headed fighters, the kind we had when we were in the Navy Seals, twenty some odd years ago. Mario smiled at me and knew that I was ready for action and that I was getting too chummy with the broads, as he looked at Christy and Julie sitting very quietly on the sofa.

Julie added what she knew about Chuck, especially what Rita told her today, and Christy was able to remember certain things about Chuck's house, his restaurant, and the apartment upstairs.

Obviously, she was invited up to his little whorehouse above the restaurant. But that was in the past. I was only too happy to see both of them safe, and maybe, away from this guy for good. I just didn't realize how big he was in stature and how many people he was associated with around the world. No wonder Rita told me that we would not be safe from him. He had spies everywhere and we were the hunted.

Dickie had gathered much material from the archives of the newspapers and magazines from all over the world. He had brought with him, certain information that would be beneficial in the conviction of Chuck and how his law firm always seemed to get him off the hook. This was the same law firm that Julie worked at. This made Julie sick to her stomach and did not realize how deep the law firm was in, and how her former boyfriend truly did a number on the partners before he was canned.

She wondered if the partners really knew what was going on and were their families threatened if they did not cooperate with Chuck and get him off the hook every time he had to go to court and fight the attorney general's office. If that was the case, the partners in her firm were also in danger. Everyone became marked for murder.

"Before I go over some facts, guys," stated Dickie, "just think in terms of how we are going to knock out his affiliates both here and overseas, one by one. Then, when he starts to lose some of his strength without the help from his associates, we will dry up his assets, go after his money which is buried in Swiss banks, and we can take down this man who will be weakened by the lack of resources he now has."

"The key is", he continued, "is that the politicians who are in his back pocket will be running to the nearest exit after seeing what is happening. They will not interfere as that is like sabotage and they can also be jailed. We have certain people in government on our side and that makes our positioning strong. So let me review some of the areas that Chuck has eluded, and how we can get to him by having him make the same mistakes, thinking that he has the total support of his allies. When he realizes that he does not, he will be all alone. Then, we nab the cock sucker."

Dickie took out different folders, some of which had the names of countries on them, while others had names of politicians, and the names of the five major families on the east coast and those throughout the country. We were witnessing the Pro in action. The journalist who took down Enron, and he was now going to take down the kingpin of them all, Chuck Manzione, who also was a part of the Enron fallout, it seemed. This list read like a storybook, and we were in the middle of something that was so much bigger than life. While Dickie started to read off his expose on Chuck, I thought, boy, could I have used a little of Christy's tongue on my own little Dickie.

"First of all," recited Dickie, "It seems that in order to get to the heart of this operation, we need to dismantle many of his sites in the Middle East, South America, and Asia.

"We need to set up a group of men at each of the locations and close them down. In the early nineties, Chuck had placed large amounts of money in Swiss Bank Accounts for some Senators and Representatives, which supported their campaigns for office. I have the account numbers and whom they belong to. We can log every dollar that was spent on their campaigns and get these Congressmen to walk away without feeling the bite of the bullet."

Dickie started to offer 'Chapter and Verse'. "They are small fry and they would not want to rock the Goddamn boat. They will know that we have them by the balls. With some editorials in the media, I can lead them to a most difficult situation where they will have to relinquish any assets they have and stay away from trying to defend all of the arms deals and space programs that they pushed forward during these past few years. I have outlined how we can do this without receiving any salutations from these whiz kids. We now have them by the balls and they will know it. This is true justice in the making."

Dickie went on and laid out each of the programs that he had put together for nearly a year. His precise and fundamental logistics were mind boggling, as I sat there listening to his plan of action. I glanced over to Christy and Julie, and they were in awe of what was happening. To think that Julie was a member of the law firm that defended Chuck and Christy was his girl who got suckered into drugs and other areas that made her a patsy in her eyes.

She could not believe what was happening, and got tired and asked to be excused. Cappy's wife, the dear housewife, who coped with one of the most intelligent men I had ever met, took Christy upstairs to one of the bedrooms and bed her down. Julie sat there and listened to all of the allegations and the history on this gangster and terrorist, Chuck Manzione.

"Let me add a few things," Moose interrupted. "From the time we left the Navy Seals about twenty years ago, there were over sixty embassies that had been blown up not counting those in Africa. The money that financed these terrorist acts came from Manzione, and these funds were funneled in to the terrorists' organizations. It was a sort of trade off. Many of the terrorist nations allowed Manzione to cultivate the poppy seeds on their land, using their people, and then selling the drugs throughout each country, using distributors supplied by Manzione.

"Each drug lord worked with Manzione's people and billions of dollars were made and split among the different organizations. Manzione, with the help of certain radical groups in the Middle East, and right here in this country, purchased large caches of weaponry and actually gave them to the terrorist groups who later were able to blow up the embassies. This became big business, and I wouldn't be surprised, based on the intelligence of the Israelis and our own secret service, that he also financed the Al Qaeda in destroying the twin towers in New York.

"Once we destroy the networks within the organization, then we can destroy the heart of the organization which operates out of his home in Pacific Palisades."

CHAPTER 8

▼

THE NAME OF THE GAME

Cappy turned to Dickie and asked to review the news reports and editorials that he had gathered from overseas, as the files seemed so huge and were broken down by category.

"Dickie," he asked. "What we need is to set up our own network to hit each of their organizations at the same time. If we could get a handle where they all are, we can go back to the Seals, The Delta Force, the Rangers and the Green Berets, and recruit enough of their best fighting men to take them down. This would have to be done quietly, so as not to alert anyone in Washington or the media. We want to do this quickly, yet quietly. I will make some calls tomorrow and either you or I would go to Washington if necessary to start the ball rolling. This operation has to have no flaws, but we, in this room, have to be instrumental in the organization of it. We will call this "<u>OPERATION BITTERSWEET</u>.""

"That could be arranged," Moose replied. "With my clout with the State Department, as well as many of our own resources, we can put together a force like no one has ever seen. This would be a most delicate operation, and should be highly coordinated by working only with the State Department and those who know what we are trying to accomplish. I will make arrangements for the men in a few days by flying to Washington and laying out a plan of attack and requesting the bodies we need to carry out the program. We should be ready within four weeks. Will you guys be ready to go at that time?"

He looked around the room and received nods from each of us. This was to be a major operation and we were getting back into the business of taking down renegades and terrorists, just like in the old days.

By nine thirty, Cappy turned to Mario and asked him to get his ass to Angelo's and check on Chuck and Rita. We sat there and saw this trusting sole run out the door and get into his car. If anyone knew how to check on a situation, it was Mario. He had the cat's eye and the wisdom of an owl. He would protect Rita and watch over our target person.

By ten o'clock, I checked my watch, and Mario should have been at Angelo's, as well as Rita, and Chuck. I could imagine what had happened as Chuck realized that Julie was not there and had to converse with his messenger, Rita. But I knew that Rita was able to handle herself; and that Mario was there just in case. After all, it was a public place, with lots of guys and gals, roaming around, trying to pick up on anything that seemed attractive and available. But it was a showdown for Chuck and Rita.

The scenario was set, and Chuck walked into the bar, with his henchmen, and approached Rita who was standing by the bar. Mario stood about fifteen feet away, just enough to hear what was going on.

I checked up on Christy. She was asleep on the bed in the guest bedroom, next to Cappy's master bedroom. The television was on, but not loud. She was most helpful in explaining the layout of Chuck's house in detail to the guys. They even drew a diagram based on what she remembered and Cappy was going to get an actual architectural drawing anyway. We wanted to search his home for documents and anything else that would nail Chuck to the wall. I personally would have liked to see him killed. Who would miss him anyway?

But our plan was to have the other families put the drop on him and to show them that he was cheating them and were going to place them in jeopardy by naming them during his testimony in court. We were going to have Sean, as an attorney, work with the prosecutor's office and be on the panel to question Chuck and having him lie under oath. Also, by checking up on his finances, we would get him on tax evasion, as well as selling arms to terrorist nations, which is a federal offense. We were either going to have enough on Manzione to put him away for life, or have him killed. Either way, he was going down, for good.

At eleven, the phone rang. It was Mario. He first noticed that Rita sat at the bar in deep thought, as if it took everything she had to come here and meet with Chuck. Rita had always been a faithful friend to Chuck, though it became more apparent that she was not enjoying the ride she was on. She became painfully aware that her life was in jeopardy, more now than ever before.

When I told her that I had connections with others to go after Chuck, she saw the proverbial red flag. There might be a hit out for Chuck and though he was not aware of this yet, his kingdom may diminish right before his eyes. What I said was that we were going to eliminate the illegal drug smuggling and other dishonest ways of this tyrant and she just did not want to be around when all this would be going down.

Mario was having a beer at the bar and saw Chuck come in and walk over to Rita, hovering his six foot frame over hers preventing her from moving or swiveling in her seat. She was sipping a martini and his voice sounded like drum threats in her ear when he found out that she was here in place of Julie.

"Listen, Rita," scowled Chuck, "I hope you understand that I had just lost a substantial amount of time on this bitch, and if you are lying to me, so help me, I will take your sorry ass to the dumps and get rid of it."

From where Mario was sitting, he noticed that the conversation was getting heated and Rita was motionless and very afraid of this man. Rita, on the other hand, noticed that Chuck smelled of old worn musk, probably lingering on his face as he looked like he had not shaved in a few days. She also remembered back when, that he used to have a nice clean breath and a much better personality, especially when he wanted her. But now, it was repulsive.

"I don't know what you want from me," she replied. "I am not wrong here. I think that David and Christy may be in Las Vegas or someplace else. I received a phone call from Julie at her office, so I suppose she is still there now. She asked me to go see you as she was called into meetings with her boss."

Rita felt no emotion about lying to Chuck.

"Rita, I want you to call Julie and I want to speak to her now," Chuck said angrily. "Just get her on the phone."

Chuck looked into Rita's eyes and there was the same anger she had seen so many times before. He always meant what he said. She could see that he would not let this go. His pride was hurt and he needed to take control of the situation. She had no choice but to take out her cell phone and dial Julie's number at work, but kept it low so Chuck could not see the phone number. She also knew that she had to contact David as soon as possible. The phone rang at Julie's office.

"Hi, yes…may I speak with Julie Williams, please." Rita spoke into the phone. The atmosphere was so crowded that it was difficult for Chuck to hear anyone on the other end of the line, which made it easier for Rita to fake the call.

"Oh, she has? Well, please tell her to call Rita when she gets back, thanks." Rita never did call Julie's office, but her own home phone number and just made believe that she was speaking to someone at her office. After all, it was after ten at night.

"She stepped out for a bit, Chuck," Rita turned to Chuck. "But I understand that she is working late tonight, so I will try again later." He seemed satisfied with her response and they moved to a table that was available.

Rita knew that she could not call David and was worried about her new friend, Christy. Chuck ordered some drinks for the table and he made some gestures with his hands to Rita as if to say that she was treading on thin ice for not being more forceful with Julie. Chuck always had to have his way and this was not going to end.

From about ten feet away, Mario was able to listen to a few words of their conversation, and heard that Chuck had to leave and go out of town for awhile, perhaps overseas or back to Las Vegas. Mario tried to find out when Chuck was leaving, but the din and the background noise made it too difficult. The place was a mad house, filled with singles, of all ages. Mario mentioned that he was even hit on by two women who wanted to share the space at the bar, but he moved them away to another area.

Being the business guru that he was, he did not want any distraction as he wanted to focus on what was happening at the table with Rita and Chuck. He also noticed two bodyguards by the table, and one at the door, plus a driver sitting in Chuck's car, parked just outside of the restaurant.

Chuck knew that he did not come to this place for the sole intention of meeting Rita. He wanted Julie. He would have loved to take Julie to his upstairs apartment over the Italian restaurant, across the street. He looked around the room and noticed a young thing he had met weeks ago by the name of Tara. She was no more than nineteen and had been a regular visitor to the bar, and Chuck had invited her to his restaurant for dinner many times. He could be quite persuasive, and tonight, he was looking for some action with her.

He got up from the table and leaned over to Rita. "I will be tied up for an hour or so. When I return, I want you to tell me that you called Julie and spoke to her. Got the message?"

Rita nodded and saw Chuck go over to the teenager and speak with her. Obviously he wanted her to go with him back to his apartment across the street. Rita started to sip her drink and hoped to have an opportunity to call David. Chuck's bodyguards had moved from the table and were not aware of Mario, standing by the bar, and watching every move.

Within moments of their departure, a figure approached the table and stood over Rita, as she was looking around the room. "May I buy you a drink?"

She looked up and saw this man who seemed to be elusive, and not making any eye contact with her. Yet, he had this most appealing smile and she asked, "Do I know you?"

"My name is Mario," he said. "I am here to keep an eye on you. Martini, isn't it?"

He waved over to the waitress and sat down next to Rita, in the same seat that Chuck had before.

"Oh, all right," Rita responded. "Were you sent here by David? I was about to call David. Is he all right?"

Mario told her that he was a friend of David's and wanted to make sure that she was safe from Chuck. He reassured her that he watched her and made sure that Chuck would not harm her in any way.

"Look, Rita," he said. "We can't be seen talking together. So I am just going to buy you a drink and go sit over there at the bar. We don't know when Chuck will be back, so let's talk later."

Mario left her to drink her Martini by herself, and went back to the bar where he had sat for over an hour. Rita wondered how long she would be sitting at that table and when Chuck would finally come back for her. She had no control of this situation and she was getting restless. She still needed the money that Chuck was paying her, at least to get out of town. He would only pay her if he believed in her, and at this point, she was not sure. She also wondered why Mario left her and went back to the bar. She did not like surprises.

What seemed like a few hours, Chuck finally returned to the table and did not see Rita. He asked the bartender and the waitress if they had seen her leave. They did not remember. His face grew red with anger and he signaled to one of his men to go outside to see if her car was still there. He knew her car. He bought it for her. Perhaps she was in the ladies' room and he was brazen enough to walk in and look around.

No one bothered to say a word as he had this huge frame of a man and the women just moved away from him. He was pissed trying to figure out where she had gone. He paged his driver and was ready to leave the place, as he was not going to hang around anymore.

I approached the bed where Christy was lying, curled up like a little doll, with her long legs exposed on top of the comforter. She was the most adorable woman I had ever met and she truly made me feel so wonderful in bed.

"David, is the meeting over?" I heard Christy speak softly, half asleep. "Could we go home now?"

I sat down next to her and told her that I would check with the guys down-stairs and come back up to her. I went back down to the room where the meeting was and the guys were all gathering their things. I checked with Julie and she was amazed as to what was going on. I told her that it may not be safe for her to go home, but she indicated that she never gave out her address to anyone.

Since she had left her old boyfriend, she moved into this townhouse in Irvine so even he did not know where she lived. Julie had lots of work to do in her office in the morning, and Cappy called his buddy, the sheriff at the Newport Beach station and asked that he send two detectives over to Julie's law firm early in the morning to keep an eye on her. Sheriff Brandon agreed to do this favor for his good friend. He would even have someone keep watch at her house this evening for safe-keeping. I knew that Julie would be in good hands as I did not want any-thing to happen to her.

Julie asked me if I had heard from Rita as she was worried about her. I told her that she was probably not in a safe position to call but that Mario would watch over her. At first, I would have loved to have Julie come back to my house but I realized that she had to go to work the next day. And I had Christy with me. So, it was best that Julie go back home to her own place and the deputies would keep an eye on her during the night. Cappy thought of everything. That's why he was our leader and was getting the big bucks as an investment broker and financial consultant.

Cappy and the guys reviewed everything that they had spoken about and he assigned each one of us to take care of a piece of the puzzle by the time we were to meet again. The key was to first get into Chuck's home and look for information that would convict him. Moose would fly to Washington and start the ball roll-ing with the State Department. Sean would meet with the prosecutors at the Attorney Generals' office, and the other guys had assignments to follow through during the week. My job was to keep an eye on Chuck, find out where he was, and what he was doing. Also, I was to get the actual architectural drawings for his Pacific Palisades home and review the layout with my friends at their design firm to make sure we know where every part of the house led to, and leave nothing to chance.

The guys started to leave, one by one, each with an assignment to get ready for the invasion, to end one of one of the biggest terrorist organizations in peacetime.

I felt good at what we had accomplished this evening, and felt confident that we would be able to succeed.

"You did well, David" Cappy remarked, as he turned to me. "I can see that you are back and are ready to be a part of our team once again. Welcome aboard, David."

"Thanks, Cappy." I acknowledged, as I walked over to Julie, kissed her on the cheek, and walked her out to her car.

I truly liked her, her composure, her intelligence, and her looks. She always looked so damn pretty no matter what she did, how she dressed, and even when she was upset. Julie was one in a million and the guys liked her too. This was way too much for her, but she now realized that this was a major undertaking by the Seals and, not only for me and Christy, and for her, but for the nation as a whole. Taking Chuck and his organization down was going to be a coup.

I said goodbye to the guys as they walked out single file, and I went back upstairs to Christy. We were going to meet one week from tonight back at Cappy's for further assignments, as Cappy gave me the chore of studying the drawings and keeping tabs on Chuck. We were to gain access to his home either before or after the next meeting, depending on where Chuck would be, and I was to make sure that Chuck would not be there. I had to find a way to make sure he was on a trip, perhaps back to Vegas to check out his other facilities. That would be a good time to get into his home. If Mario was correct, he could be gone for a while.

Christy was sitting up now and I took her by the arm and we went downstairs. We said good night to Cappy and his wife, and I drove south to Dana Point. It was close to midnight and I was wondering how Mario was making out. He had called in once at 11:00 and had things under control. I would call Rita later and find out how she was doing. My first inclination was to get Christy back to my home and give her some hot tea, and perhaps watch a nice movie on TV.

As I drove down the I-5 Freeway, I thought of the different objectives we had discussed this evening, and how one little interlude with Manzione now wound up to be a major type of invasion of the highest magnitude. I was getting excited, as I watched the diversity and interactive demeanor of the guys, all having different professions after twenty years, yet still working as a team. We were still one of the most dynamic forces around, and Cappy, our commander, knew how to make all of this work. He was still the commander, the captain, the motivator and the guy who would direct it all.

"They are all so nice, David, I mean your friends," said Christy as she took me out of my thought process once again.

"I especially like Moose and Dickie. They are so intelligent. They all knew about Chuck, and I learned an awful lot myself. I just didn't know that he was such a bad guy, and involved with so much. I got out at the precise moment before I would have been dragged down with the rest of his mob."

"Christy, you are right," I remarked. "I am glad you considered the obvious, as you started to see what was happening, not only with Chuck, but to you. For some reason, as fate would have it, I happened to come along and now, the Seals are going after the guy you nearly married. Whew. Glad it has worked out this way. God knows what would have happened if you did marry him and found yourself a widow."

Christy smiled at me and she gave me a kiss on the cheek. As I neared the street that my house was on, I suddenly turned the wheel and headed toward the harbor. "Let's sit by the ocean and listen to the waves, Christy. We need to clear our minds over what we heard this evening, and then we can go home, okay?"

We drove past Pacific Coast Highway, and turned left over the bridge leading to the ocean. It was rather quiet, with a slight chill in the air. I loved to sit by the ocean and just relax, listening to the waves hitting the rocks. We walked by the water and I put my arm around her shoulders. She just loved being here with me as I felt her body edging toward mine.

"David, I am in love with you," she said. "You are the best thing that ever happened to me in my life. I want to stay with you. Could I stay with you, David? Maybe, until all of this is over? I like it here by the ocean. I like being with you."

I didn't know if I was ready for this. I found her to be an attractive, bright and funny woman, who taught me how to make love and showed me how to enjoy a woman's love to me. Her remark was unexpected but it felt good. I liked to be loved by a woman, this woman. But my heart was also with another. I had wished those words were from Julie, not from Christy. There was no guarantee that Julie and I would ever get together but the thought was there, at least I thought it was. I decided to play it easy with Christy, not promising her anything. But she was welcome to stay with me, at least until this episode was over. I felt that we could at least enjoy each other's company for the next few weeks, intimately and otherwise. I thought, after all, where else could you find such a beautiful woman, who wants to have sex with you all of the time.

Mario and Rita were no longer at the bar. Chuck was on his way back to Pacific Palisades, first scolding one of his ladies, and then screwing another. He tried to reach Rita on his cell phone but there was no answer. He decided to forget it for the moment as he had to prepare for his trip to South and Central America. He was going to Panama, Columbia and then to some other countries to check on his facilities. It seemed that the cartels were getting greedy and wanted more money from his organization. That was a bigger problem than worrying about Christy, Julie, David and Rita. He had to take care of these issues first and foremost.

Rita had motioned to Mario that she was going to the back of the bar where the ladies' room was and left through the back door. Mario followed. When Rita went out, she was grabbed by one of Chuck's men who had been stationed at the rear of the bar just in case Rita tried to run out. Mario grabbed him and there was a scuffle. But with his martial arts training, Mario was able to get him to the ground and break his neck. He then grabbed Rita and took her into his car, and drove her to her own car that was parked a block away.

He followed her to a diner and they both went in for coffee. He wanted some information from Rita as to where Chuck was headed and how long he would be away from his estate. As they sat at a booth, Rita's cell phone rang several times. Chuck was trying to get a hold of her, but she would not answer the ring.

Instead, Rita told Mario that Chuck was leaving the next day to meet with people in Central America, and then fly on down to South America, and he would be away for at least ten days. They had some coffee and talked about what she knew of Chuck's organization. Rita was scared and wanted out of this and was most cooperative with Mario, as he had asked her many questions about Chuck's home, his restaurant, his friendships with the drug cartel, and what he was involved with. As much as Rita knew, she was only too happy to tell Mario everything, and had hoped that this thing would finally be over.

It was getting late, and I drove back to my place from the harbor. Christy was still awake and wanted to sit on the couch and have some hot chocolate. I fixed some, and we chatted awhile. She turned toward me and kissed me on the lips.

"David, you are full of surprises. I really enjoyed meeting your friends tonight, and Cappy's wife is a doll. I would like to have a family, a home, and a decent, honest life someday. You have been so wonderful to me and I am truly sorry that I got you into this mess. I am so glad that this will be over soon and I can live in peace without all of this stress anymore."

I took Christy around and gave her a big kiss on her lips. Her body always seemed to be ready for mine. She took my hands and placed them in the middle of her chest, and I felt her heart beating, and she was on fire. There was only one thing left to do this evening, and I felt that it would be better to handle this upstairs in bed, rather on the couch.

I followed Christy upstairs and we both fell on the bed. I could not escape her body as it just fell into mine. Her legs immediately wrapped around mine, and we started to caress each other as if we had not made love in a long time. I ran my hands all over her body and kept her close to me as she started kissing me all over my face, moving down to my chest, and unbuttoning my shirt. I felt her hand go inside of my pants and fumble with the belt and the zipper. I assisted her as I pulled at my shoes, and kicked them off. Then I fumbled for my belt and impatiently took off my pants.

I leaned over to her and started to undress her as well. I knew what I wanted, and I could see that she was already waiting for me to make love to her once again. The phone had rung. It was Rita.

"David, is that you?"

I pulled away from Christy, because I had to find out the status of what was going on and where Rita was. Julie was a bit nervous earlier about Rita's safety, and I did not want to ignore this call.

"Yes, Rita. Are you okay? Did you meet Mario? How did Chuck take it when he found out that you went in place of Julie?"

"Whoa, big boy," the voice on the other end of the phone muttered. "I am with Mario right now at an all night diner having some coffee. Just to let you know, Chuck is leaving for Central and South America tomorrow and will be gone for about at least a week. Here, let me put Mario on."

Mario got on the line and told me that if we ever wanted to invade Chuck's house, this week would be the time. He was going to make sure that Rita got home safely, and then he would go home as well.

Rita had thoughts of going to Vegas, but reconsidered, as she felt safer being close to me, to my friends, and would always contact us if she needed help. At least she got a reprieve from Chuck, as he would not be around. She thought about making plans to get out of her home and find another one, as this was paid for by Chuck and she did not want to be around when all this was going down. At least I had something to go on, and we could make plans to get into Chuck's home in a few days and see what we could learn from anything we could find that he may have hidden away.

I could not talk further as my mind was on making love to Christy. So I thanked Mario and told him that I would be in touch. I also felt relieved that Rita was fine and I could tell Julie that when I would speak to her the next day. I then looked back to Christy, as she was looking up at me, reaching for me to come down closer to her. I proceeded to embrace her and we made passionate love, but my mind and my heart were not connected. I felt that this was more of a desire on my part, than what I really needed at the time. But I had this caring feeling for Christy and she was a most beautiful woman, always there for me. How could I not enjoy being with her?

After our lovemaking, wet from moisture, feeling pretty good about the kind of sex we were having, I looked at Christy as she was also staring at me. She smiled and said, in her quiet manner, "David, I truly love you, and I know that this must be hard for you. But, I am so happy to be in your arms."

I did not know how to react or where to begin. Her words were like music, and the theme was full of love songs. I also knew that being in bed with Christy was truly fabulous, but my mind seemed to be elsewhere. I had so much to think about, such as my feelings for Julie, my assignments for the team, my upcoming class that I was supposed to teach at, and the overall project to eliminate Chuck and his organization. There was so much to ponder over, and everything coming all at once. I thought that it was only a few shorts weeks ago that I was a lonely man, searching for a new life, something to fulfill the emptiness I was feeling since Martha died.

Although that was two years ago, I still felt the hurt and the anger. Today, however, everything has changed. It was just a few days ago that I had found the love of my life, but she wasn't in this bed with me. Funny, how a small vacation can change a lifetime.

I turned back to Christy and indicated that I needed some space and some air. I suppose that I needed to reconnect as to who I was or was becoming. I was so caught up in other people's affairs that I almost forgot what I really wanted for myself.

"I know that it's late, Christy, but I want to get out of bed and just sit and ponder over all of the things that have happened. I can make you some tea or another cup of hot chocolate if you'd like."

I went to the kitchen and made some tea for the two of us. I stood against the counter and thought about my life. All this time, after Martha's death, I sheltered myself from others, finally realizing that it was good for me to start all over again and be with people. In the meantime, I had met with two women in a period of a week, and I had yet to understand why I was playing this charade. I also came to the realization that I needed confirmation of myself, and I knew that I wanted to be loved. But why was I getting involved with this Chuck character and getting back to the part of my life that I was trying to run away from?

I wondered if it was good to relive the past and feel like a Navy Seal again, and make my mark on the world. I certainly did not figure that I was going to be caught up in this web to eliminate a tyrant. But was I to feel like I needed a pat on the back for doing so? I asked myself if we were really ready to get back into action and do the things we had done twenty years ago, or was I kidding myself? Being away from all this for twenty years, did we perhaps lose that edge that made us the top Navy Seals in the world?

Others do this for a living, and our time was over. At least I thought it was. What would happen to us when this job would be over? Do we go back to our own little worlds and act like nothing ever happened? What will I do after this? Do I still maintain a friendship with Christy, and with Julie, and Rita, or do I look for someone who would not be involved in this episode? Someone new?

I may have felt that I was getting too involved and was wondering if I personally had any motives for doing so. I just didn't want to be caught up in this drama, over and over again. I asked myself that age-old question, of what I really wanted out of life.

I didn't want to live on the edge forever and be the savior of women for the rest of my life. This was not the plan that I had ten years ago and thought of how I was happy then, and how I could still enjoy that happiness now. My thoughts were all over the place, as I could have a future with Julie, or maybe with someone else. I just had to start all over again. I thought of taking Julie away from all of this and move to Hawaii or to one of the islands in the Bahamas, or on one of the Greek Isles. I then thought of taking Christy as well, and it wouldn't be that bad. Either one…or none of the above! God, the thought felt so good that my mind started to wander.

The pot started to scream on the stove and woke me up from my dream. At first, I did not hear it. But then after focusing on the steam coming out of the nose of the pot, I got two cups and poured some tea for Christy and me. Now I needed some sleep and perhaps after our tea, I could fall asleep in the arms of a beautiful lady.

I grabbed the cups and went back upstairs to Christy, and put aside my own personal issues for another time. Perhaps, I needed a more stable woman than Christy. Maybe she would actually be good for me, by never questioning anything, or prying into my business. As much as I wanted Julie, that too may not have worked out. I knew that I just did not want to take care of a woman like Christy for the rest of my life. I preferred someone independent, one who would be able to take care of herself, not rely on me to take care of her, time and time again. I suppose that mattered more to me than just having raw sex. I started to sound old.

I held the cups of tea by the bed, and Christy had fallen asleep already. In a way, I was somewhat glad that she did. I placed her cup down by the bed and took mine into my computer room that I had set up after Martha had passed away. It used to be her sewing room and now it made a great computer room for me, with my laptop, desktop, a couple of printers, fax machine and a scanner. I sat in front of the screen and realized that I had to send my brother, an email.

I was not tired, or perhaps, maybe I was overtired. But Derek knew me very well as I had not written to him in quite sometime. Perhaps if I had expressed my thoughts to him, he would come back with some clarification that would help me foresee things a bit better than I was. He seemed to have a knack for refocusing my life whenever I would stray.

Should I break my feelings gently to Christy, and tell Julie how I felt about her? I had not had sex with Julie, although we were close to doing that. But I certainly loved her intelligence, and her ability to blend in where it was needed the most. I thought that once we found ourselves making love, I would never want another woman. I also knew that I had to wait, and so I did. It may have taken months to bed down with Julie, but I felt that it was well worth it. I hunted through my address book on the computer for Derek's address.

Derek was four years younger them me, and followed me into grade school and then high school. He was the favored son, as he would always do what he was told. I used to be the sneaky one, and ran off with my friends to play stickball, and not do my homework. While he excelled in school more than I did scholastically, I was the one who played varsity ball and got my letters. I used to help him get out of scrapes with the tough guys, but he went on to college and became a most respected CPA in his industry.

We used to play stickball in the streets of East Flatbush, softball on the cement at our schoolyard, as we did not have any grassy playgrounds close by except at the ball fields at the Parade Grounds, that were too far to go to by bus. We played all of the Brooklyn street games, like 'Johnny on the Pony', 'Hide the Garrison Belt', and made sling shots out of thimbles that shot wooden matches in the air, and carved out wooden guns that shot pieces of oil cloths. Heck, we even threw eggs, which we had stolen from the local candy store, into the mass of students that had gathered at our high school on Tilden Avenue during the lunch break. It was nasty, but we were nasty sons of bitches, and we had a gang.

Those were the 'good ole days' in Brooklyn. We learned very quickly how to grow up and be young men at the age of fourteen. Many of us got caught by the police and were taken back to our parents for days of reckoning, but our father was a cop, a captain in the police department in Manhattan, and we got away with murder.

When I went to CCNY, during the time of the big rock stars and there were lots of drugs available, I worked at some of the greatest Ad Agencies in Manhattan and learned how to be aggressive and motivated by those who were looking for power. But in my third year of college, I was drafted and my father, knowing lots of people in politics, got me into the 6-month program of the Army Reserves, only to be called back because of my high priority.

That is how I was able to transfer into the Navy Seals as I was given a choice to go to Army Ranger School, Army Intelligence, the Delta Force or the Navy Seals. The Viet Nam War was in its heyday, and I needed to find myself in an outfit that I would be able to learn how to survive from the war. The Navy Seals taught me how. We became the best branch of the military.

Here I was, a twenty-year old, green as they come, and I had to go through the rigors of training to become a Navy Seal. If you screwed up, they really came down on the recruits and crucified them. It was 'do or die'. I decided to be the best I could be and made it into the group by training hard and learning how to survive the rigorous training. Then they moved me to the next class, where they take your soul and turn you into a machine. I had to excel in hand-to-hand combat, know how to use guns and weapons of any kind, and learn Morse code, as well as how to handle myself in different combat situations.

My first assignment was to go to Germany and see how much we could learn about the Berlin Wall, as we wanted this monstrosity to come down. Then it was to Cuba and meet with the infidels, those who opposed Fidel Castro, and learn about his dictatorship and what his weaknesses were. We were then stationed in the Mid East, Israel, Palestine and Afghanistan, and it was then that we learned about the Al Qaeda and its new program of terrorizing the west.

I learned a lot from my trips overseas. That is where I met Cappy and he liked how I handled myself. He asked me to join his team of Navy Seals. This was an honor to me, and he made arrangements for me to meet with Moose, Dickie, Sean, Mario and the rest of the group that he was forming. This was the greatest team of experts in war and peace that had ever assembled on this planet.

Cappy took me aside and told me that I would be a member of the most elite team of professional killers, if I followed the rules and understood my place on the team. It did not matter where I came from, just as long as I worked as a team member and understood my place under this commander, who took control of any situation that came up. I re-enlisted and pledged my support to the Navy Seals. I was made an officer and received all of the benefits that came with the job I got into.

We traveled all over, meeting various types of devious characters, in Europe, in Asia, in the Middle East, and I learned the many languages as well including the many customs that we embarked on. I was a full-fledged Navy Seal. Then came the assignment to get Noriega. I bit at the chance to take this guy down. He was running so many drug cartels that he was bought off, not only by the U.S Government, but also by the thugs that ran the drug operations, from nearly every country in Central and South America. I was the James Bond of the west. I felt powerful, and loved what I was doing.

Finally, it was time to leave the service. We all had had enough. I went home, found a job teaching, and met Martha. She was wonderful. It was a first time marriage for both of us. She preferred to be a 'stay-at-home-mom' but we never had kids because of a personal problem that irked her for so many years. I learned to live with it, and although I loved Martha very much, I still missed all of the excitement I found in the Navy Seals. As much as I wanted to forget about my past, I could not forget about the different countries I had visited, the shady characters I had met, and the experiences I had been in, because we were the Navy Seals, a team of experts, of professionals, a band of killers who had no fear.

All those years, living in the dream world of being married to Martha, I still missed the excitement of being a Navy Seal. I did not realize it then, but now it all came back to me as it had haunted me all of these years. Now I can become a part of the team once again. I realized what was missing in my life. I needed the excitement, the wonderful women we had in all of the countries we visited, and the fact that we were untouchable. We were the best that money could buy!

It was getting late and I needed to lie down, as I had a lot to do the next few days. I went upstairs and took a shower. I then lay down next to Christy and started to dream of how we were going to get into Chuck's house, get after his ass, conduct covert operations, and take down this bastard. We were going back into action and I was absolutely, loving every moment.

And here was Christy, a loving soul who has given me so much pleasure in the past few days that I was ecstatic over it. Just like, being back in the countries we went to. I had any piece of ass I wanted, and I screwed any kind of pussy I met. It was a dream come true, as long as I played the game and was a part of the team. I was part of the greatest group of guys, with more combined intelligence, than any national security force that was connected with the White House in Washington.

We had the State Department by the balls and we knew it. We could do just about anything we wanted, and no body would be able to stop us. We were the dream team of the government, and I was not about to let it fly away from me. I was becoming hungry for this excitement and I was ready to do my part to be the toughest hombre in the armed forces.

That is what I was trained for, and that was what I became. I was a Navy Seal, and I had the best bitches in bed with me. I was among the toughest men alive. But I was getting tired. I finally decided to lie down next to Christy and fell asleep. It was time to cool my jets and relax my brain. Here was this fabulous body next to me, whom I had laid so many times. I was feeling good inside and I needed to face reality. I had what I really wanted in life, right there next to me. I loved it.

I got up in the morning, feeling very relaxed. Christy was already up and making some coffee for herself in the kitchen. I called Cappy and told him about Chuck not being at his home for a week, and he indicated that tomorrow would be a good night to get to his house. He assigned Mario, Mike, and Billy, with himself as team leader, to be on this mission.

I contacted my designer friends who would have access to city hall in Pacific Palisades to get the blue prints of Chuck's layout. They indicated that it would take a few hours and they would have them for me by 6 pm this evening. I would then sit down with them and familiarize myself with the drawings and then head on to Cappy's house early the next evening.

Cappy would then go over all of the plans with the four of us. By ten o'clock, we would be on our way to Pacific Palisades, all dressed in black, as if we were Ninjas, ready to rummage through this large estate by the ocean. If we encountered anyone in the house, we were to take them down. There was no margin for error. We had to go through the house with a fine toothcomb.

Cappy told me that Moose was already on his way to Washington to meet with the State Department, and Dickie was back into the newspaper files to get as much information on Chuck and his entire organization as possible. Sean headed to the attorney general's office to set up a plan to get Chuck during his next testimony in Court. We were on a plan of mercy and things were starting to gel. I was getting back into my swing of being the Navy Seals officer that I enjoyed many years ago.

I showered, dressed, and headed downstairs into the kitchen, and Christy already had a cup of hot tea for me plus some dry toast. I indicated to her that I had a lot of things to do today, this evening and tomorrow, into the night and that she was to make herself comfortable in the house. She acknowledged my hospitality by telling me that she would like to walk the stores at the harbor, probably pick out some nice tops and shorts, and find a restaurant to have lunch. I would be back around five for an early dinner, but then I would have to go out again, and meet the guys at the design firm.

Christy was okay with my scheduling and would find things to do. She did promise not to go further than the harbor, which was five minutes down the street. I gave her keys to the Jeep and I would take the sports car. But first, I wanted to call Julie to see how she was doing.

"Hi Julie," I asked, while having my tea on the back patio. "Did you have enough sleep last night?"

"David, last night was a trip. Wow. I must tell you, all of the guys are great. I felt secure when I saw a deputy outside the townhouse and he even knocked on my door this morning right before I was ready to leave. And when I came to work this morning, there were two plainclothesmen, just walking around the office, as if they worked here. Everything is great. I am back to do the work I missed doing last night, and I have a big meeting with the partners in a little while."

She continued. "We are going to discuss the situation with regards to Chuck and the trials that are coming up. It seems that the partners received a call from Sean and the prosecutor's office already, and things are in the works to take our little Chuckie for a long ride."

Julie felt a bit relieved that her day was starting out just fine and that she did not have the pressure of Chuck's grip on her, at least for a while. Cappy asked me to get a hold of some friends of ours who could tap Chuck's phones today and that would be done. The only thing left was to make some of these calls, have my tea, chat with Christy for a bit, then head out. I figured that she would be safe and sound at the harbor and I didn't have to worry about her at this point.

Christy was enjoying the view from the back patio. The air was cool, as there was a low cloud cover from the ocean. I walked over to her and she looked as adorable as ever. "How are you today, Christy?"

"Oh, David, I am feeling great. I do appreciate using your car and just window shop at some of the stores at the harbor. If I see something that I feel you would like, I will buy it. It is so very quiet around here, except for the birds chirping and the foghorns from the boats. This is a nice place to relax and be away from all of the traffic and people, and just lay back."

"Yes," I replied. "I find it very pleasing and feel as if I can just sit back and take it all in when I just want to get away from everything. After I teach at school, I usually sit out back and go over my lessons and prepare for the next day. I will make sure I leave you a set of keys for the house and the car before I leave. You just go and have fun, today."

CHAPTER 9

▼

RUNNING ON FAITH

With that, I gathered my things and headed to the garage. I drove up PCH to meet with my buddies who know how to tap phones as they used to work for PAC BELL before they changed their name to SBC. Now, they just go on service calls and are on their own time. I met with Stan and Paco who are proficient in this line of work. They would go out this afternoon to Pacific Palisades and make sure that every line at Chuck's house would be tapped into, with the lines going back into their truck. They would then remain in the truck to retrieve all calls going into and out of the house. They would even call two more guys who could use the money, for some backup to relieve them at night. These guys could use the extra money and not say a word about this to anyone.

Stan had done some work for Cappy many times in the past few years, and had been very reliable and good at his job. When this was over, he would undo the lines and no one would ever know that they were tapped.

I then headed to the design firm to meet with Richard and Carlos who would get the blue prints. I told them about the house and that we needed all of the architectural drawings and blue prints by five or six that evening. I would return by then, giving them enough time to study the drawings and make notes for all of us to follow. Richard was a top-notch architect, and now he and his people have been in the business of designing estate homes for the rather wealthy, homes that run into the millions. He has designed many homes in the Newport Beach and San Clemente areas that ran from 3 million on up. His ideas simply were astounding.

I then headed out to pick up some tools, and dark clothes, the kind we used to wear on our assignments years ago. I picked up five outfits, plus many types of electrical equipment, radios, flashlights, a small copy machine, and lots of tools that we would need tomorrow evening. This was going to be a quick but thorough search and we needed to be prepared.

By mid afternoon, I headed for lunch. I had not had time to contact Christy, but as I was getting a bit hungry and looking for a place to grab a bite to eat, the phone rang. It was Stan. He and Paco were at Chuck's estate and he told me that there were about eight people in the home, in different parts of the house. That led me to believe that Chuck left some of his men behind to secure the house, and we needed to make sure we would take them out in order to search the premises. I asked him to keep me posted as to when they come and go, and who would be there during the evening.

The next call I got was from Richard. They had the blueprints and were headed back to their office to inspect them and give us all of the necessary details we would need to get into the house and search each and every room, including any hidden closets and vaults. He did indicate that this house was 6,500 square feet, and that there was a guest house in the back that was another 3,000 square feet. He suggested that we allow about six or more hours to cover both homes. I told him that I would meet him at six at his firm. I then called Cappy, and he indicated that he would join me at Richard's place, so we could at least spend some time together and learn from the blue prints as much as we could before tomorrow evening.

I headed toward a Coco's Restaurant when the cell phone rang again. This time, it was Julie. She had some information from her partners during her meeting and asked if I was available to see her at her office in Newport Beach. I grabbed a quick takeout sandwich and Coke, and drove to her office while eating in the car. When I arrived, she was paged to the lobby and we went to her office in the back. She had made copies of the past testimonials and reports that the partners had prepared, going back a year or two, and she felt that this was crucial evidence that Sean would be interested in. I took the folder and thanked her for sharing the information, although it was strictly confidential and part of the Client/Attorney privilege.

"You look great, Julie." I smiled at her and noticed her beautiful purple dress with a cute pink ascot around her neck. "No matter what you wear, you are the most attractive woman I have ever seen. I could simply cuddle up with you right now and squeeze you in my arms."

She looked at me with her usual sneer and turned her head ever so slightly away from me. "David, you are asking for trouble, although I like the compliment anyway. Now you better get out of here before we do something I will regret."

We both laughed at her comment, and I picked up the papers and left her office. On the way out, I noticed the two detectives outside the building. Of course, only I would know this, because of Cappy's request to the sheriff. Normally, two guys in dark suits would appear to be anyone out on a smoke break. They sort of fit into the group and could have passed as attorneys or law clerks. I knew that Julie would be safe if she was threatened in any way. They probably had their guns inside their jackets, on the back of their belt so as not to alarm any of the people going into and out of the building. I just nodded, as if to say hello, but did not do anything further. These guys probably realized that I was a friend of Julie's, not knowing that I was part of Cappy's team. It was better that way. No need to take this to any other level.

As I got into the car, I thought of calling Christy to see how she was doing. She still had her cell phone and I asked that she keep it with her at all times. She picked up the call and said that she was having a good day.

"David, I bought the cutest little outfits that would look so well on a sailboat. I can't wait to show them to you. Will I see you soon?"

I told her that I had more chores to do but would be back by 4:30. We would have a snack before I had to leave once again. I headed out to the freeway. Just as I left the parking lot in front of Julie's firm, I noticed a big black sedan pulling out as well. It had two guys in the front seat and I could not see who was in the back. The windows were tinted and this car looked kind of fishy to me. So I drove along the road at a moderate speed to see what it was up to.

As I approached the Freeway, it also got into my lane and was two car lengths behind me. If I had known better, Chuck had placed his men at Julie's building and probably recognized me when I came out. I had to lose them and my little sports car was able to handle the road pretty well. Now it was up to me to do some fancy driving along the 405 Freeway. Driving my little MR2 is like traveling beyond the borders of your imagination. And this car, although not as powerful as a Porsche, could handle the road quite well. But the red color could keep you in focus since Red is not a basic color in sedans and SUVs.

I would get an adrenaline rush as I pushed down on the accelerator and switched gears almost as easy as pie, pushing me from zero to 60 mph in less than 7 seconds. I got to know its sure-footed handling and was able to move this bugger in and out of the lanes with precise performance. There was no guesswork as to its extraordinary performance and I was unleashing the power of technology, as I allowed the vehicle to take off, with ease and comfort. The black car, a 450 Mercedes, was not far behind, as we raced south on the Freeway, dodging in and out the lanes. Their car managed to stay about sixty yards behind mine. Like playing Nintendo, I moved the car from one lane to another, picking up speed to eighty-five, ninety miles per hour, when the lanes were clear.

The big black car could only gradually move as mine was doing, losing sight of its maneuverability on the road, with more than twice its weight, and half the traction of my car. I was focusing on the cars before me as I kept the car in fifth gear, not once downshifting. It was handling well, and I was gaining distance from the black car that kept its pace and being not too far behind me. But being a realist, I knew that I would not leave that car too far behind and I had to plan some horrific moves, without endangering any other vehicle on the Freeway.

I was ready to begin a game of "Chicken" and get that car cornered or perhaps, caught between two cars and the cement wall that separated the diamond lane. I felt that I truly became one of the antiheroic racers who could be one of the most dangerous when it came to driving. Being behind the wheel of a fast car was kind of like putting more bullets in your gun. And the more bullets you have, the more likely you'll hit the target. My target was to eliminate this black Mercedes that was on my ass and keeping pretty close to me at that.

My experience with cars and being a driver in the Navy Seals taught me a lot. The prodigious output of a fast car is made possible by the variable valve timing with intelligence both in the motor and by the driver that optimizes intake valve timing for increased response at low as well as medium rpm ranges. The ride is always smooth, no matter how fast you go, while the handling is nearly telepathic. I added more things to the car such as a sport-tuned suspension which gave it better handling, and I had it in premier shape ever since.

We were going south, now approaching the 'El Toro Y', where the I-5 and I-405 meet and become four lanes from eight. Traffic was quite congested but I knew that I had to weave in and out of the lanes in order to lose the car. It was a game of tag and I was 'it'. I was being followed and knew that I had to lose those sons of bitches, or they would know where I lived and get Christy as well. I had about seven or eight miles to elude these bastards, and they were doing a good job in keeping on my ass. I had to keep weaving in and out, and find a spot where I can lose them entirely.

I saw an opening between two cars, but I had to get into the diamond lane where you can go if you have a passenger in the car with you, which I did not. The hell with it! I was going to do some quick maneuvering, and I needed to get there, and fast. I stepped on the accelerator and jumped into the first lane, and I had some space between my car and the one in front. These cars were doing about 80 mph, and once I would be able to reach that speed, I would again get back in the right lanes, and do some more weaving in and out of the traffic. After five minutes of this, I then hopped back in lane two and found a hole where I was able to gun the car to eighty five, move in front of a truck, and get into some daylight.

The black sedan was trying to follow but didn't have the same maneuverability as I did. Once it came into my lane, but about six car lengths behind, we were close to Crown Valley in Mission Viejo, and I thought of getting off and leaving them on the Freeway. That was my motive. I then cruised at ninety and was looking for some open space.

The sedan was gaining on me and I knew that I had to act quickly if I was to swerve three car lanes to the right and off the Freeway. The other cars were too close and I did not want to cause any accidents, so I kept my speed up and kept traveling, in and out of the second and third lanes. All the while, the sedan was trying to get closer, and I kept watching them through my rear view mirror. I weaved from one lane to another, and they did likewise. They were good. They knew how to follow at high speed and were on my tail like a fly on a horse.

I checked my side view mirrors and looked over my shoulder to see if I was clear on either side. I then moved back into the third lane and decided that I better not head down to the Bay Cities' exits because of all the traffic around the beach area.

I saw an opening and moved two lanes to the right. I was passing the exit to the Ortega Highway, one exit before the one I normally get off at to go to Dana Point, then hopped the curb and made it onto the exit. The sedan was too far to the left to get off and they had to continue on. I then headed south down the Ortega highway, known as the 74 Road, toward Lake Elsinore and that would be a thirty-mile stretch if I stayed on this road all the way. I figured to get off on one of the side roads to see if I was being followed.

After fifteen minutes, I pulled off and sat under some Elm Trees, watching the road for the black sedan. I was right. There it was, coming down the road at a moderate speed, looking off in different directions, trying to get a glimpse of my little red sports car. I let it go by, and again waited about five minutes. Before I did, I copied down the license plate number. I then slowly moved from the trees, onto The 74, and turned left, heading north, back to the Freeway.

I did not see the black sedan and knew that they would not be able to turn around so readily as I was able to, as they drove further south. I hit the express-way and headed toward the beach. I drove down the narrow streets until I hit my street, pressed the remote of the garage and parked inside. I then looked out of the garage door windows, about six feet high off the ground, by standing on a nearby foot stool. There was no sedan.

Fortunately, the Jeep was there, which meant that Christy was home. I told her what had happened as we had some Sushi that she had purchased at the harbor. We also had some white wine, joked a bit and I told her to stay put and not leave the house. I had to meet Richard and Carlos again at their design firm and go over the blue prints. Cappy would be there too. I had a few minutes, so I called Stan and Paco to see how they were making out at Chuck's house. They would be relieved by 11:00 pm and would return at seven in the morning. There was a lot of activity, of people going into and out of the estate. Chuck was not visible as he was probably off somewhere in Central America.

They reported that there must have been about fifteen people in both the main and the guesthouse, and that all of the lines were tapped. They even had a device to record conversations from within the rooms, as they managed to bug many of the rooms by placing devices through the windows, with telescopic cameras that picked up movements from within the rooms. This was a precautionary measure.

By five thirty, I gave a hug and kiss to Christy, checked out the windows, and upon seeing that the coast was clear, I took the little car out of the garage and went on to meet with Richard, Carlos and Cappy. If I encountered the black sedan again, it would be easier to elude them with the little car, rather than the 4 x 4 Jeep. I had to use some basic logic as we were just getting started in this spy business and I needed to keep my profile as low as possible. Obviously, Chuck would have his people out, looking for each of us, but without him being present, it would simply be to keep tabs on us.

I drove the ten miles to the design house. There was Richard and Carlos, already at the blueprints with Cappy. I related to Cappy, of my experience, being chased by the black sedan. He was concerned and put a call out to see if the black sedan was around the area in Dana Point. Always best to be sure. He called Lt. Ballard, chief at the Dana Point sheriff's station, and asked that he send some deputies around the city in search of the vehicle. He gave the chief the license plate number that I had written down on a small piece of scrap paper.

We then turned to Richard for some of his expertise and advice on the blue prints of Chuck's estate. It had so many rooms, including the guesthouse. The grounds were surrounded by a nine foot gate, all power electrified. It sat on five acres of prime real estate within a stone's throw from the Pacific Ocean. Docked by the waterside, was a small yacht, about eighty feet long, worth about 3 million. It also had lots of space within its three decks.

We looked at each and every room, the many floors that we would have to go to, and then, by surprise, take out the men who were situated throughout the main house and the guesthouse. There were approximately six ways to get into the small mansion, with lots of windows, all covered with an alarm system that hopefully, would be eliminated by Stan and Paco.

There was a huge living room and an even larger den with a huge bar, and billiard area. The walls were thickly lined with heavy paneling, and the carpets, except for the den, were thick, all wall-to-wall. The den had hard wood flooring, covered with Oriental Rugs, all recorded in the plans. We had to be aware of other things upon arrival the next evening, but for now, we were getting a good picture of the layout. There were two separate stair cases leading up to the eight guest bedrooms, and huge master bedroom, plus the six bathrooms, three linen closets and work out room.

Downstairs, there was a breakfast nook, a kitchen overlooking the ocean with long windows, and a few secret stairways, one leading upstairs to a room behind the master bedroom, the other leading downstairs, and out into the side of the building. There was an underground tunnel from the six-car garage, going through to the guesthouse, and that smaller building was big enough to hold about twenty-five people. The grounds had tennis courts, a bike path, a small putting course, lots of chaise lounges and chairs in the back, an area to park cars, and a gazebo, overlooking the ocean and the yacht. If we were to search this place, it would take hours, using many people.

Cappy decided to get some help. He asked for reinforcements by contacting Moose in Washington. Moose was able to bring in about fifteen more Navy Seals who were on hold in San Diego. They would fly in early in the morning, and we would have a meeting at Cappy's before we were to go to Chuck's. That would give us a total of twenty Seals to go through the house, and we would all be heavily armed.

For the next two hours, we laid out our plans that would consist of placing the twenty men inside the house at exactly ten o'clock. We planned on having four at the guesthouse, and sixteen at the main house, and Stan and Paco were to have lookouts around the perimeter of the house to watch in case others might be entering the premises. We were pretty well satisfied with the overall containment that we would have.

Finally, looking up from the blue prints, Cappy remarked. "David, I want you to lead the team upstairs, while I take the team and go through the downstairs of the house. I am going to place six men with you upstairs, and we will have a total of about eight downstairs. I will put Mario on your team, and I will take Billy on mine. We will have Mike run the team at the guesthouse. By the time we are ready to leave tomorrow evening after our meeting, we all should have our assignments, as this will take at least six hours to complete. And how is Christy doing?"

"Christy is doing well, Cappy," I answered. "I left her in good spirits and she was going to watch some TV until I returned. I believe she is fine. I also got these folders from Julie that she took from her partners. They contain some information about Chuck. Perhaps you would like to give them to Sean for the upcoming Court dates."

I gave the files to Cappy that Julie gave to me and we were now moving along with precision, so I had thought. I decided to call Christy. The phone rang and rang, and there was no response. I got a little nervous, as she should have responded. I asked Cappy to contact the deputies who were supposed to be outside of my home, keeping an eye on the place. When Cappy called them and got no response, he called Chief Ballard, and the Chief also did not get any answer from his deputies. He told Cappy that he and another deputy would go to the area and check things out.

Cappy and I decided to head down to Dana Point, he in his car, and me in mine. We thanked Richard and Carlos took all of the blueprints and the notes we made, and Cappy followed me down the Freeway. I approached the garage and used the remote to open up the door. The Jeep was there so I pulled inside. Cappy parked in one of the guest spots outside. He walked around to see if he could find the deputies, while I went inside the house with my gun drawn.

Cappy had given me one of his pistols just in case there was a problem. All of the lights were on, the TV was blaring, and there was a wine glass on the table by the couch, but no Christy. I started to walk through the lower part of the house, to the dining room, the living room, and then the kitchen. I then went outside to the back patio to see if she would be sitting there, but still, no Christy. I noticed that the back door was open, as if it was jimmied. If anyone came into the house, this is the way they entered. I then checked the hall closets, and looked inside the bathroom on the lower level.

With that cleared, I went upstairs. By that time, my phone rang. It was Cappy. "Let me in through the garage, David, as your front gate is locked."

I ran back through the den, out the door leading into the garage, and pressed the remote on the wall. Cappy came in and walked to the door.

"David, it does not look good. I found the car belonging to the deputies. They were sitting in the car, both with bullets through their heads."

Just then, a car with headlights shining into the garage, pulled in front of the house. It was Chief Ballard and his deputy.

Cappy walked with the Chief toward the car with the two dead deputies. Lt Ballard called it in and stayed outside with his deputy, waiting for the coroner and fire department, as well as the State Police.

I ran upstairs with Cappy and looked for Christy. She was nowhere to be found. There was nothing messy nor did it seem as if anything was missing. Cappy called Mario, Mike and Billy. They would be at the house within thirty minutes. I went downstairs and again went into the kitchen. I told Cappy about the back door and he went to investigate the area.

Just then, Cappy's phone rang. It was Stan, from the van across the street from Chuck's home. He told Cappy that he heard that some of the men were on the way back to the estate with a female. That female had to be Christy. They got to my home and took Christy. They probably had a few cars following me from Julie's law firm and I did not concentrate on the other cars. I was getting soft and sloppy.

When the State Police arrived, they had some detectives with them and scoured my home for fingerprints and any evidence that might lead them to whom the culprits were who broke into the home. Cappy went out to Lt. Ballard and gave his condolences to him and realized that this thing was getting a bit out of hand. Now we had our first casualties, two deputies of the Dana Point Sheriff's Department, and we hadn't even begun to start our assignments yet. I also felt sorry for the two deputies and reassured Lt. Ballard that we will find the people who did this to the two officers.

Mario first arrived and he was filled in by Cappy. Then Mike and Billy showed up, and they too were informed of what was going on. They looked at me as if I had screwed up, but knew better not to make an issue of it. I was doing my best, as it has been twenty years since I was involved with these kinds of covert operations. Maybe I was getting stale, and losing the touch of a Navy Seal. But Cappy put his arm around me and told me that I was doing the best I could and we will resolve this matter quickly. We just didn't have time to wait until the next evening to get to Chuck's home.

We all changed our clothes and put on the outfits I had gotten, and put all of the tools in my Jeep. Cappy asked Lt. Ballard to give us some of his deputies to back us up, and then we headed to Pacific Palisades to get Christy out of harm's way. There was a total of seven deputies and state police joining us and we had hoped that the twelve of us could handle the job efficiently and without any loss of life.

It was about eleven o'clock and the roads were pretty empty, so I was able to drive pretty fast, up the 405 Freeway to Los Angeles. On the way, we stopped off at Cappy's house and got into his arsenal that had an inventory of the most advanced firearms you could have imagined. He had stored away the latest weapons that consisted of automatic guns, AK 47s, firearms with telescopic lenses and lots of ammo. I chose a PPK as my weapon for my waist, and an AK 47 for an automatic rifle. We were headed for a showdown and we needed to be prepared.

The Chief would look after things with the State Police and would be responsible for closing up the house after they left. The State Police were told that it was a gang related shooting, although nothing like this ever occurred in Dana Point, since it became a City in 1989. This incident would put the City on the map and take away its 'clean city' image. Dana Point has been a city of retired individuals, senior citizens, and good families with good incomes and great scholastics. This one incident, that occurred right in my own home, would change all that forever.

Oh well, another neighborhood gone to hell, I thought. And I felt that all this was because of me, my trip to Las Vegas, meeting Julie and Christy, then being confronted by Chuck, in my hotel room at the Venetian. So who cared what the neighbors would think of me? I really didn't care. Many were just pains in the ass anyway. Typical nosy neighbors!

We were approaching Pacific Palisades, and Cappy kept in close contact with Stan and Paco. They did not leave the van, and they had more of their people scattered throughout the grounds of Chuck's estate. We parked about two blocks away and knew what we had to do. Everything had to work with precision and timing, and none of our guys was to get hurt. We had to rescue Christy, and if we needed to take down each and every one of the characters in that place, we would do so.

I thought to myself, 'Jesus Fucking Christ…what the fuck am I doing here?'

It has been twenty years since I last crawled on my stomach, climbed trees, and ran with a bunch of guys who were the elite squad in the Navy Seals. My body was not as agile as it was then, and I wondered if I still had it in me to move as quickly as I did when I was that skinny kid who was able to perform miracles with the rest of the team.

I was glad that I kept up my training by working out at the local gym on Pacific Coast Highway, lifting weights, working the machines, and going to the range for trap and skeet shooting. I wanted to keep my body in shape just in case I had to get back into this game of good guys versus bad guys. I had cataract eye surgery years ago plus a detached retina and now I was going to use my night vision to shoot at bad guys and expect to take them down. Fortunately, my comrades all seemed to be in good shape but I was not sure of myself. I just was hoping that I would not fuck it up real good and cause any harm to my buddies. They were counting on me.

"Hey big guy, are you ready for some action?" Mario managed to get me out of my dreaming and I was ready for action.

We decided to surround the house. I took the back with Mario, while Cappy, Mike and Billy surrounded the front of the grounds. We had to get over the tall gates that surrounded the grounds and that meant that Stan and Paco would have to cut the electricity. That took only an instant, which allowed us to open the gates and go through.

We timed it precisely, and as the gates opened, Mario and I headed toward the rear of the grounds, and Cappy's group spread apart, heading toward the front of the house. Mike took a few of the officers and headed to the guesthouse. There were two guards sitting by the gate, and when the gate opened, they saw these black figures coming at them, and we shot them with our weapons, and the silencers did not stir anyone up at the house.

I headed toward the back door and noticed two more men, soldiers in the Mafia as they were called, and waved to Mario. Mario snuck up on one and put a knife to his throat. There was no noise and the other soldier was not aware of what was happening. By the time he turned around, I threw a six inch blade at him, caught him in the back, and he keeled over like dead weight. We had a clearer path to enter the house in the rear. We each headed for a separate doorway.

Cappy was close to the front entrance, while Billy was to the right of him. There were the deputies behind Cappy and Billy, who had probably never fired their weapon at anyone. Mike was already at the guesthouse and looked over to us for orders.

There were two more of Chuck's men on the front lawn of the main house, discussing sports and smoking cigars. Billy lunged at one with his knife, catching him off guard, and the other guard had seen this and pulled his weapon on him. Cappy had no choice but to gun him down. There was silence. We decided to sit back as I called Cappy on my radio to see what was happening in the front of the grounds.

Mike and his men had encountered two men outside the guesthouse. Mike knew how to take them out and did not want to rely on the deputies. He shot them both with his gun, and the silencer did not alert anyone inside the guesthouse. There was dead silence and we all waited for Cappy to give the word to enter the building.

Just then, Paco called to tell Cappy that they had the woman upstairs in one of the bedrooms. She was being bound to a bed and if she were not Chuck's lady, the guys who took her to the room, would have banged her. Oh well, thank goodness for small favors. It pays to know someone high up the ladder, and nobody wanted to cross old Chuckie.

I opened the sliding door near me and went into this fairly lit room that looked like a downstairs bedroom. Mario went into another set of sliding doors that led into the den where the pool table was. There were also three guys at the bar having drinks. They would have noticed the sliding door open and close, but the phone rang. It was Chuck from Central America, calling back in response to a message he received.

"Yeah, Chuck," one of his men stated. "We got the girl. She is safe upstairs in the bedroom, all tied up, nice and tight."

The talking had halted and we waited for the man to speak once again in the phone. Then we heard him say, "Okay, Chuck, we will put her on a plane for Columbia tomorrow morning. We will call you back and tell you the flight number and time of departure and arrival in Bogotá."

There was silence once again, as he hung up the receiver. He spoke to Chuck and we got there just in time, before Christy was to find herself on a one-way flight to Columbia. Now we had to rescue her and get her out of this place.

We were just about to move in on these guys, when Cappy contacted us on his mobile phone.

"David, Mario, go slowly. We understand that there are three guys in the den, four in the kitchen, and another six or seven upstairs. You handle those in the den, and we will take down those in the kitchen. There are two stairways. You take the one closest to the den, and we will take the other. Make sure you count bodies as you go upstairs, and Stan and Pico will keep us posted as to the bodies left in the building. One more thing! There are five more in the guesthouse. Mike is there now, and Stan's people will watch to see if they decide to come close to the main house. Mike, Mario, David, we have to take them out at all costs. I don't care how you do it, just so long as you do it. Okay? So be careful and move your ass…NOW!"

I crawled on my hands and knees and could see, through the corner of my eye, Mario, who was so good at tactical diversion, that he was already half way to the bar area. As I approached the bar, I got my leg snagged on a wire and it pulled an end table, toppling a glass object that fell to the floor. The noise startled the men at the bar and they drew their weapons. We had no choice but to fire at them. I hit one, and Mario was able to hit the remaining two. It was like an instant reflex, and the three men were dead. I then heard from Cappy once again.

"David, I just got a call from Paco. The lights from your automatic weapons were seen from the men at the guesthouse. Mike and the deputies were not able to take them all down. They are on their way to the main house. Watch your ass. They are coming through the front doors. We are close to the kitchen but have to watch for them as they enter the building. You and Mario cover the guys in the kitchen, and we will take care of the men coming from the guest house."

Again, my sloppiness was causing us to lose our edge, and Mario and I had to move toward the kitchen. When we heard the front doors swing open with a thud, this caused the four men in the kitchen to run out, with guns in hand. As they did, we gunned them down, like a shooting gallery. Cappy and his crew managed to take out those coming in through the front door, as they did not know what hit them. Cappy called us and said that they hit three of the five guys from the guesthouse. The other two were probably going around back, where we came into the house.

We had to backtrack and make sure we got them. Cappy asked Stan to close down all of the electricity as we had infra-red goggles that could help us see in the dark. That was our asset, and we again had the edge. As we waited for the two to enter from the back, Cappy and Billy headed upstairs. Mike was back at the main house and stayed at the foot of the stairs to watch the action in case someone jumped out from one of the secret passages.

I laid quietly on my stomach as did Mario, until the two men came into the same sliding doors as I did, only moments before. What they failed to see, because of the darkness, were two guns facing them, as they approached. We opened fire and gunned them down. I went over to each of the bodies and took away their weapons. Mario did the same with those by the bar and outside the kitchen. So far, we were cleaning up the mess and were able to stabilize the situation as efficiently as possible.

The upstairs was dark and Cappy and Billy climbed the steps slowly. Based on Stan's information, there were still six or seven more bad guys upstairs. I knew that Cappy needed help, so Mario and I climbed the other set of steps leading to the upstairs bedrooms. We waited until we could see what was taking place. We did not want Christy to be harmed in any way so we were cautious not to do anything irrational.

We stopped by the top of the stairs and looked around to the different rooms. It was pitch black and we had these great infra-red goggles that gave us sight of any movement, whereas those in the building did not have these. We also had to make sure that Christy would not be hurt. As Mario and I moved to the top of the stairs, obviously Cappy and Billy also had reached the top of the stairs on the other side. We then heard some gunshots downstairs.

Mike and the police officers were alone at the foot of the steps, and probably more of the guys from the guesthouse had entered the main building. More shots and then silence! I then heard over the radio, the all-too-familiar words from Mike, as he used to say to us years ago.

"All's well on the western front, guys."

Thank Goodness, he was able to take out the intruders.

By then, the other men from the bedrooms were swarming about, at the top of the stairs, only to be hit with a wall of darkness. Two of them came to our side and Mario and I took them out with our automatic weapons. Cappy and Billy sat quietly and waited for any of those guys to come down their staircase. I decided to move up to the hallway and go from one bedroom to the next, looking for Christy.

Mario was guarding my back, watching for anyone coming from any of the bedrooms. I opened the nearest door and looked inside, but it was empty. I then tried the next door. There was movement inside and I spotted a figure bustling about, trying to use the phone. He had his gun by his hip and was concentrating on pressing the buttons on the phone, when he noticed the door open. He aimed high and shot three times. I was on my stomach and was able to clip him in the knees with two quick shots. He fell backward and I shot him once again. I then eyed the room and there was no one else there. I then went to the next bedroom.

In the meantime, Cappy had eliminated another one of the residents while Billy moved toward the other bedrooms, crawling on his side. All of a sudden, there was a lot of gunfire. Two other guys jumped out from one of the other bedrooms and started to shoot at them. Cappy was hit in the arm and Billy took them both down, after scattering them both with enough bullets to take down an army. I moved toward them and entered another bedroom.

The room seemed empty except for a slight noise coming from the bathroom. I moved cautiously toward that room and pushed the door open and dropped hard to the floor. Gunshots exploded in succession and I looked carefully to make sure that Christy was not being used as a shield. I then shot upward, catching the figure in the chest and the neck. He went down like a lead balloon. No one else was in the room, so I moved toward the next room where I saw this body lying on the bed. It had to be Christy.

As I approached the bed, a huge figure jumped on me and knocked me to the floor, and my AK47 went flying to the other side of the room. I reached in my back and pulled out my PPK and was about to fire, when I felt this big foot lodge in my stomach. I lost my senses for a few moments, and I heard the voice say to me that he got me.

I heard two shots and just sat there, thinking that I was going to be dead. I looked up and the big black figure was going down. Mario got into the room and took him out. I then grabbed my body, hoisted myself onto the bed, and found Christy. I untied her and grabbed my AK47 and we left the room.

Billy then investigated every room to make sure we got all of the varmints. Mike was downstairs, counting the bodies and he took all of the weapons from them. The deputies and the police called the coroner's office and the crime scene investigators, while we walked to the outside of the house. There were residents gathered outside, held back by the patrol cars, all trying to find out what had happened. Between the gunshots and the many patrol cars and motorcycles, it looked like the 1967 riots back in Harlem or Detroit.

Cappy was okay, as the bullet winged his arm and left his body. He asked Stan and Paco to put the lights back on and Mike, Mario and Billy were to go through the house and look for any kind of literature that would be evidence against Chuck and his organization. The CSI team would do their investigative work and take care of the bodies.

It was such a huge place and we had to investigate each and every room. We spent hours trying to check each drawer of every cabinet that may give us some information about Chuck's organization and who else might be involved. Stan's people also gave us a hand in the search as we double-checked everywhere, each room, and every nook and cranny. We did not want to leave any stone unturned.

Mike and Billy were to stay behind and continue their search throughout the rooms for any evidence, including the many secret passageways. If any fed officials would show up, our guys had carte blanche and had the authority to continue with their search without interference. They were to stay there for as long as it would take them, and we would send the rest of the team, the other fifteen Seals, by tomorrow evening. Stan and Paco were to keep all of their people in the shadows to watch the house and it was the chore of one of the guys who worked for Stan, to make sure that everyone had enough food to eat, cold drinks, and to be the runner to the store for anything, anyone would need.

Cappy got into my Jeep, Mario took the wheel and I sat in the back with Christy.

"Sweetheart, tell me what happened and how these guys were able to get you out of the house."

Christy started to cry, but it was a happy cry, knowing that she was safe. She started to go over the sequence of the earlier part of the evening.

"I was watching TV and was just sitting on the sofa, when I heard this crash from the kitchen. I got scared and before I was able to do anything, two guys came into the den and grabbed me, tied my arms behind my back, and put a kerchief over my eyes. I found myself being carried out but didn't know where I was going. I was placed in a car and it drove off for about forty-five minutes, so I figured I was going to Chuck's house. I was frightened."

I held Christy ever so tightly against my chest as Mario headed south to Dana Point. There, he would drive Cappy back to his house, in Cappy's car and tend to his arm. It was not a major wound and Mario also was good at first aid. He took Cappy's car to his own home and we would all meet later the next day to go back to the scene of the crime and continue to ransack the house. In the meantime, Mike and Billy would be doing some preliminary inventory work throughout Chuck's home, and if anyone would show up, we had a team of experts outside the house, watching every move, every sound, and every conversation.

It was after 1 am, and I undressed Christy, took her into the shower and washed her down thoroughly. She had a rough evening, and she needed to be tended to. I told her about the two deputies being shot at and she expressed total remorse. This was going to be a tough war, and it had not even started yet. The stakes were high, and any one of us could be killed. But I was getting my strength back as a professional Navy Seal, and any kind of error could be curtains for any of us. I did not want that to happen. We are too good at what we did, but just a little rusty around the edges.

I laid Christy down on the bed and called Julie. She was nearly asleep when she picked up the phone. I told her what had happened and wanted to make sure that she was all right.

"Thank goodness, you are okay, Julie." I said.

Two deputies were still outside of Julie's house as she peered through the curtains to look at them. I still had this uneasy feeling about leaving Julie alone, just as I left Christy. I could not be at both places at the same time, and there was no other security around my house right now. But Julie felt comfortable, and figured to herself, that if she were to be harmed in any way, by Chuck's men, the attorneys would not defend him in Court. This was her feeling. I was glad that she felt that way, although it was a ridiculous way of looking at things. With that, we hung up and Julie went to sleep.

I decided to call Rita and see what she was up to. "Rita, how the hell are you?"

Rita was half out of it, but recognized my voice. "David, do you know that it is early in the morning, and I was sleeping?"

"Listen, Rita, we had some break-ins, some fighting, and a kidnapping, and I really don't give a shit if I woke you up."

"Okay, sorry I asked." she said, as she indicated that she was getting out of bed, going for a cigarette, and taking the hands-free phone to the kitchen.

"I'm sorry, David, but my day has not been so ginger-peachy either. I was told to evict the residence in five days by an attorney who works for Chuck. Guess I didn't give him my total attention, as he wanted me to. Next, I found that my car was impounded, another title owned by Chuckie-Boy. So now, I am lacking wheels to go from one place to another. I am trying to find another place to live and it is difficult without any means of transportation."

I felt sorry for her, but this was part of life.

"Listen, Rita, suppose you pack all of your stuff, get a good night's sleep and I will be by in the morning to pick you up. You can stay at my home for a while. You can have access to one of my cars to look around for a place to rent."

Rita took a deep breath and sighed. "David, I don't know what I would do without you."

I told her to start packing that night and I would be by in the morning. I had to go back to Christy and tend to her. For a woman I had loved for just so many days, I felt that one day in the future, there was a possibility that she could become the mother of my future kids. More than likely it was not going to happen. But, with me, anything was possible.

Christy had put on one of her new outfits that she purchased at the harbor, earlier on in the day. God, she looked so beautiful. I told her that she looked like a model, as pretty as a picture, and I truly loved when she wanted to please me so. Without hesitation, I decided to take her to bed.

I put my arms around her and reached down to kiss her. Christy responded with intense passion for me. I was overwhelmed and very enthusiastic, and her body looked too damn good not to go for it. For all that had happened recently and the fact, that there was still so much passion between us, I still had enough of an urge to make love to her.

I had only hoped that she would be ready for another round of desire and intense lovemaking. She looked incredibly beautiful in her new outfit, and though my mind was ready for some more sexual action with her, I also felt a tinge of guilt. I knew how I felt about Julie, and I also knew that it meant that one day soon, I would have to make a decision as to which woman I really wanted as my soul mate. This was not going to be easy. We should all have these problems.

She looked into my eyes and thanked me again for saving her life, and would have liked us to go out soon as a couple. She told me that she wanted to show off her beautiful body by wearing one of her new outfits, more than just parading around the bedroom and displaying herself to me. I respected her choice and told her that we would. But it was kind of late and we both had a busy day. It would be nice to take Christy to the harbor and show her off to the people who knew me, or even if they didn't, it would be great to be with such a beautiful woman in public. I bent down to kiss her, and there was no pressure at this very moment. There was no gunfire, no expectations, and no life threatening activity to worry about.

I thought back to all of the fun I had had recently, and the lack of it in the past few years. I enjoyed being in bed with various beautiful women, which was making me increasingly energized. I told Christy that I was getting tired and perhaps it was time to lie down and go to sleep. I remembered that I had to call Rita in the morning and committed to pick her up and take her back to my home until such time when things would cool off.

When I mentioned this to Christy, her eyes became distant, but I reassured her that all was going to work out wonderfully. No matter what would happen, she would not be with that tyrant any longer. She would finally feel safe and that gave her lots of reassurance. Every time I would glance down at her, lying in bed, I didn't mind being her caretaker. She was absolutely so beautiful and giving, in her own way.

It was basically the times when Christy was alone, that bothered me. It occurred to me that she was extremely needy, and that a long-term commitment to her would also mean that my life would forever be committed to tend to her insecure soul. In some ways, I was getting used to it, although I truly loved the feeling of saving someone, particularly a woman. I loved it when they continually needed me around to keep comforting them and making love to them.

I also knew that Christy would be a handful, and I would forego a lot in my life to tend to her desires. I realized that I was not stupid enough to allow myself getting trapped by a needy woman, not after having experienced the love of so many women in my lifetime, especially in the last few weeks. It was truly worth it though. I was becoming a spoiled, arrogant, and sexual madman.

I felt that I would feel a bit safer with Julie, knowing that her independence meant so much to her. I always liked women who felt independent. Julie had a good job, and her tendency was to handle things in a more mature manner than Christy did. I was feeling a sense of compassion and the fact that I believed my love was greater for Julie than it was for Christy. If there was an opportunity for our passion to ever ignite, more than just a few words of flirtation, there was no telling where this was leading to. Yet, there was always that enigma that Julie may not need someone such as me, and this might eventually be an issue with me. It was hard to let go, being the savior that I had always been. But at my age, I thought it best to look at the overall picture.

All of a sudden, Christy sat up and surprisingly turned to me, with her eyes looking at mine, and asked a most interesting question.

"David, do you ever think of marrying again in your life?"

In some ways, I thought that perhaps this was one of the most intelligent, yet provocative questions she had asked in a long while. I turned to her in an unwillingly manner by expressing my feelings.

"Well, Christy, I cannot say for sure. But I do know that I am having fun being with you, and I don't know if I am ready to get serious right now. How do you feel about getting married in the near future? Have you given this any thought, yourself?"

She seemed a bit disappointed upon hearing my response, but that could have been my perception.

"I know that I was ready," she continued. "But that was when I was spending a lot of time with Chuck. At first, when he asked me to marry him, I really didn't know him as well as I thought I did. Now, I find myself feeling extremely guilty for all of this. I am getting to know you a lot, and you are so different. You are so caring, much more so than Chuck was. You give me straight answers when I ask you questions."

"Please, Christy, don't feel so guilty," I responded. "I know how much trauma you have been through, and I am here to help you. And my friends are more than willing to assist you in any way they can, as you saw when we invaded Chuck's house to get you out. Do you feel sorry for Chuck and what might happen to him?"

Christy nodded negatively to me.

The more I looked at her, in her pretty new outfit, the more I was ready to bed her down, take off her clothes, and put my lips on hers. I was ready for her now, as I felt the excitement in my body starting to rise. I was hoping that she would also feel the same way toward me. I wanted to feel the pleasure once again, of her arms and legs wrapped tightly around me, as I would enter her body, and slowly make my way up to her heaven. She turned to me and asked if we could find a private corner near the cliffs, where no one would see us, and make love outdoors. Although I was tired, I loved the idea. Thinking about it, I actually never made love outdoors.

Having lived in Dana Point for so many years, I knew of some great private places where two people can hide and not be seen. We got into the small car and drove up the hills by the harbor, overlooking all of the boats that were tied down for the night. We went around some bends in the road and drove the sports car up higher, into the hills, looking for the right turnoff. Finally, I found a small spot where I was able to hide the red car, and we could find lots of privacy, deep, under the tall trees.

We got out, and Christy walked around to me. I held her in my arms, and I told her that there was a better spot, a small area of grass, just behind the trees up ahead. I took the blanket out from behind the seat where I squeezed it in, right before we left. I was feeling new at this game, yet brave for doing it. Heck, you have to try everything at least once. And Christy was giving me that opportunity to try all sorts of love making, that I had never done before.

Having sex on a blanket, overlooking the ocean, reminded me of a movie I had seen years ago. There was Burt Lancaster making love to a married woman, his boss's wife, played by Deborah Kerr, in 'From Here to Eternity'. What a great scene on the beach. That scene was played over and over again in film clips, and now it was visible in my mind as we walked to the grassy area away from the car.

I was being adventurous, almost playful, but I also wanted to please her as well. I felt that if I made her happy tonight, she would accept the fact that Rita was coming over tomorrow, and that it was our future that was most important. We walked hand in hand as I led her to the spot that I thought would be most secretive, out of view from anyone passing by. But then again, it was after midnight, and no one walked these parks so late at night anyway. It was our 'Plum Beach', the make-out park near Brighton Beach, back in Brooklyn, where we used to take our girlfriends, as teenagers. But we only necked then, and never had actual sex. I wanted to have sex with Christy.

I spread the blanket down and pulled her down toward me. I took her in my arms and she looked ready for me. Her eyes glowed, and her body felt warm under her silk outfit. I took her top off, then one strap of her bra, and then finally, the other. I kissed her neck and with both hands, lifted her skirt over her head. The moon was a bright orange, nearly full, and the right amount of shadow made the most incredible view on her lovely face. I told her that I loved her, and although it may have been my mistake at the moment, I could not control the amount of excitement I was feeling in every part of my body.

I reached toward my feet and took off my shoes, then my shirt and pants. We then nestled down on the blanket, her naked body below mine. She just posed there, as if she had nothing or no one else on her mind. I wanted her to fondle me with my briefs on, and then in an instant, she went down on me, throwing my underwear over the cliff. At that moment, I didn't care. But I knew that later, I would be hanging a bit. In the heat of passion, you just let it all hang out and I did just that.

I reached for her breasts and brought them to my face. They were not very large, but firm and I brought her nipples to my mouth. I started to suck them, moving my tongue back and forth, and she moaned and enjoyed this. Then she placed her hand on my balls and started to move them up my penis, slowly leaning her face toward my groin. I wanted to come but held it in as I felt the blood rushing to my brain. Christy knew how to excite me and nothing else mattered except to feel the movement of her body and the feeling that I was ready to explode.

Her mouth succumbed me and she gently embraced every inch of my penis. She slid herself up on top of me and I could see the moon shining in the distance.

The fact that this was new to me, it was even more stimulating. I turned her body, by placing her down on her back and she let me enter her, but ever so slowly. We embraced as she kissed me and told me that she loved me too. I did not know how long this was going to last beyond this evening, but I did not care. I was enjoying this moment, immensely.

Christy started to scream, louder and louder, and although I was sure that no one would hear us, I felt a tinge of paranoia. She must have come several times, and then she started to relax, and turned over on her side. I pushed her on her back and mounted her, and finished myself. The ending was always the best. It was like building up a crescendo during an orchestral oration of classical music. The drums were beating and the cymbals were clashing. The moment had come when you know that the music is over. We were sweaty and I was panting, but it was a moment in time that I would never forget. I needed to rest by finally turning myself on my back and lie on the blanket. I was completely relieved, as I had given a tremendous surge from within my body. I felt that we had touched the stars. And she felt the same way.

I knew that it was time to get going, so we both started to get dressed. Christy turned to me and asked, once again. "David, do you love me?"

Well, she certainly did have a sense of asking the right questions at the wrong time, and I knew that I had to come up with something creative, as she would not take 'no' for an answer. I thought for a quick minute and in this moment of passion, even with thoughts that she would have made a wonderful mother to my future children, I knew better than to be completely honest.

"Yes, Christy, I love you. And I think that you are a wonderful woman. But I do hope that you understand that right now, although…" I stopped midway.

I looked at her as she inquisitively looked at me. I did not know what it was that I wanted to say to her, but I knew that I had to clarify what it was and what her love meant to me. I was not sure if I wanted to tell her that she was not the only one who I desired. I also did not want her to think that I was using her just for my pleasure either.

"Christy, I prefer to just take things easy, and very slowly, for now, okay? Let's not think too far ahead at this time."

That went over like a lead balloon. Another big mistake! Women don't like to be kept hanging on a wire, while the men dangle the only thing that gets them into trouble, that being their penis. I knew that by being honest was a mistake, but I could not lie to her. There was too much going on in my life, and a commitment to Christy at this time was not in the cards.

I had no choice other than to come forward with the truth, and the way I felt. This was my life, as well as her own. I had paused, and she was sitting up, looking at me, with her beautiful blue eyes, moving downward toward her feet.

"Yes, David, I do understand." she said, as she put her sandals on.

"I am not stupid you know. As much as I know you may think that I am probably an air head, and that I have been on drugs, and that I have been with a tyrant for way too long." She then looked up at me very calmly.

"I do understand that you are interested in my friend, Julie. Although you never mentioned this to me, I have known this for a while. I also know that I love you, and would do anything for you."

She turned away, and as I lay on the blanket, with only my pants on, I thought to myself, "God, I am in for quite a challenge, and only God knows how I was going to handle this!"

We finished dressing, rolled up the blanket, got in the car, and drove home.

I was hopeful that she knew of all the dangers that we were facing, and that to talk of marriage now was not a good idea. But she did sense that I felt something for Julie. You can never doubt a woman's intuition. Never in a thousand years! They seem to know when a man feels something for another woman. You just cannot deceive women. No matter how hard you try. They sense when something is wrong, and they play 'coy' by letting you think you are keeping things from them. Forget it! My wife Marsha always knew when I held things within myself and she just let me think that I was feeling as if nothing was bothering me. Somehow, she knew but she would never let on. That is scary with women.

We drove home rather quietly. We each showered in separate bathrooms, and I met her in bed. She would always look so lovely and I could never tire of her beauty, especially her long legs that always seemed to drape over the covers. I waited for a while before I said anything, but Christy was there again, beating me to the punch.

"David, I shall always love you. I know what you are going through and I will be here for you. Thank you for being by my side."

Chuck did not get a phone call with regard to Christy's flight schedule. He was in Bogotá, Columbia, meeting with the drug cartel overlords, who wanted to take over the entire operation in Central and South America, leaving Chuck and his mafia family, with a smaller percentage than he had realized for the past ten years.

His empire was crumbling, and unless he showed some strength in the negotiations, he would lose everything. He did not like being cut out of the deals, and he certainly did not like not hearing from his people back home that he may have been losing his leadership.

He sat at the huge conference table with the chiefs of the drug industry, listening to the demands on him. He was getting pissed and decided to tell them where to shove their requests. Chuck was not about to let go of his domination, nor was he going to give in to the demands of these 'spics' as he called them. He was the domineering factor, the head of many families, and his posture in the mafia rested on how he conducted his leadership.

The DEA was cracking down on the drug lords and the FARC, the largest concentration of soldiers run by the drug cartels. In the meantime, the U.S. was training a huge police force in Bogotá to go after the drug runners, and there were thousands of new forces, led by the DEA to contact and destroy any of the drug cartel's thousands of soldiers throughout the country. Columbia was the biggest hotbed in the western hemisphere, and the residents were scared, just as those in Iraq, Iran, Syria and other countries with dictatorships. The president of Columbia had had his own life threatened twelve times in twelve months. It was not a secure job, by no means. The country needed the help of the United States.

Christy was, but only a smidgeon of what Chuck was facing in Bogotá, the drug capital of the world. He had too much at stake in the middle east, the arms he was selling to the terrorists of Afghanistan and Iraq, as well as Syria and Palestine, the backing of the mafia in the United States, in Italy, in England, in Ireland, in Canada and in the many countries in Europe and Asia. He was in a most crucial position, and if he lost his leadership, he would be cremated in cement or in the river.

Chuck knew that he had to act with confidence, as he had some of the leaders in Washington on his payroll, as well as in the defense department, the executive branch, and the Senate Arms Committee. He had to take the lead and not allow these so-called rebels call his bluff, as he had too much to lose, and not enough of a support system to keep him at the helm. He watched the faces of his suppliers, and kept thinking how he was going to handle their demands.

He sat with these so-called rebels, together with his most trusted-bodyguards, around the table, each ready to react upon his command. What was happening, not knowingly, was that his own mafia family was also questioning his judgment, his rationale, and his leadership. If the other families in Chicago, Los Angeles, New York, New Jersey, Florida and Texas, saw anything that resembled weakness, they would decide to whack him and put someone else in charge.

He had to be strong and not allow these rebels threaten him, nor give him ultimatums. He was Chuck Manzione, the toughest son-of-a-bitch in the whole damn racket. He knew what he had to do and he had to do it now, today. He would not allow these bastards to assert any pressure on him that would cause him to lose any confidence and respect that the family had for him for so long. After his father, and his uncles, being involved with the family for so many years, it was up to him to show leadership and take charge.

The meeting began with a few of the drug cartel leaders telling him that they wanted 30% more for the heroin and crack, after not raising the cost for the past number of years. This was not negotiable, as Chuck told the other families back in the U.S., by guaranteeing them that he would be able to sell the drugs through HIS distribution, and continue to buy them at the same price. But the members of the drug cartel would not buy his rhetoric. They wanted more money and they didn't care about the other families. They were pushing Chuck in hopes that he would agree to their demands.

As they broke for lunch, he signaled to his people to gun down those in the room who stood up to him the most, and in an instant, three leaders of the drug cartel were gunned down. Chuck took a stand, and no one, not even the most known of the members, would ever try to go against the family again. The power play worked and the rebels were held in check.

After the bodies were taken away from the room, that consisted of nearly eighteen members of the different Columbian tribes, who were growing the drugs on their plantations, Chuck made an announcement loud and clear.

"Let me set the record straight. No one and I mean no one, will come to me and demand more money than what we offered back in the seventies. We have more expenses, and we are being pressed a lot more by the Federal Government. We also have to pay a higher price to those in the government to keep them off our backs. This is 2004, and we will not bow down to any militant group that thinks they can control the distribution of drugs in the United States."

The other drug lords just sat there, not saying a word. Chuck made his appeal and demands. There was complete silence and either they just ignored him or and they went off on their own agenda. One of the leaders got up and spoke for the rest of the group of Columbians.

"Chuck, you do not understand what we are saying here, today. You have ignored our plea, and you have walked away from our wishes. We will not be threatened by any of your firepower. We have our own. You may as well go back to your little families, and tell them that we have told you what we want. If you do not honor our desires, we will not develop the farms and output that you would need to keep all of this operational."

This made Chuck even more upset. Not having tact or any diplomacy, he merely got up, put his fist on the table, and told each of the remaining members, that if anyone goes against the organization, each and every one of their family members would be shot and killed. There would be no exceptions. He was emphatic and spoke with authority.

"No one and that includes any one of you, shall think that he will make demands from us and try to take profits from our families. We are stronger than you are, and we have all of the right people in our pockets. Without us, you are nothing. You are shit, you will not succeed, and you will fail. Hear me out, oh great warriors of the drug business. Hear me, but good. You will do what we want, or be put out of business."

It was a standoff, and both Chuck and the drug cartel members knew it. Yet, no one wanted to buck this American Gringo. They were not happy with his attitude, and would not stand by and take orders from this irresponsible Italian Mafioso who knew very little how the drugs were grown. Chuck was in a bind but he had the power and the money. They had the drugs and the cheap labor. Each side was waiting for the other to back down. It did not happen.

The meeting ended, and instead of joining his Columbian partners for dinner, Chuck wanted to find out if Christy was on the way to Columbia. Again, he added more insult to injury, but Chuck needed to find out what was happening back in California. He hated when people defied his orders and would just as easily shoot them dead than to argue with them.

He called his home only to find the phone was ringing and ringing. He then called his chief lieutenant, Ricky DePalmerio, a trusted capo in the family. Ricky organized a group of two-dozen tough gunmen, and headed toward Chuck's estate. Chuck decided to meet with some of the drug cartel and do some more lobbying. His thought was to grab a plane to Brazil, then on to Ecuador, to check on the other drug cartels, as well as the warehousing of one of the largest inventory of arms this side of the Third Army Brigade. He was planning to sell most of the inventory to groups in Syria, Afghanistan and Palestine.

Chuck had his hands in more shit than any man on earth. But he was Chuck Manzione, the best enforcer the mafia ever had in over one hundred years. By the family's standards, he was respected by more heads of families than anyone before him. This was the new wave of the capo regime in the mafia. More corporations, both in the U.S. and abroad, were involved in some way in the family business. With worldwide tension, and the need for large caches of weapons all over the globe, this was bigger business than just running Whore Houses and Casinos in Cuba and Vegas.

I left the house early the next morning, and headed north to pick up Rita. The night before was a shining example of my virility as a man, and I loved it. I was not ready for Viagra yet, but when I am, I hope to continue to have many women in my club, as I have now.

Wow! Did I strike it rich, or was I getting in deeper than I had hoped to. Did I really want to think about marriage now, with so much happening in my life? Was this woman a better bet than that one? Why was I even thinking about giving up my freedom and sexual activity to one woman, when I can have anyone I wanted, at any time, and any place?

Yet, I was still part of the Navy Seals, and to go on all of these assignments, was one of the greatest jobs in the world I felt that I was like another James Bond, the ultimate spy, and no one called the shots, but you. If you are good, you ride the waves and live the good life. If you screw up, you just die and get buried.

After about forty minutes, I arrived at Rita's house. There she was, waiting outside, smoking a cigarette.

"Give me one, dear girl," I said, as I realized that I was going to have, not only Christy in my home, but this little bitch. I felt that I would be able to keep a better eye on her. If anyone wanted to come after me, they already knew where I lived, and I was sure that we would have more action brewing at Chuck's house as the evening wore on.

"So just don't stand there like an isolated sperm, you ding-a-ling." Rita blurted out. "Give me a fucking hand with my things, you overgrown load of shit. I've been waiting for half an hour and now you decide to show up, you brainless bowl of crap."

She looked at me to see if I was going to shoot her or laugh. I walked over to her and reached in my pocket. Then I walked right up to her, staring down into her eyes, raised my hand as if I was going to smack her, and just burst out crying.

That was Rita. Sometimes, I thought she would go too far. I always felt like bopping her but I was afraid that her little brain would not be able to take the pressure. We loaded her things in the Jeep, and she did have lots of things, including junk that I did not have room for in my garage. There was no way I would bring all of her shit into my home. Not in a heartbeat.

We started to drive southbound on the Freeway, and she just chatted away about how Chuck told his people to evict her from the house, and that she did not have more than a couple of days to clear her ass out. Instead of fighting them, she decided that she had had enough, and needed a place to stay until she found something affordable. After all, this was Orange County, and the rents and property values were too far out of her range. So here I was, like a schmuck, offering her my home until she found another. Boy, did I screw up. This could take weeks, maybe months, and here she was, with Christy in the house, and I had no chance in hell to ever bring Julie over to the house. But then, there was always the possibility of going at it with a 'free-for-all'. Oh, dream on, you crazy nut! That was all I thought about at the time.

We arrived at my house early afternoon. Christy had prepared a nice lunch with some lemonade, always being thoughtful, and she always seemed to care. Christy knew that I was going to pick up Rita and she seemed rather happy about it, but deep down inside, I felt her jealousy. At least she would have someone to converse with while I was out doing my thing.

Rita brought with her, several bags of luggage and a couple of boxes, which she mentioned had some information with regards to the work she had done with Chuck over the years. I couldn't wait to go through them, and told her to make herself at home. I gave her a guest room downstairs and told her to use the downstairs bathroom to shower and change if she wanted. I took the boxes, while Christy set the table with her favorite dish of tuna melts and salads, and went into my office and started to rummage through all of Rita's papers.

I could hear Christy downstairs, talking to someone, because I knew that Rita was in the shower, as I could hear the water running. I walked to the top of the stairs to listen.

"Yeah, I know, it's just that it is so comfortable here, and I don't have anywhere else to go right now."

Christy was on the phone but I did not know with whom she was talking to. Do I dare pick up the receiver and eavesdrop? Well, it was my house and I did have that privilege, I suppose. I went into the main bedroom and slowly covered the mouthpiece, and I heard Julie's voice on the other end.

"Listen, sweetie, you'll be fine. Just hang in there, and I will come by for a late lunch with you guys. Just give me about thirty minutes."

My heart jumped a mile. Julie was coming to join us for lunch and that got my adrenalin pumping once again. I had some free time to spend with the girls this afternoon, so why not spend it with all of them. I had to leave to get to Cappy's by five for our second visit to Chuck's house later on that evening, so I did create some extra time to be with the girls. What a wonderful opportunity to see Julie again. I hung up and went back to the boxes, and waited for Christy to tell me that Julie was coming over. I had thought that this was good news. It was just about forty-five minutes later, when the doorbell rang.

"David, Julie is here. Are you hungry? I made some Tuna melt, pasta and a demi salad. Please come down when you are ready."

"Thanks, Christy," I responded. "I'll be right there."

I heard Rita downstairs, laughing at something on the television, and Christy looked incredibly cute with the red apron that she had found in the kitchen. I knew that Martha had worn that years ago, and I had not seen it since. She also had on one of the other new outfits that she had bought the day before, at the harbor. It was a short, peach skirt, and a white silk blouse. And she had her hair tied up in a bun, which made her look like she belonged on the cover of 'Babes & Cuisine.'

She had the table all set up with pretty plates and fabric napkins in the silver holders. And Rita, that crazy broad with the dark, red hair, had changed into something so incredibly outstanding, that my libido was working overtime. I thought that if given the chance, I could seduce the both of them and forego lunch, and we all could make a trip to my bedroom. The chances of that were slim. But I never knew in my entire life, what women were capable of doing. I looked across the table, and there was Julie.

"Hi David, I thought I would take a long lunch hour and check on my favorite people. How are you guys doing?"

Julie looked as beautiful as ever. She was radiant in her work outfit, as she stood there in her five foot, ten inch stature.

"Oh my, did I come at a bad time? Hope you waited for me."

I couldn't imagine Julie coming at a bad time. It wouldn't have mattered when she came, as long as I was along for the ride. I was suddenly amid three women, all in my home. Now that was a first for me.

"Oh, don't be silly, Julie. Sit down and join us." Rita said as she made a plate for her, and the girls connected as if they hadn't seen each other in years. I stood back and watched this play out and thought, 'how lucky could one guy get?'

Three beautiful women, sitting at my dining room table, all so hot and on fire! And there was I, having been to bed with three of them, possibly in love with two of them, trying to save the tall, pretty blond, while drooling over the beautiful brunette. I even thought that the redhead was pretty darn hot, as well. I couldn't believe my luck, and I decided to take my place with the ladies, and jumped into their conversation.

"How 'bout if, after lunch, we all go for a stroll by the harbor and watch the boats. We should be able to see the birds searching for food. I wish I could make it for dinner with you guys, but I have an appointment this evening."

I didn't want to say with whom or what the meeting was about, as I was not sure if Rita was truly on the level. There was still that possibility that she would go blabbing back to Chuck about what was happening at his home.

As if in unison, they all cheered at my suggestions, but unfortunately, Julie had to get back to work. That only left Rita and Christy. But, as they used to say, 'Beggars can't be choosey.' As much as I would have loved this to be an evening event, I could only settle for 'an afternoon delight'. And as luck would have it, only two of the three maidens were available. After all, where were they going anyway, except to stay with me, in my home, and I could have each of them if I wanted to. Heck, I had them before, and they were so willing. I was ready to take on the world at this point.

As I looked around the dining room table, there was Rita, looking as sharp as ever, with her tits coming out of her tight-fitted red blouse, wearing tight jeans, and a bandana around her neck. Christy had on her new outfit that made her look just like a model, and Julie was in her work ensemble, a nice, purple suit, pink blouse and a cute pair of off white, high heel shoes. Three gorgeous women, sitting in my house, and I could have them all.

During the lunch, we all talked about the times we spent in Vegas, and the kidnapping of Christy, the meeting at Cappy's, the bodyguards at Julie's firm and at her home, and of course, the 'hit and run' saga at Chuck's house last night. We spoke about the rescue of Christy, and Cappy getting a stinger from a bullet. After an hour, they each cleared the table and went in different directions. Julie had to get back to work, so she refreshed herself in the bathroom and said her goodbyes.

I sat there, watching the three do their thing, and thought, what a luck guy I was. I had three of the most beautiful women, in my home and I could fuck each and every one of them. Well, maybe two for now, but I felt confident about the third. I just sat and wondered if I could handle all of these women at once. How silly of me to think this, but at least I could try to control my wild thoughts and imagine if they would enjoy each other so much, that they might even bring this to a sexual level. I fantasized using every bit of creativity I could imagine, that I lost track of what was happening around me.

"David, are you coming?" came a voice from the den. I thought about the question, and could only respond in my own thoughts, "Not yet, but I really want to."

"Oh, yes, I am on my way," I replied, as Julie came up to me, and planted a kiss on my cheek then left to go back to work.

I saw Christy and Rita standing by the door, waving goodbye to Julie.

Christy took me aside and said, "David, you look a little distracted. Are you okay?"

I said yes, as I watched Julie get into her car and drive away. I was feeling a bit like a schoolboy, trying to get a date with the pretty girls in class, and knew that I had another horrific evening ahead of me. I decided to go with the girls to the harbor, walk around, and have a good time.

I remembered our dinner at the Las Vegas Hotel. But instead of Rita, it was Suzie, and I was having the time of my life, sitting with the three ladies, any of whom I could have bed down with, without hesitation. I knew that Christy was aware of my feelings for Julie and that she was suspecting my love for her best friend. But I also knew that she would not make a scene as she and Julie had been friends for many years, and they seemed to have an understanding of sorts.

I watched Christy and Rita as they walked and giggled together like school-girls, and I kept imagining my face in each one of theirs', and my cock jumping from one to the other. They looked back at me as they approached the beach, as Rita spoke up.

"Come on, David, stop dragging your feet and catch up."

I hurried up to them and Christy grabbed my hand as we took our shoes off and walked on the sand close to the ocean. Rita spread the blanket that she was carrying, on the sand, the same one that Christy and I had used the night before. Christy sat down while Rita and I walked down to the water and had a cigarette.

"David, I am so happy that you have allowed me to stay with you for a few days while I find a place to call my own."

Rita was being thankful for all that I was doing for her.

"It means the world to me. I just have to get my shit together and decide where I want to go, now that I have to start a new life all over again. That bastard, Chuck can really destroy one life after another."

We then walked back to the blanket and sat down next to Christy. Rita turned to her and felt sorrow and remorse.

"I am sorry, Christy, but Chuck has done a number on both of us. I realize that he was your beau, but he did try to screw you too, didn't he?"

"You are not alone, Rita." Christy replied, "But I can't stay with David forever either, although it would be so great if it were possible."

She turned to me and kissed me on the cheek, and rubbed her hand through my hair. She was teasing me but there was a hope in her remark that I would ask her to stay with me as my wife. I knew what Christy wanted.

Thinking back to Julie, I found her to be a frustration to me. I remembered at the house when she asked Christy to move in with her if she wanted to. Christy was happy to hear that her friend had offered her the guest room in her home. Did Julie want Christy out of my house, or did Christy ask her if she could move in with her beforehand? I thought that I was falling madly in love with Julie, but these women can really be pains in the ass. You never know where you stand with them.

Just then, Rita turned to me and had a serious look on her face.

"Listen, guys, I 'm really not into this right now, I mean…sitting here by the water is great, but all of that packing last night and this morning, really knocked the shit out of me. Maybe, I should head back to the house and lie down."

We folded the blanket and got back into the Jeep. I realized that I had two women in the house and it felt like a harem. From not being with any woman for two years, I now had so many, it made my head spin. And what about that giggly, busty Suzy? How come she wasn't there? Heck, I could have put a red light on the front patio and made some money.

I checked in with Cappy, and then with Stan and Paco, to see what was happening at the Manzione estate. Both Stan and Paco were on the job, day and night. It seemed that many cars had driven up to the house, and lots of guys packing rods went into both houses. It appeared as if we were going to have a BBQ that evening. I asked Cappy if we were going to get some help from those fifteen or so Navy Seals from San Diego and he gave me a definite 'yes'.

I turned back to the girls, and Rita was putting her things away in the guest bedroom. Christy was putting the dishes in the dishwasher, and I went up to my room to load my PPK and automatic rifle. I wanted to make sure that I had all of the ammo I would need for this evening. I did not want to call Mike and Billy, because, if they were hiding in one of the secret passageways, and their phone rang, that would not be a safe move. I had some time, so I decided to continue to read the papers that Rita had given to me. I then went down to the den and relaxed.

Rita came in and sat down on the couch. Within a few minutes, Christy also sat down and we just stared at each other, then we all laughed. Always count on Rita for doing something to either upset you, or get you in a funny or happy mood.

We stared at each other, feeling somewhat jovial, and laughed at anything that came to mind. Rita finally broke the ice after the giggles had stopped, and remarked.

"Let's pop in a movie on the VCR. Seems you have quite a selection, David."

She got up from the couch and walked over to the shelves that held my collection of over three hundred movies. I had more in the garage, but there were enough to choose from right in the cabinet.

"Mmm…what would be good for all of us to watch? How about a gangster movie to get us in the mood?"

Christy also got up and walked over to the cabinet, right next to Rita. I watched them chatting it up, going through the hundreds of movies, looking so sexy and hot, crouching down, next to each other, in front of the shelves. I could have passed the next hour or so, seducing these women. Instead, I asked them to wait for my return later on this evening. I wanted to know that they would be safe and comfortable, and to do anything that would make them feel good. I told them that it was in their best interest that they stay low key and to keep themselves entertained. No matter how I felt about seducing both of them, I had to behave like a gentleman, but kept the door open if they chose to take their pleasures anyway they saw fit.

I would not reject them if they decided to come on to me together, and the thought raced through my mind. I wondered how they would have felt if they were able to read my mind at that moment. My mind was on them, looking at their cute little asses, in their tight fitting clothes. I thought, the heck with the movie. Maybe we would have a little herbal tea or a small glass of wine for our midday pleasure.

"Ladies, let's watch a movie later when I get back. I will probably need to get comfy and would enjoy a good flick at that time. How about before I go, we have some wine or brandy, and sit on the back veranda. Hey, I know, we could also have some Biscotti's? I just bought a few from the new bakery on PCH. You guys will love them."

I wanted to chat with them awhile so they would have an understanding of what was going on in my mind. Christy got some wine glasses, a new bottle of Chardonnay, and Rita took the bakery box from the kitchen.

When Rita put the box on the patio table, she leaned into me.

"I know what you are up to, David, and it isn't going to work," She giggled and walked off.

I thought about her remark and said to myself, "Hmm, that's what you think, you oversexed broad."

I saw the way she looked at me and the way she moved her ass from side to side as if she was on display. I felt like grabbing it and sticking my dick all the way up. We did that before back at the hotel room and she was dynamite.

We all found our places on the patio, each holding an Italian cookie and a glass of wine. I watched them enjoy the Boscotti, and wished that they would use their mouths on me the same way they seduced the biscuit.

We sat out on the deck and chatted, and laughed, which, in one way, was good for me to recharge for the next battle out in the trenches. Chuck's house was only the tip of the iceberg. We had many more missions to accomplish as the days and weeks came. Even with this happening in the next few hours, I felt relaxed having these two lovely ladies in my presence. After all, what could be better than this? I gave a deep breath, took some wine and a bite of the Boscotti, and realized that I was also getting a hard on.

I dared not get up, but remarked. "Ladies, if you feel up to it later, why don't you set up the den in such a way for all of us to watch a move later, you know, with the big pillows I have, and something comfortable to wear? I may need a good massage and I definitely will need some tender loving care when I come home."

"David, my boy," Rita laughed. "Are you teasing us? I mean, you will be wondering what we ladies are going to be up to while you go off and fight a war. You are such a warrior, a sexy warrior at that. I can only imagine the drama that will unfold, while we ladies sit here, all nice and comfy, waiting for you to come home. Am I right in my assumption?"

She laughed some more, and Christy joined in, thinking that it was pretty amusing as well. But her eyes showed some uncertainty. I wasn't sure if she knew exactly what Rita had meant, but I knew she would catch on quickly. Christy then turned to me and said, "Is this what you want, David? Do you want us all to get together when you come home?"

Rita was pulling the plug and upsetting Christy to a point where Christy would be scared off in thinking that I would want to take them both on when I returned. I really did not want Christy to feel like this although it was a thought that I had.

"Listen girls, I have to get ready to leave soon. I want to review the papers you gave to me once again, Rita, and then I have to pack my gear and go to Cappy's house. Just make yourselves comfortable and stay in the house, please. I will call you later if I am able to, or I will just come home when I am through. I have no idea how long it will take, but I do not want to worry about you guys going out this evening."

I got up and started to go upstairs. Christy followed me.

"David, wait. I want to talk to you."

She followed me upstairs, and spoke, in her usual whispering tone. "David, I love you, and I do not want you to fool around with that bitch downstairs. I do not trust her. If she had her way, she would get you on the floor and want you to fuck around with her. I am not comfortable with that."

"I was teasing, Christy. I am not going to touch her. You are the one I want, not her. I am sorry, but I was just trying to be cute before I head off and face more danger as I did last night. I just want the two of you to remain home and out of harm's way. I may be gone until after midnight, so make yourselves some dinner and if you get tired, then go to bed. Rita will stay in the guest room away from our bedroom."

I gave Christy a kiss and smiled at her, then went into my office and reviewed the papers for about an hour. At about four, I got into my black outfit out, and left to go to Cappy's.

Chuck had called Ricky De, his trusted lieutenant, and found out that there was no sign of Christy, or any of his men he had left in charge at his estate.

"What the fuck happened to them, Ricky? Were there any signs of a struggle or was the house broken into? Could you handle the situation until I get back next week?"

Ricky De reassured Chuck that he would take care of everything while Chuck was away. He told him that the place was clean as a whistle, too clean. But obviously, there was something wrong, although he felt that the place was secure. He was not aware that in a few hours, all Hell was going to break loose.

The boys did a good job in cleaning up the mess, and the blood. Where the walls had bullet holes, the guys patched them up and painted the area, without any kind of paint odor around. The boys were good and knew how to do a hell of a cleanup after a job. And this was a job well done.

Stan related to Cappy that there were about twenty men in the main house, about five or six in the guesthouse. There were guards posted at the front gate, and many were roaming the area in the back. We were going to have our hands full, as these guys looked mean and tough. They probably suspected that there might be trouble, because of the missing men who were there the night before. They also figured that it were the other mafia families, or the drug cartel, and not the Navy Seals, who were involved, so they posted bodyguards all over the place. Ricky De also put out the request for more men to arrive later on. Stan kept Cappy posted as to the goings on, while Mike and Billy were deeply hidden in the secret passageways inside the house.

I arrived at Cappy's house about five o'clock. His home resembled a barracks full of soldiers. Each of the Navy Seals was dressed in dark outfits, all carrying automatic weapons and side arms. Mario arrived right after I did, and we started to review the floor plan of the estate. I also brought along the papers that Rita had given to me, but that was for another day. There were about fifteen Seals, Cappy, Mario, Sean, Jules and me. There were also some of Sheriff's Brandon's deputies. We had amassed a small army and now we needed to conjure up a plan of attack.

Cappy told us that Moose was able to speak to the Foreign Aid Committee and the State Department about the drug cartel operation and they had set up a plan to go after the different cartels. They knew of the meeting in Bogotá between Chuck and the cartel families, but decided to wait until Chuck left the compound before they would take them down. They wanted Chuck to lead the DEA and the other law enforcement agencies to the other drug families so they too would be taken out, and that would decrease the enormous armies that controlled the drug trade in Central America.

There were scuttlebutts coming from Congress as to what was going on, but neither Moose nor the State Department would have any difficulty from them. This was going to be a controlled operation and we had to invade the 'nests' of the mafia and the cartel in order to break the cord that held them together.

Cappy then laid out the plans for this evening. We knew that we had at least twenty-five Mafioso to capture or kill, and then we had to search the place for evidence. There was a possibility that more of them would come later, so we had to post guards all over the place. It sounded like an all night affair. Stan had called about eight thirty and told us that another fifteen mafia men pulled into the gate, and they were having a large 'powwow' in the dining room. There would be a total of about forty or more enemy soldiers in the house and we needed accuracy to get to them.

The police were not to get involved, and they were told not to interfere. Aside from the Sheriff's department, we were also getting some help from the FBI through intelligence forces from Moose being in Washington. But they may not show up in time as they were coming from Los Angeles. They would have to take a helicopter from LAX, to a nearby field, only a mile or so from Chuck's estate, in order to land. They would be met by SUVs, driven by the police department, and would be taken to Pacific Palisades to assist us. With so many different organizations involved, anything could go wrong and the entire plan could blow up in our face. We had to have precision timing or lives would be lost.

It was time to hit the road north, and we piled into our SUVs and Jeeps, including my own. We didn't want to attract any further attention by going in Hummers. They were too large and too noisy. And they could not move as quickly as the smaller vehicles. We loaded our ammo and weapons and put on our earphones. We were ready for combat.

It was dark and quiet by the time we arrived at Pacific Palisades. Most people were in their homes, and Chuck's house was sitting by itself, up on the palisades, close to the ocean, away from any other home in the area. We sent some scouts around the gated house and we all stayed in touch by phone. Each group had copies of the blue prints so they would know how to approach the house, by the doors and windows, without searching for portals that did not exist. I took the back with some of the Seals, and Mario took another group to the side. Cappy had the major thrust in the front of the gated area. We sat and waited. There is nothing worse than just waiting, and anticipating what would happen.

Again, Cappy was going to give the signal to Stan and Paco to turn off the electricity of the gate, with just enough time for us to open the gate and to put the electricity back on again, as we did the night before. At the right time, they were to turn off all of the electricity as we had our infra-red goggles, enabling us to see them, without having them see us.

It was ten thirty, the bewitching hour. We were all set in our positions. It was time to get into the compound and take our positions by the house. We also had to take out the guards by the front gate, and cover the guesthouse. Mario took five of the Seals to the guesthouse and he would hit them at the same time we hit the main house. We were counting on our precision. So far we were pretty careful, as the trained Seals were more than eager to show off their training to the commander, Cappy. For many of them, it was their first time in battle, and they were a bit nervous and had itchy fingers.

Within an instant, the electricity by the gate went out, and we were able to get inside the gates without a sign of trouble. But the guards by the gate had to go first. Cappy handled that with ease and put up two of our own men in their place.

We were getting into position, when we heard some of the Mafioso people inside the house coming out for some smokes.

We moved back into the shadows and waited. But they just stood there, having cigars and talking about the new shipment of weapons that Chuck was to check on and sell to the Syrians and the Palestinians. They did not see us, as they were preoccupied with their own private conversation. Cappy radioed to us that he was going to take them out with silencers.

When we got the okay, there was a loud crash outside the gate. It seemed that the FBI arrived and thinking that the gates were unlocked, tried to open the gates. This caused a stir from inside the main house, as a few of the Mafioso came out to see what the noise was. The two guards at the gate, our own two people, waved and indicated that it was nothing. How differently the FBI operated than we did. Too bad they came after we got into the compound.

Then, three Mafioso started to walk toward the gate. If they recognized our guys standing by as guards, it would have messed up our surprise ground attack. I took my men and moved inside the sliding doors of the downstairs den, leading into the hallway and toward the other first floor rooms. Then, more men emerged from the guesthouse and went toward the gate. We had to haul some ass if we were going to take some of these guys down and be able to search the estate.

I then heard gunfire from outside the house. Everyone was on his toes, not knowing where it came from, or who caused the shots. My guys stayed with me as we crawled through the den toward the hallway, and the steps. Cappy radioed Stan and Paco to turn off all of the electricity. This gave the FBI agents access into the front gate, and the place was crawling with feds.

The first sign of the enemy caused some of the Seals with me to cock their weapons, and be ready to fire. The Mafioso inside the house came charging down the steps, and there was a scatter of fire from the automatic weapons held by the Seals. They were able to take out three figures, but more came, and I was getting uneasy with this. No one gave the order to fire, and now we would have to protect ourselves from enemy fire, from all sides.

I came upon the staircase close to us, and started to move up the steps. A few of the Seals followed behind me, and we saw some figures coming down. There was no time to head for cover as we were on the stairwell, leading upstairs, so we just fired at the bodies coming at us. They did not see us, although we saw their figures through the infra-red goggles. Another two went down, while the rest ran back upstairs and scattered into the many bedrooms.

Cappy and his people were met with fire power as they came through the front door and shot back, hitting as many as they could, but there was no telling who was hit or not. I was hoping that our guys would be all right. But I had to stay with my own objective, and had my guys constantly move forward. We had to go upstairs and knock out those who were on the second floor. I was hoping that Mike and Billy would be able to help us from inside the walls as well. Where were they?

The rest of the Seals came through other sliding doors and windows, and kept firing at figures, hoping that they would not fire at us, as we ascended the steps to the upper rooms. More gunshots came from the guesthouse, as the Seals, the deputies, and the FBI surrounded the smaller building, trying to get inside. It was mayhem, and lots of gunshots were heard for many minutes, until silence. We waited until we had more reinforcements up the steps, then decided to go for each of the bedrooms. I chose the first one on the right, and two Seals followed me. They were to cover my ass, as I pushed the door open and fired aimlessly at space. I could see the lights of shots headed toward me and kept low on the ground. I fired back at the lights, hoping to hit anything that moved. That is how it was with each of the upstairs bedrooms.

I carried enough ammo in my waist band, that weighed me down as I tried to move. These automatic weapons can go dry on you, and you need to load them quickly. Obviously, the Mafioso did not expect us, nor did they expect such a huge force of people to attack them. My heart was pounding, as were the hearts of all of my comrades. I realized that I was not as young as I used to be, and this 'thriller stuff' was getting to be Old Hat. Thinking of the fillies I left alone in my house, to do this thing, was absolutely nonsense. The sweat was pouring off my head and I was sore all over. Luckily, I was on the attack end of this, or I would have had a better chance of getting killed. To think that twenty years before, I did this for a living.

After about thirty minutes, what seemed like a lifetime, all firing had ceased and there was silence in the main house as well as in the guesthouse. Our friendly forces had gotten into each of the rooms, and took over the facilities. I looked for Mike and Billy who were close at hand, emerging from the secret passages from one of the bedrooms. Cappy asked Stan to put the electricity back on and the lights went on again. We saw the bodies strewn all over the place, including one Navy Seal and two FBI agents. One was dead, and two were injured.

We then asked the Seals to take the bodies from the premises, and that the FBI vacate the area so that our team would be able to go through each room, each file cabinet, and search each and every part of the two buildings. This took about four more hours and we came up with lots of accounting books, letters of names, places, dates, and sales of arms, drugs, and anything else that Chuck was involved with.

We then closed the house down and asked the Seals to clean up the debris and call in the Crime Scene Investigation Unit of the detectives' squad, to take finger-prints and to take the bodies back to the morgue and do what they do best. Cappy took all of the data and placed it in his car. He thanked everyone for a job well done. I went over to Mario, Mike and Billy and we had a smoke, before I headed back to Dana Point. Sean and Jules already left and went back to their own respective cities. Thank goodness, our guys were okay. For Mike and Billy to hide in the inner sanctum for so many hours, was indeed a chore. But they came out just fine.

The ride back to the ocean was relaxing, although I was still a bit tense due to the startling gunfight we had just been involved with. But it was going to be great just to get back to Christy and Rita, and enjoy, whatever was left of the evening. I received a call on my cell phone from Cappy as he walked into his house. He told me that I did a great job as a leader of the group and praised me for handling the situation as I did.

He also told me that Moose was making headway in Washington, and formu-lated a program to go after all of the drug cartels in Columbia, Ecuador, Chile, Peru, and other countries, including Mexico. This would commence within seven days. They were keeping close tabs on Chuck as he was going from one country to another, trying to lock down all of the problems with the cartels.

Dicky was gathering lots of information through his newspaper buddies and all of this would be given to the prosecutor's office when it was time to put

Chuck on trial, if he ever made it to trial. But there were other problems. The other Mafia families were getting wise as to what was happening, as there were too many leaks in the government, and they needed to keep their positions strong. There was a possibility that they would contact Chuck and that would take the element of surprise out of this operation. Time was of the essence, as all of the plans had to be in place very soon. I wondered if Cappy would have me go on another assignment to Central America, or even to the Middle East. My mind was racing all over the place. Heck, is that what I really wanted? I couldn't bear being away from my sexy women. Not now.

But now I had to go home and see my lovely ladies who were probably waiting up for me, with baited breath. I wished.

CHAPTER 10

▼

IT'S BEEN A HARD DAY'S NIGHT

When I walked into my house, all of the lights were out, except for a small gleam of light coming from under the family room door. It was nearly two thirty in the morning and I assumed that the girls were sleeping by now. I first went up to my bathroom to freshen up, take off my gritty outfit, put my guns away, and put on my silk robe that I loved to lounge in. I looked on the bed and I did not see Christy. I then went downstairs and approached the family room door and opened it. Christy was lying on the couch, wrapped in one of my cashmere blankets, and Rita was on the chair, with her head hanging over the side.

Both of them got up when they heard me come in. Although it was late, they looked like they were both happy to see me, 'alive'. Christy jumped up off of the couch first and ran to give me a big hug.

"David, you made it!"

Her arms felt wonderful, as she had wrapped them around me, and the smell of her hair in my face was a welcoming change from my previous experiences of gunpowder, and the blood and sweat of men's fear.

"Yes, and how are you ladies doing?"

Rita lit a cigarette, and she looked like she had not moved from the chair in a long time.

"Oh, we have been keeping ourselves entertained while you were out, playing soldier boy. So what happened?"

"It all went well," I responded. "We got what we needed, and things are progressing beautifully. A few of Chuck's men didn't make it."

I just didn't want to go into all of the gory details with them.

"But that was to be expected. Hey, let's talk about that tomorrow, as it is kind of late. I'm thinking of making some hot tea before I hit the sack. Anyone interested? We still have some of the Italian cookies left, unless you ate them all."

"Oh, let me make it for you." Christy was being so obliging, and she sincerely seemed happy to see me, although she knew not to push me for more info at this time. She wanted to be with me as long as she could. Her eyes were half asleep, but she had the need to please me. I was hoping in other ways, of course, but that would have to wait. I was still winding down from the events of this evening.

Rita got up from the chair, with her cigarette in hand, and excused herself saying that she was going to bed. She just wanted to wait and see if everything worked out okay, and then she would be able to sleep restfully. I didn't blame her.

Christy and I sat at the kitchen table and drank our tea, and she told me that she and Rita had watched some movies, and talked about their lives, just plain old girl talk. But she also said that Rita was a tough broad, someone she would not normally find herself associated with. Having gotten to know Christy and Julie, Rita felt that she could not continue her undercover work for Chuck, and although she had mixed feelings, she also knew that it was in her best interest to cut out and do the right thing.

Christy told me that she felt sorry for Rita, and even though Rita had had a sexual relationship with Chuck at one time, she assumed that Rita was a woman with a lot of issues. This had surprised me, as I knew that Christy also had her own problems. It seemed incredible that she could be so forgiving and understanding of Rita.

After we finished our tea, I told Christy that I was ready to collapse and was going to bed. She looked at me in a funny way, as if she would have liked me to invite her to go to bed with her. Of course, she was always welcome, but I was still feeling the anxiety, and needed some private time to go over some things in my own mind, as this evening's gunfight was an ordeal for me. I supposed that a little sex would be welcomed, even though it was late. But I knew that I needed to keep up my peak performances for this oversexed woman. Christy loved the fire and the energy in me, but tonight I would show her another side of me that I may not have wanted to. Perhaps this low-key appearance might have been disappointing to her.

We both walked upstairs together, and she had pinched my butt as we climbed the steps. I turned around, and she winked at me, and I asked, "Christy, are you flirting with me?"

"I believe I am, David," she responded. "Are you interested in some company?"

"I think that would be fine, except that I am very tired, as you can imagine, and I might just fall asleep on you."

"Oh, that's okay," she insisted. "We can just hold each other."

As we got to the top of the stairs, I turned to look at her, and could not resist that lovely face. I took her hand and led her to the bed. She took her clothes off and slid under the sheets, and I told her that I would be right back. I went back downstairs to make sure that Rita was sound asleep and I heard her snoring through the door. Boy, did she ever cut up the logs! Sounded like a bunch of cellos during a classical composition. I just did not want Rita to listen in on what Christy and I were doing, but I had no doubt that she was asleep.

I slid under the covers, and Christy immediately wrapped her arms around me, and I could feel her body pressing against mine. She was warm and I was hard. I could not believe I was able to get so excited after so much of what had happened only a few hours before. But, there I was, in all of my glory. I felt the incredible urge to mount her and get myself in her, reach my climax, and do it quickly before I fell asleep on her. It wasn't that I did not think that she was so wonderfully hot, but just that I was so doggone tired. She continued to take her hands and moved them up and down, rubbing my thighs. She then reached for my hard anatomy.

I whispered to her in her ear. "Sweetheart, this is fabulous."

She went further under the covers and put her full mouth around me and I was feeling incredibly good. This girl was talented, to say the least, as she must have done this a million times before. She knew exactly what she was doing, and for some reason, I was becoming more awake.

But, just then, out of the corner of my eye, I saw the door slightly open. I reached for my PPK under the bed. As I got my eyes focused more steadily, I saw Rita, standing there, naked as a jaybird, except for a Teddy Bear that she was holding in both hands. She walked over to us, and though there were no words exchanged, it seemed apparent that she wanted in on the action. Christy must have heard someone come in, but she did not stop, and Rita slid into the bed.

The two women started kissing, and I felt the two of them succumbing me, each with their mouths. I had one of my hands feeling Rita's breasts, and a finger on the other hand was inside of Christy. The girls allowed me to play with both of them, and this was absolutely mind blowing. My only thought was that Rita wanted Christy to start with me, and may have planned this all along, where she would join us later. She probably pretended to be asleep, so I would not have any idea as to what they had planned, or talked about earlier.

Christy turned over and I entered her from behind, as Rita slid under her, so Christy would be able to lick her. We switched positions, and after awhile, I did not know whom I was in, or who was kissing me. I had my eyes closed, and the room was dark. But it did not matter in the least. Soon, Christy and Rita were sucking each other again, and though I was still hard as a rock, I knew I had better play with myself to keep the action going. But Christy leaned into me and forced herself on top of me once again. It didn't take too long for me to come, and I was able to tell if she did as well. She was a lot quieter than in the past. Rita lay still on one side, as I was on the other side of Christy. No one spoke for several minutes. Then Rita leaned over, and kissed each of us goodnight, and left the room.

I was stunned that there was no conversation. But I thought it best to go with the flow. And there was much of that from all of us. Christy then curled up next to me.

"Thank you, David, sweet dreams."

I was not able to question this at all. I knew that I just had the most incredible experience in my entire life. There I was, I thought, with two women in my bed, and no one said anything, but just fucked each other to kingdom come. I wondered if this would become a regular occurrence, or was I really dreaming that this had happened. Whew, now that was something I could go for again. I wondered if I would have a re-run in my dreams. I could only wish. It reminded me of the first time that Christy and I had made love. We had very little conversation, and we certainly had a wonderful experience. At least I did. She always seemed to make me wonder what was happening in that little head of hers.

The following morning, I awoke to find myself alone in bed. I must have been exhausted. But I did hear noises from the kitchen, as pots and pans were clanking, and a low sound of music was coming from the radio. I got up and showered, dressed and went downstairs, to find Christy making breakfast.

"Rita left," she said. "She told me that she was very thankful for your hospitality, and mine, and left to find herself a new life. She had called a cab company and they picked her up about an hour ago."

Christy did not stop what she was doing, while she was telling me about Rita, and she seemed a bit annoyed actually, but she laughed afterward. Then she continued.

"Are you hungry, David?"

"You mean that she got up and took a cab to go someplace?" I asked. "Where was she going to go? I mean, she had no more house, no car, nothing. Did she say anything else to you?"

"Yep," replied Christy. "She said that she was going to meet someone, but I really wasn't listening, as I had the water on, and she was running out the door, like she was in a hurry. Probably the cab pulled up and she went through the garage, as she didn't have time to take the key and unlock the gate in front. Like a shot, she was gone."

Well then, I thought, no good-bye. Just a quick, little threesome, then adios. Just like a woman. I wondered who she was going to meet later on, and if that someone was a member of Chuck's organization. Was she actually spying on Christy and me? You never knew with Rita. She was a cunning little bitch who always seemed to get her way.

Christy made a scrumptious breakfast consisting of eggs benedict over croissants, with a fruit cup, and some tea for both of us. We sat there looking at each other, and all I could think of was last night. In one day, I had accomplished a successful feat, with my Seal Buddies, and I had two women for dessert. It seemed all so surreal, yet I knew that everything happened in just one day.

"So what do you want to do today?" I heard Christy say in a sudden tone, awakening me from my thoughts.

I was about to tell her that I was going back upstairs, when she asked me if I would join her in the shower. I was thinking that maybe it was time for me to do some errands, and for her to feel free to roam and shop, or do whatever might be a good start to get her on the road to her own independence. She quickly started to clean up the kitchen. It had occurred to me that I might have a problem with her needing my company on a steady basis. I had to make it clear to her that we were not a couple, but just two people caught up in the midst of a mess, that she herself got me into.

In fact, I was starting to feel a bit smothered with her around. I still had to find out about my teaching schedule, my next assignment from Cappy, and the many things that awaited me in the days ahead. After last night, I thought that the quality of what was part of our unique bonding could only be lessened by the fact that she was okay with sharing me with another. Now, she was holding on to me so tightly, that I had to straighten this out with her, or at least discuss the possibility that I was confused about her behavior, and that I had never been in a three-some before.

Perhaps I didn't know the rules following such an act, if there were any. Being married to Martha for so many years, I could have been out of the loop for so long, that I did not know what to expect afterwards. Maybe, nothing does change between people, but it seemed to me that my feelings for her had changed to a slight degree. I did find her extremely attractive, but my heart did not feel what it felt like when Julie was in the room. I did have to contact her today as well. I felt that I missed her.

"Listen, sweetie, I have a few things to do today. Perhaps we could meet later for lunch at the Café at the Marriott Hotel or at the St. Regis, say about two-ish. Could you keep yourself occupied until then?"

"Oh, David," she responded. "Why so late? I really had hoped that we could spend the day together?"

"Christy, I have to run some papers over to Cappy's, get a haircut, and see about catching up on my mail which is still sitting at the post office. I still have things to do to get my life back in order and today is a good day to do it."

I felt odd having to explain to her, or to anyone, of my plans for the day. It was only a few days ago, when these things didn't seem like chores, but a break in my mundane lifestyle. I realized that I had to talk to Christy, but I didn't know where to start. This was not the right time to go into how I felt, and that perhaps she had to move on and do something for herself. Perhaps it was best for her to move in with Julie, but I just didn't know how well that would be for me in the long run.

"Okay," she said. "I will meet you later then. But if your time table changes, you can call me if you want."

She walked out of the kitchen and went upstairs. I followed her and saw that she was heading toward the bedroom. She sat down on the bed and looked sad. I asked her what was wrong.

She looked up at me with her saddened eyes. "I don't know, David. I'm just not sure what I am supposed to do, now that you have things under way, with the Navy Seals, and your getting back to teaching, and the fact that you seem to be preoccupied with many other things. I also know how you feel about my friend, but I love you, David, and I don't know what I am going to do without you."

I guess this may have been the opening that I needed, whether I liked it or not. She needed answers, and I didn't blame her, as she was not sure where she really fitted in my life. I decided to sit down with her and tell her my feelings.

"Sweetheart, my feelings for you are very sincere. I think that you are a wonderful woman. I have not felt this good in a long time. But, it is very new to me. I am unsure as to how I feel about where I want this to go. And yes, I do have feelings for Julie, and yes, we did have a nice time last night with Rita. And yes, there is still a lot for me to figure out right now. I don't want to hurt you, but I am not ready for any type of commitment with anyone right now. That is the truth."

Christy looked at me, with some tears emerging from her eyes.

"So, you just want to fuck all of us and think that we are not supposed to have feelings for you in other ways?"

She was getting hostile and I wondered if she was on any of the drugs she was on before. I also wondered if I could make her see that I had no intention of hurting anyone, and that I was being completely honest with her.

"I'm sorry, Christy. I don't know what you want me to say. I know that this has been hard for you. But I am not ready for any more in my life right now. I have been alone for a while now, and I don't know what I am feeling."

"You don't know WHO you want, right? Isn't that your problem? You don't know who the best in bed is yet, because you haven't had HER yet, isn't it?"

I stood up as I was getting really annoyed with this childish behavior, and where this conversation was going. I knew on one hand, that she was right. But on the other, I wasn't going to be brutally honest with her, and tell her so, even though it would be ideal to truly open up and get it all out in the open. She could hear the truth, as I could hear the truth, and then everything would be out in the open. But I did not think that she was able to handle the truth.

"Oh, by the way, Christy, did you girls plan that act last night, or did it just happen to occur all of a sudden?"

"David, we talked about it after you left, because Rita thought that it was what you wanted. Didn't you like it? C'mon, David, you did like it, didn't you?"

"Did you want it too? Christy?" I asked her. I thought that she may have been coaxed into it by Rita. That sly little Rita!

She looked at me and didn't say anything. I knew that she was coerced into believing that it would please me, but I could tell that she didn't agree initially. She hung her head down, and I sat down next to her on the bed.

"I'm truly sorry, Christy. I really am. I thought it was something that you wanted to do also. You acted so comfortable with it."

She started to cry, and put her head on my shoulder. I knew that she was in love with me, and I knew that I was going to have quite a problem with this beautiful lady. I was convinced that if anything pleased me, she would do just about anything for me. This was not a good thing for me. I would never want her to do anything that did not please her.

"How about if we discuss this when I get back later, Christy? We do need to get this entire matter out in the open as I do not want you to feel hurt, or do anything that would not please you at all, even if you thought that it would make me happy."

"No, David, I think that I am gong to pack up and go to Suzie's. I feel that it would be best for now. As much as I would love to share my life with you, it seems to me that you and Julie have some things to work out first."

This was the most intelligent thing she had told me up to this point. So I let her decide what was best for her and we parted ways that day. I prepaid the cabbie when he came by to pick her up, and she headed to Suzie's house. I went about my business, and was taking a haircut when I thought how fabulous it would be to have my tongue inside of Julie. Just then, my cell phone rang. It was Julie.

"Julie, how are you. Funny, I was just thinking about you," I said, not telling her of my risqué thoughts about she and I having sex together.

"David, what have you done? I just got a call from Suzie, and Christy is all upset. Did you throw her out of your house, David? Why are you being so mean to Christy? David, she is so vulnerable right now, that I am disappointed in you."

I had to quiet Julie down. I told her that it was Christy's idea, not mine. I would not want to force Christy into anything, but that she was questioning me as to where I was going, when I would return, and the fact that I had feelings for Julie. This made Julie a bit comprehensive as to where all of this was going.

"David, please come over after work and we can sort this entire nonsense out. I like Christy, as a friend, and I do not want her to get hurt. I realize that you were caught in the middle of this, but we have to be very careful about handling all of this. Suppose you come over about seven this evening."

We hung up and I told the barber to continue. I then headed to the school so I would be able to get my next teaching assignment, as I was now ready to resume my teaching career. There were so many things that I had to get to know as the school was into another set of text books and I did not have any of the new series. That would take some time to do. I had limited time to do this as the new schedules for classes were to begin in two weeks. I had to cram all of the assignments in, and lay out a program for the students for the next semester.

I then headed to the market, picked up some staples for the house, and some personal care necessities, and headed for home. Upon arrival, the phone rang. It was Cappy.

"David, we have a new assignment. In the next few days, we are going to move 'Operation Bittersweet' to New York so we can be in contact with the other mafia families. We have a lead on some of the drug operations going into Harlem and the garment center, and I need you, Mario, Mike Billy, and Dickie there with me. Dickie will stop off at the New York Times corporate office and get more information on Chuck and the drug cartel. Moose will be flying back from Washington next week and then we will have the information on how they intend to crack down on the cartels in Central America. Sean is working on the trial dates. So be prepared to travel and we will all meet at my home, two nights from today."

Wow, again I am called away and back to square one. I needed to find out about where my own life was headed, and I didn't mean to the Big Apple or to some far away place like Columbia or Iraq. Could it be that I just didn't have a life anymore? I also needed to see where I stood with Julie. I was looking forward to seeing her later on.

Although I still had tremendous feelings for Christy, it was my life that I was interested in right now. My groins would have to take a breather as I was getting sore and I needed to cool it for a while. As much as I loved playing around with the girls these past few days, first in Vegas, then in my own home, I was getting worn out. Maybe, just maybe, age was creeping up on me, and I was losing my stamina. Heck, I am only in my forties, so I still had lots of time to live the life of a sex maniac.

As I was putting things away, the phone rang. This time, it was Rita. I thought, now what does this bitch want?

"David, I am glad I caught you at home. How are you doing? Sorry I missed you this morning, but I had some things to do and people to see. Could you talk?"

I sat down to listen to what she had to say, and her information caught me off guard.

"David, I am at a friend's house in Tustin and was able to find out that Chuck is planning to return in five days. He is off in Peru now, and he already found out that his home had been ransacked by the FBI. He has no idea that the Navy Seals were involved, or that you were part of the operation. My friend told me that Chuck is going to meet with the families of New York, Chicago, Houston, New Orleans and Miami, for a big get-together at Pebble Beach in Monterey, and they are going to increase the drug trade in this country. He is also going to come after Christy, so I hope that she is safe with you."

I didn't tell Rita that Christy was at Suzie's, but I also wanted her to know that she was not here any longer. I did not need my home upset by Chuck's thugs again. So I told Rita that Christy was put on a plane and went out of town. She wanted to know where, but I didn't want to tell her anything. For some reason, I just did not trust this broad. She had too many ties with Chuck and could have been a plant to see what we were up to.

I asked her where she was and she told me the name of her friend. Roger Helmesby, an old friend of hers, who was a bookie for the mob, and had kept close ties with some of Chuck's people. He used to make his rounds to big corporations, selling crack and pot, and would supply some of the corporate management people with enough drugs to hold parties and sell them to their own friends. I told Rita that I would be in touch and hung up.

I called Cappy back and asked that this Roger character be tracked down, and that a tail be put on Rita. She may be the link that we needed to find Chuck's whereabouts when he came home from his travels. I then called Ricardo and Carlos for a rundown on Helmesby's home in Tustin. I figured that if we had his floor plan, we could go there and either help Rita if she needed some help, or kill that lying bitch, if that be the case.

It was nearly six and I decided to shower, change into something more comfortable and pick up a bottle of wine and some flowers for Julie. I even had the car washed. I wanted to ease the tension and maybe get lucky tonight with this woman who has been on my mind since that day we met in the parking garage of the shopping center. I got into the little red car, placed the wine and flowers on the passenger seat, and headed to Newport Beach to meet with Julie.

When I had arrived at her place, her car was not there. I thought that maybe she got hung up in traffic, so I sat in my convertible and listened to some music, and looked around the area. A sort of middle class neighborhood, with lots of people mulling around, some young children, some mothers, a few fathers wheeling carriages, an elderly couple holding hands while sitting on a park bench across the street, a commuter bus stopping at the corner, sirens in the distance, and teenagers being young and silly.

Oh, to be that young again, I thought. I was not jealous of them, but little did they know what the real life was all about. Did they taste real hot sex yet, and real hot money? Probably not! As I sat there, I thought, that I was glad I was not in that age group anymore.

I then watched the sun set, although it was still quite light outside. And though it was the end of summer, nothing much changes here on the west coast of southern California. I remembered why I had chosen to live here, and why I would not want to live anywhere else. There wasn't anything west from here, except, maybe on the islands of Hawaii, and the pace there is even slower than in California. I thought of finding a teaching job there, learn their language, drink margaritas, and be with the woman whom I dream about every day of my life.

What was I going to tell Julie? And why would she initially think that I had thrown Christy out of my home? I did tell her that it was her choice, not mine. But something in her remarks caused me to sense something else from her, perhaps that it was not all Christy's choice to leave. It would be ridiculous for her to think that I would do anything to harm Christy, even though she got me into this situation in the first place. I risked my life to save her's, and now I am going to take him down, this Chuck Manzione, one way or another. Heck, I never even heard of Chuck before we all met in Vegas. I suppose the level of Julie's trust is limited, and I wondered how much her career has played a part in her trusting anyone right now.

I circled the block several times, thinking about all of this, when I noticed Julie pulling into the driveway. She saw me and waved, shaking her head as if to say, 'damn traffic'!

"I'm so sorry, David, please, please come inside with me. Let's get cooled off with some ice cold drinks."

She still had the same tone that someone would have as if she was still working in the office. Although, having the kind of freeway traffic that we do, I could understand why she was late. She must have had a busy day, but she continued to ramble on, as we walked inside her home.

"Good to see you, David. And what have you been up to today?"

She hugged me after she put her briefcase down on the tiled floor. It felt sensational and I did not want to let her go. I told her that it was good to see her as well.

"Come, sit on the sofa while I freshen up. I will make us some cocktails. Just make yourself at home."

She disappeared into another part of the condo, and I went over to the couch. Looking around, I noticed photos of her family, and antique figures on the piano. To the left, there was a bookcase filled with law books and psychology texts, and books on poetry. I glanced at her wall hangings that I may have overlooked before when I first came to her home. She had beautiful plants and flowers in the windows, and they all looked so warm and inviting.

Now, it was just the two of us. This was a treat to me without distractions, and no emotionally wrecked woman to save. I knew that Julie had something all together different than Christy, but to what level? Would I ever be able to love this woman unconditionally? Did she have what it took to be my partner? I would hope that I would be able to find my answers that evening.

I sat myself on the sofa, and started to play with the remotes that were placed on the coffee table. When she had returned, she was dressed in a soft pastel dress, walking barefoot, and a new scent of sweet smelling perfume that lingered behind her, as she walked by me. She looked absolutely scrumptious. I wanted to tell her how much she always seemed to turn me on, but I did not want to come off as being too aggressive. She did say that we needed to discuss something and I was wondering what she had on her mind.

I could barely get up from the couch as I already had one of my huge hard-ons that forced me to remain seated a little longer.

"So David, what happened this morning?" she asked.

Oh God, another interrogation. Just what I needed right now, I thought. It was at that moment that my 'woody' started to diminish and I finally got up and responded to her question.

"Christy told me that she felt better if she would stay at Suzie's house. I suppose that tells you that I have had enough right now, Julie, and that I am not able to be with her, 24/7. She really needs to figure out what she wants to do for herself."

"We all know what she wants to do, David. She thinks that you don't want her."

She handed a martini to me and we both went back to the couch. But she then turned and sat in her favorite chair, a brown, cushioned armed chair, made of leather. I felt that she was much too far from me in that chair. I could not say anything at that moment, until she was somehow convinced that I did not throw her friend out into the street.

"I know that you and Christy had a relationship, David. And I know that when I first met you at the restaurant in Vegas, she couldn't stop looking at you. She is in love with you, David."

Julie sipped her drink and I did the same, listening to what she was getting at. I may have needed some liquid courage to speak my mind as she was speaking hers. Perhaps it would take a few more martinis, but I would eventually tell Julie that I wanted her, not Christy, in my arms. All this talk about Christy and her feelings for me was getting dull and boring. I needed to quickly settle this and move on.

"Julie, I am well aware of Christy's feelings. But, I suppose that she is also overwhelmed with everything that is happening in her life right now. I have only been a source of comfort, and I realize that she wants to please me to no end. But, honestly, it is suffocating me. I adore her as a person, but I am not in love with her. We are adults here, and she knew what she was doing from the very beginning. I also feel that she has to make up her own mind, and not expect me to think for her, decide what is best for her, and stop thinking that I am ready to settle down with her, because I am not."

Julie looked a bit perplexed at my response and with her own courtside mannerism, responded, without hesitation.

"Yes, David, I do believe in my heart that you are right. She's denying her fear, and clinging on to you for security, and I know that she is confused right now. I do believe that she will be safe with Suzie, but I do wonder about her drug problem. When she is unhappy, she takes those pills, and then who knows what?"

"I just can't go on being her keeper," I said. "I want to be her friend, but she wants more than I feel for her."

"I understand, really I do." And with that, Julie got up from her chair and came over to the couch.

I thought that this was a good sign. I was hoping that we were making progress in her mind. Her glass was nearly empty, and she asked if I was ready for another. Before I had responded, she was off to the kitchen again. She also seemed a bit nervous, and I wanted to reassure her that she didn't have to be. But I thought it was best that I just keep quiet for the moment.

I remained on the couch, and waited for her. I thought that I had better make this progress happen quickly if we were to move jointly together. I was beginning to have high hopes for us, and hopefully to her satisfaction. Julie was incredibly smart, and so sexy, that I would have done anything if she would only let me rip her clothes off.

When she returned, she stood in front of me, and looked down at me, while I sat so comfy on the couch.

"Look, I know that this is a tough situation, but I don't want my friend to be upset."

She sat down next to me and put her glass on the table. I watched her as she put her hand on my knee and continued to talk. Although she was telling me things from the heart, I could not focus on her words. I was caught up in her beauty, and I felt like I was in a vacuum without hearing anything coming from her lips. I caught the last few words…

"So this is what I think is best. Please listen without saying a word. Do you understand?"

Oh shit…what did I miss? Time to improvise, as I answered abruptly.

"Well, then, okay. Where do we start?"

"David, it's simple. You have to tell her that you don't love her, just like I said. Otherwise, she will continue to think otherwise."

I sat there, a bit dumbfounded and was truly not with the program, so to speak. I nodded, and then uttered a few possibilities, hoping for a possible jaunt with Julie.

"So, what do we do about tonight?"

I had had enough of this drama. I wanted to move on and truthfully, I wanted Julie to entertain me. I wanted to wrap myself up in her pleasures, and be inside her. I could not think of anything else, let alone how I was going to tell someone else that I didn't love her. I sat, thinking that I love this woman, the one sitting next to me. So how do I tell her that?

Before she had a chance to respond, I offered her a suggestion that we have some dinner together.

"Tonight, I thought maybe we could go listen to some music at the Beach House down at the harbor, or at one of the local joints in the neighborhood," I said, hoping that she would obligingly consent to my proposal. "They have a three man band at 9 pm and we can have some wine and cheese. Perhaps we can dance a little. Would you like to do that?"

I thought that it was a nice gesture, although what I really wanted to do was to be naked with her and to forget about all of the formalities. But I knew better with this woman, and tried to act as gentlemanly as possible, as she was too slick a babe to try to entrap her into going to bed. She replied by saying that it sounded terrific but only for a short while, as she had to head back early for an early morning meeting at her office. She decided that the local place would be best and went to put on some shoes. She had recommended a quaint little club that had some music and it was less than a mile down the road, on the other side of the complex.

When she returned, I was standing by the door, waiting for her. She leaned over to open it, and I took her in my arms. I watched very carefully to see her reaction, but she did not flinch. I turned to her lips and kissed her. She did not reject me and we kissed, making me feel warm all over, as if I had died and gone to heaven.

After several seconds, she stopped and pulled back.

"David, I am getting the impression that you have something else on your mind, and it is not the music, or the dancing. Could I be wrong?"

I looked at her and tried to act a bit debonair.

"As a matter of fact, not that I wouldn't mind dancing with you and holding you close to me, but I was thinking of some gentle way of holding you, more intimately close to me."

She looked at me and I could not figure out what she was thinking. Julie was like a closed book. Her expression was luminous, and she made it very difficult to see what she wanted to do.

"David, I think that you are one hell of a guy. I really do. But I don't think that it would be prudent right now for the two of us to get together. And I just feel that it would not work out for us right now."

I could not figure her out. I stood there waiting for her to continue to give me her sermon on what is best for me. It must have seemed to her that I was only after her for one thing. Perhaps I was, but I tried not to show it. I was not very good at the formalities as it had been years since I felt this way. I was rusty, but I was not foolish.

"Julie, I understand. I just thought that you might like a small kiss for old times sake, you know, as two friends."

I played it cool and I did not want her to think that I had it real bad for her. I wanted her to make the next move, as I felt that she liked to be in control, especially in situations where she may have thought that she was the prey. Julie needed to make the moves first, which was her style. We left and walked to the club.

We found the small lounge, was ushered to a small table surrounded by two couches, and she ordered some wine. They also served us a small plate of cheese and crackers. The band was setting up in the corner, and the place was fairly empty. She told me that not too many people show up this early in the evening, especially during the week. It was a cute little club with plush couches and some rockers, and many glass tables. The dance floor was small, but it was suitable for this size room. I could see her villas where she had her condo, through the window, since most of the residents had their interior lights on. An elderly couple walked over to the direction where she and I were sitting.

"Hi Julie," said this very friendly gentleman. "So good to see you."

The elderly gent and Julie hugged each other like old pals.

"Tom, this is David. David, I would like you to meet Tom and Gail."

I shook his hand and that of his woman friend. They continued to talk to Julie and I started to feel out of place. All of a sudden, I felt like I did not want to be here, as I really wanted to be with her alone. I started to get annoyed and uncomfortable and excused myself, by telling Julie that I was going outside for a bit of fresh air. I figured that I would grab a smoke outside and leave her with her friends. Within minutes, Julie came out on the patio where I was standing and in no uncertain terms sounded a little bitter.

"That was rude, David. We were in the middle of a conversation and you just walked away."

I was not happy with this scenario. I looked at this woman who was losing control and I did not need to be talked down to.

"You know what, Julie? I think I will go back to the house, get my car, and go home. I have not been comfortable ever since I came to your house. All you have done, all this evening, was tell me how you felt, and what I should do, and never one time asked me my feelings. You seem to like to take control of other people's lives, and I cannot be controlled by anyone, not even you. So excuse me, for taking back control of my life."

She looked perturbed at my statement and responded. "Just as I thought. You came to see me with the intent of going to bed with me, and now that I just told you that we aren't going to work out, you have to leave. Yes, you're right. It would be best if you did go home."

She started to storm off when I grabbed her by her arm.

"Listen to me. You were the one who asked me over this evening. But, you are right. I made a big mistake. I think that perhaps I have not been honest with myself, as I did not intend to hurt anyone, not you, not Christy, not anyone. I never used you or Christy, and yet, I had found myself falling in love with you, not with Christy. I had loved you since the first time I saw you in the garage. Just as fate would have it, we meet in Vegas because you are Christy's friend, and Christy and I met earlier on in the afternoon. I had not stopped thinking about you and never thought I would see you again. But, there you were, bigger than life. And there it is, out in the open. I've told you my feelings, like you told me yours."

We continued to walk back to her condo and then she stopped, and stared at me. She then continued to walk away, leaving me there with my heart buried in my chest, and a dangling cigarette burning my fingers. I had this strange feeling, one that I had not felt before. I started to walk toward my car without turning toward her, or even waving goodbye. I was unlocking the door, when I heard my name called. It was Julie.

"David, wait, I am sorry. I did not know what to say to you. All this has been very confusing to me. I don't think that it will work out because I will always be afraid that we will find ourselves in some kind of danger. Between you and your Navy Seal buddies, and me, a fighting trial attorney. Each in our own way, we are trying to save the world. We are two of a kind, David, and it does not feel like it will mesh. Do you understand what I am trying to say?"

I started to feel enthusiastic again, finding that our relationship was not over. I might still have a chance with this woman, or at least there was this window of opportunity. Perhaps we were finally able to understand the other person's feelings.

"Julie, this is what makes us work best. We each have what it takes to fight the world together. If you would be willing to give us a try, you might actually find a life with me down the road. The life may be exciting and have many unexpected twists and turns. But at least, as a team, we can fight the demons together. If you would only consider the option, you may find that between the two of us, we just might become two very happy people. Just consider it."

Well, I thought I gave the perfect line. Maybe she would be able to see through it or not. But at least I was saying something that was from my heart, and that I wanted her to believe in anyway. We were told in the Seals to trust our feelings. I was asking Julie to trust hers. I truly had deep feelings for Julie, but I saw another side of her that was domineering and abrupt. She could be a tigress as well as a dove. At this point, I wasn't sure of her true stripes.

"David, I am flattered, really I am. But I need time to think."

"Yes, you do," I interrupted. "Take as much time as you need. But I still would like to think that we could make a great team. When you are ready, I will be there for you."

I then kissed her on her forehead and got into my car. She looked at me with her beautiful face glowing in the moonlight, the one I got to know in my dreams. I could only hope that she was thinking about what I said. I knew that after this year, I wanted to re-establish myself somewhere else to teach, and live out the rest of my life with someone as beautiful as Julie. I decided to give her all of the time she needed to think about the options I laid out to her. I knew that there was no one better suited for at this stage in my life, and I drove away feeling rather satisfied with myself. I also hoped that she would feel the same way for me one day, as I had felt for her that night.

This has been quite an evening so far. Christy left to go to Suzie's house, and Julie and I were trying to work things out. So far my life had taken so many turns in the past few weeks, I wasn't sure what road I was really on.

I was not ready to call it a night, so I headed to the Beach House in Dana Point, at the harbor, where all of the boats are docked. It was fairly early for a week day night and I needed to have a drink with some real live people. I had the valet park my car and headed toward the bar. There was the usual evening crowd, just sitting around, listening to quiet music by the same trio who has been there for years, playing sounds from the mid sixties and seventies. The lead singer sounded like Neil Diamond and he was pretty good with the guitar.

I ordered a glass of wine and figured I would just have one or two, and then head back to my place and call it a night. In two days, I would have to fly to New York. God knows what I was going to do there, especially in Harlem and the garment center.

The bartender brought me a glass, and I overhead a voice say, "I'll take the same, Mike."

It was my old friend, Stephanie. She sat down beside me and we both smiled.

"Had a tough day, David?"

I told her about my upcoming trips but chose not to get into much detail. I felt that it was best not to get her involved. After all, she was a married woman, a plain and simple soul, who just needed company. She indicated that her husband had gone to visit his mother in Arizona and she was left to hold the fort. We told each other some jokes and laughed.

She was always there for me, no matter how or where I was. For some reason, I felt that she always had a crush on me. Being married to Martha, I had never considered the fact that she could have been someone I may have gone to bed with years ago. But then again, she was married and both she and her husband were friends. I thought it best not to get involved with her. So here we were, two lonely people, sipping some wine at the bar, and just enjoying each other's company.

We must have sat for hours as it was getting late. I decided to call it a night and gave my credit card to Mike, the bartender. Stephanie also got up and we walked out together. I started to notice how well she looked, about five ten, thin, nice body, and long legs. I was wondering how she would be if I invited her home with me. But she was a friend and I knew her husband quite well. I just did not have the balls to invite her to my home. But the thought was there and I was sure that she would have accepted my invitation. Again, I just would not be able to face her husband if we did screw around, even if he was traveling. I decided against this, and I just kept the thoughts to myself.

The valet went to get my car and I told Stephanie that I would wait until he got hers. She drove this beautiful, white Lexus, with all of the trimmings, and she looked good in it. I turned to her and wished her goodnight and drove the five minutes that it took to get to my home.

I parked in the garage and was about to close the garage door when I noticed two headlights coming down the street. I turned off the light in the garage and waited. The car came right up on the driveway and I panicked. I was not packing anything, so I had to be ready for anything and anyone. As I stared outside, the figure came out of the car and walked slowly toward the garage.

"David, I hope you don't mind. I am not ready to go home yet. Could we have one more before we call it a night?"

It was Stephanie. She needed some company and I was not about to close the garage door on her.

"Hi Steph. Sure, come on in. I'll make us a drink."

I couldn't believe she was there, or that she had the courage to come over this late in the evening. She followed me through the garage and I pressed the automatic button, hearing the door coming down. She was literally right behind me, and I could smell her perfume, which wasn't too bad. It was a sweeter smell than I was accustomed to, especially having Christy and Julie around.

She moved in front of me, knowing the layout of the house, and decided to take off her shoes, and flopped herself on the sofa. Looking rather attractive, as I was able to get a better view of her in the house, than in the bar, I went to my own small bar and prepared a martini for her, a glass of wine for me. When I brought the glasses back to the sofa, she already had one more button on her blouse undone, but I tried not to notice. What was she thinking? A night of wild passion? Was it something that I wanted to do? I was rejected by Julie just hours before and I was truly in love with someone, aside from Stephanie. Did it matter that I was good friends with her husband, and that we went back years, and we had history together? I thought to myself, time will tell.

We sat next to each other on the couch and she leaned over to me.

"Dave, I have been thinking. It has been a long time since we have known each other. I just wondered if you ever thought of me? I mean, in the way that would be fun for us. You know, without anyone being the wiser?"

I took a deep breath. I knew why she came here. I knew what she wanted. I also knew that I could do it in a heartbeat. But, could I? There were circumstances to every action. Her husband was one of my closest friends. But then, again, we have not been that close since Martha died.

I looked at her and imagined us in bed together. I could not get past the fact that it would be fun for me, and possibly for her, plus the possible guilt I might feel. Perhaps this one little time in our lives would not matter and we would just go on as usual. I turned toward her and gave her a kiss. She practically jumped into my arms that I had to hold her back so she would not fall over. Boy, was she ever so horny. And I thought I was bad!

We felt each other and kept a close embrace for a few minutes. I thought that perhaps if she didn't say another word, it would all go away smoothly, and she would leave without any knowledge of what may or may not have occurred. After a few drinks, she was a bit woozy anyway, and even if we did screw around, she would probably not remember a thing. At least, that is what I was hoping.

We got up from the couch, almost in unison, and walked to the bottom of the stairs, with the intention of going up to the bedroom. She stopped and turned to me.

"Dave, I am not sure if this is something that will be anymore than what it is. Are you good with that?"

I couldn't help, but hold back my laughter.

"I'm good with that, Steph, really."

We made it to the doorway of my bedroom when I heard the phone ring. I just let it ring until the answering machine went off, and I heard a familiar voice come on.

"David, are you there? Where are you? I have been trying to reach you all evening. Please call me. I miss you." It was Christy.

Stephanie stopped in her tracks and turned to me.

"New girlfriend?"

Yet, she continued to touch me, and I could not, for the life of me, remember what the question was. I grabbed her by her legs and lifted her up, and carried her to my bed.

We spent a few hours together, and to my surprise, it was an amazing time. Though it was unlike any other married woman I had been with, which of course, was Martha, it was incredible. I felt the excitement of hiding from someone, and not getting caught, although it crossed my mind as I was on top of Stephanie. I imagined her husband bursting into the room while I was banging his wife. But it never happened. We were alone and enjoying each other in bed.

Stephanie had beautiful, round breasts with large nipples that stood out like storm troopers. Unlike Christy and Julie, she was big boned, and had strong legs, and was more physical than the other girls. She had a tighter grip on my penis and moved her body faster and with more strength than I was used to. It seemed that she was in dire need of having sex and wanted everything she could get from me. From sucking my cock to fondling my balls, she then wanted me to squeeze her tits and jam my woody into her vagina with force. She pounced up and down with so much exhilaration, while I was on top of her, that I thought I was going to fall into a deep dark hole and never see daylight again. Stephanie wanted to come in the worst way and she did. It was a ride that I would not forget for a long time.

The excitement of being with someone who you can't have on a permanent basis, realizing the unimportance of it all, by not getting serious with each other, made it even more appealing. I loved the idea of being with a friend, a married friend, who truly loved her husband, but wanted a little more excitement in her life. And she came to me to provide that excitement for her.

She was somewhat tender, yet distant, as I was. Yet, I felt that we were on the same page, even as we caressed each other and our bodies were entwined in our lovemaking. We both must have been fantasizing about something else, which allowed us to bring each other to a level of passion that was unlike my time with someone I truly cared about. We did what came naturally, playing a little rough, and at times being tender with each other. It seemed to me that Stephanie had not had sex with her husband for a long while. I felt the tension, the anxiety, and the need. It was absolutely tremendous.

It felt good, and got even better as we touched each other intimately. We each reached our climax and she screamed out as if she was relieved and enjoyed the moment. When she got up to dress, she started to speak in an almost childish manner.

"Thanks, David. I hope you know that I was never here in your house, and that this never occurred."

It was amazing that we both had filled a need that we each wanted, but in our own way. This was something that I would never have thought about, prior to my trip to Las Vegas. Since then, I had grown more confident and willing to explore the deeper side of me that had been dormant for way too long. Not that I blame Martha for having boxed me in, as it had been my fault as much as hers. I felt a better me emerging, someone whom I was able to feel good about, even when I was doing something terribly wrong.

After all, Stephanie was a married woman, a friend, and her husband was also a friend. But, how often is a married woman available for a little fun in the sack? I had nothing to lose, and I really didn't care whether or not Stephanie lost what she had or didn't have, with regards to having a good, sexual life with her husband. It had nothing to do with me. If she wanted to cheat on her husband, and chose me to have sex with, that was truly up to her. If not me, she may have chosen someone else. It was she who happened to be at the Beach House this evening, perhaps looking for a mate to have sex with. I happened to be there and she followed me home. I did not even ask her. I did not lead her on. So what the hell was I concerned about?

I look at it as a mature thing, as we are all grown adults, some having a need and a desire to please another human being. And, basically, that is what we did. This will be forever etched in my mind and actually, I don't give a fuck what others think of me anymore. I am doing what I had dreamed about for years. And before I get old and fat, and not able to get it up anymore, I am going to go out and have one hell of a good time.

Stephanie left the condo and said that she enjoyed her stay. I was now alone, to think about what I needed to do for myself, from now on. I had been concerned about saving others, specifically the women I had met recently. And now I felt that I was ready to make a new person of myself. I was going to show the world that I have what it takes to be the 'David' that no one has met yet. But they soon will.

It was after midnight, and the phone rang again. It was Christy.

"Christy, I am here, but did not want to call you so late, after I heard your voice messages. How are you doing?"

She told me about her day with Suzie, and how she missed me. She hated to go to sleep by herself, without my body next to hers, and the fact that she felt warm and safe with her friend did compensate somewhat for the company that she did not have with me. I told her that I would be out of town for a few days and would contact her when I got back. She signed off by saying that she loved me and I did the same. It was short and sweet.

Two days later, the six of us were on our way to New York. We left on an early morning flight on an American 757 Jet for arrival at JFK and the flight was pleasant. Cappy sat with Dickie, I with Mario, and Mike with Billy. My favorite pastime on a long plane trip has always been to do crossword puzzles, which would eat up a lot of time. I tried to finish the book before we landed, as each puzzle usually had the same questions, whether across or down, it didn't matter. I was good at it.

The time went by and the flight was good. Dickie discussed many of the reports he had received from publishers and editors, with Cappy, from the Washington Post, to Time, and other periodicals, that made Cappy's head spin. It was a lesson in geography and history, and some of the indiscreet material put some of our own Congressmen and Senators in a position where our nation would have been at risk. This was getting much bigger than I had imagined, but Dickie kept everything relative to what our operation was all about. No need to scrutinize our congressional leaders at this point. When the dominoes would start to tumble, it could lead straight up to the National Security Office of the Executive Branch of the United States Government. There were too many connections, from one branch to another, and many heads would probably roll.

We had reservations at the Hilton New York and Towers, on the Avenue of the Americas, a hotel with over two thousand rooms, a health club, and modems for our computers, a concierge, and many other amenities. We had to meet some people up around Central Park, near Lincoln Center later that evening, along Sixty-Second Street, then on to Harlem, and back down to the garment center on thirty-fourth and Seventh Avenue. Cappy had scheduled us to spend about four days in New York. We also had a meeting in the SoHo district where we were to encounter some shady characters. Cappy always had us keep our side arms with us, wherever we went. We assumed that some of the characters were not the usual 9 to 5 office workers.

After checking in, Mario and I shared a nice room, overlooking the west side of Manhattan, not far from Fifth Avenue. It was late in the afternoon, as we had lost three hours in the time difference, plus the six plus hours it took us to get to New York from California. Our first meeting was at nine o'clock that night, first uptown, then further north, in the shady area of Harlem. I decided to go down to the lounge, and Mario would join me later, after he made some phone calls. I found a nice seat by the bar and ordered a glass of wine, my usual drink.

The place was filled with business people, mostly wearing suits, and talking loudly. This was New York. In California, you would not find a suit in a bar, but people in shorts, polo shirts, and having quiet conversations. But in New York, people had to be heard, and stand out like freaks in a sideshow. This was not my kind of relaxation. I looked around the room and saw three or four suits at any one table. Sometimes, there would be a good looking skirt seated with the men, just to look pretty, but would not speak. I scanned the room, from left to right.

My eyes stopped at one table, where three suits were yapping about a marketing project that they were working on and that they were hoping that the client would approve their creative designs. The fourth seat was taken by a sweet look-ing blond who just seemed so distracted by all of this trashy talk. She would have loved to get out of the way of these conceited bastards and find a loving guy to get into the sack with. Here I was, wearing a California sweatshirt, with the name, Pebble Beach on the back, and a pair of faded jeans. I probably looked like a country bumpkin from Arkansas.

As our eyes met, I smiled at the young gal who didn't know why she was wast-ing her time with these three assholes. Just another big deal and an advertising coup that was to motivate some corporate stud into thinking that their marketing package would bring him millions of dollars. Actually, it sounded like a piece of hogwash, and if I were the client, I wouldn't have bought it in a 'pig's eye'.

The gal caught my smile and smiled back. I felt relaxed. I just moved around on my barstool, as if I was trying to avoid her. But I kept catching up to her as she smiled at me. I finally thought to myself, that if this young lady is bored stiff over what the three schmucks were discussing, perhaps she would appreciate some company.

I walked over to the table and introduced myself to her. She acknowledged by saying that her name was Heather. I asked her about her job and the company she represented, and she told me that she was a designer. She was a pretty, thirty-year old, who seemed to have been caught up in all of this advertising pre-sentation. I also noticed her deep brown eyes, her dark brown hair, and she must have been about 5 feet, 7 inches. But she was attractive and had a lovely smile. I asked her to join with me at the bar.

Just then, one of the men looked at me and asked me what I was doing at their table. I politely told him that I was having a conversation with Heather. He became very indignant and asked me to leave the table. I told him that I was not about to, and if I did leave, I was going to take Heather with me. He suddenly got up and really became obnoxious.

These typical New Yorkers did not know how to act in this kind of situation. New Yorkers think that they are tough and can be very arrogant. Seeing my sweatshirt with the 'California' name on it, he probably thought that I was one of the usual 'air heads' that outsiders think normally come from the Golden State.

He told me to 'Get the fuck out of here' and when I refused to move, he pushed me. I took his hand and in one move, twisted his arm around his neck, and got him in a chokehold. The other two dimwits just sat there with their mouths open.

"You really are not a nice man," I told him. "If I were you, I would just let it go, and sit down."

With that, he tried to push me again. Only this time, I gave him such a punch in the stomach, that all of the martinis he had were nearly coming up through his gullet. Then, the other two guys started to rise, and I felt that I was going to defend my manhood, by taking them both down.

As they approached me, I heard Mario, who had just come into the picture behind them, ask them to sit down and not pursue this any further. I turned to Heather, and asked her to join me at the bar. As she started to walk with me, the first suit lunged at me with all of his might. I quickly grabbed his head and got him into a chokehold, throwing him on his ass about four feet from where I was standing. The other two didn't react so readily and held their positions. Mario was right in back of them, and they felt his presence, not knowing what he might do.

The young female walked to the bar and waited for me. I left the table and walked to her, leaving Mario to stand by the other two men who were sort of dumbfounded, not knowing who we were or what we were going to do next. I ordered another glass of wine for myself, and she requested a vodka gimlet. She was quite attractive as she sat on the stool next to mine.

"I am so sorry that these guys reacted the way they did. This is not the kind of attitude I would expect from them at all. I hope you don't mind if we just sit here while they re-organize and settle down."

"Not at all," I responded. "My name is David. I thought that you were getting pretty bored with those overgrown Ad people and you probably needed a break from their bragging how good their advertising campaign was."

"Hi David, and thanks for your understanding. I was hired about four months ago by the Hollensbach, Kline Agency, as their new art director and I helped put together that campaign for Struther Industries, a retail manufacturing company that is out in Long Island. They also have manufacturing facilities in the garment center on thirty Seventh Street, and cater to the department stores. It has been a complete nightmare, as these guys are just trying to outbid, outclass, and out-convince the client that our campaign is so much better than the others. Basically, I am not happy with it. It is not what I would do if I had my druthers. It lacks creativity and passion. I like to put passion in all of my work."

I looked at Heather, and if she could put passion in all of her work, then I would love to hire her myself. She was a bright and cheery female, full of life, and was not afraid to speak her mind.

"Hey, I understand, Heather. I am somewhat creative in my type of work, myself. I am from California as you can see on my shirt. I am here with a group to sort of resolve some work that we are involved with. I am staying at this hotel for the next four days and perhaps we can get together one night. My room number is 1509 and you can call me if you want. I have to leave in a little while, but maybe tomorrow evening. Are you living in town?"

"I am living over on the east side. I'm sharing an apartment with Madeline, who is a loan officer for City Bank, and we met when I opened up an account at that bank and decided to share in the expense of an apartment. I was bouncing around for a couple of years, from one Ad agency to another, until these guys offered me $65,000 to be one of their art directors.

"For a gal from a small town in Nebraska, who wanted to make it big in New York, I went from Benton & Bowles, J. Walter Thompson, to one or two others, until I was hired by this group. And you know what? I was never in California. I heard that it is a great place to live, with all of that sunshine and warm weather. I think I have had it in this city. The weather is too cold in the winter, too humid in the summer, and I hate the mind games that people play. I am just a small town, country girl."

I looked at this tall, enterprising young woman, with a great bod', a keen sense of what was happening in the world, and I liked what I saw. From Julie, who was so domineering and opinionated, to Christy who had emotional problems, I liked feeling free and independent to meet other women and get to know them. This was not bad, I thought. Perhaps I may be able to meet her and get to know her. A

Midwest type gal who was never in California might be the one type of gal that would fit well in my life. I was hoping for a miracle and that we would be able to meet again before I left.

Just then, Mario came over and put his arm around my shoulder.

"Hey big guy, can't I leave you alone for a minute without you causing mayhem in a place?"

I looked at Mario, and beyond his shoulder, to see the three suits sitting quietly in their chairs.

"So what did you tell them, Mario? They seem to have settled down a bit."

Mario laughed and replied. "I told them that we are government agents and if they felt like acting like assholes, I would take them out. Hope that is okay with you, miss?"

Heather looked at Mario and excitedly approved his action.

"I had better go back to them David. Here is my card and home phone number, if you decide you may want some company for dinner while you are still here at the Hilton. I could take you to some nice quiet restaurant in the village where the food is good, and the music is dreamy."

She walked back to the table and sat down with her three cohorts. I turned to Mario and he gave me one of his long looks.

"Hey, Mario, I just happened to see this lovely gal who looked so bored, so I thought I would strike up a conversation with her. Then this asshole jumped at me as I stood at their table and pushed me. What could I have done? Now if you are available tomorrow evening, and are nice to me, I might have a date for you with Madeline."

"David, David. You are a trip. No matter where you go, you meet women. Then we have to come and bail you out. Have you ever thought of settling down after Martha died? I mean, maybe it is about time you found a nice little Jewish girl, or even a nice Catholic or Protestant one, and think about courting her, then marrying the bitch. This way, we wouldn't have to save you from your own women problems. Hey, bartender, give me a Chivas. Thanks."

Mario was always funny, yet a bright, caring sort of guy, who was the best kind of friend to have in the entire world. We grabbed a table and sat down. Mike and Billy came into the room and joined us. We had a few minutes before we had to go back upstairs and go to Harlem, a place that has seen more drug activity than any other place in the city of New York. Mike was his usual quiet self, and Billy was the kind of guy who would venture out and take a dare, anytime.

We went up to the room and already had a message from Cappy to meet him downstairs in the lobby by 8:30. He had two cars that he already rented from Avis, waiting for us and we were to split up into two, three man teams. He wanted me to go with him and Dickie, while Mario, Mike and Billy would be in the other car. He first had to make a quick stop uptown to get some hardware for us. We then had to see this Abduhl Assisi, a leader in the streets of Harlem, who was a drug informant, but also ran the streets with the distribution of drugs and heroin.

This Haitian was a slime ball who got paid by the CIA for divulging information on his brethren, while at the same time, ran a numbers game and a drug distribution network throughout Harlem, the Bronx, Brooklyn, Queens and Statin Island. He also had an office on Sixty Third Street where he would entertain some of the Mafioso people and set them up with women when they came to town. He was dangerous and he was not to be trusted. He also was Chuck's contact for New York City. We drove up to the dark streets of Harlem, where the worst of the 1967 riots were.

We parked in front of the building where Assisi would be and we all got out. Cappy, Mario and I headed into the building. Mike and Billy stayed by the cars, and Dickie entered the building, but stayed downstairs. We took the elevator up to the top floor, and as we walked out of the elevator, there were eight tall, dark guards stationed along the hallway.

The door at the end of the corridor opened, and this tall, burly man stood there, and in his deep voice, blurted out to us.

"I have been expecting you guys. You are right on time. Come into my office, please."

We entered his office, and it was full of cabinets, desks, and lots of pictures decorating the walls of this primitive looking room. We noticed famous movie stars, fighters, race car drivers, athletes, even congressmen. This was the world of Assisi, a character who had known many of these celebrities, and who had shared his products of drugs with many of them. He was a promoter in his own way and had a cadre of customers from all walks of life. He asked us to be seated and continued to speak.

"I know why you are here. I got word from my sources that you are going to take down Manzione and for me that would not be a great loss. He is upsetting my friends in Central America, and the distribution of cocaine and heroin, is becoming a problem for me. I realize that you guys are feds, but I also understand the situation. This is my business, same as what you do is yours. I am willing to work with you and get him out of the racket. But we need certain understandings, and that is if I help you, my business stays intact. I have worked with some of your big shots in Washington for years, and they have left me alone. So before we continue, I want you to know the ground rules, and where I stand right now. You understand?"

Cappy did the talking. He and Assisi agreed to certain terms and conditions and we had a new relationship with this scumbag who had people selling drugs to kids in schools as well as to athletes, and celebrities, all over the country. But, at this point, our job was to take out the cancer, that being Chuck. We would deal with this character some other time.

We sat for an hour, and spoke about the new breed of Mafioso that was coming into play, that may or may not be good for Assisi. After all, he had control of the market, and he did not want to lose that control. We decided to work with him, and in doing so, he gave us the names of people who were destroying his network, groups of vagrants, rebels in the organization, who sought ways to take over Assisi's distribution of the drugs.

We made notes and were about to leave, when Assisi commented.

"Listen, I have had control of this distribution for a long time. We try to keep it on an upper level. If others get control, you will have bad stuff all over the place and people will die from the bad stuff. Whatever we do, we keep it clean and not dangerous. Just take out the people who will put bad stuff on the streets. If you do not, there will be lots of deaths, either from the drugs, or lots of gang wars. You can always contact me later."

We left and went back to the hotel. The next day was spent in the garment district, where we met people who were tied in with the Mafioso. They were being forced to use their trucks, pay their insurance, and to give payoffs as protection, so that their garments would not be stolen, or their warehouses blown up. We needed names, and contacts. The same thing happened in the SoHo district where restaurant owners were forced by these notorious gangs to buy their meats, fish and chickens from certain food suppliers at outrageous prices. The quality was not as good as grade A foods, but more expensive. This was a most educating process for me, as well as the other guys.

After a grueling time, traveling to all parts of the City of Manhattan, it was now dinnertime, and we all decided to have some food at a nice little Italian restaurant uptown. We still had two more days of meeting people. But tonight, we just relaxed with some great pasta, wine and small discussion on what we had experienced last evening and today. After dinner, we headed back to our hotel, and Mario and I went up to our room.

We thought about what we wanted to do during the evening, and that included hitting some nightspots in town. The phone rang. It was Heather. She wanted to know if Mario and I would like to join her and Madeline her roommate, at the Rainbow Room in the NBC Building. I believe that this was the place where Bette Midler started to do her shtick over thirty-five years ago, or was that in the Empire State Building. I was not sure. They had a nice band to dance to and Heather wanted to tell me about what happened at their meeting today with the client. She sounded a bit disappointed with the outcome of the strategy that her Ad agency presented, and how her design work was torn apart by the client.

I told her that Mario and I would join both her and Madeline at nine thirty. We put on some spiffy clothes, as I had a nice purple shirt, tan slacks, and a black blazer. Mario always looked sharp in his custom made, Italian clothes. We hailed a cab and went across town.

Upon entering the yellow cab, I looked over to Mario as he turned to me, with a gleam in his eye. By the look of it, he was ready to be with a woman, and I was ready as well. We had told Cappy that we were going slumming and he didn't care. Just stay out of trouble, he told us. Heck, we were old enough to take care of ourselves. We had also been so busy, and preoccupied with business, that a change in venue, and meeting new women were uppermost in our minds.

Sitting in the back seat, Mario remarked that it didn't matter to him which woman he would up with. He needed a good roll in the hay, and whichever one I decided to stay with, he would be fine with the other. As long as she was willing to go to bed, he didn't care, and neither did I.

Most of the better restaurants in New York indulge in gourmet dining, while you are relaxing over superb wines, soft jazz and sophisticated song stylings. Some restaurants as well as cruise ships, offer festive buffets, star-quality entertainment, and toe-tappin' dance tunes, or even dazzling floorshows. There is more to see in New York City, more to do, and more to experience than anywhere else on the planet.

New York is the Capital of the World in finance, culture, technology, entertainment, fashion, food, and much, much more. It is home to Times Square, Fifth Avenue, the Empire State Building, the Statue of Liberty, Wall Street, Central Park, Rockefeller Center, Harlem, the Brooklyn Bridge, the Bronx Zoo, the Yankees, the Guggenheim Museum, Radio City Music Hall, and the Staten Island Ferry. The Big Apple certainly is the place to visit, but I personally would not want to live there. Now that I am living in a very small town by the ocean called Dana Point, I get this uneasy feeling every time I visit New York. It may be the greatest city in the world, but to me, it was a place that I was born in years ago, and could not wait to get out of. It was all I had known until I decided to see the world.

As we rode in the cab, I still pictured New York City still being a magnet for meeting-goers, with something for everyone. A city of architectural treasures and gorgeous parks, a draw for the high rollers and the budget conscious, for lovers of art and sports, show tunes and Wagner. There are over seventy thousand hotel rooms, unique and impressive event venues, and easy-as-pie access and transportation options.

New York has been the host to the US Open tennis tournament, and where thousands of runners head to in November to take part in the New York Marathon. And of course, there is the Belmont Park Race Track, the final race of the Triple Crown where fortunes were made if a Triple Crown Winner succeeds. And that only happens about every 28 years.

There are more cabs in this city than anywhere else on earth. And about 10% of the cabbies are women. If you don't like a taxi ride, you can always take the subways, north and south, or east and west. The New York City Transit Authority operates one of the largest systems in the world, 6,250 cars, stopping at 500 stations, carrying 4.8 million passengers each day, over 685 miles of track.

Whether you spend the evening at The Rainbow Room or The Starlight Roof at The Waldorf Astoria, you will have a venue unparalleled in comfort, elegance and historic charm, the ideal setting for anyone. People come from all over the world to visit New York, for its arts, attractions, restaurants, nightlife, shopping, sports, theatre and tours.

We passed Madame Tussaud's off 42nd Street, some of the famous opera houses, the theatre district and many other spectacular places of interest, including museums, brownstones, galleries, The Lincoln Center and even the usual homeless on the streets. We saw the prostitutes along the curbs trying to earn some money from the local Johns. The streets were always alive with people, and the air is forever thick with people rushing to get from one place to another, like no other city in the world. You will find just about anything you want in New York.

You want to party? You can find any kind of nightlife you desire in this city. Mario and I may have found ours. We decided to be adventuresome and meet with two strange women and party. Why not! This is New York City!

We arrived at the NBC Building and took the elevator to the Rainbow Room. We saw Heather and Madeline sitting at a small table by the bar. The Rainbow Room was an elegant, yet comfortable place, at the top of this elaborate sky scraper, one which many famous people have visited, where you could feel important, just being there. The view from the top was outstanding.

I approached Heather and saw that her friend was just as beautiful with her long, blond hair, and an incredible smile. The girls got up from their chairs and greeted us, asking if we would be more comfortable at a larger table. They already put their names down for a reservation, just in case. We agreed to that, and just squeezed together, temporarily, at this small table, with them, waiting for the roomy one to be available. We had about a half hour wait.

I looked around the room and saw many people laughing, and could have sworn that I saw David Letterman with a few other men at the bar. What the heck was he doing at NBC, when his show was on CBS? Oh well, he was probably looking to take over the Jay Leno show as he always felt that he was passed by for this gig over ten years ago.

But our ladies looked outstanding. If it were up to Mario and me, we would have foregone the meal, since we had some pasta just a little while ago, and headed to the nearest hotel with them. We were patient men, learning that in the Seals, but we were also horny men, and loved women. We kept our cool and made conversation like gentlemen. Mario kept eyeing Heather and I could tell that he preferred her. That actually worked out perfectly for me, as I was always a sucker for blond hair anyway.

Madeline, or Maddie, as Heather kept referring to her, was a knockout. She was sweet and gentle, and she spoke with a soft poetic tongue, one that I would have liked to have all over me that evening. She laughed a lot, but not loud, and she had a tremendous sense of humor as well. She kept touching my leg, and I thought that this was a good sign. Not simply because we were sitting so close due the sheer fact that the table was unusually small, but I thought that she genuinely like to show affection.

Maddie was not overly assertive, and maintained an aura of mystery as well. This was another trait that I liked in a woman. She had on a typical New York City style tight fitting dress, with bright colors, and although it appeared to be a bit small for her, she held it very well. She was small in stature, at least compared to Heather, who was quite tall, and her makeup appeared to be a bit heavier than

I was used to. After all, in California, women hardly wear makeup because of the sun. But Maddie was definitely a beautiful creature.

Mario and I went up to the bar for a round of drinks, as we had to wait for our table in the restaurant area anyway. Mario and I did have a few words to share in private, away from the women.

"David, my boy, it looks like we hit the mother lode here. I think I am leaning toward Heather. What about you? Is Maddie the kind of woman you could find interesting to be in bed this evening?"

Mario didn't mix words, as he always went to the heart of the matter. In this case, it didn't matter to me. Although I would have liked to talk to Heather, as she did invite us to join with them, I was wondering how she would take this changing of partners. But then again, it was a group of four people, and whatever would materialize, would happen. But knowing Mario, he would get a little drunk right away, so I would have to watch how many drinks he would have. I told him to slow down and just go with the flow, or we would sink before any one of us would be able to sail into the sunset.

"Hey, David, yeah, yeah. What's the difference? We're here and they're here. They are New York chics, and typical New Yorkers don't like to wait for anything."

Mario grabbed the drinks and brought them to the table. And I thought, I was bad? But Mario didn't mince words with anyone. He gave Heather her drink and wanted to stretch his legs on the dance floor.

"Heather, would you like to dance with me. I think they are playing our song."

The music in the background was just audible, and we were able to see two other couples on the small dance floor. He held out his hand for her to take and they both went over by the piano to slow dance. I was now alone with Maddie.

"Your friend, Mario likes Heather, I can tell." Maddie started the conversation, as we both looked over at the dancing couple.

Heather looked back to us and smiled, so I guess that was settled. I was with Maddie, and Mario found his partnership with Heather. In a way, the choice was good. Either way, we were going to have a nice time, hopefully.

Mario had mentioned in our hotel room that he had met with Rita after that night at the lounge when Chuck came by, and that they briefly had sex together at her home. But Rita was not someone he would want to have more than one time. I had agreed with him and we knew from experience never to revisit a place that was spread out too thinly, and Rita was just not one you would want a second visit with. I told him of my ménage d' triple play at my home with Christy and Rita and he told me that I was just a stud in a suit. He laughed at my antics but deep down inside, he was jealous of my associations with all of the women I had met of late.

Looking back at the dance floor, he truly seemed to be enjoying himself with Heather, and after a few dances, they returned to the table. The hostess came by and told us that our dining room table was ready, so we decided to have our dinner.

It was then that Heather told us about the advertising meeting with her boss and the client. It seemed that the campaign was battered down, and the presentation was a flop. Not that her artwork was bad, she felt, but the fact that there was no chemistry between her management team and the client. They were to try another campaign or give up on the idea that their creative ability would be sufficient to win over this company as a client. Heather was somewhat disappointed, but she also felt that the guys whom we had met last night were cocky ad people, who felt that their shit didn't stink. She probably made a wrong choice in agencies, but the money was still good for the time being.

Afterward, we took the elevator back down to the street and Mario and Heather started to hold hands, indicating that they wanted to take a stroll through Central Park West. If we wanted, we would meet up with each other later, as it was still a weeknight, and the two women had to go to work. Plus the fact that Mario and I had our morning planned out already with Cappy and the rest of the guys.

I was not concerned for them, nor was I concerned about being alone with Maddie. We were hitting it off as friends, and that seemed to be as far as we were going to go. We did chat with each other through dinner, as if we had known each other for years, and I was sure that Mario was glad to be out of the restaurant and was able to get away with Heather by themselves. We said our goodbyes, and Maddie and I walked in the other direction.

"So, David, would you like to come by for a night cap. My brownstone is a few blocks from here."

"Sure," I answered. "We can take a cab if you're too tired. Or we can just walk off the food."

"Oh, it's a nice evening for a stroll, David. And I again want to thank you for a lovely dinner. Your friend seems nice and it is good that the two of them hit it off. That's great!"

I told her that the feeling was mutual and that they seemed very eager to get lost in a hurry. But Maddie and I seemed to enjoy each other's company, laughing at the least little thing that came to mind. This was easier than being with Julie, who was always so serious. Yet, I missed the culmination of an evening with Christy, as we always wound up in bed. This was different, as I had not felt this way in a long time. Julie kept creeping into my mind, and I almost called Maddie her name, but corrected myself. The worst thing I could do is to make love to Maddie and call her Julie. That wouldn't go over too well. But I was not sure if we were going to head in that direction.

I tried to focus on Maddie, who was a New York beauty, born and bred in Long Island and went to school at Hunter College, taking graduate courses at Princeton. She was a banker, and had an incredible sense of the moment, plus a great ability to make me feel quite comfortable in her presence. I did not have any reservations about saying or doing anything that might offend her, and I certainly felt at ease for the first time since, I don't know when. I suppose Martha also brought this kind of inner peace to me as well.

We approached her brownstone and sat on the outdoor steps. We both were not ready to go in yet as the night air was cool, with a slight breeze, and there was a lot of activity on the street. People were walking in all directions, couples holding hands, laughing, talking aloud, and there were many cars going by. This was New York. This was a far cry from Dana Point, where they roll up the sidewalks at nine o'clock. It was also nice to come back to the city where I grew up in. I lit up a cigarette and offered one to her. She accepted although she told me that she quit the habit many times.

"I really love it here, David," she said. "I have lived here all of my life, and it was such a blessing to find work in a big bank as I did. Of course, my schooling and experience had helped me get into the front door. I love what I do and have made many good friends in this crazy city. Heather and I met at my bank when we both were looking for apartments. It is so expensive to live here so we decided to share the apartment we now have. She is a wonderful friend. She told me that she met you last night and that you knocked her boss on his ass. Good for you. I hate that little twerp. I met him and he is an arrogant bastard who does not care about anyone else but himself. What do you think of our crazy city?"

"I think it is quite a place. I haven't been here for over twenty years and there just wasn't any reason for me to come back here. I really like California because it is a more relaxed place, close to the ocean, with lots of sunshine, good golf weather all year 'round, same for tennis as well. I do feel a little out of place here, but it is truly a good place to visit and have fun. Great restaurants, and terrific Broadway shows, that we do not have in abundance in southern California."

Just then, my cell phone went off. I looked at the number, and it was Cappy. I knew that because of the hour, it must have been important, and I also knew that my evening with Maddie was coming to a close.

Mario was probably getting the same call, if I knew Cappy. I opened the cell phone and Cappy told me to get back to the hotel immediately. I told Maddie that business was calling and that I would call her before I would leave for California. We hugged and exchanged numbers, and I hailed the first taxi coming down the street. I told the driver to hustle back to the hotel and was hoping that Mario would be there as well, and did not turn his cell phone off while trying to seduce Heather.

I went directly to Cappy's room and there was Dickie, Mike and Billy. Mario was right behind me. Too bad he was not able to score, but business before pleasure. Cappy told us that when Chuck was in Columbia and shot up some of the members of the Drug Cartel, this caused a big furor. Now, the cartel was going after Chuck and the mafia. There would be a large gang war, not only in Columbia, but also in Peru and Ecuador, and it would move into the United States. Our new friend from Harlem, Assisi also called Cappy and told him that his people were going to be in a fight for their lives and needed our help. We jumped into two cars and headed toward Harlem to meet with Assisi. He laid out the situation.

"Listen up guys." Assisi laid out the scenario to us. "Manzione did something wrong and the Columbians are going to make him pay for killing those guys at the meeting he had. Then he goes off to Peru and threatens more of the cartel. This guy is poison, and the more he aggravates these people, the more wars we are going to have. I also found out that he knows about what happened to his people at his estate. It seems that there was a big gun battle and all of his men were killed. Do you know anything about that little episode?"

We just sat there, not saying a word.

"There is something else." He continued. "One of my people told me that there is a girl, perhaps two, who may be in danger. One was supposed to be his new bride who got mixed up with some character, and she disappeared. Manzione now has his people looking for her. The other is an attorney who works for the law firm that was supposed to represent him. I have my people on the inside so that we know what is happening. This is getting to be a big problem, and I am afraid that we will be having so much bad stuff brought into the U.S. that will affect the lives of many people. I realize that I am in distribution, but I do not want to sell any of that stuff that will kill people. You understand?"

As I listened to Assisi about the part of the supposedly new bride being with some character, I turned to Mario and he winked at me. When he mentioned the part about an attorney, he was referring to Julie, or perhaps, one of the attorneys at Julie's firm. I didn't like the fact that Chuck was still trying to find Christy and Julie. They were too innocent and would be harmed by Chuck and his people.

Cappy was getting uneasy with this and told us that we had better get back to California soon. We would change our plans and leave tomorrow, late afternoon, or early evening, after our meeting in the garment center. We needed to get to meet some of the Mafia leaders who ran the trucks and tell them to lay off the merchants or we would come down on them. This would only make matters worse and we had to move quickly.

We listened to Assisi tell us that his network of people were all over the city of New York, and now they would be threatened by the Mafia and the drug cartel. After all, he got his drugs from the cartel, and that Manzione handled the distribution from the cartel to Assisi. There were too many organizations involved, and everyone wanted more and more, until the price of drugs would hit the roof, or the drugs would dry up and only the bad stuff would be on the market.

He was willing to keep us in the loop as this was his bread and butter. By assisting him, we would know what was happening in all of the hot spots. Manzione was ready to go to war and he was dragging the other mafia families into a position that was not conducive to them. Something had to happen, and quickly. The key was to take Manzione out as quickly as possible.

"Listen, I have a business." Assisi continued to dwell on his profession and how this was his way of making lots of money. "I do not want to lose it. If the bad stuff goes on the street, you will lose innocent lives, because I will not have control of that. The Columbians want to have their own distributors and I will be cut out. I need you guys to get them, or all hell will break loose. No one will win, and there will be people dying all over."

We listened to what he had to say. We knew what we had to do. Cappy had to pass this information on to the DEA, and we needed a larger force of men to go after the syndicate here in New York and other cities. We still had the possibility to get more of those Seals from San Diego, but that would not be enough. We had to block the airports, the rails, and watch the borders, as we may very well have an influx of Central and South Americans, the size of a battalion, coming into California or flying to the east coast.

The families were also going to gear up for combat, and there would be lots of killing all over the place. We needed to step in and stop this at the beginning. I could understand what Assisi was concerned about. If he lost the distribution, all of the drugs coming in would be bad, and a lot of people could die. This was not good, and although we didn't like the idea of Assisi running a distribution center for drugs, at least we knew who he was and that he would not jeopardize the lives of innocent people. After all, anyone can get drugs if they wanted to. But if the quality turned to shit, then these people would be endangering themselves. It was six of one, half a dozen of another. We needed to make sure that no one would be endangered.

What would happen if the wrong drugs got to the hospitals, where doctors give their patients certain drugs before surgery? Anything was possible, and we needed to stop this before it started. This was a major problem facing us. Of course, the best thing was to eliminate drugs entirely. But no matter how hard the government would try, they could never succeed. Realistically, the best thing was to keep a handle on the problem and watch it closely.

After we returned to the hotel, I quickly ran to my room and called Julie. Realizing that it was late, I wanted to make sure that she would be okay. The phone rang and there was no answer. I called Suzie's house, and she answered.

"David, is that you? Yeah, we're okay. Christy was worried about you. No…she is sleeping in another room. What? Okay, okay, I will check. (Minutes ticked by). David, she is fine. No, she has not left the house all day. You want me to try to contact Julie first thing in the morning? Sure. I will do that. You want me to check on her office as well? What is going on, David? Okay, I don't ask. I understand. I will make sure we stay indoors and lock all doors and windows. Yeah, sure, I will contact you if something is wrong. Goodnight."

Suzie hung up and I was nervous about not locating Julie. I paced the floor, and then went downstairs to the lounge to think about my responsibility to both girls. Did I fail? Was I going to lose any of them? Mario decided to visit Mike and Billy at their room since I left to go to the bar. Mario knew that I needed some space and wanted to be alone. I thought about all of the possibilities and what might happen if I was not there to help the girls. I asked the bartender for some wine.

"Can I buy you a glass, Sir?" I looked up and it was Heather.

Of all times, this was not a good time to be with her right now. Heck, it was after one in the morning. What was she doing out so late? But I just acknowledged her presence and let her speak.

"David, I heard that you and Mario had to get back to a meeting. I couldn't sleep and needed to talk to you. You were a perfect gentleman being with Maddie. I really wanted to spend the evening with you, but Mario kept on pursuing me and I did not want to say NO to him. He is nice, David, and he is your friend. But I wanted to spend time with you. I was hoping you would be here and decided to come on over."

"Heather," I commented. "This is really not a good time. We have some problems that we have to take care of. Secondly, the kind of work we do is not something you want to get involved with. I hope you understand."

"David, Mario got a bit drunk and told me that you guys are Navy Seals and are on a mission of mercy. That sounded exciting and I am not afraid. I wonder if we could talk as I am also thinking of leaving the ad agency and finding something else for myself. Do you guys have an opening for a creative type person?"

She then laughed at the prospect of working with us, as she was truly a fine looking gal. But her place was in an art department, not on a battlefield.

Maybe this gal wanted to go to bed with me and get her frustrations out by making love. Maybe it was something that I wanted as well. I excused myself and went to the desk to see if there was any available room. There was no way I would bring her to my room, with Mario in the next bed. The desk clerk indicated that there was one room, a junior suite, and it was $450. for the night. I told Heather and she agreed. I paid for the room and Heather and I headed to our own little sanctuary.

It was a nice room with a king size bed, a bit larger than the room I was sharing with Mario. I took Heather around and gave her a big kiss on her cheek. She wrapped her long legs around me and told me that we would not divulge this to anyone, not to Mario, or to Maddie. This would be our secret.

I then reached for her buttons on her blouse and opened each one, gently not to tear her blouse. I then felt her hand moving along my legs and inside, touching my penis and finding the zipper, then moving up to the top and unhooking the slacks. I managed to take off her blouse and she revealed her full breasts to me, while unhooking her bra. I then took my shoes off and then my pants. We got on the bed and she unhooked her skirt and threw it on the floor.

I moved on top of her, feeling her body with my hands, and she had a tall frame, with the longest legs I had ever seen. She seemed to enjoy making love to me and I had forgotten why I had gone down to the lounge in the first place. I liked the way she moved herself, this mid western girl who had the body of a model, but hot and delicious. It was a wonderful experience for me.

As we were reaching our climax, I leaned into her face, put my tongue on hers, and felt my sweat come pouring over her body. I needed this change and it felt great. As I felt myself in her and hit my highest level, I called out to her. She gave me a pert little smile and asked me, ever so gingerly, "David, who is Julie?"

I couldn't believe that I had done that. I knew she said it with slight mockery in her voice, and yet, I was totally embarrassed. There was nothing I could say to take it back, but I had to tell her something. We just had an incredibly passionate moment, and though my mind and body felt sensational, I was obviously obsessed with Julie, and had to spoil it. The fact that I had mentioned her name just as I was climaxing with Heather, sort of put me in a predicament.

"Hey, I am truly sorry, Heather. It just slipped."

"Is she your wife, David?" she asked as she looked at me with her soft blue eyes.

Although I could tell that she was curious as to whom Julie was, I didn't know how troubled she was by it. I had just met this woman last night, and if it didn't matter to me at all, I could have easily made something up, and she might have believed it. But the problem was that I didn't know how much it also mattered to me. I knew this would happen. I just couldn't control my feelings.

"No, Heather. She is someone I happen to know in California. I have been involved with Julie on a professional level, nothing sexual mind you, and I have been so preoccupied with business lately, that I have had a hard time finding time for any pleasure. I guess I was thinking about her as her life is in danger right now."

Accepting my response, Heather rubbed my torso, which led her fingers toward my balls, and I could only imagine what New York women were like these days. I assumed, once was never enough. They would want more of the same if they enjoyed it. And this babe seemed to enjoy our playtime. I had several minutes of rest before I was ready for round two. When she realized that I was ready to go at it once more, she simply held her hand in place and waited for me to react.

"I know how hard you can be David, and I am sure that I can help you find it again." She was a real trooper.

We laughed and the moment of embarrassment had passed. But I still felt like a jerk. I did not know if this was going to be the first and last time I would have with Heather, so I made it a point to focus on her and relieve myself from any guilt that I might have felt for my mistake. I went down on her and she tasted lovely. While I was there, I could only imagine what she might be thinking. I tried my best to make her feel, not only good, but also important to me, and forget what I had said earlier. We were getting hot again, and I loved the way she moved those long legs around my body.

Twenty more minutes had passed and she finally pushed me back, up to her face. And while she was holding me to her lips, she whispered those incredible words that guys usually hear at the end of the rainbow.

"David, that was incredible. But, all things have to come to an end, as I have to get more sleep and be ready for my job, early in the morning. If you don't mind, I would like to pay you back for the room, I do have an early appointment in the morning and it is getting very late. Or should I say, it is nearly three in the morning."

I was not sure if that was a brush off, as that one slip of the tongue may have changed her feelings at this point. I did not choose to argue or ask her to stay longer, and I knew that I had to go to my own room. We both got up to dress and unfortunately, we never made it to round two. She simply watched me put my clothes back on, and we got our things together to leave. She then turned to me to speak.

"David, if you have some time tomorrow, you can call me and perhaps we can meet for lunch. If you don't have any time, I would understand. Just leave me your address so I can mail a check to you for the room."

I looked at her and was taken back by her comment, and responded.

"No, don't be silly. It was my pleasure."

She was persistent, that little lightening rod who had just juggled my nuts and gave me relief and pleasure.

"No, David. I insist. This was not a paid 'Fuck'. I insist that I pay you for the room."

I let it go, and gave her my P.O. Box Number in Dana Point. Hey, if the bitch wants to pay me for the room, let her. I also gave her my cell phone number and thanked her for joining with me. I just didn't know what else to say. Maybe, that is how they do it in the Midwest. I knew that I screwed up by mentioning Julie's name and was not sure what else I could say or do at that moment.

When I got back to the room that I shared with Mario, he was sound asleep. As quietly as I tried to be, I accidentally dropped my pants on the floor and the buckle hit the corner of the night table. This startled Mario and he opened his eyes.

"Hey bud, did you have fun this evening, or what?"

"Sorry, I didn't mean to wake you," I answered.

"Hey, that's okay," he said. "I was in and out so any little noise would have gotten me up. So, did you land Maddie tonight?"

I didn't have the heart to tell Mario that I was with Heather.

"Yeah, I landed her all right. But I screwed up by mentioning Julie's name right in the middle of fucking her."

Mario just burst out laughing and tears started to roll down his face.

"Geez, what the hell…you can't even keep your women straight. What is it with you? Can't you block out one woman when you are fucking another?"

With that, Mario rolled over and went to sleep. I felt that it was okay not to tell him that I was with Heather. Why hurt his feelings although Mario would not have cared. Everything is circumstantial and whatever happened, happened. I was sure he would have understood. But the way it seemed, we would probably never see these women again, anyway.

I pulled the covers up over my head and knew that I had made a stupid mistake by mentioning Julie's name, but it was done. Although Heather sounded like she didn't mind, I knew that we would probably never see each other again. Still in all, I also felt that it was not the thing to do with anyone, and even in New York, where all of the women are hot and horny, and would go to bed with strangers. They still had their own scruples, one way or another. When I would get home, I would contact her and thank her for the lovely evening. What else could happen, being over three thousand miles away?

The next day, we all went to the garment center to meet with some of the mafia people who controlled the trucking business for the manufacturers who made the apparel for the department stores. We told them of the coming wars with the drug lords from Columbia, Panama, Peru and Ecuador, plus the matter with Manzione. It seemed like they knew what was going to materialize and they were pissed at Chuck for starting a global war that would implicate them.

Although they would have loved to see him gone from the families, there was this 'blood' thing that would not cause them to move against Chuck. They would also lay off the merchants and not force them to use their trucks, as we told them that we would also make it difficult for them if they persisted to antagonize the merchants. They would also notify the rest of the families about trying to work with Assisi's organization and try to prevent any war with the Central Americans. This would only put more pressure on the families and with the government cracking down on drugs and the numbers. They needed to conduct their business as a business, not as a street gang.

The people we saw were all gentlemen and they recognized that fact that we could be on their side if they would work with us. We had some lunch at Giordano's on 39th and ninth, right in the middle of Hell's Kitchen. The food was northern cuisine and was one of the best Italian restaurants in Manhattan. We sat on the inside patio and I enjoyed the meal. We then left to go to the SoHo district once again, followed by our last visit that was up in the diamond district.

Back at the hotel, Cappy called Assisi, and if nothing was brewing yet, he told him that we were on our way back to California.

I thought about Christy and the more I thought about our relationship, the more that I felt that this situation needed some closure as well. Her obsession with me had to stop, one way or another, even if I had to stop it myself. I could not have that looming over my head if I were to proceed with my relationship with her close friend, Julie. When I called Suzie's place, she sounded worried as Christy was having a hard time not being able to leave the house, and not hearing from me. She also told me that she was not able to reach Julie. Maybe Julie was too busy at work, or she just didn't want to be bothered.

We had an early evening flight out and we sat at the airport discussing all of the people we had met. Dickie stayed on as he had things to do at the New York Times and wanted to check all of their back issues for other information. It seemed that I had so much on my plate, that it was becoming a bit suffocating. My experiences up to this point were somewhat energizing and stimulating to say the least, and I had thought about what had happened to my simple life. I felt that I was losing myself to the outer world by taking care of everyone else, except myself.

Sure, sex with beautiful women was great, but that could become old hat, and in the long run, I would wind up with nothing and no one. I realized that I was becoming a horny bastard, by hooking up with Christy, having sex with Rita, trying to get into the pants of Julie, winding up with a tall Heather, and I was getting, not only sore, but doggone tired. If it weren't for Christy, I might not have found my life in this intriguing mess with the mob, with Assisi's network of pimps and runners, and with the drug cartel, the Mafia families, and Chuck's insanity.

But then, I would not have tied in with Cappy and the guys again, as I realized that I had missed all of this in twenty years. Now I had to go to New York, wound up with a lovely gal in my bed once again, mentioning some other woman's name, while having sex with this wonderful young lady. God, just when I was prepared to go back to teaching, my life seemed to be turning around and getting much too complicated for me. Perhaps I was just filling time until I truly found what I wanted for myself. We finally boarded the plane for that six-hour flight back to Los Angeles.

Cappy was on the phone with Moose. It seemed that the State Department was preparing to send our CIA and DEA operatives to Central America to wipe out the drug cartel. Moose recommended that we might consider going, but Cappy indicated that we had bigger fish to fry here California and New York. The borders were going to have four times as many agents to keep out those who would try to cross into Mexico, Arizona and Texas. It seemed that the President was a bit lax in tightening up the borders for obvious reasons. There were people associated with the White House that wanted catastrophes to occur so it would give the President more opportunities to charge into more wars. He was acting like 'Alexander the Great' and wanted to conquer the world so he would be the fearless leader his father was not.

Changes in personnel were taking place at the CIA and the FBI because the agents knew too much about what was going on and the president needed to put in people who would not question his authority. Even the State Department was going through an overhaul and people wanted out before they could become involved and would go down based on the domino theory. We heard about people quitting and getting fired. Many Senators and those in the House of Representatives were putting in for early retirement and moving to other locations with their wives and families.

The FBI was cracking down on the Mafia families, from New England, especially in Rhode Island, and in New York, Chicago, California, and other states across the nation. The Congress was moving toward the approval of the budget to support the crackdown on all of these activities, and the White House was preparing to make a speech to the nation on the possible wars between all of the factions. Everyone was trying to cover his ass as the 'shit was about to hit the fan'.

Sean was already getting ready to prosecute Manzione in the next two weeks, if and when we were able to capture him and take him into custody. Julie's law firm was expected to recommend to Manzione to take a plea and go to jail. All of the pieces were beginning to fall into place. There was still the matter of many possible wars between the Mafia, the drug cartel and other factions that could pop up at any time.

Cappy was organizing additional Seals from San Diego and Annapolis so we could have reinforcements whenever they were needed. In the meantime, I had to go home and find out what happened to Julie. A lot of things were going down, and it was only a matter of time before I was to be put into the thick of all of it. Maybe I was getting too old for this. Maybe we all were, but we tried not to show our age.

Cappy and Moose were the oldest, while Dickie followed, then Mario and me. Sean was in the same age bracket as Mike and Billy. We all seemed to work as a good team together, but age was showing and this was probably the last assignment for all of us. I thought about what I wanted to do after all of this was over. Did I really want to go back to teaching, find a woman to marry, and maybe have some kids before I got too old and fat to be any kind of parent?

By ten o'clock, California time, I was home and started to put my clothes away. I threw some things in the washer, made a drink for myself and reached for the phone to call Julie. Again, there was no answer. I decided to hop in the car and head out to her home. I knocked several times but no one came to the door. I walked to the back of the house and climbed over her gate. I then found a window that I was able to open and crawled in over the windowsill. The house was dark and without putting on any lights, I tried to remember the layout from my visit with Julie a few days ago.

I went into her bedroom and her bed was made. Her clothes were intact in her closets, and there was nothing on the stove. All of her dishes were put away, but then again, Julie was a 'neat nick' and hated disarray of any kind. There was no sign of any struggle and it all seemed so peaceful. I sat down on her sofa in the living room, and waited for a few minutes, hoping that she would walk through the door. It was getting late and I was a bit worried. But, then again, Julie was a big girl, and if she had other plans, that was her choosing. I would have liked to have a relationship with her, but it took two to tango.

Julie was probably keeping a low key and chose not to talk to anyone until all of this would blow over. After all, her law firm was going to defend Chuck, even though they wanted him to take a plea. I was sure that they were working on all sorts of opening and closing statements for the courtroom. I checked my watch and it was almost midnight. I started to get up to leave, when the front door opened. I hid behind the drape so I would not be seen. If it was Julie, and she was safe, I would leave the same way I came in, through the window. She would never know that I was there and perhaps, that would be best.

I saw this figure coming toward the living room, and still no light. Was it Julie, or was it someone looking for Julie? Just then, another figure came into the hallway from the front door. Now there were two people in the house. I was a bit anxious and curious as to what was going on here. Were there two of Chuck's men, looking for Julie? Were one of the shadowy figures Julie and the other Christy? I was so anxious, that I had to pee, but there was no the time for it. Anytime you want to hide, and stand perfectly still, somehow, your bodily functions tell you that you are ready to take a pee.

Suddenly, the light went on. One figure was Julie. The other figure was a man I did not recognize. They walked into the kitchen and I tried to listen in on their conversation, but it was faint. I moved closer to the kitchen, still staying low. A voice called out.

"Julie, where do you keep the coffee? Do you have any cream and sugar?"

I recognized Julie's voice, responding to the question.

"Ted, it is in the cupboard above the sink. Help yourself. I am going upstairs for a moment then I will be right down. Take the coffee into the den and wait for me."

Julie went upstairs and I tried to get a glimpse of the man who was in the kitchen. He seemed a bit tipsy, as he was trying to stand up straight, but had to hold on to the counter for support. No wonder he needed some coffee. Who was Ted? Was this her new interest? Were they both out drinking tonight and now it was time to have sex? I thought of just waiting it out and maybe I would have all of my answers very soon.

After a few minutes, Julie came down and I saw that she was wearing a white sweater and shorts. She had walked into the den where Ted was waiting for her, and remarked.

"Julie, you look like a million dollars. I am glad we were able to get together this evening. Here, I made a cup of coffee for you too. Let's sit down and talk."

Julie took the cup and sat down in her favorite chair. This guy, Ted sat on another chair and they started to converse.

"Ted, it's not that I am involved with anyone right now, but during dinner, you asked me if I had any interests with a man. I appreciate your asking and since we work at the same law firm, I really do not want us to be an item for now. There is too much going on and I am going through many things in my life right now. I hope you understand."

Ted replied. "Well, Julie, I realize that you had a relationship with one of our former partners before, but I always had my eyes on you since you joined the firm. I can really make things work out for you, and for us. We are doing well and I would like you to consider taking on more responsibilities. The firm could use a woman partner, as it would help the firm in so many different areas. Would you be interested in that?"

"Of course, I would," Julie answered. "And I do hope that it would be given to me without any loopholes or anything more than what I would do to benefit the entire law firm, not just you."

Julie was intelligent and did not want to fall into any trap with this Ted person. Obviously, he was a partner who would elevate Julie as a partner, but he also had other motives in mind. Julie wanted to earn the respect of the firm, not give up her body to this asshole who may have just wanted to bed her down and get a piece of ass from her. Heck, that is what I wanted. So far I had not succeeded. If I had my druthers, neither would he.

Ted got up from his chair and walked over to Julie. He went behind her and continued talking.

"A partnership would mean more money, a greater bonus, and you can take on your own cases and work them as you like. Your bonus from any one case would be a greater percentage than what you are earning now, and I am sure that you would make out really well. Not because you are a good lawyer, but because you would give a woman's touch to so many of our clients".

With that, Ted leaned over Julie and put his hands under her chin, kissing her on the forehead. I could not see Julie's expression, but I could hear her plea.

"Ted, please, I would rather not."

He then took his hands and moved them down the front of her chest, cupping her breasts and trying to bring her up from the chair. Julie seemed uncomfortable and immediately commented by crying out.

"Ted, please do not do that. I do not want you to touch me. This was supposed to be a professional meeting, not a sexual interlude. I think you ought to leave."

With his strength, Ted grabbed Julie and took her up from the chair and started to kiss her, bringing her body closer to his. From where I was standing, Julie seemed to be trying to move away from him, but he was too strong for her. Ted started to put his hands under her sweater, and then moved them under her shorts. Julie started to jerk backward and raised her voice. At this point, I had seen enough. I jumped into the room and grabbed Ted from behind and used my forearm to get him into a headlock, while to Julie's amazement, who was shocked at my appearance, I pushed Ted to the front door and opened it.

"Ted, if you ever try this again, I will personally kill you." With that, I threw the 'cock sucker' out into the street.

"Where the hell did you come from, David? I thought you were still in New York. And what the hell are you doing in my house? Do you realize that you are trespassing and I have the right to call the cops and put you in jail......"

Interrupting her, I took her around and gave her a big hug. She did not move. I apologized for my behavior and told her how I tried calling her from New York but got no answer. I told her how I asked Suzie to call her, but she too, received no response. I was worried, I said, so I went into the house by an open window, thinking that something was wrong here.

Julie was so frightened by my appearance, that she could not leave my arms. She stood there shaking, as if by chance, I came by on my shiny, white horse, and rescued her from being molested by one of her bosses. At first she asked me, how I could do this to her, by spying on her from another room. But then she quieted down, and realized that I only did that because I was worried about her, and that my presence probably put a damper on her getting any new position in her law firm.

"David, I don't care about the partnership deal. This Ted is a good lawyer, and he is also married. He just wanted to spend the night with me. I saw it coming for a few days, and especially at dinner. He is harmless, but he had his motives. I would not have slept with him, not for a full partnership in my firm. But, I do appreciate your coming to my rescue. You dear boy, you really care about me, don't you."

I told Julie about my trip to New York and what was happening in Central America, about the characters we met, Assisi, and the families of the Mafia. She poured a glass of wine for me, and one for herself. We went into the den and sat on the sofa and I remarked how lovely she was. She told me that I looked tired and probably needed some sleep.

"David, my feelings have not changed toward you. I still care for you, and I would not want to have sex with anyone right now, especially that stupid moron who would have tried to take me to bed, if I let him. I am grateful for your concern and glad that you had a nice trip to New York. I am sorry that I did not respond to anyone, but I have been busy, and I just didn't want to pick up the phone, thinking that it might be one of Chuck's goons. Thanks for thinking of me, you big goof."

We laughed and just stared at each other.

"Tell me, David. Did you behave while you were in New York?"

I sat back and wondered how much I really wanted to share with her, any part of my trip to New York. Behave? Now that is relative, depending on how you look at it. I told her that I was a good boy, at least in my eyes anyway. I had not implied anything but the truth to Julie.

But I chose not to mention the fact that I might have made a slight error and mentioned her name to a stranger while I was having sex with her. Thinking about it, in looking back at the situation, I believed that I was pretty darn good, if I have to say so myself.

Julie pressed me and asked me again.

"C'mon, David, you can tell me. I'm a big girl. I can take it."

She took another sip of her wine but I did notice that it was getting very late. I refrained from mentioning how late, as she too probably had to get to sleep and be at work early, as she always had done. So I just told her that I was as good as I always was, as nothing mattered to me more than putting this fiasco to bed. I was bored with her questions, and the fact that I had sex with someone else while she was trying to make up her mind about us and what she wanted to do.

I was thinking ahead and truly wanted my own life back. I knew that I wanted to be with someone who was able to give me less drama, and one whom I did not feel that I had to save again and again. I just did not want to call on my friends again to save any more women. Heck, they would have just questioned my ability to take care of my own, personal business.

I was having a blast revisiting with Cappy, and Mario, and the others, but this was only temporary. I knew that my life had to return to some kind of normalcy soon. I had my own obligations and prior commitments, my teaching for one, and my hobbies, which I had missed. Going golfing with my old buddies used to be something that I looked forward to doing on weekends. Now, I didn't have any idea where my life was going.

As I sat there and looked at this beautiful woman, a real bombshell, I knew that I had to clear up the feelings that I had for her. I could not return to my old life with this hanging over my head. I also knew that she was a challenge, and if I took a few more weeks, I probably would be able to handle it. But after that, I was sure that I would have to step back and find someone whom I would be able to get closer to.

Julie was not easy to get close to. She had her own reasons and I felt that, at times, it took a lot of work. That was something that I was not used to, as my relationships with others were simple and easy. I was never uncomfortable with Martha, although I never had the same passion for Martha as I had with these new women in my life. But what I did have with Martha was stability and I always knew where I stood. This new life of mine sure had its perks, but each and every woman was a challenge to me at times. Did I really want this kind of challenge in my life right now?

I reached over and took Julie's hand and looked into her eyes.

"Sweetheart, I have to tell you that I have not felt this way for anyone else as I do for you. I do believe that I know where you are in your life, but I want you to know that I would be willing to wait for you to decide if I will fit into your life. I just find you so beautiful and the fact that I am not interested in continuing this running around, from place to place, a habit of mine. What I mean to say is, being with my Seal buddies and going from place to place as we have been doing. This all came about because of our friend, Christy, someone who I also care about, but not in the same manner as I care for you. Christy is not someone I would choose to marry. She is a lovely girl, and yes, we have had some fun. But she isn't the woman I am looking to spend the rest of my life with. I was hoping that you and I could form a relationship."

I could not believe that I was opening up to Julie. Nor could I believe that I was spilling my guts out and taking the risk of losing her all together. I knew at that point that I had nothing to lose anyway. She did not say anything for a few minutes, but when she spoke, I had my answer. She did have feelings for me and I suppose she just needed time to sort it out.

Driving home that night, I realized how doggone tired I was. I had hoped that I would make it home without falling asleep at the wheel but I still had the memory of her lips on mine. I thought back right before I left, how she leaned into me and kissed me right before she told me that she loved me too. I could have fainted, but instead, I told her that I needed to go home and get some sleep.

If I were going to convince Julie that she was the one I wanted, I would have to wait for her to make the move. As much as I wanted to go to bed with her, I could not risk losing her by my being assertive with her, especially when I was so tired. My body would not have reacted to her making love to me, and this would have turned out to be a disaster. She liked to be in control and take the lead. If it meant waiting for her to start, I probably would have. I smiled to myself as I hit the driveway, and watched my garage door open.

As I moved the car forward, I found a note taped to the door leading into the den. I could not have imagined how anyone had gotten in. It read: 'If you know what is good for you, you will stay away from her'.

I took the note inside, just as the phone started to ring. Who would be calling me this late at night? It was Julie.

"Hi David. I just wanted to make sure that you got home okay. You seemed so tired when you left a few minutes ago."

My heart started to pump and I knew that this was a good sign, and that she cared enough to find out if I happened to fall asleep at the wheel at two in the morning.

"Hi sweetie," I responded. "Yep, I made it in one piece."

She told me that she would talk with me later on in the day but had to hit the sack, wished me sweet dreams and was too tired to talk any further. But, knowing me, Julie would be on my mind all night. I reached for the note that I found and decided what I wanted to do with it. It was probably from Ted who I saw at Julie's house, and who tried to take advantage of her. If he wanted to play a game with me, I would truly like the challenge. But how did he know where I lived and how did he get into my garage? This made me curious, but sleep was what I needed at that time.

Late in the morning, I sat in my car outside of Julie's office building. I dialed her up on my cell phone and told her that I had to see her, regarding the note that I had found. She made it down to the parking lot and read the note in my car. She too was a bit startled by the fact that I had found it on the inside door of the garage. And the puzzling thing was, how did he know where I lived and how did he get inside. I told her that I was curious and I needed a few answers.

Julie went back into the building and I waited in my car, in hopes that Ted would be coming out of the building. Julie told me that he drove a dark gray Benz. I searched the lot until I found his car, and waited for him to appear. At about one thirty, I saw Ted coming out of the building and head toward his car. I waited until he opened the door on the driver's side, then pushed him into the car and took his keys. I decided that it was time that Ted became aware of whom I really was.

"What the hell do you think you are doing?" he asked as I pushed him into the passenger seat of his car.

I then sat in the driver's seat, started the car, and drove it to a side street under some trees.

"Ted, I found this note inside my garage, pinned to the door leading to my den. Are you going to tell me how you got in and put the note on the door, or am I going to blow your fucking brains all over your nice leather seats?"

Ted was cocky and thought that I was just a hood, looking to screw his associate, Julie. He started to smile at me but when I produced my PPK gun into his face, he turned slightly chalky, and his smile turned a bit downward.

"Ted, I am not going to ask you again," I said. "If I do not get a straight answer from you, you are going to be like toast in an oven."

Ted looked at the gun, then at me. If he thought that I was kidding, he should have noticed that I had cocked the pistol and was ready to pull back on the trigger. He suddenly broke out in a sweat and knew that I was not fucking around. I again gave him an opportunity to tell me what he was doing at my home last night, and how he knew where I lived.

"Look, David, I was always trying to hit upon Julie and I felt that she was vulnerable enough to let me take her to bed. I didn't realize that you were seeing her. I left her house last night and made a phone call, and found out where you lived."

"Who did you call and why leave such a threatening note for me?" I asked him.

"Hey, I'm a married man with kids, I am also one of the partners in the firm. Manzione was paying me off to take care of certain things for him and I never told the other partners. He told me to get close to Julie and offer her a raise and a new position or he would have destroyed me, and my family. I took her out last night for dinner and just wanted to get her to have sex with me, that's all.

"When you showed up, and I left, I called Manzione on his cell and he told me where you lived. He told me to leave a note for you and scare you. I climbed over the back gate and found the kitchen door open. You probably had some company before, and the door was unlocked and the window was broken. I left the note on your den door in the garage, and left the same way I came in. My family is being threatened. I had no choice. I could be killed by Manzione."

He led me to believe that Chuck was back in town. That meant that Julie was not safe, nor was Christy. We sat in his car and he told me that Manzione would kill anyone who would get in his way. He threatened Ted into believing that his family would not be safe if he did not play ball with Chuck. I told him that some day soon, all of this would be resolved, but he was not to bother with Julie again. Ted understood, and at the sight of my gun in his face, knew that I would kill him myself. Now he had two people to contend with, Chuck and me. I think he got the message and he realized that he could not afford to screw around with me because Julie was my friend. With Chuck, he could lie a little, and not have to face him daily. The picture was clear to him as he saw me put the gun back into my shoulder holster.

We drove back to his office and I got out. Ted went on his way, saying that he was going home to have lunch with his wife. He was concerned for her safety and I could understand his feelings. He also had a better understanding that if he didn't play ball with me, his wife and his family may still be without a husband and father. I accepted his answers and went upstairs to see Julie. I told her what had just transpired and that it may not be safe for her as long as Chuck is in town. I asked her if she wanted a bodyguard at her home as she had before. Julie was cool through all of this and she was going to be on guard. I left her and called Christy.

"Hello, this is Suzie." Once again, I heard that sweet, innocent voice at the other end of the phone. "David, how nice of you to call. And how the heck are you?"

Suzie was always giggling. She had a great disposition and she also was good at taking care of Christy. It seemed that they were okay for the moment and that Chuck had no idea where Suzie lived, so I let it go. I did not speak to Christy as I told Suzie that I had to run, but would get back to her later.

I then called Cappy and told him of the incident. He told me that Sean was going to meet with the prosecutor and that they were preparing the allegations against Chuck. They were also going to court for an appearance date for Chuck as they gathered mounds of evidence against the Mafia leader. He also indicated that things were heating up once again as the drug cartel managed to get to New York and to California. The Mafia families were gearing up for a big battle. Chuck had his organized crime team ready to strike Assisi, and the Columbians, as they expected a lot of trouble in the next day or two. If Chuck would be killed, that would save a trial in Court. If he survived, he would be facing many years in the hoosegow and that would be just fine with me as well.

I was getting impatient and decided to call Mario and perhaps the two of us would go on over to Chuck's estate and see what was going on. Stan and Paco were still monitoring the house and all of the information was being fed back to Cappy. There was going to be a big 'powwow' there, the next evening, and I wanted to be there as well. It was time to get rid of this cancer and get all of our lives back to normal. I went home and waited to hear from Cappy and Mario.

The phone rang. It was none other than Heather. Her job at the advertising firm was not working out. The agency lost the big account and Heather was given two weeks notice. She wanted to come to California. I told her that I was busy for the next couple of weeks but she was persistent. I asked her about her friend, Madeline and they too had some words. It seemed that Madeline had this crush on me, but Heather did not tell her that we had sex or Madeline would have become totally pissed. I told Heather to patch things up with Madeline for a while any way, at least until I had time to spend with her if she chose to come to California. I just could not handle any more women at this point.

After talking for a while, I hung up and looked at my watch. Mario was on his way and we would then go to Pacific Palisades to watch what was happening at Chuck's house. The phone rang and thinking it was Mario, I said, "Hey, I am ready. Are you outside? I will be right there."

But it was not Mario.

"David, I am not outside, but I wish I were. How are you doing?"

This time it was Madeline. She told me about Heather losing her job, and she had missed our little fireside chat. She sounded like she cared about me but she had no idea that Heather had called me, or that Heather and I made love that same night I was with Madeline. This turn of events was getting to me. I could not keep up with the players, and the scorecard was getting filled up with lots of hits and misses. But our conversation went well, until I heard a click on the phone. This time it was really Mario. I told Madeline that I had to run, and went outside, jumped into Mario's car and we took off.

The ride to Chuck's house was amusing. Mario asked me if I had heard from Madeline and told me that he was thinking of calling Heather. Obviously he liked her. Not realizing that Heather and I had sex together, he wanted to visit her in New York in a week or when all of this was over. He was also not aware of her losing her job and her wanting to come to California. I didn't tell him that bit of news either. I was starting to lie to my friend, and it did not feel good. I sat back in his car deciding what I should tell him and how he would take it. It was time to be honest with someone who has always been honest with me.

I then leaned back into my seat and decided to confide in my friend.

"Mario, there is something that I should discuss with you."

I told him about Heather losing her job and that she wanted to come to California. I also told Mario that I had sex with Heather when she visited me at the bar of the hotel. Mario was a bit startled at first, then turned to me and started to laugh aloud.

"David, there is no way I could ever keep up with you. You are just about the biggest stud I had ever met, who always seems to get the girl that everyone else wants. Okay, okay, I understand what happened. So maybe I won't call Heather. Once you decide whom you really want, I will be happy with the leftovers. Just make sure you save your second choice for me, okay?"

Mario was indeed a good friend. There was no need to lie to him, and he truly appreciated my telling him what had happened. He too wanted to end this madness of working with the Seals once this episode came to a close. We were both getting too old for this shit and we both needed to put our lives back into their proper perspectives. Good friends are hard to find, and I had one of the best friends in Mario, one could ever hope to have. Of all of the people I had encountered in the past few weeks, I must say that Mario was the best of the lot. There was no fooling around with this dude. He was there when you needed him, and he protected your ass no matter what. He was more important to me than anyone. He was even at my wedding when I married Martha, as we hit it off in the Navy Seals together.

We got to Pacific Palisades just about nine o'clock in the evening. We parked the car about two blocks away and walked to the van where Stan and Paco had parked, still keeping Chuck's home under surveillance. They had camera lines and monitors throughout the house, and the telephone lines tapped. We could see and hear what was going on in the house. There were many people scattered about, and you could not make out what each was saying, as the voices were loud, and everyone was talking at the same time. Italians do communicate in this fashion, but you have to concentrate on one or two voices in order to get the gist of any part of a conversation. Paco turned to me and brought me up to snuff.

"David, here is what's happening. Chuck arrived last night from his trip. He was joined at the airport by about ten of his bodyguards and they all went to the estate. This morning, about twenty more thugs came, and tonight, another fifteen or so drove up. It looks like they are having some heated discussions right now, although tomorrow evening, there will be other families coming. They are preparing for a gang war with the Columbians who are threatening the families."

We looked at the monitors and there he was, all decked out in a black shirt, and white pants. He was the epitome of what a tough looking hood looked like. He had a cigar in his mouth and passed out some Cubans to his men. They lit up and it looked like an Italian Spa in Sicily, in the dead of winter. They all gathered around the large living room and some others were still in the guesthouse. There was another car pulling up at the gate, then another. Out came about a dozen or so women, wearing tightly fitted gowns and low cut dresses.

The women moved toward the main house and were led to the family room, on the other side of the house. Chuck always needed his little pieces of ass, no matter where he was, and this was no exception. The lights were dim, but through the monitors, we saw that he was giving instructions to some of the men. We also heard him say that he would be upstairs if anyone needed him.

He went into the den, picked out one of the women and she followed him up to his bedroom. As I looked at the monitor more closely, I thought that I might have recognized who that woman was, but I was not sure. Why did she look so familiar, or was it my imagination that all women were beginning to look alike to me.

Fortunately, the cameras that were placed throughout the house followed his every move. He was a big, burly type guy who spoke with a raspy voice, and walked like a clog. He weighed about two hundred and seventy pounds, although one always looks bigger on a TV monitor. But he did take on the presence of a large animal, after his prey. I turned to Mario and told him that I would really like to take out this guy who has gotten me in a place where I was now in, and I just did not want to do this any more. It was time to end this once and for all. And if there were not so many of his hoodlum friends in the house, I would probably have gone in his home, up to his bedroom, and shot him dead.

Mario indicated that Cappy and the Seals would be joining us the next evening and that was on the agenda. Our next drama in Chuck's house would be to take down Chuck and all of his hoodlum friends. And if the Mafia families were there, they would have to go too. That sounded good to me, and not soon enough. I just wanted to get back to my normal life and not get involved with all of this intrigue any more. I wanted to settle down, hopefully with Julie. If not Julie, then there was always Heather. And if not her, there was always Madeline, or even Christy.

My mind was like an axle of a vehicle, turning in circles, picking up lots of crud from the road, and not accomplishing anything substantial. I needed to find some stability in my life. It was so much easier being married and settled down. There wasn't any of this running around crap that I found myself into. Being with many women was fine for a while, but it was always nicer to spend your time with only one woman.

Just then, we heard a loud cry from Chuck's bedroom. As we looked into one of the monitors, we saw Chuck slapping this young gal around over and over again. I started to move, but Mario kept me down. There wasn't anything we could do, but watch. The house was too overpopulated with his people, and we would not last too long against the odds.

The girl obviously did not make Chuck happy. He then leaped out of the bed, put his clothes on and ran downstairs. He then charged into the room where some of the other girls were and told one of them to join him upstairs. This guy was insane but knew what he wanted, and he made sure he would always get it. The second girl, who was at the bar, followed Chuck upstairs and when they opened the door to his bedroom, the first girl ran past them toward the steps.

Chuck closed the door behind him and stayed in his room for over an hour with the second female. Mario and I decided to go home, as we did not have to watch this maze of sex and orgies by all of the others. We said our goodbyes to Stan and Paco and told them that we would see them the next evening. Mario dropped me off at my condo and I checked for messages. Not finding any, I decided to call it a day.

CHAPTER 11

▼

MEMORIES ARE MADE OF THIS

As I lay on my back, staring up at the ceiling, I thought about my life, and what had happened in the past twenty years after I left the Seals. I got married to Martha, and we tried to settle down. She did not want children right away but wanted to continue with her career. We traveled a bit, went on some cruises, visited the Grand Canyon, traveled to Lisbon, Spain and France, and spent time at Disney World and Disney Land. We also went to Corpus Christie, New Orleans, and to see the change of colors of the leaves in New England. We enjoyed traveling as we both worked, and looked forward to just going places about two or three times a year.

Martha was not a sexy woman, and did not care to have sex too often. She would rather try to make me happy in other ways such as watching me work out, and going bike riding with me. We played tennis and golf together and loved the outdoors. Our friends were few, but we always seemed to have people around us on weekends. We watched others have children, but that did not motivate Martha to consider having any, so we just hung loose and did what we could to occupy our time in other ways. When she did become pregnant once or twice, she wanted abortions and there was no argument as this was what she truly wanted.

My dear Martha even had two abortions without my knowledge, as I had found out later and did not say a word. It seemed that she was afraid of having any children but I did not know the true reason why at the time. It was something that we didn't talk about in the house or to any else. If anyone asked us when we were going to start a family, she would always get uptight and I would chime in by saying that we were so busy that it just was not the time. When the time was right, then we would try. That was acceptable for a while, but the years went on and the children of our friends started to get older, as we did. It would have been harder for Martha to conceive.

In our twelfth year of marriage, I remembered she telling me that she was beginning to feel tired and needed more rests, especially when we played some outdoor sports, or worked out in the gym. She was not eating as much, and she started to look withdrawn and pale. The doctor told us that it was probably a change in her metabolism and gave her some tests. Nothing really showed up until she had some bone marrow tested, together with a CAT scan and blood tests. Martha had the initial stages of cancer and she was advised to go through chemotherapy. She had gone through the stages for a couple of years and became more introverted and standoffish.

I was really worried that I might be losing her and made sure that I was always there for her. I took her to the doctors so she would not have to go alone. It was a time in my life that I felt helpless and was at the mercy of the doctors. But there were so many doctors, and each had an opinion that may have differed from the others. We had to see many doctors for opinions, and go to many clinics where they had special care, and every week, we went from one city to another. Martha knew that her sickness was a strain on me and told me to take some time off and just get away from the house for a while.

After much convincing, and knowing that her mother would watch over her, I took off for a week to Hawaii. I traveled to Waikiki, and then flew to Maui, on to Kauai and to Hilo and Kona, on the big island. I spent a lovely two weeks in the sun, just relaxing and finding some Karma by sitting back and figuring out what would happen if I lost Martha. It was a thought that I had had for a long time, and finally learned that the reason why Martha did not want children was because she was afraid that she would not be there for them if she had died early on.

Martha always had problems with her body, but we never knew that it would get to this stage. She never wanted to disappoint me and tried to do her best to always please me. We had become the best of friends, but I did miss having lots of sex with her. Her body could not tolerate the emotion and she would only want to please me, but would not allow me to give her all of the excitement of sexual activity.

Of all of the places I went to, I loved Hawaii best of all. Hawaii has been an American state for more than 40 years, and there are several unusual aspects of the place that still surprise me. First of all, it is composed of eight islands, namely Oahu, Kauai, Maui, Molokai, Lana'i, Hawaii, Kahoolawe and Nihau. The last two are generally off limits to visitors.

Having studied these islands of paradise, I found that there are 132 islands in the archipelago, which stretches for 1,600 miles from Hawaii (the big island), to Kure Atoll. Traveling to Waikiki, Honolulu's most famous neighborhood, I realized that it was often, wrongly referred to by tourists as being "downtown." Actually, this coastal city is about 3 miles from downtown Honolulu, the seat of commerce and government. The real downtown features unusual buildings such as Kawaiahao Church, constructed of coral blocks cut from Honolulu Harbor, and Iolani Palace, known as the "only royal palace in the United States."

Iolani was built in the 19th century by Kalakaua, Hawaii's last king, but not its last monarch. That was Queen Liliuokalani, who was forced from her throne in 1893. A prolific songwriter, Queen Lil, as she was called, composed Aloha Oe, perhaps the quintessential Hawaiian song, and it is still heard everywhere.

The Hawaiian language is regularly spoken in daily life only in one place, on Lihau, the small island just offshore from Kauai. But if you think that you are hearing Hawaiian on the streets of Honolulu, it is more likely Samoan, spoken by an immigrant population from that Polynesian Island. Yet, many islanders, young and old, take pride in speaking variations of Hawaiian pidgin—basically English, with some unusual grammatical construction and verbal inflection. Words and expressions are thrown into the mix from Hawaiian, Japanese, Chinese and other languages.

Island residents prefer not to hear expressions such as "back in the States" but refer to the rest of the country as "the Mainland." Captain James Cook, of the British Navy is credited for the discovery of Hawaii, which had been an American Territory from 1898 until 1959, when it and Alaska were admitted to the Union.

Looking around the islands, I came to realize that all of the islands were created by volcanic action, punched out, in effect, by magma breaking through from the Earth's core. The lava built higher until it eventually broke the ocean's surface. The island of Hawaii is the only place in the United States where you can safely view a live volcano. Kilauea, centerpiece of Hawaii Volcanoes National Park, has officially been erupting since 1983, and it occasionally puts on spectacular shows.

Visiting the Big Island, I found that many of the Hawaiians still believe the Kilauea and its companion crater, Mauna Loa, is the home of Pele, the goddess of the volcano. She is said to visit the roads of the island from time to time, disguised as either an old or young woman, or a little white dog. If islanders see any of these on the roadside, they will probably stop and offer a ride. It is supposedly bad luck not to do so.

What I do not like about Hawaii is one of the staples of their Polynesian diet called poi, which is the root of the taro plant that has been pounded into a brown paste or fluid. The food, usually difficult to enjoy for most mainlanders, is actually nutritious and easily digestible and is regularly used by island mothers as baby food. As far as I am concerned, it tastes like "poopy" which to me meant something else. But that is my opinion. Say this to an islander, and they will fill up their big round urns with boiling hot water, and you may find yourself as their next entrée.

One of my favorite Hawaiian dishes is mahi mahi, which is dolphin fish in English. Mahi mahi is so popular, that the seas around the islands no longer provide enough to fill the demand. Most mahi mahi is now shipped frozen into Hawaii after having been caught off Taiwan or Ecuador.

My first experience in riding along the highways is that I did not find any billboards in Hawaii. This is the result of a state law that dates to the 1920s, enacted on the theory that a beautiful landscape should not be obscured by advertising.

Nor will you find any snakes or dangerous animals in the mountains and forests, with the exception of some wild pigs, descendants of those brought by early explorers. However, there is a colony of rock wallabies living in the mountains behind Honolulu. These are descendants of a pair that escaped from a private zoo in the 1920s.

Hawaii has no squirrels, with the exception of a few in cages at the Honolulu Zoo. Sometimes called the "Hawaiian squirrel", the Indian Mongoose was imported into Hawaii in the late 19th century in a futile attempt to destroy rats that threatened the sugar cane harvest. Unfortunately, the rats are nocturnal and the mongoose diurnal. They only met occasionally at the change of shifts. The mongoose has survived mainly by eating ground-nesting birds.

And how could we not talk about the Hula, the Dance of Life! Hula continues to be an integral part of Hawaiian Life and existed as performance art or enter-tainment, as spontaneous activity for pleasure, as magic in ritual form, and in cel-ebration or honor of people or events. Hula has been described as an important and basic element that rendered melodically and rhythmically, the poetry that could be interpreted on more than on level. This dance rendered poetry into visual form by alluding to selected words, from prayer to entertainment. The dancer was essentially a storyteller...conveying the text depended primarily on the movement of the hands and arms.

Lastly, the steel guitar, sometimes called the Hawaiian guitar, was invented when a Honolulu schoolboy noted an unusual sound when he slid a comb along the strings of a conventional guitar. However, the famed ukulele was actually imported by Portuguese immigrants in the 19th century. Then it was known as the braga or the cavalquinho. It was named the uku (flea) lele (jumping) when the Hawaiians noticed the hand of its player seemed to emulate a dog scratching an itch.

I remember laying on the lounge at the hotel in Kauai when a pretty young gal took a chaise next to mine. She asked me if it was occupied and I said no. She was tanned and looked so beautiful, with a black bikini covering only a small portion of her rounded breasts, but you could see the nipples pushing through the bra. Her legs were long and her hair, if I remember, was dark brown, long and soft, and was all over the place. She was a natural beauty and I sort of gotten many glimpses of her as I sat on my lounge. It was my first day of three days on this island and the weather was wonderful. The bartender walked around the pool area and stopped at my lounge and asked if I wanted a cold drink. I decided that a Mai Tai would be great, and then leaned over to the gal and asked if I could get her one too.

"Hey, thanks," she said, as she went back to her sun tanning. Not even a glimpse up to see who I was.

"Hey guy, how about two Mai Tais for us," I said to the tanned Hawaiian who took down our order. I then turned to the gal and started a conversation. "My name is David and I am a resident of southern California. What's your name?"

The young twenty year old lowered her book and replied, "I'm Diane, and I also live in southern California. Do you know where Studio City is? That is where I live. I came down to Kauai with two of my friends for a holiday and they are here somewhere."

She reminded me that she was not alone and I had better not get any ideas in picking her up.

I looked at this pretty young gal who obviously was alone but I did not see her friends. I figured that I might as well keep the conversation going some more. After all, it was a bit lonely just sitting here in the sun and not talking to anyone.

"I am also here on a break from my work. I suppose I needed some time away to relax and not worry about what is happening back at the school. I write for a publication as well as teach in a college. What do you do, may I ask?"

"Oh, I am trying to break into the movies. I have had some bit parts but nothing so far. I only had one speaking part and that was because the director thought I looked like Demi Moore and would fit right in some particular scene. What kind of material do you write? Are you into the movie business also?"

"No," I responded. "I write essays and books on people's behaviors and get them published in magazines. Although I have dabbled in scripts, nothing really came of them. Guess I am not cut out to be a screen writer."

She smiled, and looked at the pool with its blue color and many of the hotel guests splashing in it.

"I love it here on this island and never want to go home. But, I have a few screen tests coming up next week and I have been studying the parts for them. Nothing major, but you have to start some place. My friends Holly and Erica left this morning for a tour of the island and will be back later. Are you here alone?"

It was as if she was curious to see if I was married or had come down with my friends, as she did with hers. I decided not to go into any explanation and just act accordingly.

"Actually, I am here by myself, and this is my second island I have visited. I spent the first two days on Waikiki and it was wonderful. I stayed at the Beachcomber and went to see Don Ho singing his 'Tiny Little Bubbles' song, or whatever you call it, and just enjoyed a little surfing and swimming. I will be here for three days before I move on to Maui and the big island. Are you just staying here?"

"Yes. We have a garden apartment with two bedrooms that faces the ocean. This is paradise for me after living in Studio City for a few years. I was born and raised in Sweden, as my father was an attaché for the government. We traveled around a lot, my parents, younger brother and me. I went to drama school and decided that I wanted to get into the movie business so I came to California three years ago.

"I went through all of the bullshit, you know, getting my photos taken, doing a little modeling, working as a waitress and sales clerk in a department store and anything I could just to make some money. I was given an opportunity to work at one of the TV studios in Hollywood when I get back. I have to go for an interview next week."

She seemed to ramble on, and I found her to be very amusing. She never looked at me while she spoke, but rubbed her tanned body with oils, and kept eyeing the guys walking past us. She seemed very interested in being noticed, and looked darn good in her skimpy bikini, yet I found myself becoming very interested in looking at her. I didn't want to appear like I was drooling, but I thought that by continuing a conversation, this would give me the license to keep staring at her.

I looked at this young woman who had so many high hopes ahead of her, and thought of Martha back at our home, and wondered if anyone can really picture what their future lies ahead of them. This was most frightening to me, since we all have dreams of glamour and success when we start out, and Diane was no different.

I thought of myself being a bit older than she was, and perhaps more of a father image. Well, maybe an older brother. I was around forty at the time, maybe fifteen years her senior. But I still had this very young persona about me, as I was in good shape, probably more so than many guys ten years younger than me. Perhaps, I thought, she would have liked to have dinner with me later on.

"Diane, since I am here by myself, I was wondering if you would like to join me for dinner tonight. They have a wonderful buffet and they serve right on the beach. After dinner, we can walk along the ocean, if you'd like, and see the most beautiful sunset in your life. How does that sound?"

She looked at me with her big, black eyes and smiled.

"Cool. I'll tell my friends. They would love a party tonight."

I had hoped that she would have known that I meant just her and me. But being with this beautiful young lady was a start, and her accepting my invite was a good sign.

The bartender came by and handed each of us a Mai Tai. I gave him my key and he put the drinks on my hotel tab. I actually felt strange buying this woman a drink, as it was always Martha whom I would buy a drink for. This was new for me and I was beginning to feel a bit less strained and started to enjoy the new company in the next chair. I also wondered what would happen if, after we walked on the beach, Diane would suggest coming back to my garden apartment and wanting to have sex with me? How would I respond if that happened? I guess I had to play this out and see what was going to happen.

She got up from her lounge chair and put her hair in a knot, saying, "I'm going in. It's too hot out. Aren't you hot?"

She then straightened out her bikini, and I noticed the sensual tone of her hardened, tanned form, and how the sunlight reflected in just the right shade off her beautiful legs. As she walked toward the pool, I rose to my feet and started to follow her. I wanted to keep our friendly conversation going, even if it meant following her to the cool water. I just could not resist such a young body.

We approached the pool as the other guests were also enjoying the pleasures of the crystal blue water. She then took a nosedive off the deep end that indicated seven feet. I walked over to the diving board and thought twice about it as it has been years since I bounced off one of those. Even though there was still some confidence left in my body, I took the slow road and lowered myself off the ledge of the pool.

"Oh, C'mon David, lets see you try a swan dive," she yelled from the other side of the pool.

Her laugh was becoming intoxicating and I was starting to get aroused by her presence. I thought that I had better get in the water and cool off or this sexy, beautiful young lady would start to get to me in a way I was not prepared for and tease me some more.

I got up close to the water, raised myself up on the ledge and this time, I jumped in. I swam to her and as I approached the other side, I saw this gorgeous face and her giggly nature that awakened the child in me. I was feeling lighter by the minute and knew that this trip was probably the best thing for me. I had been totally dedicated to Martha for years and having someone else being attracted to me was uplifting for my ego.

I did not feel any guilt though. After all, I wasn't doing anything except enjoying the company of this young woman. I also knew that if Martha were not ill, I would not be in this body of water with a lovely, twenty five year old. I was always a one-woman man, and I always preferred my women to be with me at all times. Somehow, this was a complete change for me, and to be acting silly with someone so much younger than I was, was something I was not too comfortable with. But, it was really my dear Martha who convinced me to go on this trip anyway. Did she know something that I didn't? Did she feel that I needed some other outside interest and that I was not honest with myself all of these years?

I usually liked being alone, but with a pretty gal such as Diane, I knew that I would have a much more exciting vacation spending time with her, than being alone. My male instincts started to move me to flirt with her, and we started to tease each other in the pool. When the moment occurred where she was close to my face, I did not hesitate to give her a slight kiss on the cheek. I didn't know what made me do it, but it just happened, and she started to giggle and swim away with the intent of having me follow her. When I caught up with her, she dove under the water and started to play with me that I felt an unexpected hardness of my penis. She came back up to the top of the water with a big smile on her face.

"Are you enjoying yourself, David?"

Diane started to giggle in a childish way, adding more excitement, as I stayed hard and erect below. This gal was getting to me, and it really felt good.

"Yes," I responded. "I am very happy to have met you. As a matter of fact, very much so."

It may have been the three Mai Tai's I had, or it could have been the simple fact that I was extremely horny, something that I had not felt for a long time. But after being in the pool a few times with Diane, I took her in my arms and hugged her, pulling her head toward mine, trying to kiss her. Finally, she pushed me away and told me that she had to leave to meet her friends, and wanted me to meet her in the lobby at six, reminding me to have my party hat on.

She then pulled herself up from the water and draped a towel around herself. I stayed back long enough to watch her, and then walked toward the main lobby. I already had a party hat on, and it was not on top of my inflated head.

As I got out of the shower, I heard the phone ring. I grabbed the towel and wrapped it around my waist and headed toward the phone. It had stopped. I could have called downstairs to see if they had left a message but I was dripping wet and it would have to wait. I thought that whoever it was, would call back. I needed to find the right outfit for this evening's fun and games, and decided to follow the natives' dress. I chose my brand new silk Hawaiian shirt with my white slacks. I was drying my hair when the phone rang again. This time, there was a voice on the other end.

"Hi, Sweetie, how are you doing?" It was Martha.

I told her that I was fine, and that I missed her dearly. I also told her that I was in the shower and was getting dressed for dinner. It was great hearing her voice, as she sounded a bit lonely, yet knew that I was here for a short while.

"Going anywhere for fun?" she asked. "Is it a Luau?"

I had never lied to Martha before, but I could not tell her that I was meeting a group of youngsters, female kids, for dinner. I also knew that there was a possibility that I would have a chance to dance with any of them, or who knew what else? I knew that it was not right but I could not tell her what I was going to do. Not now!

"Martha, sweetheart, it is so good to hear your voice. I thought I would just go and have a bite to eat and watch the fire and the dancers at the Luau. They are having one at the hotel. I do wish you were here with me. How are you feeling?"

Martha was good at smoothing things over, by not allowing herself to question anyone, including me.

"It all sounds terrific, David. I am doing great. I just wanted to call to see how you were doing. I was not checking up on you, my love."

I realized that in the pit of my stomach, I had limited time left with Martha, but I did not want to think about that now. I wanted to have fun and enjoy my time here. And since she called me, I felt that I owed it to her to make her feel that I truly missed her. In my heart, I did miss my dear wife. But something inside of me told me that I also missed being out with other people, sharing laughs with the opposite sex, and perhaps having sex with women, something that I had not done in over a year, perhaps two. It was Martha who told me to go somewhere to relax and to stop making a fuss over her. I was hoping that she didn't call to ask me to return home, as I wasn't ready to leave this paradise as yet.

Martha continued.

"Honey, I am the same, but I do miss you and hope that you are enjoying yourself. Just have some fun and I will see you when you come home. Please call me when you get a chance, and take some pictures to show me where you went, and what you did."

We hung up, and I felt a twinge of guilt about our conversation, and what may occur in the next few hours. But I had convinced myself earlier that I should not feel this way. I was sure that whatever guilt I had, would pass, and I knew that I was good at making the best out of any moment.

I walked through the lobby of the hotel, and, right at six, I saw Diane standing there with three friends. Her two girlfriends looked as pretty as she did, just like purebred American beauties. Her other friend was a young man, late teens or about twenty, by the name of Peter. He had a shaved crew cut and a go-tee, and wore loud, flowery shorts. He waved his hands a lot when he spoke and I had the distinct impression that he was gay.

"So you're David. What a pleasure to meet you, man."

Peter held out his hand for me to shake. His limp hand was not the kind I was accustomed to, and he smelled of roses and salt water. I was convinced that he wanted to be the 'gal' in charge this evening. He was flamboyant and comical, and very motherly with the girls. I watched him try to feel important, being a gay person trying to take charge, and I laughed inwardly at his very sight. Yet, under my breath, I kept saying to myself that he was a character.

Diane was thrilled to have me join with them and kept saying that I was a lucky find and would bring a new sparkle to the group. The outdoor tables were long and we sat on both sides of one of the closer ones to the stage. We chose this table so we would be close to the Hawaiian performers who were going to dance and chant.

A basic Luau may have more than one hundred Pacific Islanders from Hawaii, including Tahiti, Fiji, Tonga, Samoa, and New Zealand, and can take to the stage for about ninety minutes of traditional song and dance. The festivities may include a fire knife performance, wonderful costumes, an erupting volcano and much food and drink.

The most popular way of preparing food in old Hawai'i was to Kaula (bake) the meat, chicken, dog or fish in an imu (underground oven), and the heart of any soul of any Luau is still in the preparation and unearthing of the imu. Although dog is no longer part of the menu, current Luau food is reasonably authentic, except for such items as teriyaki steak, barbecued chicken, and macaroni and potato salads, added to suit all tastes in the buffet line. You still find pig roasted to flaky tenderness in the imu, accompanied by poi, made by pounding taro corns (roots) into a paste, sweet potatoes, marinated lomilomi (mashed) salmon with chopped tomatoes and onions, and sometimes 'opihi (a shellfish plucked from rocky shorelines and eaten raw as a special delicacy).

A word to the wise for uninitiated taste buds, I was told, that it is best to sample poi with salty lomilomi salmon or kalua pig in order to enhance the flavors and textures. But, as a Brooklyn born, city person, I preferred to grab a mai tai topped with a paper umbrella, a pineapple stick and a marinated cherry and prepare for an evening of feasting.

They started to serve drinks and there were little snacks on the table to munch on before you walked up to the buffet tables for the pig roast dinner and all of the fixings. It was indeed a terrific feast.

Peter was extremely outgoing and made it clear that he had things under control. On one hand, I liked his style, but something kept popping up in my mind about his unusual nervous behavior. I tried to ignore him and concentrate on the young ladies, Holly and Erica. I would have put them both in their early to mid twenties, each one as pretty as the next, and all three, including Diane, had these great looking tans from back home in California and some in Hawaii.

I started to hold a conversation with them, when Peter turned to me and brought up his roots in southern California.

"I hear you also live in southern California. My dad runs a big company in California and he always tells me to get lost, so I take off and travel."

After I briefly told Peter why I decided to travel to Hawaii, by taking a break in work, he just wanted to be friendly and I asked him about his dad.

"So, Peter, what does your dad do in California?"

Peter seemed like he was proud of his father but chose not to discuss his work too thoroughly or in detail.

"Oh, he runs some kind of compound, with lots of men who work for him. When he found out that I was not into women as he is, he told me to split. I told him to go to hell. I am happy to be who I am and don't need him to tell me how to behave or jump every time he calls me or asks me to do something. I have my own life and my girlfriends are awesome, not the sluts he always winds up with, and life is so much better without him."

I sat back in my chair and wondered what kind of compound he was referring to. Was it a jail, or maybe some kind of religious cult? There was always the possibility that he might have been involved in some shady operation. Who knew and who cared. But one thing I did know, and that was that Peter was the first flamer I had ever drank with.

Diane sat next to me and kept touching me. She winked several times and was very flirtatious. I enjoyed the attention but I noticed that Peter did not like it. He was getting jealous and I realized that I was taking the attention of the girls away from him. Every time Diane would pat my leg or touch my shoulder, Peter would give her a glaring, funny look. My gut feeling was not to move too fast, as I really did not want to go against her great, big body guard, even though he probably wouldn't be able to hurt a fly.

Peter then reminded us that it was time to go on the buffet line and fill our plates with the great food. I was happy that Peter felt important, which gave him something to do and not feel that I was taking away his leadership role. As we rose from our seats, I leaned toward Diane and asked to speak to her in private.

"How about a walk on the beach after the Luau? Just you and me?"

After ten years of marriage, I just could not believe my boldness. I couldn't believe that I was asking another woman to walk with me on the beach by the ocean. I tried not to think of Martha, even though her face kept reappearing in my mind. I quickly brushed it off when Diane took my hand as we headed toward the buffet. Holly and Erica followed behind us, as Peter led the way to the buffet tables.

The food was tremendous and so much of it. We tasted every little morsel from every dish, and kept refilling our wine glasses, waiting for the show to begin. Both the male and female Hawaiian dancers were great, as well as the smaller children who played a major part in the show. We sat there in awe, taking snapshots of the entire show that lasted nearly two hours. I had to make sure that when I snapped photographs that I would not get Diane, the two girls and Peter in any of them. I didn't want to face any questions when I would show them to Martha.

After the Luau, Diane and I decided to walk toward the ocean. The beach was so clean and white, and the ocean was simply beautiful. When we got closer to the water, the sun was already setting, and the skies looked so orange, with white slits of clouds shooting across the sky.

I thought to myself that California time was three hours ahead of Hawaii, and how Martha would probably be asleep by now, due to the drugs she was taking.

I stared out into the ocean and turned to look at Diane. I knew that whatever happened on this night, it would be a temporary thing. And that if I were to cheat on Martha, I would have to be very careful, and not feel any remorse for doing so. I knew the condition of my wife's poor health, but it still did not give me the license to go overboard at this time. In my mind, my brain was telling me one thing, but my small head, the one that gets emotional and excited, was screaming at the top of its lungs.

I was taken back to reality, when Diane spoke.

"So David, what do you want to talk about?"

I turned toward her and smiled, ever so gently. We walked closer to the ebbing tide and watched the white caps hit the shore. In the distance, we saw surfers running toward the waves.

"I was just curious as to what you wanted to do this evening. You asked me to join you and your friends, and here I am. Would you like to get away from Holly and Erica later and join me in my room for a nightcap? I thought that we could share some intimate moments together if that is agreeable with you."

Diane looked at me, as if I were either her big brother, or her long lost lover from yesteryear.

"Well, I suppose we could go for a midnight swim later and then we can dry off in your room. Water seems to suit us quite well."

She giggled again.

Just then, there came this whiney sound from the tables. We both looked around and saw this tall, thin character waving at us. It was Peter, waving his hands, yelling at the top of his lungs, to come back and join him and the girls. I turned to Diane and asked her what she wanted to do. She then ran back to her friends, as I stood there, uncertain of what her intentions really were. I then decided to walk back to the seating area where they were standing.

"So Peter, what do you have in mind? What great plans have you conjured up for us, this evening?" I asked, as he was ready to start on the next venture.

In the meantime, I was getting some pretty good once-overs from Holly and Erica. Obviously they seemed to like older men. I was not a threat to them and they felt comfortable being around me.

"David, we are going dancing in the nightclub," Peter responded. They have this great quartet that plays all of the wonderful Hawaiian melodies. Do you like to dance, David? I can show you some pretty good dance steps as I love to dance and just flit about."

Oh, Peter was really flitting about, as he took the two girls by their arms and headed toward the lobby. Diane stayed behind as she hung on to my arm. The Luau must have had over three hundred people, so it was slow moving away from the area. It seemed as if everyone was headed toward the lounge where the next show was about to begin. Peter found a great table off to the right, but close to the dance floor. It was only made for four people, so I grabbed an extra chair and we all had a place to sit down. The band was playing and the place was filling up fast. The girls went to the ladies' room so it was just Peter and I, all by ourselves, sitting like two buddies in the bar.

"Diane told me that you are a writer and a teacher. That is great. Looking at you, I would have thought that you were a gym instructor or an athlete, or even a businessman. In case you were wondering, I knew Erica back in Encino, in the San Fernando Valley when she attended UCLA. She was a student teacher and I was her student. We got along pretty well. And then I met Holly, who introduced me to Diane. They told me that they were going to Kauai, so I told them that I would join them at the hotel. I do this you know. I travel, just to get away from my father and his people."

I turned my head slightly, not knowing what he was referring to, and asked about his family.

"How about your mom, Peter? Do you see her at all? Do you live at home or do you have a place of your own? You are a bit young to go off and support yourself unless you have a good job or have financial needs to do all of the things you say you do."

"My mother and father are divorced. I was living with my mom, but she decided to go out with someone who I thought was a 'mench', but he always called me 'Fagala'. I got peeved at that son-a-bitch, and took off to be with my gals. We always have a blast together. It's a trip. I love them like they were my family."

"I hope you are not pissed because Diane asked me to join with you and the girls," I asked.

Peter laughed. "At first I was a bit angry when I saw you. But as I got to listen to you and realized that you are a caring person, I feel more comfortable now. By the way, where do you live in Orange County?"

I told Peter that I lived in Dana Point and he lived in Newport Coast, just off the road from the famous Pelican Hill Golf Course. He had this nice home that his father bought for him a year ago, just to keep him close to his father, yet far enough away so each of them could do his own thing. This relationship between father and son was most curious, having no children of my own. I could understand a boy missing his parents and only wanting some kind of love and respect, but he was not getting either, from his father, and probably none from his mother. This was some kind of lonely young man.

Peter told me that he was not allowed to discuss his family's business with anyone. His father was involved with so many businesses, including politicians, builders, finance people and unions, that if they found out that he had a gay son, it would not sit too well with all of the organizations. So Peter found his own way in life and realized that he could be happy if he had good friends, and was given a chance to be a part of a group. He was bright, funny, and most of all, caring.

The girls returned to the table and the place was filled to capacity. The music sounded great and Peter asked Erica to dance.

"David, watch my feet. You may pick up some of my style and become a good dancer yourself."

And off he went to center stage, showing off his charisma on the dance floor. He was pretty good at that.

"David, could you do with a drink?" asked Diane. "I know I could use a shot of Tequila. Holly, how about you?"

I ordered drinks for the table, having my usual glass of wine. I got to know Holly, who was a registered nurse and loved her job at the Huntington Medical Center in Pasadena. She was a lovely gal who came to southern California from Santa Barbara. Erica worked for a clothing chain, and was a buyer. After many glasses of wine, and dancing with the girls, the music was getting to sound a bit monotonous and I was getting a bit woozy from the alcohol. I think we all were getting tired.

We decided to take a stroll on the beach and it was so soothing to smell the cool air and watch the waves hit against the rocks. Peter was like a caretaker to the girls and had more energy than anyone I had ever known. He was a lonely boy and loved being a part of the group. If his father would only understand that his son was a decent kid who needed the love of a parent and that all it would take was a show of kindness and a paternal love to Peter. That was not the case.

We strolled the beach, picking up seashells and laughed over telling jokes and feeling good inside. Diane held my hand as we walked on the edge of the sand, as the water climbed over our feet.

"David, I could use a swim right about now. Should we all go back and change into our bathing suits? I will ask the girls. Are you ready for our midnight swim?"

I agreed, and so did everyone else. We walked back to the main building and found our own garden apartments. I quickly put on my bathing suit and chose another shirt, as it was getting chilly. I met the girls and Peter at the indoor pool and we just sat on the edge of the pool, with our feet hanging over the ledge, and into the water. All at once, Diane jumped into the water and Peter followed. I then jumped in and cooled off my warm body. It was delightful and we needed this to relax the muscles. Both Holly and Eric looked so divine in their bikinis, that it would have been a pleasure to take any of them to bed.

Peter was playing tag with the girls in the water, and Erica, who looked like a pixie in her orange flowered bikini, laughed so loud, that she inadvertently dropped her bikini top and revealed her breasts. Holly went over to Erica to help her find her top, when Peter reached down in the water and brought up his shorts. He removed his bathing shorts and waved them in the air. Diane and I looked at each other and we just became hysterical. Holly found the top and helped Erica put it on. It would have been my pleasure to help her myself, but I didn't want to spoil it with Diane.

After awhile, Diane came over to me and asked me if I still wanted company back at my room. I was delighted to hear that. I nodded, agreeably and we waved goodbye to Peter and the girls, and walked toward my room. I felt guilty but I knew that I needed to face reality if and when Martha was no longer in my life. I needed to know if I was able to make love to another woman again, and this young lady was the best thing that would have been my choice to break the ice. We entered the room and Diane turned toward me and put her arms around me, kissing me on my lips.

"Smooth, mmm…. You have sweet lips, David," she said, as she started to take her bathing suit off.

I did not say anything, as I didn't have to. I just chose to watch instead.

"So what are you waiting for?" she said, as she looked at me, but continued to undress.

And I thought to myself that this was it…either do or die.

She walked over to me, got up real close, and put her arms around my shoulders.

I felt her naked body up against mine, as she said smilingly, "Looks like you are ready for some lovin', big man."

I kept feeling like I was someone else. I thought that maybe this was a dream I was having, Although she was probably one of the most beautiful young women I had seen in a long time, she looked awfully good without her clothes. Diane seemed to want to kiss with her tongue more than I was used to, and she reached for me rather abruptly, that I was totally surprised with her aggressiveness.

I moved backward for a moment, and said to her, "Let's lay on the bed, Diane. It will be more comfortable."

"No David," she replied. "I want you to come from behind."

And she turned the other way and leaned over the desk in the room. I took her standing up and held onto her small, tanned frame. With one hand, she kept feeling my balls and made just the right amount of movements to get the rhythm together. I was impressed with her assertiveness, but I had hoped that I would not lose my hardness with all of this new and exciting activity going on around me.

She moaned and screamed, and told me that I was a "hotty man" over and over. I was hoping that what she said, in her own jargon, was good. She then turned to look at me after several minutes and went down on me, and started sucking my vital organ. Luckily, I was still firm as a brick, and she went wild on me. It did not take long for me to reach my climax, and I came, spilling all over her face.

She giggled, and said to me, "You're bad, David, so bad."

She quickly put on her bikini suit, and I told her that if she wanted to stay longer, she was welcome to.

"Oh, thanks. Anyway, I have another date...hehehe...if you know what I mean." She took my hand and said, "You're terrific. And, oh yeah, thanks for the fun. Maybe we'll hook up tomorrow...if you're still around."

I stood there trying not to look too disappointed, and had all I could do to keep my mouth shut, as I was astonished at this entire event that had just occurred. I watched her leave the room, waving goodbye, and I shook my head. That was it? Was that all there was to a fling? I must not have been doing something right. I had to figure this one out and make some drastic improvements. Then, I had to find myself another "hotty girl", one who would stay over the next time.

In the morning, I decided to find the restaurant and have some breakfast. There, in the corner, were the three lovely ladies from last evening...minus Peter.

"Hey handsome, come join us," Holly yelled at the top of her lungs, and waved for me to sit down next to them.

"Hi Ladies, did you all sleep well last night?"

I knew that I was only referring to Diane, but it was only polite to ask the entire group. Diane was busy eating her breakfast, and only looked up for a quick second. It seemed as if she liked doing things rather quickly, and that included eating, no matter what reached her lips.

"Well, we are off to do some scuba diving after breakfast. Wanna join us?" asked Holly.

Diane then glared at her, and I got the distinct impression that I was not on her itinerary, as she was not happy with the invite from her friend. So I declined and made up an excuse that I was busy this morning, but appreciated the offer. I could sense that Diane was happy with my response and I decided to tour the island by myself.

By the time my breakfast came, the girls were already paying for theirs', and said their goodbyes. Diane was the first to leave and waved to me, the same wave I saw her throw a wave to me the night before, and disappeared past the hostess.

I turned to Holly and asked her,

"Hey, Holly, is everything all right with Diane?"

"Yeah," she replied. "She didn't have a good night. Seems, some guy she hooked up with treated her real bad, but she'll get over it."

I asked her who that person was and Holly leaned into my ear so no one else would be able to hear.

"She met up with some bartender late last night and he was real rough with her. She'll deal with it. Don't worry, David, she'll be just fine."

I was alone at the table, thinking about what Holly had said. Diane must have left me to meet some bartender, and it didn't pan out too well. I knew that she was young, but I also knew that I could not get involved with her any more. It was apparent that there was an immaturity that surrounded this scenario that I was beyond, at this stage in my life, and the fact that I was still a married and horny man. I thought it best to find someone more suitable as this was only the beginning of my reawakening in life.

Just as I started to pay the check, I saw Peter coming into the dining room.

"Hey man, what's up?" I said, as he too did not look too pleased. What was with these young kids anyway?

"Hi Peter, I just finished my breakfast. You going to sit down?"

"I am not a happy camper, David, and I think you know what I am talking about," he said, looking hard into my eyes.

"No, Peter," I said. "I really do not know what you are talking about."

I could only think that he was referring to Diane and what happened to her last night, thinking that it was me who roughed her up.

"What the hell were you thinking?" he asked me, coming up to my face, with his voice sounding as whiney as it did yesterday on the beach.

"I really do not know what you mean, Peter," I said, questioning him to find out what really went on last night.

"Listen, friend, I know that you were with Diane last night, and if you like it rough, do it with someone else. I'm not happy with you right now."

"Listen, friend," I retorted. "I was with Diane, yes, but only before she went to meet some bartender who seemed to have roughed her up, as I was told by Holly just a little while ago. Physically, Diane looked fine this morning. Perhaps you ought to get your story straight."

I started to walk away and he reached out and grabbed my arm. My instincts kicked in, as I grabbed his feminine arm and twisted it around, causing him a bit of pain.

"And, by the way, my little friend, don't ever assume anything until you get your story straight. Have a nice day, Peter."

I walked away and knew that I had to find something more stimulating to do today than to get involved with this immature gargle, and ridiculous childish behavior.

As I tried to pick up speed in my footfalls, there came a voice from behind me.

"David, I am sorry. I was not sure who it was. This bartender came to me yesterday and asked me to fix him up with Diane. I told Diane about him and they probably met early in the day. Then you showed up and we all saw you and Diane go off to your room after the walk on the beach. I was not sure who roughed her up and now I feel responsible. Hey man, I apologize for accusing you, but I had to be sure."

"Do you know who this bartender is, and is he on duty now?" I asked.

"He goes on duty at two in the afternoon. He is about thirty-five and is a muscle type, who works out in the gym. He probably wanted to play rough with Diane and she refused. I found out early this morning when Holly called me in my room. At first, we didn't know if it was you or this bartender. I would really like to kick him in the ass myself."

I looked at Peter and he was sincere about what had happened. I sat down with him and had another cup of tea, while he had some eggs Benedict. We then spent the morning walking around the town and he told me a little more about his father, and how he was not accepted around his father's business because he was gay. He tried to do what other young boys did when he was growing up, but his interest was elsewhere and he decided that he needed companionship with kids who could tolerate him and not make fun of him. He learned how to shoot pool, draw well, and loved soaring, and became an equestrian as he loved horses and enjoyed the game of polo. He was an interesting young man, and we started to become friends. He was longing for a father image and I guess I was there for him at this time.

We looked into some of the tourist shops in town and they had some really great trinkets that I could buy for Martha. I did not let on whom I was buying the things for, although Peter was quite inquisitive and wanted to know more about me, and my life in Dana Point. I found some Hawaiian t-shirts and leis that Martha would love, and had them wrapped in a box for my trip back home. The streets were lined with tourists as they made their way from one store to another.

By two o'clock, Peter reminded me that this bartender would be on duty. I just didn't know what he wanted me to do, as it was not my problem and the situation was over. Diane got herself into this mess, and she got herself out. She had an option to stay with me last night, but chose to meet with this rough character and got her ass charred.

"David, could you please go with me back to the hotel? I want to meet the guy and give him a piece of my mind, okay?" Peter asked.

And I kept wondering what Peter would do if this gymnast would grapple with him and slice him into little pieces.

I then turned to him and asked him that if I said No, would he forget about it? He said, absolutely not. So we both walked back to the hotel and headed toward the bar. Peter pointed out the bartender to me. He was about six feet, two inches tall, with a large build and would probably break my neck if I were not careful. But Peter was eager to go after him and I just couldn't allow that to happen. We approached the bar and Peter opened the conversation with him first.

"Hey, remember me? I'm the one you went to yesterday and asked me to introduce you to that gal by the pool?"

The bartender looked at Peter, and smiled so cleverly, that even one so innocent would recognize a cheap grin coming from a brazen asshole. He leaned over the counter and into Peter's face.

"So what is it to you? Are you here to preach some of your gay rights to me, you little fairy. Now do you want a drink or do you just want to bother me?"

Peter reached over and grabbed a used glass from the counter and threw it at the bartender. The bartender looked startled and started to grab Peter's shirt. I then grabbed the bartender's arm with my left hand, and with a fist, gave him a punch in the face with my right hand. As he let go of Peter's shirt, I then reached across the bar and dragged his sorry ass over the counter and smashed his head on the counter until his nose was flattened, and the blood from his face splattered all over the counter. When he was in a stage where he was not able to control his emotions, I picked his head up and asked him what had happened last night.

It seemed that he invited Diane into his room and he wanted to play caveman with her, a bit more than she had wanted to. When she refused, he hit her in the face, took her clothes off and raped her. I then held the back of his head and smashed his face again and again onto the bar counter until his front teeth were lying on the floor. There was blood everywhere. I told him that he had one choice, and that was to leave the island quickly or I would press charges of rape against him. He took off and I went behind the bar and made a couple of drinks for Peter and myself.

"You are amazing, David," said Peter. "You really took care of that son of a bitch. I had everything under control, but I am thankful you took him down. Boy, you sure can handle yourself."

Little did he know that I had Navy Seal training and that it came in handy whenever an occasion like this would arise. We took our drinks and walked toward the ocean. The surfers were out and there were lots of lovely female bodies running on the sand, into the water. The ocean breeze felt good and the glass of chilled wine was the right ticket to refresh myself with. I looked down at my hands and shirt, and noticed some bloodstains from that idiot who I just put away. But it kind of felt good to get my frustrations out for a change. If it had to be that bartender, then so be it.

"You know, David, my dad would love to meet you. He has goons around him that are mean and tough. All union members, he told me. But you know how to handle yourself. I bet one day you and my Dad will meet and he will like you. You may want to work for him. He pays well and you can move up quickly in his organization."

With that, I took Peter by the arm and told him that I was not interested in being an enforcer. I just wanted to enjoy the sun and look at the scenery. I loved watching those gals with the big boobs as they soaked up the sun and swan in the ocean. This was my kind of place. I really liked the islands a lot. Perhaps, one day, I would settle in Kauai.

As we were walking, and not looking in any general direction, I tripped and fell over, landing on a blanket. There was a woman in her late thirties or early forties, sunning, trying to read her book. I landed on her thighs and looked at her and apologized. She was most gracious and helped me to my feet. She then turned to look at Peter who was also trying to help me get up, and they both smiled at my clumsiness.

I first thanked Peter, then turned toward this lovely, Sophia Loren type beauty who truly caught my eye.

"I am awfully sorry. I wasn't looking where I was going. I feel like an invalid falling all over you like this."

The woman looked up and graciously remarked to me with her gracious charm.

"Well then, if you were falling all over me as you said you did, then you deserve to make yourself comfortable and sit down next to me."

Peter was happy that I was okay and excused himself, as he had to go back to the hotel. The sun was too hot for him and he wanted to change into a bathing suit. I sat down next to this fairly, dark skinned woman who was called Leticia. She was indeed a native Hawaiian, but lived in Samoa for a while and loved to come to Kauai for relaxation. Her complexion was bright, a bit dark from her background as part Samoan and part Hawaiian, and her skin had this illustrious glow to it that radiated as the sun had shone on her.

Her features were rather unique, as she simply looked gorgeous in her one-piece bathing suit. I introduced myself as David and a resident of southern California. She was mature and was quite beautiful. I decided to sit for a while and chat with her. I just could not stop looking at her striking features and listening to her beautiful accent. Heck, this was as good a spot as any, and it couldn't get any better than this.

"My, my, we have a little blood on our shirt, don't we?"

She was being clever and sexy with me, but I was enjoying the moment anyway. I told her of my little bout with the bartender and what he did to a guest of the hotel. That must have pressed a button as Leticia became more interested in me and asked me if I would share a drink of Tequila she had in her thermos. Not being a Tequila drinker, I asked the floating bartender who happened by, if he would bring a carafe of wine to our blanket.

Leticia then asked me what I had in the box. I told her that it was a gift for some friends back home. No need to go into explanations at this point, and like yesterday, I only wanted to keep this on a 'need to know' basis.

She had this really cute accent and was slightly bronzed from the sun, but her natural beauty was in her sharp features of her face, her long dark legs, and her bright, white teeth that glittered every time she would smile. And she loved to smile. I felt comfortable being on the blanket with her and fortunately, I had shorts on so I was not too hot from the sun. The drinks came and I was happy that the glass had been chilled, and the wine was cold and dry.

After we spoke for a while, she turned to me in her soft, quiet tone.

"Tell me, David, did you leave your wife at home and come here by yourself? You look like a married man who is here on a mission of rest and recuperation."

She somehow, knew that I was married, so I decided to tell her about Martha and why I needed this deservedly, restful vacation in Hawaii at Martha's request. Leticia appreciated the honesty and told me that she too decided to get away from her husband who had been abusive to her during the past year while he went on a drinking binge. He was Samoan and they had met when she was there, visiting her family about seven years ago.

She had a little girl who was staying with her brother, and she also had some relatives in Kona, on the big Island. Leticia was a very astute woman, who was bright, cheery and mature. This was the first time away by herself as it was for me. Our related stories formed a bond between us and we both realized that it was good to open up and be honest, thereby not trying to lie to each other.

She had gone to school in Honolulu but had moved to Samoa when she was very young. Then, as a teenager, they moved back to Honolulu and she grew up on the beaches of Waikiki, swimming and surfing, and attending school on the island. She got a job as a tour guide for a travel agency and was able to travel with groups to Europe and Asia, including the small islands in the Pacific and Atlantic.

When she went to Samoa to visit her family, she met her husband at one of her staff meetings and they dated and got married a year later. They had Rosa within a year but Leticia kept working because her husband lost his job, and he became insecure, and started to drink heavily. Eventually, she needed a change and decided to come to Kauai to get away from all of her marriage problems. She was taking it very well.

We laughed at the way we were enjoying each other's company and decided to get together for dinner later. I felt very much at home being with her as we were close in age and had much in common, not like Diane and her friends who were so much younger than me.

Leticia did not smoke and I had to turn away each time I had lit up a cigarette. It seemed that her husband had smoked so much that this had become a problem with her, as the house always smelled of smoke. But she didn't mind when I had a cigarette as I respected her feelings and made sure that the smoke did not go in her direction. But the thing that really got to me was the way she looked in her bathing suit. She was an absolute beauty and I truly would have liked to get to know her better. I loved the way her full breasts sat in her top, and the muscled legs were absolutely beautiful that I could not take my eyes off of her body. She picked up on that as we sat there talking.

"You think that I am attractive, David?" she asked, as she caught my eyes roving all over her body.

"Absolutely," I said. "I will not lie to you, Leticia. You are one of the most gorgeous women I have ever seen. I just don't understand how a man would treat you as badly as you say, your husband has done. He is a foolish man, if you ask me. If it were me, I would treat you with passion and make love to you every single day."

Leticia smiled at me and turned toward the sun.

"You know, I am really getting burnt. I could listen to you all day, David, but I better get inside before I burn up. Are you ready to go back inside? I would love to meet with you for dinner and continue our conversation. It has been a long time since I was able to have a nice conversation with any one, without getting into any argument or hear yelling and foul language all of the time. Could you help me with my blanket, please?"

As I bent over to fold up the blanket, so did Leticia. Her breasts were overwhelming as they tried to fall from her bra, and I could see the beauty of her body even more than she wanted to allow me to. I was truly looking forward to having dinner with her later on and maybe she would be so inclined to join me in my room after dinner for a little sex. Heck, I thought about it and I was hoping that the evening would move in that direction. I was becoming smitten with this woman and if I was lucky, I might just have this wonderful looking Island girl share my sheets this evening.

We were scheduled to meet at eight in the evening. I was a nervous wreck as I decided what to wear, and primped myself, as if I was going on my first date. I couldn't wait to see her again. The memory of her beautiful face, together with her sweet laugh almost made me want to stay on this island longer.

She was sitting at a small table as I walked into the hotel bar. I saw her smile at me and I took a seat next to her, after giving her a small hug and a kiss on the cheek. She smelled lovely and I couldn't wait to be this close to her, hoping that it was going to be an extended amount of time.

"So good to see you again, David," she said. "I took the liberty of ordering a martini for myself before you came. I would have ordered you some wine, but I was not sure what you would like."

I was looking at her beautiful face and her body, and listened to her sweet voice. But I would have liked the evening to move at a quicker pace, hoping to get her into my bedroom. Getting to know her was important but I was still horny from last night when Diane just blew me away and left me dangling with myself. I felt that I needed to be with a real woman, someone with substance and maturity.

Diane was such a tease, and so young. Being with this mature, sexy, intelligent woman, who was flirting with me, increased my desire to be intimate with her. Leticia was simply the kind of woman I would die for. After experiencing sex with Diane, and wanting more, I now wanted someone like Leticia, and knew that this was a possibility. I already paid the ante and was waiting for the dealer to shuffle the deck. I just had to play my cards right, get a few good hands, and then walk away with the entire pot.

She coyly suggested that we have a drink and discuss where we might like to have dinner. I was already building up this tremendous appetite. After a few minutes of laughing and joking about some silly things, she took my hand from across the table. She then asked me if I might rather enjoy ordering our dinner from her room or mine. Intrigued with her proposal, I suggested that we could go back to my room if she would like. She indicated that she would prefer that we went back to her suite instead. Beggars can't be choosy. It didn't matter to me. Just being alone with her was my priority.

Leticia was not only beautiful, but very sexy, and knew how to please a man. She followed up by saying that if we were going to treat ourselves to a fine evening, we had to go in style. I liked her reasoning and her putting things on a "we" basis. Not only did I find her mature, but I was getting the sense that she was probably has horny as I was.

Once we finished our drinks, we left the small table. Somehow, I felt like a schoolboy, anxiously waiting my first kiss. We then walked to her garden apartment and, although I felt somewhat nervous, I was on cloud nine. These surprising changes of events were great for my ego as a man, and not having been in the single scene for many years, I found being with beautiful women quite stimulating and exciting.

Looking at Leticia, I would have thought that she was more conservative. But to my surprise, she seemed to have the same feelings that I did, by moving things along without hesitation.

We seemed to communicate in sync, and although all this was very new to me, I felt that this arousal made me feel like I was entering a new lifestyle all of my own. I felt as if Leticia was a golden queen, capturing me and then taking me to a den of pleasures. I had visions of being inside of her for the rest of the evening, feeling her warm body next to mine.

As we approached her room, she turned to me and asked, "David, sweetheart, could you please scratch my back?"

She then turned around and pointed with her right hand to a spot that she could barely reach. She was wearing this black, backless dress that only had a tie around her neck, revealing her entire bare back.

"I have this incredible itch. Do you mind?"

I must say that this had done it for me. There was no control left in either of us at that moment. After I started to reach toward her back and touched her body, she took my hand and slid it inside the front end of her dress, revealing that she had nothing else on underneath. She gently moved my hand over her breasts and reached up to give me a kiss on my mouth, using her tongue, and licking my lips with intense pleasure. I was surprised by her assertiveness, but I was not going to hesitate and just go with the flow. I was getting excited and felt that this woman was 'hot' and I could be her lover this evening.

It didn't take more than twenty minutes, when we lied on her bed, undressed, wet and spent on the sheets that were warm from the perspiration from both of our bodies. I was making it with this lovely woman, feeling sighs of contentment. While lying naked next to her beautiful body, I remembered the spontaneous reaction we both had after the door had closed behind us and we were alone. It felt incredible, as this woman was a vixen and a tiger all in one.

Within moments, the fireworks went off and nothing got in our way toward our much, needed desires for each other. I simply helped her out of her dress while she kicked off her shoes and pulled down her panties. I watched her reveal her body and I was taken back by all of her beauty. I had never seen such a full-breasted woman before, and I loved to watch her as she moved those breasts back and forth. I could hardly move fast enough to take my own clothes off.

Within forty seconds or so, I found myself inside of her and her beautiful face was below mine, as she kept kissing me and telling me how sexy I was. I enjoyed burying my face in her bosom and smelled the fragrance of her breasts, and realized that this woman would never need silicone breasts in her life.

She was so endowed that I thought of her as a goddess, a Venus, a female with a passion for love. She knew exactly how to arouse me by fondling my body as if her fingers were a human machine, knowing how to hit all of the right buttons, and causing an impulse that rattled my brain and excited me like no other time in my life.

"David, darling," Leticia whispered lovingly in my ear, "let's come together. You are so heavenly, I love being with you."

My adrenaline was peeking, and I just had to make sure I would not blow it, before it was time. I looked into her dark eyes, and the luscious tone of her smooth skin, and felt the way she moved gracefully on top of me, then under me. Leticia was all that I had hoped for and so much more. I finally was able to relieve myself of so much anxiety that I held inside of me for that past year, ever since Martha and I stopped having sex.

Finally, after our roll in the hay for nearly two hours, as her face and lips touched my chest, Leticia looked up at me.

"Time for some room service, a bottle of wine, cheese and fruit…yes?"

She reached for the phone while displaying those wonderful breasts. All I could say was…
Yes…Yes…Yes!

I was famished, but I was in heaven. This had been the most exciting love affair I had ever had.

We laughed at our abrupt, spontaneous behavior, within seconds upon entering her room. I could not believe that it was so easy to get this woman to bed, although she had played a major part in getting us there. After all of these months, possibly years of not having sex with Martha, I could not think of anyone else I would rather have been with tonight.

"David, I cannot believe that we were not able to control ourselves," Leticia said, laughing at the sight of our naked bodies spread over the sheets.

She started to straighten out her long, black hair and continued.

"David, you are terrific. I feel a bit unsure about what we did, as we are both married. But let's just have fun with it."

I knew that we were enjoying each other and going with the moment. I, too, thought that we jumped way ahead of ourselves. Yet, I might have been out of the loop for so long, that maybe this was how it was done now. Who knew?
What I did know was that our passionate encounter was hot and heavy, and I felt a huge sigh of relief coming over me.

Martha must have known that I needed to have sex and feel this way. She sent me on this journey so that I would feel like a whole man again, and enjoy the sexual relations that we used to have years ago. She allowed me to feel the emotions once again and knew that I, as a man in need of loving and touching, would find this on my trip to the islands.

We found some robes in the bathroom and put them on just in case there would be a knock on the door by room service, with our wine and cheese and other goodies. We started to laugh again and it felt great just to act silly and be with someone with the right attitude and disposition that Leticia had. We both knew that we were away from our spouses, yet, this felt so real and so exciting to both of us. I never thought about the prospect of having two women in two days, but what happened last night, and tonight, was something that I least expected.

Not that I did not love Martha, but I knew that I had a promising life ahead of me once Martha was gone. Gee, why did Martha have to get sick on me? We could have had this kind of life for many years to come. Martha always tried to make me happy in bed, but for the past year, she just could not perform any more. I had missed her love and affection and that was what had been bothering me this entire year.

I did not want to think of the day when Martha would pass on, but I was also feeling a bond for Leticia, unlike anything I had ever had before. It also filled my emptiness, as I probably fulfilled hers' as well. Tonight, however, I knew that I had to play it close to the vest, and do what I thought would be the right thing.

When room service arrived, we both sat at the table in the white plush robes that the hotel provided, and poured the wine from the carafe. We fed on crackers and cheese, plus some shrimp cocktails. We continued to tease each other, each enjoying the incredible sense of freedom we both had felt.

"Is this your first time?" Leticia asked.

I knew that she was referring to committing adultery, as we were both guilty as charged. I said yes, lying to her, hoping that she would never meet with Diane on this trip. I also did not know if I wanted her to know too much about me as I felt that it was best to stay clear of serious subjects and just focus on our playful relationship. She seemed to feel as excited as I was, and yet, I sensed that she was getting more emotional with me than I was with her.

I truly wanted to know more about this woman, but I was still emotionally committed to my wife. I could fall in love with this beautiful woman down the road, but the chances of us meeting again were as remote as bacon is Kosher. She was the epitome of a woman from out of the blue skies. She was beautiful, knew how to make love and satisfy her man, and she was intelligent. She would be the most exciting woman I could ever hope to meet. Yet, I asked myself why her husband acted the way he did toward her. There are always two sides to every story. Perhaps I would learn more later on.

"I have never felt this good before, David. This is such a wonderful surprise for me." she commented. "I want to thank you for being so open-minded. I have to confess that I wanted you from the first time we met, as you so clumsily fell over my body on the beach. I just did not know if you were open for this at the time. I also had to tell you that I was married, and I am glad that you told me the same thing. But, David, this is a wonderful treat for me. Hopefully for you too."

She filled our glasses again, and I sensed a slight nervousness in her tone. She seemed uncomfortable talking about our real lives. I decided to break this tension.

"Leticia, honey, being here with you is fabulous. I also want to thank you for being so wonderful. You surprised me, but it was a truly fabulous surprise."

I leaned over to her and kissed her on the lips. I placed my glass down and took her hands into mine. I then raised her hands to my lips and kissed them.

I reached into her robe and cupped her breasts with my hands. Her body was on fire and I needed to touch her again. I lifted her up off her chair and moved her toward me, opening her robe and letting it fall to the floor. Opening my robe, I walked her over to the bed. There, we made love once again until I could no longer get my penis hard. I felt that it was already in shock due to all of the excitement it had in the past few hours. I felt worn, but tired.

After we finished, we had some more wine and decided to get dressed, and take a walk on the beach. We walked slowly, watching the waves hit with the thunder of a tidal wave, and I noticed that she seemed to act somewhat differently than before. I did not know if she was feeling guilty, or simply tired, as the sun started to set. Heck, we were on vacation, and not supposed to be concerned or worry about the time, or to have stress of any kind. I loved to live in the moment. This was a brand new thing for me and it felt great.

Without hesitation, I turned to Leticia and asked, "Are you feeling okay?"

"Yes, David. I am fine," she responded. "Perhaps I am just tired. You wore me out, you devil you. Maybe we ought to call it a night. Perhaps we can meet up tomorrow and go for a bike ride or something, okay?"

I thought to myself, perhaps? What does that mean? "Don't you want to see me again, Leticia?

"Of course I do," she answered. "And I am very happy to have met you today. But I don't know what the right thing to do anymore."

I told her that it was getting late and that we could talk further in the morning. I got up to leave her room, when she started to speak.

"You are a beautiful man, and you made me feel so wonderful. Please call me in the morning. Thank you for a beautiful evening. I shall never forget you, David."

With that, she kissed me and I walked away.

By the time I got back to my room, it was late, too late to call home and see how Martha was doing. I had found a note under my door and it was from Peter. It read like a fantasy, but what do you expect from someone like 'Peter'.

"Dear David. Hope you enjoyed your evening with the beautiful woman on the beach. I went with the girls to town and enjoyed the evening. Holly and Erica wanted to go swimming in the pool and Diane went to the lounge to check out the locals. She asked for you but I did not tell her anything. I have respect for your privacy and hopefully you have the same for mine. I am leaving tomorrow for California, as my father wants me to visit with him at his home. He wants to know what is happening in my life, like he really cares. So I am off at nine for LAX. Hope you enjoy your stay in Hawaii, and here is my telephone number in case you ever want to look me up. Regards, Peter."

That young fart was a thoughtful young bastard, I thought. I wondered if he would ever find love in the true sense of the word. I suppose we all need to find what is lacking in our lives, as we all seem to go about it in our own ways. These last two nights were an experience for me and I will never forget them. Now, I suppose, it was time to move on. I had to catch the plane to Hilo on the big island in the late afternoon and then drive to Kona before I would leave for home.

I wondered what would await me on my next venture on those islands. The room felt nice and cool, and I noticed that my message light on my phone was on, indicating that I had a message. I picked up the receiver and dialed for messages. There she was, and she sounded great.

"Hi lover, this is Leticia. This has been a wonderful evening for me and you are such a marvelous person. Unfortunately we are both married and we could never be together. I am too dedicated to marriage, and no matter how badly the marriage is, I will always try to work things out. You, on the other hand, have a wife that needs you and you must go back to her. Perhaps, one day in the future, our paths may cross once again. Until then, thank you for everything and keep well. I will always remember you, my darling."

Leticia left her phone number at work and I made sure that I put it in a safe place in my wallet. I couldn't sleep so I sat on my little patio that overlooked the ocean. I decided to have a cigarette and another glass of wine. I thought about Leticia and how beautiful a woman she was. Perhaps, one day, we shall meet and we can renew our acquaintance once again. It was getting later, and I was getting sleepier and realized that I had another full day.

The flight to Hilo was about thirty minutes, and the hotel called Uncle Billy's was a bit shabby, not too exciting, and there was not much to do on this side of the island. I had dinner and listened to the music from the local band, and watched more of the young gals dance. At 7 am, I had breakfast at one of the local eateries and rented a Jeep, put my luggage in the trunk, and decided to drive over to Kona, a six hour drive along the winding roads of the big Island of Hawaii.

By two o'clock, I arrived at the Kona Maluhia Country Inn Bed and Breakfast, and was looking to enjoy the famous Hawaii Volcanoes National Park, the black sands and the blue seas, plus the waterfalls and gorges of Hawaii. I heard that the active volcano Kilauea, what the natives call 'The Power of Pele', spews a natural fireworks show on the Big Island. Handed down from generation to generation, through chants and oral tales, the language of Hawaiian, like the land, tells the islands' story. Its' soft sounds echo those found in nature...the sea's gentle splash caresses the sand, with its' light rain falling on tropical foliage, and each is equally important to the beauty of the state.

The Kama'aina, the native Hawaiians, have a familiar phrase...aloha 'aina, meaning love for the land that declares their connection with these patches of earth they call home. Kai, the sea joined with 'aina, the land, where they meet lani, the sky. The union is mimicked in the sounds given to these elements...rolling, flowing, and astounding. And it's these valleys, mountains and beaches that entice the malihini, the visitors, to fly thousands of miles to bask in what they can only term as paradise.

Even as you feast on roast pig and poi, an ocean breeze tickles the orchid that so nicely garnishes your cocktail. Dark-skinned beauties, like Leticia, adorned in ti-leaf skirts and fragrant leis appear on a stage before you, their eyes toward the sky, arms above their heads and hips swaying seductively to the melody of a plucking 'ukulele. The Big Island's color is red, the same hue as the lehua, its flower.

Each island has a different hue for their leis, Kauai's color is royal purple, and its lei is the green mokihana berry entwined with the maile vine. Lanai's color is orange, its lei features the orange blossoms of the kaunaoa. Maui takes for both its color and its lei, the lokelani, a pink cottage rose, while Molikai's color is green, its lei is the small white flower of the state tree, the kukui. Oahu uses the golden-yellow ilima for both its lei and its color. So much for the many leis I have witnessed traveling throughout Hawaii.

The smooth movements of the dancers' hands are hypnotic. Entranced and relaxed, you bite into a juicy pineapple and enjoy the show. And the rainbows and waterfalls are too numerous to count. The colorful arches, which grace lush gorges, plummeting waterfalls and even the Honolulu skyline, are provided courtesy of the goddess Anuenue. In Kealakekua Bay on The Big Island, there, nestled along the western coast, is the Captain Cook Monument.

And of all of the states in the United States, Hawaii is perhaps the most individual. Different cultures, races, religions, philosophies and lifestyles, not only coexist, but blending together. For these reasons, I chose to come here and relax and find peace and serenity. I, somehow feel at home on any of the islands, away from the hustle and bustle of any other city in the country.

As I admired the ocean from the home of one of the past Hawaiian kings, I was approached by a woman who was on a mission of mercy.

"Excuse me, sir," she commanded. "It is forbidden to drop any cigarette butts on this native ground. I hope you realize that you are on sacred ground, sir. Would you mind picking it up and placing in the butt can?"

I looked up and saw this woman who could have been a teacher or a real estate broker. She had this whiney voice and just went on about throwing butts on the ground. I just dropped my butt and stepped on it, and she saw me do that.

"You are right, ma'am," I replied. "I am going to pick it up and drop it into one of the butt cans. Thank you."

With that, she walked away. I continued to look out at the beautiful ocean and there came another voice behind me.

"Beg your pardon, sir. Why are you looking out at the ocean, when there is so much more to see on land?"

I turned around and there was another woman. This time, she was a pretty lady, about thirty-five, and had her hair up in a bun. She was about five feet ten, and pretty slim, bearing the features of a well groomed woman of leisure. I was dumbfounded as I looked at her and wondered what she wanted from me. Perhaps it was a way to get my attention to buy trinkets or sell her body to me. I just glanced at her and assumed that it was just an innocent encounter that caused me to turn away from the ocean and talk to her.

"Excuse me. I actually was trying to focus on the best scenery, this side of Kona."

She rather enjoyed my little ploy and started to joyfully play with me with puns and started to tease me for being so cute with her.

"Hey, now you are viewing the best show this side of Kona. So what do you think of your new vantage point?"

I was amused by her and asked her if I could assist her in any way. She looked at me with her blue eyes, beneath her blond hair, and spoke in a rather sexy way.

"If you are interested, my name is Kaitlin. I'm here to get away from my boyfriend who is such an idiot. I'm from Encino, in southern California. Obviously that woman was after your butt, and I don't mean your cigarette. It is kinda cute if you ask me. But, you didn't ask me, now did you? Hey, could you spare one for this lady who will not accuse you of dirtying up the sacred land of the kings? What's your name tiger, and where are you from?"

Here I go again. Why do women think that they can just reach out to me and use me for their own interests? So I decided to play the game and responded to her.

"My name is David, and I am staying at the Kona Maluhia, a few short blocks from here. I am not running away from my girl friend and I find you incredibly attractive, for one, a bit insane for the other. And perhaps someone who may want to join me in a drink at the bar."

She looked at me with her light, blue colored eyes and put her arm into mine and told me to lead the way. If I ever wanted to think about being alone, I wondered if it was all that possible to do so. I had been married for many years to the same woman and now that I was traveling by myself, I found myself being picked up by an assortment of nymphomaniacs or perhaps, lonely ladies who want company to satisfy their own needs, as I may want to satisfy mine.

So now I had another female to contend with, and wondered just where this was going to lead me next. Although, this one was funnier than the rest of them, she had the cutest sense of humor and straight forwardness, with a bunch of clichés you could shake a stick at. This entire entourage of women on the make was so sweet and bittersweet, as each one had her own stories to tell, and they were either running away from others, or from themselves. I found all of this remarkably outrageous and funny.

"So tell me, David, what is a big hunk of change like you, doing in a place like this? I mean, if you're looking for women, this is not the island you should be on. There is Waikiki, Maui, and Kauai to pick from. You are here on a mission, right? You are going to buy some property here or you are looking to get away from wherever you are coming from?"

What a talker, she was. She had a mouth that just would not stop. I walked with her the two blocks back to my hotel and we headed to the lounge. Grabbing a table overlooking the blue ocean, I asked her what she wanted to drink.

"Okay, Kaitlin, put a zipper on it and just tell me what kind of cocktail you would like. I am getting a headache and need some quiet time while I drink my wine."

She was kind of pert and pretty, with a cute figure, bright, white teeth, and long athletic legs that were so noticeable as her shorts only went down to the middle of her thighs. I liked the cutesy way about her, as she could have been fun to be with, as long as she would not drive me insane with her mouth. I could see her mouth being used for other activities rather than spouting off as she did.

"Oh, a Gin and Tonic would be great, David. And thanks for putting up with my shit all the way here. I just arrived today and have to look for a place to stay, as all of the hotels are booked. Could you suggest a place where I can lay back until I find a place of my own, or until I take the plane back to the mainland in three days? What about this hotel where you are staying? Do you think you can check it out for me? I would be indebted to you if you could."

What was I getting into? I truly did not want her to stay with me, and the sooner I found a place for this 'dodo', the sooner I would find my own space and enjoy the great spots to visit in Kona. I told her that I would ask the hotel if they could spare a room for her. While she was having her cocktail, I went to the front desk, and they told me they were booked solid for two weeks. The news did not sit too well with Kaitlin.

"Oh shit! Now what am I supposed to do?"

I told her not to worry, as it was not the end of the world. I reassured her that we could probably find something elsewhere. I tried calling many other hotels in the area but they were all booked up. I asked her if she had any luggage and she told me that she had one suitcase in her rented car that was on the street. I really had no choice but to either tell her to find her own way or leave Kona and return to California, or take in this stray and let her stay in my room which was not what I had in mind for my last few days' vacation in Kona.

I left her sitting at the table and decided to go to my room and try to sort this out. Looking at my room, which was small, yet roomy enough for two people, I felt that if push comes to shove, she could make herself a bed on the couch, which was like a love seat. Placing my hands over my head and realizing that I was in a predicament, I reached for the phone and decided to call Martha. I really needed to hear her voice and find out how she was doing.

"Martha, this is David. How is my little wife doing?"

Martha was happy to hear from me as she was just sitting down for lunch. She told me that she had gone to the doctor's office this morning and took more blood tests. She was lonely for me and was hoping that I would cut my vacation short and come home. We spoke about the tests and what she was instructed to do by the doctor whom she had a lot of confidence in, but was hoping that I would be home soon to be near her and listen to all of the nonsense that she was going through. It was something that made me feel sick inside, but I knew that I had to go home. I told her that I would change my schedule and leave as soon as I could. This made her feel better and she was looking forward to having me home the next day, if it was possible.

After I hung up, I called the airlines and changed my reservations to a flight out of Kona the next day. They would get back to me with a confirmation later on, so I had to wait for their phone call. So far it looked good, but it was the flight from Kona to Honolulu that was the problem. You had to fly out of Honolulu to the mainland, and that was the problem. I would be home to see Martha and take care of her. My duty was to take care of her, and all of the episodes that I had experienced in the past few days would be no more than just a memory.

This also solved my present problem. I would now be able to let Kaitlin stay in my room for the next few days until she departed for California. I then went to the reservation desk and told them of my change of plans and that Kaitlin would take over the room after I was gone. They did not mind since it was reserved for a few days anyway.

When I told Kaitlin of my plans, she was most pleased and understood my wanting to leave earlier than I expected to. I told her that I needed to go home and tend to some personal matters, and that my room was hers for as long as the hotel held it for me. With that scenario taken care of, I helped Kaitlin take her luggage back to my room and we just spoke about why she came to Kona to get away from her boyfriend.

It seemed that he was in the electronics industry and lost his job due to the downturn in the marketplace. This made him very uneasy as he went from earning close to $80,000 to nothing. He started to drink heavily and lost his place as a decent provider, and his company did not even give him any severance pay. He verbally attacked her as he must have lost his well-being as an IT maintenance nerd who had serviced many companies through his position with his company. I felt his anger and his frustration, but Kaitlin was scared that he might do something drastic, so she decided to leave him alone and come to Hawaii to sort things out.

It was one story after another, as each of the women I had met had gone through some sort of anger and frustration with their mates, and left them to come to a safe haven like the Hawaiian Islands. This was something that I had not experienced, although here I was, in Hawaii, escaping the doldrums of taking care of my sick wife who was dying.

This was some sort of catastrophe that we all seemed to be in, and I was in the thick of it as well. Barring the fact that I truly loved my wife and wanted to go back and be with her, I realized that most people have had problems in their relationships, only to run away and think by doing so, the problems would be resolved. But, in essence, they would not.

I took Kaitlin out to a late lunch and we then hit some of the tourist spots that I wanted to see and she enjoyed them as well as I did. By the time we were finished, it was nearly seven in the evening, so we sat at the lounge and had a few glasses of wine. She thanked me for the friendship that I afforded her and she made it clear to me that she was totally in awe of my taking charge and helping her, not only to find a place to stay, but helping her keep her sanity in tact.

We went back to the room and I started to lay out my clothes so that everything would be in order for packing in the morning. I did not have time to unpack every thing, as I was too damn busy trying to be a good boy scout by helping others in need. Kaitlin was a doll and she just kept busy chatting away and laughing at her own jokes, some of which were funny. But I was not in a comical mood. What had transpired in these last few days was something that I least expected, and was not prepared for. Although I truly enjoyed my evening with Leticia, I knew that my time had come, and that I had to get back to take care of my wife. I sat on my bed, listening to the ocean waves and relaxed.

Kaitlin had walked over to me and sat down next to me. She was a lovely woman who had the longest legs, and biggest smile one could imagine. She put her arms around my shoulder and she also knew that I had a lot of things on my mind.

"Gee, David, I did not mean to be such a pest," she remarked. "But I felt so desperate and alone, that I needed to turn to someone. I want to thank you for helping me as I did not know what to do at that point."

I turned to her and reassured her that it was not her fault, and that I was only too happy to provide her with the room. She leaned over to kiss me, and I was not ready for any lovemaking at that moment. But her legs seemed to wrap around mine, as we sat upright on the queen-sized bed, and her arms went around to my back, pulling me toward her. I felt that this was my last night before I would leave this glorious place called Hawaii, and I had a pretty woman in my room who wanted to make love to me.

I could not resist her and took her into my arms and kissed her on her lips. She responded to my actions and started to unbutton her blouse, opening it wide, away from her chest, revealing her lovely breasts. She asked me to help her unhook her bra, and once I did, I saw a marvelous body, not inches from me on the bed. I then took off my clothes and we both got under the covers, thinking that we would make passionate love to each other.

The phone rang and I picked it up. It was the airlines telling me that I had to leave Kona by eight in the morning and head to Honolulu for my plane back to Los Angeles. I really had no time to breathe in the morning, but get my ass out the door and head to the airport. I set the alarm for six and decided to have quick sex with Kaitlin before I would go off to sleep. All I remember was that she was good and I enjoyed having her in bed with me. Then the phone rang once again.

"David, are you okay? My God, man, it is nearly ten in the morning. Where the heck have you been?"

I realized that I was in a deep sleep and I had overslept. The voice on the other line was none other than Mario's. I had been dreaming about my experiences in Hawaii just before Martha died and I was so out of it. I moved the receiver to my mouth and uttered, half asleep.

"Mario, boy it is good to hear your voice. Thank you getting me up. I was in a deep sleep and I am just getting awake now. We have a busy day today, with lots of fireworks happening tonight."

Mario told me to get my ass out of bed, take a cold shower and he would pick me up for breakfast at the Brig Restaurant by the harbor. Cappy was calling a meeting at his home this afternoon and was preparing us for the fight of our lives later this evening at Chuck's estate. By eleven, we were sitting at a table at the Brig and Mario was all prepared with his weapons, which were in his SUV. I already packed my PPK and lots of ammo and knew that we had a lot to do later on.

Mario told me that all of the guys would be there, including more help from the Seals, the FBI, and the DEA. We were going to have a helluva fight this evening and there would be a lot of gun fighting, unless of course, Chuck gave up without a fight. This was going to go down in the record books as a 'shoot 'em up, smoke 'em out' party, and we were the aggressors, while Chuck was the recipient.

Mario had some notes he got from Dickie that indicated a few personal things about Chuck. It seemed that he was once married and had two children. One was a girl and the other was a boy who seemed to get into lots of trouble. He would take off and travel, and could never get along with his father. The FBI was looking for him now, as he could be a material witness against his father if Chuck would ever go to trial.

Something in my dream came back, and I recalled a boy named Peter who also had the same problem with his dad. I wondered if there was a tie-in between Peter and Chuck. But that seemed too far-fetched to me, so I forgot about it. I also remembered my encounter with Diane, with Leticia, and with Kaitlin. Boy, that happened nearly two years ago and the dream was so vivid, as if it had occurred only yesterday. I also thought of my having sex with these women.

"Hey, dream boy, are you listening to what I am saying?" asked Mario, as he suddenly got me out of my past thoughts, angrily remarking, "I must tell you, Mr. Sex Pot, you are going to be the death of me or of yourself. All you do is go off and dream about some far away place. You and your women, that's all I hear about. How about giving it a rest until we take care of business. I expect you to be on your toes tonight, or we are both going to be two dead pigeons before the night is over. You kapeesh?"

I laughed and nodded without saying a word. My life was coming around full circle and I needed to make some changes once this episode would be over. I also needed to find some peace in my life and not be on the go as I had been for the past few weeks. This madness had to stop. I wanted to start a brand new life and settle down with a nice woman, if that was at all possible.

CHAPTER 12

▼

HIGH TIME WE WENT

By two in the afternoon, we got to Cappy's house. Everyone was there. We had a few hours to go over many things to make sure that what we were going to be involved with later on in the evening would be a success. Cappy didn't like failures. A failure would mean a fatality, and he did not want to see any of the guys lose their lives. The house that Chuck built was a fortress and we had a lot of support by many outside forces.

This was 'do or die' time and I was hoping that it would be my last. After this, I wanted out, once and for all. The memories of what had happened two years ago, and of the past few weeks shed a new light on me. I was in my early forties, and I was still acting like a teenager who only thought about fucking women and getting into trouble. Enough is enough. I needed to find a life for myself.

We sat around the table, Cappy in the head seat, then Dickie, Moose, Jules, Mike, Billy and Mario. On Cappy's left, was me. Sean was handling the legalities if we ever took Chuck to trial, while Stan, Paco and their people were set up in their van around the perimeter of Chuck's estate. The other Navy Seals were to follow our lead, as we were to be the team leaders, in charge of the units consisting of two dozen Seals.

Then, there was the FBI and the DEA who were supposed to be there by eight. The local police were notified and they were the back up team, together with S.W.A.T. If we had a cavalry of about one hundred, that would have been like a battalion. But we were to be the leading squad that would take control of the situation. It was like we were planning an attack against the Al Qaeda or the Hamas, or the Jihad. This was big time and I was in the thick of it.

No one cared if Chuck would be brought down and killed. But the government wanted him alive to appear on trial for all of his crimes. There were supposed to be members of the five Mafia families at the meeting in his home at nine o'clock and we were to strike at nine thirty.

Based on reports by Stan, we expected to be up against seventy five, maybe eighty members of the families, plus there was a possibility that the drug cartel would send in Columbians as well. We were going to have our hands full and we needed to take up our positions early on, so that we would have the perimeter well surrounded.

Cappy reviewed the layout and the breakdown of the attack, and how we would cover certain parts of the building. He did not want anyone to escape and that meant total annihilation of the Mafia and the Columbians. But the real danger was the protection of the nearby residents. Although the estate sat way back on the cliffs, above the ocean and not close to any other home in Pacific Palisades, the sound of gunfire would surely scare the wits out of the neighbors. We had to have crowd control and peace officers in the streets to keep all of the residents inside until this theatre of operation was over. That was the job of the police.

We sat and listened to Cappy's strategy and what each of us needed to do in order not to lose any of our lives, or those fighting along side of us. This was a massive attack and it would not be easy. The first thing was to surround the place. The next would be to take out as many soldiers of the Mafia as possible and hope that the rest would surrender. But we had to make sure that we were all in position before we would sound the alarm and tell our adversaries that the entire compound was surrounded.

There would be too much at stake if surrender was a possibility, as each of the culprits would be facing long prison terms and for some, go up for life. That was the drawback, as we felt that they would be fighting for their lives, not knowing how many good guys were waiting outside the compound.

It was about five o'clock, and we took a break. Cappy had some sandwiches for us and we checked our cache of ammo, our weapons, and our dark Seal outfits, with goggles, and telescopes for the rifles. We were going to be a team once again, and the enemy was out there. Instead of attacking on foreign soil, we were going to create havoc right here in Southern California. This would make the news, and the media would be playing this up as a circus. But, we were government soldiers and we had the authority to take down the cancer that was spreading throughout the country.

I sat back and munched on a ham sandwich with a cold drink. Mario had a small radio with earphones and was listening to some rap and hard rock music. Moose was constantly going over the plans and was always so methodical in making sure that he was totally confident before he walked away. Dickie reviewed the news articles with Cappy that would surely put Chuck away for a long time. The other guys just sat around cleaning their weapons and loading up on ammo and sandwiches.

I was proud to serve with these guys overseas and learned how to be a good Navy Seal during my tenure in service. They were the true-blue fighters you read about, but never hear about, nor see, face to face.

They were sworn to top secrecy and they took their job seriously. This was the last assignment for all of us, and as far as missions go, this did not seem as dangerous as many of the ones we were in, years ago. This was just another day at the office and we were looking for the day of retirement for good, from this kind of work. Yet, as in any operation that involved weapons, this could have been our last days on earth, permanently. We were getting too old for this shit.

I decided to call Julie to see how she was doing and she answered right away. It was good hearing her voice.

"Oh, hi, David, how are you. I just got in and it has been so hectic at work. I am ready to crash after I make some dinner for myself. So what's happening with you, dear boy?"

I asked how Christy was doing, as well as Suzie. I also asked her if she heard from Rita, and if they had been bothered by Chuck and his people. Every one seemed to be doing well, but she did not hear from Rita at all. She did say that the attorneys in her firm were busy putting together lots of material for many different court cases, including the one for Chuck. Her suitor, Ted, one of the law partners who tried to get into her pants, was taken off the case involving Chuck as he was too close to the situation. His family has been secured and that too was neutralized.

We spoke but for a few minutes and then hung up, without my revealing to her what we were up to in the next few hours. There was no need to worry her, or for that matter, tell her anything that might put her in harm's way. Having taken a short nap, Cappy told us to get ready and we all changed into our jump suits, attached the goggles, and moved out into his van. He and Moose sat up front while the rest of us sat in the back, holding on to the weapons and ammo.

By eight o'clock, we arrived in Pacific Palisades. We parked about two blocks away and quietly moved toward the estate. It was fairly dark and the streets were quiet. Cappy and I walked into Stan's van that was hidden under the trees, about a block down the street. We discussed the layout, and how many people were in the main house and the guest house.

Just then, a slew of vehicles started to arrive at Chuck's gate. They contained the members of the other families, and there must have been about twenty cars that came up to the gate. The compound had enough room to allow all of the cars onto its premises and we just watched the parade as men in dark, black suits came out, and moved toward the main house.

As the last car entered through the gate, Mario and I took our unit forces and went to the back of the estate. We were to cover the perimeter of the back of the house. Mike, Billy and Jules took their troops and were to cover both sides of the compound, while Cappy and Dickie would take their forces and go through the front gate.

Moose would stay behind with Stan and Paco, in the van. The van had twenty monitors, eight for the outside of the estate, and twelve to cover nearly every room inside the house. We all wore small microphones and hearing devices, so we could receive and send oral messages back to the van, and to each other. This would keep us informed of what was going on, both inside and out.

We sat by the outside of the gate until nine thirty, when Stan was to close down the electricity of the electronic gates. Lookouts were ordered aloft until we were to go over the gate. Cappy ordered a complete set up as an interception course that would place all of our guys around the entire perimeter and indicated that in minutes, we should stand by our battle stations.

The first thing that I thought was that if the grounds were protected by dogs, or if the Columbians decided to attack at the same time we did, we would be facing more than we bargained for. Another problem would be if our good buddies, the FBI or DEA would get itchy fingers and fire their weapons before we had a chance to position ourselves close to the building. I was not sure if Cappy took all of this into consideration, but we had to play it by ear, and hope that everyone followed instructions. Based on what he thought was a good plan of action, may well have turned out to be a homily of sorts, and we all would have been in deep shit trouble.

I personally would not have been surprised if some young trooper who was still wet behind his ears would have moved too quickly. There was nothing more dangerous than an inexperienced zealot who loved to be a hero and come out charging before the bugle was sounded. I remembered, that while on active duty with Cappy and the guys, he drummed so much discipline into our heads that we were becoming robots and acted as if every assignment may have been our last.

I was always a little vague as to how the Seals or any other outfit were able to keep their cool and not show fear on any assignment they were on. Hell, this was never a piece of cake, but I can safely say that we were trained by the best of the best, and we fought like the best. But I was always curious as to why we did what we did, and for what reason did we risk our lives. We were in our early twenties then, and now we are in our forties. We certainly did not have the same perception or peripheral vision that we did then, and for some reason, life meant more to us now, then it did years ago.

Precisely at nine thirty, I looked back, and saw a group of FBI and DEA guys surrounding the outside of the compound and they were ready to follow us over the gate. We only had one minute to do this while the electricity would be turned off, and then it was to be turned on again. During this time, no lights would be out inside the two houses, therefore no one inside either building would know what was happening on the grounds. Then it was time. Stan de-electrified the gates.

The electricity was cut right at the second. Mario and I climbed up to the top of the gate and leaped toward the ground, moving quickly toward some of the guards. The other Seals were behind us and we were able to get about fifteen Seals over before the gate was once again electrified. The rest waited outside until we told them to come through the front gate or when the gates would be safe to climb up.

I told a third of my group to head toward the guest house, while Mario and I moved toward the guards who were milling about outside of the main house. There were about ten or more, so we had to act quickly and assuredly. Once they would be taken out, my guys would have access to the house.

I managed to get two guards down, and the other Seals took care of the rest. Mario took a few of the Seals and had his side covered as well. Cappy was waiting for my signal before he and his men would move through the front gate. I then took my group to the back of the house and started to climb up the lattice, which would enable us to get to the upstairs floors. We had to be very quiet, and carrying thirty pounds of armor and weaponry didn't make it any easier.

As I made the second level, I looked into the bedroom closest to me and saw that same girl who had been with Chuck last night. She again looked familiar to me, as she did last night, but my mind was too occupied to place her. Me and my women! After a while, they all seemed to look alike. I had more than my share to last a lifetime. I felt that I was actually becoming a male prostitute.

Just then, I heard some yelling coming from the front of the house. It seemed that some of the guards were being called by name from someone inside the main house, but were not responding. At this time, they were off in a deep, long sleep and would not return any calls. That made the other family members who were inside, a bit worried.

I contacted Cappy and indicated that we may have to move in quickly. He gave the word to Stan to cut off all of the electricity, and the gates swung open to allow the rest of the Seals to gain access onto the compound. The DEA and FBI were right behind them. A loud speaker called out to the people inside the two houses to come out with their hands up.

All of a sudden, shooting started from the front of the house that I was not able to see. Although I felt secure enough hanging onto the upstairs balcony in the rear of the house, my main thought was to break a window and go inside with the small unit that was with me. As we entered, we heard lots of gunshots coming from downstairs. Obviously, no one in the house wanted to give up telling me that this may very well turn into a fight to the finish. My first thought was to get Chuck and hopefully take him alive. But it would not have bothered me one bit if I had to shoot him dead. He was the nemesis of this operation and he deserved to feel the pain that he gave to others.

Sounds of gunfire were all over the place and we were closing in on the gangsters like wolves attacking sheep. But that did not stop them from firing back, not realizing that they were completely surrounded, or how many government agents they were fighting against. The place was built like a fortress, and I understood why this had to happen at night. We needed to take out all of the families under one roof, at the same time.

The estate was over 20,000 square feet and the sound of gunfire created echoes that came from all over the place. The cracking sound of bullets started to find their way into the windows and doors of the estate. It sounded so loud, that you could not hear yourself breathe. I heard Dickie through the earphones, and Mike and Billy explaining their positions. Then I heard Mario say that he was on the balcony on his side of the building. The conversations were short as they were all in the middle of gunfire.

I immediately went out into the dark hallway, as the lights were out, and I had to use my infrared goggles to see in front of me. The rest of the Seals were behind me as we took our positions along the hallway leading into several of the bedrooms that were along the wall. We then headed toward the master bedroom, and upon opening the door, I saw a woman lying face down on the floor. She was brutally abused, as there was blood all over her face. I looked at her and she was that same woman whom I had recognized the night before. I held her head up and moved her close to my body.

"Are you okay, miss? Could you hear me talking to you?"

The young woman nodded and was able to open her eyes. She cried out to me saying that Manzione had beaten her after he attacked and raped her. I put her in a corner with her head propped on a pillow, and told her to lie still as I had to continue on my mission and check the other rooms.

Some of the Mafia members started to come up the stairs and we just shot them down, in cold blood. They had AK47s, and the only way to stop them was to shoot them quickly. I had the other Seals stand guard as I checked the other rooms. I found more young women, some badly beaten, others lying naked on the beds and the floors, while others were sick from taking cocaine given by any one of Chuck's fiends. I made sure that they were okay before I kept moving from one bedroom to another.

After checking all of the bedrooms and bathrooms, we felt that we had the upstairs secured. It was then that I looked up and saw a familiar face coming toward me. It was Mario, followed by his crew of Seals. With our combined forces, it was time to move downstairs and help Cappy and the rest of the Seals get the rest of the mafia people without getting caught in a cross fire. We needed to find Chuck and take him alive so he would be able to get to court and receive a guilty verdict by the government.

As we moved downstairs, the fighting continued, and there were many bodies strewn across the floors of each room. Mario and I moved slowly and were able to see those who were still standing, trying to shoot their way out of this. Fortunately, they did not see us, as they didn't have the goggles we had, and the place was still dark. We tried to get as many as we could and kept looking for the big guy who would be the gold ring, once we nailed him. The rest of the Seals were in back of us, keeping us covered as we moved closer to the large family room.

It was there that we saw Chuck, standing by his safe, with some of the capos of the various Mafia families. Even if he was able to get some of his money from the safe, he knew that he was trapped, and not really sure how to get himself out of this. He wanted to take his money and thought about escaping, not realizing that there was no escape for him any longer. The Mafia leaders started to yell at each other, and Chuck was being accused of being sloppy and unorganized. He then shouted back at them and accused them of being followed and bringing the feds to his house. I counted about fifteen of them, standing in a tight circle, while their bodyguards protected them.

We surrounded the group and told them to drop their weapons. When one of the Mafia soldiers started to shoot at us, Mario gunned him down. Fortunately, he could not see us clearly in the dark and was shooting wildly. At that point, I got behind Chuck and told him to drop his weapon. He conceded. I told him to get down on his stomach and not to move a muscle. He had no idea that I was the guy in the Venetian Hotel room when he went to take Christy. After a few minutes, it was over. The shooting stopped and many of his buddies were dead. I saw Cappy coming in the front door and I gave Chuck to him as a souvenir on a platter. The King was captured and his entourage was no longer viable.

I then raced upstairs to go to the young women who were in need of help. I walked back into Chuck's room and sat down next to the girl who was beaten. Stan and Paco were told to turn on all of the lights that enabled me to remove my goggles, and I was able to see her more clearly. I also radioed in for medical assistance, as we needed CPR and ambulances to take these girls to the hospital. While helping this poor young thing until the medics came, I looked at her long legs, which were full of blood, and her face, that had been slapped around by someone. I suddenly knew where I had seen that face before. I held her in my arms and called out to her.

"Is that you, Diane? Can you hear me? This is David. Remember David on the island of Kauai?"

The girl, nearly half dead, looked at me and remembered that it had been about two years ago when we had met in Kauai. She was so pretty then, and was alive and funny. It was on that evening when she had been attacked by the bartender. And I remembered how nervous she was afterward, when I met her at breakfast. I held her head up so the blood would not rush to her brain, and she opened up her eyes and cried out, "David. Is that you? How did you find me?"

The medics took the wounded away and put all of the girls in ambulances. We had not lost a single life as the Seals did exceptionally well. The FBI and DEA did a clean sweep of both buildings, and then the police and the Crime Scene Investigators went in to do their thing. Chuck was in custody, and we did not hear from any Columbians that night.

I went home and got some sleep, and by late morning, I found out that Diane was in South Coast Medical Hospital. I hopped in my car and drove there. I entered her room and had noticed that she was cleaned up and was able to sit up and look around.

"Hey, Diane, I am back. It is so good to see you up and around this morning. The doctor told me that you are doing very well for all that you went through."

She looked at me and recognized that I was the same guy who rescued her last night, and with whom she went to bed with two years ago.

"David, I am so ashamed. I want to thank you for getting me out of that house last night. It was awful, and those guys were animals. I can't tell you what they had us do as it is too difficult for me right now."

I sat on her bed and told her not to go into details. We sat and spoke for a few minutes, when the nurse came in to check on her. She seemed to be all right, but just needed some bed rest. This poor girl had gone through hell and back, and I would have assumed that she got involved with Chuck because of Peter, not realizing who Chuck was. It all made sense now. The stories that Peter told me about his father throwing him out and the fact that his father was involved with some heavy dudes were coming around full circle.

What a circus of events this turned out to be. Little did I know what would take place two years later, while I was on a vacation in Hawai'i. I just sat and thought about how my life was coming around, and where the hell it was going.

I reached into my wallet and found Peter's card with his phone number and called him on my cell phone. I left a message as there was no response. I went back to Diane and asked her if she needed anything. She was sweet and innocent and really went through the wringer. She had some scars on her face, marks on her body, and her left eye was half closed.

Obviously, she was either punched or slapped on the eye and the impact may have affected her iris as she had difficulty seeing. Her mouth was bruised, as well as her arms and legs. This was one person who had felt the pain of animals and I felt deeply sorry for all that she had gone through. We continued to speak softly as she told me how she met up with Chuck and got involved with his people, and the threats she had to contend with.

Peter had a party at his own home one evening, and invited Diane and her friends, as well as some of his gay buddies. His father happened to come by with some of his own goons and stayed a while, circulating the party and getting to know the girls. Obviously, Diane looked favorably to him and he invited her out for dinner a few nights later. Peter was too scared of his father to tell Diane not to go. Instead, Diane went, and brought along some of her friends as well.

This led to many encounters with Chuck and a few jaunts at his estate, which included cocaine, marijuana and other drugs. Diane became addicted and soon after, relied on Chuck to supply her with drugs. She became an addict and needed her poison nearly every day. In order to get a free supply, she was asked to do tricks with Chuck's people and eventually, many of her friends were involved in this. This had been going on for nearly a year.

It got worse when Chuck told her that he was pissed when he found his fiancée with another man in Las Vegas. This made him angered, and he started to treat her very badly as he took out his anger on Diane. The last two nights were the worst. He expressed so much anger that he threatened her life and told her that unless she cooperated with him, he would kill her. How my life has touched so many others, it was too astonishing and so sad.

I could not tell Diane that the other man who he found with his fiancée was me. That would only complicate matters even more. It was not necessary. As I reached to give her a glass of water, my cell phone rang. It was Peter.

"David, is that you? My goodness…after all of these years! Wow, it is so cool to hear from you."

I listened to this poor shmuck giving me all of this flowery stuff and asked him if he heard about the ruckus in Pacific Palisades. It should have made the TV news by now and I asked Peter if he recognized the grounds on which this event took place. He had no idea that I was involved in the capture of his dad, the big Kahuna, Chuck Manzione, nor did he know that Diane was in the hospital.

"Hey, I watched the news this morning and I just couldn't believe what happened. They said that my father was involved in all of this. Yeah, David, my father is Chuck Manzione. I don't know if you knew that David. I can't believe that they finally got my dad after a tremendous shootout at his home. I also understand they got some of the Mafia heads of the largest families on the east coast. Man, what the hell happened there and why did all this happen?"

I told Peter to get down to the hospital as Diane was hurt pretty badly. He hung up and was on his way. I thought that I would wait for him and talk to him about his father and what he knew about Chuck's operation. I was also pissed that he allowed Diane to go with Chuck and be a part of his nest of women who gave up their bodies for drugs. I didn't know if I was going to bash his head in or just console him. He was a troubled kid who didn't really have all of the answers.

My cell phone rang again, but this time is was Cappy. He told me that Chuck would be arraigned in two days in the Superior Court of Los Angeles, and that if I wanted to be there, the arraignment was at ten in the morning. I wouldn't miss this for the world. He also indicated that the news spread so quickly, that the drug cartel was lining up new distributors all across the country and Assisi called Cappy to tell him that bad drugs were going to run amuck, which would be a sure death to anyone who would take them. I was to be on call once again, to go after the drug lords of Columbia. Swell!

I turned back to Diane and asked her about her friends. She told me that she was concerned about them although she did not know what happened to them. I approached the nurses' station and inquired about the other girls who were brought in and decided to pay them a visit as well. I finally found two of them in another ward and spoke with them, taking down some notes and trying to find out what happened to them as well. All of their remarks coincided with Diane's, and this left me with an empty feeling. How could these girls get involved with such gangsters and be forced to get on drugs and ruin their lives? It was something that I could not understand, but then again, Chuck could be so persuasive and forceful.

I then called Julie and asked her if she heard the news, and she replied that her office was full of media people, knowing that her firm was representing Chuck in Court. I asked if I could see her later on that evening. She told me to drop by at seven and we could have some dinner together. She sounded like someone who was working too hard and needed a rest from all of this. Julie realized that I was a part of the operation to take Chuck down and thought, that I too, might need some diversion from all of this as well. I walked back to Diane's room as I wanted to wait for Peter to arrive.

Within the hour, in walked Peter. He was wearing his Hawaiian shirt, a white beret, white pants and a pair of boat shoes. I told him that I was a Navy Seal and was on the team to take down his father. At first he looked at me with anger, and then started to cry. He knew that one day this was going to happen and perhaps it was for the best. After seeing Diane lying there, badly beaten, he realized that he was as much at fault for her injuries as his father was. He was not feeling too well.

"Life sucks, David. You try to do what you can in life, stay away from danger and from people who are tyrants, and this is what you get in the end. I am sorry that Diane and her friends got into this and I have to take some blame myself."

I took Peter around and reassured him that everything was going to be okay from here on in. I then asked him a few questions about Chuck and what he knew about his father's operation. He agreed to tell me everything he knew, starting with when he was too young to realize that he was different from the other boys in the neighborhood. Even as a little kid, he knew about the call girls and the drugs, and the numbers racket. As Peter got older, his father wanted him out of his sight because he was gay and told him to find another place to live. Chuck paid for his home and Peter just stayed away from Chuck's estate. His mother was also beaten badly by Chuck and left Southern California for Oregon to stay with her own family for a while. She also maintained an apartment on Wilshire Boulevard, and had not seen Chuck all of these years.

Peter mentioned that his grandfather, Chuck's dad, was a part of Teflon Don Gotti's mob, and before that, the Gambino Family. He had seen so many of these guys come in and out of the house as Chuck was trying to be a made man. He was first a 'button', then moved on to be a driver for Sammy the Bull, and eventually when the Gotti mob broke up, he re-organized the group and wanted to take charge.

He muscled in on the other families and took over the territory that the Gotti family had. He met with the drug lords of Columbia and became the sole distributor of drugs for the west coast and wanted to move on those mobs on the east coast by having them get the drugs from him. So he decided to work out deals with the drug cartel where he would be the main distributor for the entire western hemisphere. Chuck had dreams of controlling everyone and everything. His greed and his contempt for those in the other families would someday be his downfall.

The meeting at his house the night we pulled the raid and captured Chuck was about taking over as top 'Don' of all of the families. He was ready to give each family a larger percentage but not to the cartel. Unfortunately, the families did not want him on the top, and were ready to take him out. Our attack on his estate ended any further fighting among the families. They all lost out. Now, not only will Chuck be arraigned in Court, but many heads of the families will be by his side.

His stay in jail would not be a pleasant one as he was a marked man. The families were accusing him of being too loose and allowing the feds into his compound and taking down the entire mob. They also claimed that he was too involved with women and did not give full support to the business at hand. I found someone else, besides me, who also loved women. Good thing I was not involved with his group of friends.

"David, I hope I helped you out a bit," remarked Peter. "But say, you are pretty cool with your surprises. I never would have guessed that you were a Navy Seal. If I remember correctly, you took down that bartender in a matter of minutes. So after all this time, you are still active in government work? Are you going to put me in jail for aiding a criminal?"

I told Peter not to worry. There were many loose ends and he should be able to enjoy his life without the threat of his father on his back. He should, however, go to his mom and tell her what had happened so she too can breathe easier.

With that, I left the hospital, drove home and decided to get some wine for this evening. I was hoping that Julie would be more congenial with me and perhaps we can finally enjoy a cozy night together.

When I arrived at Julie's condo, I was just as excited as the first time she invited me into her home. I sat in my car and wondered if I would be able to reach out to her and she would accept me as more than just a friend. There was a lot of catching up to do since we had last met. But what I truly wanted was for her and me to connect in ways that we had not done in our previous meetings. We always seemed to get off on the wrong foot and we would miss that connection.

My thoughts of her were uppermost on my mind, probably more than all of the things that I was involved with in these last few weeks. What I had accomplished with Cappy and the Navy Seals, and the women I had met and had sexual relations with, were secondary. It was this woman whom I felt was the right person for me, since the death of my dear wife. May God rest her beautiful soul. If only Martha knew what I had been up to for the past few weeks, she would turn over her grave and shake her head as if to say, "David, what were you thinking about, you naughty little boy."

It seemed that I had conquered so many women up to this point, that I felt, deep down in my heart, that there was something very different about Julie than all of the others. Perhaps it was her tremendous looks, her intelligence, the way she carried herself, and the fact that I really loved this woman.

I also knew that she was not going to be as easy to get in the sack in the same manner that I was able to achieve with the others. Oh, there was Leticia who I felt this tremendous fondness for, but I will never see her again. She was definitely married and would refuse to leave her marriage for someone like me. Christy was a hot, beautiful knockout, but had too many issues! Suzie was gay! Rita was too wild and uncertain! Stephanie was an old friend and still married! Heather, Madeline and Diane were too young! And then there was Julie!

Julie was a lady, a professional, and the biggest challenge in the most obvious ways to me. I wanted nothing more than to experience loving her, to touch and to feel every inch of her naked body. Perhaps I was feeling the emotion of my being horny just thinking of her, but I had to remain in focus by being the gentleman that she always thought I was. I felt that this was really taking a lot out of me, as I was able to score so easily with others. But Julie was different! Being the only one of the entire bunch I had not had the pleasure of taking to bed, I felt a certain desire for her. Yet, she kept me at arms length and refused to allow me to have any kind of sex with her.

What the hell...Mario knew that I was a 'hound dog', and he always joked with me many times about how easy it was for me to be with a woman. He would tell me that I seemed to have trouble keeping track of them, and maybe he had a point. My memory was still good, but having had so many accomplish-ments...yeah, we'll call them accomplishments; they all seemed to blend into one another.

After Martha had passed on, I had definitely made up for lost time. I had never screwed around on Martha until the year she passed away. She sent me on a mission of mercy and that mercy was for my sanity. I found the path of least resis-tance and with every turn I made, I was able to find satisfaction. I hit one home run after another. It was as if I was the star player and scored each time I was up at bat. I was a man after all, and my genes kept telling me that I still had a craving for women, to love them probably more than most dudes I knew.

Julie was so pretty, standing in the doorway as I approached her front door. She asked me to come in, and immediately put her arms around me, giving me a great big hug. If it was a week or more, it felt like a year. She had the table set with an attractive array of goodies, small appetizers, and two bottles of my favor-ite dry Chardonnay wine.

She seemed quite relaxed and comfortable, though I sensed that she was antic-ipating my telling her the long version of the story about how we shut down the Manzione operation. She may have been anxiously waiting for my version of the brawl, but I truly did not want to go there. My mind was on her and how we were going to climatically wind up the evening.

I suppose we needed to discuss this at length since her company was supposed to represent Chuck, and maybe I was invited to Julie's for the obvious reasons. Her law firm wanted their client to go to jail as their ties with him had inter-rupted their law practice, and many of their lives had been threatened. They were to defend this animal, but they either had to quit as his law team, or go through the motions and hope to fail in their defense proceedings. For the moment, I chose to keep the conversation light and airy and wait until later to discuss the horrific details of the operation. I truly wanted to focus only on us and see where this evening with Julie would take us.

"So, sweetheart, how have you been doing?" I asked, not giving her a chance to ask me about the business of capturing Chuck or anything else.

"I have been good, David, just working away at my job. I will be glad when all of this mess will come to a close. Looking back, it has been such an ordeal." She continued. "Christy has left many messages on my machine here at home and in my office all of last week, but I have not had a minute to call her. She sounds okay, I guess. Suzie must be keeping her busy, if I know Suzie."

She laughed at the mention of Suzie as she knew that her friends had a way of keeping themselves pre-occupied. She could always count on Suzie to laugh and see everything as a funny joke. Suzie was a clever little gal and had a very high IQ, but her attitude on life was carefree and gay in many ways.

"My sister is coming into town for the weekend, as she lives in Maine. I have not seen her for two years, but we have kept in contact with each other over time. She lives a very modest lifestyle and we used to be closer than we are now. Perhaps you will have a chance to meet her."

"That sounds great," I said. "I would love to meet your sister".

I felt a sense of comfort knowing that there was going to be another time with Julie in the near future.

She kept talking on numerous topics, as she was checking on the food that was cooking in the oven. At times it was as if she was talking to herself and I was not even in the room. I have seen many people do this. Perhaps it is their way of releasing tension or idle thoughts that are on their minds, whether or not they had company. Then it was back to the conversation of her sister and her family. It was as though I had to keep up with her before I got lost in the conversation.

"David, perhaps we can all go to dinner next Saturday and you can meet Jen and her husband. They are both taking a long weekend vacation, away from their kids. I suppose all parents need a break now and then. I set them up at the Hilton in Irvine for four days so they can feel like they are on a second honeymoon. I also rented a car for them so they can get around. They might need a guide to get around town as they have never been here before. Unfortunately, I have a busy work load on Friday, and will try to spend all day Saturday and Sunday with them."

She continued to talk about her relationship with her sister.

"We were pretty close up until the time she moved to Maine, then Jennifer and Ken had a family, and I got more involved with my work. We sort have grown apart, but only in miles, not in our hearts. She is a very sweet person, and her husband was in the Marines. Perhaps you and he might share similar stories together when you meet him."

"Sounds terrific," I added. "I will make myself available on Saturday and would be happy to join you guys."

I decided to open up a bottle of wine and gave each of us a glass. I started to nibble on some chips that were in a dish and tried to feel at ease. We stayed away from heavy issues, as I needed to concentrate on her with the hope that I might have a chance to make some pillow talk with her later. If it didn't go in that general direction, I most likely would have to accept anything at that point, although not necessarily like the outcome. I thought about how wonderful she would be under the covers as I looked at her lean, perfect body.

She was wearing tight fitting, light green shorts, with an over blouse, and a cute little apron. She hated wearing shoes in her house and loved to go bare foot. Julie always seemed so content in the kitchen, concentrating on the preparation of her menu, and trying to figure out how long it would take before we would sit down at the table. There were candles lit on her dining room table and the flowers that I had brought, were placed in the middle. She also had some candles lit on the fireplace and on the coffee table. The house was immaculate.

Julie took everything seriously and very personal. I wanted to know the real juice on the preparation of the trial by her associates and perhaps she would have shared that with me a little later. I knew that there was a rule of confidentiality between lawyer and client, but Chuck was not exactly the kind of client you would want to protect.

I also would not want to share any details with anyone, especially the information that Cappy, Moose and Dickey had related to us. Perhaps, under the covers in a state of lovemaking, I might be apt to reveal things that I should not. When your emotions are pushed to the limit during intercourse, sometimes you say things that you shouldn't.

"I thought that while the chicken was cooking, we could take a quick stroll to the club house." She said as she turned away from the oven.

"I have to give a check to the gentleman who keeps an eye on things while I am away for hours on end. We have an arrangement, and I pay him weekly to keep me posted if he sees anything that is out of the ordinary while I am at work. It's only a few dollars, but he is on a fixed income and could use the extra cash. He has been very good to me, and since this case is just about over, I wanted to thank him as well. Also, I would like you to meet him."

I agreed to go with her and we headed toward her complex's clubhouse. I remembered the last encounter we had where I had to leave abruptly and was hoping that this would not happen this time around.

Her dear friend and neighbor, who was seventy years old was called Yoman Jobowsky. He was a Polish immigrant, and had lived in this area for over thirty years and in northern California for twenty years before that. He had had experience with security, and met Julie when she moved in a few years back. She introduced him to me and he still spoke in broken English. His wife had passed away many years ago, and had many small jobs around the complex, one of them checking up on Julie's welfare. She didn't mind paying him for her own security and comfort, knowing that someone was watching her place.

He smiled a lot and enjoyed feeling important to her. She invited him to join us for dinner, but he politely declined, and I was secretly glad he did. I was pleased that Julie introduced me to Yoman, and on our way back to her place, she seemed to be happy and relieved. She knew that he would be there if she needed him without any other intentions.

As we walked back, Julie had commented. "He has been a good neighbor, David, and I vaguely told him about why I needed someone to watch my place. He never questioned me, and he even took care of my little garden without my asking him to. He did call me once to say that he thought there was a strange package left on my doorstep, but didn't know whether or not I had seen it. I later found out that it was an order I had placed with Barnes and Noble. Just simple things like that. You know, it kind of made me feel better."

"He seemed very nice, Julie," I said. "I am glad that you have someone like him nearby."

Deep down inside, I also wished that I were around her more often so that I would be able to also keep an eye on her. I slowly realized that even if we did not go to bed and make love this evening, I probably would have loved her just the same, maybe even more so. As we entered her condo we heard the beeping of a timer coming from the kitchen.

"Perfect timing, David," she said, giggling, as she went to the kitchen to shut the noise off. "Are you ready to eat? Soup's on."

Her chicken was delicious. I missed homemade cooking and she was a pretty darn cook. After dinner, we sat on her back deck and I enjoyed an after dinner cigarette with another glass of wine. I started to feel a little light headed, as I was on my fourth glass, yet enjoyed the moment tremendously. I kept glancing at her beautiful smile, her sexy composure, and her long, darkly tanned legs beneath her light colored shorts. The moment could not have been better, although I would have preferred to have those lovely legs next to mine in bed. I suppose I should have been content just to be with her and talk about our lives together.

Finally, after an unbelievable amount of patience on my part, feeling that we may have established a closer relationship this evening, I was about reach over to her and kiss her.

But to my surprise, she startled me by asking, "David, would you like to spend the night?"

I nearly choked on my wine, but remained as calm as I possibly could. I slowly rose from the cushioned chair and reached for her hand. She also rose and we stood there in front of each other, looking into each other's eyes. She smiled at me, and I returned her smile. We had grown very close and we both felt a kinship that would only mean one thing. It was time for the next step. A part of me hesitated, and I wondered if it was a good idea to move to the next level.

After playing cat and mouse for the past few weeks, we both seemed to have these same feelings for each other. I also wondered if having sex with Julie would change our relationship for the better, or maybe it would be a mistake at this time. My God! I was beginning to sound like a woman!

If I told her how I was feeling at the moment, would it have impressed her? Would my words cause her to reverse her invitation? We must have stared at each other for what seemed to be about five minutes before she replied.

"Are you okay, David?"

I just kept staring at her when I finally spoke in a soft tone of voice.

"Yes I am, sweetheart. I am perfectly okay. I was just thinking that my time with you has been the best I have had in a long while. If I were to spend the night with you, I don't know if I would want to leave you ever again."

"You don't have to leave, David."

My heart felt fulfilled in a way that it had never been before. My feelings for all of the other women in the past were nothing compared to those that I felt for Julie at this moment. I also felt that the wine was talking rather than me, and I lost all perspectives as to how I should behave with her. I could sense the alcohol seething into my brain, causing my body to be limp, and I had said something to Julie that I never thought I would say again in my lifetime, especially not experiencing intimacy with her.

"Julie, I am so damn crazy about you. I do want to spend my life with you. Will you marry me, Julie?"

She looked at me with her big, beautiful dark eyes, and I noticed a tear started to roll down her cheek. I had surprised myself with what I had said and knew that she too was taken back with my sudden proposal. But I noticed that Julie was also impressed by my aggressiveness as I had not made any previous advances toward her, nor did I flirt or make any indication that I wanted to go to bed with her. I felt that she was very happy to be with me and I would take her response either way, as an indication of my future.

If she would say **no**, then I knew that she was not for me. If she said **yes,** I would then know that I would have an idea of our future plans together. We would either remain friends or become husband and wife. Instead of responding to my question, Julie turned away and closed her eyes without saying a word.

She walked to the end of the patio and looked out over the trees and into space. I felt that perhaps she needed some space to digest what I had asked her in my moment of passion and love for her. Perhaps it was out of frustration or maybe, I just wanted to find out if this was real or just a casual evening of having raw sex with a woman whom I really did not know. I also thought that maybe I should not have had that fourth glass of wine.

But what did she know about me? I met her weeks ago in a parking lot, then saw her again in Las Vegas. We shared the same interesting cat and mouse game, with Christy, Suzie, Chuck and Rita. Then it was with Cappy and the Seals at his home. She has had a budding career with a law firm, and I was trying to get back to teaching and writing. Were we ready to find love and happiness and settle down as a couple and be content to spend the rest of our lives with each other?

Perhaps I was too quick in asking her to marry me. Maybe, I should have just gone to bed with her and had the time of my life under the covers that she opened up for me. Maybe I was a complete shmuck and should have had my head examined for saying what I did. But I did and it was too late to retract. I may have made the blunder of the evening.

I thought back to when I asked Martha to marry me. It was during the time I was in training for the Navy Seals and Martha would come up on weekends and spend time with me when I had a day or two off. She didn't mind the six hour drive from New York, and I loved having her visit me so we could fool around in her motel room. It was fun and we both seemed to look forward to our intimate times together. We were young and foolish, and we seemed to enjoy the intimacy between us. It was a sort of relief for me after having gone through rigorous training to become a Navy Seal.

When I was shipped overseas to engage in combat in Eastern Europe, and then in other operations across the globe with Cappy and his team, I lost contact with her and later found out that her family had moved to Northern California. By the time I got out, I traveled around the country trying to find something that would suit me best and romanced a lot of women during my cross country tour. It was fun for a while and finally wound up in the sunshine state of California. There, I signed up as an instructor and taught at a few schools, initially in the San Fernando Valley, where the temperatures soared to 115 degrees on a hot day. I was later transferred to high schools and colleges throughout LA and Orange Counties.

I started to like my new environment and found that southern California was the place to settle down. The women were beautiful and more open than back east, with their tanned bodies and easiness, that I had to take a few months to acclimate myself to all of this.

It was in Santa Monica where I had gone bike riding one day with a few of my friends, riding along the path and meeting so many great looking women by the beach. I saw this familiar face with light hair as she was leaning on her bike, talking to some other female friends. I thought I had recognized her and walked over to her. It was Martha. She had gotten older and was much prettier. As I approached her, she looked up at me and knew immediately that it was her long, lost lover from back east. I happened to be her first lover and you do not forget who your first lover was.

At first, she was shocked to see me, and then a big smile came across her face. She held out her hands to me and I went to her and gave her a huge hug. Her friends were a bit shocked, but after introducing me to them, she seemed thankful to see me although had not heard from me in years. I told her that I was not able to write as I was always on secret missions and we were sworn to secrecy. When we were seeing each other during my basic training, we had made plans to marry but that never did happen. Her father had been transferred to an industrial company in San Jose where they were beginning to develop microchips and new components, and Martha and her mom left with her father.

Finally, she decided to go south to Los Angeles and find work in Southern California, instead of being up in the Silicon Valley where the nerds were moving into electronics and they were more interested into becoming millionaires than think about settling down and raising a family. Martha always was a homebody and wanted to raise a family. She probably thought that chances were better in Los Angels than in the northern part of the state.

We decided to go out for dinner and try to renew our relationship, if that was possible. After all, I had been with many women, and Martha had been with quite a few men. She was dating, but not seriously, and her friends were all single, and of the dating variety. They were always looking for the rich and famous, and not caring about the loving and the caring kind.

We spent many weekends together, going to Disneyland, the theatre, to the movies, to Las Vegas, and then I got a place in Orange County and she moved in with me. I had a decent job and it was steady. Once in a while I would meet with Mario and his dates, and I would speak to Cappy as well, as he lived close by. They all got to know Martha as we partied together and Martha was becoming a fixture with the group.

We married on a blistery cold day and Cappy was best man. We spent our honeymoon in Hawaii, and after a while, we found a nice condo down in Dana Point where we spent the rest of our years together. Martha was not able to have children and then her illness came.

It had been a wonderful time during the years we were together, and now, I was considering a second marriage with someone whom I just met recently, and have tried to compare the two women together. They were so different in nature except for the fact that they both had good heads on their shoulders. Both were articulate, pretty, tall, athletic, and loving women.

I was in deep thought, thinking about my past with Martha, when I noticed Julie staring at the stars and kept smiling back at me. What was she thinking and why was she smiling? I asked Martha to marry me and then it was a while before I would ever marry her. Was the same scenario going to happen with Julie? Is this the way I was to go through life, and just be a part of a mystical theory? Maybe I was not meant to marry someone until hell freezes over and things have to change so that the moon is in the right position.

What ever Julie would say to me now would be acceptable. Although I enjoyed being married once, it was also wonderful to feel free and go out with other women and get laid. Maybe variety is the spice of life after all. I had great sex with Christy, that fireball who just knew how to make me as happy as any man could ever hope for. Then there was Rita, a one-night stand with this redhead, who had an ass and a pair of legs that could choke, even Arnie Schwarzenegger.

Then I meet Heather in New York who loved to fuck and was good at it. And in Hawaii, there was Diane, that young gal who had so many boy friends, she had to keep a record and a time card. Lastly, there was Leticia, just about the most beautiful, all around woman with whom I truly enjoyed being with. It was she who had taught me that making love could be such a wonderful thing.

Leticia had a lust for sex, far beyond the reaches of any woman I had ever known. I would have loved to have her in my bed every night. But she was married. Sometimes you just can't have everything you want. Life is not built that way. Life gets too complicated and never easy to understand. Life is either great or it sucks. Life takes you down so many paths, that the latest path only seems better than the former one. Life can be great or it can be hell. Life is just sweet and bittersweet.

"David, I hope you don't think that I am avoiding you."

Julie startled me, waking me up from my thoughts of yesterday.

I suppose I too needed to catch my breath. I too had to sit back and understand where I was in life and where I may be going. I looked up at Julie who looked like she was coming out of rehab and just enjoying the cool breezes of the evening chill. I got up from the chair and decided to smoke another cigarette and take a sip of my wine that was sitting on the table. I knew that at any moment I would get some sort of reply from Julie. I was not that impatient any more.

My thoughts of what I had done in the past kept haunting me as to what I really wanted in life. Perhaps I was acting too eager for a finale, and to be with Julie. I wondered if I had to slow down and just go with the flow. Maybe, I was beginning to feel more mature.

"I don't feel as if I am being avoided by you, Julie," I replied. "I was only thinking of good thoughts and letting all of that great food go down. You sure can cook a great meal. I am happy that you had some time to spend with me this evening."

With that, Julie started to walk slowly over to me. She reached down for her wine glass and decided to bring out another chilled bottle. She came back and poured some wine for both of us and took a deep breath and was ready to tell me her thoughts and feelings about my asking her to marry me. Whatever she felt and whether or not this was a good time to get into this, I had to wait for her to speak first. I realized that I was not in that big of a hurry and I would have been content to wait a bit longer if this seemed to bother her now. So I stood there and waited for her to respond. But my emotions got in the way, as they usually did, and I felt that I had to speak first.

As Julie started to speak, I interrupted her and held my glass upward, toward hers, as if I was about to make a toast.

"Julie, you are the most wonderful woman I have met since the passing of my wife, and there is nothing I would not do to take care of you, and love you as my wife. I feel very comfortable being with you and feel that we can make a great couple and enjoy life together."

Julie stood there, not saying a word. She took a sip of wine and was waiting until I finished with what I had to say. I then walked over to her and gave her a kiss on her cheek, continuing with my sermon.

"I feel that we got together by fate. We seemed to understand everything that had occurred these past few weeks had affected both of our lives. My getting to know you through your friends has brought much pleasure into my life and I would hope that you would consider spending your life with me."

Now it was time to make it sound as if I too needed some space and tell her that it may have been too bold for me to ask her to marry me so soon, without going through a dating period.

"But, I feel that I had gotten ahead of myself. By asking you to marry me after you asked me to spend the evening with you, was simply my way of telling you that I want more than just having sex with you. I would truly want you to be in my life and that is important to me. I therefore do not want you to respond to my question right now. I would rather you give it some time and then decide if this is something you would like to do in the near future."

Julie just listened without making any facial expression. She allowed me to speak, and knew that what I was telling her was from the deepest part of my heart. She approached me and put her arm on my face and moved her head closer to mine. She then reached up and kissed me on my lips and whispered a 'thank you'. She seemed quite pleased with my comments and asked me to sit with her on the couch inside the house.

We locked arms around each other and she became passionate with me, moving her legs around mine. She then placed her right hand inside my shirt and felt around the hairs on my chest and pressed her body to mine. Julie showed her love to me for the next hour without even going to bed. She trusted me and understood my feelings for her. I would see her again over the weekend when her sister and brother-in-law would come by to visit her, and we would have more opportunities to make love and enjoy each other.

Two days later, I was sitting in the courtroom in Los Angeles with Cappy, Moose, Dickie and Mario. The lawyers from Julie's law firm, who represented Chuck, were sitting next to him. On the other side of the aisle, the prosecutor's table consisted of three assistant district attorneys and Sean, our own legal mind who had been working with them for the past few weeks. Since this was a preliminary hearing for a court date, there was no need for any witnesses, or even Julie. The D.A.'s office had a different arraignment date for the other Mafia leaders and their people.

Chuck's people were put in jail for using weapons against the authorities and there would not be a problem in prosecuting them. I looked at Chuck sitting there, wearing a dark blue suit and pink shirt. He was a big man but a wonderful dresser. He turned back to look at the four of us many times, trying to see if he knew who the hell I was. I looked familiar to him but I wasn't sure if he knew that it was me who he found in the room with Christy. But he did know that it was me who captured him at his home a few nights ago. Probably he was not able to tie both together, and looked a bit curious and stifling.

The judge came into the courtroom and proceeded to read the documents that were laid out before him. The media was kept to a minimum, while there were many TV trucks outside the building, and some newscasters in the hallway, outside the courtroom. Then the judge called out the charges and asked Chuck how he would plead to them.

"Not Guilty," was the response, and the date of the trial was to be in four weeks. Normally, a case of this magnitude would take at least six months before a trial date would be set. But both the prosecutor's office and the defense team agreed to an early date ahead of time.

At first, the bail was set at two million dollars. With some persistence and tough arguments by the assistant district attorneys, the judge agreed not to have any bail. Chuck was to be locked up for the next four weeks and placed in a very secure detention center.

As they started to take Chuck away, my Seal buddies and I rose from our seats. Chuck looked toward the four of us and called out to me.

"Hey you, Mr. Federal Agent. I want to tell you something. Yeah, you! Come here!"

I walked over to Chuck as the police held him at bay. He was looking at me very intensely.

"I know who you are, you son-of-a-bitch. I finally figured it out. You're that fuckin' pimp I found with Christy in the hotel room in Las Vegas. I knew you looked familiar. I could not forget your face. You caused me a lot of shit and I will never forget you for this."

I got up really close to Chuck and stood before him, staring into his eyes. He was a few inches taller than me and I had to tilt my head back a bit to actually look straight at this eyeballs. Then I remarked in my nearly, quiet demeanor.

"You have punished enough people in your lifetime, Mr. Manzione. Now it is time for your punishment. I will see to it that you never harm another human being again."

With that, they took him away and I felt a hand on my shoulder. It was Cappy, who just wanted to calm me down. Moose and Dickie had to get back to their respective jobs, and Cappy was off to his company. Mario asked me to go with him for an early lunch and I agreed. We sat in the restaurant and pondered over what the next four weeks would be like. We felt that this was an airtight case and there was no way, Manzione would be freed. There was too much evidence mounting up against him, including the fact that we had many witnesses, and he was caught shooting at federal officers. His days were numbered and this made me feel good. I couldn't wait to call Christy and tell her.

Mario had always been a dear friend and he was always there for me, and we protected each other like brothers. Even though he enjoyed giving me advice on just about everything, this day was no different. We munched on our sandwiches when Mario decided to give me one of his sermons.

"David, for God's sakes, you gotta take care of yourself. Don't get involved with all of these women, especially at the same time. You are going to be totally wiped out and we will just have to send you away to a silly farm, where they treat your hormones by taking away all of your desires to fuck ever again. Why not concentrate on your teaching and your writing, and stay away from the broads for awhile."

He was always so diplomatic. I could understand his frustration with me, this big, burly Italian Stallion. He had more women in secret places than you could shake a stick at. Yet, this brazen 'Goombah' was telling me to cool my own jets.

After lunch, I headed back to Orange County. On the way, I called Suzie's place to tell Christy of the arraignment and the court date. There was no answer, so I headed toward Dana Point. Upon reaching my home, I figured that I would change from my suit and put on some shorts, a polo shirt, and some tennis shoes, and head out to the ocean. Tomorrow, I would go to the school and get my assignment for my classes. Then I would put my house back in order by going food shopping, play some golf and relax for the next few days. On Saturday, I would be with my sweetheart and enjoy some good company.

I was preparing dinner when the phone rang. It was Suzie. She received my message and brought Christy to the phone.

"David, how are you? Suzie told me that you had called. Is anything wrong?"

I told her about our morning in court and that trial would begin in four weeks. She felt relieved that Chuck was in custody as she caught the news programs on TV, and even saw a picture of Chuck being taken away by the police.

Fortunately, my own picture was not shown which meant that I still was able to teach at the college without any problem. Once my cover was blown, no one would want me to be an instructor. I asked Christy how she was doing and if she found some work.

"Guess what, David. I got a job in Newport Beach, at one of the office buildings, off MacArthur and Jamboree. I was hired as an assistant to the production manager of this electronics firm. I can learn a lot and it is not far from Julie's work. Are you going back to teaching as long as this is now over?"

I told her that I set up an appointment this week to check on my status and will pick up my assignments from the school. But I did not tell her of my relationship with Julie as I felt that it was not the time to reveal my feelings. She asked me if I had some time to see her over the weekend, and I told her that I would call her back in a day or so, depending on what my schedule would be like. We hung up and I made a delicious lamp chop with veggies. But the beauty part of this was that I was eating alone and not having to cope with anyone else with their problems and conversation. This was indeed a relief. Maybe, single life was not so bad and perhaps I was just pushing a button to be with someone.

I finally got my classes, and would teach three periods a day for a week. If I wanted to, I could also have a night class, three times a week. But I chose not to at this time. I also wanted to continue with my writing, and needed some time to concentrate on the curriculum for the students. It had been a busy week and I needed to be alone for a while, at least until Saturday evening. I grabbed a book and sat in my favorite chair, and started to doze. I thought about starting a novel on my life as a Navy Seal and maybe I would simply call it 'My Life as a Zombie."

As I went into a deep sleep, I remembered my last few days with Martha. I was in the hospital, sitting by her bed, as she lay there with tubes in her nose and mouth. My favorite friend was dying and I was not able to help her except to be by her side. When the doctors told me to go home and get some rest, I refused to leave. Instead, I sacked out on the chair in the room. I had brought extra clothing, my drug articles, and some books to read, as Martha slept most of the time. This was the worst time of my life.

I also knew that she felt my presence in the room and would open her eyes to catch me napping or utter a word or two. The medication was allowing her to sleep most of the day and all I could do was to be there for her, waiting for a glimpse of her opening her eyes, or saying something to me. Sometimes, I would go outside for a smoke and start crying. I felt helpless, only to be at the mercy of the doctors and their somewhat vague consultations, which did not sit too well with me.

On one hand, I tried to take it as bravely as I could as no one wants to lose a loved one. On the other, I was helpless and could not do more than what I was already doing. Martha was my life and soul to me and I could never do enough for her. She was instrumental in my jobs, my discipline, and my loving her as a best friend, anyone could ever hope for. There was not much hope left, nor anything I, or anyone could do for her. The thought of losing her was too unbearable for me, and I was alone, trying to imagine what it would be like to be without her. I found myself sobbing constantly.

As I sat in the courtyard, I noticed some of the nurses talking among themselves. They had tremendously important jobs, working with the patients and being there for them. Martha's nurse, Amber, was a young blond in her late twenties who had just received her nursing degree. She was alert and was very pretty. She had a sweet voice, but was most conscientious about her job at South Coast Medical. The other nurses were always very sweet, but the older ones had more experience and knew how to handle nearly all types of situations.

As I sat in the partial sun, I thought about all of the things that I would have to do, if and when Martha was gone. This was a tremendous burden on me as her parents were out of the country and I was not able to notify them. They loved to travel and would do so for months at a time.

I was in deep thought, when I had seen a shadow on the ground, and noticed that there was a figure blocking the sun. I immediately looked up to see who it was.

"How are you doing, David? Have you been able to speak to Martha at all today?"

It was Amber. I saw how she had filled out her nurse's uniform with her fully rounded breasts, and her long blond hair just sparkled in the after glow of the sun. I had all I could do to keep from coming apart and sobbing, as tears started to trickle down my face. I always tried to hide my tears from others as I thought that crying by a man was not masculine.

I tried to smile at her.

"Oh hi, Nurse Amber. Thank you for asking. Martha did say a few words to me this morning and we held each other's hands while I sat on the bed. I wish I could have done more. This is all very frustrating to me."

"Martha is resting comfortably and she knows that you are with her, David. If you need me, please come to my desk." she smiled and went inside to get back to work.

I sat for a while and then went back to Martha's room. It must have been a few hours catching up on some sleep, when I heard Martha's voice. "David, are you up? I could see you but I think you are sleeping."

I immediately opened my eyes and walked over to her bed. She reached out for me once again.

"David, I want you to promise me that you will take care of yourself and go on with your life. I don't think that I will go home again so I am leaving you with a lot of responsibility. I love you, my darling, and I only want you to be happy and be brave. I shall always be there for you and love you with all of my heart."

I reached over to her and kissed her on her lips. She smiled and held on to my hand as tight as she could. Those were the last words she said to me before she passed away.

After the funeral, I tried to reach her parents, and finally left a message on their voice mail at home. They were probably traveling to France or Switzerland and could not be reached. I notified my brother and he helped me with the funeral arrangements. I also had help from Mario, Cappy and some of the other guys who were great to have around, especially during this time. I was devastated and was not able to think about what I was doing, but simply acted like a robot.

I remember going to bed, reaching over to Martha, and she was not there. I was not able to sleep, as her memories were so deep in my mind, and any noise, like the movement of the window blinds, reminded me that Martha was there. I would stay up all night, staring at the blackness of the room, waiting to hear something that told me she was in the room.

I would cry continuously, and could not function completely. My best friend was gone and I was left to live out my life without her.

Why do nice people have to die so young? Why are we subjected to pain and feel so insecure about life when things seem to be going so well? I realized that life could be so rotten when things are taken away from you without you ever having a chance to debate or counter the issue. The worst part of life is when you lose a loved one. That is the worst fate of all.

Time had passed and I was simply getting my life back in order. It was lonely without Martha but I needed to move on and plan for a new future without her. It was difficult for me as I was so much in love with her, and she meant the world to me. I gathered all of her clothes and gave them away. I sent out thank you notes to those who had helped me during this most difficult period, and went back to teaching. My life was so different as I was alone and needed time to think about how I was to carry on without my dear wife. She was not only inspirational to me but a tremendous friend.

CHAPTER 13

▼

UNCHAINED MELODY

I again returned to teaching, and the trial of Chuck Manzione was only a few weeks away. I enjoyed having a few classes and talking to students who were preparing themselves for their careers. Each day that had gone by, I was able to get more and more involved in my teaching. I finally started to sit my ass down and begin my novel. It was good to be productive and start learning how to relax once again.

My relationship with Julie was good, although I had not seen her too often, except maybe on a Friday or Saturday evening. She was so busy working on cases that her time was consumed by writing her litigations or being with clients. I had not seen Christy in nearly three weeks and somehow I felt for her, knowing that she was on a road to recovery as well.

It had been pretty quiet in my life for the past few weeks after the arraignment. We had the trial coming up and Julie and Christy had planned to be present in court. I would be there as I had made arrangements with a substitute teacher who would fill in for me so I could attend the court proceedings. I was hoping that this might be the end of all of the madness that had crept into my life.

About four days before the trial, I received a phone call from Cappy. It was something that I was hoping would not happen. The drug cartel and many of the Columbians were spreading dirty coke throughout the streets of Los Angeles, as well as New York and the major cities in the country. They were causing havoc with the DEA, and without the Mafia to keep them in line, they were using every opportunity to sell their drugs to school kids and people in business, off the street, and to other distributors who wanted to make some fast money. This was becoming a problem, and Cappy wanted us to be on call to go after these people. Now that I had a good curriculum at school, I really didn't need this headache.

"David, we have to finish this up. The State Department is counting on us to assist the DEA and the FBI, and close down this operation, once and for all. When I see you at the Court House, I will lay out all of our plans to move on this."

Cappy was ready for action. He wanted closure, the end game, and he needed us to accomplish his last goal before he would retire. I suppose I had an obligation to be a part of his team, even after all of these years. It was getting tiresome but he was there for me, and I had to do the same for him. Mario, Billy, Sean, Moose, Dickie and the rest of the guys were in it to the end. This was our way of ending our illustrious careers by doing what had to be done.

Finally, the day of the trial was here. I met the guys in court, and there was Julie and the partners from her law firm. Christy sat in the back of the room, while Chuck Manzione, the prosecutors from the district attorney's office, and many witnesses all patiently waited for the trial to begin. The room was full of radio and TV people, and the media vans surrounded the court building as if this was going to be a major event, shown all across the nation. I took a sabbatical from school as they found a really good substitute to take over my classes. Like others, I too was ordered by the government to appear in court, just in case they needed my testimony.

Every seat in the room was filled, and there were FBI agents and police officers at every doorway and exit, on our floor and in the lobby. The air was filled with anticipation and anxiety, hoping to see this kingpin sent away for a long time. It was to be the finale of this episode. All eyes were on the bench, when the judge appeared and sat down.

As the judge read the formal charges, Chuck sat in his seat, looking unconcerned, as if he knew that he would never see the inside of a jail cell or face the electric chair. The entire thing looked rather disoriented and I felt that something was wrong. It was a feeling that I always seemed to have when I sensed that something was not right. I looked over to Cappy and he had the same kind of feeling, something we were taught in the Seals. There was a feeling of uneasiness in the room and I was getting a bit nervous over it.

The prosecutor started to speak to the judge and was ready to approach the jury and give them his opening statement. It was at this moment when we noticed that the double doors in the back of the room swung open and a man in a dark blue suit, an FBI agent, came running down the aisle. He stopped at our row and asked us to walk with him to the judge's bench.

We followed him as he approached the judge and then openly gushed out the worst thing that we could have imagined.

"Gentlemen, we just received a call a few minutes ago that this building has enough explosions in it to destroy everyone and everything in it. The caller made certain demands."

Cappy and I looked at each other and turned toward the other agents sitting in the seats in back of us. Then Cappy asked the man what else the caller had said that would put some light on this new problem. The agent was informed that there were demands. Nearly out of breath, he spoke to us quietly, while the rest of the people in the room were puzzled by all of this.

"The caller indicated that we have to release Chuck Manzione within the next two hours or they will turn this building into ashes. It seems that the caller was from the drug cartel and they didn't want Chuck to be jailed, but returned to them. He owes them lots of money and they want him freed or they would kill everyone in this building. No one will be able to enter or leave the building or the explosives would go off. All entrances and exits are being watched and if anyone leaves, then tons of C4 explosives would explode. We cannot bring in the bomb squad or 'poof', there goes the building."

We had two hours to release Chuck. The court room had about two hundred people in it, including many of the Seals, the judge and his staff, some police officers, DEA and FBI agents, Julie and her law associates, including Christy and many others. There were twenty floors in the building and probably thousands of people. We had a major problem and we didn't have much time. We had to decide what to do and do it quickly.

No one was allowed to leave or enter the building or they would blow it up. We also had to consider the people in the other courtrooms, and those in the offices on the other floors. We were not bomb or explosive specialists, but we did know that we could not take a chance and have all of these people destroyed because of one man. It was not worth it. Yet, we had some time to try to figure out where the explosives were and hopefully, disassemble them. With all of our training, and all of the planning, this is something that we had overlooked. How did they get those explosives in this building anyway, and where did they put them?

The first thing Cappy did was to make the announcement about the explosions to those in the courtroom and told everyone not to panic. I ran over to Julie and then to Christy. We didn't have much choice but to comfort one another. Any movement toward the exits to leave the building could mean the end of the lives of those inside the building. I told Julie to stay with Christy, while they took Chuck to a holding cell.

Cappy and our team decided to scout around the building, from the basement to the roof. We had less than two hours to find the explosives, as they probably had been placed in various locations of the building. I told Mario to take some of the FBI agents and police officers and head to the basement, Billy to the roof with other officers, Sean and others would go to each floor and check fuse boxes and closets.

Moose called the bomb squad of Los Angeles and Dickie took care of crowd control. We wanted all the people to head to the lobby, since that would be the best place to be. Many of the police officers went to each floor to get all of the people to head down the stairs to the lobby and wait there for further instructions. Cappy and I stayed in the courtroom using it as a base as we took walkie-talkies from the police officers who were on our floor. He also radioed for assistance from within the building to see who had experience with explosives or were trained in disconnecting these types of explosives that would blow up buildings.

If we attempted to bring in others from outside the building, the explosives might go off and he didn't want to take that chance. We still had some time to find the explosives because there was no guarantee that the terrorists would not destruct the building even if we did release Chuck to them. We knew that we at least had a window of less than two hours to solve this.

Within minutes, a few FBI agents came into the courtroom and told Cappy that they were trained in dismantling bombs and many types of explosives. Seth Armstrong and Val Mason, who were on another floor, had brought in about a dozen technicians and they laid out a plan to first, find the explosives, next, to determine what kinds of explosives we were up against. Lastly, the next step would be to disconnect them. The time left was one hour, forty-five minutes. They gave us a brief history of implosions and what we were looking at in the way of locating the explosives and what to do to disengage and remove such explosive devices in buildings.

In 1998, seventeen buildings comprising the Villa Pan Americana and Las Orquideas public housing complex in San Juan, Puerto Rico made The Guinness Book of World Records when all seventeen buildings were demolished simultaneously with explosives. In that case, the seventeen buildings were of modular construction, consisting of 42 ft. x 15 ft, 1-story, light-weight concrete boxes, stacked in staggered formation, like bricks, and tied together with vertical post-tensing rods through the columns. Initially, the post-tensioning rods, containing conduits and standard reinforcing bards, were present in each individual column, which initially created problems for the drilling crews. It was determined that counter-drilling each column would set off the explosive charges to eliminate the concrete satisfactorily.

At first, the modular construction created structural control problems as it was determined that during the implosion sequence, the delayed undermining of one side of each box would create the rotation of that box as a unit, shearing out the post-tensing rotation of the next column row, thus removing support from that vertical column of boxes. It was decided to drill 7,242 holes in supporting elements of the 17 structures. A total of 1,825 pounds of explosives, 8,640 blasting caps and 37,200 feet of detonation cord were implemented to initiate this carefully timed, non-electric detonation sequence.

This created a progressive collapse that accelerated as it moved throughout the length of each structure. The buildings, up to 300 feet in length in some cases, fell quickly and the preparation of the design to coordinate this resulted in superb breakage that facilitated a fast removal of the debris that is required to meet the site clearance schedule. Again, order was for the seventeen structures to fall asymmetrically, and the carefully timed detonation sequence allowed the vibration 'waves' created by the fall of the individual structures to 'cancel one another out' to the extent possible.

During the nineteen second implosion sequence, the highest seismic readings recorded, less than 100 feet away, were less than ½" per second peak particular velocity. The implosion was orchestrated to evacuate over 1,300 local residents who lived within 500 feet of the site prior to the implosion. Of particular concern were the post-tensioned, reinforced concrete support shafts that had been added after original construction at either end of the buildings.

Acting like structural 'bookends', these shafts were designed to bolster the structures against high wind loads imposed by tropical storm systems, prevalent in the region. As these reinforcing shafts were extremely rigid, they could not be 'telescoped' like other portions of the structures. But, with the proper planning, the proper design allowed the towers to separate from the main structures, and 'lay out' in pre-determined fall areas, away from other buildings close by.

In our case, we were looking at a twenty story building in the heart of Los Angeles, and the implosion would affect the surrounding buildings if the explosives were not placed in the right manner. We still did not know what kind of explosives that were being used. As Seth and Val explained to us, Dynamite, which is one example of a chemical explosive, could be used. An explosive is anything ignited, burns extremely rapidly, and produces a large amount of hot gas that expands very rapidly and applies pressure.

Other explosives that were suggested were Nitroglycerin and TNT, and anything from gasoline to ammonia fertilizer to special plastic explosives are in the same class. Unfortunately, we did not know what was planted within the columns of the building we were in until we found them. We were doing that as we spoke.

Gasoline is what we, as Seals, were probably most familiar with, as we worked with this substance years ago. But most true explosives contain the oxygen they need for burning in the chemical reaction. Dynamite is simply some sort of absorbent material, like sawdust, soaked in acid and the absorbent material makes the nitroglycerin much more stable.

We also had experience with C4 Plastic Explosives, which are very high quality, very high velocity military plastic explosives. C4 is usually supplied in bulk drums, in a slightly powdery form. Upon manipulation, the material immediately consolidates into a rubbery fully plasticized mass that may be kneaded and pressed into any shape.

The material has excellent mechanical and adhesive properties, and may be stretched into long strands without breakage. In its original powdery form, the explosive may be poured into charge containers, and then pressed into intimate contact with the liner.

The bomb squad experts took a few minutes to explain to us how a building implosion works. They indicated that you can demolish a stone wall with a sledgehammer, and it's fairly easy to level a five story building using excavators and wrecking balls. But, when you need to bring down a massive structure, say a twenty story skyscraper, you have to haul out the big guns. That was what we were facing at that moment.

Although explosive demolition is the preferred method for safely and efficiently demolishing larger structures, we had no idea what kinds of explosives were placed around the building. By imploding the building, it collapses down into its own footprint. These types of violent blasts and billowing dust clouds that are brought about by a building implosion is one of the most precisely engineering feats known in using explosions. A well-designed implosion causes the collapsing inward because the external atmospheric pressure is greater than the internal pressure. For example, if air is pumped out of a glass tube, it might implode.

The basic idea of explosive demolition is quite simple: If you remove the support of a building at a certain point, the section of the building above that point will fall at the same time the part of the building below that point does. If this upper section is heavy enough, the lower part will have sufficient force to crumble, thus causing significant damage as the upper section tumbles down.

The explosion would be the trigger for the demolition and the gravity brings the building down. The demolition blasters load explosives on several different levels of the building structure so it would fall down on itself at multiple points. When everything is placed and executed correctly, the total damage of the explosives and the falling building material would be sufficient to collapse the structure entirely whereupon only rubble would remain.

We were told that in order to demolish a building safely, blasters must map out each element of the building ahead of time. The first step is to examine architectural blueprints of the building and determine how the building is put together. To get the blue prints of our building would take too long as we only had less than two hours. Once all the raw data is gathered, the blasters would be hammered out for the attack.

Drawing from past experiences with similar buildings that we were in, they would decide what kinds of explosions would be used, where to place them in the building, and how to time the detonations. Some of the agents made calls to City Hall to get the blue prints of our building faxed to us.

The blueprints would be made into smaller pages and would probably take over two hours to fax, and we didn't have the time. So we kept listening to the bomb experts for a determination as to which way would be best to neutralize all of the explosives.

The main challenge in bringing a building down such as the one we were in, is controlling which way it falls so that the blasting crew will be able to tumble the building over on one side, perhaps into a parking lot or an open area. Our building, a twenty story high rise, was surrounded by many other buildings, on all sides of us. This sort of blast is the easiest to execute, and it is generally the easiest way to go. Tipping the building over is something like felling a tree. To topple the building toward the north, the blasters detonate explosives on the north side of the building first, like chopping down a tree. Blasters may also secure steel cables to support columns in the building, so it may be pulled in a certain way as the building crumbles.

Sometimes, though, a building is surrounded by structures as ours was, and the blasters would proceed with a true implosion, demolishing the building so that it would collapse straight down into its own footprint. But this requires such skill that only a handful of demolition companies in the world know how to attempt it. Blasters approach each project a little differently, but the basic idea is to think of the building as a collection of separate towers.

The blasters set the explosives so that the 'tower' falls toward the center of the building, in roughly the same way that they would set the explosives to topple a single structure to the side. When the explosives are in the right order, the toppling towers crash against each other and all of the rubble goes toward the center of the building. Another option, we were told, is to detonate the columns at the center of the building before the other columns, so that the building's sides fall inward.

Seth indicated to us that The Hayes Homes in Newark New Jersey was a ten story housing project that was demolished in three separate phases, over the course of three years. Although all of the buildings had exactly the same design, blasters handled the implosions differently for each phase. Therefore, every building in the world is unique and there are a number of ways a blasting crew might bring it down.

In our case, we had no idea what methods were used, and we were running out of time. Generally speaking, blasters will explode the major support columns on the lower floors and then a few upper stories. In a 20-story building, for example, the blasters would be set in the columns on the first and second floor, as well as the 12th and 15th floors. This would blow the support structures on the lower floors that would be sufficient for collapsing the building, but loading columns on upper floors helps break the building materials into pieces as it falls. By this time, we were hoping that all of the people were safely assembled in the lobby for a fast exit out the doors.

The two towers in New York's World Trade Center stood approximately 1,360 feet (415 meters) tall, with a massive steel truss at their core. At first it seemed that they might remain standing, but in less than two hours, both towers had collapsed to the ground. Once deemed as a remarkable structural support system, the buildings eventually gave way. Compared to the twenty-story building we were in, the north tower of the World Trade Center was 1,368 feet and the south tower was 1,362 feet, 110 stories.

Each floor of the WTC was approximately 210 feet by 210 feet and held approximately three-quarters of an acre of rental space, giving the twin towers a combined 165 acres of space (approximately 7 million miles or 670,000 square meters). It cost over $1 billion to build the towers circa 1979 and would easily cost $5 billion to replace them today. It is estimated that 10 percent of the total space in Manhattan was lost on September 11th, 2001.

The impact of a Boeing 767 with a weight of approximately 400,000 pounds and carrying close to 24,000 gallons of jet fuel is like comparing a large trac-tor-trailer rig hauling gasoline that can create a tremendous fire. A 767 carries an equivalent of two tanker trucks full of fuel. A basic sprinkler system sprays water but cannot fight this type of fuel inside a building composed of 20,000 gallons of fuel. When the planes crashed, they likely took out several floors and the impact caused extensive damage to the sprinkler system, making it unable to put out the fires.

Val indicated that to implode a building properly, a blasting company would use portable field seismographs to measure ground vibrations and air blasts to get the best type of implosion. You also must inspect surrounding structures prior to the implosion, so that they can determine any future damage claims following the blast. Engineers can predict ahead of time what kinds of vibration a particular implosion may cause. On occasion, blasters have misjudged the range of flying debris and onlookers have been seriously injured. Blasters might also overestimate the amount of explosives needed to break up the structure, and so produce a more powerful blast than is necessary, or underestimate what explosive power is needed, and fail to demolish the structure.

In this case, the demolition crew would use excavators and wrecking balls to finish the job. Safety is a blaster's number one concern, and for that reason, they can predict very well what will happen in an implosion. Again, in our case, we would not know what kind of explosions the blasters used until we found them. And even then, would we have enough time to take them apart and disengage the circuits to prevent them from exploding?

We started to receive word from Mario and others that they had found some of the explosives and needed guidance to neutralize them. Many of the instructions went out over the walkie talkies from the courtroom we were in.

Normally, the blasters use detonator controls before beginning a countdown while sounding a siren at the ten minute, five minute and two minute mark, to let everyone know when the building will be coming down. Typically, the actual implosion only takes a few seconds, and following the blast, a cloud of dust billows out around the wreckage, enveloping other nearby buildings and spectators. Seth Armstrong and Val Mason did a good job in educating us and now it was up to us to find all of the explosives and time was of the essence. We moved out to each and every floor of the building. There was less than ninety minutes left and we had to move diligently and cautiously. We had to find all of the explosives.

It took just a few minutes to get down to the basement where I had met Mario as he had combed the very large room. There must have been over a hundred and fifty people looking for the explosives and we needed someone in each crew who would know how to disengage them when they were found. Within thirty minutes, over six sets of explosives were found and dismantled. We just did not have any idea as to how many were left and we kept looking, from floor to floor, inside hallway closets, within floors where there were elevators, wall spaces where air ducts were, and in each and every office. Our time limit was approaching and there would not be enough left to cover the entire building.

As I looked at my watch, it was nearly that time, about twenty minutes to go, and we were able to find many explosives on the floors where the experts told us to concentrate on. It was like finding a needle in a haystack. I then made my way back up to the control center, the courtroom where Cappy and the lead explosive experts kept a tight vigil on the situation. We were close to the end.

We heard from the men searching the building, asking for instructions, from each and every floor. The lobby was crowded with the people who left their floors, and were ready to burst out the doors leading into the courtyard. There was crowd control outside the building as well, as hundreds of police officers and over ten fire engines were ready to take out anything that looked like a fire. It was mayhem in the heart of Los Angeles.

The phone rang. It was the terrorists with their last and most critical message.

"Are you ready to turn Mr. Manzione over to us now, or do we just take you and everyone else in the building down? You have one minute to decide."

They did their best in trying to force us to turn Manzione over to them, but there would be no guarantee as to our own safety if we obliged them. We needed to succeed and get all of the explosives neutralized as quickly as possible. The streets were cleared just in case. I thought about Julie and Christy, who were in the lobby with the rest of the people, and thought about any future we may have in this world after the time expired. Would the terrorists actually pull the plunger and blow up this building over one man?

We were getting some all clear signs from the men as they located a total of twenty sets of explosives, not knowing if we even scratched the surface. But we were still moving from floor to floor, from pillar to post, from the stairwells to the elevators, searching every nook and cranny for something that resembled explosives. We were also praying.

It was time. The phone rang once again. Cappy picked it up and we could hear his voice quiver as the person on the other end was ready to pull the plunger. Cappy agreed to bring Chuck to the front door but also wanted all of the women and innocent bystanders to leave the building as well. The terrorist did not consent to his wishes. They wanted to take Chuck alone, and keep everyone inside the building for insurance. We all felt that they would also take the building down, with over a thousand people assembled in the lobby of the building. Cappy asked for more time, but that request too, hit a snag. The two hours were up.

Cappy told me to take Chuck down to the first floor and show him through the glass doors in the lobby. In the meantime, all police and FBI agents were at strategic positions throughout the building, on the roof, out of windows, and in the lobby, which had two entrances, one in front, the other on the side. Each officer had his weapon trained on anything that might move outside the building. I pushed through the crowd in the lobby, and approached the front main doors with Chuck in front of me.

He turned around to me and finally commented, in his deep toned, gravel voice.

"Well Mr. Smarty Pants, now that you screwed my girl, and turned out to be a federal agent, how does it feel being screwed yourself? You know that you will die after I am released. I am also going to be killed. This is a no-win situation for everyone. You should have let me and my boys take out the drug cartel the way I had planned. But, NO…you had to interfere and bully your way into my home, killing my people, only to find that your own lives are now in deep shit."

With that, I pulled Chuck aside. "You know, for awhile I was beginning to have feelings for you. I had met your son Peter and he only wanted you to be his father, and for you to give him your love. But you never had any respect for him, or anyone else in your life. So if they decide to shoot you, that would be fine with me. I really don't give a shit about you. But I do care about the innocent lives that are in danger as we sit and wait to see what will happen if and when I decide to release you to those Columbian scumbags. So take your piss poor attitude and decide now what it is going to be. Die by the terrorists or die by injection. At this point, Mr. Manzione, I could give two shits about you, and as far as I am concerned, I would kill you myself."

With that, I heard from Cappy through my earplugs. "David, did you release Chuck to the terrorists?"

I suddenly got a feeling that Cappy did not want to let Chuck go. I still had the handcuffs on Chuck as both of his hands were behind him. I gave him to one of the FBI agents and responded to Cappy.

"You know, I really do not think we ought to let Chuck go. I think we may have a stalemate here, and if we had cleared out all of the explosives, then we should call their bluff. They have to be in the parking lot across the street to have access to this building. Let's take that chance and rush the bastards. And if we do release Chuck, they will probably drop the hammer and blow up the fucking building anyway. You know, Cappy, I am going to take Mario and some of the FBI agents and will head toward the garage. Give us some cover as we need to run about a hundred yards to the left of the building."

The deadline came and went. Obviously, we thought we had cleared the building of all explosives, and we started to let the people out of the doorways of the lobby. Mario and I, as well as many other agents, ran toward the parking garage to look for the culprits. There was no explosion. The building was saved. We had done our job again. I made sure that Julie and Christy were out the lobby door before I headed toward the garage. Their lives were spared but mine was still in jeopardy as we headed toward the garage that was about one hundred and fifty yards to the south of the main building.

As we started to run toward the parking structure, we heard a blast from within the upper floors of the building. We may have missed one or more explosives. The sound came from a few of the upper levels, but we still had the bulk of the people heading out of the lobby doors into the street. The fire department sent in their people and those in the building were fleeing at the same time. We tried to stop the people from leaving the building as huge pieces of concrete started to fall from one or more of the upper floors and they came down fast.

The people were running for their lives and there was panic, as we still had many people left in the lobby. Fire erupted on the eighth and ninth floors as windows were blown out, and pieces of glass came flying down the side of the building like bullets. We stopped the people from running from the lobby. It was best that they stay inside until the concrete and glass stopped falling.

By the time we reached the garage, there were police officers and other FBI agents who were already outside the building. We stormed the parking garage and there were no terrorists to be found. We either missed them or they were elsewhere, in another building or from a parked vehicle in the immediate area. The two floors that had been blasted were on fire, but they were under control as the fire departments were taking out the flames as best they could. Chuck Manzione was in custody, and was taken to another jail. Both Christy and Julie were safe in a van, and all of the other people who were in the building, including those in the courtroom, were safe from any danger.

It was a harrowing experience but we pulled out of it safely. The fast thinking of the bomb squad saved hundreds, perhaps thousands of lives. Those people on the upper levels were out of the building as they all came down to the lobby level during the first hour, and we had scoured the floors to make sure that everyone was safe and secure. But we never did find the terrorists.

I found the van that had Julie and Christy, and we went back to Orange County. We dropped Christy off at Suzie's house, and then Julie and I went straight down to Dana Point for a drink. God knows, we needed a few of those! It was a harrowing experience, and we, somehow, came through without missing a beat, or losing any lives. But we still had the drug cartel to contend with, and now, the FBI and the rest of the agencies were involved.

Before I was to experience another operation with Cappy, I needed some R & R and knew just how I intended to get it. Julie and I sat at the bar at the Beach House, reliving our experience of the day. It was late in the afternoon and we were both exhausted. I took her around and gave her a kiss on the lips. She then asked me to show her my home, where we could relax and come down from this terrible nightmare.

After sipping some ice cold wine, we headed for my place. Julie was still shaking from the trauma of the day, and she needed to sit down and relax. She threw off her shoes and threw her body on my favorite chair. I fixed her a martini and poured a cold Chardonnay for me. We sat and stared at each other for a few minutes.

"So this is what I am looking forward to, my dear?" she asked with some sort of sarcasm.

I knew what she meant. It was my job as a Seal that was bothering her. I knew that if I told her that I was leaving the Seals, she would appreciate my intention. So I told her that I wanted out. I just wanted to teach and I was getting too old for this kind of shit anyway. I asked her to understand my feelings for being with the group, and this is what saved her life as well.

"David, you crazy man. Come sit beside me and hold me. I want to take you around and just love the shit out of you."

It felt so comforting to be in Julie's arms. Her words made me feel welcome and secure. Her wit and charming manner brought out all of the possibilities of optimism within me. When I looked into her eyes, I saw someone that I had hoped would be in my heart and life forever. She led me to my bedroom, as we slowly ascended the steps to the second floor.

We started to undress each other and it all seemed like an innocent moment, with all of the complexities of the last several hours disappearing at rapid speed. I saw her beautiful body by the dimming light as she slid under the covers. I knew that it was going to be an incredible experience with her. I thought that I did not want to rush into anything. But then again, I was not always controlled by the head on my shoulders, just influenced by the head between my legs.

"David, I want to thank you for all of the wonderful things you have brought into my life, and into the lives of my friends. I realize that it has been such an ordeal for everyone, especially for you. It seems that Christy is on her way in life, and if it weren't for her meeting with you in Vegas, she might not have had the opportunity to make a new life for herself."

I just loved pillow talk, but time was of the essence with me, and I did not want to lose what intense desire I had. The fact that I already had a tremendous hard on, I would have ended this chit-chat right then and there. But, out of respect for Julie, I did not want to lose the closeness that she was initiating with me.

"Yes, sweetheart," I responded. "The irony of all this is, that if it weren't for the passing of my wife, I would not have had the need to travel for excitement at that time. And I surely would not have had the chance to get involved with Christy and with you."

I did not want to sound vain with her, but the coincidences seemed to add up. As I lay next to her naked body, she rubbed my hair, and slowly moved her hand over the hairs on my chest. It seemed that Julie liked to do this and it truly felt good, especially knowing that it was Julie who was touching me. I didn't want to bring up Martha, but it all seemed relevant. I had hoped that she would not bring up the passing of my wife at all as it might have brought the moment down a few notches, even if it occurred to her that I still might have been a grieving widower.

"David, now that we are here together, feeling closer than ever, I need to ask you a very personal question that has been on my mind for several days."

"Please, Julie, feel free to ask me anything you want." I responded, although I was a bit nervous and had hoped that her question was not too difficult, or that it would take us away from this anticipated moment of passion.

"David, since Jennifer and Ken are back in town, I was thinking that, maybe we could tell them that we decided to get engaged?"

I didn't realize that her sister and husband were back in Southern California. But, was this her way of telling me…'Yes'?

I told her, of course, and we both smiled. I knew then that this was her way of responding to my proposal, without making it a dramatic event. She was sometimes all business, and as much as I adored her for her commitment to her work, often times I wondered how much romance would be taken away because of her dedication to her job. But, being a man, it may have worked wonderfully for me in the future due to my commitment to work as well. This only reassured me that she was probably the right woman for me and I looked up to the ceiling and breathed a sigh of relief.

I hugged her and whispered in her ear.

"That sounds perfect, my love."

And with that, we made incredible passionate love. Her body felt fabulous, as it entwined with mine, and for the next three hours, all I could smell, touch, taste and enjoy, were the embraces of my future wife. I reached for her body and drew it closer to mine, and we connected so quickly, that I felt the most incredible excitement of love making with her. Her breasts were against my chest, and I moved inside of her and felt her tighten up, as I started my climb to reaching my climax. I kissed her breasts and moved my hands inside her thighs and around to her back. She moved her body in the same motion as I moved mine, holding on to me as tight as she could, and it seemed that we reached heaven at the same time.

It was not like Christy or Rita, or even Heather. It was total passion! And as I caressed her lovely body, I felt that I had to touch every inch of it, slowly and passionately. First with my hands, then with my mouth! I took my tongue and moved it along the curves of her breasts. From there, I reached up to kiss her on the lips. With a sweeping turn of both of our bodies, I found her on top of me, moving her chest above my chin.

I started to lick her stomach, and every time she moved forward, my tongue kept moving lower and lower until it reached the pubic hairs on her vagina. I sucked her body until all of the fluids seemed to flow into my mouth. I then turned her over on her back and stuck it in her once again. This time, we went at it until we both cried out with pleasure. It seemed that we both got down and wanted to reach deep into the annals of our passionate love making. It became very intense but the outcome was so climatic. If two people were going to corner the market on how to enjoy sex, we would have scored rather well.

I finally made it with Julie, and I thought that I was going to do this over and over for the next fifty years.

The evening flew by and it had occurred to us that we were hungrier for more than just food, yet well satisfied with what we had experienced with each other. She glowed, as did I, and the day's events, although quite important to both of us, did not seem relevant at that moment in time. Only the feelings that we had experienced together were important.

She offered me a terry robe that she found hanging up on the back of the bathroom door. She found another robe in the closet, as I told that I had one among my clothes. We then headed to the kitchen, agreeing to make some omelets and English muffins to satisfy our hunger pains.

I was not proficient in the kitchen, and for the last two years, I never cooked big meals just for me. Yet, Julie seemed most comfortable and experienced, having been a single person, even with a very busy lifestyle.

I tried to make myself look as if I knew what I was doing, but she caught on to me, and without any hesitancy, laughed in my face.

"Sweetheart, why don't you go out on the patio and relax, and I will bring you some tea and handle the breakfast myself."

She giggled, and I smiled, knowing that she could best handle the cooking without my clumsy attributes in the kitchen. I may have enjoyed some full course meals in the past, even an occasional weekend feast, but I always preferred to have someone else do the cooking.

I decided to go to the den and found a place on the leather couch where I could plop my ass down, and turned on the television. The late news was on and they were rehashing the trial and the implosion of the building from earlier in the day. Thank God, I did not see either Julie or even me in any of the news shots, and was hoping that we would not be photographed by the news media.. The sight of Chuck being hauled away by the police, and of the entire events that unfolded, plus the idea that we all could have died today, made me feel a bit uneasy.

Yet, it brought a big sigh of relief to me as I saw the cameras panning all of the hundreds of people running from the building. What could have been a fatal explosion if we had not been able to defuse most of the bombs, could have turned out to have been one of the biggest disasters in the history of Los Angeles. We have had enough earthquakes that destroyed cities in the past, and Los Angeles certainly did not need another catastrophe on its hands.

I wished that all of this would be over soon, as I was looking forward to spending the rest of my life with Julie. I felt incredibly lucky to have friends in the Navy Seals, and tried to convince myself that it would be the last time that we would be experiencing such an operation as a team. I said the same thing years ago, when I then tried to pursue a new life with teaching and my first marriage.

But, I was drawn into this again as fate seemed to bring me back to the life of danger and intrigue. It was never to this extent that we had to fight and conquer all of the evils of the world, but it was darn close. Manzione was an evil person, to the utmost degree, and it would please me immensely if something would occur where he would not exist any longer. I would hate to think that we would be paying tax dollars to have this scumbag rotting in jail.

Julie came into the room, holding a tray of tea, and sat next to me.

"Here you go, sweetheart."

She handed the cup of tea to me and noticed that the news was just finishing the all too familiar story.

She suddenly blurted out. "Just imagine, David, if things went a different way today."

I turned to her and kissed her on the cheek, looking into her eyes. I felt an incredible love for this woman, a deep fulfillment, having saved her life as well as my own. Perhaps it was fate that we had found ourselves here in this very moment in time. Sitting on the couch, holding my cup of tea, I watched her go back to tend to the meal we probably both needed. I realized that Julie would be my wife soon, that my life would eventually change, and that she and I had come so far. All that mattered now was to put this troubled event behind us.

After our midnight breakfast, we returned to my bedroom and cuddled up under the satin sheets. She indicated that she needed to get up early, and it was understood that life would have to return to reality the next morning. But for the few hours we had left before the alarm would go off, we enjoyed each other, and agreed to discuss our future plans at a later time. We also made plans to meet with her sister and her husband on the weekend for dinner, to announce our plans. But, until then, we would wait to tell anyone else.

I was so pleased that we were on the same page with this. In a way, it still gave me a sense of freedom from the impending new life that was not only inevitable and fabulous, but also intriguing. It also meant that I would be committed to one woman, a most difficult task based on what I had experienced during the past couple of years. Even with the deep sense of love I had for Julie, my fear was with my flighty ways and all I could hope for, was that I would be faithful to her. Of course, I may think of other women, but that didn't mean that I loved Julie any less. I just had to curb my appetite for another skirt, and not act on my impulses.

It seemed like it might have been a challenging task, but one in which I was most up for. With all of this on my mind, I reached over to Julie and decided to make love to her one last time before I closed my eyes.

In the morning, when I heard the shower going in the bathroom, I made my way toward the shower door and hoped that she wouldn't mind having some company. I was still very turned on, and though we made love several times last night, I could not get enough of her. I was hoping that this new day would not change her mind and reject me. I slid into the shower and she looked surprised, but did not push me away. It was another shower play, one that brought back the memory of Christy and me, in the same shower, not too long ago.

Those damn memories just seem to get in the way. But I walked into the shower anyway, not even with a hard on, but looking hung over, without any sense of hardness, and decided to come up to Julie from behind. Her body felt wonderful and I hung on to her as the water came down on both of us. Yet, in my mind, as I moved my hands all over Julie's chest, washing her with soap, all I could think about was how crazy Christy had been in the same shower. It was the same evening that I had to take her to the hospital. Somehow, I eventually had to get Christy out of my mind. My new love, and only love, was Julie. I had to remember not to mention any other woman's name from then on.

CHAPTER 14

▼

PRETTY MAIDS ALL IN A ROW

Julie was ready to leave, and I gave her the keys to my Jeep to get to the office. She had left her car at home the day before, since she was driven by a policeman to Court. We kissed, and she left to drive off to work, thinking that being married to Julie may not be so bad. We would both be leaving for work from the same house, at the same time, once we got married. Though a part of me also felt a sense of wonder and appreciation for the beautiful woman, I still felt a slight twinge of doubt.

I could not place why I felt this way. I had made it apparent to her that I was ready to settle down and be her husband, even with the impulses I had for freedom. I felt that she would be an ideal woman to be with forever. Yet, I was also thinking that I too should get on with my day and not concern myself with the unknown, and just go do my own shtick and let things play out by themselves.

I had to check on my teaching job and schedule my time at the school. It was time to get dressed and take care of numerous things that were of importance to me, such as my job, my life, and my future. Suddenly, the phone rang. It was

Cappy. He told me that we were going to meet at FBI Headquarters in Los Angeles to discuss our next, and hopefully, our last assignment.

The next item on the agenda for the Navy Seals was to take down the drug cartel that settled in East Los Angeles. Our meeting was the next day and he expected all of the Seals to be present as he and the FBI would map out our plan of action. Another day of reckoning and I was back in action. My time was not my own anymore. This was becoming a daily routine and I was not the young upstart I used to be, when I signed up for all of this. I already told myself that once this was over, I just wanted out for good.

As I was about to leave the house, the phone rang again. I hurriedly ran over to pick it up and I heard a voice on the other end that sounded somewhat familiar.

"Is this David? I am trying to reach David."

I was not sure who the caller was at first, and responded by saying that I was David and asked who was calling.

"David, this is Leticia. Remember Leticia from Hawaii? I am here in Hollywood and was wondering if you still remembered me. How are you, David?"

I could not believe that this was the same Leticia whom I had met in Hawaii when I went there nearly two years ago.

"Leticia, how are you? What are you doing in California? Of course I remember you. My goodness, you still have my number. Of course I would like to meet with you. You want to meet today, for lunch? Wolfgang Puck's in LA? Sure, see you at noon."

Now, if I had any doubts about my getting married to Julie, I was hoping that by meeting Leticia, this would tell me that I was ready for the big step, or I still needed to soar my oats with this beautiful Samoan, whom I had made love to years ago. Leticia was the most gorgeous woman I had ever known and she made love to me like no other woman. Julie was great, but Leticia was special. But that was two years ago when there was no Julie in my life. This was when I was married to Martha and had not tasted another woman for years. Was this the right thing to do right now?

I had wondered if she finally got out of her marriage and divorced that stupid fuck who had treated her so badly. Wow, I thought! Leticia was in Los Angeles, and on the day after Julie agreed to marry me. My mind was going a mile a minute. I forgot all about Leticia and how I enjoyed making love to this woman. I was not sure how to handle this situation, but it was sure worth a try. If I could survive walking away from Leticia, then I knew that I was ready to walk down the aisle with Julie. I agreed to meet with Leticia for lunch in Los Angeles because I knew that I had to tie up some loose ends.

I first headed to the school and spoke to the Dean about my reinstatement back to class within two weeks. They understood and agreed to take me back. I figured that I still needed two weeks to work with Cappy and go on this one last assignment with the Seals. I also needed time to catch up on the assignments of the classes so that I could be up to snuff and back to a schedule with the students. It was also necessary for me to get my head together with regards to my marital plans with Julie, where we would be living, meet with her family, and now, meeting with Leticia. Something told me that I was in, up to my ears lobes.

At about eleven thirty, I headed to L.A. on the 405 Freeway thinking about how I would react meeting Leticia after all these years. She was so understanding and definitely a princess, who cared about life and would not leave her husband. But I was also married at the time, and she knew about Martha's health problems.

Just about noon, I arrived at the restaurant, and parked my little sports car in the parking lot near Wolfgang Puck's. I looked a bit older than I was two years ago and I felt like I was going on a date. I just didn't know how this was going to work out, but it was only supposed to be a simple lunch, with a former friend of years gone by. I was wondering how I would react if Julie had met an old friend from two years ago, or how she would feel if she knew that I was having lunch with a woman I had gone to bed with. It was just an honest luncheon and nothing could happen between us.

I walked into the place, and there, seated at one of the booths, was Leticia. She was more beautiful than ever. She was so radiant, that some of the men seated close by kept staring at her. I walked over to her table and smiled at her.

"Leticia, it is so wonderful seeing you again. You are still the same beautiful woman when I first met you two years ago."

She reached up to me, as I bent over and kissed her on the cheek. I then sat down and took her hand in mine.

"Leticia, you still had my phone number after all these years. It is so wonderful that you remembered me."

"Of Course I remembered you, David. I told you that once I worked out my problem, I would come visit you in California. How is your wife? Has she improved after all of this time?"

I tried to hold back my emotions, not knowing if I was really happy to see her, or if her appearance in my life was an omen of some sort.

"She had passed away two years ago. I have gone through much in two years as I am sure you have as well."

"I am sorry," she sighed. "I had left my husband a year after you and I met, as he only got worse and he became more abusive. I needed to be with my family, so I spent the next year with my sisters and brothers, and then traveled to Bermuda, the Bahamas, and the Fiji Islands, and toured California. I have been here for about six weeks, trying to find a new position. I am now working as a publicity agent for some magazines, handling their advertising and marketing. How about you, David? What have you been up to since your wife died?"

It was not likely that I was going to tell this woman what had transpired during the past few months, or that I just got officially engaged to Julie. I indicated that I was teaching, writing a book, and had gotten my act together, as a widower. Leticia accepted my response and we ordered some wine and lunch. She was so darn attractive and spoke with elegance, that I was honored to be in her presence.

Her demeanor was like that of Sophia Loren, and her beauty was astonishing, not only to me, but to all those who glanced over to our table. I felt as if I was entertaining a movie star and it was an experience. Little did the other patrons know that I already had made love to this woman and the thought of this made me want to do it again. She was so full breasted, and her dark complexion was extreme beauty in the making.

"You know, Leticia, I just can't believe that you still remembered me and decided to give me a call. I had no idea that you were in California and the thought that you are now living here is great. Where are you living, if you don't mind my asking, and what is going on in your life now?"

Leticia looked at me with her dark eyes, her lips curled up and she put her hand on mine.

"David, I had thought about you ever since we met. If I were to leave Hawaii, I would come to California and look you up. You were a gentle soul and you made me feel so good that first night we made love. I truly thought of you so many times during the past two years. I never called you, thinking that you were still married and you didn't need me to complicate your life. But, I found my way to Los Angeles, and I am living in Sherman Oaks, not far from the Galleria Shopping Center."

I thought that if she didn't want to complicate my life two years ago, then what was she doing to me now? Realizing that she was on a lunch break and didn't have too much time, and I was about seventy miles north of my home, I cut out the small talk and tried to see where she was heading with her conversation.

"What are your immediate plans, and would you want to show me your new digs in the valley?"

She smiled at me and without hesitation, asked if I was available on Friday. She had a day off and wanted to know if I would help her hang some pictures in her new apartment as well as move some furniture around. I agreed to do it, but realized that I may have to get back to Dana Point early that evening just in case Julie would need me to set up dinner arrangements for us and her sister and brother-in-law. I was crossing the line here, and had to cover my tracks. Julie wanted to meet her family on Saturday evening, which meant that I may have some time for Leticia on Friday. Without throwing a wrench in the works I had to think quickly and carefully. This was indeed getting very complicated.

On the way back down the freeway to Orange County, I thought about this new episode in my life. Tomorrow I had to go back to L.A. to FBI headquarters and find out about our plan to go after the drug cartel. Then the weekend was approaching and I started to have a busy schedule. What was I getting myself into? Did I still have a crush on Leticia, or was this causing me to have second thoughts about my marriage to Julie? I was in a quandary and I needed to sort out this picture of where I was at, what I was becoming, and with whom I was going to wind up with.

I never liked to be in a place where I was unsure of myself, and now I was heading in that direction. Looking back over the past few months, I was carefree and enjoying my single life. Now it was different. On one hand, I asked a beautiful, smart, young lady to marry me and she consented. On the other hand, I have this feeling for Leticia who was getting into my heart like an angel. This was a situation that I would have to work out and hopefully very soon, or they would be taking me away to a funny farm. Mario was correct! He did tell me that my life with women may kill me one day.

The next afternoon, I met Cappy, Dickie, Mario and the rest of the Seals at FBI Headquarters with at least 150 agents, the chief of police of LA, the deputy mayor, and other task forces, including the DEA and the CIA. It was a desperate time for the city as we were facing thousands of drug cartel insurgents and drug distributors who were passing out bad white powder and weed, that were killing people on contact. We had an epidemic on our hands and thousands of people were going to be killed unless we stopped this madness.

The plan was laid out, they knew where the headquarters of the terrorists and drug carriers were, and the time of the action would be in five days. At the same time, the DEA and other governmental agencies would hit the farms in Columbia and Ecuador, and hopefully, exterminate these pests, once and for all. The politicians were staying away from this one since many of them were on the line for money laundering.

This new theatre of action would require a lot of manpower, from all agencies, to take out and destroy these terrorists. At the same time, we were told that there was a possibility that they could be planting more bombs in buildings, as they did in the courtroom building that we were in. We had no choice but to go after all of these people and take them down.

The plans were set, and D-Day would be in less than five days. Mario and I looked at each other and only hoped that all of the other agencies would be as proficient as we were. Our lives were also in the hands of these, somewhat, inexperienced combat soldiers who didn't know what it was to attack the enemy straight on, after planning the way we had done in the past twenty years. Cappy was one of the directors and again, we were to take the lead in the operation. Everyone was put on alert, and it was going to be a bloody mess, by far.

That night, I telephoned Julie to see how she was doing. She planned a nice dinner on Saturday evening with her family and invited her friends as well. This was going to be a big thing for her, and we were to be the host and hostess, while announcing our engagement to all who would attend. She asked me if I wanted to invite Cappy and his wife, Mario and any of the other Navy Seals. I decided against it as we had another operation to perform and it was better to do it after the battle was over. No need to include my friends yet, as I felt that a separate gathering would be better. Julie agreed.

This left Friday open. By ten in the morning, I jumped in the car and headed for Sherman Oaks, in the San Fernando Valley, to visit Leticia. What I expected was still up in the air, and the thought of being with this woman had my heart pounding. I took along some small nails, picture hooks, a hammer, screw driver, and other assorted tools, just in case she did not have any. By late morning, I arrive at her complex, a gated community with condominiums that were about thirty years old.

I parked in Leticia's driveway and rang the doorbell. There she was, wearing a tightly fitted, black sweater that emphasized her breasts as if they were the only things I could see. She was absolutely beautiful and luscious to look at.

She took me into her living room and I noticed all of the pictures scattered throughout each room. I used her step stool to measure the wall space and she told me how high and how even they looked, as I held each picture against the wall. We spent the first few hours raising the pictures, placing them against the wall, and then I hammered the hooks into the wall to hang them. If they looked a bit off, I had to re-hang them. Finally, on my way down after my fiftieth climb on the step stool, I heard the most comforting words from Leticia.

"Sweetheart, how about taking a break for a while and let me serve you a nice cold drink."

She fixed a glass of cold lemonade for me and we sat on the couch, admiring the pictures. I was getting hot, climbing up and down on the step stool and decided to remove my shirt. Leticia was accommodating as she started to give me a rubdown on my neck, which was getting sweaty. She got a cold, wet towel and wiped my back, as well as my chest.

The temptation was too much to bear. I took her around by her neck and drew her close to me. I gave her a kiss on her lips and felt that warm body against my bare chest. She acknowledged by tightening her grip on mine, and kissed me with so much passion, that I started to get hot and excited. I reached under her black sweater and pulled it above her head, revealing her tremendous breasts, moving my head toward them, kissing them over her bra.

I then reached in back of her and unzipped the hooks, pulling the bra off of her body. I lost control and wanted to make love to his woman, probably from the get-go, once I saw her at the restaurant. She was absolutely the most attractive woman I had ever seen in my life, and I was not going to pass up this opportunity to have sex with her.

She led me to her bedroom and pulled her jeans down. I also took my pants off and we got into bed. We both pulled each others' briefs off, and our naked bodies touched, with the intensity of two hot bodies that were drawn together like magnets. I had no other thought but to make passionate love to Leticia and I could not think of anyone or anything else at the time. If this was heaven, I wanted to stay here for the rest of my life. I found the Garden of Eden, and here we were…Adam and Eve.

I suddenly felt that I had a fucking hard on that was reaching for the sky. The inside of my body was so excited that I didn't know what to touch first, Leticia's breasts or her pussy. I first placed my hands on her breasts and held them together, then reached for her huge nipples and slowly caressed them, watching them stand up erect. As I bent over to suck them, I moved my hands down to her thighs and placed them close to the middle of her body, every so slowly, inching toward her pussy. All the while, she was kissing me with passion, and held on to my cock and my balls, moving her fingers back and forth, keeping me as hard as a rock.

She lowered her head and moved my cock up to her mouth and started to move her lips up and down the shank of my huge boner. It was so intense, that I felt myself ready to come into her mouth. She knew that I was ready to release a large dosage and allowed me to decide where it would be, in her mouth or in her pussy. I just let it go with full force.

I put her on her back and moved down to her stomach and used my tongue to massage her belly, slowly moving my mouth down to her crotch. When my tongue found its way to her pussy, I let it move around and started to suck her clitoris, feeling all of her juices that drove Leticia to a level of wanting more of me. She was ready for me to get inside of her and move my cock around her pussy so she could also reach her climax. I accommodated her wishes and as it went inside of her, it slowly revived itself, bringing the hardness into her and generating such force.

She pumped her body, moving it up and down, from side to side, feeling the pressure of my cock inside of her. As she moved with intense force, she became faster and aggressive. Leticia wanted everything she could get from me and knew how to do it. She had reached her climatic impact and her body jumped, telling me that she was satisfied with my sexuality and my organ being inside of her. I was ready to have another climax myself and did. I was hot but not yet finished. I wanted much more.

After several hours of hot passionate lovemaking with this wonderful woman, I leaned back into one of the big down pillows that lay on the bed and stared up into space. There was nothing better than what just transpired, and it occurred to me that I had not felt this way ever before. Maybe I did, but that was when I first had sex with Leticia two years ago. But that was a long time ago.

My mind was empty, my heart was full, and as I turned to look at Leticia, I noticed how happy I felt being with her. It wasn't that I was unhappy before, or that another woman, like Julie, did not bring immense pleasure to me. It was unlike anything else I had ever experienced. Even my love for Martha did not compare to this. I reveled in this delight, and I chose not to question myself at this time. I decided that if I felt that good, I was going to feel this until the end.

Whether it ended tonight, or whether it may never end. I knew that I had to find out.

Leticia leaned over to me and brushed the sweat from my brow that had formed during our intense lovemaking. When she took a deep and comforting sigh, I immediately knew in my heart, that she felt the same way I did. There were no words exchanged between us during sex, and when I did have the urge to speak during our passionate lovemaking, I was too deeply involved in making love to this woman, that I could not say a word.

This was also new for me, as I had always felt that close proximity also meant constant communication between two people, even during intercourse. Perhaps the need for communication was to ease whatever uncertainty I may have had during my having sex with a woman. But in this case, I felt that there was no doubt about my feelings toward Leticia. The touching of our bodies and the continuous passion was enough to show our love and feelings for each other.

I reached over to her, placing my face against hers, and continued to feel her hands, first rubbing my hair, then making sensual gestures with her fingers on my body. I responded by kissing her on her beautiful lips, sensing that I wanted more of her. I just could not get enough.

We had made love four times, and each time we did, was just like the first time. I thought that I had been around the block long enough to know that in the beginning, this is how it was supposed to feel. But something else told me, deep down, that each time I would enter into Leticia, it would be brand, spankin' new. And each time I did, it would feel like the first time, only better.

She was creative and mysterious, but not coy and manipulative, or hiding behind walls of fear or insecurities. Leticia opened herself up to me in ways that I never thought had existed before. I was thankful and appreciative for having met her, and though I felt the need to tell her how I felt, I had this greater desire to show her. Leticia had brought out all of the sides of me that had been disjointed, and made every inch of my body feel as if it had been massaged with love and affection. It was as if I took my body for a tune up at some local lube joint.

Several hours had passed, and we had fallen asleep together in each other's arms. We had not realized the time when we had awoken, and panic had set in. I had a few places to go and things to do, a meeting to attend to with Julie and her family, and an announcement of an engagement that I was involved with. But, my desire to look at the clock was delayed.

As I looked at Leticia, laying there, next to me, her eyes half open, I was wondering what the hell I was doing. I carefully slipped out of bed and went to the shower. Once there, I began to realize how my life was getting more involved, and reality started to creep back into my mind. I was not happy with my situation, and although I knew that I had better get my brain back to a functional mode, it was also both frightening and frustrating to do so.

I was ready to announce my engagement to one woman, and I was falling in love with another. I truly did not want to lose the feelings that I was having for Leticia and walk away from her forever. This was troubling for me as I had felt a strong desire to just whisk her away and go somewhere where no one would be able to find us. I was getting nervous because I was in a stupid dilemma and only I could get myself out of this. Anything I would decide to do would only jeopardize any part of my relationship with either woman. There was no way I was able to take care of any one of these obligations without causing a problem with one of them and myself.

I was just drying off, with my mind a hundred miles away, when the door opened and she stood there, her beautiful naked body, so shiny and dark, and lovely, and her luscious lips, looking for mine. I grabbed her and held her close to my body. I wanted to have her again. I knew that she was longing to have me, but I also knew that time was interfering with the moment. I knew I had better get my ass in gear and get the fuck out of her place as soon as I could. What a pisser.

I turned to her, and she smiled then spoke to me in her quiet, sexual manner.

"Sweetheart, let's get some dinner later and then make our way back here for more beautiful pleasures."

Leticia then put her fingers on my already hard cock, and I started to lose control once again.

With all that I had within me, I reached down into my heart and responded.

"I'm sorry, my love, but I have a business meeting I must go to. But, I will call you first thing when it is over and we can meet later this weekend. How does that sound?"

I knew that I was lying to her, because I was going to dinner with Julie's family on Saturday. I had no idea what I was going to do on Sunday. The hours seemed like days, and the days were stretching into tiny molecules of particles that I had no control over. How could I do that to Leticia, the woman whom I was having the best love affair with in my life? Why would I want to lie to her like this? I thought that I might be able to work something out later and make it right. I looked so innocently into her eyes for her answer.

"That sounds wonderful," she said. "And, David, thank you for being so fabulous...hmmm. I shall look forward to hearing from you and hope that you have some time from your busy schedule to spend with me."

She gave me one of her great big smiles, and I continued to hold her close to me. But time was moving along and I had places to go and people to see.

As I was driving on the Freeway, back to Dana Point, my cell phone rang. I recognized the all too familiar number on the caller ID that belonged to Julie. I was fantasizing about my recent encounter with Leticia, and how perfect it was, and what I was feeling inside and out. The last thing I needed right now was a reality check, but inevitably, I knew that I had to play this out.

I did love Julie, and I did ask her to marry me. I just did not expect Leticia to come back into my life and make it more complicated than it was before. I started to feel the weight of someone who had too much on his plate. I may have gotten used to challenges like this, but it was not a major part of my life as it was becoming now. I was never in the throes of marrying another woman, while being in love with someone else.

And I kept hearing Mario's words swarming around in my mind.

"Boy, you are something else, so many women, so little time."

"Hi, my love," I said as I spoke to Julie on the cell phone. "How are you doing?"

But I kept seeing flashes of Leticia in my mind and I was becoming a bit paranoid over who I was really talking to.

"I'm doing great, sweetheart," she responded. "Are you ready for our dinner on Saturday?"

I could tell that she was smiling, as she let out a small giggle, the same laugh that I had found so irresistible so many times before.

"Oh, why...yes," I muttered, and hoped that I didn't sound doubtful. My tongue was getting in the way of my brain.

"Are you sure, David? You don't sound excited?"

I tried to compose myself and took a deep breath before answering.

"Julie, I'm actually on the Freeway and in a lot of traffic. Let me call you when I am in a better place."

I was hoping that she would understand that speaking on a cell phone while in heavy traffic on the freeway can be bad for one's health. Upon hearing my plea, Julie hung up.

Although I felt a twinge of guilt, it didn't sustain too long, as I went back to smiling for my love, Leticia. She would be waiting for me when I would call her in a day or two. I didn't like lying to Julie, nor to Leticia, but I also did not know that due to unforeseen circumstances, I would be falling in love with one woman, while being engaged to another.

Somehow, I would have to make a decision as to what I would do with each of them. Or would I? Or, I could play this out a while longer and enjoy each of them through my own disillusionment. I could very well have the best of both worlds instead of settling for just one of them. I was not sure how to handle this. I was not sure if Leticia was truly on the level. Was she also playing me so she could have a good time? Was Leticia being honest with me or was I just another notch on her belt, as she was on mine?

It all boiled down to this. Did I have to settle for one woman, or should I continue to play the role that I put myself into and act out this play to the end? And that was to bed down with as many women as I could until I grew tired of them.

The entranceway to my complex was coming up and it had occurred to me that I had too many things to do. I knew that I could handle them all if I put my mind to it, and yet, I also knew that it was much more complicated than a chess game. I felt that if I did not do what I really wanted for myself, I would lose out big time. The game was getting close to 'Check Mate', and I was going to be either the conqueror or the fallen victim of my own game playing.

I decided to call Julie back and we talked about the coming event the next evening, where we were going to meet, and whether we were all going together, or meeting her sister and brother in law, or any of her friends. I really wanted to meet Julie at the restaurant so I could have some time to call Leticia and tell her that I could still smell her on my body, even after my hot shower at her place. I could still feel her touching my body and I did not know if I really wanted to have this engagement dinner with Julie and her family after all. I also felt that it was much easier fighting insurgents than it was coping with my sanity over women.

"Julie, David. Yeah, I made it home safely. I had to go to LA today on business. About tomorrow, I hope you don't mind, but I would rather meet you at the restaurant as I have so many things to do. Where did you set up the reservations? Oh, that's in Laguna Beach. I can meet you there as it is closer to Dana Point."

Julie agreed and that was that.

I then immediately called Leticia.

"Hi. How is my lover?" I asked. "I am still feeling the effects of you all over my body and it happens to be wonderful. I must say that you are such a wonderful woman. I want to thank you for coming back into my life."

At first, there was silence. Then I heard Leticia's response.

"David, it is so wonderful to hear from you so soon. I too am thankful but I cannot talk now. I will get back to you later. I have another call on the line."

BAM!!!

I felt like I was just slapped across the face. I thought that it would be a perfect time to have some after-play, to relive some of the hot moments of pleasure. Phone sex has always been one of my favorite past times, perhaps one of those playful engagements when you just couldn't get to the woman right away. But Leticia surprised me by saying that she was too busy to talk to me. I managed to say to her that I would speak to her later, but I was not sure if she heard me.

Although I was a bit disappointed, I decided to rummage through my closet and choose an outfit that was befitting for tomorrow's occasion. I was going to meet people whom I had not met before and tell them of my attentions of marrying their sister. This seemed much more difficult than being on the Seal's squad under Cappy's definitive orders.

I also received calls from Cappy, from Mario and from Christy. I decided to call Cappy first. His remarks were that we were going to war against the Columbia drug cartel next week. It was going to be a large theatre of operation. I had to be ready at two in the morning as this was going to be coordinated by the FBI, the DEA and the State Department. We had lots of people involved in this, and we had to be in the Los Angeles area early on in the a.m.

I then called Mario and he just wanted to know what I was up to. He asked if I was getting into any kind of trouble and for the life of me, I just couldn't tell that I was. This Italian Stallion knew far too much about love and sex, and there was no need to give him any fuel to get his motor running. He was a good friend, but sometimes too interested in my social affairs. I told him that I would have more info on me, and my social calendar on Sunday. He was on pins and needles.

I then called Christy. She was not aware of my engagement with Julie as she wanted to see me. I told her that I was in the middle of some operations with the Navy Seals and she understood. She asked if I would be available Sunday evening and I told her that if I were, I would call her back. But my time, at present, was tighter than a drum and I was running out of days on the calendar.

I then decided to lie down and go over, in my mind, what had transpired yesterday and today. I decided to close my eyes and doze off, hoping that I would be able to come up with an interesting solution as to what I was looking for, whether it would be with Julie, or with Leticia, or just not with anyone at all. Somehow, I called out to Martha.

In my dreams, I saw Martha as she looked about five years ago. She was young and so pretty. She always wore nice clothes and tried to please me to no end. She was someone I always felt comfortable with and there was no pretense to our relationship. She would always know if I was happy, or sad, or just needing her warmth to lean on.

"David, you seem a bit uptight, this evening. How can I help you, my love?"

I turned upward, and opened my eyes. It was Martha. She was there in my room, or so it seemed. I looked at my beautiful wife and asked her to consider all of the options that I had, and what was the best decision I could make.

"David, you are going through many situations right now that seem to be affecting you and this is not the David I got to know. You used to be able to resolve all of the problems without even blinking an eye. You are not happy, David. There is more than meets they eye, and you are only touching the surface. Start taking control of your life and analyze the situation as you used to. You will be presented with more problems and you need to take hold."

I could feel my eyes getting teary and my thoughts were sad. I was now talking to my wife who has been gone for over two years, and I was reaching out to her for her advice. She came to me like an angel from heaven.

"Martha, I would like to go on with my life. I have two loves and I am totally lost. I am about to get engaged to Julie who is the sweetest thing I had met since you were in my life. I am comparing her to you and I find that there are many things missing that I had with you when you were with me. But, I am in love with her and appreciate her as I appreciated you. And then there is Leticia, whom I am sexually attracted to.

"I find myself falling in love with her also. But it is a different kind of love. We are so bound sexually, that it has been a tremendous feeling to make love to her.

There is still something missing in our relationship. I don't know her that well, and she is so mysterious that it makes my life crazy just thinking about her. I am lost, my dear Martha. I am not sure which road to take. I need you to guide me as you always have done. Listen to my feelings and tell me what I am to do to make things right. I am not sure what is right any more."

In my deep sleep, I could see Martha, as she always had done, looking at me and smiling ever so beautifully. She knew how to sit me down and settle my nerves, giving me alternatives that I could not imagine possible. She was simply ignoring the wrongs, but looking at all of the rights. She was not manipulative, but rather caring, and always seemed to come up with some logical response that I could never do. I always leaned on Martha before I would ever make any decision on anything in my life. I believed in her and I loved the way she used her mind to resolve any differences I may have had.

"David, what makes you think that you are ready to get married? And why is Julie your choice as your next wife?"

I thought a moment before I could even respond to her questions. I then turned my head toward space and replied.

"Martha, I have not been content with my life ever since you left me. You have always been that guiding light that kept me going and believing that we were going to spend our entire lifetime together. I never had to think about how I was to go on with my life or who would make a good wife for me. It has always been you and I miss and love you dearly."

"David, why don't you answer my question? I am no longer a part of your life, but only a memory in your soul. I have been there for you and you have been a wonderful husband to me for many years. But it is time for you to move on and choose the right woman who will make you happy and give you all of the comfort and love you could ever want out of life."

She continued.

"I ask you to consider the fact that perhaps you may not be ready for another marriage, or that you are simply trying to compare either one of these women to me. That is a mistake. Take a long, hard look at each one and what they can offer you as your life long companion. They are not me, David. You must appreciate what they have to offer you, and not compare them to me at all.

"Each can bring a lot of love into your life, and each will offer something different, that will make you want to love them and adore them. You must feel their love within your heart. Only you can determine who would make the right partner for you. I gave you my love and continue to love you but I can no longer be a part of your life. You have always been there for me as well, and I shall never leave your heart. But you must go on with life."

I could feel myself sobbing as I listened to Martha. She always knew how to put all of the pieces together. I was a spec of a man, far from being the take charge type, who needed a woman who was strong, a solid rock, and would be able to look at life like no other woman can. Now, I was reaching out to Martha for answers as to what I may expect from two women whom I really did not know enough about. Perhaps there were pieces that were missing and I needed to ask each of them to put all of the pieces together for me. Why was I feeling that there were pieces missing from this puzzle?

"Martha," I responded, "I thought I was ready for that next step of marriage. I asked Julie to be my wife and she accepted. And I feel that she would make a wonderful wife and take care of me as I would take care of her. She is intelligent, can stand up on her own two feet and face problems with the kind of methodology that you did. I can look at her and know that she would be there and handle life's situations without a doubt. She is a tremendous woman who I could love. Yet, there is something else that is bothering me. I can't put my finger on it. But it is there and I feel it, but cannot see it."

I paused for a moment, and then continued.

"Now there is Leticia. She is a complete stranger to me. Yet, when we make love, it is like heaven and earth. She makes me feel so good inside that I want more of her and I cannot get enough. I had an affair with her, my dear Martha, when you sent me to Hawaii over two years ago. I have to admit my infidelity now and hope that you will forgive me for this.

"This is what happened to me then, and what is happening to me now. She is like a torch that I want to bear, and I just can't get enough of her. Why do I feel this way and what is it about Leticia that makes me feel like a little boy who only wants her sexually and intimately? I never felt this way before?"

"David, I knew that you had an affair when you went to Hawaii. I could sense it when you came back. I did not make any accusations nor did I question you at the time, nor will I do so now. You deserved the sexual fling as I was not able to give you the kind of love any more that I had done for so many years. There is no need to apologize. All is forgiven."

I suddenly felt relieved. I cheated on my wife and finally told her after so many years. She understood. She was my angel. She had known that I had women in Hawaii but chose not to tell me. She knew, but was always a lady about it, and I could never have faced her then, on her dying bed, as I am now. All of a sudden, I felt vindicated. I felt clean and honest once again. My dear Martha still accepted me and told me that she understood my emotions and my needing to have sexual contact with another woman, as we had not done for such a long while. This is what was missing in my life.

I found the depth of my problem by listening to Martha. If you love someone, you must be honest. You must find solitude and happiness at the same time, and never try to disillusion the one you hold so dear. I never told Martha about my sexual activity in Hawaii, but she knew. And she forgave me for my sins. How do you ever try to compare one woman with Martha? It was not possible. What would Julie or Leticia have said to me if they found out that I was fooling around? How would Julie feel if she found out that I fucked another woman, the day before we were to announce our engagement? What would Leticia say if she knew that I was about to announce my engagement with another woman?

When I called Leticia, she was on another line and didn't have time to talk to me. She was rather abrupt and told me that she did not expect me to call so soon and then hung up. What was she up to? Was she having numerous love affairs and I was only one of many whom she was seeing? I just didn't know as much about Leticia as I did about Julie. Julie and I had gone through many emotional times together and she consented to be my wife. I had no idea if Leticia would feel the same way about me tomorrow as she did last night.

I was not sure of her intentions. I was falling in love with her body, rather than the woman. I needed more time with her before I could truly understand if she was the right person for me. Although she gave me the kind of love men only dream about, it may not be enough to convince me that she was the perfect catch for me. I needed to spend more time with her, but I was on the last lap and the finishing line was approaching. Either I go for the gold or find that I was left out in the cold all together. Time was not on my side.

"David, you must think about what is right and what is not. You are contemplating what may be the most important decision in your life right now. Are you ready to settle down with Julie, or do you need more time to come to terms with yourself? You really do not have to make this decision tonight. You have your entire life ahead of you if that is what you want. Don't rush into anything if you are not sure. Keep options open until you find that you are only positively sure."

Martha was right. Yet, how could I go to dinner tomorrow evening and tell Julie in front of her sister and brother in law that I decided not to go ahead with this engagement? I truly loved Julie and would do anything to be with her forever. But I had to do what was right for me. I had to reach into my heart and find the right answer and I needed time to do this.

I felt the sweat appearing all over my body, and found difficulty breathing. I tossed and turned and could not come to terms with what I truly wanted. This was too emotional for me, and I knew that only I could make that choice. I found a place where it was comfortable for me to reach out to Martha once again.

"Martha, you are always right. I will think very seriously of my choices and play these next days out without allowing my emotions get in the way. I truly believe that I made the right decision and I feel good about being with Julie. But in my heart, I must be sure, yet I will seek those answers that will guide me. I want to say that I miss you so much, and feel grateful that you are still a part of me. I only wish that you could be there for me when I need to turn to you again for your support and love. You have been and shall always be the dearest thing to me and I shall always adore you. Thank you."

With that, I fell into a deep, long sleep. I was at peace with myself as Martha came to me and tried to guide me to find answers that would affect my life. Was she really there or was I dreaming? She knew of my escapades in Hawaii two years ago and only wished me well without any question. She was truly a great woman and I missed her so much.

The morning came and I quickly awakened to the sound of the alarm. It was Saturday, announcement day, and I had a full day ahead of me. I again thought about what happened last night. Was it a coincidence that I had this image of Martha or did I dream of my wife because I knew that she was still hovering over me all of these years, protecting my every move, guiding me as she had always done.

I had to go to the restaurant this evening and be with Julie and her family. The first thing I needed to do was to call Leticia and see where I stood with her. It was at this point that I felt either she wanted to see me, or if not, then it was meant to be that way.

I reached for the phone and dialed the number. Leticia was not in. I left a message that I had to go on an urgent call and would not be able to be with her today. I hung up and decided to leave my cell phone at home just in case she would call while I was in the restaurant. I quickly got into the shower and took a cold one, just for the sake of simplicity. I was going to meet Julie's family later on and announce our engagement. This was a moment for me that should be filled with happiness. Somehow I was not sure, but I was going to attempt to go through the stages by being the future husband of Julie.

By seven that evening, after taking care of some chores during the day, I had driven to Steakhouse Restaurant in Laguna where Julie and her sister and husband were to meet with me. I wasn't sure if any of her friends would be there so I would just play it by ear. I had finally relaxed and felt more at ease with myself. The three glasses of wine that I had prior to my leaving had helped to relax me. Had I not made arrangements to be with Julie and her family, I may well have spent the time with Leticia.

I gave the car to the valet and walked into the restaurant and looked around for Julie. There she was at a corner table with just her family and no one else. I had met Ken and Jennifer the last time they were in town so they knew me. I approached, and Ken got up to shake my hand. Jennifer looked so pretty in her bright red dress, looking a little like Julie, perhaps a bit younger. I went over and gave a kiss to Julie on her cheek.

"David, I am so glad we all have this time to tell my family about our plans. Hey guys, isn't David a big, strong and handsome devil?"

I looked at Ken who was tall, about six feet, one or two, and he was dressed in a nice suit and tie. I had put on one of my purple shirts, blue blazer and tan pants. But I always made sure that I had a matching handkerchief in my pocket. That had always been my trademark. Julie looked so lovely in her tight, white sweater and light green pants, with a gold necklace, as if she was going to walk down the aisle posing for all of the other guests. She was always outstanding.

"So congratulations, David," commented Ken. "I am glad to have this opportunity to meet with you once again, having heard the news from Julie about your future plans."

He was nice and very polite. I nodded gracefully and turned toward Jennifer.

"Well, it is certainly my pleasure to share this with both of you. I do hope that you are enjoying this trip to California."

Jennifer and Ken both smiled and then got into a conversation about their children, their home and small town, and the fact that they are ready to leave our sunshine state and return to the rigors of family life back in the Midwest. Julie was pleased with the banter and we ordered some wine for the festive occasion.

The atmosphere was pleasant and the company was charming. Julie kept hitting my leg with hers in a gentle gesture that I felt like grabbing it and spreading it apart from the other one. She was enjoying the dinner and the company, and we kept it light and airy. They were very charming people and were into working out at the gym, sports for the kids, and a lot of bicycle riding and hiking.

By the time the check had come, we were stuffed and we all had our quota of cocktails. I mentioned that I was going on another journey in the coming week, which was of course, the operation with Cappy and his people against the drug cartel. I did not let on what I was going to do, although Julie had an idea of my plans. Ken offered to pay the check in celebration of our engagement and I did not argue.

Since Julie was driven in Ken's and Jennifer's rental car, I asked her to come with me into my car and I would take her back to her place, while her family would go back to their hotel room. They were scheduled to depart from John Wayne Airport, early in the morning. We drove the few miles to her home and she was smiling at me all the way home. There was this brightness about her that made me feel so good. Julie was an absolutely beautiful woman.

"So, how did you feel this evening with my family?" she asked. "You didn't feel like a stranger with them, now did you?"

I replied that I felt very comfortable and looked forward to seeing them again. As I turned to Julie while driving, I thought about Leticia and how she had felt upon receiving my message that I was not able to see her tonight. But this was best, as my time with Julie was more important. Yet, I still had feelings for Leticia and had hoped that this would not affect our newly found relationship. We approached Julie's driveway and as we entered her home, I took her in my arms and gave her a great big hug and kiss.

"This is for you, sweetheart, and you must know that I am overjoyed to be with you and have you in my life. You are truly the most wonderful woman I could ever hope to be with, and you make me so happy."

The drinks we had, and the drive to Julie's house made me feel tired. But it also felt good to think about having some time to myself as I had to prepare for my next escapade with the Seals. Although I had a wonderful time with Julie and her family, and announcing our pending marriage, I realized that I needed to have my own space back for a time. My thought was to get home and think about the next few days with Cappy and the gang, and the next few hundred years with Julie as my bride.

I also could not stop thinking about Leticia. She was everywhere. Every person I had seen on the street, at the restaurant, or in another car, reminded me of her. I secretly kept hoping that I would run into her between stoplights. After telling Julie that I had an early day coming up, we said our goodbyes for the evening, and she was very understanding. The long hug and kiss felt incredible, having tasted her soft lips touching mine. I just loved the way she smelled, and the way she smiled at me. I could only hope that I truly had what it would take to make this wonderful girl happy.

I knew that I had a few more challenges to conquer with the Seals, as well as my tempted desire to see where I was going with the lovely, dark creature whom I had been obsessed with, since she came to town. I was also tempted to call her again, but I knew that I should not do so. I was wishing that she would call me, but that too was not likely. I already told her that something had come up this evening and I would not be available to meet with her. Therefore, the likelihood of hearing from Leticia was indeed quite minute.

As I left Julie's house, I decided to take a detour back on the I-5 Freeway going north, instead of driving south to Dana Point. Something inside of me told me to drive to Leticia's home in the San Fernando Valley. Instead of a 20 mile trip to Dana Point, I was now going to drive 65 miles to the valley. I was determined to find out more about this mysterious woman. I felt like I was acting like a school kid with a crush on his teacher.

I could not believe that I was doing this, yet I could not stop myself. After an hour, I found myself pulling onto her street, but I chose not to park on her driveway, but about 500 feet away from her house. I then looked for her rented vehicle, and not seeing it, thought that it might be in her garage. I sat in my car long enough to convince myself that it was okay to go to her door and ring the bell. How could I say that I was in the neighborhood and decided to come by?

I never told her what kind of plans I had this evening, and if they took me to Los Angeles, it was closer to go to her home in the Valley, than to mine in Dana Point. Or, I could have been coy and say to her that I just had to see her, and I cut my plans short just so I could visit with her before it had gotten too late. Either way, I had to allow fate to take over and I decided to ring her doorbell. Not knowing if this was the right thing to do, I just had to act out my feelings and let nature take its course.

As I approached the door, I heard voices inside her home. I heard a man's voice and Leticia's. This peaked my interest and I tried to get a glimpse of the images inside her house by peering through the front windows.

"But I told him that I was only here for a short period of time." That was the voice of Leticia.

"That does not matter, Leticia," was the male voice. Both voices became blurred as the figures walked from the living room to the kitchen. I lost the visual of both of them, and I was not able to hear either of them at that point. Then I saw Leticia coming back into the Living Room.

I heard her once again, as she said, "I will just have to do something, I know."

"Yes, you will, darling," said the male who also came out of the kitchen and into the Living Room, and was now visible through the front windows.

Just then, the male voice came closer to the front door. I ran away from the door to get to the side of the house. I then saw this man coming out of her home. He was a big, beastly sort of a male, also with her skin color, only darker. His hair was greased back, and he carried a briefcase. I watched him walk down the street to his car that was parked about fifty feet from Leticia's house. His car was parked on the same side as mine, but much closer to her house.

I did not know what I should do next. Should I leave and go home, or do I go back to her door and knock, and find out what this was all about? Was it my business to inquire, and were they talking about me? Did I really want to get involved with this woman now? What the fuck was I doing in front of her house?

My curiosity got the best of me, so I knocked on her door. As it opened, there she stood, looking at me, with a puzzled look on her face.

"David! What a pleasant surprise! I mean...I thought, you were busy this evening."

"Hi Leticia. My plans got cut short so I thought I would come by and see you. Hope this is not a bad time or is it? I never like to go to someone's home unless I tell the person I was coming. I did try to reach you but you were not in. I left a message for you. Did you get it?"

"Oh, what a wonderful surprise! I was just on my way out to pick up a bottle of wine. Perhaps you'd like to go with me, and share some of it with me? You are such a mysterious young man, David. You seem to pop up anywhere at anytime."

She didn't act at all surprised to see me, although she said she was. Instead, she really seemed to be caught off guard, as if she wanted to hide something from me. It was too obvious. But, I just let it go.

"I would love to share some wine with you, Leticia. Let's go find a store that is open this late at night. We can always go to the nearest supermarket."

I got into her car and we left her garage, pulled down the driveway, and she drove to Ralph's Supermarket. She turned toward me with her gorgeous black eyes and spoke, in her usual soft manner.

"You know David, I was hoping to see you before I headed back to Hawaii. My family needs some assistance, and I have to cut my stay here shorter than I had hoped. I will have to take a leave of absence from my job, but since we have business in Hawaii, it will work out fine. There won't be any problem with my job. This will be for only two weeks or so."

My heart fell to the ground. I had limited time with this lovely creature and I knew that I had better make the most of it.I responded to her comment.

"Is anything wrong back home, sweetheart?"

"Well, it seems that my brother has some legal issues as he is in Los Angeles and is headed back to Hawaii. I will meet with him tomorrow and we will fly to the islands together. I was hoping that I would be able to contact you before I leave in two days. I am so glad that you are here."

She leaned over to kiss me on the cheek. I was petrified, but excited all at the same time. So it was her brother whom she was talking to earlier.

I was hoping that she would not stop there, but tell me more, without having me sound too nosy. She pulled into the parking lot of Ralph's and we sat there, staring at each other, with such intense passion. I didn't know if I could wait until we got back to her house and attempt to tear her clothes off, or just do it in the car. She seemed to have the same look in her eyes as well. But she sat back and chose to tell me more of what was happening in her life.

"David, I am not sure what to do with you."

She laughed, but I also knew that I was feeling the same way about her.

"Since we have met, I have been so smitten. I sure do love sharing time with you, but I do hope that you realize my stay in Los Angeles is only on a temporary basis, and not for any length of time. My husband has put me through such turmoil since I had left him. He has also gotten my family involved in this issue. I am not pleased with what he has done. This hurts me a lot."

I sensed that she needed a hug. So I reached for her and she looked at me in a way that I felt I was doing the right thing.

"Is there anything that I can do?" I asked.

Here I was again, in the midst of trying to help a woman, being her savior, the one who comes to a woman's rescue, finding myself in deeper than I wanted to be. Does it ever end with me, I thought? I am that 'putz', the 'schmuck', the guy who finds more ways to complicate his life than anyone I know. Mario was right. Yet, looking at Leticia, she looked so beautiful and I was deciding if I truly wanted to help her. I could have put myself back on the drawing table to see if I could be the knight in shining armor once again. Or I could have just let it ride. Leticia made the decision for me.

"No, David. I don't want you to get involved. I do have so many things to do before I leave for Hawaii. But, if we could spend a few hours together before I have to go back, that would be wonderful."

Thank God, I thought. I didn't think that I could have handled one more thing on my plate at this time.

We picked out a good Chardonnay and drove back to her house. I realized that it was past midnight, but our energy levels were high, and we sat together on the couch and drank a few glasses of wine. She told me about how much she loved being here in Los Angeles. But before she could move on in her life, she had to settle some pending matters, and would return eventually. This did not sit too well with me because I kept thinking that by the time she ever returned, I would be well into a committed relationship, perhaps married. She did say two weeks, but it had been two years since I was with her.

Perhaps this was for the best. As I thought about what might happen to our own relationship, Leticia took my hand, placed it on her breast, and asked me to stay the night. I could not resist her. It was all of a few minutes later that we were naked in each other's arms under the sheets, making passionate love.

It was like our sex had not ended, but just continued from the night before. I just had to move my hands all over her body, from the tips of her nipples, to the inside of her thighs. I reached down and kissed her nipples until they stood up tall, like two soldiers on guard. I reached down and put my tongue between her legs and got her wet and she moaned and cried out. I was ready to get inside of her and put my penis down hard between her legs and let myself go, attacking the inside of her body.

She was feeling the arousal of a woman who also wanted no less than hard sex and I was giving her the ride of her life. It was the most passionate lovemaking I had done, or at least, since the night before. Since my first encounter with Leticia over two years ago, my yearning for sex had grown and the urge had taken over my body.

I could only do this with her, as she immediately captivated my body into hers. The perspiration kept rolling off my chest, and I didn't know where to touch her next. I spread her legs so far apart, that I thought she was going to yell bloody murder. But she loved the way I was making love to her, and I yearned for this moment. I came once, twice, three times, and felt that I had more to give, but my body was becoming weak and I had to take a breather. Nothing mattered to me other than making the most of this beautiful woman. I was back in Heaven and I was with the most gorgeous creature God had ever created on earth. This was THE best fucking time I ever had in my entire life. I was THE man.

I found myself day-dreaming about her the next morning as I lay in my own bed, having showered and shaved, almost forgetting the entire day's itinerary. I left Leticia's house about five in the morning and got home around six thirty. The traffic at that time started to build up due to the Sunday drivers heading south to the shore, but I seemed to elude most of it. I was to call Julie later in the morning, meet with Cappy and the guys for a briefing session, and tend to my lesson plans.

Yet, all of this didn't matter. I could not help but wonder if I was going to be tempted to go to the place where this lovely creature was going, just so I could be with her. I thought about her beauty, our lovemaking, the sex we both seemed to enjoy, and how my body reacted each and every time I was with her. I was more than obsessed. I was extremely distracted.

I didn't know how to get myself out of this, if I even wanted to. My head was not clear, and my dick was sore as hell. This was more than I could handle, although it was fun and the fucking we were doing, was the best. I was a lucky son of a bitch, and I had the best bitch in town. I realized that I had things to do, but I just couldn't get myself out of bed. I started to feel myself down below, the soreness and the pain that comes from using your 'shmeckle' too much. I thought of Leticia touching my entire body last night and made me feel so good. I kept wondering if I would ever see this brown bombshell again.

I knew that I had to see her, one more time, one day soon. I would have to make an arrangement to go back to Hawaii after our war against the drug cartel, and tell Julie that we had business there. I had to have one last fling with Leticia before I stood under the altar next to Julie and say, "I do!" I needed to be sure if my marriage to Julie was the right thing for me to do, or if I was always going to carry a torch for Leticia.

I finally had enough strength to get up and had called Cappy.

"So what's up, Doc," I asked. "Are we on for this evening and what are the plans, Cappy? Where are we headed for now?"

Cappy responded by saying that we were to meet at his house at seven p.m. then head up north, to Carmel/Monterey. The drug cartel was going to have a big 'pow-wow' in the mountains and he had made arrangements for us to stay at the Marriott. We had the usual team and it was going to be a joint effort including the DEA, the FBI, the State Police, and more Seals from the San Diego area. Large shipments of crack, cocaine, heroin and other drugs were coming in at such great speed, that we needed to stop this immediately.

Under new leadership, the Mafia was also going to be present. Chuck was still in prison but the other families were going to be involved. We had a cache of people we had to eliminate, and that would take lots of manpower on our part.

We were to meet at Cappy's house this evening and go by private jet to the Monterey Peninsula.

At the hotel, we were to meet with the heads of the other organizations to plan out our attack against the insurgents, many of whom were staying in Pebble Beach, and the surrounding areas. Their meeting, we were told, would take place tomorrow evening, when they would be gathering in the mountains to speak with distributors from all over the country. This was big business, worth billions, and the details were still a bit sketchy. But, as usual, Cappy had a plan.

After I hung up with Cappy, I called Mario. I had to discuss my situation with someone, and Mario was a good pal to speak to. We decided to meet for lunch at Cannons Restaurant, overlooking Dana Point Harbor, and from there, we would drive down to Cappy's house together. I immediately put all of my gear in my duffle bag and checked my weapons, my night vision goggles, and dark outfits that I would normally wear at these types of operations, such as the one we were going to be engaged in the next evening.

This seemed like it was going to be a major theatre of activity and I was hoping that it would be over quickly so I could concentrate on my new life and start planning my future. I was getting too old for this shit and I wanted no more of this after tomorrow. Our guys were looking a bit ragged anyway, but Cappy always seemed to stay in shape and loved the action. It was time for him to call it quits as well, and he knew deep down, that being in his 50s, it was getting a bit tiresome. His wife also wanted him to hang up his Seals outfit and do more golfing and boating.

By noon, I was at Cannons, and Mario was already there, sipping on a cocktail. We moved to a quiet table in the corner and he noticed that I was looking a bit tired. Hell, with all of the drinking and fucking I did last night, no wonder I was still feeling pretty shitty. I decided to order some hot tea, and turned to my good buddy for the usual conversation about the Seals, girls, and the same old crap that we normally talk about.

"So Mario, what is happening?"

"You look like a piece of shit, David," he immediately remarked. "I have never seen you so worn out as you look today. Aren't you getting enough ass or are you in so deep, that it would take an optometrist to find you. What the hell have you been doing with yourself? Here, my deranged little friend, have some sour dough."

I took some of the hot tea that I ordered and the bread and started to feel a little better.

"Mario, I have some things going on in my life that have placed me in a quandary. Let me explain. Julie and I are getting married. I met her family, and we told them."

"Hey, that's good news. Are you ready to make such a commitment and settle down?" Mario asked.

"To be honest with you, Mario, I love Julie. I want to spend the rest of my life with her. But there is something else that keeps getting in the way."

Mario looked puzzled, but I continued.

"About two years ago, I met this Hawaiian gal when I went to the islands for a few days, while Martha was going through her resting period. Well, this woman showed up in California and we have been seeing each other. To tell you the honest truth, I have never felt so good having sex with any woman as I do with her. She is fantastic, Mario. I mean, I can be with her all day and still feel like I haven't had enough of her."

Mario smirked a bit and started to laugh.

"David, David, David. Your pecker is telling you one thing, and your brain is working overtime. What does your heart tell you, my friend? Are you just going to fuck every single broad you can lay your hands on for the rest of your life, or do you really want to settle down with a sweetheart like Julie? My God, man, you ought to check yourself into a shrink, instead of checking your dick into a pussy.

"If I were you, I would cool this relationship with this Hawaiian chick and concentrate on your love life with Julie. Now, if you were a good friend, you would pass along this Hawaiian babe to me and maybe I could create some interest with her. That would be my recommendation to you. But to have marriage on your mind, and go around screwing some other gal is not a good thing."

We both laughed at his crude, yet comical way of putting things in the proper perspective. I continued with my plight for Mario's compassion and his thoughts on life.

"Mario, this Leticia is a brown bombshell. She is a mysterious woman, but she has a way of making me feel so comfortable. I get absorbed with her and it is simply like, well…it's like nothing I have ever felt before. I know you must think that I am an idiot, but then again, I have to look at all sides of the equation. I love Julie and she is great to be with. But this Leticia brings out another side of me, one that I cannot explain. She captivates me with her charm, her body, and her lovemaking. Am I making sense to you?

"Look, this is not what I expected nor was I looking for it. She contacted me after two years and we sort of got into it, if you know what I mean. If you saw her, you would agree that having sex with this woman is like the ultimate for any guy. And she is so good, Mario. I hate to give up this 'Eve' and my new 'Garden of Eden.' She is off to Hawaii for awhile and I was thinking of going to Hawaii after our operation is over with."

Mario was indeed perplexed and looked downward toward the table. He asked the waitress to bring over another drink and took a deep breath before he commented.

"You know, David, you are a friend. I love you dearly. But sometimes, you can be such a shmuck. If you enjoy Julie and she feels good for you, why are you looking to get your dick wet with this other woman? Speaking from experience, being with too many women, only makes life complicated. It's okay when you are young and hitting the streets as a twenty year old. But you are getting on in the middle age portion of your life. Pretty soon, you won't be able to screw a fucking sheep, let alone a beautiful woman with tits that jump out at you."

Mario knew how to explain the facts of life like a good Italian Stallion. He made homage of the English language.

"I realize that you think this is another adventure for you, and that you are taken in by this woman. But it can get sticky. I think you should think about this before you go after her in Hawaii or before you take Julie to the wedding chapel. Tell me what makes this woman so special that you can ruin your relationship with someone like Julie. Julie is a smart woman who will come to realize that you have someone else in the wings and you could lose her because of your sexuality."

Mario made good sense and for once, he was hitting the jugular right where it was hurting the most. Perhaps I was still content acting out my fantasies of my single life as Martha only passed away two years ago. Maybe I needed to play around some more and not commit to a one-on-one relationship, let alone a marriage. On the other hand, I could feel at home with Julie and between us, we can offer each other so many good things to share together. Mario was right in saying that Julie would eventually find out sooner or later.

"Hey, lover boy," added Mario, "let me tell you what eventually killed my marriage years ago. I also felt that I needed to screw every skirt in town, even after I married Ginny. Hey, Ginny wasn't so bad. She had a pair of strong legs that could have tightened the grip on an octopus. She was a healthy bitch who loved to fuck me day and night. But she had other problems. She used to nag the shit out of me.

"It was always, 'Mario, I thought you promised to take me to the theatre. Mario, what happened to that trip to Italy to see my family? Mario, so when are you going to spend some time with me at home instead of going out with the guys? Mario, you sit in front of the TV too much, and you don't have any time to go with me to the gym. And Mario, this shit, and that shit, and this shit again.'

"Finally, I went out and found some other women to fuck around with. And wouldn't you know, women can definitely tell when you cheat on them. They can smell another women's perfume, another women's marks on your body, and another women's cigarette smoke on your clothes. They know when you are lying and they know when you are screwing."

We ordered some lunch and Mario continued.

"So one night I went out with the guys. Yeah, I remember, you were spending a lot of time with Martha at the time. So we wound up at this TGIF on a Friday evening. I found Sandra, who had the cutest little smile, the cutest little voice, and the cutest little tits you could imagine. But they were not so little after she took off her loosely fitted sweatshirt.

"But, God in Heaven, this broad jumped all over me when I took her home. She was the Wicked Witch of the West. She had this thing for jumping on you in bed. And when you are sportin' a fucking hard on, that could be the end of your genitals. Know what I mean, David? The jumpin' wasn't so bad, but the fuckin' fall could kill ya.

"She loved to first get me hard, and then swoop down like a Kamakaze Pilot and suck up my cock like it was a Peach Martini. In any case, we had a go at it for several weeks. Finally, one evening while I am sitting home on the couch, Ginny sits down on the chair next to me and tells me that she had enough. She wanted out of our marriage."

Mario started to shed a few tears, just talking about his wife finding out about his affairs.

"You know, David, women have an uncanny way of finding out what you did that night. She just blurted out to me that evening that I screwed up the marriage with my carousing around, picking up women, and leaving her home alone while I was fucking some other woman's brains out.

"Women know, my boy. They know more than we think they know. David, let me tell you a story that might help you understand life a little more than you think you do."

Mario sat back in his chair, reaching for his glass, and reflected in his past.

"I was standing against the counter, and she walked in the kitchen. It wasn't unfamiliar to see her upset, and most of the time I just didn't ask. You know how Italians are. They are always upset about something. But she initiated something, and I could barely understand her.

"'So will you be home for dinner?' I think she said. Can't remember the exact words.

Everything seems a bit fuzzy right now. Must be the alcohol. I think I'm getting blasted.

"No", I said. "I will be late tonight, which was my typical response. I took my empty glass and sat it in the sink and left. I stopped kissing her goodbye, although I really wanted to have some closure with her each day, in the event I never returned. I was running with some hard characters and you never knew what was going to happen from one day to the next. In our line of work, it was difficult telling anyone, anything, and it was best to just not have them know anything.

"David, since the Seals, I was always involved with some high energy and dramatic events with our old chum, Cappy. This time, we were finishing up a contract that was most imperative for the survival of several people. I got in my car that night, and drove away, not even thinking what Ginny's day was going to be like. We were married a long time. I lost count, and we took each other for granted. Ginny, being an Italian woman, either kept her thoughts to herself, or she would come after me like a fart in a crowded elevator.

"We met as youngsters at a football rally, or at some high school field a lifetime ago, which I may have mentioned to you years ago. To me, she was the prettiest girl in her clique, and I just had to talk to her. I played it tough though, as I hung around with a wild crowd. And God forbid if we ever led on that we still kept company with a girl and couldn't get into her pants after the first night. No one would ever let on that we couldn't score with any girl after one date."

Mario was reliving his past and I just sat there, listening to his days in school and how his marriage finally ended. He was telling me how he went through a marriage, perhaps preparing me for my second time around. He was also feeling sorry for himself as he did have a nice woman who tried to do her level best in tying him down. But Mario could never be tied down to anyone. He needed his space to roam about, going from one circumstance after another. He loved it.

"David, I saw her giggling and playing it coy with me, just like she did with the rest of the guys back then. But I knew that I had a better chance with her at a time when we were alone. That didn't happen for several weeks. But when it did pan out, our passions for each other were outrageous. We did it everywhere we could find ourselves, in the bleachers, in the restroom, in my friend's closet, even when I was supposed to be hanging with the guys. We even did it in my parents' bed when they went to a movie one night. She was a hot babe with a fire that never stopped.

"I loved the attention and enjoyed her for the pleasures we shared. I had no intention of marrying her at the time. We were too young to think about marriage. But it turned out that she found herself with a child in her belly, so my life took a different turn. That bitch got pregnant and she wanted me to marry her. Hell, I was only twenty-one at the time. I never regretted it, though I wished that I had more women to satisfy my cravings for sex before I settled down. That was not the case. So we got married.

"At first, it was heaven. We had three children in a period of six years. She was so involved with them to a point that I was almost jealous. But I knew that she wasn't one for making any money, so I had the sole obligation to tend to the practicalities of life. This is one of the reasons I was not available for Ginny and the kids, and why we started to grow apart. Her life was the kitchen, with the kids, with her small group of friends, open school week, and the PTA. She liked security and felt that this is what her parents did, so she needed the same thing in life.

"Ginny was a fine wife, David, and she made the household a haven for my children. She always had dinner ready for me whether I showed up or not and she only started to nag at me when she started to sense that I was working late or working on other women. One night, I came home around three in the morning and slowly slipped into bed next to her, not knowing that she was awake. I was hoping that she would never know what time I had come home. Instead, I was shocked when she jumped up and yelled, 'you are a scum!

"She grabbed her pillow and headed for the door, and all I could do was jump up and grab her before she left the room. I asked her what the hell she was doing, that dumb Italian broad. She turned to me and told me that she smelled someone on me and knew that it wasn't her. She yanked my arm and took off for another room. It took three days, but I convinced her that she was imagining things, and I truly believed that we were past it.

"I knew that you and Martha were going through a difficult time with her sickness, and I didn't want to bother you with my problems. But I really needed a friend to straighten out my head. I was out of control, man! Like you are now.

"So what I really want to say to you, David, is to think about what you are doing and don't make the same mistakes I did. My God, man, you are so much like me, and when it comes to pussy, we want what we want, and there's nothing wrong with that. But you have to realize, when you are married, it isn't about just you anymore.

"Time had passed, and I thought that she was more secure with me. Little did I know that she had her own agenda. She would spend her evenings at her girl-friends' down the street, and stop tending to the house. Even the kids sometimes didn't know where she was. I thought perhaps she was having an affair. Now get this! I actually had her followed by a private detective, and found out that she was having one helluva good time. She was making it with men and women. Imagine, my Ginny was carousing with some local dudes and some of her girl friends. Whew, I just couldn't handle that.

"I was concerned and pissed at the same time. But Cappy had me tied up with his business and his operations so I just couldn't concentrate on what was happening. Time had elapsed, and then one day, she called it quits. I was actually shocked, but I also offered her the option of a marriage council. You know, some therapy. If we were able to work it out with a therapist, perhaps everything would go back to the way it was. Ginny just laughed at me in my face saying that there was no therapy in the world that could cure ME. Imagine, it was ME who needed to be cured, not that bitch. What the fuck…!"

I looked at Mario and he was sobbing. That big, Italian tough guy put his hands to his eyes and started to wipe away his tears. I looked at my watch and it was approaching three in the afternoon. We had to leave soon, so I took over the conversation while he composed himself. Poor slob. I loved him dearly and he was the loneliest mug in town.

"Mario, my dear friend, I am deeply moved by your story. I hope that I don't find myself in the same scenario. Although, when I think about it, at this rate, the percentages are getting higher."

"Yes, you poor slob, they seem to be going in that same general direction," Mario responded. "Just remember what I am saying to you. It isn't all about pussy all of the time. It is about commitment, trust, integrity and love. You know, how we guys feel about each other? We wouldn't want to hurt each other, now do we? Then why would you want to hurt your lover, your wife?"

With that, we had one more round and paid up the tab. It was time that we had to drive to Cappy's house. Due to his drinking, I had Mario follow me home first and asked him to park his car on the driveway. We emptied his stuff from his car and put them in mine. Mario was too drunk to drive and we needed to catch a flight out this evening. He needed time to catch some sleep and sober up.

I wish I had more time so I could have driven to Julie's and had given her a great big kiss before we took off to Monterey. But there was just enough time to get to Cappy's and discuss our game plan. I was still troubled with my situation knowing that I had to settle a few things regarding my life after Seals. But that would have to wait.

I thought about playing this game of 'trust' with Julie. I would tell her about Leticia and see if she would understand that I would have to close one chapter, before moving on to another. I would tell Julie that I would have to go to Hawaii and end all ties with any woman that I had encountered in my life before we had met. If Julie said 'no' to my going to Hawaii, I would then tell her that I needed to do this anyway. But if she said 'yes', I would go to see Leticia and end whatever relationship I felt that I had with Leticia, and consider that Julie was the one for me, and I would marry her.

To be honest with myself, I really didn't know Julie that much. I had no idea how she would take my going to Hawaii to see another woman and telling her that our relationship was over. Then again, by seeing Leticia, would I want to come back to Julie? That was a chance I had to take and this was the only way I could justify which woman was for me.

How much does one really know about someone before we marry that person? I was analyzing so much in my head that it was giving me a headache. It was starting to drive me up a fucking wall. Oh well, I had time to think about all of this.

As we got closer to Cappy's, I thought of how great Julie was, but I also felt that there was something missing in our relationship. Was it the sex that I looked forward to from Leticia, or the rigidity that I had felt with Julie? Make no mistake about it! Julie was great, but there was something missing. I needed something that Leticia had given to me, and I was not sure if Julie would be able to satisfy my needs.

Deep inside, I knew that after this last operation with the Seals, my life would have to take a new turn. I could continue with my teaching and tending to my classes. That was one option. I also knew that this was a dead end job. With all of the activities in my life, I just didn't want a dead end job that would only seem mundane and insignificant to me. Another option would be that I could go somewhere completely different and forget my job, the women, and start all over again, perhaps in Hawaii or some other location where I could find myself.

I also knew that I was trying to make excuses for myself as I drove up the 5 Freeway, with Mario snoring so loudly, it sounded like a Howitzer in battle. But I had no choice and I felt that I had to settle this in my mind one way or another. I just imagined what would have occurred, if I had gone to Julie's house.

Women never cease to amaze me. Women were always trying to conjure up an excuse to see me for some reason or another. But, when push comes to shove, it is all the same shit. They all have some motive in mind to try and trap you.

I leaned back in the driver's seat, imagining in my mind, and saying to Julie, that I needed to talk to her about our relationship and our pending marriage.

I would first tell her that my life had been unsettling in the last couple of years and that I was willing to start a new life by leaving the Seals, and just concentrate on my teaching and writing. I could picture myself feeling uneasy and nervous about telling her that I also cared for another woman who I thought about and needed to make a clean break from her.

I then imagined myself telling Julie that I preferred a small wedding, with just her family, and a few of my buddies. I even thought about eloping, and getting married by a minister or a rabbi, in his study. This seemed like a better idea than having the entire family, lots of neighbors, and her office and friends, attend the nuptials. Perhaps the thought of being surrounded by lots of people would put me in a compromising situation. What would happen if Christy, Rita, and others would show up? I would feel totally embarrassed and shameful. That is why I thought of a private ceremony, rather than a large one.

But then, knowing Julie, I could hear her say 'okay, you got it.' And she would smile and make things all better. She would know how to soften the blow, to ease the pain, and to allow sunshine come in, during a wet and cloudy day. I would look at her, and by the time we would arrange for a Justice of the Peace, I would feel convinced that Julie was the right person for me.

I would have the rings and the certificate, and we would be on our way to a happy marriage, ready to fly off into the sunset and enjoy life together as husband and wife. I somehow knew that having Julie in my life, I could handle another marriage once again. And Martha would be proud of me, and give me all of her blessings. Julie and I would go on our honeymoon and come back to wedded bliss, start a home, and we could join the ranks of newly married couples. So what was I getting so uptight about? Julie understood! I knew she would!

I started to visualize us standing before the Justice of the Peace. He turned to us and acknowledged that we were husband and wife and that I could kiss the bride. I turned toward my new wife and started to kiss her. As I looked down, I noticed that the face was not Julie's. She was different, a little darker, with more defined features. I looked at my new bride and suddenly realized that I had not married Julie at all. The face of my bride belonged to Leticia. It was Leticia who was standing next to me at the Chapel.

"Hey, sex pot, you there, driving the fucking car. Where the fuck are we?"

It was Mario. My dear friend, Mario! He finally woke up, stretching and yawning, after an hour of sleeping off the booze. We were almost at Cappy's and I could see the familiar streets that I had taken so many times before.

"We are at Cappy's. Pull yourself together. We are supposed to meet with the guys and get to John Wayne Airport for our flight to Monterey. Are you ready to get on the flight and get into the game, Mario? You better get your head together. Sometimes you can be such a fucking pain in the ass, I wonder how you can cope with yourself sometimes."

Cappy was ready with his gear. All of the guys were standing around the living room ready to fly out. A couple of the guys got into my Jeep and three cars headed out to the airport. We spoke about the operation in the car as we drove, but my mind was on the image of the bride standing next to me on my wedding day, that being Letica, and not of Julie.

On the plane, Mario was back to his sarcastic self, cracking jokes. The flight was an hour and a half, and we finally arrived at the Marriott. I shared a room with Mario. We had to meet at seven in the morning with the rest of the group, plus the DEA, the State Department guys, and the rest of the team. My mind was not with this. If we ever got out of this alive, I never wanted to see another operation again. This was it for me.

After we finally settled in, and I showered, I decided to call Julie. She was at home after another trying day at the office.

"Hi, sweetheart," she said softly. "I was thinking about you all day. I was trying to determine that if I moved into your place, I may need to sell a lot of my furniture. We could have two places, but I would prefer to move into yours in Dana Point."

Julie was thinking ahead, while my mind was still in the past. I could not even think of the present, let alone the future.

"Julie, whatever makes you happy, would be great with me. Whatever your heart desires. Right now, I am in Monterey with the Seals for our last big hurrah and we need to go on a massive witch-hunt against the drug cartel and the Mafioso. I know that I don't have to go into details with you right now, as you would understand. Is there anything new with Chuck and his people that you can tell me? Are you still planning a defense for his case?"

Julie was surprised that I was not aware of the situation. It seemed that Chuck had made bail at a million dollars and was out. He was told not to leave the country, but he was able to come up with enough money to get him his freedom. Now he is out there, running rampant, getting his crew together, and going after what he thought belonged to him. I felt betrayed in a way, but anyone could be bought off, and I felt that the judge was on the list.

How could Chuck have made bail? Another fly in the ointment, and he could be headed our way. I wished Julie a good night sleep and ran to Cappy's room to tell him the news. He wasn't surprised. Obviously there were many people on the payroll and Chuck had greased too many officials at this point. If he was coming to Monterey, we would take him down again and this time, for good.

I decided to take Mario downstairs to the restaurant for a late dinner. We sat at a corner table and just spoke about what we had covered in the afternoon, and I told him about my dream. He just flipped out and started to laugh aloud.

"David, you are in worse shape than I was, when I was married to Ginny. You are so screwed up that you don't know which end is up. This is one thing that you, not me, will have to sort out by yourself. If you have ever been in a quandary, this is it, my friend. You have accumulated enough dust balls to create an enigma for yourself. I hope you decide who is going to be your wife, and not marry the wrong person for the right reason. Whew, glad it's you and not me. Shit, man, this is worse than being faced with Crabs after having sex with an Iranian and not checking her out for disease."

After we finished, we were to have a short meeting in Cappy's room at 10:30. It was just after 10 o'clock and I had some time to take a walk outside of the hotel. It was a nice evening, lots of stars surrounding a clear sky. I could hear music coming from the lounge area and walked around the building.

As I approached the pool area, which was closed for the evening, I noticed two people standing in the shadows inside the gate area. They were talking softly and it was apparent that the gentleman was angrily scolding the woman, who seemed to back away every time the man spoke to her. There were footfalls behind me, and as I turned around, it was Cappy. He too needed to walk and he caught up with me. I told him about the two people inside the pool area and we both walked closer to the gate. At first, there was shouting by the man, then a bit of cajoling and laughter.

Something didn't look Kosher, so I started to move closer to the area where they were, and tried to listen in on their conversation. Cappy was right behind me, and we both moved quietly and out of sight. As the conversation got louder, we could hear the man speak angrily to the female, who seemed frightened and in pain.

"If I told you once, I told you a thousand times. You are not to get involved with anyone while you are in California. You are to find out what is happening and you are to report back to me. Is that simple enough, or do I just consider you a liability and cut your freakin' arms off and call it a day?"

With that, the man walked quickly out of the gated area and toward the building. Cappy told me that he was going to follow him, and that I should check up on the woman to see if she was okay. I opened the gate, and walked toward the woman. She was looking away from me and toward the ground. It was quite dark and all I could see was the image of a person standing there in the shadows.

"Is everything all right? I heard lots of yelling and decided to see what the matter was."

As she turned around, I caught a glimpse of her face in the moonlight. I couldn't believe who was standing before me.

"Leticia, it is you. What the heck are you doing here in Monterey? I thought that….."

"Don't say another word, David. I am sorry I put you through this. I never meant to lie to you and I had no intention of going to Hawaii. I am in a screwy situation now and I don't know how to get out of it. I don't know what you want from me or what you are doing here. But for some reason, you seem to show up every time I am with certain people. What is it with you? What is it that you do and why do I feel like you are checking up on me?"

I looked at Leticia and here was this lovely woman, scared and feeling alone, accusing me of either following her or just being someplace where I was not supposed to be. I had to be vague as to why I was at the Marriott but needed to know what she was up to as well. She was not as innocent as I thought, and her presence sort of scared me a little.

"I am here for a meeting with my business colleagues, and we just had dinner. And here you are. Leticia, I think we had better sit down and discuss what is happening here before one of us finds out something that the other doesn't want revealed. It seems we both have some explaining to do. What do you say if we meet in your room in an hour?"

Leticia felt comfortable with that and walked toward the building and back to her hotel room. She told me that she was staying alone in room 310, and I told her to wait for me as I would be there soon. I then headed to Cappy's room for a brief meeting about tomorrow, after which I would go visit Leticia. This was getting a bit more complicated than I wanted it to, and I knew that I was getting in deeper because of my relationship with Leticia and with Julie. Now that Chuck was out on bail, he too may show up at any time himself. I walked into Cappy's room and the guys were just about to sit down and talk.

"David, so glad you could join us," remarked Mike.

I just ignored the childish behavior and sat down in one of the chairs. There were eight of us, plus Cappy. Then one of the FBI guys joined us, followed by the DEA leader, and Moose who was checking on something in his room. It was a high-powered meeting as we had lots to cover in so short a time. I then would have to get back to Leticia and find out what was going on with that woman.

"Listen guys," started Cappy, "we are here to take down the drug cartel. They are having their meeting tomorrow evening in the mountains, and we need to be there, prepared if you will, no later than eight pm. I have maps and diagrams of the ski resort they are staying at. I also found out that Chuck Manzione has been let out of jail on bail. He and his people have left Pacific Palisades and are headed by a fleet of limos, up to this area. They will arrive this evening.

"We will find out where they are staying and keep watch on them as well. The plan is to take out the drug cartel in one fell-swoop with as little firepower as possible. They will try to escape but we have to stop all of them. They are holding thousands of kilos of drugs in a warehouse in Salinas, and we are watching that building as we speak. We are to meet tomorrow morning at seven am in this room, grab some coffee and whatever, and then at ten o'clock, we are to drive separately to the ski lodge and wait. We were able to get some four wheelers."

Cappy then turned to Moose to give his report.

"Gentlemen, I have something important to tell all of you. One of the ring-leaders is staying at this hotel, and that is why we are here. His name is Gustavo Lopez. He seems to have his family with him including his wife Maria, and his brother, who is a notorious and vicious individual. We don't know about his wife, but his brother is just as guilty as Gustavo is as he has been linked to the drugs coming into this country. I dare say that our government wants to put them all in jail.

"I have these reports here that indicate that there is another woman who is linked to Lopez by marriage, as her husband is known as the 'The Crown Prince of Samoa.' I don't have a name but he is a ruthless killer and he kills people just for the fun of it. His wife is here and Cappy tells me that David saw her in the pool area and may have had a conversation with her while Cappy followed Lopez back to his room. We don't know where her husband is but we are sure that he is here also. This is what we are up against as of right now."

Moose was always on top of things, after which Cappy took over the rest of the short meeting. It ended with everyone now up to speed as to what was expected of us during the operation. The rest of the Seals were to meet us tomor-row night as well as the State Police, and hundreds of other law officials. I felt betrayed as I walked out of the room. I quietly walked over to Mario who was walking out with Dickie, and I pulled him aside.

"Mario, I gotta talk to you. That woman who Moose was talking about, remember? I know her. I spoke to her."

Mario looked puzzled and quickly pushed me in a corner.

"What is it, David? Who is she? What are your ties with her?"

I turned toward Mario and whispered.

"That is Leticia. The same Leticia I have been having an affair with. She is here, and she is that woman who is married to the so-called Crown Prince of Whatever."

Mario closed his eyes and then put his arm around me.

"David, you are in deep shit, you know that? What the heck are you involved with now? Don't tell me that you are going to see this broad later. If I know you, you will probably want to get a little ass before you go to sleep tonight, and then arrest the bitch tomorrow. Don't tell me that you want to see her."

"I have to, Mario," I pleaded. "I told her that I would see her later. I have to find out what Leticia is up to, and why she has been threatened by these people. She is not like them, Mario. She is scared and is being threatened to follow their orders."

CHAPTER 15

▼

NO ONE SAID IT WOULD
BE EASY

With that, Mario and I parted and he went back toward our room. I headed to the lobby area, and on the way, I reached in my pocket for a cigarette. As I did so, the pack fell to the floor. A shadowy figure passed by and reached down and picked it up for me. I hardly saw his face in that one instant but did thank him for doing it. He replied by saying, "De Nada," and walked in the opposite direction. I turned around and saw the back of a tall man hurriedly walking away.

I then found the elevator to the other side of the hotel and took it to the third floor. I walked out and looked for the signs to would lead me to room 310. I found the door and stood there motionless, listening to see if I could hear any conversation inside the room. Once I found that it was quiet, I knocked on the door. The door opened slightly and I heard the voice from inside.

"David, I am so glad you came. Please come inside and talk to me. I am frightened and I don't want to be alone."

I walked inside Leticia's room and we sat down on her bed. She told me that she came here this morning and met with Gustavo and his wife. His brother, who is a big honcho in the drug cartel, flew in from Bogotá last night. She had no idea what was going on, only that her husband was here also. He was staying in a different room, and tomorrow, they had a big meeting at another hotel or lodge. Why she was told to be there was something she could not answer, except that if she did not come, her children would be in jeopardy.

She knew that she was married to someone who was involved with drugs, only after she had married him years ago. It was too late and too dangerous to try to leave him, as he would not allow her to. She was trapped and tried to get out of the marriage many times, but was not able to.

She asked me if I was involved with all of this, or if I were a federal agent. She seemed to have a sixth sense to what was going on, and she needed to know where she stood with me as well. If I told her that I was there to take the drug cartel down, that would have blown the operation. So I lied again.

"Leticia, I am here on business. What you are telling me at this point makes no sense to me. I heard a man yelling at a woman and came to her rescue. Then it turns out to be you by the pool. You are not supposed to be here, but in Hawaii. But here you are, with enough baggage to choke a railway porter. What am I supposed to believe? But look, this is your life and we are supposed to be friends. I cannot be your judge and jury. I have no right to judge you or doubt you."

Leticia then started to cry. She was upset over all of this and only had wished we had met under better circumstances. I started to put my arm around her, when there was a loud knock on the door. It was not a good feeling. She got up startled, thinking that it could be her husband. I left the bedroom area and went into the shower in the bathroom. She then closed the door behind me leaving it ajar, so I could see into the bedroom. Then Leticia walked to the room door and asked who it was.

"Let me in, bitch. It's Ramon."

"I am not dressed right now Ramon and I am very tired. I would rather you not come into my room right now."

Ramon sounded like he was getting ready to break the door down by rapping loudly on the outside of the door.

"If you don't open the fucking door, I am going to break the Goddamn thing down and you will be sorry, bitch."

With that, Leticia opened the door and Ramon hurriedly entered the room. I was able to peek out, from behind the shower curtain, and saw Ramon push Leticia onto the bed. He then leaned over her and started to yell.

"Look, you are in enough hot water as it is. One word from Gustavo and you are worth less than a piece of hog on a spit. What do you think you are doing? You know why we are here? You gotta play by the rules and don't screw around. I told you this before. Once this meeting is over, I'm taking you back to Bogotá where you belong.

"No more Hawaii and no more California. You have walked out on me enough. Now you are going with me wherever I go. And the kids are going with me too. You want to see the kids, you gotta go with me. That's the way it is, my little bitch. Now give me some sex or else."

With that, Ramon started to pull off Leticia's top and she started to scream, while trying to push him away. He grabbed her neck and slapped her face, knocking her to the bed. With that, I jumped out of the shower, pushed the bathroom door wide open, and jumped on his back, getting him off balance.

I immediately took my arms and put them around his neck and squeezed as hard as I could, stopping the circulation of his blood. He fought back, knocking me on my side. He then reached for his knife that was tucked away, under his pants leg. I kicked him in the groin, jabbed at his neck with my fingers, as if they were small knives, then lunged forward, snapping his head sideways, as if I was going to dislodge it from his neck.

For an old fart, I still knew my moves, and my quick reaction was enough to put him out. I turned to Leticia to see if she was okay, and saw that she was slightly bruised from his slapping her. There was another rap on the door and I heard an old familiar voice on the other side.

"David, let me in. It's Mario."

I quickly opened the door and there he was, my good buddy.

"Mario, what the hell? What are you doing here?"

"I just followed you from the time we parted company in the lobby," Mario replied. "I knew you would probably need someone to watch over you, knowing how you always seem to find trouble wherever you go. Oh, you must be Leticia?"

Mario turned to Leticia and she nodded, acknowledging his question. He then reached down to Ramon and placed his arms in back and tied his hands and legs. He immediately called Cappy, and within minutes, Cappy and a few DEA men came rushing into the room. They took Ramon away, and I sat down with Cappy and Mario and told them how I knew Leticia. I explained to them that Ramon was her husband, and why I was in her room. Cappy, being understanding as he always was, told me to clean up the mess, take care of what I had to do, and that he expected to see me at seven in the morning, for our briefing. He left the room, and Mario had called me outside, into the hallway.

"David, this happened to turn out all right. We got this ass-hole, as he is one of the henchmen we were looking for. He is also the guy Cappy followed from the pool area. You did okay, my friend. Cappy will interrogate him now and see if we can get any information out of him. You tend to Leticia and everything will be all right. If you need me, just call me. I will be in the room. But do me a favor, and don't get into any more brawls, will you? I need my sleep."

With that, Mario left. I walked back into the room and locked the door. Leticia had put on a robe and was sitting on the bed looking up to thank me for coming to her aid. She was so beautiful, sitting there, with her great big smile, not saying anything. Her great big gorgeous eyes just stared at me as I approached the bed. I just could not resist her.

"David, you are so wonderful. Come sit down beside me. I need your warm body next to mine."

I finally told her that I was a Navy Seal, here on a mission to take down the drug cartel and the Mafia. She understood and did not mention anything about her husband and his business associates after that. She just looked at me with her big, beautiful, dark eyes. I was taken in by this woman once again, and made love to her. By two o'clock, I went back to my room and found Mario fast asleep. I quietly undressed and lay under the covers, waiting for our big day that would begin in a few hours.

Julie was lying in her bed thinking about her future with David. There was something that she had to tell him or this relationship with him would never be right. She had deceived David and she thought about the time when she first met Chuck at his home. She had played a game with David and she felt awful about it. She thought about the incident and it was time to come clean with David and tell him what had happened and what the circumstance was, plus how they actually met in the parking lot, and in Las Vegas. Because of this, David was risking his life, not aware of why he was doing it. Julie realized that she had not been truthful to David all this time.

Flashback: Three Months Ago...

In the moderate size office where she sat, day after day, Julie's mind began to wonder towards more pleasant things. Her workload was enormous, and she dreamt of faraway places, or even a small vacation to get her out of the same, old routine she was strongly attached to. She enjoyed her work, but she longed to escape.

Her thoughts kept bringing her back to the time she had with Joe only a year before. Julie thought of the two of them, lounging on the beach drinking margaritas, and soaking up the hot Hawaiian sun. That relationship fizzled soon after that, but it wouldn't stop her from going alone on a vacation to the sun and the ocean, or even with a girlfriend or two.

She flipped through her Rolodex and stopped at a name. She had not seen Christy in many months, although they had kept in touch by phone, every few weeks or so. She had known that her friend was involved with a powerful man and that they were thinking of getting married. Christy's life was now strictly consumed with her new relationship, as he was a most demanding individual with Mafia ties, but she didn't know too much about them. Whenever she had spoken to Christy on the phone, she preferred not to go into details, and Christy told her many times that she was not privy to many of her new boyfriend's dealings, and the work he was involved with.

Christy indicated that she would love to join her for a great escape, if her boyfriend would approve, of course. He was so domineering, always telling her what to do, how to dress, where to go, and how she should be whenever she was in his presence. Julie knew that Christy was under his thumb, as Chuck kept a close eye on her, and her every move. Being an attorney, Julie had heard of Chuck from the papers and the fact that he was being pursued by the district attorney's office.

As a matter of fact, there was talk in her firm, of representing him by one of the partners. Yet, not all of the partners of the law firm were in favor of this. As recently as a few weeks ago, Chuck Manzione's name had appeared on some paperwork that had crossed her desk. Julie knew that it might be a good time to touch base with her friend.

"Jules! So good to hear from you," the voice on the other end of the phone responded.

Christy was always cheerful and looked up to her friend as a big sister.

"What's shakin', girlfriend?"

Julie sat back in her chair and was happy to hear from Christy as well.

"Hi sweetie. I was just sitting here and dreaming about getting away for a week, even a long weekend, and I thought that perhaps you could get away as well. Say, in about two weeks, maybe three? Do you think you could take a break from your boyfriend?"

"Wow! That sounds fabulous!"

Christy did sound sincerely excited, but Julie knew that she had to give her plenty of notice because she would need Chuck's approval. Besides, the airline fares would be cheaper if they bought the airlines tickets, and reserved hotel rooms that far in advance.

"I was thinking perhaps, Aruba, or some other island in the Caribbean? What do you think about my idea?"

"Terrific," remarked Christy. "Let me know when and I will work on it."

What Christy actually meant, and what Julie was to understand, was that Christy had to gradually and subtly bring it up in a conversation to Chuck for his approval. And this may take days or even a week, as Christy was not one to move mountains and make waves. She was under the thumb of this gangster, and whatever he said, she would do. She accepted this way of life, although she resented, to some degree, that she could not be completely spontaneous with her life. She had sacrificed this for the enormous mansion that she now had access to, plus a bank account and credit cards that Chuck had given to her for play money. She knew that Chuck was one of the most powerful men on the west coast.

"Christy, I will not make arrangements until I hear from you. Please get back to me as soon as you can."

With that, she hung up, as Christy had to run, and Julie had to get back to her work. As far as Christy could imagine, this was an opportunity for her to get out of her 'cage', if only for a week, and the thought of going away was an exciting one.

Over the next week, Christy made it her priority to mention to Chuck that her lawyer friend wanted Christy to join with her on a vacation to one of the islands. At first, Chuck was not interested in listening to her, and her wanting to be with her girl friends. One morning, out of the blue, he brought up her trip while she was in the bathroom.

"So, you want to go on a vacation?"

"Yes, Chuck. My girlfriend told me that she can get some good rates to the islands and I am thinking of going with her."

"You, know, Christy," Chuck pondered, "I think that it is a good idea. You say her name is Julie Williams? Your lawyer friend? The same Julie who works in the law firm that I am trying to get to represent me, down there in Newport Beach?"

"Yes, Chuck, that's the same Julie."

Christy's heart skipped a beat, as if Chuck was ready to give her permission and send her on her way.

"How about if we have her over for lunch next weekend, and I will make the arrangements for you," asked Chuck as if he had something else up his sleeve. Christy was actually happy that Chuck was going to let her go on a trip without him.

The following Saturday, Christy, feeling excited over the visit by her dear friend, asked Chuck's servants to prepare a fabulous lunch. The dining room table, in this big house in Pacific Palisades, was decorated with expensive China dishes and Italian crystal glasses, encompassing fancy finger sandwiches. Not that Christy was unfamiliar with this type of setting as Chuck usually used his good China dinnerware whenever he had many of his associates over the house. But Christy wanted to impress Julie, as she was proud to show off the expensive China and silver.

After all, Chuck, the Don of a huge Mafia organization in Southern California, and one of the most powerful individuals in the country, always did things in a big way. This was Chuck's way of showing his authority and his wealth, and hopefully, the girls would be more acceptable with the arrangement plans he had in store for them. Expensive China and crystal were not new to Julie, as she had been invited to the homes of congressmen, the partners of the law firm, and to many homes of their clients. But it is always nice to be the guest of someone who tries to take that extra step in the preparation of a meal.

Julie arrived right on time. She was never late for anything. She kept a dedicated schedule for most of everything she did in life, even in the most mundane, domestic duties where she had certain days to do many of her household chores. The women hugged each other as if they had not seen each other in so long. Christy could not contain her excitement, and whispered in Julie's ear.

"I am so thrilled you called me to go on a vacation with you. I need to get away from here, between the hostility of Chuck and the terrifying people he associates with. I am truly beside myself."

During lunch, the girls were chatting it up, and discussing the kinds of things they would do on their trip. Julie remarked that another gal would be coming along, as she too needed to take a break from her boring life. Julie liked the idea of this being a girl's only vacation.

Just as the servants were about to take their plates away, Chuck made his entrance. He walked right over to Julie, as she stood to shake his hand.

"Nice to see you, Mr. Manzione." she said.

Chuck, in his overpowering, gruff manner, told Julie to sit and had the servant bring some coffee and cake. He wore a white, button down shirt, with his black velvet vest and black pants, carrying a cigar that he started to light up. He did not sit until the coffee arrived, and Julie could see that Christy was becoming a bit nervous.

"Listen ladies, I think your plan to go on a vacation together is a good idea. I have a few projects that will take me away for a bit, and maybe, we can all meet together at the end of your vacation. I was really hoping that you could help me with one of the projects that would require a woman's touch while you are having a great time on your vacation. Julie, you would be perfect for this."

He winked at Julie, and though she was a little embarrassed, and a bit flattered, she was not getting the full picture from Chuck. She wanted to take Christy and vacation in the islands, Aruba or some other exotic place. What was Chuck talking about with regards to getting involved with a project that would require a woman's touch? Why was this becoming more of a project of Chuck's, rather than a vacation for the girls?

"Let me explain," Chuck continued. "I have a friend who I might be interested in hiring. His wife had recently died from a terrible sickness and I think that he may need a new environment, a new job, and start a new vocation."

Christy, feeling sympathetic for the person, and for his wife, jumped in.

"Oh, how sad."

"Hush, I am not done, Christy," barked Chuck, as he never liked to be interrupted while he was talking.

"As I said, he would be perfect for the job I have in mind for him. He may need some coaxing, though, as he is very distraught over his wife's death, and the last thing he needs is to think that I am trying to interfere with his life right now. Ladies, let me just say that time is of the essence. What do you say, girls?"

Chuck did not want to tell the girls the truth, but he needed them to have compassion for this person, nonetheless.

Chuck had found out that one of his drug suppliers, Ramon, had a beautiful wife who took some time off in Hawaii over a year and a half ago. On her trip, she met this young man and they had sex together. When this man left the Hawaiian Islands, he was followed back to Southern California. That young man turned out to be, none other than me, David of Dana Point.

And the woman, Chuck was referring to, was Leticia. This Ramon asked Chuck for a favor, and that was to put a contract out on me without my ever knowing it. I was a marked man and now Chuck found a way to take care of this favor for his good friend who was a main supplier of drugs from Columbia. They found out that I was planning to go to Las Vegas and that is where he wanted to send the girls, not to Aruba or the Bahamas or the Mediterranean, or any of the other islands. He wanted to use the girls to entrap me, and then find the right time to kill me.

"What I need from you is to get close to him and to win him over. I want you to do what you have to, to make him happy. I will pay for your entire trip if you do this thing for me. I don't care what you have to do, but it would mean a lot to me plus a substantial gift for each of you. The only thing is that I want you to go to Las Vegas, not to the islands."

Julie knew that she was being manipulated. All she wanted was a peaceful escape from her routine, which was now turning into a risky proposition. What happened to her rights as a person? But then again, if they would not go to Vegas, Christy would never have been given permission to go with Julie to the islands. Perhaps, Julie thought, it may turn out to be fun anyway, but she had no idea what she was getting herself into. She was just learning what kind of power this man had and how he was able to maneuver things in his favor.

Also, by going along with this, she would have a better chance of getting more information for her colleagues back at the law firm, thereby making a better name for herself in her work. This could very well mean a promotion, perhaps a partnership in her firm, if she was able to play her cards right.

"Julie, I would like you to do me a special favor before the trip. I would like you to meet with this young man, so you will know who he is. But under no circumstances, are you to let on that you are meeting, and keeping tabs on him for me."

Julie sat back in her chair contemplating all of this and thought that this entire thing was crazy. Why was she even considering doing this, and why go to Las Vegas, when she had her heart set on going to the islands? Then once again, Chuck jumped in with his glorified way of enticing the girls by offering them a free trip to Las Vegas. He lit up his cigar and sat back in his chair, looking first at Julie, then at Christy. He then got up and paced the room, as the girls sipped their coffee and looked at each other, first rather puzzling, then, as if to say, "why not?"

The next Monday, Julie was back at her office, bewildered about her lunch with Christy and Chuck. Of course, she could change her mind, but that may not be good for Christy. After all, she was not obligated to do anything. But in her heart, she also felt that her friend was now in some trouble and needed Julie to sort things out. If she declined to go to Vegas, she felt that she may never see Christy again, as Chuck was a bully and he could do harm to her.

When she returned from lunch that afternoon, there were several phone messages waiting for her. One of them was from Chuck, and the message was that his friend, 'David', was on his way to the mall on El Toro Road, and that she should coincidentally and accidentally meet him in the garage. From the description Chuck left her, Julie would easily recognize him, as a man in his 40's, average built, dark gray hair, and he was driving a silver gray Jeep.

For the past two years, I was being followed and had no clue that I was on a hit list. I also didn't know that everywhere I happened to go, that I was being tailed by people who worked for Chuck.

Julie was to report back to Chuck after the meeting in the garage took place. So she left her office in a hurry, and waited in the parking lot adjacent to the mall and found my vehicle, a 1995 Jeep Cherokee Limited, with the license plate NS 4USA. When I was walking to my vehicle, there was Julie, looking around as if she had lost her car.

In a period of three days that followed, the arrangements for the trip to Vegas were made. It seemed that Chuck knew what hotel I was staying at, and he wanted this to work out well so he and his cronies could take me out at the hotel. Chuck didn't hesitate to send someone else to Vegas to keep a close watch on me as well as the girls. The person he also sent to watch my every move was one of his women associates, Rita.

He made it clear that Julie and Christy had to play this game right to the limit, and that meant anything the girls thought necessary, including inviting me to dinner or to a show at the hotel. Under no circumstances did Chuck ever think that his future wife would have sex with me.

Christy was okay with dinner and playing the game, as she never realized that she would have fallen for me and like me as a friend, then go to bed with me. She was getting burnt out with Chuck anyway. Julie had never thought that her good friend would find comfort in the person they were to set up for a fall. Her main concern was to support her friend.

The next morning, Mario got me up. It was time to head to Cappy's for a briefing and then on to the mountains, to await further instructions. To put together a well-planned operation, we needed to know the terrain. Monterey County refers collectively to the coastal towns of Monterey, Carmel, Salinas, Big Sur, Pebble Beach, and Arroyo Seco. We were headed for Big Sur where the drug cartel and mafia were to hold their big "pow-wow".

Here, sixty-seven growers maintain 45,000 acres of wine grapes comprising of seven appellations. The region is especially well known for Chardonnay and Pinot Noir, which visitors can sample in the county's twenty tasting rooms. I just loved this great, little town and had dreams of moving to Pebble Beach, on Seventeen Mile Drive, one day.

By heading into Big Sur, this meant that there would be a lot of tourists, heavy traffic, and very few roads going into and out of this tourist town. We were to look for a glass-covered conservatory, sort of a large, three story cabin, with lots of windows and balconies, hidden by tall trees, in the mountains not far from where they conduct tours for groups of any size. Finding a house like this one was like finding a needle in the haystack. But, we had our ways to find anything.

During certain times of the year, tourist events included grape stomps and the Galante Vineyards, and Rose Gardens' elegant outdoor amenities that would also include group gatherings of up to 2,000 that overlooked the Cachagua Valley. I was familiar with the contemporary Covey Restaurant in the Quail Lodge Resort and the Golf Club that served high-end cuisine.

Group lodging is easy to find in Monterey such as Cannery Row's Monterey Plaza Hotel and Spa with ocean view facilities, or the famous five star Inn at Spanish Bay, located on the famous Seventeen Mile Drive. We were staying at the Marriott, and some of the DEA and government boys were at the Double Tree and The Hotel Pacific nearby.

Big Sur was only twenty minutes south of us but we had to quietly creep into the wooded area and not be seen. There were many of us and we had to surround the large mountain cabin where the enemy was going to be. If there was ever a chance to cause a fire because of the gunshots, this was a place that would become a deadly firetrap, as it had dead trees within the thickly covered forest. We were not about to start a fire in these woods, although using our automatic weapons was not ruled out either.

By early afternoon, looking like tourists, we scattered into the mountains, some of us as hikers, others as wine tasters, and still others as tourists of Big Sur, looking to spend a quiet afternoon, just admiring Mother Nature. This was how we had to proceed with the initial stages of the operation. Many of the agents were women, so there were couples scattered about so as not to look too suspicious. We had to be in place by nightfall, and the weather would go down into the thirties. In preparation, we had to dress warm to prevent hypothermia. This did not seem like an easy operation to get a handle on, and the Seals were not as young and energetic as we used to be. Hopefully, this would be easier than I imagined, yet I still had my doubts.

Many of us sat in our cars, keeping warm, while the rest were scattered about, looking like tourists. Mario and I quietly admired this beautiful area as we had many hours to kill, and this was indeed a lovely location to pass the time away. I reached into my duffle for a book on Big Sur, and realized that the name, "Big Sur" was derived from the original Spanish language "El Sur Grande", which translates as "The Big South". And so it seemed to early settlers in Monterey.

The coastal area to the south was huge and unexplored, and its coastline was especially treacherous to ships. This Big Sur region, about ninety miles in length, along California's coastal Highway 1, lies between the San Francisco Bay area and the Los Angeles area. The Big Sur region's northern end, where we lay unnoticed, was at Carmel, approximately 130 road miles south of San Francisco and adjacent to Monterey. We could not have picked a more perfect spot to spend a chilly afternoon.

Its southern end is at San Simeon, where the Hearst Castle is, approximately 240 road miles north of Los Angeles and near Cambria, Morro Bay and San Luis Obispo. Since we estimated an amount in excess of three hundred State and Federal officers in the operation, it was advantageous to us that this Northern Big Sur Region extended between the Carmel River Bridge and Point Sur Light Station State Historic Park, away from where most of the locals and tourists would be.

I did notice quite a few tourists coming up here on the way. The Atlas described The Central Big Sur Region extending from Andrew Molera State Park, which includes the mouth of the Big Sur River, through the Big Sur Valley, and south as far as Esalen Institute.

The Southern Big Sur Region extends from Big Creek to San Simeon. Big Sur's rocky coastline goes as far as Hurricane Point. Driving up to this location, I noticed signs that pointed out so many attractions including Point Lobos State Reserve, the Carmel Highlands, Garrapata State Park, Abalone Cove, Rocky Point, Palo Colorado Road which goes to Bottcher's Gap, Rocky Creek Bridge, Bixby Creek Bridge, Little Sur River Bridge Point, and the Sur Light Station State Historic Park.

"David, what you thinking about," asked Mario, interrupting my deep thoughts.

"You know, Mario," I answered, "this is one of the most beautiful spots in California. It is so quaint, with all of its historical beauty, that I wouldn't mind living here one day. After all this is over, I may consider the change."

Mario sat in the car, drinking his coffee and a bran muffin, then looked at me and remarked.

"David, if you intend on marrying Julie, you should think about her career, her job at the law firm, and what would please her as well. It is probably a great place to settle down in, and raise a family, but knowing you, you would probably tire of the boredom."

Just then, there was a knock on the car window. Cappy was outside the vehicle and told us that many Columbians were spotted driving up the narrow road to the cabin where the meeting was to be held. He figured that there would be a couple of hundred people at this meeting with many from the Mafia families around the country. This was big business and everyone wanted in on the action. There was a slight chance that Chuck Manzione would be there as well. It seemed that he had pissed off many of the drug cartel and they wanted to kill the bastard.

Nevertheless, we had to expect anything, and now we had to be on alert. We decided to get out of the car that was hidden in a parking area within the trees and by a picnic area, and find a position close to the cabin. It was difficult to spot all of the agents as they were scattered all over the area, like tourists, and not all of them had arrived as yet. Just being there, on that cold afternoon, with many hours to kill, was not only a boring thing to do, but we had to stay alert and not cause anyone to suspect us as agents of the government.

Hours had passed, and after finding a roadside diner, I ordered enough sandwiches and drinks for a few of the guys. I then hiked back to the spot with the sandwiches, and settled down under a tree. I then decided to check my weapons and the cache of bullets that I had in my knap sack. I noticed Dicky and Cappy were checking maps, and conversing with other DEA and State Department honchos, while the agents were pretty well hidden from view.

I thought about my time in Hawaii, and the people I had met there, including Leticia, and how she was involved by marriage, to one of the top drug cartel people. I went over in my mind how she had deceived me, and how I had started to fall in love with this woman. She was absolutely the best woman I had ever had in the sack, and the experience was, without a doubt, simply tremendous. If I had not met Julie, I probably would pursue Leticia and want to spend my life with this woman. With her husband under wraps by the federal government, Leticia may be willing to start a new life once again. My thoughts kept going from Julie to Leticia, and the kinds of relationship I could have with each of them.

On the other hand, I had met Christy, a great little piece of ass, I thought, but not too smart. I liked Christy, for the moments we had shared together, but it was wearing thin, and I had to get out of that relationship. Then Rita came into my life, that little weasel, but she sure knew how to give good head, and boy, was she a wild thing in bed. I didn't think that I would have lasted too long with her. But she had something that I liked, and that was moxie. She was a tough little bitch and knew how to wrap you around her finger. But when the chips were down, she folded up like a newspaper.

Aside from Susie, Christy's lesbian friend, there was Julie. One of the prettiest women I had ever met, who looked like a model. After courting her for some time, we were now preparing for our marriage. This undoubtedly was a coup for me to capture such a woman, or I was being taken in like a rabbit in a stew. Yet, I felt that there was still something wrong, something that bothered me, and I had not yet put my finger on it. But I felt that sooner or later, it would come to me.

I thought about how we met, first in the garage and then in Las Vegas. I felt as if these two incidents were too coincidental, as if she was following me. How did she wind up in Las Vegas the same time I did, and then again, how did Chuck Manzione know that I was fucking his girlfriend? There were too many iffy questions, and I just didn't have all of the answers. But something told me that I was being set up, and I had the suspicion that Julie was involved.

When I would finally get back to civilization, I had to confront Julie and find out if my suspicious mind was correct in its analysis, or was it only playing tricks on me. I needed to get the facts straight and did not want to go into a marriage with so many doubts left up in the air. If I was set up to meet Christy, were Julie and Christy involved with Chuck Manzione?

There had to be a tie-in there, somewhere. This entire episode made me feel uneasy. Normally, when I have second thoughts about something, they are usually true. I felt that I was actually set up and was being used.

"Hey guys, let's stay on our toes," interrupted Cappy, as he made his rounds to each of us.

"It is close to six and night is starting to fall upon us. Listen up, now! Many people have entered the cabin and they are getting ready to start their meeting. Mario, you and David try to get as close to the cabin as possible."

Cappy was making sure that we understood the game plan, and he was acting the part of the drill sergeant that was so fitting to him.

"We have the other Navy Seals on the back end of the cabin. We need some coverage on the east side. Make sure your 'walkie-talkies' are working, and you have the sound plugged into your ear. We need silence but we need to converse at all times when necessary."

Cappy was very methodical and knew how to get the troops ready for anything. He was already in his fifties but he still had the stern, rigid sense to lead a pack of wolves into battle. When this operation was finally over, I knew that he would surely miss the adventure and the daring feats that he thrived on through most of his life. But he could at least enjoy life once again with his wife and family. I always looked up to Cappy, but after so many years as my leader, I was getting tired of all of this.

Mario and I moved closer to the side of the cabin, and we could hear voices coming from inside the large building. More and more cars drove up to the front, and lots of Columbians and Mafioso left their vehicles and walked to the front steps of the cabin. There were guards standing outside, around the perimeter, and they had to be taken out quickly. They carried AK-47 automatic rifles and were ready for anything. Little did they know that it was going to be the last time they would ever shoot that weapon again. Hopefully, I was thinking the same thing for myself. I too never wanted to be in this position ever again. When this was over, I wanted to put all of my outfits and weapons in a crate and seal the damn thing.

As we lay prone on the ground, listening through our headsets for orders, and the whispers of our agents around us, I thought again of the people I had met in Hawaii, including Chuck's gay son. I was glad that we met once again at the hospital and realized that he hated his father and just wanted to live a different kind of life in Santa Monica. He was a nice young man and realized that being gay, would be a detriment to Chuck, so he just left the area to live out his own life in his own way. When we met at the hospital, he realized that I was on the side of the law and that it was my job to get his dad. I was glad that he took all of it in good spirits instead of hating me for doing my job.

Then, there were the other young girls, the ones who we met at the last operation we had at Chuck's house. They were used as prostitutes and hopefully, had found their own way in life. What they went through was horrendous and they were nearly killed. Sooner or later, all of this shit catches up with you and you find yourself looking at different paths in life.

At that moment, we got the order. It seemed as if all those who were supposed to be present, were in the cabin, which was a huge structure, three stories high, and must have had hundreds of people, packed into it. The trees were so tall, and full of heavy leaves, with lots of brush around the house, that it prevented us from seeing the top floor of the cabin. We had to be on our toes as the agents were already set up around the house and the fireworks were about to begin.

A bullhorn suddenly sounded out.

"All those in the cabin, come out with your hands up. The place is surrounded."

Mario and I, with some of the other agents, had climbed up the trees to try to see the upper floors and have a better view of what was happening inside. The guards, outside of the cabin started to fire into the woods and all hell broke loose. The agents fired back, having their sights on the guards who numbered about ten. Then, there were shots coming from inside the cabin, aimed at the trees. Many of the agents resembled dark figures that appeared as shadows under the moonlight. We tried to prevent this from happening, as any spark from a fired weapon could have started this tinderbox to go up in flames. Our major concern was that the area could very well have been swallowed up in a firestorm.

It was too late for any kind of peaceful negotiations. The sound of gunfire erupted from within the cabin and from the trees where the agents hid. There was no way we could get any air support, so we had to start and finish the job on the ground. They may have had a couple of hundred people inside the cabin, but we also had a similar amount of agents around the house. We also had the advantage of the darkness, as we had infrared lens, plus the brush cover.

Overlooking the upper level of the cabin, we were able to swing the branches close enough to jump onto the balconies and go through the sliding glass doors that led into the bedrooms on the third floor. Mario and I had a cadre of about eight agents, and with some acrobatic maneuvering, we finally made it inside.

With lots of noise, firepower, and yelling, coming from the floors below, we moved cautiously toward the hallway and crept along the wall, leading to the stairwell. We could hear a lot of Spanish being spoken and there were arguments between the Mafioso and the drug cartel warlords.

Each group blamed the other for allowing the federal agents to find out about the meeting, not realizing that we also had some plants within the cabin, which the government set up.

There were two airborne rangers who were part of the drug cartel and had slipped into the ranks unnoticed. They were there to slip us the information that we needed and hopefully, they would also help us secure the building. I didn't know who they were or what they looked like. I was counting on them to find us first before we shot them.

While Mario and I stood guard on the top of the stairs, the other agents searched the rooms on our floor to make sure that they were cleared. Then we heard people rushing up the steps to reach the upper level to have a better advantage out of the windows. We were ready for them. As they started to get to the third level, we fired upon them and took them out. Little by little, we made our way down the steps to get to the second level. More agents had come in through the balconies on the second level and then the lights went out. Our plan was to cut all of the electricity and leave those in the house without light, while we wore our infrared lenses and were able to see the figures moving about in the building.

As we reached the second level, we were faced with a few armed men who had trained their weapons on us. For an instant, I thought that it was all over for us. Just then, shots rang out and the gunmen were gunned down.

I looked up and saw two men waving at us.

"We are on your side. We are federal agents."

Mario and I, and the two men proceeded to move down the stairs and were close to the first level while the other agents secured the second and third floors. There was a lot of activity as the drug cartel and Mafia people were hopelessly fighting a battle that they would not win. Our troops outside the building were closing in and we were moving closer to the Columbians and had them in a cross-fire. The constant barrage of gunshots continued, but we were winning the battle. Now, we had to also win the war.

The cartel people were fearless fighters, and chose to do battle with us in a do or die situation. The group of Mafioso also fought, but was searching for exit doors to get out of the building. The bullets were flying in all directions, and the noise was unbearable. I kept low on my stomach and crawled along the balcony rail, trying to move downstairs. It was like a shooting gallery as I kept firing my weapon, then reloading, and then shooting once again. There seemed to be no end to this.

I fired blindly into bodies that were mulling about on the lower level. The house was being riddled with more holes than a package of Swiss cheese and there was lots of yelling and screaming. In a way, I felt sorry for many of the insurgents who were trapped in the crossfire. But it boiled down to their lives or mine. I wanted to live, and whether they were killed or not, just did not bother me in the least. I was used to this and I had no emotions when it came to preserving my life.

I must have killed or wounded at least a dozen people in this battle. As long as I kept my head low, I felt that I would be able to survive. It is great to have the advantage, and when your opponent is without knowledge of the force they are facing, there is no way they can beat you. That made all the difference in the world, and why we always won the wars.

Cappy and his crew slowly moved into the building by the front door and the DEA and state troopers were right behind him. They all wore goggles and could see any movement in the dark. The bullets were flying all over the place but we always had the advantage. As Mario and I and the two agents hit the main floor, we were careful not to hit any of our guys. We finally saw Cappy and his people forming an arc around the people we came to take down.

Finally, after nearly an hour of battle, we managed to contain the area and there was a cease-fire. I turned to Mario and he was hit in the shoulder by a bullet, but was okay. We counted the casualties, and almost sixty Columbians and Mafia soldiers laid dead, and another one hundred fifty taken into custody. We did not find Chuck as I suspected, but we found thousands of kilos of crack and cocaine in one of the rooms on the lower level.

It was pretty dark outside when we finally emerged from the building. I helped Mario into an ambulance that was standing by just for that reason and he thanked me for taking care of him. We lost three agents in the battle, and ten were wounded. None of our guys were seriously hurt, except Mario. We got the drug lords and their drugs, all neatly wrapped in a nice package for our government to sort out. Cappy was pleased with the outcome although we lost one agent who was struck down by the wielding knife of a Columbian. It was a shame, as we all came here to do a job and hoped that none of us would get in harm's way. Mario was lucky, and I was glad that this episode was finally over.

I went with Mario in the ambulance and saw to it that he was taken care of at the nearby hospital. Cappy took care of the Navy Seal who was killed, and the other agents loaded the bad guys onto trucks and buses, for the nearest state prison up in San Francisco. We did our job and now it was time to go home and get back to some normalcy for a change.

By the next morning, Mario was patched up and we all piled into the same private army plane for our flight back to John Wayne Airport. We drove back to Cappy's house, and I retrieved my vehicle. Mario and I said our goodbyes to the other Seals, and then drove back to my home in Dana Point. Mario smiled at me, got into his own car and left for his home. He has always been a great buddy to me and this friendship would never cease. I loved him like a brother.

I called Julie at her office and she was glad to hear from me. I told her that the episode was over and now I wanted to see her and discuss our future plans. I did not go into details as to how I felt about the secrecy that loomed over our relationship and decided to wait until I saw her. We were to meet at her house that evening. I took a hot shower, put my army surplus clothes back in the closet, unloaded my weapons, cleaned them with linseed oil, and put them in a safe place. I thought at that point, that I would never have to use them again.

Since I had some time before I would meet with Julie, I decided to lie down and rest. I did not feel comfortable. And all of a sudden, I had this funny feeling that perhaps, I was being set up for some reason. I knew that it did not feel right, and perhaps Julie could answer many of my perplexing questions.

About seven o'clock, I got dressed and drove to Julie's house. She was anxiously waiting for me at her front door when I arrived. She first greeted me with a great big hug and kiss, then handed me a glass of wine. Before I had a chance to say anything to her, Julie was the first to open up on the topic about how we had "accidentally" met in the garage of the shopping mall, and then in Las Vegas. I just sat there in awe, trying to take everything in. I was angry at first, and then I just put all of the pieces together.

"Please, David, let me explain."

"If I hear you correctly, Julie, you were asked by Chuck, the guy who the Seals have been trying to take down, to find me? So Chuck would kill me?"

"I was so worried about my friend, as Christy and I go way back. If I did not do what Chuck asked of me, I thought I would never have seen her again. Believe me, David. In no way does it change the way I feel about you now."

Julie sat down on her favorite leather chair and lowered her head. She looked shameful and disappointed in herself, but I still had my doubts about her. I was also very disappointed in her for playing such a game with me, and though the pieces of the puzzle were starting to fit, my head started to spin. I didn't realize that she was capable to do such horrible things, especially to someone she did not know. She actually set me up for a death squad.

I shook my head and was very tempted to get out of her house and never see her again. I looked at her with slight disdain, but somewhere in my heart, I knew that I could forgive her. I just did not know where exactly that place was yet.

"I am so sorry, David. It didn't occur to me that I would fall in love with you and that this entire mess would come full circle, and…"

I took a deep breath and faced up to her, my future bride, my lifetime friend, my Benedict Arnold.

"Let me ask you something, Julie, and please tell me the truth. Did it ever occur to you that perhaps, maybe one day, you were going to tell me the truth, or were you going to wait until after we got married? Or, perhaps, you were just going to wait and see what would happen to Chuck before you decided to tell me anything?"

Julie was literally shaking and could not utter the right words. And for the first time, she had lost control of her emotions.

"Oh David," she started to cry.

I was tempted to go over to her, but I was so angry that all I wanted to do was scream.

I became impatient and I didn't know how much longer I could have taken all of this. Julie started to say that she was going to tell me, but Christy's welfare became an issue. Christy, noted Julie, started to go on a suicidal mission with all of the drugs she was taking, which she got from Chuck. Julie tried to help her once or twice, but was only pushed away by Christy. Things started to progress so rapidly that Julie was not able to come to grips with this and tell me what had happened. She was not able to tell me why I was drawn into this scenario, both in the garage or in Las Vegas.

"David, I truly wanted to tell you when I first met with you, but I couldn't. I am so sorry I have hurt you."

I decided that I needed to somehow absorb all of this before I would make any rash decision that would involve Julie and me. Chuck was still out there so no one was completely safe from this madman. He could still go after Julie, or Christy, or even me. The next thing for me to do was to go after him and destroy him.

"Okay, Julie, I need time to think things through, so I will leave you for now. When I can make sense of all of this I will call you. Until then, thank you for being honest with me. I suppose it is better late than never."

I abruptly got up and made for the door. Julie ran after me and tried to stop me. I truly felt for Julie and perhaps I still loved her so much that I could not face her with the hurt that I had. Being in love with her also was the reason why I chose not to question her any more than I had to. She was already hurt. There was no need to push her to the limit.

I turned to her, and with the hurt feelings from within me, I told her how I truly felt at that moment.

"If you were honest with me from the beginning, I could have helped you, Julie. Perhaps I could have resolved this in a different manner and avoided both of us from this entire 'god damn' mess as we have it now. We could have prevented many things that we had done, and some of my friends would not have been hurt. Perhaps, a few of them may still be alive today as well. To tell you the truth, I am not feeling so good right now. I feel as if I was used, by you, your law firm, and your friends…and for what? Did you use me to get to the top of the ladder in your company? Or did you truly fall into a trap because of Manzione and could not get out of it?"

As I drove home afterward, I realized that I was not as physically tired as I was mentally exhausted. What I learned from Julie about how she had to find me in the garage, and then seduce me in Vegas, and getting caught with Christy, was just a ploy to have me killed. It was for the pleasure of a Mafia Don who owed a favor to his Columbian drug pal because I had an affair with his wife nearly two years ago. Leticia, whom I grew so fond of, was the lady on the blanket. She was my 'Sophia Loren', my beautiful Hawaiian who I adored so very much. Her husband knew all along what I did.

My God, when will I ever learn? Perhaps I was not as experienced as I thought I was, and more naive then I should have been. I was married to Martha, living a very simple home life, without having to deal with relationships with different women. Perhaps, I should have limited my time to just saving strange women at the supermarket, and just keep putting those chocolate cookies back on the shelf. Heck, I can handle that. That is enough excitement for me.

I certainly found out that once you get involved with more than one woman, one thing leads to another and you certainly can get your ass in a sling. I may not be the most experienced lover or the smartest guy when it comes to relationships, but I still have a brain. Now that brain, no matter how it sits in my cranium, shall tell me how to settle this mess once and for all. Whatever decision I had to make, would affect my life and my future. I knew one thing for sure, and that was, and still is, 'Love is so damn sweet and bittersweet'. That's for damn sure!

I arrived home as the phone was ringing. It was Julie. She was apologetic and was sobbing her heart out. I still loved this woman but I needed time to sort things out. Maybe it was just not meant to be, I mean between Julie and me. Julie was conned by Chuck, together with his antagonistic attitude, being the big shot of the Mafia world. This was not my world. I wanted a simpler life, a life where I could go back and teach the young kids, and come home to a loving wife who would be content to take care of the house and our kids. I didn't need any more complications in my life. I had too many in the past, and I realized that I created some of the complications myself. Now, it was time to think about me for a change. What was best for me?

"Julie, I still care for you," I told her. "I have a lot of love for you. But right now I need to get my head on straight. Perhaps in a few days we can talk some more and then we can meet and see if anything of this relationship can be salvaged. Right now, I want to just be by myself and get back into teaching, and put all of the Navy Seals activities behind me. Please don't cry. We both need our own space now. I will call you in a few days. Yeah, I love you too."

I hung up the phone. That was the easy part. The difficult part was what was going on in my head. I felt as if I was having a massive brain injury and it was hurting like crazy. As I sat on the couch and poured a glass of wine for myself, my time of reflection didn't last too long. The phone rang again. This time, it was Rita.

"Rita, how the hell are you? I haven't heard from you in a while. What's happening in your life?"

Rita told me that Chuck was back in action, having heard about the stake out and fire power that occurred in Big Sur. He was organizing a group of hit men to come after me since he found out that I was a Navy Seal and that it was my outfit that had been putting him out of business. Each time that he tried to regain momentum with the under bosses of the Mafia and the drug cartel, he was getting clobbered. He was out for blood and I was on top of his 'shit list'.

I kinda figured that I was a marked man, and I thanked Rita for her warning. I called Cappy and told him what was happening and he immediately sent a squad of Seals over to my home in Dana Point. Mario came over that evening and spent the night with me, as we chugged down some beer and talked about my love life, and what was left of it. The Seals were outside in their cars just in case there would be a disaster waiting to happen. My neighbors would never forgive me for the racket.

At about eleven, I decided to retire and Mario took the couch downstairs. I took a long, hot shower and got into bed.

Then the phone rang again. This time, it was Julie. She told me that she heard from Christy and she was doing just fine. Being out of state was the safest thing for her as she went back to her family's ranch. We spoke of the issues that were discussed at her house and we managed to laugh at many of the things we encountered in the past. The garage incident with the partner in the law firm was funny, and the way we ran from Chuck and his men in Vegas became nothing less than hysterical. At least we were able to find some light through all of this. I wished Julie happy dreams and decided to go to sleep.

About three in the morning, there was a hand on my shoulder, and I awakened in a flash. I immediately grabbed the big claw and was about to toss it over the bed. It was Mario! He woke me up to tell me that he was told by one of the Seals outside in the car that there were three strange cars circling the street.

I got dressed and waited until we got further word. There was none. The cars took off, probably noticing our friendly Seals' cars parked outside. This was not good. I could not go on with life like this. I told Mario that I needed time to get away.

The next day, I secretly drove to the Mission Viejo Shopping Mall, where I had a friend pick me up, and drive me to John Wayne Airport. I got on a plane for Honolulu, Hawai'i. Six hours later, I was at the Outrigger Hotel in Waikiki, in a nice cozy room. I told Cappy and Mario where I was going so they would not worry about me. Later that day, I took a cab to the Bishop Museum, the State Museum of Natural and Cultural History of Hawai'i.

This Bishop Museum was really a beautiful place to visit. It was founded in 1889 by Charles Reed Bishop, in honor of his late wife, Princess Bernice Pauahi Bishop, the last direct descendant of the royal Kanehameha family. Being the largest museum in the State, it was established to house one of the largest collections of Hawaiian artifacts and royal family heirlooms of the Princess.

Just by walking through the building, I had experienced over 2,000 years of Polynesian history and cultural heritage. Amazingly, it was built of volcanic rock and it features a grand staircase made of rare koa wood, a full sized replica of a Hawaiian grass house, and a fifty-foot Sperm Whale Skeleton. The grounds were built to house the original Kamehameha Schools for boys, and were established by Princess Pauahi to educate children of Hawai'i.

Interestingly, I learned that Princess Bernice Pauahi was designated the heir apparent to the kingdom of Hawai'i, but declined to take the throne so that she could devote herself to the cause of educating Hawaiian children. She was originally betrothed to Prince Lot but went against her family's wishes and married her true love, Charles Reed Bishop, who came to Hawai'i from New York, my home town. So much for the history of Hawaii! It was fun just to get away.

At night, I went to the Royal Lu'au, the only true lu'au on Waikiki Beach, on the grounds of The Royal Hawaiian. With Diamond Head in the background, The Royal Luau is a feast, and the show was fit for a king. I was treated with a lei and a refreshing Mai Tai, and then I had some Luau Punch, and listened to the Hawaiian melodies. After digging into the island style buffet, munching on Teriyaki Beef and Island Fish, I went back to my room at the Outrigger.

The next day, I climbed aboard the Maita'i Catamaran and took one of their four daily sails out of Waikiki Beach, reaching speeds of up to 20 miles per hour. I listened to CD sounds of Hawaiian music, sunbathed, and sipped some champagne, wine, and some of their delicious fresh island juices, and of course, more Mai Tais.

I was really enjoying the mood of Hawai'i and not thinking about my last few days in California. That night, I dined at the Ocean House Restaurant with its panoramic open-air view of Diamond Head, Waikiki Beach and the Pacific Ocean. I had to try the 'Hawaiian Salt', the slow roasted prime rib au jus, which was roasted in an electric imu, plus a taste of their Crab Stuffed Mahi Mahi and the Mac Nut Crusted Opakapaka, Cold water Lobster Tail and Mac Cane Ahi Chops. Then it was back to the Beachcomber where I saw the old, but famous Don Ho doing his usual Tiny Little Bubbles, while sitting on a chair and talking into the phone. He had been performing for over 40 years and still drew large crowds. Just being by myself felt wonderful.

The next day I went to the Polynesian Cultural Center Ali'i Lu'au which transports you to days gone by. Upon my arrival, I was welcomed with a fresh flower Lei, and the Polynesian people were eager to share their culture with me, as well as the many guests who attended. Before dinner, I experienced the kalua (steamed) pig being lifted off the steaming rocks of the imu (underground oven). The blowing of the conch shell announced the arrival of Hawaiian Royalty, the Ali'i Court, who were believed to manage the affairs of the land and people on behalf of the gods.

As Hawai'i's most authentic lu'au began, hula dancers performed the hula kahiko, or ancient dances, that tell stories of old Hawai'i. Next, the hula dancers took me on a nostalgic tour of Hawaiian musical styles, including songs of the 1930s and 40s, and the classic sounds of the Hawaiian steel guitar. This is what I needed, and by experiencing the traditional lu'au in such a paradise part of the world, was more than one can imagine. I was relaxed and enjoyed the beautiful cultural experience, which was a far cry from the guns, the mafia, the drug cartel, the Navy Seals, and the women who crept into my life in this past year.

I headed back to the Outrigger and found a cozy spot at the bar and decided to have one last drink before I headed to my room. My last three days here had been great and did a world of good for me. As I sat down, I heard my name mentioned and turned around, only to find that same beautiful face I had seen so many times before.

"Leticia, what in the world are you doing here? I came here to get away and bam, you show up again."

Leticia was as beautiful as ever. She was wearing a Hawaiian dress with flowers in her hair. She sat down beside me.

"David, it is so good to see you. I came to Oahu to visit my family and decided to take a stroll in downtown Waikiki. I thought I had recognized you as you entered the Outrigger so I just walked over to see if it was really you. Oh David, this is a complete surprise. I am so glad you are here at the exact same time that I am here."

Leticia was so much the lady, so complimentary, and so gorgeous. How did she find me? But she was there, sitting next to me on the bar stool, with her arm through mine. And I could feel the warmth of her lovely body as it radiated affection and love. She looked absolutely beautiful. I could not believe my eyes. And the beautiful part of all this was, she was mine for the asking. I was at another crossroad in my life. I needed space from Julie, only to find myself in the arms of Leticia.

We sat at the bar and had a few drinks. I was beginning to have that urge again, to make love to this woman. She was her usual charming self, and I was like a young stud, who needed her right about now. So I persuaded her to join with me in my room. It didn't take much persuasion. Leticia was not only willing, but she was hot. She knew that she was free of her husband and we were going to make it together, without any cause to worry.

As soon as we opened the door, I grabbed her and held her close to my body. I could feel her breasts as they pressed against my chest, and her lips were glued to mine. She reached for my open shirt and unbuttoned it and pushed it off my body, while I pulled down her dress. I then reached in back of her and unhooked her bra, while she was grappling with the button and zipper of my pants. We threw ourselves on the bed and I could feel the heat from her body as we bounced on the mattress, my body on top of hers.

It was just like poetry, the way we created our own sounds of delight, in a chorus of moans and groans, methodically beating the drum to a passionate conclusion of metaphors that would have driven both of us into ecstasy. I found myself feeling excruciating pain in the lower part of my body as I kept moving in and out of her, while enjoying the tremendous excitement, finally reaching our conclusion.

But we didn't stop, only to start all over again, until the nerve endings of my body started to tingle. And I felt myself getting exhausted, but forced myself to continue on and on. I could feel the sweat pouring off my forehead, and my chest was soaking wet. She felt so moist and hot that I could not stop what I was doing. She cried out for more and I gave it to her. I heard her tell me that she loved me and I responded by telling her that I wanted her and wanted to love her. It may have been two hours later, when I suddenly realized that I had come at least four times. This was an amazing feat for me but it was well worth it. Leticia was the most exciting and amazing individual I had ever known.

She reached for a bottle of wine and I grabbed two glasses. I put on my pants and headed to the outside balcony and had a cigarette while she poured us both a drink. I felt great, although my loins were a bit sore. Yet, I had never experienced such emotion as I just did with her. It was good...no, better than good. It was the best. I felt manly and realized that I had accomplished a feat that I had not experienced in my entire life. The only other time I ever came close was with Leticia in Hawaii two years ago. But this was especially good because we both wanted it, and needed it. Not only had I felt that she was so right for me, that I completely forgot about Julie and why I had come to Hawaii in the first place.

"My sweetheart," came a voice from the sliding doors. "Here's your wine, my darling. You were so forceful and so wonderful. I am still feeling the tension and the emotions in my body. I am so happy that we met today."

Leticia was absolutely gorgeous, standing there with a bath towel wrapped around her body. All of her five foot, 6 inch frame was shaped by the white cotton terry that seemed to bring out her lines. Not only did she seem to glow with passion, no matter how she was dressed, she was still the most beautiful woman I had ever seen.

I took the glass of wine and drank a toast to both of us. We raised our glasses and clinked them, then sipped some of the Chardonnay, while giggling like two school children, touching each other on the ass, sticking out our tongues to each other, and trying to step on each other's toes. We were in heaven, and if anyone had any doubt about the existence of such a place, I can honestly say that I found it in that room that day.

"Do you feel like having some food, David? I am hungry. I am also hungry for your body but I need more stamina to keep up with you. I never knew that you were so passionate. I am learning so much about you, my darling."

We decided to take our showers and get dressed, and head down to the restaurant for a light snack. We found a menu that had the most wonderful appetizers and we munched on crab cakes, some shrimp cocktails and Hawaiian Sweet Bread. We ordered some more wine and just looked at each other as if we were lovers on a date, and this was to be the night of our first lovemaking. I couldn't wait to go back to my room, with Leticia in my arms, and start all over again.

While we were sitting there, Leticia noticed someone at the entranceway of the restaurant and became disturbed.

"David, don't look up. Keep your head down. I recognize that man by the hostess's table. He used to work with my husband. All of a sudden I just got a cold chill up my spine. David, we better get out of here, quickly."

We finished our wine, and I grabbed the waitress, asking her for our check. We walked out to the rear of the restaurant, to the kitchen, and through the back door. Leticia was afraid, and I felt her body shaking. That man whom she saw truly frightened her and she wanted out of the place, immediately. We found a street that ran parallel to the hotel but it backed up to another hotel. I held her hand as we entered the lobby and we both looked around to see if anyone was following us.

We decided to walk around the building until we came upon the door leading back into the lobby of the Outrigger so we would get back into the elevator and speedily go to my room. As we approached the elevator, we saw two other men that she recognized.

They may have seen us as the doors opened, and we moved into the elevator, quickly pressing the button to the tenth floor. The car started to go up and I held Leticia closely against my body. As we got to my floor, we raced to my room, opened the door and we jumped into the room.

"Who were those fucking guys?" I asked her. "And why are you so shaken by them? Are they in with the drug cartel?"

She sat on the bed, and looked downward toward the floor.

"David, those guys are killers. They used to talk to my husband about drugs and the cartel, and they are also involved with the Mafia. If they are here, then there must be many more in the area. I am afraid, David. They know me and since my husband is dead, they may want to kill me as I know too much."

Leticia was frightened and that told me that I had better get some help from the mainland.

I reached for my phone and thought about calling Cappy. But he was home in Orange County, Southern California, and we were in Waikiki, Hawai'i. How would Cappy be able to help us? I called him anyway and sought his advice.

"Cappy, how are you? Yeah, this is David. I am at the Outrigger in Waikiki. Guess what! I believe that I am surrounded by a few gunmen from the drug cartel who are probably looking for me. Right! I am with Leticia right now! She recognized them. I may need assistance to get out of here. I think they saw us and Leticia feels that there must be quite a few of these guys in the hotel."

Although I told Cappy that I needed some time away and he knew that I was going to Hawai'i, he reminded me that no secret getaway is completely secretive. When I told Cappy that Mario also knew of my trip to Hawai'i, he then told me that he had not been in contact with Mario since the Monterey operation. At the mention of Leticia being with me, that was when I heard a thump in his throat. He then told me to just listen and not to talk so Leticia would not know of the conversation. He still did not feel comfortable with Leticia always showing up when I went someplace.

He told me that I was probably in danger and would send some of the Seals and special op guys here to get me out. It seemed as if our friend Chuck Mazione was also hunting me down, and he felt that he may have found me. I held onto Leticia as he spoke, and I realized that it may have been Leticia who warned them of my presence. But after making love to her, why would she do this to me? I was just not sure. Yet, it also could have been just a coincidence. My entire life had been one coincidence after another lately.

We had about six or seven hours to kill before we would receive some help from the good guys. We just sat on the bed as Leticia told me stories of how her husband would leave for days, perhaps weeks at a time, and just come home as if he had never left their house. His demeanor would change after a long trip and she would ask him where he went, only to be shut out of his private life.

She did meet some of his cronies, as they would chat in the house or on the phone, and sometimes at restaurants. But Leticia was out of the loop as far as what kind of business he was actually involved with. All she knew was that he was tied in with drugs, killings, and tough men who were only interested in one thing…money and more money.

While he was away, she had found duffle bags in the closet containing guns and ammunition, plus airline stubs to Columbia, New York, California, and other South and Central American countries. This was the kind of business he was involved with and she did not like it. It was too dangerous and against the law, and something that she wanted to get away from. Leticia felt that one day, he would be hunted down like a wild animal and she too, may get caught up in this.

Many times, she would go to Hawai'i to visit friends or family and she needed time alone to sort all of this out. But he would always find her and scold her, perhaps hit her excessively for her taking off as she did, and she was deathly afraid of him. Upon his death, she felt that she would be able to have the freedom to get out from under this charade and start a new life. That is why she came to Waikiki and think things through until she decided what she really wanted. She thought of calling me but needed to give this some time. Meeting me today was a godsend, and she was very happy that we did meet. I was not only happy to see her, I also missed having her beside me, in bed and making love to her.

It must have been a few hours, perhaps five or six, when we heard the phone ring. It was about one in the morning, and I was lying in bed, while Leticia was fast asleep. I decided to pick it up and asked who it was.

"David, how the hell are you? This is Mario. I am here at the Honolulu airport and will be in Waikiki within the hour. Hey, I know that it's late, so let's get together first thing in the morning. I'll meet you for breakfast at 8 am at the Outrigger restaurant, okay?"

I agreed, and was just about to lie down and go back to sleep, when I looked at the clock once again. It was fifteen minutes before one in the morning. Leticia was asleep and I thought back to when I had called Cappy. That was about ten minutes past seven. It would take at least 5 hours to get to Hawaii from Los Angeles, plus a couple of hours driving to the airport and going through security. How did Mario get here so soon?

I got up, quickly changed my clothes and awakened Leticia.

"Sweetheart, get up. We gotta get out of here now."

Leticia opened her eyes and was curious as to why I wanted to leave so suddenly. I told her that Mario had called.

"Leticia, Mario couldn't have made it to Honolulu so fast. He was probably here before I called Cappy. Something doesn't seem right. Let's leave the room now because I don't want you to be in this room if we get company soon. I have a strange feeling and I usually have a good sense about things. We're heading out the back door and into another hotel for the time being."

I packed my luggage and Leticia and I headed down into the hallway, down the ten flights of steps to the lower level where the kitchen was located. We walked slowly, through the dark kitchen, and out the back door and headed toward another hotel down the street. I checked in under an assumed name and found a room for us. I took my two pieces of luggage, but Leticia left hers in her own hotel room, the Waikiki Beach Marriott Resort and Spa, as it wasn't safe to go there either. We grabbed another two hours sleep as we were exhausted. I got up at 7:30 and told Leticia to stay put in the room while I would sneak back to the Outrigger and see what Mario was up to.

There he was, the big Italian Stallion, sitting at one of the tables, drinking his black coffee and eating a muffin. I waited, and watched him as he was looking out for me.

Across the room I noticed a table that had two men who looked like the two we saw last night. This was beginning to smell rotten, and I was smart enough to pack my gun just in case I needed to get out in a hurry. I grabbed a tray off the shelf, then found a white jacket hanging nearby, and put some dishes on the tray. I walked toward Mario's table, as if I was a busboy waiting to clean tables, and stopped in back of Mario. I then leaned forward and whispered in his ear.

"Good to see you, Mario. Let's get up slowly and head toward the kitchen."

Mario was surprised at my sneaking behind him and obeyed my request. He had no idea why I was doing this, only if he thought that I was trying to be cautious. I asked him to go to the service elevator and we headed toward the tenth floor. I still had my room key and we went into the same room I had occupied just a few hours before. The room was literally messed up as if a tornado had swept through the room with a gusty wind of over a hundred miles an hour.

"Mario, what is going on here? Why did you call me last night, and why do you want to see me this morning?"

Mario looked inquisitively at me as if he didn't understand why I was so edgy.

"David, look at your room. Someone did a job on it. Were you out walking when this happened? And where is Leticia?"

I knew then that he had me followed, and he also knew that I was with Leticia.

"Mario, what are you up to? Why are you so curious as to what I am doing and whom I am seeing? Are you working for the other side? Tell me before I put a fucking hole in your head. Things are falling into place, my dear friend. You knew exactly what I was doing, and it was you who warned Chuck that we were going to raid the house in Monterey. That is why he never showed up there. You are working for the Mafia, aren't you?"

Mario turned around and saw the gun aimed at his head. He had been a long time friend of mine but I also knew that every time we tried to do something, there was always a hitch. He was tipping them off so we never really got the big guys. It was Mario who got Chuck free and clear, and it was he who knew how to find Rita and Julie. It was also Mario who had me followed back in Dana Point, and it was Mario who nearly got Leticia killed. Things were starting to add up.

"David, I wanted to tell you, but I was in too deep. I saw a way to make more money and this shit with the Seals was getting to be old hat."

He sat down on the bed and decided to open up and tell me how he got involved with the guys we were to take out. He told me that after his divorce, he had not had a decent job, and needed to get back in the circuit. He met with Chuck and became his informer. He didn't mean to screw up my life, but he knew me well enough to convince Chuck to have Julie set me up in the garage, in Vegas, and in Dana Point. Only he knew where I lived in Dana Point so that is why I was tailed and almost killed.

It was not Mario in the car, but some of Chuck's button men who tried to get me. He was on Chuck's bankroll now but did not want to see any of the Seals guys get hurt, including me. But he was paid big bucks to keep me out of the way, and on the other hand, protect me as a friend. It was Mario who warned Chuck of the plan to take down the drug cartel in Big Sur. It was his idea to become intimate with Rita and gain her trust. That is how Rita knew of Chuck's plans. Mario would spill the beans when he drank too much. Since Rita had a soft spot for me, she called me to warn me of the upcoming plans by Chuck.

"So there, you have the picture, David. I crossed the line. I am not what you think I am. Basically I am a disappointment to you, I know. But that's life! You have the entire story now. Only thing is, you are still in danger."

I asked Mario who got into my room after I left with Leticia, and he told me that he guided the two guys up here. He was hoping that I would realize that he was in Hawai'i and that is why he called me when he did. He wanted me out of the room before the Mafia guys would get there. They were looking for something that I didn't have, but Leticia did.

They believed that Leticia had a key to a safe deposit box that she took from her husband. The box contained over five million dollars in large bills. Leticia was holding out on me, but I could accept that, as she too could not trust anyone any more. They actually wanted me to lead them to Leticia, and Chuck would not have cared if I got in the way and stopped a bullet. I felt sorry for Mario, yet he truly was a disappointment to me. He was not my friend any more, but I still cared for him. He was in deep shit trouble and I knew that I had to turn him in to the authorities. Cappy would be pissed when he would find out.

After I tied him up with some cord I took from the curtains, I left him on the bed. I also took his revolver from his holster and I told him that I would return for him after I took care of the two characters downstairs, who were looking for me. Mario also indicated that Chuck was in Honolulu with some his Mafia buddies and they were going to find me as well as Leticia if we weren't too careful.

I was happy to have contacted Cappy and decided to call him again and tell him of the new situation that we had. But I didn't want to do this in the room with Mario listening. I told Mario to stay out of this and that I would handle the problems at this point. He seemed to be secure, having tied him tightly to the bed, and I left.

I hit the stairwell and called Cappy on my cell phone. After hearing about Mario, he was fit to be tied. Of all people, Mario was his top honor student, the one he truly relied on. I could tell that he was totally pissed. He would be on the next plane out with the DEA and the FBI. He also told me that the six Seals and Special OP boys were in the Outrigger Hotel now and that I would find them on the fourth floor in room 428. I immediately went to the room and chatted with the guys.

We devised a plan to first get the two men in the lobby, after which they would question Mario to find out where we would find Chuck and his people. With the two thugs out of the way, and Mario spilling the beans to all of us, I left them and headed back to Leticia. She was fully dressed and had already ordered up some breakfast. I told her of the latest developments and asked her about the mysterious key.

"David, I did not want you to get involved with this. I did steal the key but have not had a chance to go to the safe deposit box. I have no idea what is in the box but I know that it has to be something important. I thought that it could be lots of money or even drugs. I am willing to give you the key because I want you to take the contents and return it. If it is blood money, I don't want it."

With that, I took the key and put it into a small compartment in my luggage. I decided to once again believe in her, but that I needed to put all of what happened in a proper perspective and protect Leticia from any harm. We sat and talked for a while, trying to figure out our next move. I was also in contact with Cappy by cell phone as he was boarding a private government jet with over fifty agents. They seemed to know where Chuck was staying. It was going to be the culmination of what had started in the mall garage so many weeks ago.

Waiting for Cappy to arrive, I decided to get Leticia out of the hotel room and head for Pearl Harbor. We decided to tour the many ships and submarines that were docked and just walk around the area, feeling some remorse for my friend Mario. I had some distant thoughts of Julie, and what we had to do in the next few hours to make peace with ourselves. We needed to end all of this so we could go back and lead a normal life once again, without the fear of being shot at by a band of killers. No matter how this worked out, my main thought was to protect Leticia as well as myself.

I found myself taking charge and feeling good about it. I was not that yellow-faced kid who was wet behind the ears of yesterday. I was maturing and was learning how to think like a leader while handling all sorts of problems as they arose. Leticia, in her own way, was also helping me become the man I chose to be. I realized that my past was becoming a vague memory of indecision and immaturity. My goal was to move forward, and finally take control of my life, even if that meant becoming the leader, not the follower. My destiny was to lie in what I was able to accomplish on this last mission, and whom I would prefer to be with in my life.

I learned that people will follow you only when you have earned their trust and respect. I was beginning to develop a common vision, trying to influence people to give their best, in any situation. I remembered a statement by President John F. Kennedy, when he said: 'The great enemy of the truth is very often not the lie, deliberate, contrived and dishonest, but the myth, persistent, persuasive and unrealistic'.

I was in a maze of comprehension. What was required of me? What was in it for me? How was I doing as a man?

Another great quotation that came to mind truly hit me on the head: 'Nothing is so simple that cannot be misunderstood'.

I realized that in order for me not to fail, I had to leave the comfort zone. I had to develop and use the power that was given to me, that would change the course of my destiny.

We decided to stop off at the Harbor in Pearl and have some lunch. Again, it was always a pleasure to be with Leticia. We held hands under the table and she started to tell me about her life growing up in Hawai'i and how she met her husband. It was interesting to listen to her as she was so much the intimate type of woman who could make anything sound so perfect. She told me how she was related, as a great, great granddaughter to Queen Lili'uokalani and her stories were fascinating to listen to.

You can almost imagine how the explorers found these tiny islands in such a vast ocean over centuries ago. Leticia spoke about the history that was taught to her, how the early Polynesians discovered Hawai'i through impressive feats of celestial navigation, and how those brave explorers crossed the uncharted ocean in huge sailing canoes, using the stars, winds and currents as navigational aids. They arrived in Hawai'i with their families, animals, plants, and everything they needed to survive in an uninhabited island.

In 1778, British navigator Captain James Cook 'discovered' the Hawaiian Islands, known then as the 'Sandwich Islands' and found that each island was its own kingdom, organized in a feudal manner with chiefs, priests and commoners. The first maps of Hawai'i, known as the world's most isolated land mass, was credited to Cook, William Bligh, the master of Cook's ship, the Resolution, and Henry Roberts, a mate and assistant to Bligh.

By 1810, Kamehameha I, King of Hawai'i Island, had united all of the Hawaiian Islands. He and his descendants reigned until 1872, and were followed by other families. In 1893, Queen Lili'uokalani, a great, great grandmother of Leticia's, was overthrown by prominent businessmen and the U.S. military. Hawai'i was suddenly under the jurisdiction of a United State provisional government.

The Republic of Hawai'i came into existence on July 4th, 1894, with Sanford B. Dole, a missionary descendant, as president. The islands were annexed by the United States in 1898 and made a territory in 1900. Between annexation and World War II, sugar and pineapple industries flourished and the number of immigrants brought in to work the plantations increased. The military's interest in the islands resulted in the construction of numerous bases, including the huge Naval base at Pearl Harbor where we were enjoying a nice lunch at that moment. This was the same site of the December 7th, 1941 surprise attack by the Japanese.

Finally, in 1959, Hawaii became the 50th state, ending the campaign for statehood that had begun at the turn of the century. Today, Hawai'i's population exceeds one million and Honolulu is the country's eleventh largest city. And here Leticia and I sat, waiting for our fate.

Were we to succeed and put this behind us? Would we go our separate ways, or would be wind up with each other for the rest of our lives? My mind was going in all directions. Yet, I was still able to keep my eyes open, and watch the area for any danger. And in that one instant, I noticed that some men in the distance were approaching us.

It was Cappy and some of the DEA and Special Op guys.

"David, I am glad that you are looking well and in good hands. Hi Leticia. I am Cappy of the Navy Seals, and we are here to get you guys out of Hawai'i and back to the mainland."

I looked up at Cappy, smiling from ear to ear, and shook his hands.

"How'd you know where to find us? I mean, er.. I was going to call you on your cell phone after lunch. And why do you want us back on the mainland? I am still part of your team, aren't I?"

"David, I need you in California. I need you to take Leticia away from here and keep her safe. I had two of the Seals follow you guys to Pearl Harbor, and report in to me when I arrived. I wanted to make sure that you were safe from harm's way. Now that we know where Chuck is, we can get him. And, by the way, we also kept an eye on Mario for some time."

I knew that Mario's little games could never get past Cappy. He was too good to allow Mario to play both ends without getting caught.

"I never chose to tell you, David, as he has been your friend for years. But we knew that he was involved in the other side and that he was in Hawai'i all this time. I am sorry to say that we will have to press charges against him for his part in playing both sides and for risking the lives of our men in a few of the operations. Three men died during our actions and that will play harshly on his conviction.

"But I can tell you, David, that you have been a faithful Seal and a good man. I am relieving you of your duties and you can go home to California. We will take it from here."

With that, Leticia and I were escorted back to her hotel where she picked up her luggage and then to the Oahu Airport where we caught a plane back to John Wayne Airport. I dropped Leticia off at my place in Dana Point and I went to the store for some groceries. When I got back, we made love all over again. I was beginning to feel so close to her. I almost forgot about the key that she gave to me and decided that I would follow through on this the next day.

CHAPTER 16

▼

AS IF WE NEVER SAID
GOODBYE

It was late morning and Julie was not sure that she had the energy to go to work. She had worked a very long, grueling eighty-hour week and hoped for some time to herself to catch up on some work at home. She laid her morning newspaper next to her favorite chair and turned to the news on the TV. She had brought in a cup of tea and occasionally, thoughts of David had crept into her mind. Why had she been so infatuated with him, and why didn't she just forget this man? She could not help herself.

She was annoyed for having gone so far with him on one hand, and on the other, he certainly turned out to be a good catch. David felt good to hold on to and be close to. She knew what she had been doing from the start, and that she had hurt him, feeling a twinge of guilt all over again. She quickly brushed it out of her mind and thought it best to put the entire thing behind her for a while. Though, in her heart, she knew that there was no way she would find out what would happen to David in the end. She may never see him again and he may never return.

Julie always had an attraction to him. Even from the beginning, in the mall garage when they first met, when it started out to be fun and games. There was something about David that was pure and honest. And she followed through with her escapade since she did not want to be a disloyal friend to Christie, and what repercussions that might have followed if she did not do what she was told to do by Chuck.

She did not want to jeopardize her position at the law firm. But her attraction to Chuck at the time was always a prominent force that hindered her from being with anyone else for the long haul, especially David. What was it about these two men that put her in such a position?

She remembered when she first met Chuck, and the way he looked at her with his deep dark eyes. She was introduced by Christy, who was so smitten with Chuck that she had to contain her excitement when she looked into Chuck's eyes. Julie thought about the several conversations with him during the past few months, but never did she once succumb to his physical propositions.

Julie was very tempted, but felt that she would be a terrible friend to Christy if she followed through with this. She adored Christy, and the last thing she wanted to do was to hurt her, or for that matter, hurt herself, as Christy had the tendency to go off the deep end when she was disappointed.

Just as Julie was taking some last sips of tea, her cell phone rang from upstairs. She heard the ring over the TV but hesitated to run upstairs to answer it. It could have been work or it could have been someone important. She decided to let it ring and would catch the message later. She finished watching the news, took a shower, felt more relaxed, and then decided that it was time to take a ride to her office.

Although she was going to be a few hours late, it didn't matter as she had been working late for so many weeks now. She just couldn't resist the temptation to work. After all, she didn't have someone to rub her back, or make her breakfast, or take her to a movie. She didn't have someone to come home to, or a partner to have sex with. She probably had blown any chances she had with David. And now that Chuck may be jailed or even killed, her prospects with any man at the present seemed lost. She realized that she was the culprit, not David.

Upon reaching her office, she saw the little red light blinking on her phone and she muttered to herself, as she reached for the handset.

"My God, don't they ever leave me alone?"

One message, in particular, sat her down on her leather chair in such a quagmire, that she had to replay it several times.

"Julie, sweetheart," it began.

She knew that voice, and every time she heard it, her heart leaped an extra few beats.

"I have been trying to reach you all morning. Please call me ASAP. It is urgent."

It was the way he lowered his voice, and sounded so coy and seductive, in a manner that she had grown vulnerable to. Julie pictured his strong features talking into the phone and she did not move from her chair for what seemed to be a very long time. She had to think this through before she returned the call, and gathered her paperwork to do her daily legal work. She said to herself that she would call him when she felt more secure and less panicky. She just did not want to get any more involved with him, but she kept thinking of her 'friend' and the thought occurred to her that perhaps she was using Christy as an excuse to not get close to him after all.

She had put in another long day, and when she returned home, she heard her cell phone ring again. Only this time, she answered the call, knowing full well whom it was going to be.

"Well, it is about time I reached you, 'my little darling'?"

"I'm sorry, Chuck, for not getting back to you sooner. I have been busy with work, errands, and so many things. How can I help you?"

Finally, after a long and shocking conversation, trying to settle down after hearing what Chuck asked her to do, Julie decided to make arrangements to meet with Christy for dinner. She knew by the tone of Chuck's voice, and from the feelings she had for Christy, she needed to make sure that her girl friend was perfectly comfortable with what Chuck had demanded both girls to do. It was as if Julie was trying to avoid further complications for Christy, but was doubtful of Chuck's contempt for the life of others. Chuck was looking for justice and he was putting both Christy and Julie at risk.

After all, all of the events leading up to this were inevitable.

Julie met with Christy in a small café located a few miles from where Christy was living with her new roommate, so as not to inconvenience her. Both girls were excited to see each other, especially Christy, who had been out of the loop for quite some time. She had not seen Julie in quite a few weeks, and was thrilled when she had called.

"So what's been happening with you?" asked Christy.

"But before you say anything Julie, let me first say that after spending a few wonderful months with my parents, I decided to come back to southern California, find a job, a new roommate, and start a new life."

After an hour and a half of telling Julie about her parents, renewing her relationship with her family, and being out in the country air, Christy wanted to know all the dope on Chuck, David, and what was happening. Even as she spoke, Julie only heard a partial of what Christy was saying. Each was so occupied with herself, they did not truly pay attention to what the other had to say, nor did they absorb the conversation of the other. Finally, Julie turned to Christy and started to get on another subject, the one that caused her to contact Christy in the first place. This was the request made by Chuck over the phone to her.

"Christy, I have another project that I think we might enjoy doing together. I hope you can handle it as I am counting on you. Are you game to do something that might be fun and adventurous?"

Christy could not contain her excitement and although she was busy with some mundane things, like her job, and trying to distance herself from some of the past surroundings, she was looking to enlighten her self worth with some new and exciting activity. Julie was at first hesitant to ask her friend to assist her, but she had no other option.

"It seems that our friend, David has been not been happy with the Navy Seals, and wants to do something outside of the government. He probably needs a 'rude' awakening. Our mutual friend has contacted me and has informed me that David has found himself a new lover and is planning on leaving his Seal buddies to be a part of the team...Chuck's team."

Christy, having been out of touch with what has been going on, was stymied to learn that David had a new lover. She thought that David and Julie were an item and were going to be married. All of this didn't make sense to her. Also, Christy wanted out of all that had happened in the past, and truly did not want to be bothered with Chuck and his conniving ways any more. At first she seemed a bit disappointed in finding out that David was seeing someone else as she was still infatuated with him, in her own twisted little mind. She had hoped that David would come back to her and resume a relationship with her, not with Julie.

Julie, on the other hand, believed that Christy would be more inclined to help her once she found out that David was two-timing everyone and that he was playing each of them for fools. This was Julie's motive to get to Christy to help her.

"Christy, I heard that David is seeing some Hawaiian woman named Leticia, an ex-wife of one of the drug cartel members, and David had him killed so he could take his wife. They are both in Hawaii now, and Chuck wants us to go there to settle a few things, if you know what I mean. It seems that David has been deceived by one of his own loyal Seal buddies who is now working for Chuck, and either David gets on board with Chuck, or becomes history, together with his girl friend.

"Christy, I realize that you moved away from this and probably don't want to get involved. But, it would be a tremendous favor to me if you would just do this one thing for me. I promise that this would be the last time you would get involved."

Julie had to lie a bit to get to her friend. Upon hearing that David was with another woman, this truly pissed Julie, as well as Christy off to no end. Although they had some disagreements and they may have lied to him, to find out that

David chose an ex-wife of a criminal over each of them, really made them both angry. Chuck's call to Julie really got to her and she was out for blood. If she couldn't have David, then this Leticia would not have him either.

Julie felt cheated, even though she initially cheated on David from the beginning by not being honest with him. But to have it thrown back in her own face was something that she never experienced before. Julie was a spoiled brat who always got her way. Now, the partners in her law firm were not giving her entry into a partnership. With Chuck out of the picture, and Julie's experience with Chuck not painting a good picture of her with the partners, her bright star was a bit faded. She thought that having David ditch her for someone else was not only hurting her ego, but she started to feel in denial. She wanted revenge against her fiancée.

When Julie had spoken to Chuck earlier that evening, her ears began to ring, and the tightening of her throat was becoming more and more evident. She listened most attentively to Chuck, when he told her that it was most important to have Christy become a part of this plan as David would be more accessible this way. Julie was reminded that David always had a weak spot for assisting the ladies, and if Christy needed him, he would most certainly be there.

Based on his past, David was more vulnerable when he knew that a woman was in trouble, and needed his help. Therefore, Chuck told Julie to get tickets for Hawaii and convince Christy to help, and she would be generously compensated. Then Christy would be forever left alone once this was over.

Christy heard Julie explain the details to her and thought long and hard about the plan. She knew that she could use extra money, and if Chuck would not bother her ever again, that was something she truly wanted, although she never believed Chuck and his promises. She knew that if Chuck wanted to find her, he would. She also knew that her life would never be the same until he stopped bothering her. At this point, she was damned, one way or the other.

She decided to go along with Julie, and it was then that she found out that Chuck offered each of them one hundred thousand dollars to do this one last job for him. Unfortunately, what they failed to learn was that David and Leticia were back in California and that the FBI and the Navy Seals were in a hot pursuit of Chuck and his people.

As they were about to leave the restaurant, Christy asked Julie one last question.

"Julie, why are you getting involved? You have a good job, and you are moving up in your profession, whether at this law firm or any other. By doing this, you are going to jeopardize every thing that you had worked for these past few years? Are you sure that you want to do this?"

Julie turned to Christy and sternly responded, like a defiant woman who had been scorned.

"Christy, my entire life has been to get to the top. I had to do many things to get to where I am at now, and it was necessary to do the things I had done to get me there. I am still looked upon at my firm as a young, woman lawyer and not a partner. I am still making a measly $120,000 and I should be making more. I pulled a stunt on a strange guy who I never met before and he fell in love with me."

Julie continued to vent her problems to Christy.

"Then, when he found out that I played with him, he ditched me. He ditched me for a Hawaiian woman who was the wife of a member of the drug cartel. Do you know how that makes me feel? I am pissed, Christy. I am nothing to him now. He will never take me back. Why then should I care about him? I fucked him and he fucked me back. I don't like that feeling. I am too smart to be fucked."

Julie started to cry and Christy took her around. Obviously they had feelings for each other, and never really meant to hurt anyone else. They were put into situations by chance, not by choice. They each found love, only to realize that they were the ones who allowed love to slip away from them. They realized that life could be so awful at times, that no matter how they felt, they would be harboring this for the rest of their lives.

Leticia was rubbing baby oil on my bare back at the pool in the gated community that I had been living in for many years. She remarked how I had acquired such a beautiful bronze tan, and perhaps she should put oil on more parts of my body so I would not burn any more from the sun. We giggled together and were enjoying a lovely, lazy afternoon in Dana Point. It was nice to be away from the aggression that had presented itself to both of us, and this quiet moment was just what the doctor ordered. The pool was nearly empty except for a few older women, and it seemed as if we had the best of both worlds.

Our running from the hostility in Hawaii was over and we were now simply relaxing and enjoying the pleasures of each other's company. I was enjoying this beautiful moment with Leticia, and as I stretched my aching body on the chaise, I started to daydream once again. I thought that of all of the many months of passion and desires I had had with so many women whom I had encountered, it was becoming more apparent that all of that had led me to this point in my life.

Before this, I was a simple man, interested only in tending to my class instructions. I tried to be a good husband to a wife of frailty who would not be able to spend a lifetime with me. I found myself making mundane conversations with strangers in supermarkets and parking garages. Before I knew it, one thing led to another, and I got involved with total strangers.

I started to reinvent myself, by touching base with my Seal buddies and found myself trying to capture a mob boss, some drug lords, a drug cartel ring and Mafioso. My life had taken more twists and turns than my sports car on the thirty-mile strip of the winding road commonly known as the Ortega Highway, down to Lake Elsinore from Dana Point.

I found myself trying to screw every pretty face I could, as it became a passion and possibly a sickness. I even played games with their emotions and found myself hurting some of those whom I enjoyed being in the sack with. There I was, telling one woman that I wanted to marry her, while telling another that I can't live without her.

I lost a good friend in Mario, which came as a big surprise to me. All this would not have happened if I had not gotten involved with the Seals again. What Mario chose to do on his own time was his business. He was a friend and I had no right to question him. I never would have known about Mario's past and his present involvement with the mob.

While I pondered over my past, even with a beautiful woman at my side, I was also blaming other beautiful women for putting me into situations that changed me into someone I never thought I was. Perhaps I was weak after all, not having experienced these kinds of pleasures in my early years. And perhaps, if I had gone through such a period in my life, I would not have had the desire that I had during these past few months. Maybe I was just a late bloomer in life.

Thinking back, I must admit that both Christy and Julie were dreams made in heaven. And there was Rita, with her bouncing tits, giving head like it was going out of style. It was Christy, though, who opened the door for me. Our first nights in Vegas were heaven. But when I think back, two years prior, I had experienced the loves of Diane and Leticia. And now Leticia sits by my side as if this angel of heaven came back to my life for a reason.

But, before meeting Leticia here in California, I thought that I would never have the opportunity to find a better catch than someone like Julie. Of course, I cannot forget the mindless bedding of Rita and Stephanie, and the many others in between. What was I thinking at the time? Was it my way of proving to myself that this middle age Don Juan still had what it took to score with many mindless women who came into my life? Or was I the mindless person?

Somehow, I have to admit, that if it were not for these women, I may not have built a more suitable confidence level for myself as I felt I now had. The downside to all this was that I was wondering if I was able to control myself now, being with Leticia. I started to feel that maybe I was finally relieved to actually say to myself that I was ready for one woman.

Maybe I would still be able to have some children. I always wanted a daughter, and I would call her Toni. That was a name I always had in mind for my little girl. Perhaps there was a chance with Leticia to have children.

Suddenly, my cell phone rang. As I reached for it, I looked at my Leticia next to me, thinking that she was not only the most beautiful woman I had ever met, but I was enjoying her company, her kindness and the fact that she was now in my life.

"Hello, this is David. Wha...why are you calling me, and how did you..." The caller started to ramble on.

I thought twice about who was on the phone and why I was being contacted. The voice on the other end of the phone sounded a bit nervous, yet she had an insight as to what I had done in Hawaii, and knew that I was with Leticia. But the caller had no idea that I was in California, as I was asked how I was enjoying the Hawaiian sunshine. I thought twice about what I wanted to say and decided not to allow Julie, who was waiting for me to speak, ruin my passionate moments with my beautiful Leticia.

"I'm sorry, David," Julie continued, "but I have a serious situation. I don't mean to bother you on your vacation. But, for your information, Chuck notified me and told me how to locate you. He told me that you are with a woman called Leticia who was married to a drug cartel leader. You must know by now that he can find anyone he wants to, and he keeps me informed of your whereabouts. This should not come as a surprise to you, David. You know that I was on his payroll before and he relies on me to do things for him. He wants to have a meeting with you to discuss your situation with your joining him, as your friend Mario did. I suppose I also want to know if we have anything left between us."

Julie was either warning me of some danger, or was actually setting me up in a sting. What she failed to realize was that Chuck was being hunted down like a rat in Honolulu, and that I was right here in Dana Point. Why spoil it and tell her? I wanted to hear her entire story. If she was involved with Chuck, then she too would have to be dealt with.

"David, it seems as if I am smack in the middle of a crisis with my law firm and I think that they are aware that I may have been secretly dealing with Chuck. I really need your help and if you could talk to him about my getting out of this, I would truly appreciate it. Please do this for me."

I got up from the chaise and walked to the far side of the pool. Leticia sat there not knowing who had called and patiently waited for me to return, hoping that I would tell her what was happening.

I told Julie that I had nothing to say to him and if she got in the middle of something that was hurting her, then she should find a way to get out of it by herself. I thought carefully before I told her absolutely no, as she told me how she was threatened by Chuck, and how he always had a grip on her, as well as

Christy. I finally indicated to her that I would consider this and that I would contact her in a few days since Leticia and I were moving on to another island. I just didn't want her to call the hotel and find out that I checked out.

After ending the call, I was thinking that any day soon, Cappy and his boys would take down Chuck and this would close the book on Julie. I had to think carefully as to what her motives were and if she again was trying to lure me into a trap. Knowing Julie, she only wanted what was best for her, but she was a good person and I had to read between the lines.

I walked back to the chaise lounge where Leticia was sitting and told her that it was just a call about my teaching job. There was no need to tell her about this, as I did not want to worry her. As I looked at her tanned body and how her bathing suit gripped the right areas of her body, I knew that I wanted to get more intimate with her again, continuing to seduce her and enjoy her body next to mine. I was truly attracted to Leticia and I felt that she was attracted to me. I didn't mind having her spend some time with me in my home, as it was safe and secure for both of us.

Back in my condo, I checked the mail and messages from the last few days. Then my cell phone rang once again. It was Cappy.

"David, we have made some inroads with our search and seizure, together with the DEA and the FBI. We had captured the ring of hoodlums including Chuck, and the Mafioso working with Chuck are now in custody."

Cappy was elated and I felt relieved. He told me that Mario was also being arraigned but they would be lenient with him as he was a good Seal who had just gone off on the wrong track. His work against the bad guys was to be considered and he would receive a fair punishment. I was happy to hear the good news.

I felt relaxed and had informed Leticia of the latest events. I was beginning to see some light at the end of the tunnel. The only problem I had was with Julie. She chose a course that was not going anywhere and she was not going to be happy. Perhaps when she found out that Chuck was captured, she and Christy could go on with their lives once again, without the fear of Chuck and the power he had over them.

I turned toward Leticia and told her how happy I was that she was with me. I moved closer to her and kissed her on the lips. She responded by moving her body close to mine, placing her hand on the back of my neck, moving her body from side to side, so I could feel her breasts against my naked chest.

I reached in back and untied her straps and let her bathing suit drop to the floor. We inched toward the sofa in the den and I pulled down my shorts. She immediately lay down and pulled me on top of her. Her body was not only hot, but heaving with sex. I knew that I had to get inside of her as I started to get the urge of my penis needing someplace to go.

I found the opening and moved in on her as if I was going to explode. Leticia responded so rapidly that it did not take long before we both reach our conquest at the same time. It was the angel in her, and the devil in me. We drove each other wild with love making until we had no more strength to do it again. Her body was genuine and made me feel like a god.

Leticia and I enjoyed a few more days together by hitting some wonderful restaurants in Laguna Beach and touring the small beach towns. We loved to take advantage of the beautiful ocean breezes by watching the surfers do their thing on the waves, and doing what two lovers normally do. I felt that it was time to close out all past business and decided to see what road I would take that would lead us to happiness. I surely did not want to go back to what I had with the Seals, the other women in my life, and being alone. Leticia gave me the comfort of a lover and a friend. Was this going to lead to a marital pact between us? Only time would tell.

We finally decided to go to the Amtrak Train Station in Los Angeles and open one of the lock boxes in the terminal. I had thought that the key was for a safe deposit box, but after checking it out at the local FBI headquarters, it was actually a key for a locker at the terminal. We searched the entire terminal until we finally spotted the locker with the right number. I took along a suitcase just in case we needed it to deposit the goods from the locker.

Leticia and I opened up the locker and found three satchels that were also locked with combination locks. We took the satchels, placed them in the suitcase, and went to the car. Driving back to Dana Point, we spoke about what might be in the bags and what we were going to do with whatever we found. After all, was this drug money, and could the Feds confiscate this from us? Would we become felons if we kept any of it? These thoughts crossed our minds.

Back at my garage, I found a tool that enabled me to open up the bags, and lo and behold, we found lots of money. It seemed that there was nearly ten million dollars worth of drug money in all three satchels. This was illegal for us to have but we decided to hold on to it for a while. Leticia was totally surprised to see more money than she had first realized.

She asked me to call Cappy and return the money to the government. I agreed and counted every last dollar in the bags to make sure that I would account for every single dollar that was present. The denominations were in hundreds and thousands, and the bags weighed a ton. Luckily we had a luggage carrier in the car when we went to the terminal, and the large suitcase also had wheels. There was no way we would have been able to carry these bags by ourselves.

I then hid the bags in the attic of my home and waited until the moment was right before I would contact Cappy. In the meantime, Leticia and I started to talk about some serious things that involved both of us. It sounded like she was contemplating spending her life with me, but it was still a little too early and difficult to know how we both felt about this.

There was still some unfinished business I had to take care of and I decided to contact Christy by phone. I asked her to meet me at the mariner in Newport Beach so we could talk alone as I wanted to find out all about her role with Julie in getting me to meet with Chuck.

I did not let on that Chuck was in custody or that Mario was also a good Seal who turned bad. Fortunately, Christy kept her cell phone number so I was happy that I was able to contact her.

We met at a restaurant and we hugged and kissed, had some wine and tried their catch of the day. I asked her how she was doing and everything seemed to be coming together, until she met with Julie about a week before.

"David, Julie wanted me to set you up with Chuck, and she told me that I would make a lot of money. I just don't know what got into her. She seemed angered because you were seeing that Hawaiian gal who was married to the

Columbian drug cartel gangster. I am so glad you called me because I really do not want to do this and I need your help."

I reassured Christy that she would not have to get involved with Julie and that she was safe from Chuck. Christy was not only a special gal to me, but she looked more beautiful than ever. She was happy at her new job, started to meet new friends, and was into a new lifestyle, away from the hideous times she had had with Chuck. She was on her way to a new life, and her encounter with Julie had definitely disturbed her.

Christy always looked up to Julie like a big sister and admired Julie's business sense, including her statuesque appearance, and the way she handled herself. This meeting they had was not something that Christy wanted, and she was not sure what was happening to her best friend.

I assured her that I would take care of it and that she should just go back to her present life and not worry about it.

"Christy, I am so very proud of you. You are doing so well and you don't need to get involved with this nonsense any more. Whatever happens with Leticia and me is something that I have to think about, as time will tell. Leticia is a wonderful lady and we seem to have hit it off. There are no strings attached right now but I certainly like being with her. You and I have had our moments of pleasure and many good times. But we have to move on in life. I thought I would have liked to share my life with Julie but I found too many gaps in our relationship. To find out that she is working with Chuck on his game plan does not make me too happy, as she is allowing herself to be associated with known criminals. You and I both know that this is not good for Julie."

I asked Christy if she kept a friendly relationship with Suzie or if she happened to meet Rita on occasion.

"David, Suzie is fine, as we meet for lunch once in a while. She dropped her friendship with Julie as they parted friends a while back. Julie didn't have time for her and Suzie, you know, is a lesbian, so she has her own group of friends. I have not seen or heard from Rita since our days back in Las Vegas. I asked Julie about Rita, and all she said was that she never heard from her."

With that, I told Christy that I would contact Julie and straighten out this problem. We parted and I left for home. On the way, I decided to stop off at Irvine, where Julie had her office. When I went inside and inquired about Julie, she was not in. So I took a ride to her home. I rang her doorbell and the door opened. There was Julie, surprised to see me, as she seemed to be puzzled why I would come to her house in the middle of the afternoon.

"Why, David, what are you doing here? I thought you were traveling in Hawaii. I am totally surprised to see you here."

"May I come in, Julie? We have lots to talk about. There seems to be a problem and I want to get to the bottom of it."

I walked into her home and it was as neat as it ever was. We went into the living room and I sat on the sofa while she grabbed her favorite chair. She then offered me a drink and I declined. I wanted to get down to business and find out why she was turning into a vamp who seemed to be destroying, not only her life, but those around her.

I started the conversation by confronting her with the news that Chuck had told her that he wanted to see me and why she was working with him to make trouble for others. I also wanted to know why he still had a grudge against me. What I didn't tell her yet, was the fact that Chuck was in the hands of the authorities and he was out of commission.

"David, you should know right now, that I truly loved you and wished that this would be different. I got in too deep and liked the fact that I can be whomever I want, and not have you or any partner of a law firm tell me what to do and how to be in life. I was passed over by the law firm and was not made a partner. I resented the fact that they have a click of men who don't recognize me as an equal and therefore, I cannot move up in this lousy law firm."

Julie spilled her heart out to me and I could see that she was frustrated.

"But why are you so set on having Chuck come after me, Julie? What have I done to you that provoked you to seethe with anger? It was you who deceived me from the beginning, and it was you who kept your many secrets from me. I may not have been perfect and I did have a sweet time with many women, including you. But that should not put so much hatred in you or try to get me killed. Why are you going in this direction?"

Again, Julie could not truthfully face the fact that she was doing anything wrong, but only tried to justify her actions because of her inability to become a top-notch attorney by getting the recognition that she felt she deserved.

"David, I am good at what I do. Chuck gave me an opportunity to prove myself with my firm, and be a part of something that I found exciting and out of the ordinary. You happened to come along and I fell for you, even though I was setting you up. Then, with the help of your navy buddies, you had become stronger and you kept surprising me with your ability to outfox Chuck and his cronies. You got wise to me and then you got involved with a woman, whose husband was also a killer. She must be worth it, David. You must really love her to toss me out on my ear."

Julie was talking like a lady scorned. She was trying to justify herself as to her wrong doings, and therefore put some of the blame on me. Although I felt that I was open to much of her criticism and deserved some of her wrath, I never put her in danger, nor did I allow Chuck to harm her or Christy. Yes, I did love Leticia, as she was always kind and considerate. She too had not told me the entire truth when I was with her, but she never placed me in harm's way. I let Julie continue with her comments and just sat, listening to her hurt and anxiety through all that had taken place.

"And to think, that we had something going between us. I felt like I was tossed out for another woman and that you didn't care how you hurt me. You are nothing more than a pimp, David. You tell me you love me. Then you go out and get laid by another woman. How did that make me feel? You are just like Chuck, and you are just like me. We all want something out of life and we take it when it comes along. That is what life is all about, David. Like you once told me, Life is Sweet and Bittersweet. If it's there for the taking, we take it. We don't care if we hurt others, because we are all after the same things in life. Life is up for grabs."

Julie was expressing her feelings and she was probably right in so many ways. I realized that I had become a pimp in heat and I loved every minute of it. She reminded me of my sexual drives with other women and how I enjoyed the passion, the challenge, and the sex. In a way, I did commit adultery by having relationships with many women, trying my best to get many of them in bed. It just happened, and when the opportunity came, I lured them and I succeeded. I even tried to get Julie in bed, and it took some time. But, here too, I finally got her ass in the sack and we fucked all night.

Our conversation at her home opened up the Pandora's Box, as Julie was spitting her guts out how she felt jilted, not only by me, but by her company, her friends, and herself. I felt sorry for her, yet I did not approve of her trying to get me killed, or putting anyone at risk. I told her that I was always there for people, and I didn't put anyone in danger.

I was there for her until I found out that she used me for her own satisfaction. I did not approve of her lack of conscience, her "Me" attitude, and the fact that all of this was a game to her. We all had feelings and we were all searching for something in life. But unlike Julie, I would not place any one at risk. Unlike Julie, I had a conscience and morals. And unlike Julie, I could love someone.

"David, you are too self righteous and so innocent. You really don't know what is going on, do you? You come into my home and expect me to apologize to you for my actions, when you are so naïve about life that you are truly a stupid man. You think that I only did this for the money? Do you think that all this was for my ego and my stature in life?"

It was time for Julie to show her importance and put the blame on others. She sat in her chair, sipping a martini and felt that it was time to allow herself some breathing room by explaining to me who she truly was and to explain her purpose in life. This was the same Julie who was the beautiful model I had fallen in love with. This was the Julie who I felt was like a dream come true, the kind of woman I would be proud to spend the rest of my life with.

"Let me tell you, that there is more than you realize. I am not who you think I am, David. Yes, I am an attorney, only because I studied law in college. I am a former model and learned how to walk as tall as the rest of them. Everyone wanted to get into my pants, and at the beginning, I allowed them to, just to move ahead in business. The only one I never went to bed with was Chuck. He truly scared me, and he also had something going with Christy. I didn't want to cross her path, and move in on her boyfriend. Although I had thoughts of having sex with him, I never did. He was exciting and rough, and he knew what he wanted out of life. Just like me."

Julie continued and I just sat listening to her.

"And then there is you, the young man on the white horse, who comes into my life and woos me to a point where we are in the throes of getting married."

At this point, I got up and went for a glass of wine. The plot was thickening and I knew that I was going to have my head handed to me. Julie started to preach as if she was in Court, addressing the jury in a criminal matter.

"I have you meet my relatives and we announce our engagement and you think that everything is rosy. But you still have temptations to go out and fuck other women while we are so-called, engaged. You are something else, my boy. I know all about you and how you spent your time with this Leticia. Mario told me, as he and I also became lovers. You didn't know that, did you?"

Julie continued to spill it all out. She was hurting me to no end, even the part about Mario.

"He was on Chuck's payroll and he told me everything. Just give him some alcohol and he would tell you anything you wanted to know. I suppose you think that Leticia is a better woman than I am and you can get more enjoyment from her than from me. You also crossed the line, David, and you are no better than I am. We are both the same kind of people."

I sat back and listened, as Julie read me the riot act. In a way, she was right. I did play the field and found that I was happier with someone else, rather than with her. There was something very devious about her that I was not able to detect until she told me that she used me and followed me to Vegas. I could overlook that but not the fact that she was involved with a gangster whom we were trying to capture. She was toying with all of us, warning him of the plans we had, by working both sides of the fence.

Having a love affair with Mario was a new tidbit that I did not know. I was hoping that Mario enjoyed her as much as I did. She was cool, all right. Right down to the fucking details. I took all of this into its proper perspective and then raised the question as to why.

"Julie, you should not have used me or worked for Chuck. As far as Mario is concerned, he and I came to odds when he tried to give me up to the mafia. I caught on to him and he is now in custody."

It was time to let the cat out of the bag. I felt that Julie had a right to know what had happened to Mario and Chuck.

"Also, Chuck is in jail, as he too was taken down by the FBI. So that leaves you, all alone, to wallow in your own mud. As an accomplice to a gangster, you have stepped over the line. I could understand your feelings on trying to get ahead, and accusing me of deceiving you by making love to other women. But you did the same with Mario. Why did you think that you could get away with this? Did you feel that you had a lock on how to get ahead by screwing others? Didn't you ever think about the circumstances you would be facing once all of this would come to an end? Now what the hell are you going to do with your life?"

Julie looked at me and then started to laugh.

"David, you are missing the point. You think that Chuck is in jail and that you are safe from him? Well, you are wrong. I want you to know that he is out there somewhere and he is coming after you. The man they think is Chuck, and is in jail, is someone who looks like him. He was very careful to find an exact double, and with a little scar tissue and some rework, he created an exact duplicate of himself. He created a clone. That is who is in jail, not Chuck. No one truly knows Chuck, and until they understand that he has outsmarted them time and time again, he is out there, lurching in the shadows. And he will get his revenge, one way or another. I told you that you are so naïve."

At that moment, my heart dropped. If Chuck was truly out there, would he be back in California, searching me out? Would he go to my house and find Leticia? Was he sitting outside, knowing that I was in Julie's house? Or was this just another one of my screw-ups and Julie was just testing me once again, to see where I would go with this?

"Well, David, you better understand your prey before you think that you have won the game. It is not over yet. And you and your little girlfriend are in trouble. He is after the millions of dollars that Leticia took from her husband. He told me that if I would help him, he would give me one million dollars. I told Christy that her share would be much less. I deserve some of that money, David. I worked hard for it. I suppose you know that your little Leticia took the key from her husband. Well, that money was stolen from Chuck when he paid for the dope and he never received it. Now you know the real reason why he is after your little Hawaiian girl friend. He wants his money, David. Do you know where it is?"

I suddenly panicked, realizing that Leticia is at my home and I left her unguarded. If what Julie was saying was correct, I had to get to my home in Dana Point and protect Leticia as soon as possible. I didn't want Julie to know that Leticia was there so I did not want to rush out of her house. I told Julie that I would be on my way and I appreciated her candor with me. Unfortunately, I did not have time to call the police and have them take her into custody. Instead, I told her to consider turning State's evidence and inform the authorities about Chuck. With that I left for Dana Point and Leticia.

As I drove frantically down the 405 Freeway, I was hoping that she was alive and well. Yet, the other part of me cynically wished that all of this was a dream, and when I would wake up, I would find Martha, my wife, lying next to me. Perhaps I wanted out of all of this. Maybe I was hoping that I could continue on with my life where I left off months ago.

That was a simpler life for me. What was I thinking! I realized then, that I was actually in love with another woman who was in my home and could be in danger. Now that I have experienced the raw desires and pure pleasures of so many lovely women, I fully believed that I would not trade Leticia for any of them.

On the way, I contacted Cappy on his cell, about this latest turn of events. I asked him to get the police over to my home as soon as possible. He told me that he would take care of this. Cappy would contact the sheriff's office in Dana Point and the FBI, plus he would get the Seals to move on a dime. Cappy was good at this. He knew how to respond at a moment's notice. I was counting on Cappy to get help and be at my home by the time I got there.

As I got off the freeway, I stopped at a light and I could see a man in a car next to mine, holding a cell phone to his ear. He looked distraught, shaking his head, and with his small, thin lips, wavered angry words into the receiver. Was this what I was becoming? Was I becoming an angry person, a paranoid, and feeling hatred for people? I didn't like the feeling. That was not me in that car that day. God, it better not be me.

Yet, I could be that man, driving like a lunatic, trying to save someone or something from the perils of death. In fact, that was what I was doing right then. I was speeding home to save the woman in my life. I didn't feel angry, nor did I feel paranoid. I was cool headed, and sorting everything out in that thirty minute drive from Julie's to my home. And I somehow managed a smile at the thought that I may have brought something special into my life. I was hoping that I could spend the rest of my life with Leticia. Here she was, having experienced a life as the wife of a killer, a drug lord, and a brutal husband who beat her when he wanted to. And here I was, trying to race home to save her life from Chuck.

"Martha", I asked "Are you proud of me? Or are you disappointed in how my life was turning out?"

Martha had not returned to me since we last spoke in a dream. Perhaps she was upset with me for screwing around as I did. Maybe she is not happy with the choice I made with Leticia. But she did tell me that she wanted what was best for me. And, although in death, there is no jealousy or possessiveness, I almost wished that she was jealous and possessive, so I could finally tell myself that I had had enough. Perhaps it was silly to think that I could get help from a dead woman. But I truly loved Martha and treasured our life together. All I really wanted now was a sign from her to help me do the right thing.

What would I do when I finally meet up with Chuck, I thought? Do I shoot him between the eyes? Would I plead for mercy so that he would not harm Leticia? Was I going to save her from him, or was this the end of my love?

I saw a black hole of an empty soul and putting him down for good would make me feel like I finally saved the world from an evil person. I was ready for it.

When I arrived home and pulled the car into the garage, I noticed that the house was quiet. I looked cautiously around the house, and did not see anything suspicious. I quickly opened the door in the garage, leading into the house, and looked around. I had not seen any strange cars parked on the street, as the house is in a gated community in lovely Dana Point. After checking in the kitchen, I ran upstairs hoping to find Leticia safe and sound. I did not see her nor had I heard any sound that would tell me that she was okay. She was not lying down on the bed, nor was she in any other room. I finally charged into my office and called out her name.

"Leticia, Leticia. Where are you?"

Finally, as I turned to go back downstairs, I heard a wimpy sound coming from the master bedroom. I ran toward the room, and there, emerging from the vanity room inside the master bathroom came Leticia. She had not heard me as she was probably running the shower or the commode. My heart was racing a mile a minute and there she was, as beautiful as ever, safe and sound.

"Whew! Am I glad to see you! Are you okay? I was worried when I didn't see you downstairs. I just wanted to make sure that you were okay."

"Oh, honey, I was in the bathroom. Sorry if I startled you. I took a nice hot shower, made some coffee for myself and decided to read one of your wonderful books that I found in the library. You certainly have a great collection of novels. Why are you panting so? You seem out of breath. Is everything all right, David?"

I told Leticia about my encounter with Christy, then with Julie, what I learned about Chuck, and how he was determined to go after the money that Leticia took from her husband's closet. She became a bit frightened, but after living with her husband among the thieves, the killers, the drug cartel and the mafia, she learned to take things slow and easy.

I decided to call Cappy again to find out where he and the police were. He was on the way over and had already notified the police and the Seals to get to my home as fast as they can. He then spoke as he was flying on the freeway.

"David, you have been a busy beaver, and your comments were well taken. Upon hearing what you said, I contacted the FBI and told them about this 'other' Chuck Manzione. Just to let you know, that upon examining the so-called "Chuck" we picked up in Hawaii, we realized that we had an imposter. We also sat down with Mario and got the scoop on what he did and whom he was in touch with in the last few months."

I knew I could count on Cappy. He had everything under control. As he spoke on his cell phone, I ran to my office and pulled out my 38 Special, making sure that it was loaded. Just in case my house would become a target, I wanted to make sure that both Leticia and I were well protected. I also gave her a small hand gun just in case she needed to use it.

Cappy continued.

"Mario was being most cooperative and we believe that we can work things out for him that would get him off. I will send some of the guys over to Julie's and pick her up for questioning and since she did not do anything unlawful, we may only hold her for a day or so and let her go. No need to keep her any longer. I am sorry the two of you didn't work out but perhaps it was for the best." He was beginning to sound more like family.

"All I can say is to keep Leticia safe until I get there. The FBI and the police are probably in the neighborhood now, looking for Chuck. By the way, you did say that you had the bags full of money, didn't you? Make sure that they are in a safe place and don't even think about it. Talk later."

Cappy was short and to the point. He knew how to get right down to the basics and not waste time. It would take only a few minutes to get some of the boys here to keep an eye on the house. In the meantime, I sat down with Leticia and we each had a glass of wine. No time like the present to mellow out for a while, until reinforcements came. It was late afternoon, and the sky was light blue, the sparse clouds scattered the horizon, and there was a chill in the air. I again made sure that my gun had a full chamber. I also loaded my pockets with extra bullets. With Chuck loose, I had no idea what would happen, even in my own house.

I kept checking the back yard and the front to see if there were strange cars lurking about. I was getting paranoid again, and I had to protect the woman I now realized that I was in love with. Leticia, on the other hand, was sitting on the couch, reading her book and enjoying her glass of wine. I went to the cabinet to pour both of us another glass, when I heard a tapping noise on the front door.

This door had a screen door in front of it, and I had thought I had locked the gate in front of the house.

As I peered through the small, vertical windows along side the door, I noticed two guys in suits. I could only see one face as the other looked away from the doorway. He held up a shield with his name on it and the letters, FBI. I waved at him and he walked toward the gate with the other gentleman.

I went back to the cabinet to continue to pour our wine, when the bell rang. I again walked back to the door and this time, he asked to speak to me, and if I wouldn't mind opening the door. With that, I told Leticia to go upstairs and stay there. No telling who these guys were, I placed my hand on the gun that was hanging on to my pants, in back of my sweater. This 'FBI' agent could be any-one, other than whom he claimed to be, and why did he shield me from seeing who the other cat was?

I opened the door and we spoke through the screen door.

"Yeah, what do you want?" I asked

He introduced himself as Jeff Canby, an FBI agent sent by Cappy, and his partner was Todd Olsen. I asked to see the face of Todd. As Todd turned around, Jeff pulled a gun and demanded that I open the screen door or he would blow my "Fucking Brains Out".

I felt for the old trick. Guess I wasn't that polished enough to know a con when it hit me. I unlocked the screen door and in they walked, both holding Magnum Forty Fives. Todd was none other than Chuck himself.

They had found the two FBI agents and took away their badges, climbed over my personal gate and tried the oldest trick in the book by showing me someone else's credentials. They asked me to sit down on the couch and asked to see Leti-cia. Chuck turned to me and announced his demands. He was determined to get that money and probably shoot us both anyway. I was hoping that Cappy and the other Seals and police were close by and would come to the door at any time.

"If you don't bring Leticia down here, I will personally go upstairs and shoot the broad in the fucking head. You understand, David?"

Upon hearing that from the upstairs stairwell, Leticia walked down the steps and came into the living room. She sat next to me on the couch. Chuck asked Leticia for the money and she told him that it was probably still in the terminal locker where it had been for many weeks. He asked for the key and told us that he would take us to the terminal and release us once he had the satchels in his hot little hands.

I looked at Leticia and we both realized that the key was left at the terminal, as it normally stays in the locker once you open it. Leticia had to stall for time and looked to me for suggestions.

I immediately replied.

"Chuck, I have the key. Leticia gave it to me. I put the key in a safe place and it is not in this house. You can understand that I would not want the key in this house. I would probably be under suspicion if the police found the key on me or in my home. So, do we talk about getting the key or what?"

I had to play with Chuck's emotions and the fact that he wanted the money more than killing Leticia or me. I also had to think the way he did, as he was quick witted, and sharp as a tack. If I screwed up at all, he would kill us both immediately. Chuck never liked to be outsmarted by anyone.

"Okay, David, where is the fucking key? I don't have all day. You have one answer and it better be right. I am sure that your place is being watched and before I destroy it, and your lovely bitch, I want you to play it smart with me and tell me what I want to hear."

I eyed him directly, and watched the other guy, 'Jeff, getting edgy with his gun as if he was ready to take my head off. I told Chuck that the key was in the clubhouse across the way. Perhaps that would give Cappy more time to get here. And maybe, I could find a way to get either Jeff or Chuck to go with me to the clubhouse, offering me a better chance to disarm him. I still had my 38 tucked into my pants as they never even bothered to search me. I thought that if I pulled it out right here in the house, he would shoot Leticia and I didn't want to take that chance.

I told Chuck that if all he wanted was the key, I would get it for him and he can go and get the money from the terminal. I figured that he would send Jeff with me and he would watch over Leticia until we both returned. I was thinking that at best, on the return trip from the clubhouse, only one of us would be walking through the door. At this point, Chuck did not have too many options, and we were each trying to outsmart the other. Either way, one of us was going down.

He agreed to send Jeff with me to get the key and we had to walk through the front gate, across the road, to the clubhouse. I also knew that if anything occurred along the way, he would not hesitate to shoot Leticia. The clubhouse key was hanging on a key rack in the laundry room by the front door. I was also hoping that Cappy and the rest of the guys would see us as we left my house and walked to the clubhouse. There were no signs of anyone anywhere, and I was getting a bit uncomfortable. Where in the hell was Cappy? Why wasn't he here yet? Was he hiding in the bushes?

Once inside the clubhouse, I walked over to the fireplace and told Jeff that the key to the locker was behind a loose brick. He told me to go get it and bring it to him. I reached into my pocket and felt the keys to the house, plus other keys that were on the same key chain. I turned away from Jeff and pulled the keys from my pocket and reached behind the brick and told him that I had the key. I showed him the set of keys and he was satisfied.

I thought twice about trying to disarm Jeff, as any struggle that was seen by Chuck would cause him to shoot Leticia. I decided to try to kill time and play all of this out, hoping that Cappy was out there, waiting to make his move.

We started to walk toward the clubhouse door. I then locked the door from the outside, and we both headed back to my townhouse. Just then, a car pulled up. It completely came out of the clear blue sky. I looked inside the side window and recognized the driver. It was Julie.

What the hell was Julie doing here? Now she would also be in danger. This was not the right time to be courageous and I would have thought that Julie would be next in line on his hit list. I did not expect her to drive to Dana Point and get involved with Chuck. But there she was, in her sporty looking car, pulling over to one of the parking spots near my condo.

"Julie, what are you doing here? You came at a bad time. Get in your car and get out of here."

Julie got out and saw that Jeff was behind me.

"I came to let you know that I want out of this, David, and I don't want Chuck to hurt you. I made a terrible mistake and I am sorry for all of the trouble I had caused you."

This turned out to be a bad time for Julie. Of all times to decide to become a good little girl and finally want out of the mess she ultimately got herself into. She had no idea that Chuck was in the house, or who this guy was standing beside me. Still, I did not see Cappy's people and that worried me even more so. Where the heck were those guys?

Sensing that Jeff was getting anxious and irritated with Julie now in the fold, he grabbed Julie's arm and told her to join us in the house. She was confused by the appearance of Jeff and the fact that he had his Magnum pointed at my back. Julie then walked with me inside my house with Jeff pointing the gun at both of us.

Chuck was surprised to see Julie and had laughed at her appearance, then remarked, in his usual sarcastic tone.

"So, the little fish is turning on me once again. Julie, I never trusted you and although you may have been a good piece of ass, you are simply not my kind of woman. So, welcome to the party and sit on the fucking couch while we look at the key to millions of dollars."

Julie got more than she bargained for, and sat down next to Leticia who was already on the couch. All of a sudden, I realized that the two most beautiful women in my life were face to face for the first time. These two women had been my lovers and they had never met each other before. Julie knew about Leticia, but Leticia did not know about Julie. Somehow I knew that I was going to have to explain to Leticia who Julie was and what she was doing in my home.

If this is what happens to contestants on the 'Dating Game', then I was becoming the 'booby' prize. I first looked at Leticia, then back to Julie. I took a deep breath and wondered what was going on in their minds.

I then walked over to the Chuck and Jeff and told Chuck to take the key and get out before the place was going to be surrounded by FBI agents. He laughed and said that he did not see a key that would work in a terminal locker.

"What are you trying to do, Mr. Navy Seal? Do you think that I will fall for your shit? Now I am pissed. You just wasted my time. Who shall get it first, Julie or Leticia?"

With that, we heard many cars pulling up around the house and the posse had finally arrived. What the fuck took them so long? In any case, there was a sound of a bullhorn, and the voice told Chuck and Jeff to throw down their arms and come out peacefully. Chuck would not think of surrendering and just pointed his gun at the two women. I knew that he would shoot one of them just for spite and it didn't matter who was first on his list. For that matter, it could have been me.

I had no choice but to take action and try and save some lives here. If anyone was to get shot, it should be me and not the women. Realizing that Chuck was not going to throw down his gun, I had to do what I was trained for.

I gathered all that I was able to muster from my tired limbs and leaped at Chuck, knocking him down on the floor. I reached in back of my pants and grabbed my gun and tossed it to Leticia. I knew that I would not be able to find the trigger as I had to concentrate on keeping this massive body down on the ground. Chuck was a big son of a bitch and was much more powerful than I was. Knowing that I could not give up, I grappled with him and we rolled over and over on the floor.

As Jeff was aiming his weapon at me, Leticia picked up my 38 and fired one shot at Jeff, hitting him in the arms, and knocking him down on the floor. The FBI, Cappy, and the Seals came rushing into the house as I kept Chuck from reaching for his weapon. It had been a close call and Leticia came through for me.

Julie went with Cappy to headquarters, and after some questioning, was released. Jeff was taken into custody and would be charged for attempted murder. Chuck was finally on his way to prison…the real Chuck Manzione.

Mario was given a suspended sentence, as he was the one who told the FBI and the Seals where the gangsters and the Mafia were in Hawaii. Christy was on her way to becoming a top-notch PR person and started to develop great programs for her new firm. Suzie was into writing books and was never heard from again. Peter, Chuck's son, opened up an art studio with his friends in Newport Beach and it became a successful business. Julie got another position with a law firm and finally became a partner, with all of the benefits.

The surprise was that Rita finally emerged as an undercover agent for the CIA and she had moved on to other assignments in Israel and Iraq.

Leticia and me, well, we found other things to do with our lives. First thing we did was to return the three satchels of money to the government, unexpectedly finding out that there was a ten percent reward of one million dollars for its recovery. Oh well, it pays to be honest, I suppose. We all learned our lessons in the bitter end.

The next thing I did was to take Leticia to the supermarket and she watched as I looked after the senior citizens who seemed to love to put high carb and high cholesterol items in their cart, and I would go around, taking them out. This seemed to amuse her immensely and she was actually enjoying my nonsensical behavior as well as living in Dana Point.

Months later, we found out that she was pregnant and carrying a girl. We decided to name her Lila, after her great, great grandmother Queen Lilu'uokalani. We were married at the South Shores Church two months later with a reception at the Beach House on Dana Harbor Drive, one our favorite hangouts.

Cappy and his wife attended, and Mario was our best man. Also in attendance were Christy, Suzie, and of course, Julie, who came with a boyfriend, one of the junior partners of her law firm. Funny thing was, Julie looked happy, and even winked at me after the ceremony.

It was a wonderful time in our life and we looked forward to many happy years ahead. We celebrated our honeymoon in none other than Kona, the big Island of Hawaii, where it all began.

As they had written in the storybooks many years ago, Hawaii, which had experienced internecine warfare and political upheavals, did not merely survive, but prospered in an aura of equality. The edifice that became a society of equal people was not built in a day, nor was it always easy. But in the end, people of goodwill were able to be neighbors and business partners and to court future spouses from a variety of other races as Leticia and I had done.

I did not feel like a foreigner in Hawaii any longer. With Leticia by my side, I felt that I belonged to this wonderful culture of new and sometimes, curious ideas that were strange to those who never visited Hawaii before. I began to appreciate, as well as love the music, the festivals, the foods and the customs. Lila will grow up and be a part of that community and its history, as it was her mother's, and grandmother's and the rest of her family's. Only then will she be able to appreciate the people and their activities in order to get a sense of time's footfalls.

From the early thirteenth century, the coasts of the main islands started to have permanent settlements, through the 1600s when they started to build a civilization. Hawaii has since been altered by human inhabitants, as people began to recognize the beauty and the peaceful evolution that has taken place. Once you set foot on the islands, can you truly appreciate this miracle. For the islands of Hawaii have become more than a beauteous and busy mid-ocean crossroads; but rather a model for a world in which racial equality and racial acceptance can be a prerequisite for world peace.

A century ago, on Waikiki Beach, on the island of Oahu, stood the home of Hawaii's last reigning monarch, Queen Liliuokalani. On that day in Kona, while we enjoyed our time away from the mainland, stood our daughter Lila, who one day may decide to live on the islands and take that voyage through time as her great ancestors once had done.

It was on our first evening in Kona when I had that dream. Martha had once again appeared and I had seen her so vividly smiling down at me.

"David, I am proud of you. It is time for you to go on with your life and enjoy your beautiful family. You have my blessing, always."

I turned toward my bride and smiled. I had come full circle and can now rest peacefully in my new life.

Oh yes, I finally got my class back as a professor in journalism and I started to write a book on my experiences as a Navy Seal. It has been quite an experience for a Brooklyn kid, born and raised on the east coast, and settling down in a small, yet beautiful city called Dana Point. Henry Richard Dana, the author of 'Two Years Before The Mast' had given me something that I never would have imagined. This was indeed a life that was Sweet.

The Beginning...

0-595-33532-2